BRI
MYT

## The Burrowers Beneath
## The Transition of Titus Crow
## The Clock of Dreams

### 'MARVELS . . . STRANGE AND TERRIFIC.'

'The nethermost caverns are not for the fathoming eyes that see; for their marvels are strange and terrific. Cursed the ground where dead thoughts live new and oddly bodied, and evil the mind that is held by no head. Wisely did Ibn Schacabao say, that happy is the tomb where no wizard hath lain, and happy the town at night whose wizards are all ashes. For it is of old rumour that the soul of the devil-bought hastes not from his charnel clay, but fats and instructs *the very worm that gnaws*; till out of corruption horrid life springs, and the dull scavengers of earth wax crafty to vex it and swell monstrous to plague it. Great holes secretly are digged where earth's pores ought to suffice, and things have learnt to walk that ought to crawl . . .'

ABDUL ALHAZRED, the *Necronomicon*

By the same author

# BRIAN LUMLEY'S
## MYTHOS OMNIBUS

## *The Burrowers Beneath*
## *The Transition of Titus Crow*
## *The Clock of Dreams*

## BRIAN LUMLEY

**HarperCollins***Publishers*

HarperCollins*Publishers*
77–85 Fulham Palace Road,
Hammersmith, London W6 8JB

This paperback edition 1997

1 3 5 7 9 8 6 4 2

First published in Great Britain in three volumes:

*The Burrowers Beneath* published by Grafton 1988
Copyright © Brian Lumley 1974

*The Transition of Titus Crow* published by Grafton 1991
Copyright © Brian Lumley 1975, 1991

*The Clock of Dreams* first published by Jove/HBJ 1978
Published by Grafton 1992
Copyright © Brian Lumley 1978

This one-volume edition copyright © Brian Lumley 1997

The Author asserts the moral right to
be identified as the author of this work

ISBN 0 00 649937 6

Set in Times

Printed and bound by in Great Britain by
Caledonian International Book Manufacturing Ltd, Glasgow

# Contents

## The Burrowers Beneath

## The Transition of Titus Crow

## The Clock of Dreams

# THE BURROWERS BENEATH

This one
with special thanks,
for the memory of August Derleth,
who sanctioned it; and for all those
splendid scriveners of macabre tales
who, over the years, have enlarged
upon or borrowed from the
*Cthulhu Mythos*
of H. P. Lovecraft.
In so doing, they have helped
to keep the Mythos alive
for the rest of us
to enjoy:

*That is not dead which can eternal lie,*
*And with strange aeons even death may die.*

# 1
## The Nethermost Caverns

*(From the Files of Titus Crow)*

Blowne House
Leonard's-Walk Heath
London
18th May 196–

Ref: – 53/196–
G. K. Lapham & Co.
Head Office, GKL Cuttings
117 Martin Fludd St
Nottingham, Notts.

Dear Mr Lapham,
   Please alter my order as it stands to cover only the most outstanding cases, on which your continued cooperation would be appreciated as ever. This action not to be misconstrued as being all but a cancellation of my custom, on the contrary, but for the time being I would rather you concentrate your efforts on my behalf to *full* coverage of one special line. I require *all* cuttings, one copy of each, from all forty-three dailies normally covered, of current occurrences involving earthquakes, tremors, subsidences, and like phenomena (and backdated to cover the last three years where at all possible), to continue until further notice. Thank you for your prompt attention.

Yrs faithfully,
T. Crow

Ref: – 55/196–
Edgar Harvey, Esq.
Harvey, Johnson & Harvey, Solicitors
164–7 Mylor Rd
Radcar, Yorks.

Dear Mr Harvey,
  I am given to understand that you are the literary agent
of Paul Wendy-Smith, the young writer of tales of roman-
tic and/or macabre fiction, and that following his mysterious disappearance in 1933 you became executor to the
estate. I was only a very young man at that time, but I
seem to remember that because of certain special circumstances publication of the writer's last story (showing, I
believe, strange connections with the disappearance of
both the author and his uncle, the explorer-archaeologist
Sir Amery Wendy-Smith) was held in abeyance. My query
is simply this: has the work since seen publication, and if
so where may I obtain a copy?

I am, sir, hopefully
expectant of an early
answer, Yrs sincerely,
T. Crow


Harvey, Johnson & Harvey
Mylor Rd
Radcar, Yorks.
22nd May

Blowne House

Dear Mr Crow,
  Regarding your inquiry (your reference 55/196– of 19th

May), you are correct, I was executor to the estate of Paul Wendy-Smith – and yes, there was a tale held in abeyance for a number of years until the Wendy-Smiths were both officially pronounced 'missing or dead' in 1937. The story, despite being a very slight piece, has seen publication more recently in an excellently presented and major macabre collection. I enclose proofs of the story, and, should you require the book itself, the publisher's card.

Hoping that this covers your inquiry to your complete satisfaction, I am, Sir,

Yours sincerely,
Edgar Harvey

Blowne House
25th May

Ref: – 58/196–
Features Reporter
*Coalville Recorder*
77 Leatham St
Coalville, Leics.

My dear Mr Plant,

Having all my life been interested in seismological phenomena, I was profoundly interested in your article in the issue of the *Recorder* for 18th May. I know your coverage was as complete as any man-in-the-street could possibly wish, but wonder if perhaps you could help me in my own rather more specialized inquiry? Tremors of the type you described so well are particularly interesting to me, but there are further details for which, if it is at all possible you can supply them, I would be extremely grateful. Calculations I have made suggest (however inaccurately) that the Coalville shocks were of a linear rather than a general nature; that is, that they occurred on a line almost directly south to north and in that chronological order – the most southerly occurring first. This, at least, is my guess, and I would be grateful if you could corroborate, or (as no doubt the case will be) deny my suspicion; to which end I enclose a stamped, addressed envelope.

Sincerely and appreciatively<br>
Yrs, I am, sir,<br>
Titus Crow

Blowne House<br>
25th May

Ref: – 57/196–
Raymond Bentham, Esq.
3 Easton Crescent
Alston, Cumberland

My dear sir,

Having read a cutting from a copy of the *Northern Daily Mail* for 18th May, I would like to say how vastly interested I was in that article which contained certain parts of your report on the condition of the west sections of Harden Mine's old workings, and feel it a great pity that Sir David Betteridge, scientific adviser to the North-east Coal-Board, has chosen to look at your report in so unenlightened and frivolous a manner.

To me, while admittedly knowing little of yourself or your job, it would seem rather irresponsible on the part of so large and well-founded an industrial board to employ for twenty years an Inspector of Mines without, during that time, discovering that his 'faculties are not all that they should be!'

Now, I am not a young man myself, indeed at sixty-three years of age I am far and away your senior, but I have complete faith in *my* faculties – and, since reading certain of the things in your report which I can (in a rather peculiar way) corroborate, I am also sure that you were *quite correct* in the observations you made in the complex of the discontinued Harden workings. Just how I can be so sure must, unfortunately, remain my secret – like most men I am averse to derision, a point I am sure you will appreciate – but I hope to offer you at least some proof of my sincerity in writing this letter.

Thus, to reassure you beyond any doubt that I am not simply 'pulling your leg', or in any way trying to add my own sarcastic comment to what has already been made of your report, I return your attention to the following:

Other than mentioning briefly certain *outlines* which you say you found etched in the walls of those new and inexplicable tunnels which you discovered down there cut (or rather 'burned', as you had it) through the rock a mile below the surface, you seem reluctant to describe in detail the content or actual forms of those outlines. Might I suggest that this is because you did not wish to be further ridiculed, which you feared might well be the case should you actually describe the etchings? And might I further *tell* you what you saw on those unknown tunnel walls; that those oddly dimensioned designs depicted living creatures of sorts – like elongated octopuses or squids but without recognizable heads or eyes – tentacled worms in fact but of gigantic size?

Dare I lay my cards on the table yet more fully and mention the *noises* you say you heard down there in the depths of the Earth; sounds which were not in any way the normal stress noises of a pit, even given that the mine in question had not been worked for five years and was in poor repair? You said *chanting*, Mr Bentham, but quickly retracted your statement when a certain reporter became unnecessarily facetious. Nonetheless, I take you at your original word: you *said* chanting, and I am sure you meant what you said! How do I know? Again, I am not at liberty to disclose my sources; however, I would be obliged for your reaction to the following:

> Ce'haiie ep-ngh fl'hur G'harne fhtagn,
> Ce'haiie fhtagn ngh Shudde-M'ell.
> Hai G'harne orr'e ep fl'hur,
> Shudde-M'ell ican-icanicas fl'hur orr'e G'harne.

Restricted as I am at this time regarding further illuminating my interest in the case, or even explaining the origin of my knowledge of it, but still in the hope of an early answer and perhaps a more detailed account of what you encountered underground, I am, Sir,

Yrs sincerely,
Titus Crow

*Coalville Recorder*
Coalville, Leics.
28th May

Blowne House

Dear Mr Crow,

In answer to your 58/196–, of the 25th:

The tremors that shook Coalville, Leics., on the afternoon of the 17th, were, as you correctly deduced, of a linear nature. (And yes, they did occur south heading north; have in fact continued, or so I believe, farther up-country.) As you are no doubt aware, Coalville is central in an area of expanding mining operations, and doubtless the collapse of old diggings was responsible, in this area at least, for the peculiar shocks. They lasted from 4:30 until 8:00 P.M., but were not particularly severe – though, I am told, they had a very bad effect on certain inmates of the local Thornelee Sanatorium.

There were, too, other slight surface subsidences, not nearly so bad, almost a year ago. At about that time also, five miners were lost in the collapse of a very narrow and unproductive seam which they were working. The twin brother of one of these men was in a different part of the mine at the time, and much sensational publicity was given his subsequent condition. I did *not* cover his case, though it was done up pretty distastefully in a hack contemporary of the *Recorder* under the heading: 'Siamese Mining Horror!' Apparently the living twin went stark staring mad at the very instant his brother and the other four men were killed!

You should be interested in a series of articles which I am at present planning for the *Recorder*, 'A History of the Midlands Pits', to be published later this year, and I would be pleased to send you the various chapters as they appear if you so desire.

Yours faithfully,
William Plant


Alston, Cumberland
28th May

Blowne House
Dear Mr Crow,

I got your letter yesterday afternoon, and not being much of a writing man, I'm not sure how to answer it, or even if I can find the right words.

First off, let me say you are quite right about the pictures on the tunnel walls – and also about the chanting. How you could know about these things I can't possibly

17

imagine! So far as I know, I'm the only one to have been down that shaft since they closed the pit, and I'm damned if I can think of any other spot on or under the earth where you might have heard sounds like those I heard, or seen drawings the like of them on the tunnel walls. But you obviously have! Those crazy words you wrote down were just like what I heard . . .

Of course, I should have gone down there with a mate, but my No. 2 was off sick at the time and I thought it was going to be just another routine job. Well, as you know, it wasn't!

The reason they asked me to go down and check the old pit out was twofold – I'd worked the seams, all of them, as a youngster and knew my way about, and of course (to hell with what Betteridge says) I am an *Experienced* inspector – but mainly someone had to do the job to see if the empty seams could be propped up or filled in. I imagine that the many subsidences and cave-ins round Ilden and Blackhill have been giving the Coal-Board a bit of a headache of late.

Anyhow, you asked for a more detailed account of what I came up against underground, and I'll try to tell it as it happened. But can I take it that everything I say will be in confidence? See, I have a good pension coming from the Coal-Board in a few years' time, and naturally they don't much care for adverse stuff in the press, particularly stuff to worry local landowners and builders. People don't buy property that's not safe, or ground that's liable to subsidence! And since I've already had one ticking off as it is, well, I don't want to jeopardize my pension, that's all . . .

I think what really annoyed the bosses was when I went on about those tunnels I found down there – not old, timbered seams, mind you, but *tunnels* – round and pretty smoothly finished and certainly artificial. And not just one, as they said in the *Mail*, but half a dozen! A proper maze, it was. Yes, I said those tunnel walls were burned rather than cut, and so they were. At least, that's how they looked, as though they'd somehow been coated on the inside with lava and then allowed to cool!

But there I go running ahead of myself. Better start at the beginning . . .

I went down the main shaft at Harden, using the old emergency lift-cage which they hadn't yet dismantled. There was a gang of lads at the top just in case the old machinery should go on the blink. I wasn't a bit worried, you understand; it's been my job for a long time now and I know all the dangers and what to look for.

I took a budgie down with me in a little cage. I could hang the cage up to the roof timbers while I looked about. There are some of the old-fashioned methods you still can't beat, I reckon. The old-timers used canaries – I took a budgie. That was so I'd know if there was any firedamp down there (methane to you). A heavy gas knocks a bird out in a wink, which lets you know it's time to get out! I wore protective gear and high boots in case of water – Harden's not all that far from the sea, and it's one of the deepest pits in the country. Funny thing, but I *expected* water, yet as it happened I was quite wrong; it was dry as a bone down there. I had a modern lamp on my helmet with a good, powerful beam, and I carried a map of the galleries and seams – standard procedure but hardly necessary in my case.

Well, anyway, I got down the shaft all right and gave the old handset at the bottom a twirl to let the boys on top know that everything was well, and then I set out along the horizontal connecting-shaft to the west-side galleries and coal-seams. Now, you have to understand, Mr Crow, that the main passages are often pretty big things. Some of them are almost as large as any single tube-tunnel in London. I mention this to show that I wasn't shut in, like, or suffering from claustrophobia or anything like that, and it wasn't as if I hadn't been down a pit before – but there was, well, *something*!

It's hard for me to explain on paper like this, but – oh, I don't know – I had this feeling that – it was as if – well, did you ever play hide-and-seek as a child and go into a room where someone was hiding? You can't see him, it's dark, and he's quiet as a mouse, but you know he's in there all the same! That's what it was like down there in that deserted mine. And yet it *was* truly deserted – at that time anyway . . .

Well, I shook this feeling off and went on until I reached the west-side network. This is almost two horizontal miles from the main shaft. Along the way I had seen evidence of deterioration in the timbers, but not enough to explain away the subsidences on the surface. So far as I could see, there had been no actual cave-ins. The place did *stink*, though, like nothing I'd ever smelled before, but it wasn't any sort of gas to affect the budgie or me. Just a very unpleasant smell. Right at the end of the connecting-shaft, at a spot almost directly under Blackhill, I came across the first of the new tunnels. It entered into the shaft from the side away from the sea, and frankly it stopped me dead! I mean, what would *you* have made of it?

It was a hole, horizontal and with hard, regular walls, but it was cut through *solid rock* and not coal! Now, I like to keep slap-up-to-date on mining methods, but I was pretty sure right from the start that this tunnel wasn't dug using any system or machinery I knew of. And yet it seemed I must have missed something somewhere. The thing wasn't shown on my map, though, so in the end I told myself that some new machinery must have been tested down there before they'd closed the mine. I was damned annoyed, I'll tell you – nobody had told me to expect this!

The mouth of the tunnel was about eight feet in diameter, and although the roof wasn't propped up or timbered in any way the bore looked safe-as-houses, solid somehow. I decided to go on down it to see how far it went. It was all of half a mile long, that shaft, Mr Crow; none of it timbered, straight as a die, and the neatest bit of tunnelling work I've seen underground in twenty-five years. Every two hundred yards or so similar tunnels would come in from the sides at right angles, and at three of these junctions there had been heavy falls of rock. This warned me to be careful. Obviously these holes weren't as solid as they looked!

I don't know where the thought came from, but suddenly I found myself thinking of giant moles! I once saw one of these sensational film things about just such animals. Possibly that's where the idea sprang from in my mind. Anyway, I'd no sooner had this thought than I came to a spot where yet another tunnel joined the main one – *but this one came down at an angle from above!*

There was a hole opening into the ceiling, with the edges rounded off and smoothed in some way I don't understand, as if by heat like I said before. Well, I went dead slow from then on, but soon I came out of the tunnel into a big cave. At least, I took it to be a cave, but when I looked closer at the walls I saw that it wasn't! It was simply a junction of a dozen or so of the tunnels. Pillars like stalagmites held up the ceiling. This was where I saw the carvings, those pictures of octopus-things etched in the walls, and I don't think I need add how much *that* put the wind up me!

I didn't hang about there much longer (apart from anything else the stench was terrible), but long enough to check that the place was all of fifty feet across and that

21

the walls were coated or smoothed over with that same sort of lava-stuff. The floor was flat enough but crumbly, almost earthy, and right in the middle of the place I found four great cave-pearls. At least, I *think* they're cave-pearls. They're about four inches across, these things, very hard, heavy, and glossy. Don't ask me how they got down there, I don't know, and I can't see how they might have been formed naturally, like other cave-pearls I remember seeing when I was a kid. Anyway, I put them into a bag I carried and then went back the way I'd come to the terminal of the west-side workings. By then I'd been down there about an hour and a half.

I didn't get far into the actual coal-seams. The first half dozen were down. They had collapsed. But I soon enough found out what had brought them down! In and out of the old workings, lacing them like holes in Gorgonzola, those damned smooth-lined tunnels came and went, literally honeycombing the coal and rock alike! Then, in one of the few remaining old seams that still stood and where some poor-grade coal still remained, I came across yet another funny thing. A tunnel, one of the new ones, had been cut right along the original seam, and I noticed that here the walls weren't of that lava substance but a pitchy, hard tar, exactly the kind of deposit you find bubbling out of hot coal in the coke-ovens, only set as hard as rock . . . !

That was it. I'd had enough, and I set off back towards the main shaft and the lift-cage. It was then I thought I heard the chanting. Thought? – like hell I thought – I *did* hear it; and it was just as you wrote it down! It was distant, seeming to come from a very long way away, like listening to the sea in a shell or hearing a tune you remember in your head . . . But I knew I should never have been hearing things like that down there at all, and I took off for the lift-cage as fast as I could go.

Well, I'll keep the rest of it short, Mr Crow. I've probably said too much already as it is, and I just hope to God that you're not one of those reporter fellows. Still, I wanted to get it off my chest, so what the hell care I?

I finally arrived at the shaft bottom, by which time the chanting had died away, and I gave the lads on top a tinkle on the old handset to haul me up. At the top I made out my report, but not as fully as I've done here, and then I went home . . . I kept the cave-pearls, as mementos if you like, and said nothing about them in my report. I don't see what good they'd be to anyone, anyway. Still, it does seem a bit like stealing. I mean, whatever the things really are – well, they're not mine, are they? I might just send them off anonymously to the museum at Sunderland or Radcar. I suppose the museum people will know what they are . . .

The next morning the reporters came around from the *Daily Mail*. They'd heard I had a bit of a story to tell and pumped me for all I was worth. I had the idea they were laughing at me, though, so I didn't tell them a deal. They must have gone to see old Betteridge when finally they left me – and, well, you know the rest.

And that's it, Mr Crow. If there's something else you'd like to know just drop me another line. Myself, I'd be interested to learn how you come to know so much about it all, and why you want to know more . . .

Yrs sincerely,<br>R. Bentham

PS

Maybe you heard how they were planning to send two more inspectors down to do the job I'd 'messed up'? Well, they couldn't. Just a few days ago the whole lot fell in! The road between Harden and Blackhill sank ten feet in places, and a couple of brick barns were brought down at Castle-Ilden. There's had to be work done on the walls of the Red Cow Inn in Harden, too, and there have been slight tremors all over the area ever since. Like I said, the mine was rotten with those tunnels down there. I'm only surprised (and thankful!) it held up so long. Oh, and one other thing. I think that the smell I mentioned must, after all, have been produced by a gas of some sort. Certainly my head's been fuzzy ever since. Weak as a kitten, I've been, and damned if I don't keep hearing that awful, droning, chanting sound! All my imagination, of course, for you can take it from me that old Betteridge wasn't even partly right in what he said about me . . .

R.B.

Blowne House
30th May

To: Raymond Bentham, Esq.

Dear Mr Bentham,

I thank you for your prompt reply to my queries of the 25th, and would be obliged if you would give similar keen attention to this further letter. I must of necessity make my note brief (I have many important things to do), but I beg you to have the utmost faith in my directions, strange as they may seem to you, and to carry them out without delay!

You have seen, Mr Bentham, how accurately I described the pictures on the walls of that great unnatural cave in the earth, and how I was able to duplicate on paper the weird chant you heard underground. My dearest wish now is that you remember these previous deductions of mine, and believe me when I tell you *that you have placed yourself in extreme and hideous danger in removing the cave-pearls from the Harden tunnel-complex!*

24

In fact, it is my sincere belief that you are constantly increasing the peril every moment you keep those things!

I ask you to send them to me; I might know what to do with them. I repeat, Mr Bentham, *do not delay but send me the cave-pearls at once*; or, should you decide against it, then for God's sake at least remove them from your house and person! A good suggestion would be for you to drop them back into the shaft at the mine, if that is at all possible; but whichever method you choose in getting rid of them, do it with dispatch! They may rightly be regarded as being infinitely more dangerous than ten times their own weight in nitroglycerin!

Yrs v. truly,
Titus Crow

Blowne House
5 P.M., 30th
May

To: Mr Henri-Laurent de Marigny

Dear Henri,

I've tried to get you on the telephone twice today, only to discover at this late hour that you're in Paris at a sale of antiques! Your housekeeper tells me she doesn't know when you'll be back. I hope it's soon. I may very well need your help! This note will be waiting for you when you get back. *Waste no time, de Marigny, but get round here as soon as you're able!*

Titus

# 2
## Marvels Strange and Terrific

*(From the Notebooks of Henri-Laurent de Marigny)*

I had known this strange and inexplicable feeling for
weeks – a deep-rooted mental *apprehension*, an uneasiness of psyche – and the cumulative effect of this near-
indefinable atmosphere of hovering hysteria upon my
system, the sheer tautness of my usually sound nerves,
was horrible and soul-destroying. I could not for my life
fathom whence these brooding fears of things unknown
sprang, or even guess at the source of the hideous
oppressiveness of air which seemed to hang in tangible
heaviness over all my waking and sleeping moments alike,
but the combination of the two had been more than
sufficient to drive me from London to seek refuge on the
Continent.

Ostensibly I had gone to Paris to seek out certain
Eastern antiques at the House du Fouche, but when I
discovered that my flight to that ancestral city had gained
me no respite from my sickening, doom-fraught mood of
depression, then I was at a complete loss as to what to do
with myself.

In the end, after a stay of only four days, having made
one or two small purchases – simply, I suppose, to justify
my journey – I determined to return to England.

From the moment my plane touched down in London I
felt somehow that I had been *drawn* back from France,
and I considered this peculiar prescience proven when,
upon arriving at my home, I found Titus Crow's summons
waiting for me. His letter had lain on a table in my study,
placed there by my housekeeper, for two days; and yet,
cryptic as that note was, its message lifted my spirit

instantly from the constant gloom it had known for so many weeks, and sent me flying to Blowne House.

It was midafternoon when I reached Crow's sprawling bungalow retreat on the outskirts of the city, and when the leonine occultist opened his door to me I was frankly astonished at the alterations which had taken place in his countenance over the three months since last I had seen him. He was more than tired, that was plain, and his face was drawn and grey. Lines of concentration and worry had etched themselves deep in his high forehead; his broad shoulders were slumped atop his tall, usually energetic frame; his whole aspect betrayed the extensive and sleepless studies to which he must needs have lent himself, making his first words almost unnecessary:

'De Marigny, you got my note! Thank goodness for that! If ever a second head was needed it's now. I've just about knocked myself out with the thing, driven myself to distraction. A clear mind, a fresh approach – By God, it's good to see you!'

Crow ushered me inside, led the way to his study, and there indicated that I should take a seat. Instead I simply stood gazing unbelievingly about the room. My host poured me a customary welcoming glass of brandy before flopping wearily into a chair behind his great desk.

Now, I have said that I gazed unbelievingly about the study: well, let it be understood that Titus Crow's study (incorporating as it does his magnificent occult library), while yet being the apple of his eye, is more often than not the scene of at least a minimal activity, when my friend involves himself within those strange spheres of research which are his speciality; and let it be further understood that I was quite used to seeing the place in less than completely tidy order – but *never* before had I seen anything like the apparent chaos which reigned in that room on this occasion!

Maps, charts, and atlases lay open and in places over-lapping, littering the floor wall to shelved wall, so that I had to step on certain of them to reach a chair; various files, many of them fastened open at marked or paper-clipped places, stood at one end of the cluttered desk and also upon a small occasional table; numbered newspaper cuttings were everywhere, many of them discoloured and plainly faded with age, others very recent; a great note-book, its pages covered top to bottom with careless or hurried scrawlings, lay open at my feet, and rare and commonplace tomes alike on various obscure or little known semimythological, anthropological, and archaeo-logical themes were stacked willy-nilly in one corner of the room at the foot of Crow's great four-handed grand-father clock. The whole was a scene of total disorder, and one that whetted my curiosity to a point where my first astonished outburst sprang as naturally to my lips as might any commonplace inquiry in less bizarre surroundings:

'Titus! What on earth . . . ? You look as though you haven't had a wink of sleep in a week – and the state of this place!' Again I stared about the room, at the apparent disruption of all previous normality.

'Oh, I've been getting my sleep, de Marigny,' Crow answered unconvincingly, 'though admittedly not so much as ordinarily. No, this tiredness of mine is as much a mental as a physical fatigue, I fear. But for heaven's sake, what a *puzzle*, and one that *must* be solved!' He swirled his brandy in its glass, the tired action belying his momen-tarily energetic and forceful mode of expression.

'You know,' I said, satisfied for the moment to let Crow enlighten me in his own time and way, 'I rather fancied someone could use a bit of help, even before I got your note, I mean. I don't know what's been going on, I haven't the faintest inkling what this "puzzle" of yours is, but do you know? Why, this is the first time in weeks that

I've felt at all like tackling anything! I've been under some sort of black cloud, a peculiar mood of despair and strange ennui, and then along came your note.'

Crow looked at me with his head on one side and ruefully smiled. 'Oh? Then I'm sorry, de Marigny, for unless I'm very much mistaken your "peculiar mood of despair" is due to repeat itself in very short order!' His smile disappeared almost immediately. 'But this is nothing frivolous I've got myself into, Henri, no indeed.'

His knuckles whitened as he gripped the arms of his tall chair and leaned forward over the desk. 'De Marigny, if I'm correct in what I suspect, then at this very moment the world is faced with an unthinkable, an unbelievable horror. But *I* believe in it . . . and there were others before me who believed!'

'*Were* others, Titus?' I caught something of the extra weight he had placed on the word. 'Are you alone, then, in this belief of yours?'

'Yes, at least I think I am. Those others I mentioned are . . . no more! I'll try to explain.'

My gaunt-looking friend sat back then and visibly relaxed. He closed his eyes for a second and I knew that he pondered the best way to tell his story. After a few moments, in a quiet and controlled tone of voice, he commenced:

'De Marigny, I'm glad we're two of a kind; I'm damned if I know whom I might confide in if we weren't so close. There *are* others who share this love of ours, this fascination for forbidden things, to be sure, but none I know so well as you, and no one with whom I've shared experiences such as we have known and trembled at together. There's been this thread between us ever since you first arrived in London as a boy, straight off the boat from America. Why! We're even tied by that clock there, once owned by your father!' He indicated the weird, four-

29

handed, strangely ticking monstrosity in the corner. 'Yes, it's as well we're two of a kind, for how could I explain to a stranger the fantastic things I must somehow explain? And even if I could do so without finding myself put away in a padded cell, who would give the thing credit? Even you, my friend, may find it beyond belief.'

'Oh, come now, Titus,' I felt obliged to cut in. 'You couldn't wish for any more inexplicable a thing than that case of the Viking's Stone you dragged me in on! And how about the Mirror of Nitocris, which I've told you of before? What a threat and a horror there! No, it's unfair to doubt a man's loyalty in these things before you've tried it, my friend.'

'I don't doubt your loyalty, Henri – on the contrary – but even so, this thing I've come up against is . . . *fantastic!* There's more than simply the occult involved – if the occult is involved at all – there's myth and legend, dream and fancy, hideous fear and terrifying, well, *survivals!*'

'Survivals?'

'Yes, I think so; but you'll have to let me tell it in my own way. No more interruptions, now. You can question me all you want when I'm done. Agreed?'

I grudgingly nodded my head.

'Survivals, I said, yes,' he then continued. 'Residua of dark and nameless epochs and uncounted cycles of time and existence. Look here; you see this fossil?' He reached into a drawer in his desk and held up an ammonite from the beaches of the Northeast.

'The living creature that this once was dwelt in a warm sea side by side with man's earliest forebears. It was here even before the most antediluvian Adam walked, or crawled, on dry land! But millions of years before that, possibly a forebear of this very fossil itself, *Muensteroceras*, an early ammonite, existed in the seas of the lower

Carboniferous. Now to get back to survivals, Muensteroceras had a more mobile and much more highly developed contemporary in those predawn oceans, a fish called Coelacanthus – and yet a *live* coelacanth, its species thought to have been extinct since early Triassic times, was netted off Madagascar in 1938! Then again, though I don't refer specifically to these sorts of things, we have the Loch Ness monster and the alleged giant saurians of Lake Tasek Bera in Malaya – though why such creatures *shouldn't* exist in a world capable of supporting the very real Komodo dragons is beyond me, even if they are thought by many to be pure myth – and even the Yeti and the West German Wald-Schrecken. And there are lesser, absolutely genuine forms, too, plenty of them, come down the ages unaltered by evolution to the present day.

'Now, such as these, real and unreal, are what you might call "survivals", de Marigny, and yet Coelacanthus, "Nessie", and all the others are *geologic infants* in comparison with the things I envisage!'

Here Crow made a pause, getting up to wearily cross the book- and paper-littered floor to pour me another drink, before returning to his desk and continuing his narrative:

'I became aware of these survivals, initially at least, through the medium of dreams; and now I consider that those dreams of mine have been given substance. I've known for a good many years that I'm a highly psychic man; you are of course aware of this as you yourself have similar, though lesser, powers.' (This, from Titus Crow, a statement of high praise!) 'It's only recently, however, that I've come to recognize the fact that these walking "senses" of mine are still at work – more efficiently, in fact – when I'm asleep. Now, de Marigny, unlike that long-vanished friend of your late father's, Randolph Carter, I have never been a great dreamer; and usually

31

my dreams, irregular as they are, are very vague, fragmentary, and the result of late meals and even later hours. Some, though, have been . . . different!

'Well, although this recognition of the extension of my psychic powers even into dreams has come late, I do have a good memory, and fortunately – or perhaps unfortunately, depending how it works out – my memory is supplemented by the fact that as long as I can remember I have faithfully recorded all the dreams I've known of any unusual or vivid content; don't ask me why! Recording things is a trait of occultists, I'm told. But whatever the reason I seem to have written down almost everything of any importance that ever happened to me. And dreams have always fascinated me.' He waved his hand, indicating the clutter on the floor.

'Beneath some of those maps there, you'll find books by Freud, Schrach, Jung, and half a dozen others. Now, the thing that has lately impressed me is this: that all my more *outré* dreams, over a period of some thirty years or more, have occurred simultaneous in time with more serious and far-reaching happenings *in the waking world!*

'Let me give you some examples.' He sorted out an old, slim diary from a dozen or so at one end of his desktop, opening it to a well-turned page.

'In November and December, 1935, I had a recurrent nightmare centring about any number of hideous things. There were winged, faceless bat-things that carried me nightly over fantastic needle-tipped peaks on unending trips towards some strange dimension which I never quite reached. There were weird, ethereal chantings which I've since recognized in the *Cthaat Aquadingen* and which I believe to be part of the *Necronomicon*; terribly deadly stuff, de Marigny! There was a hellish place beyond an alien jungle, a great scabrous circle of rotting earth, in the centre of which a . . . a *Thing* turned endlessly in a bilious

32

green cloak, a cloak alive with a monstrous life all its own. There was madness, utter insanity in the very air! I still haven't deciphered many of the coded sections in the *Cthaat Aquadingen* – and by God I don't intend to! – but those chants I heard in my dreams are delineated there, and heaven knows what they might have been designed to call up!'

'And in the waking world?' I felt bound to ask it, even remembering that I was supposed to bide my time. 'What was going on in the real world throughout this period of strange dreams?'

'Well,' he slowly answered, 'it culminated in certain monstrous occurrences on New Year's Eve at Oakdeene Sanatorium near Glasgow. In fact, five of the inmates died that night in their cells; and a male nurse, too, on a lonely road quite near the sanatorium. The latter was apparently attacked by a beast of some sort . . . torn and horribly chewed! Apart from these deaths, all of them quite inexplicable, one other nurse went mad; and, perhaps most amazing of all, yet five more inmates, previously "hopeless" cases, were later released as perfectly responsible citizens! You can read up on the case from my cuttings-file for that period if you wish . . .

'Now, I'll agree that from what I've told you these occurrences seem to have damn all to do with my dreams; nevertheless, after New Year's Eve, I wasn't bothered again by those dreams!

'And that's not all, for I've checked, and rumour has it that prior to the hellish happenings that night the worst inmates of Oakdeene gave themselves over to some form of mad chanting. And I think I can hazard a guess as to what that chanting was, if not what it was for.

'Anyhow, let's get on.

'Over the next thirty years or so,' Crow continued after closing the first book and taking up a more recent diary,

'I had my share of lesser nightmares – no more than two dozen in all, all of them of course recorded – one of which especially stays in my mind; we'll get on to it in detail in a minute. But in late 1963, commencing on the tenth of November, my sleep was once more savagely invaded, this time by dreams of a vast underwater fortress peopled by things the like of which I never want to see again, in or out of dreams!

'Well, these creatures in their citadel at the bottom of the sea, they were – I don't know – ropy horrors out of the most terrible myths of pre-antiquity, beings without parallel except in the Cthulhu and Yog-Sothoth Cycle. Most of them were preoccupied with some obscure magical – or rather scientific – preparations, assisted in their submarine industry by indescribable blasphemies more heaps of mobile sludge than organic creatures . . . hideously reminiscent of the Shoggoths in the *Necronomicon*, again from the Cthulhu Cycle of myth.

'These Shoggoth-things – I came to think of them as "Sea-Shoggoths" – were obviously subservient to their ropy masters, and yet a number of them stood guard over one certain member of the former beings. I had the mad impression that this . . . this Odd-Thing-Out, as it were – which was, even in its absolute alienage, obviously demented – consisted in fact of a human mind trapped in the body of one of these sea-dwellers!

'Again, during the period through which I experienced these dreams, there were occurrences of peculiarly hideous aspect in the real, waking world. There were awful uprisings in lunatic asylums all over the country, cult gatherings in the Midlands and Northeast, terrible suicides among many members of the "arty set", all coming to a head in the end when Surtsey rose from the sea off the Vestmann Islands on the Atlantic Ridge.

'You know, of course, de Marigny, the basic theme of

the Cthulhu Cycle of myth; that at a time yet to come Lord Cthulhu will rise from his slimy seat at Deep R'lyeh in the sea to reclaim his dry-land dominions? Well, the whole thing was horribly frightening, and for a long time I morbidly collected cuttings and articles dealing with Surtsey's rising. Nothing further occurred, however, and Surtsey eventually cooled from its volcanic state into a new island, barren of life but still strangely enigmatic. I have a feeling, Henri, that Surtsey was only the first step, that those ropy things of my dreams are in fact real and that they had planned to raise to the surface whole chains of islands and oddly-dimensioned cities – lands drowned back in the dim mists of Earth's antiquity – in the commencement of a concerted attack on universal sanity . . . an attack led by loathly Lord Cthulhu, his "brothers", and their minions, which once reigned here where men reign now.'

As my friend talked, from his very first mention of the Cthulhu Cycle of myth, I had put to use an odd ability of mine: the power of simultaneous concentration in many directions. One part of my mind I had turned to the absorption of all that Crow was telling me; another followed different tracks. For I knew far more of the Cthulhu Cycle than my gaunt and work-weary friend suspected. Indeed, since suffering certain experiences when, for a brief time, I had owned the accursed Mirror of Queen Nitocris, I had spent much of my time in correlating the legends and pre-human myths surrounding Cthulhu and his contemporaries in the immemorially handed-down records.

Among such 'forbidden' books, I had read the unsuppressed sections of the British Museum's photostat *Pnakotic Manuscript*, allegedly a fragmentary record of a lost 'Great Race', prehistoric even in prehistory; similarly reproduced pages from the *R'lyeh Text*, supposedly written by certain minions of Great Cthulhu himself; the *Unaussprechlichen Kulten* of Von Junzt and my own copy of Ludwig Prinn's *De Vermis Mysteriis*, both in vastly expurgated editions; the Comte d'Erlette's *Cultes des Goules* and Feery's often fanciful *Notes on the Necronomicon*; the hideously revealing and yet disquietingly vague *Revelations of Glaaki*; and those uncoded sections of Titus Crow's priceless copy of the *Cthaat Aquadingen*.

I had learned, somewhat sceptically, of the forces or deities of the unthinkably ancient mythology; of the benign Elder Gods, peacefully palaced in Orion but ever aware of the struggle between the races of Earth and the Forces of Evil; of those evil deities themselves, the Great Old Ones, ruled over by (created by, originating from?) the blind idiot god Azathoth, 'the Bubbler at the Hub', an amorphous blight of nethermost, nuclear confusion from which all infinity radiates; of Yog-Sothoth, 'the all-in-one and one-in-all', coexistent with all time and conterminous in all space; of Nyarlathotep the Messenger; of Great Cthulhu, 'dweller in the Depths' in his House at R'lyeh; of Hastur the Unspeakable, a prime elemental of interstellar space and air, half-brother to Cthulhu; and of Shub-Niggurath, 'the black goat of the woods with a thousand young', fertility symbol in the cycle.

There were, too, other creatures and beings – such as Dagon, fish-god of the Philistines and Phoenicians, ruler over the Deep Ones, ally and servant to Cthulhu; the Tind'losi Hounds; Yibb-Tstll, Nyogtha, and Tsathoggua; Lloigor, Zhar, and Ithaqua; Shudde-M'ell, Glaaki, and Daoloth – many, many of them. Of some of these beings much was made in the mythos, and they were given ample space in the books. Others were more obscure, rarely mentioned, and then only in a vague and indecisive manner.

Basically the legend was this: that in an epoch so remote

in the past as to make Crow's 'geologic infants' statement perfectly acceptable, the Elder Gods had punished a rebellion of the Great Old Ones by banishing them to their various prisoning environs – Hastur to the Lake of Hali in Carcosa; Cthulhu to R'lyeh beneath the Pacific Ocean; Ithaqua to dwell above the ice-wastes of the Arctic; Azathoth, Yog-Sothoth, and Yibb-Tstll to chaotic continua *outside* the geometric design of which the known infinite forms but one surface; Tsathoggua to cthonian Hyperborean burrows, and similarly Shudde-M'ell to other lost labyrinths beneath the earth – so that only Nyarlathotep the Messenger was left free and unprisoned. For in their infinite wisdom and mercy the Elder Gods had left Nyarlathotep alone that he might yet ply the currents between the spheres and carry, one to the other in the loneliness of their banishment, the words of all the evicted forces of evil.

Various magical sigils, signs, and barriers kept the Great Old Ones imprisoned, had done so since time immemorial (again an inadequate cliché), and the books, particularly the *Necronomicon* of the mad Arab, Abdul Alhazred, warned against the removal of such signs and of possible attempts by deluded or 'possessed' mortals to reinstate the Great Old Ones as lords of their former domains. The legend in its entirety was a fascinating thing; but as with all the world's other, greater primal fantasies, it could only be regarded as pure myth, with nothing in it to impress any but the most naïve souls of the possible actuality of its surmises and suggestions. So I still thought, despite certain things Crow had told me in the past and others I had stumbled across myself.

All these thoughts passed in very short order through my head, but thanks to my ability to give many things my full, simultaneous concentration, I missed none of Titus Crow's narrative regarding his dreams of over thirty years

37

and their implications as applied to actual occurrences in the real, waking world. He had covered certain monstrous dreams of a time some years gone, when his nightmares had been paralleled in life by any number of disastrous losses of oceangoing gas- and oil-drilling rigs, and was now about to relate the details of yet more hideous nightmares he had known at a time only some few weeks ago.

'But first we'll go back to those dreams I skipped over earlier,' he said, as I banished all other pictures from my mind. 'The reason I did that was because I didn't want to bore you with duplication. You see, they first came to me as long ago as August, 1933, and though they were not so detailed they were more or less the same as my most recent, recurrent nightmares. Yes, those dreams, until recently, have been coming nightly, and if I describe one of them, then I shall have described most of them. A few have been different!

'To make it short, Henri, I have been dreaming of subterranean beings, octopus-things apparently without heads or eyes, creatures capable of organic tunnelling through the deepest buried rocks with as little effort as hot knives slicing butter! I don't know for sure yet just what they are, these burrowers beneath; though I'm pretty certain they're of an hitherto unguessed species as opposed to creatures of the so-called "supernatural", survivors of a time before time rather than beings of occult dimensions. No, I can only guess, but my guess is that they represent an unholy horror! And if I'm correct, then, as I've already said, the whole world is in hellish danger!'

Crow closed his eyes, leaned back in his chair, and put his fingertips up to his furrowed forehead. Plainly he had said as much as he was going to without prompting. And yet I found myself no longer truly eager to question him.

38

This was, without a doubt, a much different Titus Crow from the man I had known previously. I full knew the extent of his probing into various strange matters, and that his research over the years in the more obscure corners of various sciences had been prodigious, but had his work finally proved too much for him?

I was still worriedly staring at him in sympathetic apprehension when he opened his eyes. Before I could hide it, he saw the expression on my face and smiled as I tried to cover my embarrassment.

'I . . . I'm sorry, Titus, I – '

'What was it you said, de Marigny?' He stopped me short. 'Something about doubting a man before trying him? I told you it was going to be hard to swallow, but I don't really blame you for whatever doubts you have. I *do* have proof, though, of sorts . . .'

'Titus, please forgive me,' I answered dejectedly. 'It's just that you look so, well, tired and washed out. But come on – proof, you said! What sort of proof do you mean?'

He opened his desk drawer again, this time to take out a folder of letters, a manuscript, and a square cardboard box. 'First the letters,' he said, handing me the slim folder, 'then the manuscript. Read them, de Marigny, while I doze, and then you'll be able to judge for yourself when I show you what's in the box. Then, too, you'll be better able to understand. Agreed?'

I nodded, took a long sip at my brandy, and began to read. The letters I managed pretty quickly; they drew few conclusions in themselves. Then came the manuscript.

39

# 3

## Cement Surroundings

### (Being the Manuscript of Paul Wendy-Smith)

### 1

It will never fail to amaze me how certain allegedly Christian people take a perverse delight in the misfortunes of others. Just how true this is was brought forcibly home to me by the totally unnecessary whispers and rumours which were put about following the disastrous decline of my closest living relative.

There were those who concluded that just as the moon is responsible for the tides, and in part the slow movement of the Earth's upper crust, so was it also responsible for Sir Amery Wendy-Smith's behaviour on his return from Africa. As proof they pointed out my uncle's sudden fascination for seismography – the study of earthquakes – a subject which so took his fancy that he built his own instrument, a model which does not incorporate the conventional concrete base, to such an exactitude that it measures even the most minute of the deep tremors which are constantly shaking this world. It is that same instrument which sits before me now, rescued from the ruins of the cottage, at which I am given to casting, with increasing frequency, sharp and fearful glances.

Before his disappearance my uncle spent hours, seemingly without purpose, studying the fractional movements of the stylus over the graph.

For my own part I found it more than odd the way in which, while Sir Amery was staying in London after his return, he shunned the underground and would pay extortive taxi fares rather than go down into what he termed 'those black tunnels'. Odd, certainly, but I never considered it a sign of insanity.

Yet even his few really close friends seemed convinced of his madness, blaming it upon his living too close to those dead and nighted nigh-forgotten civilizations which so fascinated him. But how could it have been otherwise? My uncle was both antiquarian and archaeologist. His strange wanderings to foreign lands were not the result of any longing for personal gain or acclaim. Rather were they undertaken out of a love of the life; for any fame which resulted – as frequently occurred – was more often than not shrugged off on to the ever-willing personages of his colleagues.

They envied him, those so-called contemporaries of his, and would have emulated his successes had they possessed the foresight and inquisitiveness with which he was so singularly gifted – or, as I have now come to believe, with which he was cursed. My bitterness towards them is directed by the way in which they cut him after the dreadful culmination of that last, fatal expedition. In earlier years many of them had been 'made' by his discoveries, but on that last trip those hangers-on had been the uninvited, the ones out of favour, to whom he would not offer the opportunity of fresh, stolen glory. I believe that for the greater part their assurances of his insanity were nothing more than a spiteful means of belittling his genius.

Certainly that last safari was his *physical* end. He who before had been straight and strong, for a man his age, with jet hair and a constant smile, was now seen to walk with a pronounced stoop and had lost a lot of weight. His hair had greyed and his smile had become rare and nervous while a distinct tic jerked the flesh at the corner of his mouth.

Before these awful deteriorations made it possible for his erstwhile 'friends' to ridicule him, before the expedition, Sir Amery had deciphered or translated (I know little of these things) a handful of decaying, centuried shards known in archaeological circles as the *G'harne Fragments*. Though he would never fully discuss his findings I knew it was that which he learned which sent him, ill-fated, into Africa.

He and a handful of personal friends, all equally learned gentlemen, ventured into the interior seeking a legendary city which Sir Amery believed had existed centuries before the foundations were cut for the pyramids. Indeed, according to his calculations, Man's primal ancestors were not yet conceived when G'harne's towering ramparts first reared their monolithic sculptings to predawn skies. Nor with regard to the age of the place, if it existed at all, could my uncle's claims be disproved; new tests on the *G'harne Fragments* had shown them to be pre-Triassic, and their very existence, in any form other than centuried dust, was impossible to explain.

It was Sir Amery, alone and in a terrible condition, who staggered upon an encampment of savages five weeks after setting out from the native village where the expedition had last had contact with civilization. No doubt the ferocious men who found him would have done away with him there and then but for their superstitions. His wild appearance and the strange tongue in which he screamed, plus the fact that he had emerged from an area which was taboo in their tribal legends, stayed their hands. Eventually they nursed him back to a semblance of health and conveyed him to a more civilized region whence he was slowly able to make his way back to the outside world. Of the expedition's other members nothing has since been seen or heard. Only I know the story, having read it in the letter my uncle left me, but more of that later . . .

Following his lone return to England, Sir Amery developed those eccentricities already mentioned, and the merest hint or speculation on the part of outsiders with reference to the disappearance of his colleagues was sufficient to start him raving horribly of such inexplicable things as 'a buried land where Shudde-M'ell broods and bubbles, plotting the destruction of the human race and the release from his watery prison of Great Cthulhu . . .' When he was asked *officially* to account for his missing companions, he said that they had died in an earthquake; and though, reputedly, he was asked to clarify his answer, he would say no more.

Thus, being uncertain as to how he would *react* to questions about his expedition, I was loath to ask him of it. However, on those rare occasions when he saw fit to talk of it without prompting, I listened avidly; for I, as much if not more so than others, was eager to have the mystery cleared up.

He had been back only a few months when he suddenly left London and invited me up to his cottage, isolated here on the Yorkshire Moors, to keep him company. This invitation was a thing strange in itself, as he was one who had spent months in absolute solitude in various far-flung desolate places and liked to think of himself as something of a hermit. I accepted, for I saw the perfect chance to get a little of that peaceful quiet which I find particularly beneficial to my writing.

One day, shortly after I had settled in, Sir Amery showed me a pair of strangely beautiful pearly spheres. They measured about four inches in diameter, and, though he had been unable to positively identify the material from which they were made, he was able to say that it appeared to be some unknown combination of calcium, chrysolite, and diamond-dust. *How* the things had been made was, as he put it, 'anybody's guess'. The spheres, he told me, had been found at the site of the dead G'harne – the first intimation he had offered that he had actually found the place – buried beneath the earth in a lidless stone box which had borne upon its queerly angled sides certain utterly alien engravings. Sir Amery was anything but explicit with regard to those designs, merely stating that they were so loathsome in what they suggested that it would not do to describe them too closely. Finally, in answer to my probing questions, he told me that they depicted monstrous sacrifices to some unthinkable cthonian deity. More he refused to say but directed me, since I seemed 'so damnably eager', to the works of Commodus and the hag-ridden Caracalla.

He mentioned that also upon the box, along with the pictures, were many lines of sharply cut characters much similar to the cuneiform and dot-group etchings of the *G'harne Fragments* and, in certain aspects, having a disturbing likeness to the almost unfathomable *Pnakotic Manuscript*. Quite possibly, he went on, the container had been a toy-box of sorts and the spheres, in all probability, were once the baubles of a child of the ancient city; certainly children, or young ones, were mentioned in what he had managed to decipher of the odd writing on the box.

It was during this stage of his narrative that I noticed Sir Amery's eyes were beginning to glaze over and his speech was starting to falter, almost as though some strange psychic block were affecting his memory. Without warning, like a man suddenly gone into an hypnotic trance, he began muttering of Shudde-M'ell and Cthulhu, Yog-Sothoth and Yibb-Tstll – 'alien *Gods* defying description' – and of mythological places with equally fantastic names: Sarnath and Hyperborea, R'lyeh and Ephiroth, and many more.

Eager though I was to learn more of that tragic expedition, I fear it was I who stopped Sir Amery from staying on. Try as I might, on hearing him babbling so, I could not keep a look of pity and concern from showing on my face which, when he saw it, caused him to hurriedly excuse himself and flee to the privacy of his room. Later, when I looked in at his door, he was engrossed with his seismograph and appeared to be relating the markings on its graph to an atlas of the world which he had taken from his shelves. I was concerned to note that he was quietly arguing with himself.

Naturally, being what he was and having such a great interest in peculiar ethnic problems, my uncle had always possessed, along with his historical and archaeological source books, a smattering of works concerning elder-lore and primitive, doubtful religions. I mean such works as *The Golden Bough* and Miss Murray's *Witch Cult*. But what was I to make of those *other* books which I found in his library within a few days of my arrival? On his shelves were at least nine works which I knew were so outrageous in what they suggest that they have been mentioned by widely differing authorities over a period of many years as being damnable, blasphemous, abhorrent, unspeakable, literary lunacy. These included the *Cthaat Aquadingen* by an unknown author, Feery's *Notes on the Necronomicon*, the *Liber Miraculorem*, Eliphas Lévi's *History of Magic*, and a faded, leather-bound copy of the hideous *Cultes des Goules*. Perhaps the worst thing I saw was a slim volume by Commodus which that 'Blood Maniac' had written in 183 A.D. and which was protected by lamination from further fragmentation.

And moreover, as if these books were not puzzling and disturbing enough, there was that other thing . . .

What of the indescribable droning *chant* which I often heard issuing from Sir Amery's room in the dead of night? This first occurred on the sixth night I spent with him, when I was roused from my own uneasy slumbers by the morbid accents of a language it seemed impossible for the vocal cords of man to emulate. Yet my uncle was weirdly fluent with it, and I scribbled down an oft-repeated sentence-sequence in what I considered the nearest written approximation of the spoken words I could find. These words – or at least *sounds* – were:

> Ce'haaie ep-ngh fl'hur G'harne fhtagn,
> Ce'haaie fhtagn ngh Shudde-M'ell.
> Hai G'harne orr'e ep fl'hur,
> Shudde-M'ell ican-icanicas fl'hur orr'e G'harne.

Though at the time I found the thing impossible to pronounce as I heard it, I have since found that with each passing day, oddly, the pronunciation of those lines becomes easier – as if with the approach of some obscene horror I grow more capable of expressing myself in that horror's terms. Perhaps it is just that lately in my dreams, I have found occasion to mouth those very words, and, as all things are far simpler in dreams, my fluency has passed over into my waking hours.

But that does not explain the tremors – the same inexplicable tremors which so terrorized my uncle. Are the shocks which cause the ever-present quiverings of the seismograph stylus merely the traces of some vast, subterrene cataclysm a thousand miles deep and five thousand miles away – *or are they caused by something else?* Something so *outré* and fearsome that my mind freezes when I am tempted to study the problem too closely.

## 3

There came a time, after I had been with him for a number of weeks, when it seemed plain that Sir Amery was rapidly recovering. True, he still retained his stoop, though to me it seemed no longer so pronounced, and his so-called 'eccentricities', but he was more his old self in other ways. The nervous tic had left his face completely and his cheeks had regained something of their former colour. His improvement, I conjectured, had much to do with his never-ending studies of the seismograph; for I had established by that time that there was a definite connection between the measurements of that machine and my uncle's illness. Nevertheless, I was at a loss to understand why the internal movements of the Earth should so determine the state of his nerves. It was after a trip to his room, to look at that instrument, that he told me more of dead G'harne. It was a subject I should have attempted to steer him away from.

'The fragments,' he said, 'told the location of a city the name of which, G'harne, is known only in legend and which has in the past been spoken of on a par with Atlantis, Mu, and R'lyeh. A myth and nothing more. But if you give a legend a concrete location you strengthen it

47

somewhat – and if that location yields up something of the past, centuried relics of a civilization lost for aeons, then the legend becomes history. You'd be surprised how much of the world's history has in fact been built up that way.

'It was my hope, a hunch you might call it, that G'harne had been real; and with the deciphering of the fragments I found it within my power to *prove*, one way or the other, G'harne's elder existence. I have been in some strange places, Paul, and have listened to even stranger stories. I once lived with an African tribe whose people declared they knew the secrets of the lost city, and their storytellers told me of a land where the sun never shines; where Shudde-M'ell, hiding deep in the honeycombed ground, plots the dissemination of evil and madness throughout the world and plans the resurrection of other, even worse abominations!

'He hides there in the ground and awaits the time when the stars will be *right*, when his horrible hordes will be sufficient in number, and when he can infest the entire world with his loathsomeness and bring about the return of those others more loathsome yet!

'I was told stories of fabulous star-born creatures who inhabited the Earth millions of years before Man appeared, who were still here, in certain dark places, when he eventually evolved. I tell you, Paul' – his voice rose – *'that they are here even now – in places undreamed-of!* I was told of sacrifices to Yog-Sothoth and Yibb-Tstll that would make your blood run cold, and of weird rites practised beneath prehistoric skies before Old Khem was born. These things I've heard make the works of Albertus Magnus and Grobert seem tame; De Sade himself would have paled at the hearing.'

My uncle's voice had been speeding up progressively with each sentence, but now he paused for breath and in a more normal tone and at a reduced rate he continued:

'My first thought on deciphering the fragments was of an expedition. I may tell you I had learned of certain things I could have dug for here in England – you'd be surprised what lurks beneath the surface of some of those peaceful Cotswold hills – but that would have alerted a host of so-called "experts" and amateurs alike, and so I decided upon G'harne. When I first mentioned an expedition to Kyle and Gordon and the others I must surely have produced quite a convincing argument, for they all insisted upon coming along. Some of them, though, I'm sure, must have considered themselves upon a wild-goose chase. As I've explained, G'harne lies in the same realm as Mu or Ephiroth – or at least it did – and they must have seen themselves as questing after a veritable Lamp of Aladdin; but despite all that they came. They could hardly afford *not* to come, for if G'harne was real . . . why! Think of the lost glory! They would never have forgiven themselves. And that's why I can't forgive *myself*. But for my meddling with the *G'harne Fragments* they'd all be here now, God help them . . .'

Again Sir Amery's voice had become full of some dread excitement, and feverishly he continued:

'Heavens, but this place sickens me! I can't stand it much longer. It's all this grass and soil. Makes me shudder! Cement surroundings are what I need – and the thicker the cement the better! Yet even the cities have their drawbacks . . . undergrounds and things. Did you ever see Pickman's *Subway Accident*, Paul? By God, what a picture! And that night . . . that *night*!

'If you could have *seen* them – coming up out of the diggings! If you could have felt the tremors – The very ground rocked and danced as they rose! We'd disturbed them, do you see? They may have even thought they were under attack, and up they came. My God! What could

49

have been the reason for such *ferocity*? Only a few hours before I had been congratulating myself on finding the spheres, and then . . . and then – '

Now he was panting and his eyes, as before, had partly glazed over; his voice, too, had undergone a strange change of timbre and his accents were slurred and alien.

'*Ce'haiie, ce'haiie* – the city may be buried but whoever named the place *dead* G'harne didn't know the half of it. *They were alive!* They've been alive for millions of years; perhaps they can't die . . . ! And why shouldn't that be? They're gods, aren't they, of a sort? Up they come in the night – '

'Uncle, please!' I interrupted.

'You needn't look at me so, Paul,' he snapped, 'or think what you're thinking either. There's stranger things happened, believe me. Wilmarth of Miskatonic could crack a few yarns, I'll be bound! You haven't read what Johansen wrote! Dear Lord, *read the Johansen narrative!*

'*Hai, ep fl'hur* . . . Wilmarth . . . the old babbler . . . What is it he knows that he won't tell? Why was that which was found at those Mountains of Madness so hushed up, eh? What did Pabodie's equipment draw up out of the earth? Tell me those things, if you can! Ha, ha, ha! *Ce'haiie, ce'haiie – G'harne icanicas* . . .'

Shrieking now and glassy-eyed he stood, with his hands gesticulating wildly in the air. I do not think he saw me at all, or anything – except, in his mind's eye, a horrible recurrence of what he imagined had been. I took hold of his arm to calm him but he brushed my hand away, seemingly without knowing what he was doing.

'Up they come, the rubbery things . . . Good-bye, Gordon . . . Don't scream so – the shrieking turns my mind – but it's only a dream. A nightmare like all the others I've been having lately. It *is* a dream, isn't it? Good-bye Scott, Kyle, Leslie . . .'

Suddenly, eyes bulging, he spun wildly around. '*The ground is breaking up! So many of them . . . I'm falling!*

'It's not a dream – dear God! *It's not a dream!*

'No! Keep off, do you hear? Aghhh! *The slime . . .* got to run! Run! Away from those – voices? – away from the sucking sounds and the chanting . . .'

Without warning he suddenly broke into a chant himself, and the awful *sound* of it, no longer distorted by distance or the thickness of a stout door, would have sent a more timid listener into a faint. It was similar to what I had heard before in the night and the words do not seem so evil on paper, almost ludicrous in fact, but to hear them issuing from the mouth of my own flesh and blood – and with such unnatural fluency:

> 'Ep, ep-eeth, fl'hur G'harne
> G'harne fhtagn Shudde-M'ell hyas Negg'h.'

While chanting these incredible mouthings Sir Amery's feet had started to pump up and down in a grotesque parody of running. Suddenly he screamed anew and with startling abruptness leaped past me and ran full tilt into the wall. The shock knocked him off his feet and he collapsed in a heap on the floor.

I was worried that my meagre ministrations might not be adequate, but to my immense relief he regained consciousness a few minutes later. Shakily he assured me that he was 'all right, just shook up a bit', and, supported by my arm, he retired to his room.

That night I found it impossible to close my eyes. I wrapped myself in a blanket instead, and sat outside my uncle's room to be on hand if he were disturbed in his sleep. He passed a quiet night, however, and paradoxically enough, in the morning, he seemed to have got the thing out of his system and was positively improved.

Modern doctors have known for a long time that in certain mental conditions a cure may be obtained by inciting the patient to relive the events which caused his illness. Perhaps my uncle's outburst of the previous night had served the same purpose – or at least, so I thought, for by that time I had worked out new ideas regarding his abnormal behaviour. I reasoned that if he had been having recurrent nightmares and had been in the middle of one on that fateful night of the earthquake, when his friends and colleagues were killed, it was only natural that his mind should become temporarily – even permanently – unhinged upon awakening and discovering the carnage. And if my theory were correct, it also explained his seismic obsessions . . .

4

A week later came another grim reminder of Sir Amery's condition. He had seemed so much improved, though he still occasionally rambled in his sleep, and had gone out into the garden 'to do a bit of trimming'. It was well into September and quite chilly, but the sun was shining and he spent the entire morning working with a rake and hedge-clippers. We were doing for ourselves and I was just thinking about preparing the midday meal when a singular thing happened. I distinctly felt the ground *move* fractionally under my feet and heard a low rumble.

I was sitting in the living room when it happened, and the next moment the door to the garden burst open and my uncle rushed in. His face was deathly white and his eyes bulged horribly as he fled past me to his room. I was so stunned by his wild appearance that I had barely moved from my chair by the time he shakily came back into the room. His hands trembled as he lowered himself into an easy chair.

'It was the ground . . . I thought for a minute that the ground . . .' He was mumbling, more to himself than to me, and visibly trembling from head to toe as the after-effect of the shock hit him. Then he saw the concern on my face and tried to calm himself.

'The ground, Paul, I was sure I felt a tremor – but I was mistaken. It must be this place. All this open space. The moors. I fear I'll really have to make an effort and get away from here. There's altogether too much soil and not enough cement! Cement surroundings are the thing . . .'

I had had it on the tip of my tongue to say that I too had felt the shock, but upon learning that he now believed himself mistaken I kept quiet. I did not wish to needlessly add to his already considerable disorders.

That night, after Sir Amery had retired, I went through into his study – a room which, though he had never said so, I knew he considered inviolate – to have a look at the seismograph. Before I looked at the machine, however, I saw the notes spread out upon the table beside it. A glance was sufficient to tell me that the sheets of white foolscap were covered with fragmentary jottings in my uncle's heavy handwriting, and when I looked closer I was sickened to discover that they were a rambling jumble of seemingly disassociated – yet apparently *linked* – occurrences connected in some way with his weird delusions. These notes have since been delivered permanently into my possession and are as reproduced here:

HADRIAN'S WALL.
122–128 A.D. Limestone Bank. (Gn'yah of the *G'harne Fragments?*) Earth tremors interrupted the diggings, which is why cut basalt blocks were left in the uncompleted ditch with wedge-holes ready for splitting.

53

*W'nyal Shash.* (MITHRAS?)

The Romans had their own deities – *but it wasn't Mithras* that the disciples of Commodus, the Blood Maniac, sacrificed to at Limestone Bank! And that was the same spot where, fifty years earlier, a great block of stone was unearthed and discovered to be covered with *inscriptions and engraven pictures!* Silvanus the Centurion defaced it and buried it again. A skeleton, positively identified as Silvanus' by the signet ring on one of its fingers, has been lately found *beneath the ground* (deep) where once stood a Vicus Tavern at Housesteads Fort – but we don't know *how* he vanished! Nor were Commodus' followers any too careful. According to Atullus and Caracalla they also vanished overnight – *during an earthquake!*

AVEBURY.

(Neolithic A'byy of the *G'harne Fragments* and *Pnakotic Manuscript???*) Reference Stukeley's book, *A Temple to the British Druids* – incredible! Druids, indeed! But Stukeley was pretty close when he said snake worship! *Worms, more like it!*

COUNCIL OF NANTES. (9th Century.)

The Council didn't know what it was doing when it ordered: 'Let the *stones* also which, deceived by the derision of the *demons*, they worship amid ruins and in wooded places, where they both make their vows and bestow their offerings, be *dug up* from the very foundations, and let them be cast into such places as never will their devotees be able to find them again . . .' I've read that paragraph so many times that it's become imprinted upon my mind! *God only knows what happened to the poor devils who tried to carry out the Council's orders . . . !*

DESTRUCTION OF GREAT STONES.

In the 13th and 14th Centuries the Church also attempted the removal of certain stones from Avebury, because of *local superstitions* which caused the country folk to take part in *heathen worship* and *witchcraft* around them! In fact some of the stones *were* destroyed – by fire and douching – 'because of the *devices* upon them'.

INCIDENT.

1320–25. Why was a big effort made to bury one of the great stones at Avebury? An *earth tremor* caused the stone to slip, trapping a workman. *No effort appears to have been made to free him . . . !* The 'accident' happened at dusk and two other men *died of fright!* Why? And why did other diggers flee the scene? And what was the titanic *Thing* which one of them saw wriggling away into the ground? Allegedly there was a smell . . . *By their SMELL shall ye know them* . . . Was it a member of another nest of the timeless ghouls?

THE OBELISK.

Why was the so-called Stukeley Obelisk broken up? The pieces were buried in the early 18th Century but in 1833 Henry Browne found burned sacrifices at the site . . . and nearby, at Silbury Hill . . . *My God! That devil-mound!* There are some things, even amid these horrors, which don't bear thinking of – and while I've still got my sanity Silbury Hill had better remain one of them!

AMERICA: INNSMOUTH.

1928. What actually happened and why did the Federal Government drop depth-charges off Devil Reef in the Atlantic coast just out of Innsmouth? Why were half Innsmouth's citizens banished – *and where to?* What was the connection with Polynesia and what also lies buried in the lands *beneath the sea?*

WIND WALKER.

(Death-Walker, Ithaqua, Wendigo, etc.) Yet *another* horror – though of a different type! And such *evidence!* Alleged human sacrifices in Manitoba. Unbelievable circumstances surrounding *Norris Case!* Spencer of Quebec University literally *affirmed* the validity of the case . . . and at . . .

But that is as far as the notes go, and when first I read them I was glad that such was the case. It was quickly becoming all too apparent that my uncle was far from well and still not quite right in his mind. Of course, there was always the chance that he had written those notes before his seeming improvement, in which case his plight was not necessarily as bad as it appeared.

Having put the notes back exactly as I found them, I turned my attention to the seismograph. The line on the graph was straight and true, and when I dismantled the spool and checked the chart I saw that it had followed that almost unnaturally unbroken smoothness for the last twelve days. As I have said, that machine and my uncle's condition were directly related, and this proof of the quietness of the Earth was undoubtedly the reason for his comparative well-being of late. But here was yet another oddity: Frankly I was astonished at my findings, for I was certain I had felt a tremor – indeed I had *heard* a low rumble – and it seemed impossible that both Sir Amery and myself should suffer the same, simultaneous sensory illusion.

I rewound the spool and then, as I turned to leave the room, I noticed that which my uncle had missed. It was a small brass screw lying on the floor. Once more I unwound the spool to find the countersunk hole which I *had* noticed before but which had not made an impression of any importance upon my mind. Now I guessed that it was meant to house that screw. I am nothing where mechanics are concerned and could not tell what part that small component played in the workings of the machine; nevertheless I replaced it and again set the instrument in order. I stood then, for a moment, to ensure that everything was working correctly and for a few seconds noticed nothing abnormal. It was my ears which first warned of the change. There had been a low, clockwork hum and a steady, sharp scraping noise before. The hum was still attendant, but in place of the scraping sound was a jerky scratching which drew my fascinated eyes to the stylus.

That small screw had evidently made all the difference in the world. No wonder the shock we had felt in the afternoon, which had so disturbed my uncle, had gone unrecorded. The instrument had not been working correctly then – *but now it was!*

*Now it could plainly be seen that every few minutes the ground was being shaken by tremors which, though they were not so severe as to be felt, were certainly strong enough to cause the stylus to wildly zigzag over the surface of the revolving graph paper* . . .

I felt in a far more shaken state than the ground when I finally retired that night. Yet I could not readily decide

56

the cause of my nervousness. Just why should I feel so apprehensive about my discovery? True, I knew that the effect of the now – correctly? – working machine upon· my uncle would probably be unpleasant, might even cause another of his 'outbursts'; but was that knowledge alone sufficient to unsettle me? On reflection I could see no reason whatever why any particular area of the country should receive more than its usual quota of earth tremors.

Eventually I concluded that the machine was either totally at fault or simply far too sensitive – perhaps the brass screw needed adjustment – and so finally I went to sleep assuring myself that the strong shock we had felt had been merely coincidental to my uncle's condition. Still, I noticed before I dozed off that the very air itself seemed charged with a strange tension, and that the slight breeze which had wafted the late leaves during the day had gone completely, leaving in its passing an absolute quiet in which, during my slumbers, I fancied all night that the ground trembled beneath my bed . . .

5

The next morning I was up early. I was short of writing materials and had decided to catch the lone morning bus into Radcar. I left the cottage before Sir Amery was awake, and during the journey I thought back on the events of the previous day and decided to do a little research while I was in town. In Radcar I had a bite to eat before calling at the offices of the *Radcar Mirror* where a Mr McKinnen, a sub-editor, was particularly helpful. He spent some time on the office telephones making extensive inquiries on my behalf. Eventually I was told that for the better part of a year there had been no tremors of any importance in England, a point I must obviously have challenged had not further information been forthcoming. I learned that there *had* been some minor shocks and that these had occurred at places as close as Goole, a few miles away (that one within the last forty-eight hours), and as far as Tenterden near Dover. There had also been a very minor tremor at Ramsey in Huntingdonshire. I thanked Mr McKinnen profusely for his help and would have left then but, as an afterthought, he asked me if I would be interested in checking through the paper's international files. I gratefully accepted and was left on my own to study a great pile of interesting translations. Of course, as I expected, most of the information was useless to me, but it did not take me long to sort out what I was after.

At first I had difficulty in believing the evidence of my own eyes. I read that in August there had been quakes in Aisne of such severity that one or two houses had collapsed and a number of people had been injured. These shocks had been likened to those of a few weeks earlier at Agen in that they seemed to be caused more by some *settling of the ground* than by actual tremors. In early July there had also been shocks in Calahorra, Chinchon, and Ronda in Spain. The trail went as straight as the flight of an arrow and lay across – *or rather under* – the straits of Gibraltar to Xauen in Spanish Morocco, where an entire neighbourhood of houses had collapsed. Farther yet, to . . . But I had had enough; I dared look no more; I did not wish to know – not even remotely – the whereabouts of dead G'harne . . .

Oh! I had seen more than sufficient to make me forget about my original errand. My book could wait, for now there were more important things to do. My next port of call was the town library, where I took down Nicheljohn's *World Atlas* and turned to that page with a large, folding map of the British Isles. My geography and knowledge of England's counties are passable, and I had noticed what I considered to be an oddity in the seemingly unconnected places where England had suffered those 'minor quakes'. I was not mistaken. Using a second book as a straight edge I lined up Goole in Yorkshire and Tenterden on the south coast and saw, with a tingle of monstrous foreboding, that the line passed very close to, if not directly through, Ramsey in Huntingdonshire. With dread curiosity I followed the line north and, through suddenly fevered eyes, saw that it passed *within only a mile or so of the cottage on the moors!*

With unfeeling, rubbery fingers I turned more pages, until I found the leaf showing France. For a long moment I paused – then I fumblingly found Spain and finally Africa. For a long while I just sat there in numbed silence, occasionally turning the pages, automatically checking names and localities.

My thoughts were in a terrible turmoil when I eventually left the library, and I could feel upon my spine the chill, hopping feet of some abysmal dread from the beginning of time. My previously wholesome nervous system had already started to crumble.

During the journey back across the moors in the evening bus, the drone of the engine lulled me into a kind of half-sleep in which I heard again something Sir Amery had mentioned – something he had murmured aloud while sleeping and presumably dreaming. He had said: 'They don't like water . . . England is safe . . . have to go too deep . . .'

The memory of those words shocked me back to wakefulness and filled me with a further icy chill which got into the very marrow of my bones. Nor were these feelings of horrid foreboding misleading, for awaiting me at the cottage was that which went far to completing the destruction of my entire nervous system.

As the bus came around the final wooded bend which hid the cottage from sight – *I saw it!* The place had collapsed! I simply could not take it in. Even knowing all I did – with all my slowly accumulating evidence – it was too much for my tortured mind to comprehend. I left the bus and waited until it had threaded its way through the parked police cars and others of curious travellers before crossing the road. The fence to the cottage had been knocked down to allow an ambulance to park in the now queerly *tilted* garden. Spotlights had been set up, for it was almost dark, and a team of rescuers toiled frantically at the incredible ruins. As I stood there, aghast, I was approached by a police officer. Having stumblingly identified myself, I was told the following story.

A passing motorist had actually seen the collapse; the tremors attendant had been felt in nearby Marske. The motorist, realizing there was little he could do on his own, had driven on at speed into Marske to report the thing and bring help. Allegedly the house had gone down like a pack of cards. The police and the ambulance had been on the scene within minutes and rescue operations had begun immediately. Up to now it appeared that my uncle had been out when the collapse occurred, for as of yet there had been no trace of him. There *had* been a strange, poisonous odour about the place but this had vanished soon after the rescue work had started. The floors of all the rooms except the study had now been cleared, and during the time it took the officer to bring me up-to-date even more debris was being frantically hauled away.

Suddenly there was a lull in the excited babble of voices. I saw that the sweating rescue workers were standing amid the ruins in a gang looking down at something. My heart gave a wild leap and I scrambled over the debris to see what they had found.

There, where the floor of the study had been, was that which I had feared and more than half expected. It was simply a hole. A gaping hole in the floor – *but from the angles at which the floorboards lay, and the manner in which they were scattered about, it looked as though the ground, rather than sinking, had been pushed up from below* . . .

## 6

Nothing has since been seen or heard of Sir Amery Wendy-Smith, and though he is listed as being *missing*, I know that in fact he is dead. He is gone to worlds of ancient wonder and my only prayer is that his soul wanders on *our* side of the threshold. For in our ignorance we did Sir Amery a great injustice – I and all the others who thought he was out of his mind – all of us. Each of his queer ways, I understand them all now, but the understanding has come hard and will cost me dear. No, he was not mad. He did the things he did out of self-preservation, and though his precautions came to nothing in the end, it was fear of a nameless evil and not madness which prompted them.

But the worst is still to come. I myself have yet to face a similar end. I know it, for no matter what I do the tremors haunt me. Or is it only in my mind? No, there is little wrong with my mind. My nerves may be gone but my mind is intact. I *know* too much! *They* have visited me in dreams, as I believe *they* must have visited my uncle, and what *they* have read in my mind has warned *them* of *their* danger. *They* dare not allow me further to investigate, for it is just such meddling which may one day fully reveal *them* to men – *before they are ready!*

God! Why hasn't that folklorist fool Wilmarth at Miskatonic answered my telegrams? There must be a way out! Even now *they* dig – those dwellers in darkness . . .

But no – this is no good! I must get a grip on myself and finish this narrative. I have not had time to tell the authorities the truth, but even if I had I know what the result would have been. 'There's something wrong with all the Wendy-Smith blood,' they would say. But this manuscript will tell the story for me and will also stand as a warning to others. Perhaps when it is seen how my *passing* so closely parallels that of Sir Amery, people will be curious; with this manuscript to guide them perhaps men will seek out and destroy Earth's elder madness before it destroys them . . .

A few days after the collapse of the cottage on the moors, I settled here in this house on the outskirts of Marske to be close at hand if – though I could see little hope of it – my uncle should turn up again. But now some dread power keeps me here. I *cannot* flee . . . At first *their* power was not so strong, but now . . . I am no longer able even to leave this desk, and I know that the end must be coming fast. I am rooted to this chair as if grown here and it is as much as I can do to type!

But I must . . . I must . . . And the ground movements are much stronger now. That hellish, damnable, mocking stylus – leaping so crazily over the paper!

I had been here only two days when the police delivered to me a dirty, soil-stained envelope. It had been found in the ruins of the cottage – near the lip of that curious hole – and was addressed to me. It contained those notes I have already copied and a letter from Sir Amery which, if its awful ending is anything to go on, he must have just finished writing when the horror came for him. When I consider, it is not surprising that the envelope survived the collapse; *they* would not have known what it was, and so would have had no interest in it. Nothing in the cottage seems to have been deliberately damaged – nothing *inanimate*, that is – and so far as I have been able to discover the only missing items are those terrible spheres, *or what remained of them!*

But I must hurry. I cannot escape and all the time the tremors are increasing in strength and frequency. No! I will not have time. No time to write all I intended to say. The shocks are too heavy . . . to o heav y. Int erfer in g with my t ypi ng. I will finis h this i n th e only way rem ain ing to me and staple S ir Amer y's lett er to th is man usc rip t no w.

Dear Paul,

In the event of this letter ever getting to you, there are certain things I must ask you to do for the safety and sanity of the world. It is absolutely necessary that these things be explored and *dealt with* – though how that may be done I am at a loss to say. It was my intention, for the sake of my own sanity, to forget what happened at G'harne. I was wrong to try to hide it. At this very moment there are men digging in strange, forbidden places, and who knows what they may unearth? Certainly all these horrors must be tracked down and rooted out – but not by bumbling amateurs. It must be done by men who are ready for the ultimate in hideous, cosmic horror. Men with weapons. Perhaps flamethrowers would do the trick . . . Certainly a scientific knowledge of war would be a necessity . . . Devices could be made to track the enemy . . . I mean specialized seismological instruments. If I had the time I would prepare a dossier, detailed and explicit, but it appears that this letter will have to suffice as a guide to tomorrow's horror-hunters.

You see, *I now know for sure that they are after me* – and there's nothing I can do about it! It's too late! At first even I, just like so many others, believed myself to be just a little bit mad. I refused to admit to myself that what I had *seen* happen had ever happened at all! To admit that was to admit *complete* lunacy – but it was real, all right, it did happen – *and will again!*

63

Heaven only knows what's been wrong with my seismograph, but the damn thing's let me down in the worst possible way! Oh, *they* would have got me eventually, but I might at least have had time to prepare a proper warning.

I ask you to think, Paul . . . Think of what has happened at the cottage . . . I can write of it as though it had already happened – because I know *it must! It will!* It is Shudde-M'ell, come for his spheres . . .

Paul, look at the manner of my death, for if you are reading this then I am either dead or disappeared – which means the same thing. Read the enclosed notes carefully, I beg you. I haven't the time to be more explicit, but these notes of mine should be of some help. If you are only half so inquiring as I believe you to be, you will surely soon come to recognize a fantastic horror which, I repeat, the whole world must be *made* to believe in . . . The ground is really shaking now but, knowing that it is the end, I am steady in my horror . . . Not that I expect my present calm state of mind to last. I think that by the time *they* actually come for me my mind will have snapped completely. I can imagine it now. The floor splintering, erupting, to admit *them*. Why! Even thinking of it my senses recoil at the terror of the thought. There will be a hideous *smell*, a *slime*, a *chanting* and gigantic *writhing* and . . . and then –

Unable to escape I await the thing. I am trapped by the same hypnotic power that claimed the others at G'harne. What monstrous memories! How I awoke to see my friends and companions sucked dry of their life's blood by wormy, vampirish *things* from the cesspools of time! Gods of alien dimensions! I was hypnotized then by this same terrible force, unable to move to the aid of my friends or even to save myself!

Miraculously, with the passing of the moon behind some wisps of cloud, the hynotic effect was broken. Then, screaming and sobbing, utterly broken, temporarily out of my mind, I fled, hearing behind me the droning, demoniac chanting of Shudde-M'ell and his hordes.

Not knowing that I did it, in my mindlessness I carried with me those hell-spheres . . . Last night I dreamed of them. And in my dreams I saw again the inscriptions on that stone box. Moreover, *I could read them!*

All the fears and *ambitions* of those hellish things were there to be read as clearly as the headlines in a daily newspaper! 'Gods' they may or may not be but one thing is sure: the greatest setback to their plans for the conquest of Earth *is their terribly long and complicated reproductive cycle!* Only a handful of young are born every thousand years; but, considering how *long* they have been here, the time must be drawing ever nearer when their numbers will be *sufficient!* Naturally, this tedious buildup of their numbers makes them loath to lose even a single member of their hideous spawn – *and that is why they have tunnelled these many thousands of miles, even under deep oceans, to retrieve the spheres!*

I had wondered why they should be following me – and now I know. I also know *how!* Can you not guess how they know where I am, Paul, or why they are coming? Those spheres are like a beacon to them; a siren voice calling. *And just as any other parent – though more out of awful ambition, I fear, than any type of emotion we could understand – they are merely answering the call of their young!*

*But they are too late!*

A few minutes ago, just before I began this letter, the things hatched! Who would have guessed that they were eggs – or that the container I found them in *was an incubator?* I can't blame myself for not knowing it; I even tried to have the spheres X-rayed once, damn them, but they reflected the rays! And the shells were so thick! Yet at the time of hatching those same shells just splintered into tiny fragments. The creatures inside were no bigger than walnuts. Taking into account the sheer *size* of an adult they must have a fantastic growth rate. Not that those two will ever grow! I shrivelled them with a cigar . . . *and you should have heard the mental screams from those beneath!*

If only I could have known earlier, *definitely*, that it was not madness, then there might have been a way to escape this horror. But no use now. My notes – look into them, Paul, and do what I ought to have done. Complete a detailed dossier and present it to the authorities. Wilmarth may help, and perhaps Spencer of Quebec University. Haven't much time now. *Cracks in ceiling*.

That last shock – ceiling coming away in chunks – the floor – coming up! Heaven help me, they're coming up. I can feel them groping inside my mind as they come –

Sir,

Reference this manuscript found in the ruins of 17 Anwick

Street, Marske, Yorkshire, following the earth tremors of September this year and believed to be a 'fantasy' which the writer, Paul Wendy-Smith, had completed for publication. It is more than possible that the so-called disappearance of both Sir Amery Wendy-Smith and his nephew, the writer, were nothing more than promotion stunts for this story: it is well-known that Sir Amery is/was interested in seismography and perhaps some prior intimation of the two quakes supplied the inspiration for his nephew's tale. Investigations continuing.

Sgt J. Williams
Yorks County Constabulary
2nd October 1933

# 4

## Cursed the Ground

### (From de Marigny's Notebooks)

It soon became obvious that the occultist, despite his denials, was far more tired than he admitted, for he did in fact doze, closing his eyes and drowsing, breathing deep and rhythmically where he sat in his chair, while I read the letters and the – fantasy? – of Paul Wendy-Smith.

I admit quite frankly that when I was finished with that document my mind was in something of a whirl! There had been so many factual references in the supposed 'fiction', and why had the author deliberately chosen to give his characters his own, his uncle's, and many another once-living person's names? Considering the letters I had read prior to this disturbing document, the conviction was rapidly growing in me that Crow's assertions – so far at least – stood proven. For while my friend had not directly said so, nevertheless I could guess that he believed the Wendy-Smith manuscript to be nothing less than a statement of fantastic fact!

When I had properly done with my reading, and while I checked over again the contents of certain of the letters, Crow still nodded in his chair. I rustled the papers noisily as I put them down on his desk and coughed politely. These sudden sounds brought my friend back in an instant to full consciousness.

There were many things for which I would have liked explanations; however, I made no immediate comment but remained intently alert and thoughtful as Crow stirred himself to pass me the box containing . . . what?

I believed I already knew.

I carefully removed the cardboard lid, noting that my guess had been correct, and lifted out one of the four beautifully lustrous spheres the box contained.

'The spawn of Shudde-M'ell,' I quietly commented, placing the box back on the desk and examining the sphere in my hand. 'The eggs of one of the lesser known deities of the Cthulhu Cycle of myth. Bentham did send them to you, then, as you requested?'

He nodded an affirmative. 'But there was no letter with the box, and it seemed pretty hastily or clumsily wrapped to me. I believe I must have frightened Bentham pretty badly . . . or at least, *something* did!'

Frowning, I shook my head, doubt suddenly inundating my mind once more. 'But it's all so difficult to believe, Titus, and for a number of reasons.'

'Good!' he instantly replied. 'In resolving your own incredulity, which I intend to do, I might also allay the few remaining doubts which I myself yet entertain. It *is* a difficult thing to believe, Henri – I've admitted that – but we certainly can't afford to ignore it. Anyhow, what reasons were you speaking of just now, when you voiced your reluctance to accept the thing as it stands?'

'Well for one thing' – I sat back in my chair – 'couldn't the whole rigmarole *really* be a hoax of some sort? Wendy-Smith himself hints of just such a subterfuge in that last paragraph of his, the "police report".'

'Ah!' he exclaimed. 'A good point, that – but I've already checked, Henri, and that last paragraph was *not* part of the original manuscript! It was added by the author's publisher, a clever extract from an actual police report on the disappearances.'

'Then what about this Bentham chap?' I persisted. 'Couldn't he have read the story somewhere? Might he not simply be adding his own fancies to what he considers an intriguing mystery? He has, after all, admitted to a certain interest in weird and science-fiction cinema. Perhaps his taste also runs to macabre literature! It's possible, Titus. The Wendy-Smith story may, as you seem to suspect, be based on fact – may indeed have been drawn from life, a veritable diary, as the continuing absence of Sir Amery and his nephew after all these years might seem to demand – but it *has* seen print as a fiction!'

I could see that he considered my argument for a moment, but then he said: 'Do you know the story of "The Boy Who Cried Wolf", Henri? Of course you do. Well, I've a feeling that Paul Wendy-Smith's last manuscript was dealt with on a similar principle. He had written a fair number of macabre stories, you see, and I'm afraid his agent and executor – despite some preliminary doubts, as witness the delay in publishing – finally saw this last work as just another fiction. It puts me disturbingly in mind of the Ambrose Bierce case. You know the circumstances to which I refer, don't you?'

'Hmmm?' I murmured, frowning as I wondered what he was getting at. 'Bierce? Yes. He was an American master of the macabre, wasn't he? Died in 1914 . . .?'

'Not "died", Henri,' he quickly corrected me. 'He simply disappeared, and his disappearance was quite as mysterious as anything in his stories – quite as final as the vanishment of the Wendy-Smiths!'

He got down on his hands and knees on the floor and began to collect up some of the books and maps. 'But in any case, my friend, you've either not been listening to me as well as you might, or' – he smiled up at me – 'you have very little faith in what I've sworn to be the truth. I'm talking about my dreams, Henri – think about my dreams!'

He gave me time to consider this, then said, 'But there, just supposing that by some freak those nightmares of mine were purely coincidental; and suppose further that

Mr Bentham is, as you suggest, "a hoaxer". How do you explain away these eggs? You think perhaps that Bentham, who appears to be a reasonably down-to-earth Northeasterner, went down to his workshop and simply put them together, out of a bucket or two of common-or-garden chrysolite and diamond-dust? No, Henri, it won't wash. Besides' – he stood up and took one of the things from the box, weighing it carefully in his hand – 'I've checked them out. So far as I can determine they're the real thing, all right. In fact *I know they are!* I've had little time to test them as fully as I would like to, true, but one thing is sure – they do defy X-rays! Very strange when you consider that while they're undeniably heavy there doesn't appear to be any lead in their makeup. And something else, something far more definite . . .'

He put down the egg, neatly stacked the books and papers earlier picked up from the floor, and returned to his chair. From the centre drawer in his desk he took a certain surgical instrument. 'This was lent to me by a neighbour friend of mine, that same friend who tried to radiograph the eggs for me. Care to eavesdrop, de Marigny?'

'A stethoscope?' I took the thing wonderingly from him. 'You mean – ?'

'This was something Sir Amery missed,' Crow cut me off. 'He had the right idea with his earthquake-detector – I've decided, by the way, to obtain a seismograph as soon as possible – but he might have tried listening for small things as well as big ones! But no, that's being unfair, for of course he didn't know until the end just what his pearly spheres were. In trying the stethoscope test I was really only following his lead, on a smaller scale. Well, go on,' he demanded again as I hesitated. 'Listen to them!'

I fitted the receivers to my ears and gingerly touched the sensor to one of the eggs, then held it there more firmly. I imagine the rapid change in my expression was that which made Crow grin in that grim fashion of his. Certainly, in any situation less serious, I might have expected him to laugh. I was first astounded, then horrified!

'My God!' I said after a moment, a shudder hurrying down my spine. 'There are – *fumblings!*'

'Yes,' he answered as I sat there, shaken to my roots, 'there are. The first stirrings of life, Henri, a life undreamed-of – except, perhaps, by an unfortunate few – from beyond the dim mists of time and from behind millennia of myth. A race of creatures unparalleled in zoology or zoological literature, indeed entirely *unknown*, except in the most doubtful and obscure tomes. But they're real, as real as this conversation of ours.'

I felt an abrupt nausea and put the egg quickly back into its box, hurriedly wiping my hands on a kerchief from my pocket. Then I shakily passed the stethoscope back across the desk to my friend.

'They have to be destroyed.' My voice cracked a little as I spoke. 'And without delay!'

'Oh? And how do you think Shudde-M'ell, his brothers and sisters – if indeed they are bisexual – would react to that?' Crow quietly asked.

'What?' I gasped, as the implications behind his words hit me. 'You mean that already – '

'Oh, yes.' He anticipated my question. 'The parent creatures know where their eggs are, all right. They have a system of communication better than anything we've got, Henri. Telepathy I imagine. That was how those other, earlier eggs were traced to Sir Amery's cottage on the moors; that was how they were able to follow him home through something like four thousand miles of subterrene burrows! Think of it, de Marigny. What a task they set themselves – to regain possession of the stolen

71

eggs – and by God, they almost carried it off, too! No, I daren't destroy them. Sir Amery tried that, remember? And what happened to him?'

After a slight pause, Crow continued: 'But, having given Sir Amery's portion of the Wendy-Smith papers a lot of thought, I've decided that he could only have been partly right in his calculations. Look at it this way: certainly, if as Wendy-Smith deduced the reproductive system of Shudde-M'ell and his kind is so long and tedious, the creatures couldn't allow the loss of two future members of their race. But I'm sure there was more than merely that in their coming to England. Perhaps they'd had it planned for a long time – for centuries maybe, even aeons! The way I see it, the larceny of the eggs from G'harne finally prodded the burrowers into early activity. Now, we know they came out of Africa – to recover their eggs, for revenge, whatever – *but we have no proof at all that they ever went back!*'

'Of course,' I whispered, leaning forward to put my elbows on the desk, my eyes widening in dawning understanding. 'In fact, at the moment, all the evidence lies in favour of the very reverse!'

'Exactly,' Crow agreed. 'These things are on the move, Henri, and who knows how many of their nests there may be, or where those nests are? We know there's a burrow in the Midlands, at least I greatly suspect it, and another at Harden in the Northeast – but there could be dozens of others! Don't forget Sir Amery's words: ". . . he waits for the time when he can infest *the entire world* with his loathsomeness . . ." And for all we know this invasion of 1933 may not have been the first! What of Sir Amery's notes, those references to Hadrian's Wall and Avebury? Yet more nests, Henri?'

He paused, momentarily lost for words, I suspected.

By then I was on my feet, pacing to and fro across that

72

part of the floor Crow had cleared. And yet . . . Once more I found myself puzzled. Something Crow had said . . . My mind had not had time yet to adjust to the afternoon's revelations.

'Titus,' I finally said, 'what do you mean by "a Midlands nest"? I mean, I can see that there is some sort of horror at Harden, but what makes you think there may be one in the Midlands?'

'Ah! I see that there's a point you've missed,' he told me. 'But that's understandable for you haven't yet had all the facts. Now listen: Bentham took the eggs on the seventeenth of May, Henri, and later that same day, Coalville, two hundred miles away, suffered those linear shocks heading in a direction from south to north. I see it like this: a number of members of the Midlands nest had come up close to the surface – where the earth, not being so closely packed, is naturally easier for them to navigate – and had set off to investigate this disturbance of the nest at Harden. If you line up Harden and Coalville on a map – as I have done, again taking my lead from the Wendy-Smith document – you'll find that they lie almost directly north and south! But all this in its turn tells us something else' – he grew excited – 'something I myself had missed until just now – there are no adults of the species "in residence", as it were, at Harden! These four Harden eggs were to form the nucleus of a new conclave!'

He let this last sink in, then continued: 'Anyhow, this Coalville . . . *expedition*, if you like, arrived beneath Harden on or about the twenty-sixth of the month, causing that collapse of the mine which Bentham commented upon. There, discovering the eggs to be missing, "abducted", I suppose you could say, the creatures picked up the mental trail towards Bentham's place at Alston.'

He paused here to sort out a newspaper cutting from a small pile on his desk and passed it across for my

73

inspection. 'As you can see, Henri, there were tremors at Stenhope, County Durham, on the twenty-eighth. Need I point out that Stenhope lies directly between Harden and Alston?'

I flopped down again in my chair and helped myself liberally to Crow's brandy.

'Titus, it's plain you can't keep the eggs here!' I told him. 'Heavens, why even now – unseen, unheard, except perhaps as deep tremors on some meteorologist's machinery – these underground octopuses, these subterranean vampires might be on their way here, burning their way through the bowels of the earth! You've put yourself in as much danger as Bentham before he sent you the eggs!'

Then, suddenly, I had an idea. I leaned forward to thump the table. 'The sea!' I cried.

Crow appeared startled by my outburst. 'Eh?' he asked. 'What do you mean, "the sea", de Marigny?'

'Why, that's it!' I slapped a clenched fist into the palm of my hand. 'No need to destroy the eggs and risk the revenge of the adult creatures – simply take them out to sea and drop them overboard! Didn't Sir Amery say that they fear water?'

'It's an idea,' Crow slowly answered, 'and yet – '

'Well?'

'Well, I had it in my mind to use the eggs differently, Henri. To use them more *constructively*, I mean.'

'Use them?'

'We have to put a stop to Shudde-M'ell once and for all, my friend, and we have the key right here in our hands!' He tapped the box with a fingernail. 'If only I could conceive a plan, a system that might work, discover a way to put paid to the things for good. But for that I need time, which means hanging on to the eggs, and that in turn means – '

'Titus, wait,' I rudely interrupted, holding up my hands.

There was something in the back of my mind, something demanding concentration. Abruptly it came to me and I snapped my fingers. 'Of course! I knew there was something bothering me. Now, correct me if I go wrong, but surely we've decided that this Shudde-M'ell creature and his kind feature in the Cthulhu Cycle?'

'Yes.' My friend nodded, obviously at a loss to decide what I was getting at.

'It's simply this,' I said. 'How come these creatures aren't *prisoned*, as their hideous brothers and cousins were in the mythology by the Elder Gods untold millions of years ago?'

I had a point. Crow frowned, quickly moving out from his desk and crossing the room to take from a bookshelf his copy of Feery's *Notes on the Necronomicon*.

'This will do for now,' he said, 'at least until I can get it fixed for you to check through the *Necronomicon* itself at the British Museum. And this time we'll have to fix it for you to read the *whole* book! It's a dangerous task, though, Henri. I've read it myself, some time ago, and was obliged to forget most of what I learned – it was that or madness! In fact, I think we'd better limit your research to selected sections from Henrietta Montague's translation. Are you willing to help me in this?'

'Of course, Titus,' I answered. 'Just pass on your orders. I'll carry them out as best I can, you know that.'

'Good, then that's to be your special task in this,' he told me. 'You can save me a lot of time by correlating and summing up the whole Cthulhu Cycle, with special reference to Shudde-M'ell in the mythology. I'll list certain other books which I think might be helpful later. Right now, though, let's see what Feery has to say on it.'

We were hardly to know it at that time, but things were not to be in any way as Crow planned, for events yet to come would surely have confounded *any* plans he might

75

have made. As it was, we could not know this, and so my haggard friend flipped the leaves of Feery's often fanciful reconstruction of Alhazred's dreadful book until he found the page he was looking for.

'Here we are,' he eventually declared, 'the passage entitled: "Ye Power in ye Five-Pointed Star".' He settled himself in his chair and began to read:

'"Armour against Witches & Daemons, Against ye Deep Ones, ye Dools, ye Voormais, ye Tacho-Tacho, ye Mi-Go, ye Shoggaoths, ye Ghasts, ye Valusians, & all such Peoples & Beings that serve ye Great Olde Ones & ye Spawn of Them, lies within ye Five-Pointed Star carven of grey Stone from ancient Mnar; which is less strong against ye Great Olde Ones Themselves. Ye Possessor of ye Stone shall find himself able to command all Beings which creep, swim, crawl, walk, or fly even to ye Source from which there is no returning. In Yhe as in Great R'lyeh, in Y'ha-nthlei as in Yoth, in Yuggoth as in Zothique, in N'kai as in Naa-Hk & K'n-yan, in Carcosa as in G'harne, in ye twin Cities of Ib and Lh-yib, in Kadath in ye Cold Waste as at ye Lake of Hali, it shall have Power; yet even as Stars wane & grow cold, even as Suns die & ye Spaces between Stars grow more wide, so wanes ye Power of all things – of ye Five-Pointed Star-Stone as of ye Spells put upon ye Great Olde Ones by ye benign Elder Gods, & that Time shall come as once was a Time when it shall be known:

That is not dead which can eternal lie,
And with strange Aeons even Death may die."'

'"In Carcosa as in G'harne,"' I repeated when Crow had done. 'Well, there we seem to have it!'

'Yes,' he answered drily, frowning at the open book, 'but I'm pretty sure that this is a different version from the one in the Museum copy of the *Necronomicon*. I wish to God Feery was still alive! I've often pondered his knowledge regarding the *Necronomicon* – to say nothing of many another rare book. Still' – he tapped with his fingernail on the page with the relevant passage – 'there's part of your answer at least.'

'So it appears that Shudde-M'ell *was* prisoned at G'harne.' I frowned. 'Which means that somehow he managed to escape! But how?'

'That's something we may never know. Henri, unless – ' Crow's eyes widened and his face went grey.

'Yes, what is it, Titus?'

'Well,' he slowly answered, 'I have a lot of faith in Alhazred, even in Feery's version. It's a monstrous thought, I know, but nevertheless it's just possible that the answer lies in what I've just read out: ". . . so wanes ye Power of all things – of ye Five-Pointed Star-Stone as of ye Spells put – "'

'Titus!' I cut him off. 'What you're saying is that the spells of the Elder Gods, the power of the pentacle is past – and if that's true . . .'

'I know,' he said. 'I know! It also means that Cthulhu and all the others must likewise be free to roam and kill and . . .'

He shook himself, as if breaking free from some monstrous spider's web, and managed a weak smile. 'But no, that can't be – no, we'd know about it if Cthulhu, Yog-Sothoth, Yibb-Tstll, and all the others were free. We'd have known long ago. The whole world . . .'

'Then how do you explain – '

'I make no attempt to explain anything, Henri,' he brusquely replied. 'I can only hazard guesses. It looks to me as though some years ago, anything up to a century ago, the spells or star-stones – whichever applies in Shudde-M'ell's case – were removed from G'harne by some means or other. Perhaps by accident, or there again, perhaps purposely . . . by persons in the power of the Great Old Ones!'

'Maliciously or inadvertently – by "persons in the power

77

of the Great Old Ones" – these I can understand,' I said, 'but accidentally? How do you mean, Titus?'

'Why! There are all kinds of natural accidents, Henri. Landslips, floods, volcanic eruptions, earthquakes – natural quakes, I mean – and any single one of them, occurring in the right place, could conceivably carry away the star-stones keeping one or more of these diverse horrors prisoned. This all provided, of course, that in Shudde-M'ell's case star-stones were the only prisoning devices!'

Listening to the occultist my mind suddenly whirled. For a moment I actually felt sick. 'Titus, wait! It's . . . too *fast* for me . . . too fast!' I made a conscious effort to calm myself.

'Look, Titus. My whole concept of things, everything, has turned upside down for me in one afternoon. I mean, I've always had this interest in the occult, the weird, the macabre, anything out of the ordinary, and at times it has been dangerous. Both of us, over the years, have experienced hideous dangers – *but this!* If I admit the existence of Shudde-M'ell – a lesser deity in a mythology which I believed could never exercise over me anything more than a passing interest – which now' – I glanced in loathing fascination at the box on the desk – 'it seems I *must* admit, then I must also believe in the existence of all the other related horrors! Titus, until today the Cthulhu Cycle of myth, granted that I've looked pretty deeply at it, was quite simply *myth*; fascinating and even, yes, dangerous – but only in the way that all occult studies are dangerous! Now – '

'Henri,' Crow cut in. 'Henri, if you feel that this is something you can't accept, the door is open. You're not involved yet, and there's nothing to stop you from keeping out of it. If you do decide, however, that you want to be in on this thing, then you're welcome – but you should know now that it may well be more dangerous than anything you ever came up against before!'

'It's not that I'm afraid, Titus; don't misunderstand,' I told him. 'It's simply the *size* of the concept! I *know* that there are extramundane occurrences, and I've had my share of experiences that can only be described as "supernatural", but they have always been the exception. You are asking me to believe that the Cthulhu Cycle of myth is nothing less than *prehistoric fact* – which means in effect that the very foundation of our entire sphere of existence is built on alien magic! If such is the case then "occult" is normal and Good grew out of Evil, as opposed to the doctrines of the Christian mythos!'

'I refuse to be drawn into a theological argument, Henri,' he answered. 'But that is my basic concept of things, yes. However, let's get one or two points quite clear, my friend. In the first place, for "Magic" read "Science".'

'I don't follow.'

'Brainwashing, Henri! The Elder Gods knew that they could never hope to imprison beings as powerful as the deities of the Cthulhu Cycle behind merely physical bars. They made their prisons *the minds of the Great Old Ones themselves* – perhaps even their bodies! They implanted mental and genetic blocks into the psyches and beings of the forces of evil and all their minions, that at the sight of – or upon sensing the presence of – certain symbols, or upon hearing those symbols reproduced as sound, those forces of evil are held back, impotent! This explains why comparatively simple devices such as the Mnaran starstones are effective, and why, in the event of such stones being removed from their prisoning locations, certain chants or written symbols may still cause the escaped powers to retreat.'

For a moment this explanation mazed me even more than before, but then I suspiciously asked: 'Titus, did you know all of this earlier, or is it just something you've freshly dreamed up?'

'The theory has been my own personal opinion for quite a long while, Henri, and it explains so many hitherto "inexplicable" things. I believe, too, that it is alluded to in a certain somewhat less than cryptic passage in the *Cthaat Aquadingen*. As you know, the book has a short chapter dedicated to "Contacting Cthulhu in Dreams"! Mercifully the actual devices required to perform this monstrously dangerous feat are given only in code – in practically impossible ciphers – and concern themselves in some unknown way with Nyarlathotep. Still, in the same chapter, the author makes a statement very relevant towards proving my own beliefs regarding the Elder Gods as scientists. I have a note here somewhere that I copied for easy reference.' He searched atop his littered desk.

'Ah! Here it is. It has quite definite parallels with much that's rather better known in the Cthulhu Cycle, and certainly seems to lend itself well to the most recent Christian mythos. Anyway, listen:

'"Ye Science as practised by a Majority of ye Prime Ones was & is & always will be that of ye Path of Light, infinitely recognized throughout Time, Space & all ye Angels as beneficent to ye *Great All's* Continuation. Certain of ye Gods, however, of a rebellious Nature, chose to disregard ye Dictums of ye Majority, & in ye constant Gloom of ye Dark Path renounced their immortal Freedom in Infinity & were banished to suitable Places in Space & Time. But even in Banishment ye Dark Gods railed against ye Prime Ones, so that those Followers of ye Light Path must needs shut them *Outside* of all Knowledge, imposing upon their Minds certain Strictures & ye Fear of ye Light Path's Ways, & impressing into their Bodies a Stigma defying Generation; that ye Sins of ye Fathers might be carried down through Eternity & visited upon ye Children & ye Children's children for ever; or until a Time should come as was once, when all Barriers crumble, & ye Stars & Dwellers therein, & ye Spaces between ye Stars & Dwellers therein, & all Time &

80

Angels & Dwellers therein be falsely guided into ye ultimate Night of ye Dark Path – until ye *Great All* close in & become One, & Azathoth come in His golden Glory, & Infinity begin again . . ."'

Crow paused at the end of his reading before saying, 'There's quite a bit that's obviously not relevant, of course, but in the main I believe – '

'Why didn't you tell me all this when I first arrived today?' I cut him off.

'You weren't ready for it, my friend.' He grinned mirthlessly. 'You're hardly ready now!'

I gave the matter some more thought. 'Then what you're really saying is that there is no such thing as the supernatural?'

'Correct!'

'But you've so often used the word, and recently, in its recognized context.'

'Purely out of habit, Henri, and because *your* concept of existence still admits its use – will do for some time, as will my own – until we get used to the idea.'

I mulled the matter over. 'The magic of the Elder Gods was a sort of psychiatric science,' I mused. 'You know, Titus, I can far easier face an alien concept than a supernatural one. Why! It all breaks down quite simply to this: that the combined forces of evil, the Great Old Ones, are nothing more than alien beings or forces against which it will be necessary to employ alien weapons.'

'Well, yes, basically. We shall have to fight these things with the weapons left us by the Elder Gods. With chants and incantations – scientifically implanted mental and genetic blocks – with the power of the pentacle, but mainly with the knowledge that they are *not* supernatural but simply *outside* forces.'

'But wait,' I still countered. 'What of the, well, "supernatural" occurrences, in all their various forms, which we've encountered in the past? Did they, too, spring from – '

'Yes, Henri, I have to believe they did. *All* such occurrences have their roots in the olden science of the Elder Gods, in a time before time. Now, how do you say, de Marigny – are you with me or – ?'

'Yes,' I answered without further hesitation; and I stood up to firmly grasp his outstretched hand across his great desk.

# 5

## Evil the Mind

*(From de Marigny's Notebooks)*

I did not get away from Blowne House until very late that
night, but at least I had an idea (for some reason still
more than somewhat vague) of the task before me. Crow
had not gone lightly on me, on the contrary, he had
always been a hard taskmaster, but I knew that on this
occasion he had taken by far the majority of the work
upon his own shoulders. As it happened, I was never to
commence work on that portion of the overall task
appointed to me; it would be pointless therefore to set it
down in detail.

This aside, then, we had worked out a system, apparently foolproof in its simplicity, whereby Shudde-M'ell
(or whichever of his brood led the English nests) would
be given more than a hard time, indeed an *impossible*
time, retrieving the four Harden eggs. Crow had written
three letters to trusted friends of his. One to an ancient
and extremely eccentric recluse living in Stornoway in the
Hebrides; another to an old American correspondent with
whom over the years he had exchanged many letters on
matters of folklore, myth, and similarly obscure anthropological subjects, a man his senior by a number of years,
the extremely erudite Wingate Peaslee, until recently
Professor of Psychology at Miskatonic University in
Massachusetts; and finally the third to an old charlatan of
a medium, known and endeared to him of old, one
Mother Quarry of Marshfield near Bristol.

The plot was this: without waiting for answers to the
letters, we would send the eggs first to Professor Peaslee
in America. Peaslee would of course receive his airmail

letter fractionally earlier than the air-parcel containing the eggs. Titus had more than enough faith in his friend to be satisfied that his instructions would be followed to the letter. Those instructions were simply to send the eggs on within twenty-four hours to Rossiter McDonald in Stornoway. Similarly McDonald was instructed to send them on without too great a delay to Mother Quarry, and from that 'talented'. lady they would eventually come back to me. I say 'back to me', because I took the box with me, neatly parcelled and ready to be posted, when I left Blowne House. I was to be instrumental in forging the first link in the postal chain. I also posted the letters on my way home.

I had agreed completely with my knowledgeable friend that the eggs must be out of Blowne House that night – indeed I had insisted upon it – for they had been there long enough already, and Crow had obviously started to feel the strain of their presence. He had admitted to nervously starting at every slightest creak of the floor-boards, and for the first time since moving into his singular and oddly-atmosphered bungalow dwelling he had started to jump at the groans of certain vociferous trees in his garden.

But knowing what he knew, and believing what he – no, what *we* – now believed, his nervousness was nothing if not natural. In fact, the presence of those eggs in his house above all else, quite apart from the fact that he had lately been grossly overworking, was responsible for the rapid deterioration of his general well-being since I last saw him. It would, I believed, not have taken very much more to start him on that same degenerative path taken by Sir Amery Wendy-Smith!

It may readily be understood why I hardly slept a wink that night, but lay in bed in my grey-stone house tossing and turning and chewing over in my mind the bulk of the new concept I had been asked to accept. In fact I *had* accepted it, but its details still needed thinking on, if only to clarify the overall picture and remove any remaining fuzz from its edges. Truth to tell, though, my mind did seem more than slightly foggy, as if I were suffering from some sort of hangover. But of course there was another, more immediate reason for my insomnia – the box with the lustrous spheres lay on a small table beside my bed!

Restlessly pummelling my pillow (which I found myself doing every half hour or so), I turned things over in my mind a dozen times, looking for loopholes and finding none – neither in Crow's immediate plot to stop the burrowers beneath from regaining possession of their eggs, nor in the premises of his incredible fears themselves – and yet I knew that there was something basically *wrong*! I knew it. The fault was there, submerged at the back of my mind, but would not rise to the surface.

If only this brain-fog would lift. My mood of crushing depression had vanished, true, but now I had this god-awful mental smog to wade through!

Of course, I did not know Crow's correspondents, his friends of old, personally; but he had tremendous faith in them, and especially in Peaslee. In his letter to the professor Crow had outlined his entire perception of the fantastic threat against Earth – hypothetically and yet strongly enough to hint of his personal involvement – and in my own opinion, putting myself in the position of a vastly intelligent man on receipt of such a letter, Crow had endangered his whole case. I had bluntly pointed out to him, after listening to a reading of the hastily scrawled letter, that Peaslee might see it as the ravings of a deranged mentality. As Crow himself had said: 'I'm damned if I know whom I might confide in . . .' But he had only chuckled at the suggestion, saying that he thought it unlikely, and that in any case, if only for past friendship's sake, Peaslee would comply with his requirements regarding the box of eggs.

He had reckoned on a maximum period of three weeks for the round trip of the eggs, but had taken the trouble to request in addition confirmatory letters with regard to their safe dispatch. I thought on this, and –

*There it was again!*

Now what *was* this twinge I kept getting at the back of my mind whenever I thought of the journey the eggs would commence in the morning?

But no, whenever I tried to nail the thing down it faded away, back into the mists of my mind. I had known this frustrating sensation before, and recognized the unsatisfactory solution: simply to ignore it and let the thing resolve itself in its own time. It was, nevertheless, annoying – and more than worrying in the circumstances.

Then, turning in my bed, my eyes would light on the box with its enigmatic contents, and I could picture those contents in my mind's eye, faintly luminous with that pearly sheen of theirs in the darkness of their cardboard coffin. That would set me off tangentially on yet another mental tack.

I had asked Crow about that *other* box, the 'incubator', discovered by Wendy-Smith at the site of dead G'harne. Why, I had wanted to know, had there been no similar receptacle in the tunnel-cave at Harden? But the tired occultist (should I call him 'occultist' or 'scientist'?) had been almost equally at a loss. He had finally hazarded, after giving the matter some thought, that possibly conditions in that deep dark place had been more nearly perfect for the incubation of the eggs than in the shallow hatchery at G'harne.

But what of the *pictures* on that box, I had further probed? – at which my learned friend had simply shuddered, saying that he might only direct me, as Sir Amery had once directed his nephew, to the works of Commodus and the hag-ridden Caracalla. The pictures in his dreams had been more than enough without dwelling on the horrors others had known; for there had been more than simply blind, cephalopod obscenity to those nightmares of his. Likewise he believed that Bentham's cave-pictures had contained far more than the man had cared to mention – and perhaps understandably! This had whetted my curiosity all the more, so that I had pressed Crow until finally he had given in to me and described, all too clearly, some of those pictures of his dreams.

In some of them, he had told me, there had been an almost symbolic reaching towards the surface, a group-stretching of hideous tentacles; and in others, plainly surface scenes as opposed to subterrene – in those there had been sheer horror!

Vividly I remembered Crow's mode of *expression*, the cracked hollowness of his voice as he had said: 'There were four of them in one dream-fragment, de Marigny, rearing like caterpillars on their haunches, mouths agape – and they had a woman between them, pulling her to pieces and slobbering while the blood gushed and slopped . . .'

'But how,' I had morbidly demanded, my voice a whisper, 'could creatures without heads have . . . *mouths*?' Even asking my question I had known that I would not like the answer.

'Try thinking in less routine terms, Henri,' Crow had quietly advised. 'But whatever you do don't think on it too long, or with too great an attention to detail. They're so very – *alien* – these things.'

The memory of Crow's words and the way he had said them saw me reaching from my bed in one convulsive instant to switch on the light. I could not help it but a line from Ibn Schacabao's ancient and cryptic *Reflections* had sprung unbidden to my mind, a line I knew had been repeated by Alhazred in the *Necronomicon*: 'Evil the mind that is held by no head!' Ye gods! Minds and mouths without heads!

I am not normally a nervous man – God knows that if such were the case I should long ago have given up certain of my more *outré* interests – but with those eggs in their box beside my bed, and with the knowledge that somewhere, far away or perhaps not so far, deep down in the earth, monstrous burrowers *even now* burned and bubbled in the ground – well, who could say that merely illuminating my bedroom was an act of cowardice?

But in any case, even with the light on, I found myself no less apprehensive. There were shadows now where none had been before – thrown by my wardrobe, my dressing gown hanging on the door – so that before I knew it I found myself calculating how long it would take me to get out of bed and through the window in the event of –

I reached out again to switch off the light, purposely turning my back on the cardboard box in an attempt to put its contents from my mind . . .

Perhaps I did sleep then for a little while, for I remember a merging of my own drowsing thoughts with Crow's descriptions of some of his dreams as I recalled their telling; and when this brought me sweatingly back to wakefulness I also remembered his explanation of how he had first been alerted to the existence of the cthonian menace.

It had been those chants heard in his latter dreams of the burrowers; those chants containing the tell-tale name of a legendary city – G'harne! Remembering Wendy-Smith's expedition in search of that place, and something of the disastrous results, and then tying in certain of the newer contents of his voluminous cuttings-file and the details of his underground nightmares themselves, Crow had been led on to the Wendy-Smith document. That document, along with the letter of explanation obtained from Raymond Bentham, had clinched the thing in his mind. The remainder had been merely his normal follow-through of intelligently applied, if weirdly-inspired, logic.

We had also talked on the spread of Shudde-M'ell and his kin, and had given more thought to the horror's release from the prison of the Elder Gods. Crow was inclined to the belief that some natural cataclysm had freed the horror-deity, and I could see no better explanation, but *how long ago* had this convulsion of the Earth occurred – and how far had the cancer spread since then? Wendy-Smith had seemed concerned with the same problem, but Crow had seen Sir Amery's suggestions regarding a means of combating the creatures as ludicrous.

'Think of it, de Marigny, ' he had told me. 'Just *think* of trying to destroy the likes of Shudde-M'ell with flamethrowers! Why, these beings themselves are almost volcanic. They must be! Think of the temperatures and pressures required to fuse carbon and chrysolite and whatever else into the diamond-dust composition of those eggshells! And their ability to burn their way through solid rock. Flamethrowers? Hah! They'd delight in the very flames! It truly amazes me, though, the changes these beings must go through between infancy and adulthood. And yet, is it really so surprising? Human beings, I suppose, go through equally fantastic alterations – infancy, puberty, menopause, senility – and what about the amphibians, frogs, and toads . . . and the lepidopterous cycle? Yes, I can quite believe that Sir Amery killed off those two "babies" of his with a cigar – but by God it will take something more than that for an adult!'

And on the secret, subterranean spread of the horrors since that tremendous blunder of nature which he believed had freed them, Crow had likewise had his own ideas:

'Disasters, Henri! Look at the list of disasters caused by so-called "natural" seismic shocks, particularly in the last hundred years. Oh, I know we can't blame every tremor on Shudde-M'ell – if he, or *it*, still survives as godhead to its race – but, by heaven, we can certainly tag him with some of them! We already have the list put together by Paul Wendy-Smith; not big stuff, but costing lives nevertheless. Chinchon, Calahorra, Agen, Aisne, and so on. But what about Agadir? My God, but wasn't *that* a horror? And Agadir is not far off the route they took to England back in 1933. Look at the *size* of Africa, Henri. Why! In the other direction the things could have spread themselves all over that great continent by now – the entire Middle East even! It all depends on how many they were originally. And yet, there couldn't have been too many, despite Wendy-Smith's "hordes". No, I don't think that the Elder Gods would ever have allowed that. But who knows how many eggs have hatched since then, or how many others are still waiting to hatch in unsuspected depths of rock? The more I think of it, the more hideous the threat grows in my mind.'

Finally, before I had left him, Crow had tiredly scribbled for me a list of books he believed I should research. The *Necronomicon* of course headed the list, for the connection of that book with the Cthulhu Cycle of myth was legendary. My friend had recommended the expurgated manuscript translation (in a strictly limited edition for scholarly study only), by Henrietta Montague from the British Museum's black-letter. He had known Miss Montague personally, had been by her side when she died of some unknown wasting disease only a few weeks after completing her work on the *Necronomicon* for the Museum authorities. I knew that my friend blamed that work for her death; which was one of the reasons why he had warned me time and time again regarding too comprehensive a study of the book's contents. It was therefore understood that I should merely extract those sections directly concerning Shudde-M'ell and beings like him but keep, as far as possible, from becoming too involved with the book as a whole. Crow himself would arrange for a copy of Miss Montague's scholarly work to be put at my disposal.

Next on the list had been Ibn Schacabao's *Reflections*, also at the British Museum but under glass because of its short life expectancy. Although the museum had taken the usual precautions – chemical treatment had been applied, photostat copies made (one of which I would have to read, and more thoroughly than at that time some years previously) – still the venerable tome was gradually rotting away.

The list continued with two little known books by Commodus and Caracalla respectively, simply for the sake of their authors having been given mention by Wendy-Smith, and directly after these there followed the translated sections of the almost unfathomable *Pnakotic Manuscript* for the same reason. Similarly was Eliphas Lévi's *History of Magic* listed, and finally, this time from Crow's own shelves (he had carefully wrapped it for me), his copy of the infamous *Cultes des Goules*. He had scanned the latter book so often himself that he was fearful of missing something important in a further personal perusal. On my inquiring, he told me he did, however, intend to give special personal attention to the *Cthaat Aquadingen*; there was much in that hideously bound book – particularly in the two middle chapters, which Crow long ago had had separately bound – that might very well apply. Most of these writings, as I have previously stated, I had read before, but without a definite purpose other than occult and macabre curiosity.

It could, I suppose, be reasoned that my itinerary should also include the *G'harne Fragments*, and of course it would have, if that mass of crumbling, centuried shards had been in any one of the four languages with which I am familiar! As it was, there had been only two supposed authorities on the fragments: Sir Amery Wendy-Smith, who left nothing of his decipherings behind, and Professor Gordon Walmsley of Goole, whose 'spoof notes' contained what purported to be whole chapters of translations from the *G'harne Fragments*' cryptic ciphers, but which had been mocked as absurd fakery by any number of reliable authorities. For these reasons Crow had omitted the fragments from his list.

All these and other thoughts flew around in my strangely misty mind, until eventually I must have drowsed off again.

My next remembered thought was that of hearing, seemingly close at hand, the dreadful droning and buzzing of monstrously alien voices – but it was not until I found myself awake and leaping from my bed on wildly trembling legs, my hair standing up straight on my head, that I realized I had only been dreaming. The sun was already up, filling the day outside with light.

And yet even then there echoed in my ears those loathsome, monotonously buzzing tones of horror. And they were in my mind exactly as they had been in Wendy-Smith's document:

> Ce'haiie ep-ngh fl'hur G'harne fhtagn,
> Ce'haiie fhtagn ngh Shudde-M'ell.
> Hai G'harne orr'e ep fl'hur,
> Shudde-M'ell ican-icanicas fl'hur orr'e G'harne.

As the thing finally faded away and disappeared, I shook my head and numbly moved back over to my bedside table to pick up the cardboard box and feel its weight. I examined the box minutely, still more than half asleep. I honestly do not know what I expected to find, but I found nothing. All was as it had been the night before.

I washed, shaved, and dressed, and had hardly returned from mailing the parcel of eggs to Professor Peaslee from a local post office – all done very lethargically – when the telephone rang. It was quite insistent, clamouring like mad, but for some reason I hesitated before picking it up to put the receiver timorously to my ear.

'De Marigny? It's Crow here.' My friend's voice was urgent, electrical. 'Listen. Have you sent off the eggs yet?'

'Why, yes – I just managed to catch the morning post.'

'Oh, no!' he groaned; then: 'Henri, do you still have that houseboat at Henley?'

'Why, yes. In fact, it's been in use until recently. Some friends of mine. I told them they could have it for a week just before I went to France. They're off the boat now, though; I got the key back in a little parcel in last night's mail. But why?' Despite my question I felt oddly listless, growing more disinterested by the second.

'Pack yourself some things, Henri, enough to live with decently for a fortnight or so. I'll pick you up within the hour in the Mercedes. I'm just loading my stuff now.'

'Eh?' I asked, completely uncomprehending, not really wanting to know. 'Stuff?' The mists were thick in my mind. 'Titus' – I heard myself as if from a hundred miles away – 'what's wrong?'

'Everything is *wrong*, Henri, and in particular my reasoning! Haven't you heard the morning news or read the newspapers?'

'No,' I answered through a wall of thickening fog. 'I'm just up. Slept badly.'

'Bentham is dead, de Marigny! The poor devil – a "subsidence" at Alston. We're going to have to drastically revise our thinking. The houseboat is a godsend.'

'Eh? What?'

'The houseboat, Henri! It's a godsend! Like Sir Amery said: "They don't like water." I'll see you within the hour.'

'Titus,' I gropingly answered, barely managing to catch him before he could break the connection, 'not today, for God's sake! I . . . I really don't feel up to it. I mean . . . it's a damned nuisance – '

'Henri, I – ' He faltered, amazement in his voice; then, in a tone full of some strange understanding: 'So, they've been at you, have they?' Now he was deliberate and calm. 'Well, not to worry. Be seeing you.' And with that the line went dead.

I don't know how much later it was when the infernal banging came at my door, and the ringing at my doorbell, but for quite a long time I simply ignored it. Then, despite an urge to close my eyes and go back to sleep where I sat in my chair, I managed to get up and go to the door. Yawningly I opened it – and was almost bowled over as a frenzied figure in black rushed in.

It was of course Titus Crow – but his eyes were blazing in a strange and savage passion completely alien to his character as I had previously known it!

# 6

## That is Not Dead

*(From de Marigny's Notebooks)*

'De Marigny!' Crow exploded as soon as he was inside
and had the door shut behind him. 'Henri, you've been
got at!'

'Eh? Got at?' I sleepily replied. 'No such thing, Titus –
I'm tired, that's all.' Yet despite my odd lethargy I was
still slightly curious. 'How do you mean, "Got at"? By
whom?'

Quickly taking my arm and leading me, half dragging
me to my own study, he answered: 'Why, the burrowers
beneath, of course! Your place isn't protected as Blowne
House is. I might have expected as much. To leave you
with those things all night. Even my place hasn't got full
protection – far from it.'

'Protection?' My brief interest was already on the wane,
so that when I flopped down again in my easy chair I was
hardly bothered whether he answered me or not. 'Really,
you do make a fuss, old man!' (I had never before in my
life called Titus Crow 'old man'; I probably never will
again.) I felt my eyes closing, listening to my own voice
almost abstractedly as it rambled slowly, falteringly on:

'Look. I've had a bad night, got up too early. I'm very
tired – very tired . . .'

'Yes, that's right, you have yourself a nap, Henri,' he
told me in a soothing voice. 'I can manage what needs to
be done on my own.'

'Manage?' I mumbled. 'Something needs to be done?'

Peering through half closed lids I saw that Crow had
already started – but what was he doing? His eyes were
wide, blazing fanatically as he stood in the centre of my

95

room with his arms and hands held open and up in a typically sorcerous stance. This time, however, Titus Crow was not conjuring anything, but rather *putting something down* – or at least, holding something back, if only temporarily.

I have since recognized the alien syllables he used then, in Feery's *Notes on the Necronomicon* (I still have not read any other copy of the work, in any form), where they appear as follows:

> Ya na kadishtu nilgh'ri stell'bsna Nyogtha,
> K'yarnak phlegethor l'ebumna syha'h n'ghft,
> Ya hai kadishtu ep r'luh-eeh Nyogtha eeh,
> S'uhn-ngh athg li'hee orr'e syha'h.

When he had done with the Vach-Viraj Incantation, for his fantastic utterances had consisted of nothing less, Crow proceeded to take from his pocket a small vial of clear liquid which he sparingly splashed about the room. Still splashing, he went out into the other rooms to continue this cryptic occupation until my entire house had been cleansed; I knew, of course, that my friend's activities were exorcismal.

Nor were his thaumaturgies pointless or to no effect, for, already feeling more my old self, I knew that Crow had been right – I *had* been under the influence of Shudde-M'ell, his brothers or minions.

As soon as he reentered my study Crow saw that I was back to normal and grinned in a self-satisfied if nervous manner. By that time, shaken though I naturally was, I was already packing books and papers into a large case. My mazed mind, as if vacuum-cleaned, had been emptied of all enfeebling thoughts and ideas by my friend's 'White Magic'; or rather, by the 'Science' of the Elder Gods!

It took me only the matter of a further half hour or so to complete my packing (I made certain to include a favourite fetish of mine, a rather old and ornate pistol, once the property of the witch-hunting Baron Kant), lock the house up, and accompany Titus out to his Mercedes with my cases. Moments later we were on our way.

We made three stops on our way out to Henley, the first of which was to allow us to get off hurried telegrams to Mother Quarry, McDonald, and Professor Peaslee, warning them in no uncertain manner to send off the parcel of eggs *as soon as it arrived* without first opening it, and hinting strongly of grave dangers should they delay even in the slightest. This of course had been made necessary by the death of Bentham; an explanation may be in order and I will give it later. The second stop was for lunch at Beaconsfield, where we found a friendly pub and sat out in a small sunny garden to enjoy cold beer with chicken sandwiches. The third call was at an adequate library in Marlow, where Crow was obliged to become a member in order to borrow a number of anthropological works supplementary to those we already had with us.

By 3:30 P.M. we were aboard *Seafree*, my four-berth houseboat, and getting ourselves settled in. Where I had her moored, at a spot some distance out of Henley itself, the Thames is quite deep and Crow seemed satisfied that we were safe there for the moment from any physical manifestations of the burrowers. After we had made the place immediately livable and packed our stuff away, we were able to sit down and talk seriously of the fresh developments. The drive down to Henley, apart from our stops, had in the main been quiet; Crow dislikes being distracted while driving, and I had had time to sort out fresh points to raise and questions to ask during the journey.

Now I could learn the hows and whys of my friend's earlier obscure exorcismal activities on my behalf at my house. Crow told me of the Black-Letter Text *Necron-omicon* – notably the Kester Library copy in Salem, Massachusetts – which contains the following passage, incomplete in Feery's notes but known to Titus Crow of old:

Men know him as the Dweller in Darkness, that brother of the Old Ones called Nyogha, the Thing that should not be. He can be summoned to Earth's surface through certain secret caverns and fissures, and sorcerers have seen him in Syria and below the Black Tower of Leng; from the Thang Grotto of Tartary he has come ravening to bring terror and destruction among the pavilions of the great Khan. Only by the Looped Cross, by the Vach-Viraj Incantation and by the Tikkoun Elixir may he be driven back to the nighted caverns of hidden foulness where he dwelleth.

Thus, as a protection against this Nyogtha, I could well understand the use of the Vach-Viraj Incantation – but against the burrowers . . .? Crow explained that he had used the chant at my house because he believed *all* the Cthulhu Cycle Earth deities to be related, either physically or mentally, and that any charm having definite power against any one of them must be capable of at least *some* influence over the others. Indeed, the immediate effect of his – occult? – remedies had been to clear my place (not to mention my mind) of the influences exerted through dreams of Shudde-M'ell or his deputies; which was more really than Crow had expected. However, he also explained that he believed the chant and elixir to have no lasting strength, except against Nyogtha – who or whatever he may be! – but he has never explained to me just what further 'protections' there are about Blowne House. I suspect, though, that these are far superior to any signs, sigils, runes, or cantrips of which I am ever likely to become aware.

* * *

The next four days passed quickly at Henley, and were taken up mainly in making *Seafree* more livable and in long think-tank sessions between Crow and myself on our various problems. Had I not been around at that time to supply the obvious words of exoneration, I believe Crow might well have started to blame himself for Bentham's death. I pointed out that knowing as little of the burrowers as we knew, which had been even less at the time Crow last wrote to the Northerner, his advice to Bentham in the matter had been expert. In fact, looking back on it, I was now surprised at the amount of time it had taken the Cthonians (the name Crow eventually settled on for the subterranean spawn) to seek Bentham out and deal with him! Harden is not all that far from Alston. Crow had insisted, however, that there had been a direct parallel – one which he had missed in what, according to him, had been tantamount to criminal neglect.

He referred of course to Paul Wendy-Smith's disappearance – that vanishment which we now knew must be laid at the door, or burrow, of the Cthonians – following that of his uncle, and which had occurred *after* the discovery of their cigar-murdered infants by the Cthonians. It was all too apparent now that one did not need to be in actual possession of those crystal spheres to attract adults of the species. Having *been* in possession – even in close contact – seemed reason enough to provoke hideous retaliation; which explained, naturally, Crow's haste in getting himself out of Blowne House and both of us out of London in the first place! Too (I had realized immediately), this had been the elusive something flickering at the back of my mind that night before the Cthonians first 'invaded' me; by token of which I knew that, if blame existed at all, I must hold myself equally to blame alongside Crow. The simple fact that Paul Wendy-Smith had never actually possessed the eggs, but the Cthonians had nevertheless taken him, should have made itself apparent to both of us sooner.

And yet, even in my houseboat on the Thames, which Crow had at first proclaimed safe, over the last few days my erudite friend had grown ever the more nervous and far from happy regarding our continued well-being. The Cthonians could still find us, or so he seemed to believe, through dreams. In this, as in so many things, Crow proved to be absolutely correct.

Because of the possibility of our eventual discovery, we had early decided that our first task would be to see if we could find any *positive* counterspells (Crow referred to them as 'devices' – I preferred to think in the old 'magic' terms) against an attack. We could not, after all, remain on the houseboat indefinitely; in fact we had already taken to relaxing for an hour or so each evening in the bar of a pub not one hundred yards away down the river bank, well within sprinting distance of *Seafree*! In the furtherance of this project I had given over most of my time to correlating all the written knowledge at my disposal on the pentacle, the five-pointed Star of Power, whose design had been originated by the Great Elder Gods in the construction of their evil-imprisoning star-stones.

Now, to my mind it is not surprising that much is made of the pentacle or pentagram in so-called 'cabalistic' works – the paperback junk which clutters so many modern bookstalls, supposedly culled from the great forbidden books – but quite apart from such references I found many disturbing tangential allusions in fairly contemporary verse, in literature, even in art. Admittedly, such works as contained these oblique or obscure references were generally by persons deeply attracted to things mysterious or macabre – mystics, mages, and usually (broadly speaking) persons gifted with rare imaginations and paradoxically *outré* insight – but nevertheless the 'pentacle theme' seemed, at one time or another, to have captured the imaginations of an inordinately large number of these artistic people.

Gerhardt Schrach, the Westphalian philosopher, has said: 'It fascinates me . . . that such a perfect figure can be drawn with only five straight lines . . . five triangles, joined at their bases, where they form a pentagon . . . perfectly pentameral . . . *powerful* . . . and fascinating!' It was Schrach, too, in his *Thinkers Ancient and Modern*, who pointed out for me the Hittite practice of spreading the fingers of one hand before the face of an enemy or evil person and saying: 'The Star upon thee, Dark One!' – which was recognized as a certain protection against the evil intentions of any person so confronted.

Other than Schrach and many other contemporary writers and philosophers, there were also a number of painters whose works, I knew, had from time to time featured the star motif: noticeably Chandler Davies in many of his designs for *Grotesque* before that magazine folded; particularly his full-page black and white 'Stars and Faces', so strangely disturbing and horrific that it was now in itself a valuable collector's item. William Blake too, the painter, poet, and mystic, had not neglected the theme, and had used it strikingly in his 'Portrait of a Flea' – in which the central horror is actually *prisoned by five-pointed stars!* And while I knew the point could be argued, still, remembering Blake's stars, I found them disturbingly akin to my own mental picture of the star-stones of ancient Mnar.

On the other hand, in Edmund Pickman Derby's book of nightmare lyrics, *Azathoth and Other Horrors*, there was one clearly blatant reference to the five-pointed star as a weapon against 'Greater Gods by far', whatever gods he alluded to; and such were the other many references to be discovered that I soon found myself interested in my task almost beyond the present requirement.

It was on the fourth night, while I was making notes of this sort and trying to find in them some sort of order or clue, that Titus dozed off. He had been working hard all that day – not physical work but intense mental concentration – and had actually fallen asleep over his copy of the *Cthaat Aquadingen*. I noticed the fact and smiled. It was good that he should get some rest: I was already fatigued myself, both physically and mentally, and Crow had been familiar with the problem far longer than I.

Shortly before midnight I too must have dozed off, for the first thing I knew was that someone was shouting.

It was Crow.

I came awake immediately from monstrous dreams (mercifully unremembered considering what was soon to come), to find my friend still asleep but locked in the throes of nightmare.

He was sitting in his chair, his head forward on his folded arms where they rested on the open *Cthaat Aquadingen* atop the small table at which he had been working. His whole body was jerking and twitching spasmodically and he was shouting snatches of incomprehensible occult jargon. I hastened from my chair to waken him.

'Eh? What?' he gasped as I shook him. 'Look out, de Marigny – *they're here!*' He jumped to his feet, shaking visibly, cold sweat glistening upon his face. 'They . . . they're . . . here?'

He sat down again, still trembling, and poured himself a glass of brandy. 'My God! What a nightmare, Henri! They've managed to get through to me this time, all right – picked my brains clean, I imagine. They'll know where we are now, for sure.'

'The Cthonians? It was . . . them?' I breathlessly asked.

'Oh, yes! Definitely. And they made no pretext, didn't bother to hide their identity. I had the impression they were trying to tell me something – attempting to, well, *bargain* with me. Hah! That would be like making a pact with all the devils of hell! And yet there were tones of desperation, too, in the messages I received. Damned if I know what *they* could be frightened of. I simply had the feeling that we're not alone in all this, that reinforcements are being rushed up to the front, as it were! Damned peculiar.'

'I don't follow you, Titus,' I said, shaking my head. 'You're being a bit vague, you know.'

'Then I'd best tell you all my dream contained, Henri, and then we'll see what you make of it,' he replied.

'First off, there were no pictures, no visual hallucinations – which, it could be argued, are what dreams are really made of – but merely . . . *impressions!* I was floating in a greyness, the colourless substance of the subconscious psyche, if you like, and these . . . *impressions* . . . kept coming to me. I knew it was the Cthonians – their thoughts, their mental sendings, are so very alien – but I couldn't shut them out of my mind. They were telling me to stop interfering, to let sleeping dogs lie. What do you make of that?'

Before I could answer, even if I had an answer, he hurriedly continued:

'Then I got these fear-impressions I mentioned, a nameless dread of some obscure, ill-defined possibility with which I was somehow involved. I don't know for sure, but I don't think it was intended that I should read these fear-impressions. I'm a fraction more psychic than these horrors are used to, I suspect – a fact well in our favour. But overall it was, I don't know, as if they were trying to *bribe* me! "Get out while you can, Titus Crow, and we'll leave you alone," sort of thing. "You don't have our eggs any more and so we're willing to lose interest in

103

you – provided you'll leave us alone and not go meddling where you're not wanted!"'

'Then we're on the right track, Titus,' I broke in. 'We've got them worried!'

He looked at me, more under control now, and slowly grinned. 'It certainly seems so, de Marigny, but I wish to God I knew what it is they're so worried about! Still, as you say, we must be on the right track. It's good to know that, at least. I'd love to know, though, where Peaslee and the others fit in –'

'What's that, Titus?' I asked. Again he had lost me.

'I'm sorry, Henri, of course you can't follow me,' he quickly apologized. 'You see, there were in these impressions *references* – don't ask me to clarify – to Peaslee and certain others; like Bernard Jordan, the skipper of one of those seagoing drilling-rigs I was telling you about. He was a very lucky man, according to my cuttings. The lone survivor when his rig, *Sea-Maid*, went to the bottom off Hunterby Head. And there was mention of someone else, someone I've never even heard of before. Hmm,' he mused, frowning. 'Now who on earth is David Winters? Anyway, I had the feeling that the Cthonians were far more afraid of these other chaps than they could ever be of me! I was warned, in effect, to keep away from these other people. Rather astonishing, really. After all, I've never met Professor Peaslee in the flesh, and I couldn't even guess at where to begin looking for this Jordan chap. And as for David Winters, well . . .'

'You were screaming, Titus,' I told him, holding his shoulder. 'You were shouting something or other which I couldn't quite make out. Now what was all that about?'

'Ah! That would have been my denial, Henri. Of course, I refused their ultimatum. I tried to throw spells at them, particularly the Vach-Viraj Incantation, to get them out of my mind. But it didn't work. En masse, their minds were too strong for such simple devices. They overcame them easily.'

'Ultimatum?' I questioned. 'There were . . . threats?'

'Yes, and horrible threats,' he grimly answered. 'They told me – that they would "show me their powers", in some sort of way or other, which was when you woke me up. Anyway, they're not rid of me yet, not by a long shot, but we may have to move on from here. Three or four more days is about as much time as we can afford to stay, I should think, before moving on.'

'Yes,' I answered. 'Well, frankly, I couldn't move tonight at gunpoint. I'm dead on my feet. Let's get some sleep, if they'll let us, and make fresh plans tomorrow.'

For myself, I did get to sleep áll right – I *was* quite 'dead on my feet' – but I can't speak for Titus Crow. I know that I seemed in my slumbers to hear his voice, low and muttering, and that it seemed a very long time before the echoes of the Vach-Viraj Incantation and certain other runes of elder spheres faded in the caves of my subconscious.

Strangely, by noon the next day we were better settled in our minds, as if the knowledge that the Cthonians had found something to fear in us had lifted momentarily the bleak veil of strange dread, nervous tension and mental fatigue that had been hanging over us.

It had not been difficult to reason out just why it had taken Shudde-M'ell's nightmare brothers so long to discover our hideaway. Up until the previous night, Crow had been using the Vach-Viraj Incantation and the Tikkoun Elixir nightly, when, at last, he had run out of the latter. Evidently the liquid which compounded that strange and potent brew (I was later to learn just what it was) had had much to do with keeping the Cthonian dream-sendings and -searchings at bay, Plainly, this late

105

deficiency in our defences had been sufficient to allow them to find our subconscious minds and thus discover our location.

Later it was to become plain why the knowledge that our whereabouts was known to the Cthonians did not panic us; why Crow's dream, rather than startling us into headlong flight, had served instead – after the initial shock – to calm us down.

As it was, we reasoned that if the burrowers did indeed intend to make an attack, well, they still had the water of the river to combat, and in any case they were unlikely to attempt anything in the daylight hours. The obvious trick, if the Cthonians could manage it, would be to lure us from *Seafree* of an evening after dark, an eventuality against which we made precautionary plans. At last light each evening, until we left the houseboat for good, we would simply lock the cabin-cum-sleeper door (equipped with a stout padlock on the inside), and, since I seemed more susceptible to the dream-sendings of the Cthonians, Crow would keep the key. It now seems amazing to me that once again we both failed to see a parallel which, obvious as it should have been, proved us both totally at fault in our reasoning; simply that Paul Wendy-Smith had been taken *in daylight*, or dusk at the very latest! However, our plan, faulty as it was, meant that we would have to deny ourselves the occasional evening trip to the Old Mill Inn.

Now, I don't want to give the impression that we two were alcoholics – though we might have had very good reasons to become such – but Crow did like his brandy of a night, and I am not averse to a noggin myself. We had already stocked up with provisions for a fortnight, and so decided we had best do the same regarding liquid refreshments. With this in mind we decided on lunch at the Old Mill Inn, when we would also purchase a bottle or two.

Our timing was perfect, for we had no sooner seated ourselves in the smoke-room when the ex-Guardsman proprietor came over to our table. We had of course met him before, but on this occasion he introduced himself properly and Crow reciprocated on our behalf.

'Ah! So you *are* Mr Crow! Well, that saves me a walk down to the houseboat.'

'Oh?' Crow's interest picked up. 'Did you want to see me, then? Do sit down, Mr Selby. Will you join us in a drink?'

The huge proprietor thanked us, went over to the bar and poured himself a half-pint from a bottle, then returned with his glass and sat down. 'Yes,' he began, 'I had a telephone call for you this morning – very garbled and hard to understand – from someone who was checking on your being here. Told me you'd be using the houseboat *Seafree*. I said I wasn't sure of your names, but that there were two gentlemen on the houseboat.'

'Did he say who he was?' Puzzled as to who might know of our whereabouts, I got the question in before Crow. I could see that my friend was equally at a loss.

'Yes, sir,' he answered me. 'I wrote his name down on a scrap of paper. Here we are.' He dug into his waistcoat pocket. 'Said he'd drop in on you this evening – if you were still here. The conversation was a bit confused, but I gathered he was calling from a booth somewhere nearby. Anything wrong, sir?'

Titus had taken the slip of paper and read it. His already tired face, at a stroke, had gone deathly white. His hands shook violently as he passed me the slip. I took it from him and smoothed it down on the tabletop.

I took a sip at my drink – *and then choked on it as the meaning of what was scrawled on the paper finally drove home!*

It was, as Selby had said, simply a name:
Amery Wendy-Smith!

# 7

# *Not from His Charnel Clay*

## *(From de Marigny's Notebooks)*

All afternoon and until 10:30 that night – earlier on deck, later in the light of a paraffin-lamp in the cabin – Crow and I talked in awed whispers on the fantastic vistas opened by the totally unpredictable 'message' we had received at the inn.

It made no difference that all day long the sun had blazed roastingly down on the river from the glorious June sky, or that small river-craft had been purring upstream and down by the dozen while lovers walked on the green banks and waved to us at our mooring. For us the physical warmth of the sun had been chilled by the fearful knowledge of that horror which lurked deep beneath England's unique green; and though the songs of the birds and the laughter of the couples had been loud enough, we had talked, as I have said, in hushed whispers.

For Crow had made no bones of his firm belief that Sir Amery was indeed dead, and that therefore this latest . . . *manifestation* . . . was nothing less than another gambit of the Cthonians. Had there been a third player in our game – that is, someone who like Crow and myself knew of the dreadful activities of the burrowers beneath – then we *might* have been able to lay the blame for this latest shock at that person's feet; but there was no one. In any case, the telephone call would have been a pretty gruesome leg-pull.

And of course Crow was absolutely right in his assertion. He had to be. The unknown caller could not possibly be Sir Amery Wendy-Smith; I knew that as soon as I was able to give the matter a little reasonable thought. Why,

Sir Amery had been anything but a young man back in 1937. Now? He would be well on his way towards his centenary! Few men live so long, and fewer still manage to *live and hide themselves away*, for no apparent reason, for over a third of their century!

No, I was as sure as Titus Crow that this was simply another ruse of the Cthonians. How they had pulled it off was another matter. Crow had pondered the possibility (very briefly), that his closest neighbour, an ecclesiastical doctor who lived a hundred yards or so from Blowne House, might have been responsible for the stunning 'message'; for apparently he had given the good reverend our forwarding address prior to leaving Blowne House. He had also asked this same gentleman to accept transferred telephone calls for him, which had been agreed, but had warned him to divulge our whereabouts only to bona fida persons. It seemed that the doctor had assisted him on a number of ticklish occasions before. But this time not even that worthy had known of Crow's reason for rushing off to Henley, and he had probably never even heard of Sir Amery Wendy-Smith. In fact, *no one* knew of our reason for being at Henley – except, since last night, the Cthonians themselves!

And yet, what could the burrowers possibly hope to gain from so transparent a ploy? This was a question I had put to my friend, to which he had answered:

'Well, Henri, I think we'd better ask "how" before we ask "why" – I like to see the whole picture whenever it's possible. I've been giving it some thought, though, and it seems to me that our phantom telephone caller must be a person "under the influence" of the Cthonians. I imagine they must have such – assistants, a point we'd best look out for in the future. We've been thinking in terms of horror and hideous death at the hands – the tentacles – of monstrous subterranean beings, but we can just as easily

109

die from gunshot wounds! Now then, taking all that into account, we can ask ourselves why did the Cthonians use so transparent a ploy, as you had it, and I believe I know the answer.'

For once I foresaw his conclusion: 'I think I see what you're getting at.'

'Oh?'

'Yes. We've both stated over the last few days that we think we're pretty safe here on the houseboat, though you have had your doubts. Now, just suppose that *They* think so too; that *They* can't touch us physically while we're here. Why, the obvious solution would be to get us out of here, scare us into abandoning the boat and taking to dry land!'

'Right,' he answered. 'And this impossible telephone call serves as a second persuasion, to follow up the warning dream the Cthonians sent me last night. Go on, de Marigny.'

'Well, that's it!' I cried. 'That's all there is to it. Following your dream, this message – which we know must have its origin with the Cthonians – was simply to give their warning substance; to let us know that we're far from safe here, and that our best bet is to – '

'To get the hell out of it?'

'Yes.'

'So what do you suggest?'

'That we stay *right where we are!*'

'Yes,' he answered, 'and that's exactly what we're going to do! It begins to look more and more to me as though we're as safe here as we can be. As you say, this makes the second Cthonian attempt to get us away from the river – which is, I agree, a damn good reason for us to stay put! So, for the time being at least, we'll stay. We have at least two weapons against them: the river and the Vach-Viraj Incantation.' He frowned thoughtfully. 'We should have more of the Tikkoun Elixir shortly, by the way, if the Reverend Harry Townley keeps his promise. Townley's the neighbour I told you about. He said he'd send me on a supply; and he's never let me down before.'

'The Reverend Townley?' I frowned. 'The Tikkoun Elixir . . . ?'

The answer slotted itself neatly into place in my mind. 'You mean that the elixir is – '

'Yes, of course,' he answered, nodding his head, surprise showing on his face. 'Hadn't I mentioned it before?' He tossed me the empty vial, the contents of which had been used so well. 'Oh, yes! Holy Water, what else? We know already of Shudde-M'ell's hatred of water, so naturally water which carries in addition a blessing – well, it's potent against many a horror besides the Cthonians, believe me!'

'And how about the Looped Cross?' I asked, remembering the three forces potent against Nyoghtha as delineated in the *Necronomicon*. 'Does the Crux Ansata indeed have similar powers?'

'I believe so, yes, to a degree. I had meant to mention it to you earlier, last night when you were working on the star-stone theme. What do you have, Henri, if you break the loop at the top of the Crux Ansata?'

I pictured the image his words conjured in my mind – then snapped my fingers. 'Why! A symbol with *five* extremities, a crude representation of the Elder Sign, the prisoning star of the Cthulhu Cycle of myth!'

'Indeed, and the looped Tau Cross in Olden Khem was also a symbol of power – and a great symbol of generation! It was the *Ankh*, Henri! The very word means "soul" or "life" – a protection of life and soul. Oh, yes, I should certainly believe that the Crux Ansata has power.' He grinned wanly. 'I rather think, though, from your question, that your powers of observation can't be all that they used to be.'

'Eh? How do you mean?' I asked suspiciously, a trifle daunted.

'Why, if you look, you'll see!' he replied. 'On our first day here I nailed a tiny silver Crux Ansata to the door!'

For a moment, despite our situation and the seriousness of our conversation, I believed Crow was having me on. I had noticed no such thing. I got up quickly and crossed to the cabin door, opening it to peer at its contours in the glow of the deck- and cabin-lights. Sure enough, Crow's Looped Cross was there, at the very top of the door.

I had just turned back into the cabin, an exclamation of admiration on my lips, when the smell hit me. I say 'hit' me, and in all truth the cliché is quite void of exaggeration, for a positively vile *stench* was issuing from somewhere behind me on the midnight-black bank of the river.

There came footfalls . . .

Crow must have smelled it, too, and perhaps he heard the soft sounds from the quiet river bank. I saw him out of the corner of my eye as he jerked to his feet, his face pale in the flaring light, and then I concentrated on the darkness outside. I crouched there in the door, peering with bulging, fearful eyes into the shadows beyond the railed gangway.

Something moved there, a shape; and a low, clotted cough sounded – which was followed by a guttural, barely human voice!

'Ah, I see you're not . . . *glug* . . . expecting me, my friend! Didn't you get my message, then?'

I fell back as this reeking, awfully shadowed figure swayed up the gangplank. 'Please turn down the light, sir,' the clotted voice continued, 'and for God's sake . . . *glug* . . . have no fear of me. All will be explained.'

'Who – ?' I gulped, my voice barely audible. 'What – ?'

'Sir Amery Wendy-Smith – or at least his mind – at your service, sir. And would you be Titus Crow, or are you . . . *glug* . . . Henri-Laurent de Marigny?'

I fell back even more as the man-shaped, stinking black shadow stepped slowly closer; and then Crow's arm swept me aside and back into the cabin as he took my place at the door. In his hand he held my pistol, which had once belonged to Baron Kant.

'Stop right there!' he called out harshly, brokenly, to the black figure, now more than halfway up the gangplank. 'You can't be Wendy-Smith – he's dead!'

'My body, sir – the body I used to have – is dead, yes . . . *glug* . . . but my mind lives on; at least for a little while longer! I sense that you are Titus Crow. Now, please turn down the deck-light . . . *glug* . . . and the lamp in the cabin, and let me talk to you.'

'This gun,' Crow countered, his voice shaking, 'fires silver bullets. I don't know what you are, but I believe I can destroy you!'

'My dear . . . *glug* . . . sir, I have *prayed* for destruction!' The figure took another lurching step forward. 'But before you . . . *glug* . . . attempt to grant me any such merciful release, at least let me tell you what I was sent to tell – let me deliver *Their* warning! And in any case, neither your gun, nor the Crux Ansata there on the door, not even your elixirs or . . . *glug* . . . chants can immobilize this body. It is the stuff of which Cthulhu himself is made, or very close to it! Now . . .' The clotted, almost slopping voice grew more articulate, speeding up in some sort of hideous hysteria: 'For God's sake, will you let me deliver the message I was sent to deliver?'

'Crow,' I nervously blurted, my hand trembling on his shoulder, 'what is it? *What in hell is it?*'

Instead of answering me, he leaned out of the door to

turn down the wick of the lamp we had hung near the head of the gangplank. He left the very smallest flame glowing there in the dark. The shadow became an inky namelessness swaying almost rhythmically on the gangplank.

'Titus!' I gasped, almost rigid with dread. 'By all that's holy – are you trying to get us killed?'

'Not a bit of it, Henri,' he whispered, his shaky voice belying its message, 'but I want to hear what this – *thing* – has to say. Do as you're bid. Turn down the lamp!'

'*What?*' I backed away from his figure framed in the doorway, almost willing to believe that the strain of the last few days had been too much for him.

'Please!' the guttural voice of the vile-smelling thing on the gangplank came again as its owner took another lurching step forward. 'Please, there is little enough time as it is. They won't let . . . *glug* . . . this body hold together much longer!'

At that Crow turned, thrusting me aside and hurrying to the paraffin-lamp to dim its hissing glare. This done, he placed a chair near the door and stepped back as the stars in the night sky were blotted out by the bulk of the nameless speaker when it appeared in the doorway. Stumblingly it half sat, half fell into the chair. There was a quite audible squelching sound as its contours moulded to the wooden frame.

By this time I had backed up to the bunks. Crow had perched himself on the small desk, feet firmly on the floor. He looked very brave in the dim, flickering light, but I preferred to believe he sat there because his legs were no longer capable of holding him up! Not a bad idea. I sat down abruptly on a lower bunk.

'Here,' my friend whispered, 'you'd better have this if you're so nervous. But don't use it – not unless you have to!' He tossed Kant's pistol over to me.

'Please listen.' The nodding blackness on the chair spoke again, its stench wafting all about the cabin in thick gusts, blown by the warm breeze from the open door. 'I have been sent by Them, by the horrors beneath, to deliver a message . . . *glug* . . . and to let you see what hell is like! They have sent me to – '

'Do you mean Shudde-M'ell?' Crow cut in, his voice a trifle stronger.

'Indeed.' The horror nodded. 'At least, by his brothers, his children.'

'What are you?' I found myself asking, hypnotized. 'You're not a . . . man!'

'I *was* a man.' The shape in the chair seemed to sob, its lumpy outline moving in the flickering shadows. 'I *was* Sir Amery Wendy-Smith. Now I am only his mind, his brain. But you must *listen*! It is only Their power that holds me together – and even They . . . *glug* . . . cannot keep this shape solid much longer!'

'Go on,' Crow said quietly, and I was astonished to discover a strange – compassion? – in his voice.

'This, then, is Their message. I am Their messenger and I bear witness to the truth of what They have to say. It is this: If you leave well enough alone, as of now, They will let you go in peace. They will bother you no more, neither in dreams nor in your waking moments. They will lift all . . . enchantments . . . *glug* . . . from your minds. If you persist – then in the end They will take you, and will do with you what They have done with me!'

'And what was that?' I asked in awed tones, still trembling violently, peering at the horror in the chair.

For while the voice of – Wendy-Smith? – had been speaking, I had allowed myself the luxury of simultaneous concentration, taking in all that was said but thinking equally clearly on other matters, and now I found myself straining to see the thing in the chair more clearly.

It looked as though our visitor was clad in a large black overcoat, turned up about his neck, and it looked, too, as if he must have something covering his head – which perhaps accounted for the clotted, distorted quality of his voice – for I had caught not a glimpse of any whiteness to suggest a face there atop the oddly lumpy body. My mind, I discovered, allowed freely to ponder other things, had trembled on the verge of a mental chasm; the mad observations of Abdul Alhazred in his *Necronomicon* as reported by Joachim Feery: '. . . Till out of corruption horrid life springs, and the dull scavengers of Earth wax crafty to vex it and swell monstrous to plague it . . .'

I hastily brought my wandering mind back under control.

The thing in the chair – which had allegedly been a man – was answering my question, telling what it was that the Cthonians had done to him, what they would do to Crow and me if we refused to do as they ordered.

'They . . . *glug* . . .' the clotted voice gobbled, 'They destroyed my body – *but kept my brain alive!* They housed my mind in a living envelope of Their manufacture; a shapeless, immobile mass of filth; but with veins and . . . *glug* . . . capillaries, and a heart of sorts – with all the machinery needed to keep a human mind alive! Don't ask me how They . . . *glug-glug* . . . did it. But They've had practice, over the centuries.'

'Go on,' Crow prompted when the horror that housed Wendy-Smith's mind paused. 'Why did they keep your brain alive?'

'So that They could . . . *glug* . . . milk it, drain off its knowledge bit by bit. I was known as a learned man, gentlemen. I . . . *glug-glug* . . . had knowledge of all sorts of things. Knowledge which They wanted. And my knowledge was immediately to hand. They didn't have to . . . *glug* . . . employ dreams to get what They wanted.'

116

'Knowledge?' I prompted, steadier now. 'What sort of knowledge? What did they want to know?'

'. . . *Glug* . . . locations. The locations of mines – especially inoperative mines – like those at Harden and Greetham. Drilling operations, like the Yorkshire Moors Project and the North-Sea search for gas and oil. Details of city and town populations . . . *glug* . . . of scientific progress in atomics, and – '

'Atomics?' Crow again cut in. 'Why atomics? And another thing – Harden has only become inoperative *since* your . . . transition. And in your day there was no North-Sea search in progress; nor was there a Yorkshire Moors Project. You're lying!'

'No, no . . . *glug* . . . I mention these things because they are the modern counterparts of details They wanted at that time. I have only learned of these later developments through Their minds. They are in constant contact. Even now . . .'

'And atomics?' Crow repeated, apparently satisfied for the moment with the initial answer.

'I can't answer that. I only . . . *glug* . . . know *what* They are interested in, not *why*. Over the years They have drained it all from my mind. All I know, everything. Now I have nothing . . . *glug* . . . that They are interested in . . . *glug* . . . and this is the end. I thank God!' The horror in the chair paused. Its swaying and nodding became wilder in the flickering light.

'Now I must be . . . going.'

'Going? But *where*?' I babbled. 'Back to – Them?'

'No . . . *glug, glug, glug* . . . not back to Them. That is all . . . *glug* . . . over. I feel it. And They are angry. I have said too much. A few minutes more and I'll be . . . *glug* . . . free!' The pitiful horror climbed slowly to its feet, sloping somehow to one side, stumbling and barely managing to keep its balance.

117

Titus Crow, too, started to his feet. 'Wait, you can help us! You must know what they fear. We need to know. We need weapons against them!'

'*Glug, glug, glug* – no time – They have released Their control over this . . . *glug* . . . body! The protoplasm is . . . *glug, glug, ggglug* . . . falling apart! I'm sorry, Crow . . . *gluggg, aghhh* . . . I'm sorry.'

Now the thing was collapsing in upon itself and waves of monstrous, venomous fetor were issuing from it. It was swaying from side to side and stumbling to and fro, visibly spreading at its base and thinning at its top, melting like an icicle beneath the blast of a blowtorch.

'Atomics, yes! *Glugggg, urghhh, achhh-achhh!* You may be . . . *gluggg* . . . right! Ludwig Prinn, on . . . *gluggg-ughhh* . . . on Azathoth!'

The stench was now intolerable. Fumes of black vapour were actually *pouring* from the staggering, melting figure by the open door. I followed Crow's lead, hastily cramming a handkerchief to my nose and mouth. The horror's last words – a gurgled shriek – before it collapsed in upon itself and sloped across the planking of the floor, were these:

'Yes, Crow . . . *glarghhh, arghhh, urghhh* . . . look to Prinn's *De Vermis Mysteriis*!'

In a matter of seconds then, there was merely a spreading stain on the floor – but, God help me, within the pattern of that stain was a hideously suggestive lump!

*A human brain in an alien, protoplasmic body!*

I was paralysed, I don't mind admitting it, but Crow had leaped into action. Already the paraffin-lamp was back to full power, filling the cabin with light, and suddenly my friend's commands were echoing in my ears:

'Out, de Marigny. Out on to the gangplank. The stench is positively poisonous!' He half pushed me, half dragged me out through the door and into the clean night air. I sat down on the gangplank and was sick, horribly sick, into the obscenely chuckling river.

Crow, though, however affected he was or had been by the occurrences of the last half hour, had quickly regained control of himself. I heard the latticed cabin windows being thrown open, heard Crow's strangled coughing as he moved about in the noisome interior, heard his footsteps and laboured breathing as he came out on deck and crossed to the other side to fling something – something which splashed loudly – into the flowing river.

Too, as my sickness abated, I heard him drawing water and the sounds of his swilling down the cabin floor. I thanked my lucky stars I had not, as had once been my intention, had the cabin carpeted! A fresh breeze had sprung up to assist greatly in removing from the *Seafree* the poisonous taint of our visitor, and by the time I was able to get back on my feet it was plain that the houseboat would soon be back to normal.

It was then, just before midnight, as Crow came back on deck in his shirt sleeves, that a taxi pulled up on the river path level with the gangplank. Crow and I watched as the passenger alighted with a large briefcase and as, in the glow from the rear lights, a suitcase was taken from the boot. Plainly I heard the newcomer's voice as he paid his fare:

'I thank you very much. They're in, I see, so there'll be no need to wait.'

There was the merest trace of cultured, North American accent to that dignified voice, and I saw the puzzled look on Crow's face deepen as the second visitor of that fateful night made his way carefully to the foot of the gangplank. The taxi pulled away into the night.

'Hello, there,' the newcomer called as he stepped up the sloping walkway towards us. 'Mr Titus Crow, I believe – and Mr Henri-Laurent de Marigny?'

119

As he came into the light I saw an elderly gentleman whose grey hair went well with his intelligent, broad-browed head and wide, searching eyes. His clothes, I saw, were cut in the most conservative American style.

'You have us at a disadvantage, sir,' said Crow, carefully holding out his hand in greeting.

'Ah, of course.' The stranger smiled. 'Please forgive me. We've never met, you and I, but we've found a number of occasions in the past on which to correspond!'

For a moment my friend's frown deepened even further, but then the light of recognition suddenly lit in his eyes and he gasped as he gripped the other's hand more firmly. 'Then you'll be – '

'Peaslee,' the newcomer said. 'Wingate Peaslee of Miskatonic, and I'm delighted to make your acquaintance.'

# 8
## Peaslee of Miskatonic
### (From de Marigny's Notebooks)

Never before in my life had I experienced a night of such revelation.

Peaslee had flown in from America as soon as he got Crow's first letter, setting out from the university in Arkham even before the arrival of the eggs, which would now be put to certain as yet unspecified *uses* in America. Upon his arrival in London, he had tried to get in touch with Crow by telephone, eventually contacting the Reverend Harry Townley. But even then he had had to present himself at the reverend's residence, with such credentials as he had with him, before he could learn of Crow's whereabouts. Our ecclesiastical doctor friend was not one to neglect a trust!

'Solid as a rock,' Crow said when he heard this. 'Good old Harry!'

Once the reverend had cleared Peaslee, then he had told the professor of my own involvement in Crow's 'mysterious' activities. Though one of his prime objectives in journeying to England was to see Crow, he was not displeased at my presence or at my participation in my friend's adventures. He had heard much of my father – the Great New Orleans mystic, Etienne-Laurent de Marigny – and assumed correctly from the beginning that much of the paternal personality, particularly the love of obscure and macabre mysteries, had rubbed off on me.

He had come, he told us, among other things to welcome us into the membership of an organization, or rather, a 'Foundation', the Wilmarth Foundation. The direction of this unofficial institute was under Peaslee's own control – his and that of an administrative board formed by certain of Miskatonic's older, more experienced professors – and the Foundation's formation proper had been initiated after the untimely death of the sage for whom it was named. Its prime aim was to carry out the work that old Wilmarth, before his death, had stated he wished to commence.

Peaslee recognized immediately and was amazed at Crow's erudition regarding the Cthulhu Cycle of myth (mine to a lesser degree); and, once Titus had mentioned them in conversation, pressed him for details of his prophetic dreams. It appeared he knew of other men with Crow's strange brand of 'vision'; a somnambulant psyche, as it were! But the professor's own revelations were by far the night's most astounding, and his fascinating conversation was to carry us well into the early hours of the next day.

Before he would even begin to explain in detail, however, his unforeseeable arrival at the houseboat, seeing our obvious state of distress, he demanded to know all that had passed since the Harden eggs came into Crow's hands. In the earlier occurrences of the night in particular, Peaslee was interested – not in any morbid sense or out of grotesque curiosity, but because this was a facet of the Cthonians of which he knew nothing: their ability to preserve the identity of their victim by prisoning the brain in living tissues of their own construction. He carefully made notes as we told him of our awful, pitiful visitor, and only when he knew the most minute of the horrific details was he satisfied.

Then, and with considerable attention to detail – if occasionally prodded by our eager questions – he told us of the Wilmarth Foundation; of its inception at the deathbed of his one-time companion in dark and legendary arcana; of its resultant recruitment of scores of dedicated men – the 'horror-hunters' as foreseen by Sir Amery Wendy-Smith – and of their now almost worldwide organization aimed at the ultimate destruction of all the extant Cthulhu Cycle deities.

But before I go into Peaslee's fantastic disclosures too deeply, I feel I should make plain the truly astonishing sensations of *relief* enjoyed both by Titus Crow and myself from the moment the professor set foot aboard *Seafree*. If I had thought before that Crow. had 'freed' me with his chantings and splashings on that morning when the Cthonians had held me in their mental grasp – well, what was I to make of this new and fuller feeling of mental and physical freeness? The harsh lines on the face of Titus Crow lifted in less than half an hour, his unaccustomed nervousness gave way to an almost euphoric gayness quite out of character even in his lightest moments; and as for myself – why, I had not known such sheer joie de vivre for years, for longer than I could remember, and this despite my surroundings and the horror they had known only a few short hours earlier. Without Peaslee's explanation for this mental uplifting – which did not come, except as a hint, until later – it was far from obvious whence these sensations sprang. He did eventually clear up the matter for us (after my friend and I had remarked once or twice upon this remarkable and sudden exhilaration) with an explanation both enlightening and gratifying. At last, it seemed, Crow and I were to have the penultimate protection against the Cthonians, and against their mind- and dream-sendings. For although we had not known it, even with Crow's expert use of the Vach-Viraj Incantation and the Tikkoun Elixir, the Cthonian mastery of dreams and subconscious mind and mental telepathy had still held over us at least the echoes of their evil influence. Only the Elder Gods themselves had ultimate

123

power – and, even if it were known how, what man would dare conjure *them*? Would they even permit such a conjuring? Everyone, Peaslee had it, was subject to the influence of the forces of evil to one degree or another, but there was a solution to such moods and states of psychic depression. We were, as I have said, later to learn what that solution was.

The professor's reason for coming to England, as he had already half stated, was not wholly to invite Titus Crow into the company of the Wilmarth Foundation; but on receipt of Crow's letter he had realized at once that its author desperately needed his help – his *immediate* help, if it was not to be Wendy-Smith and Wilmarth all over again!

He explained how Professor Albert N. Wilmarth, long interested in and an authority on Fortian and macabre occurrences, especially those connected with the Cthulhu Cycle of myth, had died quietly following a long illness many years ago. At the height of this illness Wendy-Smith was sending Wilmarth imploring telegrams – telegrams which, because of his comatose condition at the time, the ailing professor was never able to answer! On his partial recovery and not long before his relapse, slow decline, and eventual death, he had blamed his English colleague's monstrous demise on himself. Then, while he was able, Wilmarth had gathered to him all references available in literature to the subterranean beings of the Cthulhu Cycle. Upon receipt of a copy of the Wendy-Smith manuscript (before its first publication in alleged 'fiction' form), he had taken it upon himself to form the nucleus of that Foundation which now secretly spanned the greater part of the Earth. Shortly thereafter he died.

Peaslee told us of the Foundation's early years, of the scepticism with which Wilmarth's posthumous report was at first met, of the subsequent explorations, scientific

124

experiments, and researching which had gone to prove the elder 'eccentric's' theories, and of the gradual buildup of a dedicated army. Now there were almost five hundred of them – men in every walk of life, who, having chanced upon manifestations of subterranean horror or other signs of alien presences, were members of the Wilmarth Foundation – a body sworn to protect its individual members, to secretly seek out and destroy all the elder evils of Avernus, to remove for ever from the Earth the ancient taint of Cthulhu, Yog-Sothoth, Shudde-M'ell, Nyogtha, Yibb-Tstll, and all the others of the deities, their minions, and spawn.

The great occult books had early been researched, studied endlessly by sincere and single-minded men until each clue, every pointer, all references and allusions were known to the horror-hunters by heart – and then the hunt had begun in earnest.

But before all this had got under way those Demogorgons of the mythology, the Cthonians, had spread into many areas (although Africa was still their true stronghold), until the spawn of Shudde-M'ell was seeded far and wide, throughout all Asia, Europe, Russia, even China and Tibet. Finally, as lately as 1964, and against all the efforts of the Wilmarth Foundation, the Americas themselves had been invaded. Not that this invasion constituted the first dealings of these beings of elder myth and their minions with the Americas. On the contrary; the United States particularly – and especially the New England seaboard – had known diverse forms of the horrors many times, and Their presence in the domed hills and wooded valleys of that area was immemorially recorded and predated the very Indians and their forebears. This was the first time, however, that Shudde-M'ell's kind had gained a foothold upon (or rather, *within*) the North American landmass!

Crow had found this invasion just a fraction too hard to understand, until Peaslee reminded him of the Cthonian ability to get into the minds of men. There were, beyond a doubt, people temporarily and even permanently in the employ of the burrowers beneath – usually men of weak character or low breeding and mental characteristics – and such persons had transported eggs to the United States for the further propagation of the horrors! These mental slaves of the Cthonians had, on a number of occasions, attempted to infiltrate the Foundation – had even tried to get inside Miskatonic University itself. But again the as yet unspecified 'protections' of Foundation members had been sufficient to ward off such deluded men. After all, their minds were in effect the minds of the Cthonians, and therefore that same power which worked against all Cthulhu Cycle deities worked against them!

The main trouble in dealing with Shudde-M'ell's sort (Peaslee was quite matter-of-fact in his treatment of the theme) was that any method used against them could more often than not only be used once. Their telepathic contact with one another – and, indeed, with others of the mythology – was of course instantaneous. This meant that should a means be employed to destroy one nest of the creatures, then it was more than likely that the other nests knew of it immediately and would avoid any such similar treatment. Thanks to Miskatonic's technical theorists, researchers, and experimentalists, however, an as yet untried plan had been formulated to destroy certain of the earth-dwelling types of the CCD (Peaslee's abbreviation for Cthulhu Cycle deities) without alerting other of the horrors. This plan was now scheduled for use both in England as well as America. Preparations had already been made for the initial American experiment, which would now have to be delayed until arrangements could be made for a simultaneous attack upon the Cthonian nests of Britain. Crow and I, as members of the Wilmarth Foundation, would see the results of this project.

While the professor was sketching in the details of these facts for us, I could see Crow growing more restless and eager to speak by the second. Sure enough, as soon as Peaslee paused for a breath, he put in: 'Then there *are* known ways of killing these things?'

'Certainly, my friends' – the professor looked at us both – 'and if your minds hadn't been so fogged over these last few weeks I'm sure you would have discovered some of them for yourselves. Most of the earth-dwelling types – such as Shudde-M'ell and his lot – can be done away with simply by the use of water. They corrode, rot, and evaporate in water. Their internal organs break down and their pressure-mechanisms cease to function. Their makeup is more alien than you can possibly imagine. A sustained jet of water, or immersion for any appreciable length of time, is quite fatal; and there's damn little left to look at afterwards! It's strange, I know, that Shudde-M'ell's ultimate striving is towards freeing Great Cthulhu – which the Foundation, in Wendy-Smith's footsteps, believes – for Cthulhu would appear essentially to be the greatest of the *water*-elementals. The fact of the matter is, though, that R'lyeh once stood on dry land, possibly has on a number of occasions, and that the ocean now forms the very walls of Cthulhu's prison. It is the water, thank God, that keeps down his monstrous dream-sendings to a bearable level. Even so, you'd be surprised how many inmates of the world's lunatic asylums owe their confinement to the mad call of Cthulhu. Of course, dreaming as he is in Deep R'lyeh – wherever that hellish submarine city of distant aeons hides – he is served in his slumbers by Dragons and the Deep Ones; but these in the main are creatures more truly of the great waters. Water is their element.'

'Cthulhu in fact lives, then?' Crow asked.

'Most assuredly. There are some occultists who believe him to be dead, I am told, but – '

'"That is not dead which can eternal lie . . ."' Crow finished for him, quoting the first line of Alhazred's much discussed couplet.

'Exactly,' Peaslee agreed.

'I know a different version of it,' I said.

'Oh?' The professor cocked his head at me.

'"That which is alive hath known death, and that which is dead yet can never die, for in the Circle of the Spirit life is naught and death is naught. Yea, all things live for ever, though at times they sleep and are forgotten."'

Crow raised his eyebrows in question, but before he could speak I said: 'From the ninth chapter of H. Rider Haggard's *She*, from the lips of a hideous phoenix in a dream.'

'Ah, but you'll find many allusions and parallels in fiction, Henri,' Peaslee told me. 'Particularly in that type of fiction so marvellously typified in Haggard. I suppose you could say that Ayesha was a fire-elemental.'

'Talking of elementals' – Crow entered the conversation – 'you say that many of the earth-types rot in water. Now, you say it as if you'd actually seen such a . . . a *dissolution* – but how can you be so sure?'

'Dissolution, you say. Hmmm,' Peaslee mused. 'No, more an incredibly rapid *catabolism*, I would say. And yes, I have seen such a thing. Three years ago we hatched an egg at Miskatonic.'

'What?' Crow cried. 'Wasn't that a very dangerous thing to do?'

'Not at all,' Peaslee answered, unflustered. 'And it was quite necessary. We had to study the things, Crow – as much as Earthly knowledge would allow. We still are studying them. It's all very well to theorize and conjecture, but practice is the only way. So we hatched an egg.

We've done it often since then, I assure you! But this first one: we had it in a large boxlike room, a pentagonal room with an imprisoning device set in the centre of each of the five walls. Oh, the thing was well and truly prisoned, both physically and mentally; it could neither move from its room nor communicate with others of its kind! We fed it mainly on soil and basaltic gravel. Oh, yes, we tried it on the flesh of dead animals, too, which produced a hideous blood-lust in it – and so it was obviously safer to feed the thing on minerals. At only six months old the creature was as fat as two men around and nine feet long; like a great grey ugly squid. It wasn't full-grown by any means, but nevertheless we were satisfied that it was at least big enough to accommodate our experiments. We had a good idea that water might do the trick. Even old Wendy-Smith' – he paused momentarily to peer with horror-shrouded eyes, nonetheless wonderingly, even calculat-ingly, at the now faint stains on the floorboards – 'knew that much, and so we left the water-test until the last. Acids didn't seem to worry it in the slightest, or any but the most extreme degrees of heat – and we used a laser! Nor, as we'd expected, did pressure, shock, or blast affect it; even powerful explosives set off *in contact* with the thing didn't bother it unnecessarily, other than forcing it to fill in the gaps blown in its protoplasm! Water, though, did the trick beautifully. But before that there was one other thing we tried, and it worked so well that we had to stop the treatment or simply kill the thing out of hand.'

'Oh?' Crow questioned. 'Might I hazard a guess before you tell us?'

'Certainly.'

'Radiation,' my friend said with certainty. 'The thing did not like radiation!'

Peaslee seemed surprised. 'Quite correct. But how did you know?'

'There are two clues,' Crow answered. 'One, the eggs of these creatures are shielded against radiation; and two, there was that which Sir Amery – or rather his brain in that monstrous body – told us before he . . . it . . . died.'

'Eh?' I cast my mind swiftly back.

'Yes,' said Crow. 'He said that we might "try Ludwig Prinn on Azathoth." And of course Azathoth is the "Nuclear Chaos" of the Cthulhu Cycle.'

'Good,' said Peaslee, obviously appreciative of my friend's grasp of the matter, 'and do you know the passage in *De Vermis Mysteriis* to which Wendy-Smith referred?'

'No, but I'm aware that there's a so-called "invocation" in the book for raising Azathoth temporarily.'

'There is indeed' – Peaslee nodded his head grimly – 'one which bears out your theory – and that of the Wilmarth Foundation, incidentally – that the "magic" of the Elder Gods was in fact super-science. It is a spell involving the use of an unspecified metal, one which, to use Prinn's own words, "may be found only by the most powerful use of extreme and dangerous thaumaturgies." He even gave the required amount of this metal, but in cryptic terms. We sorted out his symbols, though, using the university computer, and discovered his principal measurements. The rest was easy. Prinn had in fact specified a critical mass of highly fissionable material!'

'An atomic explosion!' Crow gasped.

'Of course,' Peaslee agreed.

'But there are many such "invocations" in the great Black Books – the *Necronomicon* and others of its kind,' Crow protested.

'Yes, and some of them are vocal neutralizers of the mind-prisons of the Elder Gods. In most cases, thank God, their pronunciation is a veritable impossibility. Yes, we can count ourselves as damned lucky that the ancients, particularly Alhazred, didn't have a system of getting the pronunciation of many of these things down on paper – or papyrus, or stone, or whatever. Also, it's fortunate that man's vocal cords are not naturally given to the use of such alien syllables!'

'But wait,' Crow cried in apparent exasperation. 'Here we have decided that Azathoth is nothing more than a nuclear explosion, a destructive device *against* the CCD. But surely he was the original *leader* of the Great Old Ones, including Cthulhu, in their rebellion against the Elder Gods? I don't follow.'

'Don't take the old writings too much at their face value, Titus,' the professor told him. 'For instance: think of Azathoth as he/it is described – "an amorphous blight of nethermost confusion which blasphemes and bubbles at the centre of all infinity"; that is, central in time and space. Now, given that time and space support each other's existence, they therefore commenced initially simultaneously; and because Azathoth is coexistent with all time and conterminous in all space *he was there at the beginning!* This is in effect how he became the first rebel – he altered the perfect negative-structure of a timeless spacelessness into the chaotic continuum which we have today. Consider his nature, Titus: a "nuclear chaos". Why, he was – he *is* – nothing less than the Big Bang itself, and to hell with your Steady-State theorists!'

'The Big Bang,' Crow repeated, patently in awe of the vision Peaslee had conjured.

'Of course.' The professor nodded. 'Azathoth, who "created this Earth", and who, it is foretold in books predating mere man, "shall destroy it when the seals are broken." Oh, yes, Titus – and this isn't the only mythos that has us going in flames next time!' He paused to let this last sink in, then continued:

'But if you insist on looking at the Cthulhu Cycle literally, without admitting this sort of cryptic reference, then consider this: following the failure of their rebellion, the Great Old Ones were served punishments. Azathoth was blinded and bereft of mind and will. Now, a madman is unpredictable, Titus. He rarely recognizes either friend or foe. And a *blind* madman has even less recognition. How unpredictable, then, a blind, mad chaos of nuclear reactions?'

While Peaslee had been talking, it had grown plain to me that something else was bothering Crow. He let the professor finish, then said:

'But listen here, Wingate. I accept all you say, *gladly*; I thank our lucky stars that you're here to help us out of a hole – but surely all we've done up to now is alert the CCD of your presence! All this talking, particularly what's been said about water and atomics as weapons – surely we've been giving the whole show away?'

'Not at all.' The erudite Peaslee smiled. 'True, in the beginning, when the Foundation first got started, we did give lots of information away in this manner – '

'What manner?' I cut in, having been lost by the conversation. 'Do you mean that the Cthonians can listen in on our discussions?'

'Of course, Henri,' Crow answered. 'I thought that was understood. They're good at "receiving" as well as "sending", you know!'

'Then why didn't they know where we were without first having to find you in that dream last night? Why didn't they pick your plans to come down here to Henley right out of your mind?'

Crow sighed patiently and said: 'Don't forget that we have had the use of certain protections, Henri – the Tikkoun Elixir, the Vach-Viraj Incantation. Nevertheless,' he continued, frowning, 'that's just exactly what I was getting at!'

He turned to Peaslee. 'Well, how about it, Wingate?

Here in the houseboat, while admittedly I've been using the Vach-Viraj Incantation pretty regularly, well, we've lately run out of the Tikkoun Elixir. So what's to have stopped the Cthonians from listening in on us?'

'These devices you mention are poor protections, my friend,' the professor answered. 'Perhaps they helped a little, but obviously the burrowers were still getting through to you – both of you – at least partially. It's my guess that they've known where you were all along. They are *not* getting through now, however, as witness your alert minds and, despite lack of sleep, your newfound feelings of psychic and physical freedom. Now listen:

'As I was saying, when first the Foundation got under way, we did give away lots of information in this manner, and with the passage of time the would-be hunters almost became the hunted!

'In 1958 no fewer than seven recruits of the Wilmarth Foundation met untimely, unnatural deaths, and the remaining members immediately sought protection. Of course, it had long been known that the star-stones of ancient Mnar formed the perfect barrier – certainly against their minions, to a lesser degree against the CCD themselves – but these stones were so few and far between, and usually only accidentally acquired. A definite source and supply became imperative.

'In '59 Miskatonic's kilns actually commenced manufacturing the stones – or rather, soapstone-porcelain duplicates – a process perfected by our young Professor Sandys, and by 1960 all members of the Foundation were equipped with them. The very first man-made stones were useless, by the way, but it was soon discovered that by incorporating fragments of a few damaged original stars in the composition of the manufactured ones, as many as a hundred new star-stones – each as effective as the originals – could be made from one of the old!'

Peaslee paused here to dig into his great briefcase. 'Here, by the way, are the reasons you no longer have anything to fear from the Cthonians, neither physically nor mentally . . . so long as you're careful, that is! Always remember – they *never* stop trying! You must carry these things wherever you go from now on, but even so you must try not to venture anywhere below the surrounding ground-level. I mean that you're to keep out of valleys, gulleys, quarries, mines, subways, and so on. As I've said, you needn't fear a direct attack, but they can still get at you indirectly. A sudden earthquake, a fall of rock – I'm sure you follow my meaning.'

He produced two small packages which he carefully unwrapped, passing the contents of one to Crow and the other to me. 'I have many more of them. These two, however, are yours personally from now on. They should keep you out of trouble.'

I examined the thing in my hand. It was of course a star-stone, featureless, grey-green; the thing might easily have been a small, fossil starfish. Crow, too, gave his stone a thoughtful examination, then said: 'So these are the star-stones of ancient Mnar.'

'Yes,' Peaslee agreed. 'Except you couldn't call *these* stones exactly ancient. They are samples from Miskatonic's kilns – but for all that, they're just as powerful as the real things.'

Crow carefully placed his stone in the inside pocket of his jacket, hanging by his bunk, then turned to thank Peaslee for what could only be called a priceless gift. He followed this up with: 'You were talking about the Wilmarth Foundation and its work. I was very interested.'

'Of course,' the professor agreed. 'Yes, we'd better get through as much as we can of basic explanations and details for tonight' – he glanced at his watch – 'or rather, this morning! We'll have to be on our way later today. Now where was I? Ah, yes!

'Well, 1959 was a momentous year for the Foundation, for as well as our discovery of a means of manufacturing these protective devices, we also sent out our first real expeditions since the 30s. The new expeditions were, though, less well advertised – almost secretive, in fact, and necessarily so – and fronted with fictitious objectives. We were particularly interested in Africa, where it was known that at least one Cthonian species – namely the kith and kin of Shudde-M'ell – were free and roaming loose. There, on the borders of that region explored by the ill-fated Wendy-Smith Expedition, our horror-hunters discovered two tribes whose members wore about their necks exhumed star-stones, protections against "evil spirits". Their witch doctors, the only members of the tribes allowed into the taboo territories, had been digging up the stones immemorially, and the *Mganga* with the greatest number of stars to his credit was reckoned a very powerful witch doctor indeed. Witch doctors, it may be added, did not have a great life expectancy in that area. Inevitably they would dig where they ought not!

'Incidentally, this ritual collecting of the star-stones explains Shudde-M'ell's original escape from those prisoning environs, and how his brethren were liberated to pursue their aeon-old policy of regeneration, infiltration, and their efforts to free even worse horrors throughout the world. The throne-nest had remained in G'harne for some time after the general exodus, it seemed, but it was members of the nest that followed Wendy-Smith back to England. Now, of course, as you are only too well aware, England has its own loathsome complement of the Cthonians.

'Wendy-Smith was a bit confused as to their propagative rate, though. He speaks of "hordes", then of "extremely slow procreative processes". In fact, the creatures *are* slow in producing – but not all that slow! We can reckon on a cycle of thirty years, with a female laying two to four eggs at a time. The trouble is that once they've reached this thirty-year stage of maturity they can lay every ten years. By the time a female has reached her century she may very well have littered thirty-two pups! Fortunately, so far as we've been able to ascertain, only one in every eight of these monstrous "children" is female. I rather fancy that one of the G'harne eggs which Wendy-Smith unknowingly took was just such a female!' The professor let this ominous thought sink in, then added: 'Overall, I should think we can take it that some hundreds of the beings are now alive and spreading.'

'This is fascinating,' Crow murmured. 'How do you track them down, Peaslee – what system do you employ to detect the beasts?'

'Initially, as your English professor suggested, we tried specialized seismological equipment, but the system wasn't accurate enough. For example: how might one tell a "natural" from an "unnatural" tremor? Of course, we also have a worldwide news service, and our headquarters at Miskatonic is ever on the lookout for inexplicable disappearances or anything else suggesting the involvement of the CCD. For the last few years, though, we've been using people gifted as you yourself, Crow, are gifted.'

'Eh?' My friend was taken aback. 'Gifted like me? I fail to see what you're getting at, Peaslee.'

'Why, your *dreams*, my friend! Even though you were not then "on the books", as it were, of the CCD, still you picked up impressions from their monstrous minds. To a degree – certainly on the Cthonian thought-levels – you're telepathic, Crow! And, as I've said, you're not alone in your ability.'

'Of course,' I cried, snapping my fingers. 'But that explains why I came back from France, Titus! I could sense that something was wrong; I knew that somehow I was being *called* back to England. Furthermore, it explains my moods of depression in the weeks prior to your inviting me in on this thing – I was picking up the echoes of your own gloom!'

Peaslee was immediately interested, and made me relate to him all of my doom-fraught sensations throughout the period leading up to my return from Paris, 'as though drawn back', to London.

When I was done, he said, 'Then it seems we must acknowledge you, too, de Marigny, as being something of a telepath. You may not be able to project your thoughts and emotions, as Crow here obviously can, but you can certainly *receive* such sendings! Good – it seems that the Foundation has recruited two more extremely valuable members.'

'Do you mean to say,' Crow pressed, 'that you're using telepaths to track these creatures down?'

'Yes, we are. It is easily the most successful phase of all our operations,' the professor answered.

'And yet' – Crow seemed puzzled – 'you haven't discovered the whereabouts of R'lyeh, Cthulhu's seat at the bottom of the sea?'

'What? You surprise me!' Peaslee seemed shocked. 'Do you really think we'd risk men by asking them to contact Cthulhu?' He frowned. 'And yet, in fact . . . there was one of our telepaths who took it upon himself to do just that. He was a "dreamer", just like you, and he was on a nonaddictive drug we've developed to induce deep sleep. But on one occasion, well, he didn't follow orders. Left a note explaining what he was trying to do. All very laudable – and very stupid! He's in a Boston asylum now; hopeless case.'

'Good God . . . of course!' Crow gasped as the implications hit him. 'He *would* be!'

'Yes,' Peaslee grimly agreed. 'Anyhow, this method of ours of using telepaths didn't evolve properly until two years ago, but now we've developed it fully. I flew over here yesterday in the company of one of our telepaths, and later today he'll be off to look up a British colleague – a pilot, ostensibly in "Ordnance Survey". They'll hire a small aeroplane, and tomorrow or the day after they'll start quartering England, Scotland, and Wales.'

'Quartering?' I asked.

'It's our term for dividing into a series of squares an area to be "prospected",' Peaslee explained. 'David Winters – that's the telepath's name – can detect a CCD up to a distance of twenty-five miles; he can *pinpoint* them from five miles away! In a matter of a week or two we'll know the location of every nest and each individual horror in all three countries – if all goes according to plan.'

'And Ireland?' I asked.

'We have no reason to believe that the Emerald Isle has yet been invaded,' the professor answered. 'Ireland will, though, be checked over at a later date.'

'But they can *move*!' Crow protested. 'By the time your telepath has done with his job, his early, er – sightings? – could be a hundred miles away from where he first plotted them!'

'That's true,' Peaslee agreed, unperturbed, 'but we're after *numbers*, mainly, and large concentrations. We have to know the best spots to start drilling, you see?'

Crow and I, both equally baffled by this new phase of the professor's revelations, looked at one another in consternation. 'No,' I eventually answered. 'I don't think we do see.'

'Let me explain,' Peaslee offered. 'We have men with the big companies; with Seagasso, Lescoil, the NCB, ICI,

Norgas, even in govermental circles. Now a few of these men are Americans, trained at Miskatonic and slotted in over here when opportunities presented themselves, but most are of course natives of Great Britain contacted and recruited over the years through the machinery of the Wilmarth Foundation. We have, too, interested parties in certain ministries: such as the Ministry of Land and Development, Agriculture and Fisheries, National Resources, etc.

'The "Great Britain Operation", as we call it, has been planned for some years now, but when this opportunity came along – that is, the opportunity to do a bit of incidental, valuable recruiting, as well as to intervene in what might well have turned out to be a very nasty affair – well, it seemed to me that this was the perfect time to put the plan into operation.

'I will in fact supervise and coordinate the project in its entirety. You two gentlemen will no doubt be able to help me tremendously in this, and learn a lot about the Foundation's workings at the same time. For instance, though these may seem relatively minor points to you, I don't like the idea of driving on the left, I'm not at all sure of your British road signs, and I'm damned if I'll be driven around for the next few months in a cab! The latter's out of the question, anyway, for we'll be seeing some pretty strange things before we're through, and the presence of a cabdriver is just not acceptable. Obviously, the public must be kept in the dark about all this. We'll need a large automobile – '

'I have a Mercedes garaged at Henley,' Crow hastily put in.

'And of course I'll need someone with a good knowledge of British geography, topography, and so on. All of which is where you gentlemen should come in very nicely,' Peaslee finished.

'But wait,' I dazedly protested, one part of my mind following the conversation, another groping at what had gone before. 'You were talking about *drilling*!'

'Ah, yes! So I was. I'm often guilty of a little mental wandering when I'm a bit weary. You'll excuse me, de Marigny, but I've a lot on my mind and these details are just routine to me. Drilling, yes – well, the plan is this: once we've ascertained where the nests are, we'll choose two or three centrally situated drilling sites as far out of the way of the general public as we can manage, and then we'll commence the drilling of our star-wells – '

'Star-wells?' this, again, was from me.

'Yes, that's what we call them. Deep shafts to accommodate star-stones. We drill five equally spaced star-wells in a great circle some hundreds of yards across, and one central hole to take the eggs. The idea is that once we let the eggs down the central shaft – until which time, incidentally, they'll be kept "prisoned" by the proximity of star-stones so that local adults will not know of their whereabouts – we can expect the adults to come burrowing to the rescue. Of course, their rescue attempt will fail! As soon as our telepaths and instruments tell us of the arrival of a sufficiently large number of the adult creatures . . . then we'll let down the star-stones into the perimeter wells. All the Cthonians within the circle will be trapped.'

'But these creatures can move in three dimensions, you know, Wingate,' Crow pointed out. 'Surely your star-stones will be lying on a strictly two-dimensional plane? What's to stop the adult Cthonians from simply burrowing straight down – or worse still . . . *up*?'

'No, the circle ought to be sufficient, Titus. We've experimented, as I've said – you remember what I told you of the eggs we hatched? – and we're pretty sure that our plan is sound. What we might do, if we're lucky enough to be able to get our hands on them at the right time, is this: instead of using eggs we'll use young female creatures! They'll provide a sure draw. And then, well, even if the adults do try to make an escape after we lower the star-stones, it will be far too late!'

Crow held up his hands and shook his head. 'Hold on a minute, Peaslee! First off, where will you get your young females; and secondly, why will any attracted adults be "too late" to get away?' Doubt was showing on my friend's face again.

'As to your first question,' the professor answered, 'we have a regular hatchery at Miskatonic. We took two dozen eggs from G'harne, and we've collected others since then. That's where your four eggs are destined for, by the way. Your second question? Well, as soon as the adults appear on the scene and after we've set the star-stones in place – then we flood the whole underground area by pumping water down the shafts under high pressure!'

For a moment there was silence, then Crow said: 'And you say there'll be a number of these sites?'

'Yes, and the timings for the operations will of course be perfectly synchronized – simply to ensure that if the Cthonians do manage to get "distress signals" out past the star-stones, well, at least we'll have cleaned out a large number of them at one swipe. In that event, it would mean searching for a new plan of attack for later projects, but. . .' Peaslee frowned thoughtfully for a moment, then added: 'But anyway, after we've had this initial bash at the burrowers – then we'll be able to turn our attentions to the other British CCD.'

'*Others?*' I exploded. 'What others?' I noticed that Crow seemed less surprised.

'Well, we know that there are a number of different types of these beings, Henri, these dwellers in the deep earth,' the professor patiently explained. 'And therefore

141

it's a fair bet that Great Britain has her share. Some, though, are apparently far more vulnerable to orthodox weapons. One of our men – an Englishman, by the way – has had a certain amount of personal experience with just such a being. This same chap is a drilling expert; a fellow known as "Pongo" Jordan, who used to be with Seagasso's oceangoing rigs. Now he's a member of the Foundation – but it took a lot of persuasion. Ostensibly, he works for Land Development. He'll be supervising the positioning of the star-wells once David Winters' report is in.'

'Jordan . . . ?' Crow mused, then looked startled. He frowned. 'Not the same Jordan who . . . And your telepath, David Winters! Well, I'll be – '

'Go on,' Peaslee said. 'Do you know Jordan and Winters?'

'I know that the Cthonians fear them desperately, as they fear you,' Crow answered. Then my friend proceeded to tell the professor of his dreams during the period when the seagoing rigs were stricken with that series of puzzling disasters, following this up with his latest nightmare wherein the Cthonians had tried to 'buy him off'.

When Crow had done, Peaslee excitedly dug into his great briefcase. 'You know, you two,' he said, 'when I first decided to fly over here, I had no idea it would be so easy to convert you to the Foundation's cause. Because of my uncertainty I gathered together certain testimonials which I hoped would help to convince you. One of these is a letter Jordan wrote to one of his superiors shortly after he lost his rig, *Sea-Maid*. Ah! Here it is. I'm sure you'll be interested to read it.'

# 9

## *The Night* Sea-Maid *Went Down*

### *(From the Files of the Wilmarth Foundation)*

Queen of the Wolds Inn
Cliffside
Bridlington, E. Yorks.
29th Nov.

J. H. Grier (Director)
Grier & Anderson
Seagasso
Sunderland, Co. Durham

Dear Johnny,

By now I suppose you'll have read my 'official' report,
sent off to you from this address on the fourteenth of the
month, three days after the old *Sea-Maid* went down.
How I managed that report I'll never know – but anyway,
I've been laid up ever since, so if you've been worried
about me or wondering why I haven't let on further about
my whereabouts till now, well, it hasn't really been my
fault. I just haven't been up to doing much writing since
the . . . disaster. Haven't been up to much of anything
for that matter. God, but I hate the idea of facing a Board
of Inquiry!

Anyhow, as you'll have seen from my report, I've made
up my mind to quit, and I suppose it's only right I give
you what I can of an explanation for my decision. After
all, you've been paying me good money to manage your
rigs these last four years, and no complaints there. In fact,
I've no complaints period, nothing Seagasso could sort
out at any rate, but I'm damned if I'll sink sea-wells again.

In fact, I'm finished with *all* prospecting! Sea, land . . . it makes no real difference now. Why, when I think of what might have happened at any time during the last four years! And now it *has* happened.

But there I go, stalling again. I'll admit right now that I've torn up three versions of this letter, pondering the results of them reaching you; but now, having thought it all out, frankly, I don't give a damn what you do with what I'm going to tell you. You can send an army of head-shrinkers after me if you like. One thing I'm sure of, though, and that's this – whatever I say won't make you suspend the North-Sea operations. 'The Country's Economy', and all that.

At least my story ought to give old Anderson a laugh; the hard, stoic, unimaginative old bastard! And no doubt about it, the story I have to tell is fantastic enough. I suppose it could be argued that I was 'in my cups' that night (and it's true enough, I'd had a few), but I can hold my drink, as you well know. Still, the facts – *as I know them* – drunk or sober, remain simply fantastic.

Now, you'll remember that right from the start there was something funny about the site off Hunterby Head. The divers had trouble; the geologists, too, with their instruments; it was the very devil of a job to float *Sea-Maid* down from Sunderland and get her anchored there; and all that was only the start of the trouble. Nevertheless, the preliminaries were all completed by early in October.

We hadn't drilled more than six hundred feet into the seabed when we brought up that first star-shaped thing. Now, Johnny, you know something? I wouldn't have given two damns for the thing, except I'd seen one before. Old Chalky Gray (who used to be with the Lescoil rig, *Ocean-Gem*, out of Liverpool) had sent me one only a few weeks before his platform and all the crew, including Chalky himself, went down twelve miles out from Withnersea. Somehow, when I saw what came up in the big core – that same star-shape – I couldn't help but think of Chalky and see some sort of nasty parallel. The one he'd sent me came up in a core too, you see? And *Ocean-Gem* wasn't the only rig lost that year in so-called 'freak storms'!

Now regarding those star-shaped stones, something more: I wasn't the only one to escape with my life the night *Sea-Maid* went down. No, that's not strictly true, I was the only one to live through *that night* – but there was a certain member of the team who saw what was coming and got out before it happened. And it was because of the star-thing that he went!

Joe Borszowski was the man – superstitious as hell, panicky, spooked at the sight of a mist on the sea – and when he saw the star-thing . . . !

It happened like this:

We'd drilled a difficult bore through some very hard stuff when, as I've said, a core-sample produced the first of those stars. Now, Chalky had reckoned the one he sent me to be a fossilized starfish of sorts, from a time when the North-Sea used to be warm; a very ancient thing. And I must admit that with its five-pointed shape, and being the size of a small starfish, I believed him to be correct. Anyway, when I showed this second star to old Borszowski he nearly went crackers! He swore we were in for trouble, demanded we all stop drilling right away and head for land, insisted that our location was 'accursed', and generally carried on like a mad thing without explaining why.

Well, I couldn't just leave it at that; if one of the lads was around the twist, you know (meaning Borszowski), he could well affect the whole operation, jeopardize the whole thing; especially if his madness took him at an important time. My immediate reaction was to want him off the rig, but the radio had been giving us a bit of bother so that I couldn't call in Wes Atlee, the chopper pilot. Yes, I'd seriously thought of having the Pole lifted off by chopper. The gangs can be damned superstitious, as you well know, and I didn't want Joe infecting the other lads with his wild fancies. As it turned out, that sort of action wasn't necessary, for in no time at all old Borszowski was around apologizing for his outburst and trying to show how sorry he was about all the fuss he'd made. Something told me, though, that he'd been quite serious about his fears – whatever they were.

And so, to put the Pole's mind at rest (if I possibly could), I decided to have the rig's geologist, Carson, take the star to bits, have a closer look at it, and then let me know what the thing actually was. Of course, he'd tell me it was simply a fossilized starfish; I'd report the fact to Borszowski; things would be back to normal. So naturally, when Carson told me that it *wasn't* a fossil, that he didn't know exactly *what* it was – well, I kept that bit of information to myself and told Carson to do the same. I was sure that whatever the trouble was with Borszowski, well, it wouldn't be helped any by telling him that the star-thing was not a perfectly ordinary, completely explicable object.

The drilling brought up two or three more of the stars down to about a thousand feet, but nothing after that, so for a period I forgot all about them. As it happened, I should have listened a bit more willingly to the Pole – and I *would* have, too, if I'd followed my intuition.

You see, I've got to admit that I'd been spooky myself right from the start. The mists were too heavy, the sea too quiet . . . things were altogether too queer all the way down the line. Of course, I didn't experience any of the troubles the divers or geologists had known – I didn't join the rig until she was in position, ready to chew – but I was

146

certainly in on it from then on. It had really started with the sea-phones, even before the advent of the stars.

Now, you know I'm not knocking your phones, Johnny; they've been a damn good thing ever since Seagasso developed them, giving readings right down to the inch, almost, so's we could tell just exactly when the drill was going through into gas or oil. And they didn't let us down this time, either . . . we simply failed to recognize or heed their warnings, that's all.

In fact, there were lots of warnings, but, as I've said, it started with the sea-phones. We'd put a phone down inside each leg of the rig, right on to the seabed where they sat 'listening' to the drill as it cut its way through the rocks, picking up the echoes as the steel worked its way down and the sounds of the cutting rebounded from the strata below. And, of course, everything they 'heard' was duplicated electronically and fed out to us through our computer. Which was why we believed initially that either the computer was on the blink or one of the phones was shaky. You see, even when we weren't drilling – when we were changing bits or lining the hole – we were still getting readings from the computer!

Oh, the trouble was there all right, whatever it was, but it was showing up so regularly that we were fooled into believing the fault to be mechanical. On the seismograph, it showed as a regular blip in an otherwise perfectly normal line; a blip that came up bang on time once every five seconds or so – *blip* . . . *blip* . . . *blip* – very odd! But, seeing that in every other respect the information coming out of the computer was spot on, no one worried overmuch about this inexplicable deviation. The blips were there right to the end, and it was only then that I found a reason for them, but in between there came other difficulties – not the least of them being the trouble with the fish.

147

Now, if that sounds a bit funny, well, it was a funny business. The lads had rigged up a small platform, slung twenty feet or so below the main platform and about the same height above the water, and in their off-duty hours when they weren't resting or knocking back a pint in the mess, you could usually see one or two of them down there fishing.

First time we found anything odd in the habits of the fish around the rig was one morning when Nick Adams hooked a beauty. All of three feet long, the fish was, wriggling and yellow in the cold November sunlight. Nick just about had the fish docked when the hook came out of its mouth so that it fell back among some support-girders down near where leg number four was being washed by a slight swell. It just lay there, flopping about a bit, in the girders. Nick scrambled down after it with a rope around his waist while his brother Dave hung on to the other end. And what do you think? When he got down to it, damned if the fish didn't go for him! It actually made to *bite* him, flopping after him on the girders, and snapping its jaws until he had to yell for Dave to haul him up.

Later he told us about it; how the damned thing hadn't even tried to get back into the sea, seeming more interested in setting its teeth in him than preserving its own life! Now, you'd expect that sort of reaction from a great eel, Johnny, wouldn't you? But hardly from a cod – not from a North-Sea cod!

From then on, Spellman, the diver, couldn't go down – not *wouldn't*, mind you, *couldn't* – the fish simply wouldn't let him. They'd chew on his suit, his air-hose . . . he got to be so frightened of them that he became quite useless to us. I can't see as I blame him, though, especially when I think of what later happened to Robertson.

148

But of course, before Robertson's accident, there was that further trouble with Borszowski. It was in the sixth week, when we were expecting to break through at any time, that Joe failed to come back off shore leave. Instead, he sent me a long, rambling explanatory letter; and to be truthful, when first I read it, I figured we were better off without him. The man had quite obviously been cracking up for a long time. He went on about *monsters*, sleeping in great caverns underground and especially under the seas, waiting for a chance to take over the surface world. He said that those star-shaped stones were seals to keep these monster beings ('gods', he called them) imprisoned; that the gods could control the weather to a degree; that they were capable of influencing the actions of lesser creatures – such as fish, or, occasionally, men – and that he believed one of them must be lying there, locked in the ground beneath the sea, pretty close to where we were drilling. He was frightened we were going to set it loose! The only thing that had stopped him from pressing the matter earlier was that then, as now, he'd believed we'd all think he was mad! Finally, though, he'd had to 'warn' me, knowing that if anything *did* happen, he'd never forgive himself if he hadn't at least tried.

Well, like I say, Borszowski's letter was rambling and disjointed – and yet, despite my first conclusion, the Pole had written the thing in a rather convincing manner. Hardly what you'd expect from a real madman. He quoted references from the Bible, particularly Exodus 20:4, and again and again emphasized his belief that the star-shaped things were nothing more or less than prehistoric pentacles laid down by some great race of alien sorcerers many millions of years ago. He reminded me of the heavy, unusual mists we'd had and of the queer way the cod had gone for Nick Adams. He even brought up

149

again the question of the shaky sea-phones and computer; making, in toto, an altogether disturbing assessment of *Sea-Maid*'s late history as applicable to his own odd fancies.

In fact, I became *so* disturbed by that letter that I was still thinking about it later that evening, and about the man himself, the superstitious Pole.

I did a little checking on Joe's background, discovering that he'd travelled far in his early days to become something of a scholar in obscure mythological matters. Also, it had been noticed on occasion – whenever the mists were heavier than usual, particularly since the appearance of the first star-stone – that he crossed himself with a strange sign over his breast. A number of the lads had seen him do it. They all told the same tale about that sign; that it was pointed, one point straight up, two more down and wide, two still lower but closer together. Yes, the Pole's sign was a five-pointed star! And again I read his letter.

By then we'd shut down for the day and I was out on the main platform having a quiet pipeful – I can concentrate, you know, with a bit of 'baccy. Dusk was only a few minutes away when the . . . *accident* . . . happened.

Robertson, the steel-rigger, was up aloft tightening a few loose bolts halfway up the rig. Don't ask me where the mist came from, I don't know, but suddenly it was there. It swam up from the sea, a thick grey blanket that cut visibility down to no more than a few feet. I'd just shouted up to Robertson, telling him that he'd better pack it in for the night, when I heard his yell and saw his lantern (he must have lit it as soon as the mist rolled in) come blazing down out of the greyness. The lantern disappeared through an open hatch, and a second later Robertson followed it. He went straight through the hatchway, missing the sides by inches, and then there came the splashes as first the lantern, then the man hit the sea. In two shakes of a dog's tail Robertson was splashing about down there in the mist and yelling fit to ruin his lungs, proving to me and the others who'd rushed out from the mess at my call that his fall had done him little harm. We lowered a raft immediately, getting two of the men down to the water in less than two minutes, and no one gave it a second thought that Robertson wouldn't be picked up. He was, after all, an excellent swimmer. In fact, the lads on the raft thought the whole episode was a big laugh . . . that is until Robertson started to scream!

I mean, there are screams and there are *screams*, Johnny! Robertson wasn't drowning – he wasn't making noises like a drowning man!

He wasn't picked up, either. No less quickly than it had settled, the mist lifted, so that by the time the raft touched water visibility was normal for a November evening . . . but there was no sign of the steel-rigger. There *was* something, though, something we'd all forgotten – for the whole surface of the sea was silver with fish!

Fish! Big and little, almost every indigenous species you could imagine. The way they were acting, apparently trying to throw themselves aboard the raft, I had the lads haul themselves back up to the platform as soon as it became evident that Robertson was gone for good. Johnny – I swear I'll never eat fish again.

That night I didn't sleep very well at all. Now, you know I'm not being callous. I mean, aboard an ocean-going rig after a hard day's work, no matter what has happened during the day, a man usually manages to sleep. Yet that night I just couldn't drop off. I kept going over in my mind all the . . . well, the *things* – the odd occurrences, the trouble with the instruments and the fish, Borszowski's letter again, and finally, of course, the

151

awful way we lost Robertson – until I thought my head must burst with the burden of wild notions and imaginings going round and round inside it.

Next afternoon the chopper came in again (with Wes Atlee complaining about having had to make two runs in two days) and delivered all the booze and goodies for the party the next day. As you know, we always have a blast aboard when we strike it rich – and this time the geological samples had more or less assured us of a good one. We'd been out of beer a few days by that time – poor weather had stopped Wes from bringing in anything but mail – and so I was running pretty high and dry. Now you know me, Johnny. I got in the back of the mess with all that booze and cracked a few bottles. I could see the gear turning from the window, and, over the edge of the platform, the sea all grey and eerie-looking, and somehow the idea of getting a load of booze inside me seemed a damn good one.

I'd been in there topping-up for over half an hour when Jeffries, my 2IC, got through to me on the telephone. He was in the instrument cabin and said he reckoned the drill would go through to 'muck' within a few more minutes. He sounded worried, though, sort of shaky, and when I asked him why this was, he didn't rightly seem able to answer – mumbled something about the instruments mapping those strange blips again, regular as ever but somehow stronger . . . closer.

About that time I first noticed the mist swirling up from the sea, a real pea-souper, billowing in to smother the rig and turn the men on the platform to grey ghosts. It muffled the sound of the gear, too, altering the metallic clank and rattle of pulleys and chains to distant, dull noises such as I might have expected to hear from the rig if I'd been in a suit deep down under the sea.

It was warm enough in the back room of the mess

there, yet unaccountably I found myself shivering as I looked out over the rig and listened to the ghost sounds of machinery and men.

That was when the wind came up. First the mist, then the wind – but I'd never before seen a mist that a good strong wind couldn't blow away! Oh, I've seen freak storms before, Johnny, but believe me this storm was *the* freak! With a capital 'F'.

She came up out of nowhere – not breaking the blanket of grey but driving it round and round like a great mad ghost – blasting the already choppy sea against the Old Girl's legs, flinging up spray to the platform's guard-rails, and generally creating havoc. I'd no sooner recovered from my initial amazement when the telephone rang again. I came away from the window, picked up the receiver to hear Jimmy Jeffries' somewhat distorted yell of triumph coming over the wires.

'We're *through*, Pongo!' he yelled. 'We're through and there's juice on the way up the bore right now!' Then his voice took the shakes again, going from wild excitement to terror in a second as the whole rig *wobbled* on its four great legs!

'Holy heaven – !' His voice screamed in my ear. '*What was that*, Pongo? The rig . . . wait – ' I heard the clatter as the telephone at the other end banged down, but a moment later Jimmy was back. 'It's not the rig,' he told me; 'the legs are steady as rocks – *it's the whole seabed!* Pongo, what's going on? Holy heaven – '

This time the telephone went completely dead as the rig moved again, jerking up and down three or four times in rapid succession, shaking everything loose inside the mess storeroom. I was just able to keep my feet. I still had the telephone in my hand, and just for a second or two it came back to life. Jimmy was screaming something incoherently into his end. I remember that I yelled for

153

him to get into a life jacket, that there was something awfully wrong and we were in for big trouble, but I'll never know if he heard me.

The rig rocked yet again, throwing me down on the floorboards among a debris of bottles, crates, cans, and packets; and there, skidding wildly about the tilting floor, I collided with a life jacket. God only knows what the thing was doing there in the storeroom – there were normally two or three on the platform and others were kept in the equipment shed, only taken out following storm warnings, which it goes without saying we hadn't had. But somehow I managed to struggle into it and make my way into the mess proper before the next upheaval.

By that time, over the roar of the wind and waves outside and the slap of wave-crests against the outer walls of the mess, I could hear a whipping of free-running pulleys and a high-pitched screaming of revving, uncontrolled gears – and there were *other* screams, too.

I admit that I was in a blind panic, crashing my way through the tumble of chairs and tables in the mess towards the door leading out on to the platform, when the greatest shock so far tilted the floor to what must have been thirty degrees and saved me any further effort. In that moment – as I flew against the door, bursting it open, and floundering out into the storm – I knew for sure that the old *Sea-Maid* was going down. Before, it had only been a possibility, a mad, improbable possibility; but now I knew for sure. Half stunned from my collision with the door, I was thrown roughly against the platform rails, to cling there for dear life in the howling, tearing wind and chill, rushing mist and spray.

*And that was when I saw it!*

I saw it . . . and in my utter disbelief I relaxed my hold on the rails and slid under them into the throat of that banshee, demon storm that howled and tore at the trembling girders of the old *Sea-Maid*.

Even as I fell a colossal wave smashed into the rig, breaking two of the legs as though they were nothing stronger than matchsticks. The next instant I was in the sea, picked up, and swept away on the crest of that same wave. Even in the dizzy, sickening rush as the great wave hurled me aloft, I tried to spot *Sea-Maid* in the maelstrom of wind, mist, and ocean. It was futile and I gave it up in order to save all my effort for my own battle for survival.

I don't remember much after that – at least, not until I was picked up, and even that's not too clear. I do remember, though, while fighting the icy water, a dreadful fear of being eaten alive by fish; but so far as I know there were none about. I remember, too, being hauled aboard the lifeboat from a sea that was flat as a pancake and calm as a mill pond.

The next really lucid moment came when I woke up to find myself between clean sheets in a Bridlington hospital.

But there, I've held off from telling the important part, and for the same reason Joe Borszowski held off: I don't want to be thought a madman. Well, I'm *not* mad, Johnny, but I don't suppose for a single moment that you'll take my story seriously – nor, for that matter, will Seagasso suspend any of its North-Sea commitments – but at least I'll have had the satisfaction of knowing that I tried to warn you.

Now, remember if you will what Borszowski told me about great, alien beings lying asleep and imprisoned beneath the bed of the sea – evil 'gods' capable of controlling the weather and the actions of lesser creatures – and then explain the sight I saw before I found myself floundering in that mad ocean as the old *Sea-Maid* went down.

It was simply a gusher, Johnny, a gusher – but one such

155

as I'd never seen before in my whole life and hope never to see again! For instead of reaching the heavens in one solid black column, it *pulsed* upward, pumping up in short, strong jets at a rate of about one spurt in every five seconds – and it wasn't oil, Johnny! Oh, God, it wasn't oil! Booze or none, I swear I wasn't drunk; not so drunk as to make me *colour-blind*, at any rate.

For old Borszowski was right, there was one of those great god-things down there deep in the bed of the ocean, *and our drill had chopped right into it!*

Whatever it was, it had blood pretty much like ours – good and thick and red – and a great heart strong enough to pump that blood up the bore-hole right to the surface! Think of it, that monstrous giant of a thing down there in the rocks beneath the sea! How could we possibly have known? *How could we have guessed that right from the beginning our instruments had been working at maximum efficiency, that those odd, regular blips recorded on the seismograph had been nothing more than the beating of a great submarine heart?*

All of which explains, I hope, my resignation.

Bernard 'Pongo' Jordan
Bridlington, Yorks.

# 10

## The Third Visitor

### (From de Marigny's Notebooks)

The early morning was quite close, uncomfortable almost, so that by the time Titus Crow and I had finished with the astonishing Jordan document Peaslee had taken off his coat. He had adopted a very businesslike look, donning small-lensed spectacles, rolling up his shirt sleeves and busying himself with a number of files, notebooks, and various other papers from his briefcase. He was past his tired peak, he told us, and having slept on the plane coming over, he had also now just about managed to adjust his body-clock. He looked forward, though, to a short nap in the Mercedes on the way back to London and the British Museum; a nap en route, he assured us, should put him completely to rights.

'London and the British Museum'; the normal world seemed light-years away. And yet, through the latticed windows, dawn was spreading her pale fingers over the distant capital in what seemed a very normal fashion, and the new day was well on its way. Crow and I were now very tired, but such were those feelings of general well-being engendered by the protective proximity of the star-stones, that neither of us minded the heaviness of our bodies – at least we were completely clear-headed; our minds were free of morbid Cthonian undertones.

It was as I went into the galley to cook bacon and eggs for an early breakfast, as I passed down the short joining corridor between the bunkhouse and the galley proper, that I was thrown against the galley door when the houseboat suddenly rocked violently. From the bunkroom came the clatter of falling glasses, the thud of books, and Crow's startled query: 'What on earth . . . ?'

I opened the galley window and looked out on deck and across the river. The sun's edge was just showing above the horizon of trees and distant roofs. There was a very slight breeze up, but the river was white with mist.

Mentally echoing Titus Crow, I wondered: 'What on earth . . . ?' Had some lunatic gone up the river in a large motorboat at speed? But no, that could hardly be, I had heard no engine. In any case, it would have taken an ocean liner to create a wake like that! Even as these thoughts passed through my head *Seafree* keeled again, this time to an angle of about twenty degrees. Immediately, I found myself thinking of the Jordan document.

'De Marigny!' Crow's shout came from the open window even as I heard him skidding about on the momentarily sloping deck. 'Henri.' His feet clattered. 'Get that damned pistol of yours, quickly!' There was urgency in his voice, unnatural strain – and horror!

'No, no!' came the professor's shouted denial as the boat dipped and swayed. 'That's not the way, Crow. Silver bullets are no use against *this* thing!'

What thing?

I scrambled back through the galley door and down the corridor, across the bunkhouse floor, and up the three steps to the deck. There, clinging to the rail, their faces drawn and white, stood the two men. As the boat steadied itself, I joined them. 'What is it, Titus? What's wrong?'

'There's something out there, Henri, in the water. Something big! It just now made a rush at the boat – stopped about fifty feet short and sank down again into the water – a Sea-Shoggoth, I think, exactly like those dream-things I told you about.'

'Yes, a Sea-Shoggoth,' Peaslee breathed. 'One of the Deep Ones. All the way from Deep G'll-ho to the north,

158

I imagine. It can't harm us – ' He sounded sure enough of his facts, but nevertheless I noticed that his hushed voice trembled.

The mist was thick on the river, its milky tendrils and eddies coming almost up to the deck of the houseboat, making it seem as though we stood aboard a mere raft. I could hear the *chop* as the disturbed waters slapped the hull, but I could see nothing. I felt my pulse start to race and the short hairs prickling at the back of my neck. 'I'll get my pistol,' I said, intending to go back down into the boat.

As I turned from the rail Peaslee grabbed my arm. 'Useless, de Marigny,' he snapped. 'Pistols, no matter what kind of ammunition they take, are useless against this type of creature!'

'But where is the thing?' I asked, peering again at the misted waters.

As if in answer to my nervous question, indeed, as the last word left my lips, an iridescent, blackly shining column of what looked like mud or tar embedded with fragments of broken, multicoloured glass rose up out of the swirling river mist. Eight feet wide and all of twenty feet tall, dripping water and bobbing like some great sentient cork, the thing towered above the water . . . and the sun glinted from its surface and from its myriad eyes!

The creature – stank! There is simply no other way of expressing the nauseating stench that issued from it. Lines from Alhazred again leaped into my mind: 'By their smell shall ye know them,' and I knew exactly what the so-called 'mad' Arab had meant! It was the very smell of evil. Twice in a matter of hours my senses had been thus assaulted, and this time the worst! Thank the Lord that the houseboat was upwind, what little wind there was, of the horror; we received only a minimum, but even then too much, of that miasmal, deep-sea effluvium.

159

It had mouths, too, many of them, but I caught only a glimpse. As the thing made a frantic, nodding rush at the boat I threw myself down the steps after Kant's pistol. No matter what Peaslee said, I refused to stand undefended against *that*! Any weapon seemed better than none at all. In my panic I had completely forgotten the fact that we were not at all weaponless, that in fact we had the best possible protection! In any case, I couldn't find the pistol. Where had I put the thing?

The houseboat rocked again, yet more violently, and I scrambled back up the steps to the deck empty-handed. Fighting to keep his balance while hanging on to the rail with one hand, Peaslee was holding up a star-stone and shouting at the horror in the water. The thing was already rushing back in yet another monstrous, bobbing charge. My concentration divided itself equally between the professor and the creature bearing down upon the boat. Peaslee was rapidly chanting: 'Away, slime of the sea, back to your dark and pressured seat. With the authority of the Elder Gods themselves I command you. Away and leave us in peace!' The tremor had left his voice and his old, slim frame seemed somehow tall and powerful against the backdrop of iridescent horror sprouting beyond him from the river mist.

Before Peaslee's chanting and his showing of the star-stone there had been no sound from the Deep One other than the natural noise of the water rushing past its nightmare shape as it charged. Now –

It was screaming, apparently in rage and frustration, certainly in a manner suggesting some sort of alien mental agony. Its – voice? – had been just too far up the sonic scale before; there had been a high, almost inaudible whine in the air. Now, though, the professor's chanted words, repeated over and over again, were almost drowned out and I had to grit my teeth and slam my

160

hands to my ears as the creature lowered its hideous cries. Never before in my life had I heard so unbelievable a cacophony of incredible sounds all in one, and it was my fervent prayer that I never hear such sounds again!

The screaming was still in the main high-pitched, like a steam engine's whistle, but there were grunted undertones, throbbing gasps or emissions such as the reptiles and great frogs make, impossible to put down on paper. Two more bobbing, water-spraying, abortive attempts it made to breach the invisible barrier between its awful body and the houseboat – and then it turned, sank, and finally left a thrashing, thinning wake in the rapidly clearing mist as it headed for London and the open sea beyond.

For a long time there was an awkward hush, wherein only the subsiding slap of wavelets against the hull, our erratic and harsh breathing, and the outraged cheeping of momentarily quieted birds disturbed the silence. Peaslee's voice, a little less steady now that it was all over, finally got through to me after a second asking of his question:

'How about breakfast, Henri? Won't it be spoiling?'

Crow laughed harshly as I explained that I had not yet managed to get breakfast started. He said: 'Breakfast? By God, Peaslee, but you won't catch me eating on this boat! I won't be here long enough – not now!'

'Perhaps you're right,' the professor hurriedly agreed. 'Yes, the sooner we get on our way, the better. We were perfectly safe, I assure you, but such things are always unnerving.'

'Unnerving!' *Ye Gods!*

It took us half an hour to get packed up; by 9:45 we were on our way in Crow's Mercedes.

We breakfasted at 10:30 in a pub on the approaches to the city proper. Guinness and ham sandwiches. We all were very hungry. As we finished off a second bottle each

(Peaslee's surprise at the black brew's pick-me-up quality was apparent) we also saw an end to our conversation regarding the morning's monstrous visitor.

Miskatonic and the Wilmarth Foundation, the professor declared, had long suspected a deep-sea citadel north of the British Isles, peopled by such creatures as only the Cthulhu Cycle of myth might spawn. They had good reasons for such suspicions; apparently G'll-ho was given mention in a fair number of the great works of named and anonymous occult authors. ('Occult' is a natural part of my vocabulary; I doubt if I shall ever learn how to leave it out of my life or thoughts, written or spoken.) Abdul Alhazred, in the *Necronomicon*, had named the place as 'Sunken G'lohee, in the Isles of Mist', and he had hinted that its denizens were the spawn of Cthulhu himself! More recently, Gordon Walmsley of Goole had recorded similar allusions in his alleged 'spoof' death-notes. Titus Crow, too, considering his dreams of a vast underwater fortress somewhere off the Vestmann Islands, where Surtsey belched forth in the agony of volcanic birth in 1963, concurred with the possibility of just such a submarine seat of suppurating evil.

Assuredly, the professor had it, the creature we had seen that morning had originated in G'll-ho. It had been sent, no doubt, on the telepathic instructions of Shudde-M'ell or his kind, to deliver the death-blow to two dangerous men. If Peaslee had not presented himself when he did . . . it did not bear thinking about.

While the professor's explanation regarding our visitor's origin seemed reasonably satisfactory to me, Crow was far from easy about it. Why then, he wanted to know, had similar beasts not been sent to deal with *Sea-Maid* when that rig had been drilling its inadvertently destructive bore off Hunterby Head? Again Peaslee had the answer to hand. Some of these horrors, he reminded us,

162

were in direct opposition to one another – such as Cthulhu and Hastur. The type of creature as called up those cyclonic forces which sent *Sea-Maid* to the bottom, while it was not necessarily an enemy of the Lord of R'lyeh, was certainly inferior in the mythos; it was simply too lowly for Cthulhu, or any other of the greater powers of the CCD, to bother with. True, it had had the capacity to partly control the elements, and lesser creatures such as fishes, but the experience of the Wilmarth Foundation (which had dealt with such beings before) was that these were the least harmful of all the inmates of the Elder Gods' prisons.

The theory was, in fact, that such creatures were nothing more than low-order minions of the Great Ones proper, but that they had been imprisoned separately because of their huge size – in much the same way as large animals are kept in separate cages in zoos while smaller creatures are housed together. Certainly Shudde-M'ell had not been prisoned alone, as witness the G'harne eggs and the monstrous spread of the Cthonians through-out the world. Peaslee quite expected, before we were through with the Great Britain Project, that we should see an end put to any number of such beings. (Eventually, we were, in fact, witness to many such 'kills', and one which sticks in my mind quite vividly still, though I have at times tried to forget it. But I must keep that horror for later.)

The Deep Ones, though, quite apart from these appall-ing subterrene giants, came in a number of sorts and sizes. Their name, in fact, was a group heading, under which fell all manner of fishlike, protoplasmic, batrachian, and semi-human beings, united together in the worship of Dagon and the anticipated resurrection of Great Cthulhu. Neither Crow nor I was totally ignorant of these Deep Ones; we had both heard, over a period of time and from diverse sources, mad whispers echoing down the years of frightful occurrences at Innsmouth, a decaying seaport on the New England coast of America. Indeed, such was the macabre nature of the stories that leaked out of Innsmouth in the late 20s that certain of them, almost a decade later, were fictionalized in a number of popular fantastic magazines. The theme of these rumours (no longer rumours, for Peaslee assured us of their established *fact*; he positively asserted that Federal files were extant, copies of which had long been 'acquired' by the Wilmarth Foundation, which detailed the almost unbelievable occurrences of 1928) was that in the early 1800s certain traders of the old East-Indian and Pacific routes had had unsavoury dealings with degenerate Polynesian islanders. These natives had had their own 'gods', namely Cthulhu and Dagon (the latter having seen earlier worship by the Philistines and Phoenicians), and worshipped them in disgusting and barbaric ways. Eventually the New England sailors were inveigled into taking part in just such practices, apparently against the better judgement of many of them, and yet it seemed that the ways of the heathen Kanakas were not without their own doubtful rewards!

Innsmouth prospered, grew fat and rich as trade picked up, and soon strange gold changed hands in the streets of that doomed town. Esoteric churches opened – or rather temples – for purposes of even darker worship (the many seafarers had brought back strangely ichthyic Polynesian brides), and who could say how far things might have gone if, in 1927, the Federal Government had not been alerted to the growing menace?

In the winter of 1927–28, Federal agents moved in, and the end result was that half Innsmouth's inhabitants were banished (Peaslee had it that they had been sent off to scattered naval and military prisons and out-of-the-way asylums) and depth-charges were dropped off Devil's Reef in the Atlantic coast. There, in the untold depths of a natural rift, existed a weed-shrouded city of alien proportions and dimensions – Y'ha-nthlei – peopled by the Deep Ones, into which 'select' order many of the New England traders and their hideously blasphemous offspring had been admitted since contact was first established with the Polynesians a century earlier. For those islanders of one hundred years gone had known far more than a close liaison with the Deep Ones of Polynesia – *and therefore so eventually did the New Englanders*.

The seafaring traders paid dearly for their adoption of the Kanaka 'faith' – and for less mentionable things – for by the time the Federal agents took control of Innsmouth hardly a single family existed in the town untainted by the shocking disfigurations of a stigma known locally as 'the Innsmouth Look'.

The Innsmouth Look! Frightful degenerations of mind and tissue . . . scaly skin, webbed fingers and toes . . . bulging fishlike eyes . . . *gills*!

And it was the Innsmouth Look that heralded the change from land-dweller to amphibian, from human to Deep One! Many of the town's inhabitants who escaped the horrified government agents did so by swimming out to Devil's Reef and diving down to Y'ha-nthlei, there to dwell with the Deep Ones proper, 'in wonder and glory for ever'.

These, then, were members of that seething submarine sect – but there were others.

There *were* others, more truly alien (Crow's 'survivors'), leftovers from an abyss of time and aeons before their aquatic phase, when the Earth knew the semiprotoplasmic tread of them and their masters and none other. It was one of these latter beings that had attempted the

165

attack upon *Seafree* – which only Peaslee's star-stones and chantings had held at bay.

With all talk over, our meal done, and feeling the better for it, we left the pub and continued on our way. The journey was uneventful and quiet, with Crow driving while I relaxed in the back of the car. Beside me, Peaslee nodded and drowsed, no doubt making final subconscious adjustments to his body-clock.

That night, after the professor had paid a long, lone afternoon call to the British Museum, we all three congregated to sleep at Blowne House. For the first time in what seemed like years I slept peacefully, dreamlessly; so that not even certain vociferous trees in the garden, creaking through the dark hours, could disturb my slumbers in any other than a tiny degree.

# 11

## *Horrors of Earth*

### *(From de Marigny's Notebooks)*

Many & multiform are ye dim horrors of Earth, infesting her
ways from ye very prime. They sleep beneath ye unturned stone;
they rise with ye tree from its root; they move beneath ye sea,
& in subterranean places they dwell in ye inmost adyta. Some
there are long known to man, & others as yet unknown, abiding
ye terrible latter days of their revealing. Those which are ye
most dreadful & ye loathliest of all are haply still to be declared.

Abdul Alhazred: Feery's
*Notes on the Necronomicon.*

Some months have passed; they seem like years. Certainly I have aged years. Many of the things I have seen
have proved almost too much to believe – too fantastic
even to retain – and, indeed, I actually find the pictures
fading from my memory. As the days go by, I have more
and more trouble focusing my mind upon any set instance,
any individual incident; and yet, paradoxically, it is
undeniable that certain things have left livid scars upon
the surface of my mind.

Perhaps this reluctance of mine to remember is simply
a healing process, and who can say but that when I have
'healed' completely the entire episode might well have
vanished for ever from my memory?

It is because of this – because there is a very real chance
of my 'forgetting' all that has gone since the advent of
Professor Wingate Peaslee of Miskatonic – that now,
without any conscious attempt to stress the horror in any
way, in an earnest effort to get the thing down as
unemotionally as possible, I make the following entries in
my notebook.

Possibly my *rejection* began before Peaslee and the subsequent horrors, for I find that those monstrous occurrences aboard *Seafree* before his coming are also dimming in my mind's eye, and to recall them in any sort of detail I find it necessary to resort to a reading of my earlier notebooks. Yet this, surely, is a mercy. Who was it said that the most merciful thing in the world is the inability of the human mind to correlate all its contents? And yet, if only to retain the following as an *account* as opposed to a memory, I find that I must now correlate at least certain occurrences . . .

It was late August. The three of us, myself, Crow, and Peaslee, were looking down from a low bramble- and gorse-girt hill across an area of wild open moorland. Of course, it is not my intention to divulge our exact whereabouts as they were, but we were well 'out-of-the-way'. Three weed-grown and neglect-obscured tracks led out of the area, and each of them, from a distance some four miles out from the hub of the operation, carried warning notices such as: *Danger, Unexploded Bombs,* and *Government Property, Keep Out,* or *Tank Range, Firing in Progress!* Such notices had had Crow somewhat perturbed for a time, until Peaslee reminded him of the Wilmarth Foundation's influence in high places – even in certain governmental circles! To reinforce the posted warnings a number of Foundation men with guard dogs prowled the perimeter of the area. It would be disastrous to allow the leak of any untoward tales into the mundane world outside.

No more than a mile away, and in a central, strangely barren area, the superstructure of a great drilling-rig towered up to clear but grey skies. Beneath that threatening pylon of girders and gears, fourteen hundred feet down in the bedrock, one of those monsters met before by Pongo Jordan and his ill-fated rig *Sea-Maid* slumbered in its ancient prison. That the Cthonian was in fact prisoned had long been ascertained; the telepath who first tracked the thing down had recognized well-known mind-patterns and had picked up mental impressions implying great size. It was indeed one of those outsize, low-order minions of the Old Ones which, in Peaslee's own words, 'were the least harmful of all the inmates of the Elder Gods' prisons.'

Despite a warm sun the afternoon breeze, seeming to spring from somewhere down in the direction of the drilling-rig, was surprisingly chill. We had the collars of our coats turned up against it. Peaslee was in walkie-talkie contact with a British telepath, Gordon Finch, whose mental images – relayed to us as he received them and as the climax drew to a close – came over the air loud and clear. The huge Cthonian (possibly undisturbed for millennia) had started to emerge from its comalike slumbers some hours before and was now becoming more alert, its monstrous mind forming rather clearer pictures for Finch to 'tune in' on. Crow, powerful binoculars about his neck, peered intently into lenses sighted on the matchstick people and Dinky-Toy vehicles moving about down in the distant spider web of paths and tracks cut through the greyly withered gorse and heather.

A Land Rover, churning sand and browned gorse flowers, issued blue exhaust smoke as it powered through dry, scanty foliage at the foot of our hill. The bright yellow bandanna of the driver identified him as Bernard 'Pongo' Jordan himself. He was on his way up to our vantage point, from which he hoped to photograph the kill. This in no way reflected a morbid 'thing' of Pongo's, on the contrary, for any and all information on the CCD was of the utmost importance to the Wilmarth Foundation. After death most of the Cthonians rotted so fast that

169

identification of their matter was literally impossible – and very few of the various species had anything even remotely approaching similarities of makeup! Even the count of the heartbeat – or the beat of whatever organ the creature possessed which might stand for a heart – would prove of value; and it was that chiefly, the gory spurt of alien juices, that Pongo intended to film.

In a matter of minutes the Rover had bumped its way up to the crest upon which we stood. Pongo slewed the vehicle about and parked it none too carefully beside Crow's big black Mercedes. Before the motor coughed itself out the huge Yorkshireman had joined us. He pulled a hip-flask from the pocket of his denim jacket and took a deep draught before offering the whisky to Crow, who declined with a smile.

'No thanks, Pongo – I prefer brandy. We have a flask in the car.'

'You, de Marigny?' The big man's voice, despite its roughness, was tense, nervous.

'Thanks, yes.' I took the flask from him. I hardly needed the drink really, but Jordan's jumpiness was infectious. And little wonder, for there was something . . . wrong . . . somewhere. We could all sense it, a disturbing feeling of impending, well, *something* in the air. The lull before a storm.

Gordon Finch's voice came louder now, clearer over the walkie-talkie, which Peaslee had turned up full volume for our benefit.

'The thing's not quite fully aware yet, it's still half asleep, but it knows something's up. I'm going to go deeper into its mind, see what I can see.'

'Careful, Finch,' Peaslee said quickly into his handset. 'Don't alert the creature whatever you do. We can never be certain – we don't know what it's capable of.'

For perhaps half a minute there was an almost audible

silence from the walkie-talkie. Then, simultaneous with Jordan's reminder that there were only six minutes left to penetration, Finch's voice, ethereal now as his mind entered deeper into the Cthonian's miasmal mentality, sounded again from Peaslee's handset:

'It's . . . *strange!* Strangest sensations I've ever known. There's pressure, the weight of countless tons of . . . rock.' The voice trailed off.

Peaslee waited a second, then snapped: 'Finch, get a grip on yourself, man! What's wrong?'

'Eh?' I could almost see the telepath shaking himself. Now his voice was eager: 'Nothing's wrong, Professor, but I want to go deeper. I believe I can get *right inside* this one!'

'I forbid it – ' Peaslee railed.

'Never forbid an Englishman anything.' Finch's voice hardened. 'A few more minutes and the thing'll be finished, gone for ever – and it's millions of years old. I want . . . I want to *know*!'

Again the silence from the handset, while Peaslee grew more agitated by the second. Then –

'Pressure . . .' The voice was fainter, trancelike. 'Tons and tons of crushing . . . weight.'

'Where is he down there?' Crow asked sharply, never for a second taking the binoculars from his eyes.

'In the control shack by the rig,' Jordan answered, his camera starting to whir in his hands. 'The others should be clearing out now, moving back – all bar the lads on the rig itself – and Finch should get out too. He'll get drenched in muck when she goes through; and when they shoot off the bomb – ' He left his thoughts unspoken.

By 'the bomb' I knew he meant the explosive harpoon set in the head of the great drill. As soon as the bit went through into the softer *stuff* of the Cthonian, the bomb would automatically fire, shooting itself deep into the guts

171

of the monster before exploding. Finch was supposed to break contact with the creature's thoughts before then.

'Four minutes,' Pongo said.

'*Trapped!*' came Finch's voice again. '*Trapped down . . . HERE! Nothing has changed – but why do I wake? I have only to flex the muscles of my body, arch my back to break out, to be free to go – as I went free so long ago – in search of the little creatures – to slake this great thirst with their red –*

'*Ahhh! I can see the little ones in my mind as I remember them, when once before, following the great roaring and crushing and shifting of the earth, I went free! With their little arms, hairy bodies, and futile clubs. I remember their screams as I absorbed them into myself.*

'*But I dare not, CANNOT, break free! Despite my strength, a greater power holds me, the mind-chains of THEM and their barriers – the Great Elder Gods who prisoned me so long, long ago – who returned to prison me again after but a brief freedom when the earth tore itself and their sigils were scattered.*

'*I am STILL prisoned, and more, there is . . . danger!*'

'Finch, come out of there!' Peaslee yelled frantically into his handset. 'Let the thing be, man, and get out!'

'*DANGER!*' Finch's now alien voice continued, coarse and slurred. '*I can sense . . . little ones! Many of them . . . above me . . . and something approaches!*'

'Just over two minutes!' Jordan blurted, his voice cracking.

Now there was only a harsh gasping from the walkie-talkie, and above it Crow's sudden, amazed exclamation: 'Why, *I* can feel the thing, too! It's sending out mind-feelers. It knows what we're up to. It's more intelligent than we thought, Peaslee, superior to any of the others we've so far done away with.' He let his binoculars dangle and put his hands up to his ears, as if to shut out some dreadful sound. His eyes closed and his face screwed up in pain. 'The thing's frightened – no, *angry*! My God!'

'*I am not defenceless, little ones!*' Finch's horribly altered voice screamed from the handset. '*Trapped, true, but NOT defenceless. You have learned much in the passage of time – but I, too, have powers! I can't stop that which you send burrowing down towards me, but I have . . . powers!*'

Crow screamed harshly and fell to his knees, rocking to and fro and clutching madly at his head. At that moment I was very glad that my own psychic or telepathic talents were as yet undeveloped!

'The sky!' Peaslee gasped, turning my attention from the now prostrate Titus Crow. 'Look at the sky!'

Black clouds boiled and tossed where only grey skies had opened scant moments before, and lightning played high in the cauldron of suddenly rushing air. In another second a great wind sprang up, whipping our coats about us and snatching at Jordan's yellow bandanna. Down in the depression gorse bushes came loose from the sandy earth to swirl into the air as if at the mercy of a whole nest of dust devils.

'Get down!' Jordan yelled, his voice barely audible over the wild rush of wind, flying sand and bits of gorse, heather and bracken. 'There's little over a minute to go – down for your lives!'

We all fell to the ground immediately. Crow now lay there quite still. I grabbed at thick heather roots and flung an arm about my friend's motionless body. The wind was icy now, seeming to rush up at us from the rig, and angry thunder boomed while flashes of lightning lit up the sky, etching in outlines of jet the rig's distant structure upon the gaunt backdrop of moor and low bleak hills.

Screams had begun to echo up from the declivity, barely heard over the mad, pandemoniac roar of tortured air and sky, causing me to reach through suddenly slashing rain for Crow's binoculars. I freed them from his neck and held them to my face, drawing the structures in the declivity closer with quick, jerky movements of my trembling hands.

'*The thing in the ground comes closer,*' screamed Finch's voice (or was it Finch's voice?) from Peaslee's handset. '*And I sense its nature. So be it! I die – but first feel the might of (. . . ?) and his wrath, and let my arms reach out for the surface that my mouths might drink one last time! Now know the LUST of (. . . ?), little ones, and his power over the very elements! Remember and tremble when the stars are right and Great Lord Cthulhu comes again!*'

I had finally managed to focus the binoculars on the rig and the small shacks surrounding it. In one of those buildings the telepath Finch sat, his mind still in contact with that of the great beast down in the bowels of the earth. I shuddered uncontrollably as I pictured the man down there.

Lorries and smaller vehicles were now moving away from the perimeter of the work area, and running figures, fighting the buffeting wind and squalling rain on foot. Then came horror!

Even as I watched, the lightning began to flash with more purpose, great bolts striking down accurately at the rig and its appurtenances. Running figures burst into electric flame and crumpled while lorries and Land Rovers, careening madly about, roared up in gouting fire and ruin. Girders melted and fell from the now blazing rig, and great patches of the scant vegetation surrounding that structure hissed and steamed before crackling into red and orange death.

'Time's up,' yelled Jordan in my ear; 'the bomb should fire any second now. That ought to put a stop to the bastard's game!'

Even as the Yorkshireman yelled the voice of the thing that had been Gordon Finch screamed from Peaslee's handset:

'*I am STRICKEN! – Na-ngh . . . ngh . . . ngh-ya – Great Ubbo-sathla, your child dies – but give me now strength for a final drinking – let me stretch myself this one last time – DEFY the sigils of the Elder Gods – na-argh . . . ngh . . . ngh! – Arghhh-k-k-k! – Hyuh, yuh, h-yuh-yuh!*'

As these monstrous, utterly abhuman exhortations and syllables crackled in hideously distorted cacophony from the walkie-talkie, so I witnessed the final abomination.

Dimly I was aware of Peaslee's incoherent cry as the very ground beneath us jounced and slipped; in the corner of my consciousness I knew that Jordan had attempted to get to his feet, only to be thrown down again by the dancing ground – but mainly my eyes and mind were riveted on the nightmare scene afforded me by Crow's accursed binoculars, those glasses that my nerveless fingers could not put down!

For down in the valley depression great rifts had appeared in the earth – and from these seismic chasms terrible tendrils of grey, living matter spewed forth in awful animation!

Flailing spastically – like great, mortally wounded snakes across the battered, blistered terrain – the tendrils moved, and soon some of them encountered the fleeing men! Great crimson maws opened in grey tendril ends, and –

Finally I managed to hurl the binoculars away. I closed my eyes and pressed my face down into the wet grass and sand. In that same instant there came a tremendous crack of lightning, the incredible flickering brightness of which I could sense even with my eyes closed and covered, and immediately there followed such an explosion and a

175

rushing, reeking *stench* as to make my very senses temporarily depart . . .

I do not know how long it was before I felt Jordan's hand upon my shoulder or heard his voice inquiring as to my condition, but when next I lifted my head the sky was clear once again and a freshening breeze blew over the blasted hill. Peaslee was sitting up, silently shaking his head from side to side and gazing down at the scene below. I followed his gaze.

Fires still raged down there, emitting columns of blue smoke among the shrivelled gorse bushes and brittle heather. The rig was a twisted mass of blackened metal, fallen on its side. One or two scorched trucks still moved, making their way tiredly towards our hill, and a handful of tattered figures stumbled dazedly about. Moans and cries for help drifted up to us. Grey, vile ichor steamed and bubbled in liquid catabolism, filling the newly opened cracks in the earth like pus in hellish sores.

'We have to help them,' Jordan said simply. I nodded and climbed weakly to my feet. Peaslee, too, stood up. Then, remembering, I got down on one knee and gently shook Titus Crow's shoulder. He came to a moment later, but was incapable of aiding us in the work we now had to do; his mental encounter, though brief, had been too shattering.

As the three of us walked towards Jordan's Rover, I picked up the walkie-talkie from where Peaslee had left it. In a moment of thoughtlessness I turned up the volume – and understood why the professor had left the handset behind. There were . . . *noises*: low, incoherent mouthings, snatches of childish song, giggles of imbecile laughter . . .

* * *

We lost six dead, five missing – and one, poor Finch, hopelessly insane. There were injuries, but in the main these were minor: burns, cuts, and bruises. The fact that another Cthonian – one of the 'least harmful of all' the subterrene species – was dead seemed hardly ample justification for such losses. Still, these were the first casualties the Foundation had suffered in the whole Great Britain Project to date.

The newspapers the next day were full of the earth tremors that had rocked the entire Northeast seaboard – to a lesser degree the titanic blast of ignited gases 'inadvertently released from beneath the surface of the earth by members of a scientific drilling project'. Too, ground rumblings had been heard and felt in the Cotswolds, and Surtsey had flared briefly forth again to send up clouds of volcanic steam. Freak storms vied for space with these items in the press: hailstones as big as golf balls in the South; freak lightning over many parts of England, particularly Durham and Northumberland; lashing, incessant rain the whole afternoon in the West. Lunatic asylums had also been affected, alarmingly so, by the Wilmarth Foundation's machineries that day. Reports of uprisings, mass rebellions, and escapes were legion. 'Moon, tide, and weather cycles', alienists and psychologists vaguely had it . . .

Of the form, type and characteristics of the Cthonian we destroyed that day little yet is known. That it was 'a child of Ubbo-sathla' seems as much as we are ever likely to learn. Within hours of the final explosion of its body-gases (gases which must have been closely related to methane, and under pressure at that), its tendril-substances – indeed, so far as is known, its entire body – had rotted and disappeared. Subsequent soundings of the space it had occupied underground have shown that the

177

thing was almost *a quarter of a mile long and a third that distance across!*

We do not even positively know what the creature's name was. We heard it spoken, certainly, by Finch in his telepathic trance, but such was its sound and the arrangements of its consonants that human vocal cords cannot emulate them. Only a man in actual mind-contact with such a being, as poor Gordon Finch was, might be able to approximate such intricacies. The nearest we can get to it in written English is: Cgfthgnm'o'th.

Regarding that forebear mentioned by the Cthonian in its death agonies: it would appear that Ubbo-sathla (Ubbho-Shatla, Hboshat, Bothshash, etc.) was here even before Cthulhu and his spawn first seeped down from the stars; that (if we can take Finch's mind-interpretations as a true translation), Ubbo-sathla was drawn into kinship with Cthulhu after the latter's domination of pre-Earth. These conclusions, such as they are, seem borne out by the following fragment from the disturbing *Book of Eibon*:

. . . For Ubbo-sathla is the source and the end. Before the coming of Zhothaquah or Yok-Zothoth or Kthulhut from the stars, Ubbo-sathla dwelt in the steaming fens of the new-made Earth: a mass without head or members, spawning the grey, formless efts of the prime and the grisly prototypes of terrene life . . . And all earthy life, it is told, shall go back at last through the great cycle of time to Ubbo-sathla . . .

It took a fortnight to clear up the mess, physical and administrational, and to cover our tracks – not to mention another week of fast talking in high places by Peaslee and other senior American members – before the operations of the Wilmarth Foundation in the British Isles could continue. In the end, though, the long-laid plans went ahead.

# 12
## Familiarity Breeds
### (From de Marigny's Notebooks)

On this occasion, some weeks gone, Crow and I were travelling in the Mercedes down from the Northwest. A few days earlier, in the Scottish Southern Uplands, the Wilmarth Foundation had forced a Cthonian – one of the last of the static or prisoned forms 'indigenous' to Great Britain and her waters – from its burrow deep beneath a mountain cleft. The being, a small one of its kind, had then been hosed down (literally hosed down *to nothing!*) with powerful jets of water. This had been at a place central in the Uplands; a sparse, very underpopulated area between Lanark and Dumfriesshire. The sight of the creature's violent thrashing as it melted beneath the sustained jets of lethal water, until finally it lay inert, a pool of awful, semiorganic putrescence bubbling off in vile evaporation, was one which had seared itself upon the retina of my very being. I was in fact still seeing the awful thing in my mind's eye as Crow drove the car south away from the scene of the 'kill'.

Following this latest offensive, Peaslee had flown from Glasgow to London to meet friends and colleagues coming in from America. These Americans were bringing freshly devised seismological equipment with which they hoped to follow the tracks of Shudde-M'ell's mobile Cthonian 'hordes' if the remainder of that species in Britain should make a dash for it, as certain of the Foundation's telepaths seemed to suspect they might. Of late the latter subterrene group, nests and individual members alike, had apparently developed a means of shielding their minds (and therefore their presence or

179

whereabouts) from all but the most powerful of the telepaths. Crow's limited telepathic power, following the horror of the moor, had seemed to leave him. He was, though, he had assured me privately, otherwise as 'physically aware' as ever.

It was about noon. We were, I remember, passing through a lonely region some miles to the east of Penrith. For quite some time Titus Crow had driven in what I had taken to be silent thoughtfulness. At the very edge of my consciousness, I had been taking in something of the terrain through which the big car passed. Automatically, as is sometimes its wont, my mind had partly separated its attentions – between monstrous memories of the dissolving horror in the hills and, as I have said, the country through which we passed – when suddenly, for no apparent reason, I found myself filled with an as yet obscure inner concern.

The area was bleak. A steep and rocky hillside tilted jaggedly to the right of the road, fell abruptly away to the left. The road itself was narrow and poorly surfaced, faintly misted in front and behind, and the mist was thickening as it rolled down off the hills marching away southward.

I had just noticed the peculiarly ominous aspect of the place when it dawned on me that I had a headache, something I had not known for months, since first Peaslee joined us from America. The recognition of this fact came hand in hand with the abrupt, shocking memory of the professor's warning: 'Always remember – they *never* stop trying! You must carry these things wherever you go from now on, *but even so you must try not to venture anywhere below the surrounding ground-level. I mean that you're to keep out of valleys, gullies, quarries, mines, subways, and so on. They can get at you indirectly – a sudden earthquake, a fall of rock . . .*'

'Titus!' I gasped out loud. 'Titus, where the hell are you going? We're not on the route we intended to take. We ought to have turned *across* country miles back, following the A-Sixty-Nine to the Northeast coast as we planned!' I gazed fearfully out of my window at the steep declivity falling away, and on the other side of the car, the now almost vertical wall of rock reaching up into misty heights.

Crow had jumped nervously as I commenced my outburst, and now he applied the brakes and brought the car to a halt. He shook his head, dazedly rubbing at his eyes. 'Of course we should have followed the A-Sixty-Nine,' he eventually agreed, frowning in concern. Then: *'What on earth . . . ?'* His eyes lit feverishly, strange understanding, horrible recognition showing in them.

'De Marigny – I think I understand why the Foundation has recently been plagued with an inordinately high percentage of freak "accidents", suicides, and deaths. I think I understand, *and I think that we're the next on the list!'*

No sooner had he spoken when, with a suddenness that caused the hair of my head to stand up straight and the shorter hairs of my neck to bristle and prickle, the ground beneath our stationary vehicle trembled; the rumble was audible even over the noise of the idling engine!

The next instant, I admit it, I screamed aloud; but Crow was already in action, releasing the handbrake, revving the engine, throwing the car into reverse gear. Nor were his instantaneous reactions any too soon. Even as the car lurched backwards on spinning wheels a great boulder, followed by smaller rocks, pebbles, and tons of earth, smashed down from above on to the road where the Mercedes had been but a moment earlier. At the same time, too, we heard (with our minds if not actually

181

with our ears) the morbid, alien dronings of an all too recognizable chant:

> Ce'haiie ep-ngh fl'hur G'harne fhtagn,
> Ce'haiie fhtagn ngh Shudde-M'ell.

'Nowhere to turn,' Crow gasped, still reversing, 'but if I can back her up far enough – '

Shattering his hopes and the unspoken prayers of both of us, the mist, as if answering some hellish call (which I can readily believe it was), fell in opaque and undulating density all about us.

'My God!' I gasped, as again Crow brought the car to a halt.

'Can't see a thing,' my friend shouted, his face grey now as the surrounding wall of ghostly gloom without. 'You'll have to get out, de Marigny, and quickly! The windows have misted over completely. Put your hand in the centre of the rear window, and walk down the middle of the road until you find a spot where I can turn the car around. Can you do it?'

'I'll damned well try,' I croaked, my mouth dry with nameless fear.

'You'll need do more than try,' he grimly told me as I opened the door. 'If not . . . we're done for!'

I slammed the door behind me, ran around to the back of the car, and pressed my right palm to the damp glass of the rear window. The engine roared and Crow's shout came to me from his open window: 'Good, Henri – now walk up the road, or better still sit on the boot, and guide me by moving your hand left or right as the road bends. Good, that's it, we're off!'

I continued as I had been instructed, sitting on the boot and moving my hand behind me over the glass of the window, directing Crow as he reversed the big car carefully along the mist-shrouded, narrow road. On three or four separate occasions rocks tumbled down from above, dislodged from the unseen heights by continued subterranean tremblings; and all the while I could sense, at the back of my mind, *Their* awful, droning chanting!

After what seemed like several ages the mist seemed to lift a little, the road widened, and there appeared a shallow, weed-choked reentry in the cliff-face just wide enough to accommodate the car. With a warning cry to Crow, I slid from the boot, ran around to the front, and directed him as he began to swing the rear end of the Mercedes off the road and into the cleft.

At this point I came very close to disaster. For suddenly, without any sort of warning, there came a low rumble from deep in the ground and the whole section of road where I stood jerked and shook violently. I was pitched backwards, off balance, over the edge of the road and head-over-heels down the steep decline beyond. Fortunately I did not fall far, no more than twelve feet or so, but I landed jarringly on my shoulder. Dazedly I struggled to my feet. I was on a wide natural ledge, beyond which the ground fell away and down to the unseen valley below. Again the mist had thickened and now there was a perceptible and rapidly increasing aura of dread and hideous expectancy in the damp air.

'Crow!' I yelled, trying vainly to scramble up the steep incline to the road. 'Titus, where are you?'

The next instant I was faced with something so monstrously terrifying that for a moment I thought my heart must stop. To my left, at a distance of no more than fifteen feet, the very limit of my vision in the mist, the face of the pebbly incline *burst outward* in a shower of stones and earth – and then –

– *Horror!*

I backed away, unashamedly babbling, screaming

Crow's name repeatedly as the – *Thing* – came after me. It was octopoid, this dweller in the earth . . . flowing tentacles and a pulpy grey-black, elongated sack of a body . . . rubbery . . . exuding a vilely stinking whitish slime . . . eyeless . . . headless, too . . . Indeed, I could see no distinguishing features at all other than the reaching, groping tentacles. Or was there – yes! – a *lump* in the upper body of the thing . . . a container of sorts for the brain, or ganglia, or whichever diseased organ governed this horror's loathsome life!

But it was closer, this spawn of Shudde-M'ell, it was almost upon me! I felt somehow rooted to the spot – fixed immobile, as if my feet were stuck in mental molasses, a fly in the ointment of the Cthonian group-mind – hearing the dreadful droning chant, my eyes wide open and popping and my mouth slack, my hair standing straight up on my head . . .

*My star-stone!*

Automatically, through all the shattering terror of my fear, I found myself reaching for that talisman of the Elder Gods – *but my jacket, with the star-stone safe in the inside pocket, was still in the Mercedes where I had left it.*

I was conscious of the ground beneath the pulpy horror before me *flowing* like water, flowing and steaming in the heat that the hellish Cthonian generated, and of those areas of the creature's body that touched the ground glowing and changing colour constantly. My God! It was upon me! Tentacles reached . . .

'*De Marigny!*' It was Crow's voice, and even as I heard his cry through the hypnotic chanting and the high-pitched screaming (which I hardly recognized as my own), even as his shout came to me, a star-stone – my own or Crow's, I didn't care – fell from above directly in the path of the looming star-spawn . . .

The effect was immediate and definite. The huge, alien

184

slug of a being before me reared back and almost toppled from the ledge; the mind-chants turned instantaneously to mental mewlings and gibberings with overtones of the utmost fear, and with incredible agility the thing finally turned in its slimy tracks to slither and flop away from me along the ledge. At what it must have taken to be a safe distance, with its tentacles whipping in a fearsome rage, the Cthonian turned in towards the cliff-face and moved forward, passing *into* the wall of earth and rock. For a few moments liquid earth and stone flowed like water from the hole the being left, then that part of the steep incline collapsed and I was left with only the abominable smell of the thing.

It was then I realized that I was still down on my knees with my hands held out before me; I had frozen in that position when it seemed certain that the Cthonian must take me. At the same time, too, I heard Crow's voice again, calling me from above. I glanced up. My friend was flat on the road, his face white and staring, his arms outstretched with my jacket dangling from his hands.

'Quickly, Henri, for God's sake! Quickly, before they have time to reorganize!'

I got to my feet, snatched up the precious star-stone, and put it in my trouser pocket, then caught hold of the dangling jacket and scrambled frantically, with Crow's assistance, to the tarmac surface of the road above. I saw that Crow had managed to get the car turned about, and breathed a sigh of relief as I slipped into the front passenger seat.

The ground trembled again as Titus put the car into gear, but a second later we were away, tyres screaming and lights cutting the curtain of mist like a knife. 'A close one, de Marigny,' my friend offered.

'Close! By God – I never want it any closer!' I told him. Half a mile later there was no trace of the mist, and wherever it had gone my headache had gone with it. Once more under control, I asked Crow what he had meant earlier when he mentioned the Foundation's recent plague of accidents, suicides, and deaths

'Yes,' he answered. 'Well, you remember how of late our telepaths have been having difficulty contacting the Cthonians; I think I can guess what those monsters have been up to. It dawned on me back there when first we realized something was wrong. I think that the burrowers have been concentrating their powers, massing their minds, overcoming the protective powers of the star-stones to a degree and *getting through* to Foundation members – just as today they got through to us. They've been dealing with us one at a time, which would explain our recent losses. It's no coincidence, de Marigny, that those losses have been such as defy any sort of accounting, and it's this new ability of theirs to get through to us that's deadened the Foundation's awareness of what's been going on! The sooner we let Peaslee and the others know, the better.' He put his foot down on the accelerator and the car sped us safely on our way.

# 13

## *The Very Worm That Gnaws*

### *(From de Marigny's Diary)*

8th Oct.

The threat posed by the Cthonian ability to get at us in
mass mental-sendings is at an end; a special delivery of a
great number of star-stones from the United States has
seen to that. Also (and as our telepaths have suspected
for some time), the remaining Cthonians are attempting a
sort of exodus back to Africa; indeed, they have already
commenced the move. It was a nest of them, on their way
down- and across-country to the coast, that waylaid Crow
and me in that hill pass. They had obviously massed their
minds against the two of us – perhaps helped by others of
their shuddersome species, possibly even Shudde-M'ell
himself, wherever he might be – and unbeknown to us,
having overcome the shielding powers of our star-stones,
they had thus learned of our plans to drive south to
Dover. After that, it had only remained for them to make
a special mental effort to lead us away from the route we
had intended to take, and then intercept and ambush our
car at a favourable spot. We had been meant to die in
that initial avalanche of dislodged earth and boulders.
The plan had gone astray and they had been forced to try
other methods. Overcoming the power of the star-stones
*in a direct confrontation*, however, had proved a far
different kettle of fish to doing it en masse and at a
distance; and there they failed, when, as it has been seen,
the sigil of the Elder Gods had the final say. They had
doubtless been members of the same nest (the barest
nucleus of a nest, thank God, and comparatively young
ones at that) that Williams the telepath reported when

187

first he quartered Scotland from his plane; the nest that subsequently seemed to disappear into thin air – or earth, as the case is. We have two telepaths tracking them even now as they burrow in the deep earth.

10th Oct.

Peaslee caught a man last night trying to break into his hotel room in London, where he has set up his HQ. He threatened the intruder with a pistol, whereupon the fellow started to froth at the mouth and threw himself over the balcony rail. Peaslee's quarters are on the fifth floor! The professor escaped involvement in the subsequent police investigations.

11th Oct.

Jordan has quickly set up his wells in the now familiar pattern at a spot not far out of Nottingham. He hopes to catch the nest of nightmares Crow and I had dealings with in the hills up north. We are lucky in that the site is an old extensive army barracks complex – 'Government Property' – and that the whole area for half a mile around is Out-of-Bounds to the general public, as it is being demolished. The place is scheduled for redevelopment; possibly the construction of a power-station. I have a feeling it's just as well the place is coming down – particularly if what has happened at some of the other star-well sites should happen there.

13th Oct.

Regarding the exodus of the Cthonians: the British Isles are obviously too restricting for the horrors. What with Peaslee and the Wilmarth Foundation – why, the beings are no less prisoned now than were their prime forebears millennia ago in Dead G'harne; for here they are being slowly but surely tracked down and destroyed! If those of them that remain – damn few now – can make it back to Africa they stand a good chance of losing themselves completely in that vast continent, later to begin the insidious threat elsewhere. Many of them have already made the crossing beneath the Channel, but that hardly means that they've escaped. The Frenchies are doing their bit. The Foundation has men in France, and Peaslee has very big friends in power over there. He gets a lot of confidential letters with the Bibliothèque Nationale postmark.

There are still a number of the burrowers here in England, though, and during the last few days there have been tremors and minor subsidences all down the country, converging into three definite tracks towards Tenterden. Looking back I see that it was a week ago, on the sixth, that the Foundation trapped and exterminated no less than a dozen of the horrors on Salisbury Plain; and already, of the prisoned, 'harmless' species, these islands have just about been cleansed.

16th Oct.

The last few weeks have seen a number of arrests by Foundation members of so-called 'suspicious persons'. Usually these arrests have been made in areas directly occupied by the members concerned, often on actual star-well sites or in other planned locations. There was that one Peaslee got on the tenth, and two others were picked up in the barracks complex in Notts. Invariably persons thus arrested try to escape, but just as surely if they fail or if they are caught a second time they become instantly bereft of mind and will: the burrowers beneath have no time for failures! For these people are of course under the influence of the CCD – unsound men and women, usually of frail bodies and even frailer minds – but these last few

189

days the numbers of such incidents have seen a sharp decline.

The insidious, crawling inundation of the British Isles by Shudde-M'ell's kin is at an end. Jordan's wells in their Nottinghamshire locations are being dismantled. That last nest must have got wind of our plans. It made no difference, however, and the end result was the same. They were picked up by a telepath as they made a panic-dash out from Bridlington under the North-Sea. They could hardly have chosen a worse route from their own point of view. There is a deep rift, a fault in the submarine strata, fifteen miles out from Bridlington. Our guess was that the horrors would not be too deep in the rocks when they passed beneath the fault. With the Royal Navy's assistance – ostensibly the command ship and its two submarine subordinates were on 'manoeuvres' – the place was quickly rigged with very powerful depth-charges; on this occasion there was no trouble from the Deep Ones in any form. At 3:30 this morning, on the instructions of Hank Silberhutte (one of the best of the American telepaths), the bombs were set off by radio signal from a fishing vessel out of Hull. Silberhutte reports complete success! The Admiralty, as a cover against any leakage of the facts, will put out a press item tomorrow on the supposed discovery of a sunken German World War II warship and the destruction of its huge and dangerously explosive cargo by depth-charge. It would appear that the arms of the Wilmarth Foundation continue to be far-reaching!

So far as is known not a single member of any of the diverse Cthonian species remains as a potential horror within Great Britain or her territorial waters. They have all been either destroyed or chased out. From the beginning there have been confusion reports from a number of our telepaths on impressions they seemed to be getting from a certain area deep beneath the Yorkshire Moors; but these 'reflections', as the telepaths term such false impressions, have now been discounted. Certainly there is nothing down there of the Cthonians as we have come to know them.

Here, however, a note of unique interest – 'Nessie' is a plesiosaur! Scotland has the world's last prehistoric monsters; five of them in fact, two adults and three young ones. A final telepathic check of the entire landmass, from John o'Groats to Land's End, brought this information to light. Nothing malignant in Loch Ness, on the contrary, but nevertheless the telepaths did pick up the weak, placidly watery thoughts of Earth's last dinosaurs. God! What wouldn't I give to be able to break the news to the press . . . ?

28th Oct.

*Vive la France!* I'm proud to be called de Marigny! Three underground atomic tests in the Algerian Desert in the last twenty-four hours! A few more of the damned horrors that won't be making it home.

30th Nov.

Word has just come in from Peaslee, now back at Miskatonic, that those phases of the American Project which were carried out simultaneous with certain of the major operations in Great Britain were more than moderately successful. It must be admitted, though, that in the United States and South America the task is far greater and the horrors apparently far more diverse and not confined alone to subterranean planes of existence. Certain wooded and mountainous regions (chiefly the Catskills, the Adirondacks, and the Rockies), the Great Lakes and other, more remote or obscure stretches of water; vast areas in and about New England, Wisconsin, Vermont, Oklahoma, and the Gulf of Mexico; and a dozen other places along the Andes in South America (there'll be trouble there), are all scheduled for the most minute mental and physical investigation and eventual 'pest control', to put it in the professor's own words.

And yet Peaslee's report is encouraging, for it appears that the incidence of free, mobile agencies is less in proportion to what it was here in England. The Americas do have a big problem, though, in the numbers of humans (and in some cases, particularly in New England, *semi-humans*) 'in Their employ!' Again, as in 1928, special agents are infiltrating certain of the backwater seaports on the New England coast.

6th Dec.

Cthulhu strikes back! Angered beyond endurance (Peaslee has it), Cthulhu has finally lashed out, proving once and for all his definite continued existence and potency here and now on Earth. How the Foundation and its many worldwide departments have managed to cover it all up – what chains they've put on the free world's presses – I don't suppose I shall ever learn.

Alerted by powerful telepathic currents emanating from somewhere in the Pacific, five Foundation telepaths – receptive where others mercifully are not, it appears – tuned in on the fringe of the most terrifying mental waveband of all. Great Cthulhu, dreaming but not dead, has for the past six days been sending out the most hellish mental nightmares from his House in R'lyeh. He has turned his wrath on all and everything. The weather, even for this time of the year, has never been quite so freakish, the sudden virulent outbreaks of esoteric cult activities never more horrible, the troubles in insane asylums the world over never more numerous, and the suicide rate never so high. Sunspot activity has for the last two days been so bad that radio and television reception is worse than useless; meteorologists and other scientists in general have no answer for it. Last night top vulcanologists in four different countries issued warnings that at least seven volcanoes, four of them thought to have been long extinct and most of them many thousands of miles apart, are on the point of simultaneous eruption – 'Krakatoa will have been as a firecracker,' they warn. I admit to being terrified.

7th Dec.

Amazingly, this morning – after a night of tossing and turning, monstrous dreams, and morbid fear for the whole world's safety and sanity – all seems back to normal.

Later.

Crow has been around after receiving a trans-Atlantic telephone call from Peaslee explaining all. It was the buildup of Cthulhu's fury that decided Miskatonic's tele-pathic quintet – the same five which discovered the source of the trouble on its initiation a week ago – in their final course. Deliberately they set themselves against the Lord of R'lyeh, cutting in on his dream-sendings and matching their mental powers with his; and though (God-only-knows *how*) they seem to have done the trick, they've paid for their idiotic bravery in no uncertain fashion. They left a note for Peaslee, 'In case anything should go wrong!' Pityingly, but with no mean respect, the professor likens them to cabbages – alive, but only just, utterly mindless vegetable entities.

Following a lull in operations the Foundation seems to be back in full swing again. Crow and I have been offered status positions with Oil & Minerals International, an obscure but apparently well-financed mining and drilling concern – with headquarters in Arkham, Massachusetts! We have both declined these positions; Crow has his interests, I have my writing and my antique business to attend to; and besides, we know that Peaslee has many more irons in the fire, he in no way depends upon us. Specifically we were to have joined with other 'executives' of O & MI in Ankara, to organize what has been loosely termed 'The Turkey Operation'. We have agreed, however, to head Great Britain's Chapter of the Foundation here in England. Peaslee in turn has promised to keep us up-to-date on the state of things in Turkey. It should be most interesting; the frequency of severe Turkish earthquakes would seem to determine – quite apart from any dissertations on continuing continental drift or the widening of basic subterranean faults – that Turkey is literally crawling with Cthonians. In Titus Crow's own words: 'Well, it's a very nice offer, de Marigny, but discretion tells me that for the time being at least, we have done enough.'

5th Jan.

The last of the present series of French and American underground atomic tests have now been carried out, with more than merely military success I'm sure.

2nd Feb.

Peaslee, in a recent letter from Denizli, Turkey, informs us of the loss of a Foundation plane, its pilot, two crew members, and Hank Silberhutte. They were last heard of ten days ago somewhere in the Mackenzie Mountains, only a hundred miles or so south of the Arctic Circle. Silberhutte, it seems, has had a 'thing' about Ithaqua ('The Snow Thing', 'The Thing that Walks on the Wind', 'The Wendigo', etc.) of the Cthulhu Cycle, ever since a cousin of his vanished under mysterious circumstances in Manitoba some years back. In poor Wendy-Smith's time, too (during his *normal* lifetime, I mean), as witness his document and other credible contemporary papers, Spencer of Quebec University produced ample evidence of human sacrifice to Ithaqua by degenerate worshippers in Manitoba. Silberhutte was working on a long-term personal project of his, with the Foundation's blessing, to track this powerful air-elemental down. Peaslee believes that the telepath might have strayed – or been drawn – too far north, into the Wind Walker's domain; for it was to the Arctic regions that Ithaqua was banished for his part in the uprising of the Great Old Ones against the Elder Gods. Personally, I thank the Lord that I myself am not 'gifted' with any extraordinary degree of telepathic power.

11th Feb.

Crow has an interesting theory, one that can't be proved as yet but which certainly seems sound enough. Nyarlathotep, the Great Messenger of the Old Ones, the only prime member of the CCD left unchained by the Elder Gods at the unthinkably distant time of the prisoning, is not a being or deity as such at all but more truly a 'power'. Nyarlathotep is in fact Telepathy (Crow points out that the two words come quite close to being anagrammatical, but this must be purely coincidental), truly a 'Great Messenger', and certainly we know that the CCD do in fact communicate in this fashion. Of certain reported physical manifestations of Nyarlathotep, Crow says that he has little doubt that given the right type of mind to work upon the Great Old Ones could produce by telepathic means a very real tridimensional image – that such an image might even be in the form of a man!

15th Feb.

Following the initial success of the Turkey Project, Oil & Minerals International has secured contracts in Rhodesia and Botswana. Three of Pongo Jordan's most trusted and highly skilled engineering lieutenants, along with two of Peaslee's more experienced telepaths (in great demand now), are going out to Africa to organize the first stages of the operation.

28th Feb.

With the continuing success of the Apollo moon-shots comes disturbing news from Miskatonic. Along with all the other equipment deposited on the moon by America's epic adventurers were certain seismological instruments – and it now appears that Miskatonic's science laboratories had more than a small hand in the design of two of them! Quite apart from what NASA has learned of the moon's interior construction from such instruments, Miskatonic too has been 'listening in' – but for nothing so common-place as moonquakes! The report has it that eventually it will be discovered that there is life *in* the moon; but by then (it is to be hoped) we will know just what that life is and how to deal with it. Could this be, I cannot help but conjecture, the source of those hellish radiations which, in their season, turn men's minds to those hideously aberrant acts that we classify as lunacy?

27th March.

In support of a letter from Peaslee received over a month ago – regarding the strengthening of the African force in an attempt to track down and extirpate Shudde-M'ell himself in his as yet undiscovered stronghold (G'harne is

196

now deserted) – comes the following item, copied direct
from yesterday's *Daily Mail*:

## THE INNER-SPACE RACE!

Prior to the commencement of an Ethiopian 'Mohole' project,
planned for a time some years in the future, the United States
of America's Miskatonic University has jumped the gun on the
British-led team at present carrying out survey work from Addis
Ababa. There, below the tremendously hostile Danakil Desert
where temperatures have been known to exceed more than 138°
Fahrenheit in the shade, the three greatest rifts or natural faults
in the Earth's crust meet, and it is there that the British scientists
hope to bore a hole right through the crust to the never before
pierced mantle.

This is not the first time that such a titanic feat has been
attempted – the Americans have already known one failure in
the Pacific Ocean near Hawaii in 1966. On that occasion the
project was abandoned because of escalating costs. Similarly the
Russians were defeated in the Arctic Circle's Koda Peninsula.
But quite apart from depleted funds both projects met, too,
with immense technical difficulties.

Professor Norman Ward, however, head of the Geology
Department of Medham University and chief adviser to the
British project's sponsoring authorities, seems unconcerned by
the advent of the American group on the scene. 'They are way
out in their calculations,' he says, 'if they believe that they have
found the ideal spot in or near the area where they are at
present encamped. The Afar Depression,' he goes on to explain,
'is far more suitable as a site for the project, but for some reason
the Americans have chosen a spot well out of the way; and from
what I have seen of their equipment – unless they intend to use
previously untried methods – then I give them little chance of
success. They are, though, a closemouthed lot, and I am given
to suspicions that they have far more in mind than they let on.'

'Far more in mind than they let on,' indeed! Of course
they have! They're after one of the biggest horrors the
world has ever known – an incalculable evil which only

197

Great Cthulhu himself might surpass. I wish them luck, but I'm surely glad I'm out of it.

10th April.

Crow has been round about a communication from the Wilmarth Foundation. The Ethiopian thing is well under way and the three Foundation telepaths out there believe that they've found what they were looking for – Shudde-M'ell himself! They have, too, devised a 'lure' for that supreme burrower – a number of fresh-hatched and presumably very precious (ugh!) females – and with his awful tribe so depleted over this last year or so it's believed the horror *must* make a bid for the release of these would-be nest-mothers. There is one well, a shaft three-quarters of a mile deep, and down this shaft in four days' time the females will be lowered – along with an explosive device set to disseminate a mass of one of the most deadly radioactive materials known to science. Experiments at Miskatonic have already shown that materials of only one-tenth of the radioactive potency of the stuff will kill a normal (normal?) Cthonian. This could well mean the end of one of the greatest CCD.

15th April.

Disaster! Horror! The newspapers are full of it; but as of yet, no official word from Peaslee or the Foundation. Severe earthquake near Addis Ababa and tremors in the surrounding towns and villages – Miskatonic's entire Ethiopian team, all bar one man who managed to get away in a blazing vehicle – *wiped out!* The man who got away (no particulars yet) is on the danger list in an Addis Ababa hospital. Severe burns and shock. The story of what really happened hinges on whether or not he survives.

I have read Professor Ward's appraisal in the *Mail*; he appears to be of the amazed opinion that the Americans succeeded in their attempt to break through the Earth's crust, and that in so doing they somehow released the lava-stream which so far has obstructed all attempts by observers to get into the immediate vicinity of the site. He says that from the air the site is now a great molten crater a mile across – a crater with a slightly raised rim through gaps in which a lot of lava has escaped. All 'volcanic' activity has now stopped, apparently, but the place is still too hot to approach on foot or by surface vehicle. There is not the slightest sign or trace of the men who inhabited the place only a few short hours ago, and of the machinery they used only a metal spar from the great derrick itself has been found – hundreds of yards *outside* the northern rim of the crater, where it was presumably thrown by the force of the short-lived 'eruption'. Ward considers that he was correct in his initial theory – that the Americans were trying out new, quick-drilling methods – for this would seem the only satisfactory explanation for so rapid and disastrous a penetration of the Earth's crust. My God, if he only knew the truth! I imagine Miskatonic will soon put out a cover story.

2nd Aug.

My collection and correlation, over the last quarter or so, of my own notes and some of Crow's papers and documents into a record of sorts (as suggested by Peaslee some time ago) regarding our experiences with the burrowers beneath, has left me precious little time to spare; but I have managed to keep in touch with Crow himself, and with the Wilmarth Foundation. The receipt of occasional communiqués from America has helped to keep me fairly well up-to-date, despite the fact that I am no longer personally involved – or at best only partly involved, and then only in the now limited administrational duties of the organization's British Chapter. I cannot help but wonder, though, how long this anonymity of mine can last. Crow is at present in Oklahoma, and his letters hint of suspected subterranean wonders the lure of which I cannot hope to resist for long. He talks about 'embarking upon the greatest speleological expedition in history', but as yet has not explained himself. Now what in heaven . . . ? Pot-holing – ?

In the meantime the members of Miskatonic's august, inspired, and dedicated body abroad are making great strides in their concentrated efforts to track down and exterminate the remaining lesser agents and minions of the CCD. It seems generally recognized now that the greater of these horrors – such as the space-spawn of Cthulhu, Yibb-Tstll, Yog-Sothoth, Ithaqua, Hastur, and some half dozen others; notably the Lloigor, whose disembodied subterranean race-mind is still apparently exercised and felt most strongly in Wales – are here to stay; at least until our growing knowledge of them permits us a safe attempt at their expulsion. Their destruction, an actual *end* to them, now seems out of the question; if they were ever capable of being destroyed, then why were such merciful executions not undertaken by the Elder Gods themselves aeons ago? This, at any rate, is a question which Miskatonic's theorists have now started to chew over.

13th Aug.

In relation to my last entry regarding the CCD: whether or not *all* the greater beings are immortal may never be known – but Shudde-M'ell, at least, has shown himself to be almost indestructible! This has come out following the

200

recovery of Edward Ellis, the sole survivor of the Ethiopian horror. Fortunately Ellis is – or *was* – a telepath, the most accomplished of the ill-fated trio sent out from America to Addis Ababa, and now that his extensive skin-graft operations and general therapy (mental as well as physical) are over and he is back on his feet, he has finally managed to tell what happened when the Prime Burrower went to the rescue of his doomed little females. He has confirmed beyond any reasonable doubt that those female creatures died in the incredibly destructive blast of hard radiation released by the present explosive device – but their lord . . . ?

Through the lull left by the instant shutting off of infant Cthonian thoughts, the telepath had picked up – had been almost blasted by – the most fearful waves of angered and agonized telepathic sendings as Shudde-M'ell reacted to the hard radiation. Wounded that great abomination may well have been, indeed Ellis' continued evidence guarantees it, but at the last – as witness the complete destruction of the well-shaft trap and of the men who set and baited it – he was very much alive!

I say that Ellis has told what happened when Shudde-M'ell surfaced, but I realize now that I may have given the wrong impression. As a telepath Edward Ellis is finished (it is a wonder they managed to save his sanity, let alone his telepathic powers), but he gave up what he knew of the thing under the inducement of certain special drugs taken voluntarily.

I have listened to copies of tape recordings made while Ellis was under the influence of those drugs. He babbles pitifully of 'a great grey thing a mile long chanting and exuding strange acids . . . charging through the depths of the earth at a fantastic speed, in a dreadful fury . . . melting basaltic rocks like butter under a blowtorch!' He gibbers of the explosion which released what ought to

201

have been radiations ultimately inimical, indeed deadly to all known forms of life – particularly Cthonian life – and of the instantaneous blotting out of the mind-patterns of the young female creatures. He gabbles almost inarticulately of the injured, partly dissolved monstrosity which yet lived to bore its way to the surface, to turn its massive storehouse of heat and alien energy loose in a frenzy of molten destruction! Finally he sobs weakly of the horror's retreat, of its crash dive straight down into the bowels of the earth, until it achieved that which man still has not accomplished. For Ellis' mind was *with* Shudde-M'ell when, in blind agony and indescribable rage, the Prime Burrower *broke through the crust of the Earth – broke through to swim away deeper yet, into the inner magma, against strange tides of molten-rock oceans, those oceans which hold these lily pads we call continents afloat!*

There it was that Ellis lost the horror's trail, and there too he lost consciousness, but not before he managed to throw himself from his careening, blazing vehicle into the lifesaving waters of an oasis pool.

24th Aug.

Crow is coming home again to England!

It will be good to see him again – it will be good to *talk* to him! He has written to me of things almost beyond imagination: subterranean horrors totally outside man's sphere of knowledge, even beyond the combined ken of the Wilmarth Foundation, existing in the bowels of the earth beneath Oklahoma. His writing includes mention of the 'blue-litten world of K'n-yan', of the 'Vaults of Zin', of monstrous ruins of eldritch civilizations in a still deeper 'red-litten world of Yoth', and of undisclosed but apparently indisputable evidence in respect of his theories (and the Foundation's) regarding the unbelievable antiquity of the Cthulhu, Yog, and Tsathogguan Cycles of myth, legend, and cult. Finally he has hinted awesomely of the deepest abyss of all, 'Black N'kai, whose singular stone troughs and burrows are sufficient in their very *ancientness* to turn the minds of men away shrieking!'

I gather that no speleological expedition has actually been undertaken as was originally planned, and that all these allusions have their origin in telepathically inspired dreams; but knowing something of the workings of the telepathic mind I now find myself asking a terrifying question: if these places are so fearfully deep underground – *through what mental eye have such visions been relayed to the surface . . . ?*

But at any rate, the whole thing has been seen as far too dangerous for earnest investigation – certain Indian legends of unguessed lineage have come down through time; more recently, other serious investigators have met with strange disappearances and weird displacements of time and matter – and so massive charges of dynamite have been used to seal off these buried places for ever from our sane upper world. The horrors of K'n-yan, Yoth, N'kai, and kindred vaults are not truly of the magnitude of those we within the Foundation are pledged to fight – but they are still far too terrible to contemplate or correlate within a so-called rationally ordered universe.

29th Aug.

A letter from Peaslee: he asks if I would care to join him in co-leadership of an Australian 'expedition'. There are, he says, certain things in the Great Sandy Desert in which he has a very special interest. I know that he once accompanied his father out there back in 1935, and I believe he later published a very limited edition regarding some odd discoveries; but in any case I have had to turn him down. My antique business demands I take a hand

203

here in England, and I still have certain administrational duties in respect of the Foundation's British Chapter.

3rd Sept.

Crow gets into London airport some time this evening. His last letter, received yesterday, is full of excitement; something to do with his discovery at Miskatonic University of a book containing fragments in an ancient glyph with corresponding paragraphs in Latin. He mentions his great old clock (that weird, four-handed, chronologically impossible monstrosity which once belonged to my father), relating the fantastic configurations on its dial to this latest 'Rosetta Stone' discovery of his. It's plain he believes that he can now decipher the legend of the clock, perhaps even discover the thing's purpose, for I've known for some time that he thinks the clock is in fact a space-time machine – a device come down from predawn days of extra-dimensional 'magic' – literally a toy of the Elder Gods themselves, or of others like them.

Crow's excitement, his prescience in this matter, is hardly unfounded. I recall something he told me some years ago, or rather something at which he hinted, about a pair of burglars who broke into Blowne House one night – and who stayed! Apparently one of these gentlemen-of-the-night found a way to open the clock, something Crow had never managed to do on his own, but thereafter my friend's story was vague indeed. I recall him saying something about frightening dimensions, 'a gateway to hideous times and spaces', and his mention of 'a lake of elder horror, where nightmare entities splash by a cloud-wave shore as twin suns sink in distant mists . . .' I must remember to have him relate the story in full. I'm sure he mentioned something about his 'visitors' *vanishing into* the clock! But there again, as I recall it, he was very reticent about the whole thing. In those days, though, we hadn't shared so many horrors.

There are other reasons, too, whereby Crow might just prove himself correct regarding the clock's purpose and origin. I can still remember – though I was just a lad at the time, living away from my father – a curious affair involving an East Indian mystic; one Swami Chandraputra, I believe his name was, who also disappeared in strange circumstances connected with the clock. Titus Crow has researched all this and knows far more of such matters than me. It will be interesting to see just what he has dug up.

# 14
## *Winds of Darkness*

H. L. de M.
11 The Cottages
Seaton Carew, Cѻ. Durham
28th September

Blowne House

Dear Titus,

Just a note to explain my absence should you try to contact me at home. I've been up here three days now, staying with friends, trying to recover from a rather severe attack of 'The Morbids'. It was quite sudden – I simply decided one morning (Tuesday last) to get out of London for a bit. The fog and all depresses me. Not that it's much better up here; the mist comes rolling off a sullen, dirty sea and . . . I don't know . . . I seem to be more depressed than ever. I've had some funny thoughts about this mood of mine, I don't mind telling you, though Britain is surely safe now – but in any case, I have my star-stone with me. I tried to talk to you before I left, but your telephone was out of order. I also tried calling you from up here, but – same story.

I got your note before I left, though, and I'm delighted you're finally cracking the code on that old clock of yours. I expect that by now you've just about got it beaten . . . ?

Damned annoying thing, but Sunday night before I came up north I had a burglar! God-only-knows what he was after, but he gets full marks for stealth; quiet as a mouse! Took a few pounds, but I couldn't discover anything else to be missing.

I think I shall probably stay here for a fortnight; perhaps I'll take a run up to Newcastle next week and see how old Chatham's antique shop is going. Last I heard he was doing quite well for himself.

All for now; do drop me a line when you get the chance –

Henri

Blowne House
1st October

Henri-Laurent de Marigny, Esq.
11 The Cottages
Seaton Carew

Dear Henri,

Your note is in; I'm pleased we're in touch again. Yes, my phone *is* on the blink – damned destructive hooligans, I should think! No sooner do I get the thing repaired than it's *kaput* again!

Strange that you should mention this depression of yours – I, too, have been feeling a bit under the weather – and what a coincidence, for I have also had a burglar! Same night as yours, too. There seems to be a glut of criminals in the city nowadays.

Regarding that old 'clock' of your father's: I have, as you say, 'cracked it', I've got it beaten. It's tremendously exciting! Night before last I actually *opened* the thing on my own for the first time. The whole front of the frame swings open on some principle of motion previously outside my knowledge, beyond human technology. There are no hinges, no pivots, and when it's closed there's not even a crack to show where a door might be! But that aside: if I'm correct, the clock will prove to be *literally* a door on fantastic worlds of wonder – whole worlds! – past, present, and future, to the very corners of space and time. The problem will be, of course, in controlling the thing. I am in the position of a Neanderthal studying the operational handbook of a passenger-carrying aircraft – except I have no handbook! Well, perhaps not *so* extreme, but it's difficult enough by any standard.

Had a letter from Mother Quarry – apparently she's had one of her 'visions'; says we're both in terrible danger, you and I. I'd say she's just a bit late, wouldn't you? But she's a dear really, and I often put a lot of faith in what she says.

On your proposed trip up to Newcastle: there's always the chance (remote I'll admit) that Chatham has managaged to find some stuff I asked him to look out for long ago, especially certain very old textbooks that Walmsley mentions in his *Notes on Deciphering Codes, Cryptograms, and Ancient Inscriptions*. I'd be obliged if you'd check this out for me.

Yes, a trip sounds a good idea – I find I've a bit of a wanderlust on myself. I think I might take the car over to have a look at Stonehenge or Silbury Hill; I always find the contemplation of such monolithic relics calming somehow – though just why I shouldn't be calm is hard to say. Nevertheless, as I said before, it's true that I haven't been feeling my best of late.

All for now; best, as always,
T.C.

PS URGENT!

Henri: drop everything and get back down to London as quickly as you can. We're both either blind or daft – or both! WE'VE BEEN GOT AT, the two of us, and it's a race against time now. I haven't the time to write more, and telephoning now will be no use for there are powers ranged against us. I must catch the post and then I'll have to be at the renewal of my protections. Oh, and you can throw away that damned 'star-stone' of yours! I'll explain all when I see you, but WASTE NO TIME IN RETURNING TO LONDON!

T.C.

## ADDENDUM

The foregoing fourteen chapters of this work (the last of which, Chapter 14, I have constructed myself from letters discovered in the ruins of Blowne House following London's 'freak storm' of 4th October) were penned and put together in their present order by Mr Henri-Laurent de Marigny, who introduces himself amply in the body of the work as the son of a great American mystic, as a collector and dealer in antiques, and lately as a member of the Wilmarth Foundation. The manuscript – complete apart from the preface, chapter titles, and headings, which I have appended for their obvious relevance – accompanied the letters in a locked metal box which Titus Crow had labelled and addressed to me.

The manuscript in its entirety should stand as an admirable if in parts sketchy record – to say nothing of a *warning* to present members of the Foundation – of de Marigny's and Crow's involvement prior to and following my first meeting with them (so amply chronicled), and their subsequent membership within the Foundation.

Strangely, I feel little concern over the apparent end of the affair; I have a feeling that for Crow and de Marigny it is *not* the end. As corroborative evidence in support of this feeling of mine, I offer the final note which Crow left for me in the metal box – a note which I found atop the other documents and manuscripts when the British police delivered the box to me earlier this year:

Peaslee, the storm gathers.

This note, I feel, will be brief – and I think I know which of the CCD has been given the final honour, that of removing de Marigny and myself from the surface of the Earth.

God, but Henri and I have been fools! You'll see from the two letters here that we had ample warning: the first feelings of increasing depression following those staged break-ins, 'burglaries' which served one and only one purpose, the removal of our protective star-stones and their replacement with useless duplicates; the unreasonable urgings to visit places which even Wendy-Smith had warned of as being dangerous since a time God-only-knows how long ago in the past – Stonehenge, Silbury Hill, Hadrian's Wall at Newcastle (you'll need to have another look at Britain, Peaslee!); the plan to split us up and deal with us separately, de Marigny up north and me in London. Oh, there's been enough of warnings!

I don't know how I tumbled it, really. I think it must have been Mother Quarry's letter of warning – and she was so right! How by all that's holy have they managed it, eh, Peaslee? How did they contrive to steal our star-stones? De Marigny thinks he has the answer, and possibly he's right. He reasons that our 'burglars' were not truly dupes of the CCD (or the Cthonians specifically), as we have come to understand such; that they were in fact genuine burglars, but that the CCD had implanted in each of their minds the merest germ of a notion to rob us – to steal the star-stones! The rest, of course, would be easy: typically weak-willed moronic types, such as we've already had to deal with, would have been used to deliver false, duplicate stones into the hands of the rather more clever criminals, possibly with some story or other to reinforce the previously implanted belief in the value of the real things. A further mental jab at the minds of these criminals and . . . and the rest would be up to them!

But whichever way it was done, Peaslee, the storm gathers now and I haven't much more time. I have renewed my protections around Blowne House – the Tikkoun Elixir, the chant against the Cthonians (the V. V. Incant.) and certain other 'occult' devices, but I know of no positive charm against *this*!

De Marigny is with me and we are facing the thing together. The storm rages outside; strange winds tear at the house and lightning flashes ever brighter. A few moments ago the radio mentioned the 'local storm' on the outskirts of London. Good Grief, but they don't know the half of it!

It is Ithaqua, of course. Not the Wind Walker himself but his minions, elementals of the air, ranged against us from all corners of the sky. They mean to have us, Peaslee, make no mistake – and yet . . . there is a chance. It's a pretty slim chance, but one we may be forced to –

Not much time now, Wingate. Three times the house has been struck. I have seen trees ripped up by their roots from the garden. The howling is indescribably ferocious. The windows are being blown in one after the other. I hope to God old Harry Townley is saying one for us now! He should be able to see Blowne House from his place.

I tried to get around to the British Museum earlier; if I remember right you left a number of your star-stones there . . . ? But in any case, my car has been sabotaged – it's patent *They* still have their followers here in England, Wingate – and of course the phone is out of order again.

That last blast of lightning!

Shapes form beyond the broken windows . . . they are fighting to be in . . . de Marigny is solid as a rock . . . the clock stands open and greenly illumined from within . . . this is our way out, but God-only-knows where it may lead . . . Randolph Carter, grant I have the formulas right . . . don't despair, Wingate, and keep up the fight.

The roof –


My hopes for the two comrades are further bolstered by the fact that, despite the incredible extent of the damage to Blowne House, the bodies of the two were nowhere to be found in the ruins – which to me is hardly surprising. It only remains for me to say that during that 'freak storm' Crow's ancient clock seems likewise to have vanished; for no single trace of that – conveyance? – could be found, neither a splinter nor even the tiniest fragment; and I think I know what Crow meant when he wrote: '. . . this is our way out, but God-only-knows where it may lead . . .'

Wingate Peaslee
Miskatonic University
4th March 19–

211

# THE TRANSITION
# OF TITUS CROW

This novel
was written in open
admiration of the greatest
macabre author ever,
Howard Phillips Lovecraft,
and is dedicated to the
tremendous concepts
of his now famous
*Cthulhu Mythos*.

# Author's Note

In respect of Art Meyer's Prologue to this work: he is in fact mistaken on one point, though of course he could hardly be expected to have foreseen it! For where he has it that, 'no single word of the author's original text has been altered', I personally would beg to differ.

When I originally submitted *Transition* to DAW Books back in 1973 or '74, it ran about 25,000 words too long for Don Wollheim's editorial tastes. He asked me to cut it and gave me a deadline. Alas, I was a comparative newcomer, a beginner, still learning the business of writing. And I don't suppose anyone ever learns all of it . . . but, instead of a scalpel I used a hacksaw, and then compounded the crime by losing or destroying the excised material. The novel suffered as a result, which was my fault entirely.

What's more, now that Grafton Books see fit to reprint *Transition*, I've been at it again – but this time I hope my surgery has been somewhat less brutal. Assuming that many or most readers of this current novel will have read the previous book, *The Burrowers Beneath*, I've removed several lengthy discussions of that earlier work to allow for a faster pace and 'tighter' read. All of which will meet, I hope, with your approval . . .

Brian Lumley,
Brixham, Devon –
Dec. 1986

# LONDON OCCULTIST
# BACK FROM THE DEAD!

Mr Henri-Laurent de Marigny, son of the great New Orleans mystic Etienne-Laurent de Marigny, is literally 'back from the dead', having been pronounced missing or dead in 1976 along with his friend and colleague Mr Titus Crow, late of Leonard's-Walk Heath. Speculation is now rife as to whether Titus Crow may also still be alive following Mr de Marigny's amazing reappearance after an absence of almost ten years, since the freak lightning storm of 4 October 1969 that utterly destroyed Blowne House, Mr Crow's residence. Until now it was also believed that the storm had killed the two friends. An element of doubt has always existed with regard to their 'deaths', for no bodies were ever found in the ruins of the house following the storm, despite the fact that the occultists were believed to be in residence.

De Marigny's return yesterday morning was as dramatic as his disappearance. He was fished out of the Thames at Purfleet more dead than alive, saved from almost certain death by drowning by Mr Harold Simmons of Tilbury, who dragged him aboard his barge from the precarious refuge of a buoy. Mr Simmons reports how, despite de Marigny's battered and bruised condition and the fact that all his limbs were broken, the occultist clung to the buoy like a limpet, even making an exhausted, delirious attempt to fight his rescuer off. 'He looked like he'd been hit by an express train,' Mr Simmons reports, 'but he certainly wasn't ready to give in!' Mr de Marigny, identified initially through certain documents he carried, is now recovering in hospital . . .

The *Daily London News*
5 September 1979

# *Prologue*

At Miskatonic University, the morning of 20 March 1980, just six days before the Fury, Professor Wingate Peaslee, then head of the Wilmarth Foundation, called me into his office for a final briefing on Foundation affairs before he left for Innsmouth, where he intended to supervise personally what was then Project X, since known as Project Cthylla.

As vice-president of the Foundation (and in my capacity as Peaslee's right-hand man and understudy) I was of course already very well informed in all aspects of Foundation work; therefore my briefing was not protracted. Wingate was uneasy. Though at that time our organization had already enlisted the aid of many 'sciences' of previously dubious authenticity, we were only beginning to investigate precognition; in this lay the source of the professor's disquiet. Within the space of the last week he had received no less than three separate warnings from psychically endowed persons within the Foundation, all of them forecasting doom – forecasting, in fact, the Fury! Could he afford to ignore them?

The question with prognostication is of course this: Will the foreseen event come about as a direct result of external and uncontrollable influences, or will it be brought about by internal forces attempting its avoidance? Would Project X bring about a disaster, or would the disaster be brought about by the abandonment of the project? Another problem is this: How does one avoid what will be, what has been foreseen? There again, and perhaps on the brighter side, there was always the chance

217

that those warning visions of doom had been deliberately planted by the CCD in the minds of the three Foundation psychics in an attempt to hold up the Innsmouth operations. These were some of the problems that worried Wingate Peaslee; they were among the reasons for his deciding to supervise Project X personally.

That same morning he had received by airmail a parcel from London containing a number of notebooks, various documents and tape recordings. The parcel was from a personal friend of the professor's and a former member of the Foundation, Henri-Laurent de Marigny. Similarly that morning a communication had arrived from the British chapter of the Foundation consisting of a brief and cryptic note from the psychic Mother Eleanor Quarry. Peaslee showed me the note. It said simply this: 'Titus Crow has been back. He is no longer here. I believe that this time de Marigny has followed him. Wingate, I think we are in for terrible trouble.'

Typical of the brilliant British psychic and cryptic as it was, nevertheless the first three sentences of this note meant much to both Wingate Peaslee and to myself; the last sentence was more obscure, unless it was yet another warning of approaching doom.

Peaslee then told me how he would dearly love to explore the contents of the parcel from de Marigny himself but simply had no time at present to do so. I was given that task. Perhaps, in retrospect, it would have been better if Peaslee had not gone to Innsmouth but had attended to the parcel instead. Who can say?

First I read the notebooks, a task I completed on the morning of 24 March. I began to listen to the tapes late on the night of the 25th, pressure of work keeping me from them until then. I had barely started when, just after midnight, there came the first subterranean rumblings, the first grim warning that this was to be the day of the Fury!

Fortunately, before the Fury struck with its full force, I was able to place manuscripts and tapes alike in my office safe. When I retrieved them from the debris of Miskatonic four days later, the notebooks and documents were still intact; the tapes had suffered somewhat.

So much for a prologue. As background material toward an understanding of the forces behind the Fury, and as a personal account of his own involvement with the CCD and with Titus Crow, Henri-Laurent de Marigny's work is required reading. In it, as in the transcriptions from the tape recordings of Titus Crow's narrative, which follow it – and as in de Marigny's recently reprinted earlier account of the Wilmarth Foundation's work, *The Burrowers Beneath* – no single word of the author's original text has been altered.

Arthur D. Meyer<br>
New Miskatonic,<br>
Rutland, Vermont

# 1

# *But What of Titus Crow?*

## *(From de Marigny's notebooks)*

My first thought on awakening, particularly on finding
myself in a hospital bed, was that it had all been a
nightmare, a horrific dream perhaps engendered of whichever drugs I had been given to assist in my recovery
from –

My recovery from what?

Plainly I had suffered some terrible accident or attack
of incredible ferocity. My arms and legs seemed to be in
splints; I was bandaged top to bottom and barely able to
move my head. There was a lot of pain, so much that I
could specify no single area of my body for its origin, it
was everywhere. I was patently lucky to be alive! Exactly
what, then, had happened to me? I could remember
nothing. Or was there . . . something?

Yes, there was something. I could remember water
pulling me down, and strange hands tugging at me.

Then, turning my head as far as my various wrappings
and bandages would allow, I saw the vase of flowers by
my bed, close enough for me to read the message on the
attached card:

> To a dear and valued friend,
> long lost but found again –
> get well very soon,
> W. Peaslee

*Peaslee!* Professor Wingate Peaslee, head of the Wilmarth Foundation! Fragmentary visions of past events
tumbled chaotically in my painfully fuzzy mind as I read

the man's name. But at least I knew now that they had been no nightmares, those horrible scenes reviewed subconsciously by my mind's eye immediately prior to waking – no dreams but *memories* of my past experiences as a member of the Wilmarth Foundation. My eyes, peering through slits in swathing bandages, went again to the vase of flowers, finding propped against its base a curious star-shaped stone like some fossil starfish from Silurian coral beds, a stone that went far to calming my abruptly whirling mind and fluttering heart.

And suddenly I remembered. I remembered it all! And with the memory a name sprang spontaneously to my lips.

'Crow!' I cried, 'Titus Crow! *Where are you?*'

His name, and my question, seemed to echo hollowly in the white room about me, hanging in the air. Particularly the question.

Where indeed . . .?

I must have slept then, for when I opened my eyes next it was night, or rather late evening. The shadows were long in my room and beyond the windows the first tendrils of a gray mist were rising. There was the smell of the country in the less than antiseptic air flowing into the room from a ventilator fan in the opposite wall. The room was pleasantly cool. I guessed that I was not in London, but wherever I was I knew that Peaslee was not far away, and that therefore I was safe from . . . *them!*

Them – the burrowers beneath and all the other horrors of the Cthulhu Cycle – I shuddered at the thought of them, then made a conscious effort to thrust them out of my mind. First I must think about myself.

At least I was feeling much better. That is, my pains were noticeably less and the bandages had been removed from my head and neck, allowing me at least sufficient freedom of movement to peer about my room. Above my bed, on the wall, I saw a button with the – from my position – inverted legend RING. How I was supposed to comply, even if I had wanted to, was quite beyond me. My arms were still in plaster. No matter, for the moment I desired no company.

At least this time I seemed wide awake, capable of thinking clearly and reasonably. And indeed I had a lot to think about. I cast a few cursory glances about the room, sufficient to assure myself that I was definitely in a hospital, probably a private institute, if the impeccably delicate decor and my clinically immaculate immediate surroundings were anything to go by. Then I settled down to the more serious business of getting my thoughts – my memories of what had gone before, leading up to this present as yet unexplained confinement – sorted out in my mind into some sort of recognizable order.

Those memories still had many nightmarish aspects. Indeed, they were unbelievable to a point which might only suggest – to anybody mercifully less well informed – an incredible degree of gullibility, even insanity in any believer. And yet I knew that I believed, and that I was certainly not mad . . .

No, I was alive, sane and safe – but what of Titus Crow?

The last time I'd seen him had been at Blowne House, his sprawling bungalow retreat on Leonard's-Walk Heath; that had been on the 4th Oct. 1969, when Ithaqua's elementals of the air had attacked us in all their massed might. We had been trapped there, and no way out; we faced certain death; Crow's home was being reduced to rubble around us! At the last we were left with no other alternative but to put our faith in the grandfather clock: that old (*how* old?) coffin-shaped device, yes, which had once belonged to my father, for which Crow had named it 'De Marigny's Clock'.

But 'clock'? A misnomer that, if ever there was one. No timepiece at all but a device come down from predawn days of extradimensional magic – literally a toy of the Elder Gods themselves! As for its history:

First, tracing the clock's line as far back as possible in the light of my limited knowledge, it had belonged to one Yogi Hiamaldi, a friend of the ill-fated Carolina mystic Harley Warren. Hiamaldi had been a member, along with Warren, of a psychic-phenomenalist group in Boston about 1916–18. He had sworn that he alone of living men had been to Yian-Ho, that crumbling revenant of aeon-shrouded Leng, and that he had borne away certain things from that lost and leering necropolis. For a reason unknown, the Yogi had made a gift of the clock to my father, though I am unable to recall ever seeing the thing as a child before I was sent out of America. I can only suppose that my father kept it at his New Orleans retreat, a place that had always fascinated me but that my poor nervous mother had always done her best to keep me away from. After my father died the clock was sold, along with many of his other curiosities, to a French collector. Titus Crow had been unable to discover how the thing had suddenly turned up so many years later at an auction of antique furniture in England, but his subsequent attempts to trace the previous French owner had failed miserably; it was as though he had simply vanished off the face of the Earth!

I remembered, too, a curious affair involving an East Indian mystic, one Swami Chandraputra, I believe he called himself, who had also allegedly 'disappeared' in strange circumstances connected somehow with the clock. At the time, though, I was only a lad living largely away from my father. Crow knew the story more fully, for he had researched all of these things. Even with all his research my friend had been unable to discover where or when or by whom the peculiarly ominous thing had been made, or even why. Plainly its weirdly meandering hands moved in sequences completely alien to any earthly chronological system, and at best its ungovernably aberrant ticking must drive anyone of less than iron fortitude and unbending resolution to distraction.

In Crow's case, however, it was this very lack of an easily discernible purpose, and similarly the unfathomable mystery of its origin, which had served to endear the clock to him; and he had spent many years in intermittent, frustrated and invariably vain study of the thing. Then, as a guest of Professor Peaslee at Miskatonic University, Crow had finally recognized in one of the library's great old occult volumes a curious sequence of odd glyphs which he had been delighted to note bore a striking resemblance to the figures on the dial of his huge clock. Moreover, the book bore a translation of its own hieroglyphed passage in Latin!

Armed with this Rosetta Stone knowledge, my friend had returned to London where he was soon at work again uncovering many of the strange machine's previous mysteries. And he had been right, for it was indeed a vehicle – a space-time machine of sorts with principles more alien than the center of a star, whose like we can at least conjecture upon. Titus Crow, however, was never a man to be denied anything once he set his mind after it. And so he had persevered. Once he had written to me to say of his work on the clock: 'I am in the position of a Neanderthal studying the operational handbook of a passenger-carrying aircraft – except I have no handbook!' Though of course he was exaggerating, the weird device's functions were certainly obscure enough to baffle anyone.

And yet when the final choice presented itself – between the clock and those hellish winds of darkness sent by Ithaqua to destroy us – full of trepidation and dread though we were, nevertheless we entered into the vehicle's strangely huge, greenly illumined interior . . . and then everything seemed to turn upside down and inside out! Amid the whirling, rushing, dizzying motion of that experience I had yet been somehow aware of the final destruction of Blowne House; while from the depths of a shrieking purple mist that rushed ever faster into a gaping hole in the fabric of the universe itself, I heard Titus Crow's distant, fading voice:

'Follow me, de Marigny – with your *mind*, man – with your mind!'

Then he was gone and a Stygian darkness closed about me, buffeting, crushing, squeezing me like toothpaste from a tube out of that . . . that place . . . where I had no right to be. And finally, after an eternity of torture and tissue-rending pressures, there had been those sensations of falling, of water and then of strange hands tugging at me . . .

Then the white sheets of the hospital bed. And the flowers. And the comforting star-stone, left no doubt by Wingate Peaslee to guard me from the anciently malign horror of the CCD. Something about the professor's card bothered me, however. What had he meant by 'long lost but found again'? Didn't that imply the passing of a considerable amount of time? Well, I could always ask him when I saw him.

Until then, while far from sound in body, I was at least sane . . . and safe.

But what of Titus Crow?

# 2

## *Of Dreams and Ten Years Lost*

### *(From de Marigny's notebooks)*

It must have been early morning before I managed to get to sleep, but even then my slumbers were not peaceful. Everything that I had chewed over in my mind before finally sleeping kept rising to the surface of my subconscious, and the result could only be called nightmarish!

I dreamed – or nightmared – about the Cthonians, those monstrous subterraneans alive even now and burrowing in the Earth's secret places, threatening the very sanity of the world with a resurgence of hellish magic and mayhem and plotting the release of worse horrors yet, such as loathsome Lord Cthulhu and others of his Cycle.

I read again, or at least was allowed shuddering glimpses of, the books and documents of an unthinkably ancient 'mythology': works such as the *Pnakotic Manuscripts*, supposedly a fragmentary record of a race lost before history began; and the *R'lyeh Text*, purporting to have been written by certain minions of Great Cthulhu himself. And dreaming still, I averted my eyes from the pages of such tomes as the *Unaussprechlichen Kulten* of Von Junzt, and Ludwig Prinn's 'cornerstone' *De Vermis Mysteriis*. All of these books, or copies of them, I handled again as I had in reality handled them: the Comte d'Erlette's *Cultes des Goules*, Joachim Feery's *Notes on the Necronomicon*, even Titus Crow's own priceless copy of the anonymous *Cthäat Aquadingen* . . .

In books such as these, under Crow's guidance, I had first studied the legend of the Cthulhu Mythos: of Beings seeped down from the stars in Earth's youth, and prisoned here by greater Beings yet for blasphemies of cosmic enormity. The alien names of these forces rang again in my sleeping brain – Cthulhu, Yog-Sothoth, Ithaqua, Shub-Niggurath – and I felt a fever's heat grip me as if I had uttered some demoniac invocation to open the gates of hell!

Then for a moment I was back in Crow's study – in the reeling, tottering shell of Blowne House – with that ancient, madly ticking clock standing there, its door open, issuing a swirling, throbbing green and purple light – and my friend's face wax as he held me by the shoulders and shouted some instruction which was drowned in the tumult of winds!

'Titus!' I shouted back. 'For God's sake – *Titus*!' . . .

. . . But it was *not* Titus Crow's face, and it was not waxen. It was instead Peaslee's face, worried and drawn; Peaslee's arms reaching down to me, his veined old hands holding me firm; Peaslee's voice, calming, soothing me.

'Easy now, Henri! Easy! You're safe now. Nothing can harm you here. Easy, de Marigny.'

'Wingate! Professor!' I was barely awake, drenched in sweat, my whole body trembling and shuddering in reaction. Wildly, despite the restrictions of my various dressings, I tore loose from his restraining hands to peer fearfully about the room.

'It's all right, Henri,' he repeated. 'You're safe now.'

'Safe?' The nightmare was quickly fading; relief abruptly flooded my whole being. I let my head fall back against the damp pillows. 'Peaslee, what happened?' I stupidly asked.

The frown on his face turned to a wry, wrinkled grin. 'I was hoping you could tell me that, de Marigny!' he replied. 'The last I heard of you was in Crow's letter, retrieved from the ruins of Blowne House. Of course, I've never given up hope, but ten years is a long time, and – '

228

'What?' I cut him off. 'Did you say *ten years*?' I blinked the blurred edges of sleep from my eyes and at last saw Peaslee clearly where he bent over my bed, the smile fading again on his old face. And it was an *old* face, older by far than I remembered it and by my reckoning certainly older than it ought to have been.

'Yes, Henri, it's been ten long years since I last heard of you.' He frowned. 'But surely you know that? You *must* know it! Where have you been, Henri? And where is Titus Crow?'

'Ten years!' I slowly repeated it, suddenly exhausted, utterly washed out. 'My God! I remember . . . nothing. The last thing I recall is seeing – '

'Yes?'

'The clock, Crow's great clock. We went inside the thing, Crow and I, him first, myself following immediately behind him. We were somehow separated then. I remember Crow calling to me to follow him, and then . . . nothing. But ten years! How could such a thing be?'

For the first time then, I saw that my visitor was holding someone back from my bed. Finally this stranger exclaimed, 'Really, Professor, I must protest. Mr de Marigny is your friend, I understand that, but he's also my patient!'

The voice was female, but so aloof as to be almost harsh; the face atop the tall figure that finally pushed itself past Peaslee was hawklike and severe. It came as a shock, then, to find that the hand whose fingers searched for my pulse was surprisingly warm and gentle.

'Madam,' Peaslee replied, his New England accent barely showing, 'my friend is here at my request, and I am paying for his treatment. You must understand that his mind is the only key to certain very important problems – problems I have waited ten years to solve.'

'All that is as it may be,' the matron answered, quite

unperturbed, 'but no amount of money or pressure over-rules my authority here, Professor. The only way you may do that is to take Mr de Marigny out of my nursing home, which would not be in his best interests. In the meantime his welfare is my concern, and until he is well, or until you decide to terminate his stay here, I will care for him as I see best.' She paused, then acidly added, 'You are not, I believe, a professor of medicine?'

'No, madam, I am not, but – '

'No "buts", Professor, I'm quite sure that Mr de Marigny has had enough excitement for one day. You may see him again the day after tomorrow. Now I'm afraid you must leave.'

'But – '

'No, no, *no!*' she insisted.

Peaslee turned his seamed, angry face to me. His vastly intelligent eyes flashed furiously for a moment, but then he grinned a moment later, his natural good nature showing through all his impatience.

'Very well,' he finally agreed; and then to me: 'It will all have to wait until later, Henri. But she's right, you'd better rest now. And try not to worry. You'll be perfectly safe here.' He grinned again, wickedly casting a quick glance at the matron where she stood now at the foot of my bed penciling a line on a graph, before bending over me to whisper, 'I doubt if even Cthulhu himself would dare to brave this place!'

After Peaslee had gone I slept again, this time peacefully enough, until about midafternoon. When I awakened it was to find a young doctor at work removing the splints and casts from my arms. Matron Emily, as she insisted I call her, was assisting him, and she seemed genuinely delighted when at last my arms lay bare over the sheets.

230

'You wouldn't believe it,' she told me, 'if you had seen how badly mangled your arms were. But now . . .'

Now there were one or two minor scars, nothing much to show that my arms had suffered anything but superficial cuts and abrasions. 'Your friend the professor,' she continued, 'brought in the world's finest surgeons and specialists.'

She allowed me to sit up then, making me comfortable with pillows for my back. I was given a mirror, too, and allowed to shave myself. I soon learned not to move my arms too quickly; the bones were still very sore. By the growth of hair on my face I judged that it must have been all of a week since last I had seen a razor. Matron Emily confirmed this, moreover informing me that she had shaved me twice herself at similar intervals. I had been in her nursing home for three weeks.

I asked for the day's newspapers then, but before I could settle to read them a second doctor came in to see me. He was a bespectacled, bald little man with a busy, bustling attitude. He gave me a thorough going over: chest, ears, eyes, nose – everything. He *harrumphed* and grunted once or twice during his examination, made copious notes in a little black book, had me clench my hands and bend my elbows repeatedly, painfully, then *harrumphed* some more before finally asking me my age.

'I'm forty-six,' I answered without thinking; then, remembering that ten years had inexplicably elapsed since the world had last seen me, I corrected myself. 'No, better make that fifty-six.'

'*Harrumph!* Hmm, well, I prefer to believe your first statement, Mr de Marigny. Despite your injuries you're in a remarkably good state of preservation. I would have said forty-two, perhaps forty-three at the outside. Certainly not fifty-six.'

'Doctor,' I eagerly cried, grasping at his arms (and at a

231

straw at the same time) as I sought his eyes with mine. 'Tell me – what year is this?'

'Hmm?' He peered at me through the thick lenses of his glasses. 'Eh? The year? Ah, yes, you're having some trouble with your memory, aren't you? Yes, Peaslee mentioned that. Hmm, well, the year is 1979. Does that help any?'

'No, that doesn't help,' I slowly answered, dismayed to discover Peaslee's statement with regard to my lost ten years corroborated, even though I had known it would be. I shook my head glumly. 'It's strange, I know, but somewhere I seem to have mislaid ten years. Only I'm pretty damned sure I haven't *aged* ten years!'

He looked at me steadily for a moment, seriously, then grinned. 'Oh? Then you must count yourself lucky, er, *harrumph*!' He started to pack his instruments away. 'Years seem to hang like lumps of lead on me. Each one weighs that much heavier and drags me down that much faster!'

I spent the rest of the afternoon vainly attempting to formulate some sort of answer to this problem of the time lapse, giving it up in the end when I remembered the daily newspapers. They lay on a low chair to the right of my bed, within reach but out of sight, which was why I had forgotten them. But no sooner had I picked up the first newspaper than the enigma presented itself yet again – in the date at the top of the first page. Ten years . . .

Deliberately then, and with a genuine effort at concentration – something which should have come far easier to me – I forced the recurring problem from my mind and began to read. What I expected to find, what modern wonders had been wrought in this 'future' world, I really do not know. And so it was with a definite sense of relief that I discovered very little to have changed. The Big Names of the day were different, certainly, but they featured in the same old headlines.

Then I came upon an article about the Mars program in an illustrated scientific journal of recent date, noting that space probes had already been sent around Mars and recovered, and that they had been brought down under their own power on dry land. Progress! The title, by no means purely speculative, was 'The Exploration of Space – Men on Mars by '85.' But no sooner had I come across this article than I remembered what the Foundation had found on the moon: the secret that not even the American astronauts themselves had known. Nevertheless, certain of their instruments had transmitted back to Earth the fact that life did exist beneath that stark, cruel surface, a life even more cruel and stark. The octopoid spawn of Cthulhu was there, imprisoned on Earth by the Elder Gods *before* the moon had been hurled into orbit from the Azoic Pacific, molten again following that terrific battle which the forces of evil had lost. Little wonder that the full moon has driven men to madness and caused dogs to howl down the centuries . . . And then I wondered just what new horrors the first men might find on Mars . . .

Just how widespread throughout the universe were the prisons of the Elder Gods, wherein they had chained the malignant powers of the CCD? The great occult books had it that Hastur was imprisoned near Aldebaran in the Hyades, and that the Elder Gods themselves were palaced in Orion. So very far away! I was no mathematician, but I still knew the definition of a light-year, and while no man could ever hope to visualize such a distance, nevertheless I could at least conceive of thousands of such units. So very far . . . What hope then for little Mars, mere millions of miles away, in the selfsame star system as the home planet of Man, a system which had actually formed part of the inconceivably ancient battleground?

Puzzling just such disturbing questions as these, with that scientific journal still in my hands, I eventually felt myself nodding. In fact it had been growing dark in my room for some time. Matron Emily had looked in once or twice but had steadfastly refused to put my light on, saying that it was best I should get some sleep. Perhaps it was simply the added psychological effect of her words, or it just could have been the result of too much eyestrain in the steadily darkening room, but whichever way it was I soon succumbed to sleep, and it seemed that I began to dream almost immediately.

Now I have never been what you might call a great dreamer. In fact those dreams from which Peaslee had so mercifully rescued me were as strong and stronger than any I had ever previously known. By this I mean to say that it was extremely rare for me to dream so vividly; and yet no sooner had I closed my eyes when, for the second time in one day, I found myself assailed by strange nightmares and fantasies.

I floated in a region of weird forces outside yet forming a part of space and time; and I saw the great, coffin-shaped clock hurtling toward me out of even weirder nether regions while Crow's voice called out to me. But this time it was no exhortation to follow him that I heard but more a cry for help – an urgent request for assistance which I could not quite make out in its entirety before the clock drove on along paths unknown in nature into the distance of lost temporal wildernesses. And though the clock – or space-time ship, or whatever the thing was – had gone, still there sounded in my ears the eerie echo of Crow's lost cry for help, the tormented SOS of a soul in distress. That, at least, is the way it seemed to me, and I was later to learn that this interpretation of my friend's telepathic communication was not far short of correct.

Again and again, recurrently, this vision of the clock driving through hyperspace-time came to me; and over and over again I threw myself in its path only to be flung aside, left to swim frantically in its wake, vainly attempting to rescue my friend from whatever horrors threatened him. But who may swim against the tides of time?

Finally I woke up, and it was night; the room was still and quiet; my star-stone gleamed whitely against the flower vase in a stray beam of moonlight.

For a long time I simply lay there, feeling the cool of the sheet against my hot, naked arms, and the rapid beat of my heart within my chest. And in a short while my thoughts turned again to wondering about the plight of my poor friend, lost from men for ten long years. . . . And I admit that I despaired.

# 3

# Of Peaslee and the Wilmarth Foundation

### (From de Marigny's notebooks)

Two mornings later, bright and early and just as he had
promised, Peaslee came to see me. It seemed that I was
no sooner awake and shaved, just starting in on a very
ample breakfast brought in by Matron Emily (my meals
had been growing progressively larger and more regular
over the past two days) when he opened the door to walk
in unannounced.

'De Marigny, you look well!' He came and sat by my
bed. 'God, man, do you intend to eat *all* of that? Still, I
suppose it's more substantial than all that muck they've
had to pump into you over these last weeks. How do you
feel?'

'Fine,' I mumbled around a mouthful of bacon and egg,
'and I'll feel even better after they get my legs out of this
concrete tomorrow. Listen, you talk and I'll eat, then I'll
talk. Not that you'll get much out of me, I'm afraid, for
I've nothing really to tell. But how about you? What of
the Wilmarth Foundation?'

'The Foundation?' Peaslee smiled broadly, deep wrin-
kles forming in his aged face. 'All's well within the
Foundation, Henri, in fact things could hardly be better.
We haven't got them all yet, the minions of the CCD, not
by any means – but their numbers decrease every year,
and that's the important thing. Oh, there are still certain
problems, many of them in the USSR, but even the
Soviets are starting to come around to our way of
thinking.'

'And the organization retains its cloak of secrecy?'

'Certainly. More people in high places know of the Foundation's work now, yes – that was necessary for our expansion and continuation – but mundane mankind strolls blindly by. It has to be that way. To let people know what has been going on, what still goes on, would be to invite disaster. There are still . . . beings . . . that could be called up. The last thing we want is an upsurge of interest in such matters. The fear of large-scale panic is not so great these days; there are too many wonders to see, too many marvels to behold. A handful of ghosts and nightmares from a time already lost when the Cambrian was the veriest baby of an age would no longer drive the world to madness, but to have people *alerted* to these things, to have them seeking out and reading the great old books again, and perhaps dabbling . . . Oh, no. We can't have that, de Marigny. And so the Foundation remains secret, and its work carries on as before.'

I nodded, then inclined my head toward the vase of flowers and the curiously shaped stone at its base. 'For all your reassuring words,' I said, 'I see you're not about to take any chances with my life!'

'Indeed we're not!' he declared. 'For we've already lost you once too often. And you're honoured, de Marigny, for that's a very special stone. It is one of the originals, excavated with a handful of others when the Foundation killed a Cthonian recently, one of the biggest and worst yet. That was during a supposed archeological expedition to the region of Sarnath the Doomed in what was once the Land of Mnar, Saudi Arabia to you. That stone was manufactured by the Elder Gods themselves, whoever or whatever they were.'

I leaned across to take the object of our conversation in my hand, peering at it intently. There appeared to be fine lines drawn on its surface, whorls and squiggles, curious glyphs that seemed to defy my eye to follow their intricacies. 'There are . . . markings!'

'Do you recognize them?' the professor asked at once, vastly interested.

'Yes, I think I do,' I answered. 'They're very similar to the hieroglyphs on Crow's clock, his space-time machine. Do you think there could be some connection?'

'It would certainly seem that there is,' he answered wryly. 'I've kicked myself a thousand times since I first saw that clock at Crow's place when I stayed there. I knew then that it was a very important thing, but who could have guessed just how important? I should have taken notes, photographs. Why, Crow even told me he believed the thing to be – '

'A toy of the Elder Gods themselves?' I finished it for him.

'Yes, exactly. Of course, all is not quite lost: we have the books at Miskatonic which supplied Crow with his first really important clue to, well, how to drive the damned thing! But I dearly wish now that I had photographed the clock itself. Every fragment of information is of value in the overall picture, like a piece in a jigsaw puzzle, and this must surely be one of the basic puzzles of the universe itself.'

'But what else of the Foundation?' I impatiently asked when he was done. 'How far have you gone in ten years? What successes, what failures? What new knowledge? Have you found R'lyeh in the Pacific? And Shudde-M'ell – what of the Prime Burrower now? God, Peaslee, but I'm dying to know everything. Ten years – I've lost ten years!'

'Whoa!' The professor held up his hands. 'Slow down. I'll tell you everything, of course, but it's best if I start with what we have *not* done. For instance, we have not found

R'lyeh, no, and that in turn leads us to believe that the Johansen Narrative is at fault – not in its premise that a fantastic city of alien dimensions, angles and proportions exists beneath the Pacific – but that the specific island which rose up from the ocean floor in 1925 was R'lyeh, and that its hellish denizen was Cthulhu. That it was *one* of the Cthulhu spawn seems a certainty, but Great Cthulhu himself? We doubt it. You may research it for yourself, Henri. The Foundation did long ago. Basically Johansen's story is this:

'On March 23rd, 1925, at latitude 47°9′ south, longitude 126°43′, the *Alert*, under Johansen's command and in those waters following a series of complicated misadventures that had left her wildly off course, landed on a small island where an island had never been sighted before. Now the sea in that area is two thousand fathoms deep. It is on the very edge of the Pacific-Antarctic Ridge, which falls away to three thousand fathoms and even deeper. The area is not noticeably volcanic, and in any case a cataclysm of sufficient force to bring even a small area of the ocean floor to the surface would without a shadow of a doubt have been recorded. So it would seem we might throw out the fanciful Johansen Narrative forthwith, except that the Foundation, like Charles Fort, prefers to make its own decisions!

'The buckling of the Pacific floor, in places more a stretching, as Australia tends northward in the continental drift, has been very pronounced in the area of the Pacific-Antarctic Ridge since early Miocene times. The island that rose in March, 1925, was in fact a phenomenon of this geologically prolonged buckling, and its disappearance again shortly thereafter may be put down to similar seismic forces.'

'I've read Fort too,' I remarked dryly, 'and I think he'd have taken exception to what you just said, Wingate.'

'Eh? Oh, of course, so he would – if we hadn't sent

239

down bathyspheres at that precise point just three years ago, and if we hadn't discovered what we did.'

'Go on,' I said, putting my plate aside at last. 'What did you find?'

'Our first bell was simply, well, a diving-bell, nothing more. A device lowered into the sea to record with cameras whatever it saw. It hit bottom at only two hundred fathoms, at the very peak of the submarine range, which is now, incidentally, quickly sinking back into the deeps. But before we lost it we were afforded fantastic glimpses the like of which – '

'Lost it?' I interrupted.

'Yes.' He nodded grimly. 'We lost it. Cables wrenched loose, bell smashed to smithereens – and a structure capable of withstanding thousands of tons of pressure at that! We recovered fragments later, fantastically dented, gnawed and crushed. A sea-shoggoth, we're inclined to believe, perhaps a number of them, about their immemorial task of protecting and worshiping their dreaming masters, the spawn of Cthulhu.

'I went down in the second bell myself – '

'You did *what*?' Again I cut him off, marveling that he could so blandly admit what seemed like the most colossal lunacy.

He offered me an ancient, wrinkled grin and leaned over to tap a fingernail on the surface of the star-stone where I had replaced it by the flower vase. 'Aren't you forgetting something, Henri? Yes? Well, then, as I was saying . . .

'It was three months later. We were ostensibly charting the Pacific-Antarctic Ridge. I went down with two younger men from Miskatonic in a powered bathysphere that was really more of a submarine. We had the protection of a number of star-stones, of course, but nevertheless the weather was bad and we'd been dogged by troubles all the way out from Boston: storms, mists, accidents, etc. Mind you, we were not so naïve as to believe that such troubles were merely coincidental. We've learned a lot since the old *Sea-Maid* days . . .

'There was a particularly heavy swell on the sea and an ominous mist that morning, but our telepaths on board the mother ship were all alert. Besides, we had massed what protective devices we could against any possible interference by the dark forces. Our little vessel fell away from the *Surveyor*, on loan to Miskatonic University from the American Oceanographic Society, and sank slowly down in a controlled, spiraling dive to the bottom. That bottom was in fact a top, the top of a range which may one day rise again, and permanently. If so, it will stretch from somewhere about three thousand miles west of Freemantle – or where Freemantle is now – to Easter Island, over ten thousand miles away. Indeed Easter Island, New Zealand, the Pitcairns and certain other island groups may well form its highest peaks. Somewhere in that vast range R'lyeh may rise too, and other cities of the Cthulhu spawn, like the one we found there two hundred and fifty fathoms down beneath the *Surveyor*.

'The place was . . . fantastic! We saw it in the beams of our powerful searchlights almost as it must have been in its Azoic heyday over a billion years ago. It was crusted, certainly, with millions of centuries of oceanic growths, but its sheer unthinkable size had defied all but a minimal obliteration of outline through the aeons.

'We saw the immense carved doors with their symbols of the Cthulhu spawn, the great squid-dragon bas-reliefs mentioned in Johansen; we noted and grew sick and dizzy at the madness of elusive angles that refused to stay either convex or concave but seemed to alter of their own accord, as in optical illusions. Despite our protective star-stones, we shuddered at the lurking menace, the morbidly insane horror still inherent in these colossal, monolithic structures of non-Euclidean architecture.

'The extent of these upper ramparts of the city – for want of a better word – was perhaps nine or ten acres, and this was without doubt that same shockingly alien buttress which had formed Johansen's island. But the crazy staircases and mammoth monoliths falling away on all sides, swimming down in seemingly endless tiers . . . Without descending to greater depths yet, even our powerful searchlights could only hint at the outlines of these leviathan levels. That city – if I may still apply a word which smacks of teeming, mundane life to such a nighted necropolis of the undead – must have been immense beyond words, reaching down into the roots of the Pacific-Antarctic Ridge itself.

'Myself, I believe I might have stayed longer, explored further and deeper, but the third member of my crew, young Ridgeway, had worked himself into such a state that to extend our visit was plainly out of the question. Ridgeway is a telepath, you see, which helps considerably in his work at Miskatonic, where he's a professor of psychology. Down there in the depths, however, with God-only-knows-what lurking behind those colossal stone blocks and hideously carved doors, well, he just couldn't take it. Without the star-stones there can be little doubt that he'd have been a mindless jelly in a matter of minutes. As it was he was hard enough put to keep from screaming. You remember what happened to poor Finch when he deliberately went deep into the mind of that horror beneath the Yorkshire Dales? This would have been just as bad, except Ridgeway was doing his best to keep the telepathic sendings of the Cthulhu spawn out of his mind, while yet trying to gauge their mood. And their mood was ugly, you may depend upon it.

'So finally we set out for the surface and poor Ridgeway, his face horribly screwed up, unable to speak coherently, sank into a corner of our craft. And then we saw them. The guardians of the tombs, the watchers through the immemorial night of the Cthulhu spawn, the most blasphemous shapes you could ever imagine! Sea-shoggoths, dozens of them, held back by our star-stones just as we once held off that smaller specimen from your boat *Seafree* at Henley. But these were giants of their type, de Marigny, the royal guards of the kings of evil. Mountains of protoplasmic filth floundered and wallowed in the depths like cosmic corks in the whirlpool of Andromeda! And even knowing that we were safe, still I was relieved that they kept their distance, and even more relieved when at last the keel of the *Surveyor* opened to receive us.

'Our excursion into the deeps had been brief, but we had seen enough. Since then, of course, the Foundation has – '

'Let me guess,' I quickly interrupted. 'A further series of atomic tests in the Pacific, particularly in that region?'

'No, no, out of the question. We're no longer allowed to toss atomics around willy-nilly, Henri. No, but there's more than one way to skin a cat. We simply peppered the entire submarine range with radioactives of a very short half-life, quite definitely sufficient to destroy most of the shoggoth cultures, but not of a duration to permanently damage other marine life. We couldn't hope to get all of the shoggoths, of course – there are too many millions of square miles of ocean. And it's very likely that we didn't get a single one of the Cthulhi within their incredible vaults and sepulchers, but certainly we must at the very least have raised all hell down there. Cthulhi, by the way, is our most recent name for the Cthulhu species itself, as opposed to the CCD in general. No, there was little

243

chance of getting them all, and of course our actions were governed considerably by the laws of ecology; that is, we had no desire to sterilize the entire Pacific! And so, as I've said, we simply peppered that known range and other suspect places, doing our best at the same time to avoid harming areas of exotic marine life. But, in any case, there's not a great deal of life as we normally think of it at that depth.'

'Oh?' I showed my surprise. 'Three hundred fathoms?'

'Very little lives down there, de Marigny,' he insisted, 'and there's less the deeper you go. You have to remember that Johansen's island was only the veriest tip of a great peak. The rest of that particular city just went down and down and down, to regions where there could not possibly be any other life but . . . theirs. We calculate that there could be anything up to half a million square miles of city under the Pacific, and maybe as much again in other oceans! While we still don't dare let our telepaths play about too much with the Cthulhi, nevertheless we have reason to believe that there could be as many as five hundred individuals of that species imprisoned in the great deeps. Cthulhu, the prime member himself, the race-father of course, is only one of them, though in all probability he's the oldest, the most powerful and the nastiest. Possibly he was the very first of them to arrive on Earth when they seeped down from the stars, long before the soup of terrene life felt the first stab of generative sunlight.'

I heard the professor out, but in effect he had left me behind over a hundred words earlier. 'Half a million square miles.' I eventually repeated the statement that held me in so much awe. 'A whole damn continent of sunken tombs. But that's' – I made rough, rapid calculations – 'some five times the size of Great Britain!'

'My dear Henri,' the professor sighed, inclining his

head at me, 'much as it pains me to belittle your Great Britain, in the so much vaster scheme of things she's a tiny pebble in a very large pond. Any one of a hundred trenches in the floor of the Pacific could swallow her whole, without raising the merest ripple on the surface. We are talking about an ocean that covers tens of millions of square miles – hundreds of millions of cubic miles of water!'

I knew that he was right, of course, but nevertheless my mind boggled at the figures. I whistled softly and echoed him yet again: 'A pebble in a pond – Great Britain!'

# 4

## Of the CCD in England

### (From de Marigny's notebooks)

Then I turned my mind to other questions. 'While we're on the subject of Britain, what about Crow's warning that you'd need to take another look there? I remember he mentioned Silbury Hill, Stonehenge, Avebury, Hadrian's Wall and certain other places in the Severn Valley and the Cotswolds. Did you ever get around to them?'

Peaslee frowned. 'Yes, we did take another look at the British Isles, and we found various trouble spots that we'd somehow overlooked before. In the vicinity of Hadrian's Wall, for instance, not all that far out of Newcastle, there is a gate to an outer dimension, to one of the more remote prisons of the Elder Gods. This gate is, well, locked, I suppose you'd say. Lollius Urbicus in his *Frontier Garrison* tells us that it was opened at least once in his time, probably on a number of occasions. Urbicus wrote that circa 183 A.D., "the barbarians were wont to call out devils which they sent against us; they called them out from the air and beneath the ground, and one such which they sent killed half a centuria of soldiers before falling to their swords."

'Now what do you make of that? Plainly these barbarians Urbicus mentions must have been early British – Scottish? – dupes of the CCD. Not so rare or strange, really. There are records to show that the Ptetholites were similarly employed by the CCD thousands of years before Urbicus. They, too, were adept at calling up dark forces. Oh, yes, your witches and warlocks were real enough, Henri, but their magic was simply a vastly alien science.

'Titus Crow had a copy of *Frontier Garrison*, to say

246

nothing of certain far more conclusive and damnable *reliquiae* of those times; it surprises me he never mentioned the subject to you.'

'He did, come to think of it,' I answered with a frown. 'In fact I believe he wrote a short piece of macabre fiction around just such a creature as Urbicus mentions. Now what was the story called . . .?'

'*Yegg-ha's Realm*,' Peaslee promptly answered.

'Yegg-ha!' I snapped my fingers. 'Of course, I remember now. Titus once told me about a skeleton he'd dug up near Hadrian's Wall between Housesteads and Briddock – he was something of an archeologist on the quiet, you know – and he hinted that its owner must have been other than human. Yes, and I remember that he tied his discovery in with Lollius Urbicus, too.'

'Right,' Peaslee agreed, 'and he wrote his story pretty much as it must have happened, though of course he presented it as fiction. Even so it was pretty realistic. I've read it since and I can quite understand the stir it caused when it was first published in *Grotesque*. As for the bones he dug up, they were, as you say, other than human. Indeed, they were monstrous! Mind you, I never saw the actual remains, the great featureless skull or the *archaeopteryx*-like wing fragments. For some reason Crow destroyed them not too long after he found them, but he showed me photographs. Those pictures were definitely of something from . . . outside.'

'From what I know of Titus Crow,' I put in as Peaslee paused, 'it rather surprises me that he didn't go looking for this gate himself.'

'Ah, but he was much less well informed in those days, Henri. We all were. No matter, he had the right idea in the end. As I've said, it was because of what Crow told me that we did finally track this gate down. We actually found it, a door to an imperfect, synthetic universe, manufactured by the Elder Gods to imprison beings the Earth couldn't bear to harbor! We found it, and now we've locked it once and for all.

'Of course the thing was not physically a gate or a door; it was, rather, a place where our space-time continuum occasionally overlaps with another. The CCD knew this and telepathically fed the barbarians sufficient knowledge to allow them to open the way for the beings beyond. But the prisons of the Elder Gods are not so easily broken open. Only the minions, the underlings of those imprisoned powers of evil managed to break out, hideous but nevertheless flesh-and-blood creatures like Yegg-ha, while the actual inmates of the prison-dimension were obliged to remain in their timeless bondage. And that in turn leads us to the following questions: which of the Great Old Ones did Yegg-ha and his sort serve? And would it be possible for modern, rather more sophisticated dupes of the CCD to call them out?

'Of the latter question, there's little to fear of that now. We've put the most powerful locks we know of on that gate; we have literally welded it shut with our developing science, which was once the magic of the Elder Gods. If ever the gate is tampered with again, it will have to be by men who know as much as we do, and you may only find such men within the Foundation.'

'Don't forget, Wingate,' I reminded him, 'that there was once a so-called mad Arab, one Abdul Alhazred. *He* knew as much as we do, probably more.'

'Alhazred,' the professor answered, 'was the greatest dreamer, seer and mystic of all time. Aleister Crowley was a nobody by comparison, Dee a pewling babe, Eliphas Levi a mere dabbler and Merlin, if he ever existed, a first-year apprentice. Certainly there was an Alhazred; there was also a da Vinci, a Van Gogh and an Einstein. Such men occur once, and in the case of

Alhazred we may thank all that's merciful for that! And I think, too, that he really was more than a little mad. That way he would have been an ideal receiver for the telepathic sendings of the CCD. Did it ever occur to you to ask yourself just *where* Alhazred came by all of his occult knowledge in the first place?'

'No,' I answered truthfully, 'that's something I never thought about.'

'Hmm! Well, don't worry, there are thousands of questions that no man has yet thought to ask; questions are meaningless anyway until the answers are at least half known.'

'And have you decided or discovered which of the Great Old Ones Yegg-ha served?' I asked.

'Not for certain, but we have our ideas.

'One proposal is that this outer dimension is compartmented, that is, it is divided between various imprisoned beings. For example, we know that Yog-Sothoth is conterminous with all space and coexistent in all time, or at least we are told this in the old books and documents. But how can this be? And if it is so, why isn't he here now and ravaging? Well, we believe that he is only omnipresent insofar as his universe borders on both the time and space fabrics of our own continuum. The concept is that one edge of his place lies parallel with our time while another impinges upon our space. At that point near Hadrian's Wall the two universes overlap, and with a little help it is possible for certain of these lurkers at the threshold to step over to this side. You'll recall, of course, that Yog-Sothoth is actually known in the Cthulhu Cycle as the Lurker at the Threshold?'

'Yes, of course. Then it's Yog-Sothoth who bides his time behind the barriers of this synthetic universe?'

'Compartmented, I said, de Marigny. We believe that Yog-Sothoth is imprisoned in one compartment – but there are many others! What of Yibb-Tstll and Bugg-Shash, for example? They, too, are supposed to inhabit prisons in other dimensions. And Azathoth, before we discovered him to be simply the definition of a nuclear explosion, was also supposed to be omnipresent. Nor can we say that he is not, for certain nuclear theorists have it that the fabric of space-time is momentarily ruptured at the center of an atomic explosion. Who can say what horrors and nightmares man himself has visited upon the dwellers in yet more distant dimensions with his use of that lunatic weapon? This is one of the reasons why the Foundation supports the ban on all nuclear tests.

'However, I seem to have sidetracked a bit. I was answering your questions about the remaining CCD-inspired problems in Great Britain, wasn't I? Yes, well, after Hadrian's Wall we moved on to Salisbury Plain. With the permission of the British Archeological Society we checked Stonehenge out, as Crow had hinted we should. Nothing was there now, but there certainly was at one time in the remote past. We found star-stones there, deep in the earth, as old as any we've ever seen; in fact Schneider of archeology at Miskatonic believes that the monument itself was once in the shape of a great five-pointed star. Moreover, the *G'harne* Fragments bear him out. The outer points are long gone, but the hub of the thing remains. God only knows what horror the Elder Gods incarcerated down there that they required such a monumental tombstone to keep it down! The *G'harne* Fragments have it that when the early Cimmerians invaded Gunderland, some twenty thousand years ago, they destroyed the Great Elder Sign's pointed outer ramparts and thus set free the Being of the Great Star, and of course Gunderland covered that southern part of England in which Salisbury Plain lies. As to what became of the monster after that . . .' He shrugged.

'It may seem fantastic, but as for Stonehenge itself . . . well, despite what all your so-called experts may say to the contrary, the pyramids are the veriest babes of buildings when compared with Stonehenge!'

'You mentioned the *G'harne* Fragments,' I said, choosing that focal point from the mass of information the professor had presented. 'Poor Wendy-Smith once worked on those shards, didn't he? And Professor Gordon Walmsley of Goole, too. Do you mean to say that we finally have a translation? I thought the fragments were supposed to be unfathomable, that their ciphers and glyphs were quite beyond understanding?'

'Oh, yes!' he exclaimed. 'We have a translation, all right. In fact we know almost all there is to know about the fragments now, except perhaps how they survived the centuries. Mind you, the Foundation can't claim the first translation or even the second, not by any means. Wendy-Smith must have translated quite a bit -- and all power to him for that – but we took our lead mainly from Walmsley. I don't know if you're familiar with his book, *Notes on Deciphering Codes, Cryptograms and Ancient Inscriptions*, but if you are you'll recognize Gordon Walmsley of Goole as the greatest ever in his field. Little good his knowledge did him in the end, though.'

'So Wendy-Smith and Titus Crow were wrong about Stonehenge, were they? The monument is safe then?'

'Yes, but we can't say the same for certain other parts of Great Britain, Silbury Hill, for example, and Avebury. These places harbor an ethereal taint going back untold centuries. You must understand, there is little physical about this rare brand of evil. It is as vague and ill-defined as a picture drawn on quicksilver, transient as the phases of the moon, but just as surely recurrent. There were days, weeks even, when our telepaths and mediums gave these places spotless certificates of safety, as it were. And

251

there were other times when the telepathic and parapsychological ethers were crammed with presences that simply brooked no interference. It's no mere coincidence, I may tell you, that the Society of Metaphysics now has its headquarters in Tidworth; we intend to keep a close watch on the whole Salisbury Plain area.

'Similarly, we have agents permanently stationed in such towns as Marshfield, Nailsworth and Stow-on-the-Wold in the Cotswolds; and we are particularly interested in certain backwaters and centers of malign influence such as the decaying hamlets of Temphill and Goatswood along the Severn Valley.'

'The Cotswolds,' I repeated him, 'and Marshfield! Don't tell me that you've found something in Marshfield? Why, Crow's old confidante, Mother Quarry, used to live there. It was her letter which warned Crow of the danger when he and I had fallen into that last trap of the CCD. She had had one of her visions, I remember. The way Crow used to talk of her, I always saw her as some old charlatan.'

'Then you wronged her, Henri,' Peaslee said. 'Mother Eleanor Quarry is one of the best mediums we've yet discovered. We employ such people now as frequently as we used to employ our telepaths in your day. Often the two talents complement each other; they go hand in hand. Mother Quarry heads a very effective group in the Cotswolds, and she still lives in Marshfield at her old home, which is now the group headquarters.'

'You employ mediums,' I mused. 'Isn't that carrying things a bit far? I mean, the Foundation's operational center at Miskatonic is a world-renowned seat of learning and science. Surely metaphysics and the like has little in common with – '

'De Marigny, you've much to catch up with, I fear,' he said, cutting me off, 'and there seems to be a lot you've

252

forgotten, too. Metaphysics has *everything* to do with our work! Why, didn't the Elder Gods themselves use the occult arts, and weren't those same occult arts their sciences? We're looking at all such sciences today, Henri, in as enlightened a way as our bigoted human minds will allow. At Miskatonic right now there are groups of specially talented people seriously studying such subjects as telekinesis and levitation . . . to say nothing of mere crystal-gazing, divination and necromancy. Why, certain of our seminars read like a shaman's thesaurus! Oh, yes, you've much to catch up on.'

'Well,' I answered, 'that's what you're here for, Wingate. You may as well tell me as much as you can, for I've damn little to tell you.'

'You remember nothing at all of your lost ten years, then?'

'Nothing.' I shook my head. 'Except . . .'

I made myself a little more comfortable on my pillows before continuing. 'Oh, it's nothing really, just that I have an idea.'

'Oh? Well, go on, Henri.'

'Yes, I have this . . . idea. You see, Wingate, I don't seem to have aged at all in ten years, not by a single day, and I can't help wondering if . . .'

'Yes?'

'Well, when Titus and I entered that great old clock, when we fled Blowne House before Ithaqua's air elementals could get in at us, I remember Crow saying something about a trip into time, a journey into the future.' I paused.

'That is very interesting, Henri,' Peaslee said, his old eyes wide and staring at me intently. 'Go on.'

'I was wondering if . . . if perhaps Crow had indeed managed to pilot his craft into time, into the future, and if I –'

253

'If you had fallen overboard, as it were, before he got his ship properly out of port?'

'Yes, something like that,' I answered.

'Of course it's possible,' the professor told me after a moment's silence, 'and it would certainly explain why you haven't aged, to say nothing of your amnesia. How might a man remember ten years that never happened?'

'And you don't find the concept of time-travel too fantastic?'

'Not at all, Henri. I've seen far too much of the so-called fantastic to be awed by mere concepts. And after all, we're all time-travelers when you think about it.'

'Eh? How do you mean?'

'Why, aren't we all traveling into the future right now? Of course we are, except that we're traveling at a speed of only one second per second. From what you've told me, I'm beginning to believe that Titus Crow found a way to travel faster, that's all.'

After a while I said, 'Matron Emily tells me that when I was taken off the buoy at Purfleet I didn't even need a shave. Titus and I, we must have journeyed those ten years overnight! And since then, since my return, it's been almost two months. How far into tomorrow, then, is Titus Crow right now?'

Peaslee turned his suddenly troubled face away. 'That's something we may never know, Henri. There's still hope, of course. There will always be hope, but – '

'I know,' I said, and abruptly there passed before my mind's eye a scene remembered from a dream, of a coffin-shaped meteor plunging endlessly through nightmare vast-nesses of space and time. 'I know . . .'

# 5

## *Cthulhu's Cosmic Miscegenation*

### *(From de Marigny's notebooks)*

For a long while we were silent. Then, deliberately changing the subject and entering into a long, informative narrative, Peaslee rapidly brought me up to date on all of the more recent successes of the Wilmarth Foundation – its successes, and a few of its failures. It would take too long to detail the professor's complete discourse, and in any case I doubt if my memory is up to it, but I can at least outline a few of the things that he revealed to me.

For instance, he talked about the translation of the *G'harne* Fragments and the great boost that those ancient, decaying shards had provided to the impetus of the Wilmarth Foundation. He talked about the submarine destruction of Deep Gell-Ho and its shoggoth inhabitants, of the collapse of rotting Kingsport on the New England coast and the fact that the gray sea was now eating away at certain previously unsuspected caverns of maggoty loathsomeness and ages-old decay. He talked of Lh'yib, mentioning what men had done to Ib's sister city beneath the Yorkshire Moors in lowered tones; then he brightened as he related the advances made against blue-lighted K'n-Yan, red-lighted Yoth, and Black N'kai. I remember, too, that he mentioned a certain Moon Bog of Irish myth and legend, in dark connection with the so-called nameless city of olden Turkistan.

Much of what I heard was completely new to me, only recently fathomed or discovered by the Foundation, so that I thrilled to such *outré* names as Sunken Yatta-Uc, a city drowned in the forgotten inner cone of Titicaca's volcano; Doomed Arkan Tengri, a derelict aerie of mist-obscured peaks and icy pinnacles in the white wastes south of the Kunlun Mountains; and the Jidhauas, savage nomads of Mongolia's Gobi Desert and worshipers of Shudde-M'ell.

All of these things were fascinating to me, but one subject in particular that Peaslee touched upon toward the end of his long narrative completely absorbed me. It was in connection with Shub-Niggurath, yet another weird name from the Cthulhu Cycle of myth. Yes, Shub-Niggurath, 'the black goat of the woods with a thousand young', occasionally called the Ram with a Thousand Ewes or, as Peaslee preferred to refer to the mythological figure, Cthulhu's Cosmic Miscegenation!

I knew that previously Shub-Niggurath had been looked upon as a symbol of fertility, a being locked away with the CCD by the Elder Gods, and that in the *Necronomicon* it was recorded that 'he shall come forth in all his (her?) hideousness when again the Great Old Ones are freed to walk the world as once they walked long ago.' Recently, however, the Wilmarth Foundation had interpreted all of this somewhat differently. Students of the Cthulhu Cycle pantheon had finally explained away certain conflicting statements as to Shub-Niggurath's sexual characteristics. For an example of the latter ambiguities, the Ram with a Thousand Ewes was often mentioned as being the *wife* of Hastur; and, even more confusingly, in the *Cthaat Aquadingen* Shub-Niggurath is referred to as 'Father & Mother of all Abominations, & of Others worse yet which will not be until ye Latter Times.'

Father *and* mother . . .?

The answer, Peaslee told me, is simply that Shub-Niggurath is the greatest fertility symbol of all, and in fact much more than a mere symbol. He/she is nothing less than the power of miscegenation itself, amazingly inherent in the majority of the CCD. He/she is their ability to mate with the daughters of Adam and the sons of Eve, and with others of this wide universe somewhat less human.

Thus, along with Azathoth and Nyarlathotep, Peaslee had relegated Shub-Niggurath, too, to a symbol of power proper as opposed to a physical, alien being. And of that monstrous cosmic miscegenation of the CCD the professor had much to say. He talked of the unthinkable consequences and results of the matings of them with human beings, mentioning that such vague reports as are occasionally heard of blasphemous offspring are often known to have direct links with the CCD. The Foundation, he went on, had collected and collated many valuable and damning data, but he feared that only the surface had been scratched.

From a host of hideous cases he quoted a few facts. He mentioned the twins born to an unmarried illiterate albino woman at Dunwich in north-central Massachusetts; the loathsome *serpentes* children whose mother hacked her husband to death in a lunatic fit nine months before her family was – spawned? – in Caddo County, Oklahoma; the Irish half-wit woman who gave birth to a boy with stubby, vestigial wings after her medium mother had been plagued with nightmares of a flying demon, and so on. The cases were seemingly endless.

I remember having stopped Peaslee at about that point in his narrative to question him with regard to his term Cthulhu's Cosmic Miscegenation: wasn't 'cosmic' just a trifle ambiguous or superfluous? It was then that he told me what little he knew of a certain shadowy intelligence deep in the sub-oceanic vaults of Y'ha-nthlei beyond Devil Reef. Basically what he said was that man was not alone in intelligence in the universe, and that the CCD had not confined their spawnings to human flesh and blood alone.

He had said more or less the same thing before, but now he was more explicit.

Before the Great Uprising, Peaslee told me, Cthulhu himself fathered three sons 'upon a female sentience from remote, ultra-telluric Xoth, the dim green double sun that glitters like a dæmonic eye in the blacknesses beyond Abbith . . .' This quote is taken from the *Ponape Scripture* which, according to Peaslee, is a primal document brought back from the Isle of Ponape by an Arkham merchant-skipper, Captain Abner Ezekiel Hoag, in about 1734. Circulated privately, the manuscript finally ended up in the Kester Library in Salem, where the Wilmarth Foundation first became interested in it.

From that book and one or two others, particularly the *Zanthu Tablets*, the Foundation had culled most of its knowledge with regard to Cthulhu's progeny, before setting themselves to the task of verifying or condemning such accounts. Considering the history of the *Zanthu Tablets*, it is not really surprising that the Foundation had only looked at that source seriously in comparatively recent years. Purported to be the work of a prehistoric Asian shaman or wizard, the tablets were allegedly discovered by Professor Harold Hadley Copeland in Zanthu's stone tomb in 1913, and a translation was published by Copeland three years later in a quickly suppressed brochure of 'fragmentary and conjectural content, seeming deliberately contrived to undermine all recognized authorities, especially science and theology.'

Well, people had called Sir Amery Wendy-Smith a madman, and they had scorned Gordon Walmsley of Goole and many others whose work was later to prove invaluable to the Wilmarth Foundation, and the Foundation had learned a lesson from such examples. After a number of years of hard work, Peaslee's researchers had been able to state quite conclusively that both the *Ponape Scripture* and the *Zanthu Tablets* were works which, along with those other monstrous books passed down the ages, had a firm foundation in fact and unthinkably distant prehistory.

This is what was finally brought to light: that until such evidence was discovered to suggest otherwise, it must be accepted that Cthulhu *had* fathered three miscegenetic sons upon an extraterrestrial being, and that these creatures were still mercifully imprisoned in black and shrieking abysses of earth.

The three sons were: Ghatanothoa, 'the monster on the mount', interred in crypts beneath a primal mountain, now lost in depths of ocean at the southern edge of the southeastern Pacific Plateau, about a thousand miles south of Easter Island; Ythogtha, 'the abomination in the abyss', lying chained by the Elder Sign in Yhe, which location the Foundation has not yet pinpointed; and Zoth-Ommog, 'the dweller in the deep', dreaming insanely in unfathomed gulfs off Ponape. There were three sons . . . *and a daughter*!

Cthylla was her name, the Secret Seed of Cthulhu. Her presence had been carefully edited from all the ancient texts except in the most oblique references; the minions of the CCD had even removed her likeness from the Columns of Geph in the coastal jungles of Liberia before attempting to destroy the columns themselves, to keep word of the Secret One safe. Cthylla, a name Von Junzt was heard to scream out in supplication just once, before dying in 1840 in a locked and bolted Dusseldorf chamber with the marks of taloned fingers upon his throat; a name Alexis Ladeau, Von Junzt's closest friend, wrote upon a stone floor in tottering letters of his own life's blood after reading certain sections of his friend's insane *Unaussprechlichen Kulten*. He had burned the book to ashes before slicing his throat through with a razor. Cthylla, of whose existence no other trace, no single clue remains extant in any form recognizable to mundane mankind, Cthylla *nevertheless exists and is worshiped in the world today*!

Knowing in the end that he was beaten by the Elder Gods, and seeing that his lore would be handed down through the æons by his worshipers and that eventually other rulers of Earth and the universe might try to seek him out and destroy him, Cthulhu was determined not to let his daughter, his secret spawn, fall into any such peril. Whatever Cthulhu's own future fate, his seed must be protected. The existence of his sons, too, he had tried to obscure; but his daughter, who would be the spawn-mother of distantly future generations, her concealment *must* be complete . . .

This was no mere fatherly concern for his child, as one might expect in a human being; Cthulhu was in no way human, knowing nothing of emotions as man might understand such. So where, then, did he get this desire to provide safety in obscurity for his daughter? Certain rites telepathically received and recorded by Foundation telepaths in Innsmouth held the abominable answer.

In 1975, in fact during the last week of October of that year, particularly Halloween itself, a hideous mental babble, emanating from tremendous depths beneath the bed of the gulf beyond Devil Reef, was picked up by a special team 'vacationing' in Innsmouth. Unaware that they were listening in on rites lost in every other instance in unbelievable antiquity, the Foundation people recorded the oft-repeated liturgies, discovering them to be the bicentennial incantations of Mother Hydra and Father Dagon to Cthylla, daughter of Cthulhu. They perceived that these ancient rituals had last been practiced in 1775; then, to mark the occasion, Dagon and his Deep Ones had taken hold on the minds of certain Innsmouth seafarers, thus influencing their participation in dark Polynesian religions and the eventual reunion of an alliance lost before the first coelacanth swam in Earth's seas – the liaison between the tomb-guarding Deep Ones of the Pacific and their kin in Y'ha-nthlei, whose nether vaults held dreaming Cthylla!

The Deep Ones were dead and gone now, those semi-human hosts of Y'ha-nthlei, and all the shoggoths of that sunken city with them, wiped out to the last by the Wilmarth Foundation during a second purging of Innsmouth in 1974; but deeper still beneath the bed of the gulf, in vaults which man might never have hoped to guess at, there, tended by faithful Hydra and ministered by Dagon, there Cthylla slumbers yet, awaiting . . . what?

Yet again, relying upon their telepathic and psychic fraternities, the Foundation's researchers think they have discovered the answer.

It all has to do with Cthulhu's enigmatic symbol-statement: '*Ph'nglui mglw'nafh Cthulhu R'lyeh wgah'nagl,*' which, translated from the R'lyehan, reads: 'In his house at R'lyeh dead Cthulhu waits dreaming,' and in that conjectural couplet from Alhazred's *Necronomicon:*

> That is not dead which can eternal lie,
> And with strange æons even death may die.

That Alhazred, that great dreamer and mystic, plucked the latter lines direct from the minds of the Cthulhi can no longer be doubted, for it is known now that there is a second couplet, used in conjunction with the first in

261

Cthylla's rites; and these further lines may be interpreted as follows:

> The dreamer dying faces death with scorn,
> And in his seed will rise again reborn!

Cthulhu the phoenix, rising up from the ashes of his own destruction in the spawn of his daughter's darkling womb . . . *reincarnation*!

To bear out this chilling concept, by no means far-fetched in the light of what is already known of the CCD and particularly of Cthulhu, the Foundation's researchers have returned again to Alhazred in yet another cryptic passage from the rarest *Al Azif* of all:

'Tis a veritable & attestable Fact, that between certain related Persons there exists a Bond more powerful than the strongest Ties of Flesh & Family, whereby one such Person may be *aware* of all the Trials & Pleasures of the other, yea, even to experiencing the Pains or Passions of one far distant; & further, there are those whose Skills in such Matters are aided by forbidden Knowledge or Intercourse through dark Magic with Spirits & Beings of outside Spheres. Of the latter, I have sought them out, both Men & Women, & upon Examination have in all Cases discovered them to be Users of Divination, Observers of Times, Enchanters, Witches, Charmers or Necromancers. All claimed to work their Wonders through Intercourse with dead & departed Spirits, but I fear that often such Spirits were evil Angels, the Messengers of the Dark One & yet more ancient Evils. Indeed, among them were some whose Powers were prodigious, who might at Will *inhabit* the Body of another, even at a great Distance & against the Will & often unbeknown to the Sufferer of such Outrage.

Moreover, I have dreamed it that of the aforementioned most ancient of Evils, there is *One* which slumbers in Deeps unsounded so nearly Immortal that Life & Death are one to *Him*. Being ultimately corrupt, *He* fears Death's Corruption not, but when true Death draws nigh will prepare Himself until, fleeing *His* ancient Flesh, *His* Spirit will plumb Times-to-come

& there cleave unto Flesh of *His* Flesh, & all the Sins of this
Great Father shall be visited upon *His* Child's Child. I have
dreamed it, & my Dreams have been *His* Dreams who is the
greatest Dreamer of all . . .

Cthulhu, then would be reincarnated in the womb of
his daughter, to be reborn as her child. To Dagon would
go the honor of fathering this blasphemy, Hydra would
be nurse and handmaiden, Cthylla herself would raise the
hybrid horror with Cthulhu's monstrous mind and psyche.
Then in the waxing strength of a young adult – pointless,
horrible even to conjecture what *characteristics* this thing
might have! – he could again commence the influencing
of men's minds, and this time from a location very close
indeed to vast centers of human life.

Cthulhu, alert again, powerful, would be sending out
his hellish dreams from the deeps beneath Devil Reef,
*unsuspected* – for of course officially he would be dead!

Having told me so much, even though I pressed him for
further details, Peaslee would say no more on the subject
of Cthulhu's reincarnation. It seemed to me that there
was more he could have told me, certainly, but that it was
of such importance and of so ultimately secret a nature
that he simply dared not mention it, not even to me.
Furthermore I could see that he was biting his tongue,
presumably for having said too much already. In any case,
the lateness of the hour saved him from any further
embarrassment: he used it as an excuse to take his
departure.

# PART TWO

# 1

# *Of Visions and Visits*
## *(From de Marigny's notebooks)*

Less than a week later Peaslee visited me again, this time to wish me luck for the future and to say farewell for the time being. There was work waiting for him in America. Before he left we talked of Titus Crow once more and then, finally, the old man asked me if I had any plans with regard to the Wilmarth Foundation. Did I want to come back into the organization? If so, there would always be a place for me. I thanked him but turned his offer down. I had my own interests, my own discoveries to make in this 'new world'.

It was only after a further period of six weeks in the hospital, with at least half of that time taken up with physiotherapy, the retraining of my poor, unaccustomed muscles, that I was finally allowed to sign myself out and go my way as a free man. In fact the last few weeks had seemed like a sort of imprisonment, and I was very glad when I was at last able to get back into the world, albeit a world with which I was greatly out of touch.

During those frustrating weeks there had been one regular visitor at the hospital, however, a lady whose presence helped combat the tedium of waiting out my time until the doctors would give me a clean bill of health: my dear old part-time housekeeper, Mrs Adams, who could only ever speak of Titus Crow as 'that dreadful Crow person', for in her eyes Titus had always been to blame for dragging me into whatever adventures overtook us. My hospital, I had discovered, was on the outskirts of

Aylesbury; Mrs Adams, when she finally knew my where-abouts, traveled up daily from London just to spend an hour or so with me. She had kept my place going all this time, visiting the house twice a week for ten long years in my absence. As she herself put it: 'I knowed you'd be back sooners-laters, Mr 'Enri, sir.' And now, though I was still using a walking stick, now I *was* back.

Fortunately I had all but dissolved my small but lucrative antique business some time after joining the Foundation, and so very little had wanted or wasted for my absence. I intended now to revive my lifetime interest in beautiful old books, pottery and furniture, but first I would spend a few days simply getting used to the feel and atmosphere of my old home again.

While the house itself was the same as ever, the district had seemed to change enormously. 'Progress', as they call it, waits for no man – not even a time-traveler. Indeed, *especially* not a time-traveler! Out walking in a neck of the city I'd once considered my own, it was as if I trod the streets of some strange, foreign place. New buildings, alleys, posters; a well-remembered old cinema had been replaced by a shopping arcade; even the faces were different, where shops I'd once used had now passed into new hands or disappeared completely, demolished. The underground was the same, and yet was not the same, but that didn't bother me much: its system had always been beyond my comprehension. And in all truth I had not used the tube since first learning of the existence of the burrowers beneath; and because of them, despite all Peaslee's assurances, I did not intend to use it again . . .

Not that I ventured far from my house during those first few weeks out of the hospital. I did not, except to make one very special trip to Leonard's-Walk Heath late in November. Blowne House, Crow's strange, foreboding bungalow retreat, had once sprawled on the heath. All I could find now was a shattered ruin, a drab and desolate skeleton of a house. The bricks of the old chimney were crumbling onto rotten floorboards; the creepers of wild brambles made slow but steady incursions throughout the surrounding gardens; nettles grew in threatening clumps along the drive. In another five or six years it would almost seem as if the place had never been . . .

And it was there, standing in those ruins with my nostrils pricking in painful nostalgia, lost in memories of days spent with Crow in arcane study and esoteric discussion, it was there that I experienced for the first time during waking hours a dizzying assault on my senses which was to occur ever more frequently during the following weeks. As the world started to spin around me and the gray November sky turned black, I hastily sat down on the old, bare floorboards with my back to the base of the crumbling chimney. No sooner was I seated than I experienced a wild rushing sensation, a dizzy tumbling as if I had fallen from some primal cliff into the blackness of a pit that reached down to the Earth's very core. I seemed to fall for ages, until I began to think that the sickening descent would never end. It was altogether a nauseating, stomach-wrenching, mind-numbing experience; and yet, as I sensed the approaching end or climax of this nightmare fall, even as my senses began to right themselves, I knew that what was occurring was nothing new to me. I had known this before, but only in dreams.

Well, dream or developing psychosis or whatever it was, I finally recognized my surroundings. Whereas a moment before I had seemed to whirl and plummet in blackest depths, now in a mere instant my numbed senses had become super-sensitive. I smelled the strange winds that roar between the worlds, bearing the odors of darkling planets and the souls of sundered stars; I felt about me the emptiness of remote and infinite vacuums of space, and their coldness; and I saw, blazing on a panoply of jet, unknown constellations and nameless nebulæ stretching out and away through the light-years into unthinkable abysses of space. Finally, winging through the nearer voids, I spied that enigmatic coffin shape recognized of old, and again, as in delirious dreams, I heard my lost friend's voice.

He made no new demands that I follow him, but as on a previous occasion simply called out to an empty void: 'Where are you, de Marigny? Where are you?'

'Here, Titus!' I yelled in spontaneous response, hearing nothing of my own voice above the roar of the wind blowing between the worlds. '*Here!*' I screamed again, at which the great clock seemed to swing a little, hesitantly turning toward me in its hurtling flight across the heavens. And I heard Crow's answering cry ringing out in amazed exultation:

'De Marigny! Where? *Where are you?*'

I would have answered again at once; but then, swelling out of the blackness in the wake of Crow's weird craft – bloating up in a green and rotten glow of corruption, filling my entire view in an instant and reaching with slimy tentacles – there came a shape . . . the shape of utmost lunacy!

Cthulhu! I knew him at once. Who could mistake him?

First the tentacles, seeming to reach back infinitely to the face from which they sprang; and that face itself, evil rampant, express and implied in a single glance; and to the rear, dwindling away in distant abysses of the void, the vast arched wings supporting an impossibly bloated body. Cthulhu, even now reaching to wrap fearsome face-tendrils about the toy coffin-ship!

'*Look out!*' I finally managed to scream, flinging my hands up before my eyes . . .

. . . And then I again felt the stomach-wrenching

sensation of falling as from a vast, immeasurable height, and all my senses fought for stability in the headlong rush of my psyche back to its home in material flesh.

Cold daylight rushed in upon my startled eyes. The dampness of rotting floorboards touched me through my clothes and my back felt the hard chimney bricks behind me.

Strangely fatigued by an experience which could hardly be called physical, I eventually forced myself to my feet and left the ruins of Blowne House. But I could not shut out of my mind that hideous vision of Cthulhu pursuing Crow's clock, a vastly loathsome bulk against a background of leering stars and nighted nebulæ. Thus I went my way oppressed by a gloom springing not alone of the bleak November skies, a gloom which seemed to weigh tangibly upon my shoulders.

Some few weeks later these terrible attacks had become so frequent – each one occurring without the slightest warning – that it was almost unbearable. I had just about made up my mind to see a doctor, a psychiatrist, frankly, about the problem. Then, just ten days before Christmas, I received a most disturbing, indeed an astounding communication. Having slept late on that particular morning, I found this letter waiting for me with my morning newspaper:

Marshfield

Dear Mr de Marigny –

Do please make yourself available at home on the afternoon of the 16th; I shall be traveling down to see you. I should get into London about 3 P.M. – and no need to meet me, I'll know where to find you. I may come by car. *And please, no mention of this to anyone from the Foundation.* As you know, I am just as much a member of that organization now as you yourself were ten years ago – I mention this simply to assure you that my visit goes in no way against our own and the Foundation's mutual interests – but I want to talk to you about Titus Crow, and I have reason to believe that he would not want what I have to tell you to go any further.

Until we meet then,<br>
Sincerely,<br>
Eleanor Quarry

P.S. Do not look for me in the telephone book. I have no telephone. I abhor the things.

EQ

Upon first reading this completely cryptic note my mind simply went blank; I frankly did not know how to react. Only after a second hurried reading did the implications begin to dawn on me, and then a whole host of suddenly galvanized emotions brought me quickly to what must have been a sort of mental hysteria.

Eleanor Quarry, 'Mother' Quarry, was the medium whose timely letter had warned Titus Crow of the CCD's insidious trap ten years earlier; it had sent us fleeing for our lives from stricken, doomed Blowne House in the doubtful confines of an alien time machine whose shape was that of a hideous grandfather clock. While I had never met her, I had always looked upon her peculiar psychic practices very dubiously, despite the fact that Titus Crow had seemed to have the utmost faith in her. Anyway, here she was, this woman, as good as telling me that Crow was alive, almost implying that she had been in communication with him, and that the substance of that communication was for my ears only!

Well, what was I to make of it? My mind flew in several directions at once, quite uselessly, completely out of control. Questions piled themselves up in my head, unanswered but demanding attention, whirling madly about in my mind until I had to force myself to sit down and think the problem out as calmly as possible.

If Crow *was* alive, where was he now, and why the secrecy? Could it be, perhaps, that he was in some terrible peril, maybe even a prisoner of the CCD? No, that last seemed out of the question. The CCD would never hold Titus Crow a prisoner; they would simply kill him out of hand as soon as the opportunity presented itself. He had been far too dangerous to their cause, a thorn in their sides. So had I, for that matter.

But just think of it – Titus Crow alive!

My mood leaped from one of worried tribulation to wild speculation. *Crow alive!* Could it really be? Had we indeed traveled into time, he and I, and was that really the reason behind my apparent loss of ten years? And had he then gone on into the future while, incapable of understanding the time-clock's principles, I had fallen overboard almost at the onset of our flight?

On the other hand, why was it important that he now remain incognito, as it were? Again my spirits tumbled. How much confidence could I place in this woman, this Eleanor Quarry? And could this possibly be yet another ploy of the CCD? I did not care at all for the woman's demand that I should not mention her proposed visit to anyone from the Foundation.

But the sixteenth! Why, that was tomorrow, and today was already well into the afternoon. In just twenty-four hours I would know as much as there was to know of this mystery. All my questions would be answered . . . but it would certainly be the longest twenty-four hours I had ever known in my life . . .

# 2

## Mother Quarry

### (From de Marigny's notebooks)

The knocking at my door brought me bolt upright in my chair, startling me from unquiet but mercifully unremembered dreams. A glance at my watch showed me that it was three P.M. exactly.

I realized what had happened: finally exhausted, having paced the floors of my house all through the previous evening and night, mentally juggling with the infinite possibilities in connection with Eleanor Quarry's visit, I must have fallen asleep right after an early lunch. And now, now here she was and I was still unshaved, blinking the sleep from my eyes, clutching my star-stone tightly in one hand for fear it was *not* Eleanor Quarry at the door at all but something else.

Not knowing what to expect, still half asleep, I went to the door. The knocking came again, more decisively, and a voice, not loud but penetrating the door quite clearly called, 'Mr de Marigny, I am *not* a shoggoth, I assure you, so do please open up and let me in!' That voice had the instant effect of dispelling most of my doubts and fears, so that I immediately threw open the door.

Eleanor Quarry was tiny and old, elegant in a smartly modern matching jacket and skirt; she was gray-haired, with gray unfaded eyes that twinkled despite their age through ancient pince-nez glasses. She took my hand firmly and pumped it as I stepped aside to let her in.

'I'm Eleanor Quarry,' she said, making the introduction formal, leading the way to my study as though she had lived in my house all her life, 'but please call me Mother. Everybody does. And do please stop thinking of me as an

272

old charlatan. I am a perfectly respectable, quite genuinely psychic person.'

'I can assure you, er, Mother, that I – ' I began.

She cut me off. 'And don't lie, young man. You've always considered me to be a charlatan, I know you have. Doubtless it's due to the way that rascal Titus Crow has spoken of me. And yet he always had more than a fair share of the old sixth sense himself, you know.'

'Er, yes, indeed he had,' I answered, beginning to feel more at ease. In my study she turned to face me, smiling when she saw the star-stone in my hand.

'I wear mine around my neck,' she leaned forward to whisper, a mock frown drawing her eyebrows together.

'Oh! Er, I just – '

'No need to explain.' She smiled, drawing up a golden chain from her bosom. At the end of the chain a star-stone dangled. 'A damned uncomfortable thing,' she remarked, 'and yet very comforting, too, in its way.'

My last doubts were finally dispelled. I smiled at my visitor and rubbed ruefully at the stubble on my chin. 'I had intended to shave before you arrived,' I started to explain, 'but – '

'No, no, you were right to have a little nap,' she said, cutting me off yet again. 'No doubt your mind is all the fresher for it, and that's important over all, that your mind be fresh, I mean. Anyway, I like my men rugged!'

She began to laugh and I joined in, but I sobered quickly as I thought back over the preceding few minutes to some of the rather weird correct guesses this lady had made. She had been more or less right when she hinted that perhaps I pictured something other than a human knocking on my door; she had been right to accuse me of believing her an old fraud (though I was already changing my mind) and finally she had correctly – to my confusion and embarrassment – named me a liar, albeit a white one.

273

Perhaps she was a fraud even now, but if so then she was a very clever one.

'I *am* psychic, Mr de Marigny,' she said, breaking into my thoughts, 'though in the main my powers should really be relegated to the lower levels of ESP, and even there they are limited. Primarily I am telepathic, a one-way receiver, a mind reader. If I could only *project* as well . . . ah, but then Titus Crow wouldn't need you!'

So fascinated had I become with this remarkable old woman that I had almost forgotten the purpose of her visit. 'Titus!' I gasped, suddenly remembering. 'Titus Crow! But is he . . .?'

'Alive?' She raised her eyebrows. 'Oh, yes, he is alive. He is close, too, and yet far away. Frankly, I do not understand as much as I would like to understand. Although I have received his messages, I could not tell where they originated. I mean that, well, for one thing, I don't believe him to be here on this planet.'

She stared at me for a moment as if waiting for some reaction, then nodded. 'Good. You don't find what I just said strange, so obviously I must be on the right track. You know more of his situation than I. No, Titus Crow is not on Earth, and yet he is distant in more than one sense, almost as though – '

'As though,' I finished it for her, 'he were also remote in time?'

Her mouth fell open and her eyes widened even as I spoke the words. Obviously she had read my thought an instant before I voiced it. 'But that is exactly it!' she cried. 'It surprises me I didn't think of it that way myself.'

'Oh?' I said. 'I hardly find it surprising. Time-travel is something out of science fiction, surely? Not something for merely mundane speculation.'

'And what of telepathy?' she returned, smiling.

I had to allow her that. 'It's my belief, at any rate,' I

continued, 'that Titus is indeed lost in time. Peaslee and I have talked about it; the professor agrees with me. But I suppose I'd better tell you the whole story. That way perhaps – '

'No need,' she quickly answered, stretching out a trembling hand to touch my forehead, 'simply let yourself think back on it.'

Her eyes clouded over and she swayed. Belatedly remembering my manners I steadied her and sat her down in a chair, and all the while her cool, trembling hand rested upon my forehead. Finally her eyes brightened and she withdrew her hand.

'So that is how it was,' she said. 'That old clock of his. Until now I had not known . . .'

Now it was my turn to express surprise. I had been on the point of telling her about Crow's departure from Blowne House into time, but should that really have been necessary? Surely, as a member of the Foundation . . .? Her last statement, if she was all she made out to be, struck me as being more than peculiar. 'But that's strange,' I said. 'I should have thought that you, of all people, would be the very one to know such things?'

She looked at me searchingly, questioningly for a moment, and then her eyebrows knitted in a frown of displeasure. 'I said I can receive the thoughts of others, young man, not that I *steal* them. I would not dream of looking into the mind of another uninvited either by word or gesture. That would be a hideous curiosity. I would no sooner do that than enter another's house unbidden or read another's diary.'

'But when you first knocked at my door – ' I started to protest.

'Do you think you are the only one who fears the CCD?' she quickly asked. 'When I came to your house I instinctively checked that it was a man waiting for me

275

behind the door. I merely brushed your mind, sufficiently to read your own fear.'

'But it's been ten years since we departed. Surely, as a member of the Foundation, and as a personal friend of Titus Crow you – '

'About the Wilmarth Foundation,' she answered. 'I accept what I'm told; I don't probe where I'm unwelcome. This is an unspoken rule among all telepaths who work for the Foundation. If Peaslee had wanted to tell me about you and Titus he would have done so. I respect his leadership and where work is concerned I only interest myself in those projects and experiments which he authorizes. This does not mean, however, that the Foundation governs me utterly; on the contrary, I retain my own private interests. I have my own friends and I am loyal to them, as I hope they are to me. Titus Crow has been a friend for many years.'

'And you say that he has . . . contacted you?'

'He has, yes, and now that I know his predicament I am sure that I was right to come and see you. You were correct, he is lost in space and time, trying to find his way home. He is like a sailor of the old times, lost on alien seas, compass gone and the stars unreadable. I think you have some link between you, you and Titus, some sense perhaps akin to ESP, by which you feel for each other without being truly telepathic. He needs to home in on you, Mr de Marigny. He wants you to hold out a light in the darkness, one that he can follow back to his own time and space.'

I thought about what she had said for a moment, trying hard to understand. 'Are there no others with better qualifications?' I finally asked. 'Surely there are telepaths within the Foundation who – '

'But he does not want the Foundation to know,' she answered. 'And in any case, this link between you two is not truly telepathic. It is something grown of long and close friendship, closer even than my own with Titus. Are you not aware of this psychic affinity? Have you not experienced anything of it before?'

I nodded. 'At the very start of all this, when Titus first discovered the burrowers, I was in Paris. Suddenly I had to get back to England. I came home and I knew as soon as I found Crow's letter waiting for me that somehow he had unconsciously called me back. Since then the occasion has not arisen when –'

'Well, now he is calling you again.' She nodded decisively. 'This time consciously, knowing what he is about. Has it not been apparent to you? Has there been no hint that he has tried to contact you? No phenomena, dreams perhaps, or –'

'*Dreams!*' I cried, snapping my fingers. 'There have been the most terrifying dreams, of Crow in his great coffin of a clock, hurtling through endless alien universes and crying out to me, searching for me, *wanting to know where I* –' Finally the last piece of the puzzle had dropped into place. 'Good Lord! And I thought I needed a psychiatrist!'

I thought about it for a moment longer before slapping my thigh with an angry hand. 'But why the devil haven't I realized before just what the dreams meant?'

'The devil indeed,' she answered me, her eyes narrowing. 'It occurs to me that you may well, though perhaps inadvertently, have answered your own question. Perhaps Peaslee told you that for some time now there's been a decided slacking off of specific CCD interference? While the telepathic output of the CCD has not noticeably lessened, for some time they have not been directing their hatred at any recognizable target, neither at specific groups nor any individuals that we have been able to discover. It has been almost as though Cthulhu were

shielding his damned dreams from the Foundation, as
though he were intent upon matters very important to
him and that he feared the Foundation's interference.
Could it be, I wonder, that Cthulhu and the other prime
members of the CCD are expending this awful mental
energy of theirs in an attempt to – '

'To foul Crow's return to Earth?'

'I wonder,' she answered.

'And my failure to realize that Crow needed my help,
you see that also as evidence of CCD interference?'

'It's possible, but I don't think that they're aiming at
you in particular. If that were so the Foundation would
soon know about it. On the other hand, one of our top
psychics at Miskatonic has a theory that the CCD have
effectively thrown a mental belt about the whole world, a
belt so tenuous as to be telepathically undetectable! And
if such is the case, well, there must be a purpose behind
it.'

'Titus Crow is only one man,' I said. 'Would his
attempting a return out of time and space warrant such
furtive CCD activity? I know that he's provided them
with a bit of a headache from time to time, but . . .'

'That would rather depend upon where he's been, I
think,' she answered. 'And what he's seen and done. Who
knows what knowledge he may be bringing back with
him?'

After a moment's thought I shrugged my shoulders
impatiently. 'This is all very well, but mere speculation
will get us nowhere. The only way to make anything
concrete out of all this is to get Crow back here. You said
he needed me to . . . to "hold out a light" for him or
some such. What did you mean by that?'

'Only that you must *think* of him,' she immediately
answered. 'Never let him out of your thoughts, not even
for a moment. We know that you are not truly telepathic,

278

Mr de Marigny, but obviously there is this . . . this *something* between you two, like the psychic link between Siamese twins. He seeks the way home, into safe harbor, and you must be the lighthouse by which he pilots his ship.'

I nodded. 'Come to think of it, the dreams only come to me when he is on my mind, when I am suddenly reminded of him or when he is strong in my thoughts.'

'Yes,' she answered. 'That would be when your psychic contact with him is at its most powerful.'

I turned to her in consternation. 'But Cthulhu himself often features in these dreams of mine. I see the monster, reaching out for Crow's plummeting coffin-clock, face-tentacles lashing through black light-years of space and infinite abysses of time to fasten upon the vessel, reaching back to a bloated body that fills the cosmos with its evil . . . Would Titus Crow send me dreams such as these?'

'No, I don't suppose he would, but don't forget that he is not alone in his ability to send dreams! Cthulhu might certainly superimpose his own sendings on top of those of Titus. Why, for all we know that may well be the reason for Cthulhu's planet-encircling mental blanket: a jamming device to confuse Crow's calls for assistance!'

For a second or two I considered her answer, then said, 'I'll do as you suggest; I'll not let Crow out of my thoughts for a second. If he wants my mind to be a beacon, then I'll make it one. I'll recall to mind the adventures we've known together, deliberately dwell upon the horrors and perils we faced together as members of the Wilmarth Foundation. If that's the way to get him back, then I'll get him back.' I looked at her. 'Suppose I succeed. Should I contact you?'

She shook her head. 'No, that won't be necessary, I shall know. But until then, from this moment on, I'll have my crowd keep a watch on you, on this place.' She indicated with a movement of her head the room, the house about us. 'If the CCD are trying to stop Titus from returning, then you never can tell when – '

'When they'll turn from purely mental methods to more direct ones, you mean?' I finished it for her. 'Perhaps physical ones?'

She nodded gravely, then smiled. 'But that's looking on the black side. Somehow I don't feel in the least pessimistic. But anyway, come on, young man.' She stood up and held out her hand to me. 'Show me where your kitchen is. We've a lot to talk about yet, and already I'm dry as a bone! What do you say to a cup of coffee?'

# 3

## *Of the Return of Titus Crow*

### *(From de Marigny's notebooks)*

Some three hours later Mother Quarry told me that it was time she left; transport was already arranged. I took her to the door but she insisted on walking down the garden path on her own. As she reached the gate a car drove up and pulled to a halt. She waved as she climbed in beside the unseen driver and then the car whisked her away. I was left alone to consider the things she had said.

Earlier, over our coffee and cake – a delightful home-made confection left for me by Mrs Adams – our conversation had covered a number of facets of the Foundation's work, reiterating much of what Peaslee had told me. At the time the incongruity of the situation struck neither of us, but now I smiled grimly at the thought of it: the two of us sitting there in my living room, carrying on a conversation whose tone was in direct contrast to the 'Olde Worlde' atmosphere of the beautiful eighteenth-century table at which we sat, the Irish silver we used, the simple meal itself.

Of our entire conversation, however, the part which had proved of greatest interest to me was the lady's description of the manner in which Titus Crow had 'spoken' to her, how awareness of him had first come to her during a self-induced psychic trance. She had not been sure of his identity at first but had guessed that it might be Titus. He had said simply this, 'Find de Marigny . . . tell him I'm coming back . . . I need his help . . . Can't manage on my own . . . Tell him I'm coming, and tell him – ' But that was all. Somehow Crow's psychic or telepathic sending had been cut off short.

A few days later she had received a second message, differing only very slightly from the first. It was then, in her own words, that she finally recognized Titus Crow's psychic aura and knew for certain that the two messages had been from him. However cryptic the substance of those messages, nevertheless they conveyed more than enough meaning to Eleanor Quarry. She had wasted no more time but determined to look me up immediately.

She was already aware of the circumstances of my own rather spectacular return – it had been amply chronicled in the newspapers, and further details had reached her through the machinery of the Wilmarth Foundation – and so, allowing no time for an answer, knowing in her way that I would be there to receive her, she simply dropped me that vague note of hers and then visited me in accordance with its perfunctory arrangements.

And now the rest was up to me.

I showered, put on my robe, returned to my study and got out certain documents, photographs and manuscripts of special relevance to any attempted – evocation? – of Titus Crow. Night had already settled when, comfortably in my chair and puffing at a fragrant cigar, I deliberately set upon a more than merely nostalgic trip along the often dim and elusive, occasionally exceedingly dark, byways of memory.

At first it was hard work. I was making a very physical business of what should have been a purely psychical task, and in less than an hour I had developed a splitting headache. Once, as a boy, greatly interested in certain of my father's parapsychological experiments, I had tried to move a tiny feather with my mind. Telekinesis, I believe he termed this purely hypothetical ability. In the end, having developed just such a headache as I now suffered, I had blown the feather away with the merest exhalation of breath. And here I was after all these years still doing it the wrong way, attempting to fit a physical solution to a wholly psychic problem, forcing my mind where it simply would not go, not under stress, at any rate.

Pushing aside Crow's photograph, I stacked his letters and the remaining memorabilia neatly to one side of my desk. Then I took a deep breath, leaned back in my chair and closed my eyes . . .

. . . And my soul was immediately sucked into that whirlpool between the worlds for a single instant that yet seemed to last a thousand years. The howling, tearing winds of the void, winds no waking man should ever hear or feel, carried to me the dying screams of mortally wounded worlds and the waking cries of newborn nebulae. Stars rose like bubbles as I descended into the seas of space, time itself caressing me as I drifted with its tides. The alien energies of darkling dimensions washed my being with sensations experienced by no other man before me, except perhaps Titus Crow!

And I heard then that well-remembered voice, bringing with it a steadying, a slowing of pace, a return to slightly less ethereal awareness. That voice echoing desperately out of limitless, unthinkable vastnesses:

'De Marigny – where are you?'

'I'm here, Titus!' I cried in answer, and the sickening spinning of my psyche lessened further, as if my answer to Crow's mental cry for assistance had helped anchor me and orient my being amidst the hell of this extrasensory chaos. And my being, my Id, whichever part of myself it was undergoing this experience, now indeed seemed to rock briefly before jarring finally to a halt.

Spread all about me then, so intensely bright as to be painful, I perceived a panorama of hurtling stars, rocketing spheres as colorful as precious stones thrown on a vast satin cushion. At first they appeared almost as coruscating bubbles, then they rapidly expanded to flare past me, finally disappearing in a distant haze of light. And I thought I had reached a halt! Why, if the universe itself were not mad, then in fact it was I who hurtled headlong down these alien starlanes, for surely these stars must in reality be hanging comparatively steady in the void?

Bodiless though I was, nevertheless the chill of outer space and the loneliness of infinity gripped me, but could I really be alone? 'Titus!' I shouted again, shrinking instinctively as certain stars swelled far too quickly and much too close, blooming fantastically to roar by with furnace breath. 'Where – ?'

'Here, de Marigny!' The answer came from close at hand, but where . . .?

*There!* Directly behind me, driving me before it along its path like an insect pinned to the windshield of a car, was the coffin-shaped clock, Crow's time machine!

In times of stress, in fearfully dangerous situations or when faced with wonders or evils of apparently insurmountable magnitude, moments of utter import, the human being is likely to say the most ludicrously inept things.

I felt in no way inept when I asked Titus Crow, 'Where . . . where are you taking me?'

'I'm not taking you anywhere, Henri,' came his answer. 'You're taking me! We're following a direct course between you and your body.'

How to answer that? In my bewilderment I felt a wave of returning dizziness; the rushing stars began to blur.

Crow sensed my difficulty immediately and cried; 'Just keep talking, Henri! You're doing fine!'

'I . . . I didn't understand what you said,' I finally managed, steadying up, fighting a lunatic urge to duck as the solid-seeming whirls of a great spiral nebula loomed ahead. In another instant we were into the expanding mass of stars that comprised one of the nebula's arms –

and out the other side – and in the next instant the whole magnificent catherine wheel had dwindled in our wake.

'You are returning to your body,' Crow answered, 'doing it at a speed I can match.'

'What?' Still he was not getting through to me.

'It's like this: by an effort of will, using the sympathetic psychic link between us, we got you out here; I pulled and you pushed. The rest is automatic. At the moment you're heading back to Earth, back to your own space and time, back to your body where you belong. But you are also maintaining your contact with me, something you've never managed to do before, and so I'm able to follow you.'

'You're not shoving me along?' Crow's concept still eluded me.

'No, *you* are pulling *me*! But don't stop talking to me. The moment your attention wavers you're liable to snap straight back to your body and I'll lose you. This must be the twentieth time I've picked you up, and it's by far the most successful connection yet. Just keep it up, Henri!'

'But those other times there was . . . Cthulhu!'

'A mental projection, that's all,' he answered, confirming Mother Quarry's excellent guess. 'The CCD are doing all they can to stop me from getting back.'

'And yet they haven't gone for me,' I told him. 'Not directly, at any rate.'

'There may well be good reasons,' he answered. 'I think you'll find that they've erected some sort of mental barrier about the Earth, an almost impenetrable barrier. Also, I know that they're keeping a pretty close watch on me. And of course they must still be under pressure from the Wilmarth Foundation. I don't suppose this leaves them with a great deal of power to play with. They haven't caught on that I've managed to contact Mother Quarry and yourself because I've kept my sendings brief. If they

285

try hard enough they can still get into my mind with their hellish dreams, but as for anything else – well, that's a different story. Briefly, they no longer *dare* interfere with me, not directly. I have a weapon, one that – '

'Yes?' I waited for him to continue.

'De Marigny, we're very close now! I think that perhaps this time . . .' I could feel his excitement, and was about to answer that I, too, sensed an early end to our fantastic flight, when I saw that one of the stars ahead was black . . . and that it was swelling and expanding as we closed with it in a manner altogether different from the others. In another instant the thing had assumed a shape, one which was not that of any star or planet.

'Titus!' I screamed. 'We have a visitor. And, my God! *I know him!*'

'I see it, de Marigny, but are we seeing the same thing?'

'How's that again?' I cried, astonished. 'What do you mean, are we seeing the same thing? It's Ithaqua, the Wind-Walker – and damn it, *he's close!*'

'Don't leave me now, Henri!' I heard Crow's frantic cry. 'We're almost home. It might take a very long time to pick you up again.'

I heard Crow's desperate argument and determined to stick it out with him come what may; but the living shape before me finally bloated into monstrous, definite being. It was huge, anthropomorphic, with carmine-star eyes glowing in Hell's own face, a shape of stark terror, striding splay-footed up the star winds, reaching with great taloned hands that visibly twitched in their eagerness to –

Again the universe seemed to spin and blur about me, but just as quickly Crow cried, 'Remember, Henri, it's just a mental projection! It's not really there, a telepathic image sent by the CCD. Don't let go now, man, we're almost home and dry!'

And then, even among all these fantastic events, came

yet another wonder. I heard a second voice, a *female* voice, one of such beauty and strength, rich and warming and yet delicate as finest crystal, that I knew its owner must be a most remarkable woman even before I realized just what her words meant. '*No, no, Titus. Not this time,*' that golden voice cried. '*This is Ithaqua; it is him and not one of Cthulhu's dreams. Take care, my love . . .*'

'*Look out, de Marigny!*' Crow yelled too late, as fingers of ice closed about me. '*Look out!*'

He need not have worried, for already his voice was fading and the stars were blurring again. In my terror I had lost my mental grip, stretching the thread of psychic contact too fine, until at last it had snapped! The hurtling clock and the man it carried, the monstrous beast-thing that but a moment before held me in its foul hands, these things and the very stars themselves now rushed away from me, receding in a twinkling. Yet still, over vast distances, I could somehow see that dreadful scene.

In a rage that his victim should so escape him the Wind-Walker turned from a short-lived, futile pursuit of myself to an awesome attack on Crow in his space-time machine. Moreover, before the scene dwindled away completely and the winds between the worlds once more claimed me, to whirl me off to my house of flesh on Earth, *I saw Crow fight back!*

He had said that the CCD dared not interfere with him directly, and now I saw what he meant. As the Wind-Walker reached for the coffin-clock, his burning carmine eyes full of blood lust and his whole attitude one of mad bestial fury, there shot out from the dial of that fantastic vehicle a pencil slim beam of purest light. The beam struck the striding god-thing square in his monstrous chest. Though I personally could never claim to be endowed with anything much greater than the usual sense perceptions, even I heard the telepathic shriek of most terrible agony that Ithaqua uttered before turning and bounding away, seeming to stagger now as he fled for the farthest stars.

My last conscious act was an abortive attempt to hang on as there came from dark and rapidly receding deeps Crow's fading, aching cry: 'Wait for me, de Marigny. I'm trying to follow you . . . wait for me . . .'

Finding myself once again in my physical body was a painful affair, far more so than on any previous occasion. For though I had left my body sitting in an easy chair before my desk, (while my psyche had been busy dodging hurtling stars and nebulæ out in the farthest reaches of space,) that supposedly empty shell had apparently reacted to my psychical danger in a similar manner right here in my study! In fact, just as one often wakes up from a nightmare still fighting the horrors of the subconscious until the moment of total awakening and awareness, so I now found myself engaged in a desperate struggle with my Boukhara carpets. My chair lay on its side; a bookshelf and its contents had been brought down by my kicking, scrabbling feet.

Mercifully I had not knocked over my reading lamp; that still stood on my desk, holding the shadows back in my study. My robe was torn, drenched with cold sweat.

I got to my feet and crossed unsteadily to the bay window overlooking my garden. Night had fallen, black and cold, but the sky was clear and all the stars shone brightly down. Opening the windows, I looked up at those stars and shuddered, then instinctively shielded my eyes as, suddenly, the whole sky blazed with an incredibly brilliant flash of lightning!

I had time for one thought only – lightning? From a clear sky? – before feeling the effects of a tremendous rushing blast of air. The windows slammed in on me, throwing me to the floor; a rising wind howled wildly in the eaves; my reading lamp dimmed and almost went out, then burned bright again; and finally there came a clap of thunder to end all thunderclaps!

In another second the acrid reek of ozone filled the air of the room. My God! I thought. *It's hit the house!* But then, lifting my aching head up from the floor for the second time in the space of only a minute or so, I realized that nothing had hit the house, but perhaps something had *entered* it! For two sources of illumination now lit my study. My reading lamp was one of them, burning a steady electric yellow upon the desk; and the other . . .

The other was a purplish throbbing glow whose source lay in a corner of the room hidden from view by my desk. I climbed to my feet again, stumbling as I sought to recover from the combined effects of that blinding flash of lightning and its colossal accompanying thunderclap. And then, as I tottered forward, my jaw fell open in awed amazement and delight.

I had guessed what I would see, certainly, for I recognized that pulsing purplish glow of old. Nevertheless, there in the far corner of my study, charred, blackened, strangely steaming and peculiarly scarred, its frontal panel open to emit that eerie oscillating glow, stood the great coffin-shaped grandfather clock that once belonged to my father. And sprawled at its foot, his head even now lifting from the floor and his arms pushing his shoulders up and back, was Titus Crow, a grimace of pain upon his face as he tried vainly to rise.

'Titus!' I cried, starting forward. 'Is it you?' For indeed I had already noted strange inconsistencies. For one thing, this seemed a much younger man than the one I had known. But then, looking up at me and finally managing a grin – oh, yes, this was Titus all right, despite the fact that he looked young enough to be my brother!

'Any – *ah*! – coffee in the house, de Marigny?' he groaned painfully. 'Or perhaps – *oh*! – a spot of brandy?' Then his eyes rolled up and his shoulders sagged, and with a sigh he collapsed unconscious in my arms.

# 4

## *A Universe for the Taking!*

### *(From de Marigny's notebooks)*

Toward morning Crow came around briefly, long enough to take a sip of coffee before lapsing again into deep sleep. Fatigue was all that ailed him, and this much I was sure of for I had called in a certain ecclesiastical doctor immediately after Crow's collapse in my study. The doctor was none other than the Reverend Harry Townley, a friend, confidant and former neighbor of Crow's in the old days. Now retired and having been out of the country for some months, only recently returning, Harry had known nothing of my own remarkable return until my telephone call got him out of bed. The last he remembered of Crow and myself was in connection with a night some ten years ago, when he had watched from his house the so-called freak localized storm that ripped down Blowne House brick by brick and, as far as Harry Townley knew, destroyed the two of us utterly, leaving no traces.

My call must therefore have been doubly shocking to the old doctor. Not only was he receiving a call for assistance from a man he had every right to believe dead, but on behalf of a second dead man! And yet the urgency in my voice had got through to him immediately, that and the fact that I was not simply some rather grim hoaxer. It was only after he had given the unconscious man a thorough going over, when finally we left Crow sleeping in a comfortable spare bed, that I noticed the doctor's bemused expression. Of course I asked him what was wrong.

'It's as well I've known Crow for so many years,' he

answered. 'I don't think there's much he could do now, or anything that could happen to him, to surprise me. And that's as well, too, for this time . . .' He shook his head.

'Go on then,' I prompted him.

'Well,' he slowly continued, 'first let me say that there can be no doubt about his identity. This *is* Titus Crow. And yet, there are places on his body where he should be marked but isn't, places where I remember small scars to have been, which now seem to have vanished. It would take the most brilliant plastic surgeon in the world half a lifetime to do such a beautiful job! And that's only the beginning. He is . . . younger!'

'I thought so, too,' I answered. 'But how can that be?'

'I have no idea.' He stared at me blankly. 'I don't see how it can be. I can only say that his is the body of a man of, say, thirty-eight years. Somewhere he's lost a quarter of a century. And even that is only part of it. The rest is completely . . .' He shook his head, at a loss for words.

'The rest?' I pressed him.

'Where have you been, you two, and what have you been up to?' he answered with questions of his own.

I shrugged. 'Myself, I've been . . . nowhen!'

'Eh?'

I shook my head negatively. 'Hard to explain. I just haven't been *here*, that's all. And as for Crow, don't ask me where he's been. If I told you what I believe you'd probably think I was a madman. I really think, though, that now that he's back he wants his presence here kept secret.'

He nodded. 'You can rely on me to say nothing about tonight. And I'm not the curious type. There's nothing you need tell me.'

'Fine,' I answered, 'but there's something I would like to know. What is it you've found out about Crow that's so fantastic?'

'It's his heart,' he answered after a moment.

'His heart? Why, what's wrong with his heart?'

'Oh, nothing much,' he answered, putting on his coat and starting for the door. 'Hadn't you noticed that there's no heartbeat?'

That good old English reserve indeed! 'No heartbeat?' I cried after him. 'My God! But if his heart's not working, then – '

'God?' he tossed over his shoulder, frowning as he cut me off. 'Yes, I suppose He must have had something to do with it, but who said anything about Crow's heart not working? It most certainly *is* working, and very efficiently at that, but it's not *beating*! It's humming, purring away like a satisfied kitten in his chest. Or rather, like a very well oiled machine!'

The doctor was right of course. As soon as he left I went back to Crow and stood watching him for a few moments. His respiration seemed fairly normal; he had a normal body temperature; but when I laid a hand upon his chest . . . his heart purred, 'like a very well oiled machine'!

All that had been twenty-four hours ago. Now night was upon the house again and I had dozed briefly in a chair beside my friend's bed. It was hardly surprising that I myself was tired: I had watched over Titus Crow's recumbent form continuously, taking a break only to grab a bite to eat.

I awoke feeling cramped and clammy. Crow's bed was empty, the blankets thrown back. I realized what had roused me – noises from my kitchen, recurring now, the clatter of plates, my kettle whistling, the dull thud of the refrigerator door closing.

'Titus?' I yawned, leaving the spare bedroom and making for the kitchen. 'Are you all . . . right?'

The last word fell flat from my mouth as I reached the kitchen door. He certainly looked all right! Two plates on top of the open refrigerator were piled with cold meat sandwiches, coffee steamed in a large jug and Titus Crow, with a leg of chicken in one hand, was methodically searching the cupboards for an elusive something. He was even mumbling to himself through a bite of chicken about civilization going all to hell!

'If you're looking for the brandy,' I said, 'I don't keep it in here.'

He turned and saw me, put down his chicken leg and bounded over to me, gripping my hand in a firm if greasy greeting. 'You old dog!' he rumbled, his voice showing a strength and vitality rare in the older man I had previously known. Then he grinned, his eyes brighter than I remembered them, and said, 'No, no, Henri, I've *found* the brandy.' He showed me the neck of a bottle protruding from a pocket of the robe I had left for him on his bed. 'I'm looking for the corkscrew!'

He began to laugh and I joined him, the two of us roaring with laughter until it hurt, literally laughing till we cried. Then we ate and drank and laughed some more, remembering old times. The night flew by as we reminisced, often in more somber moods but inevitably in delight at this reunion, the two of us, fit and well. Much later, slightly drunk and filled to capacity with food, I sat back and watched him carry on alone as if he would empty my pantry. Finally replete, one might almost say bulging, he stood up and stretched and asked me where his cloak was.

For a moment I misunderstood. 'Your cloak? You mean that rag you had thrown about your shoulders when you . . . arrived? That and your Arabian Nights trousers are stashed in a box under your bed.'

'The Arabian Nights!' he answered with a grin. 'Not

too far wrong, Henri. That cloak of mine is fitted with an antigravity device. Makes all your flying carpets look clumsy!'

'An anti – ?'

'And the old clock? Do I remember falling out of it into your study?'

I nodded. 'You do, after raising a storm I thought was going to do for me, yes.'

'Then let's go in there where I can have a look at Old Faithful. He's looking a bit battered, I imagine, the old clock, but there's more work for him yet. One more trip at least. That is, if I gauge my man right.'

'Your man?'

'You, de Marigny, you yourself!' he answered.

That started it off! Here he was, the living answer to every question I had asked myself since waking with a broken body in my hospital bed, and though we had talked and laughed and reminisced together all through the night, I had not once thought to put these all-important questions to him. Now, however, the dam was broken and I began to gabble uncontrollably. Words tumbled out of my mouth, questions piling themselves one on top of another until, comfortably seated in my study, with dawn already spreading pale fingers over the horizon beyond the bay window, Crow held up his hands to quiet me.

'I'll tell you all, Henri,' he said, 'all, but all in good time. I'm tired now and I can tell that you are, too. The journey was long and fatiguing. I've rested and the food and drink have done me good; this reunion of ours here on Earth, safe and sound and hardly the worse for our various adventures, is marvelous. But once I make a start I don't want my story to lag through weariness. It's a tale that will take a long time in the telling anyway. Right now, however' – he got up and moved over to the

295

enigmatic clock in the corner, reaching to wipe a smudge of some sooty deposit from the great dial – 'now I just want to check over the Old Fellow here, then take a shower, and then it's me for bed for the rest of the day. I'll sleep like a baby, and this time for the sheer luxury of it, not just because I'm exhausted. If you get some rest, too, we'll be able to take all this up again this evening.'

Disappointed though I was I saw his logic. 'All right.' I nodded. 'Just answer me one thing. What did you mean when you said that the clock would be making at least one more trip, a trip involving myself?'

He seemed surprised, then cocked his head on one side to look at me in a curious attitude that I well remembered of old. 'Why, can this be that same lover of mysteries I once knew?'

Puzzled, I opened my mouth to ask his meaning but he cut me off before I could get started. 'De Marigny, I've been to the veriest corners of space and time, I've known a diversity of alien worlds and dimensions. I've lived in the pavilions of Ghengis Khan, journeyed to distant Yuggoth on the Rim, talked with incredible intelligences spawned in the hearts of suns. I've hunted on the mammoth plains of Northumberland, fourteen thousand years ago, with King Conan's own forebears, wandering the very forests and wilds where, twelve thousand years later, Hadrian would build his wall – and I was there, too, during that wall's construction!'

He paused to study the erratic sweep of the four hands about the dial of his clock. '. . . I've been trapped on the shores of a prehistoric ocean, living on my wits and by hunting great crabs and spearing strange fishes, dodging the flying dinosaurs which in turn hunted me. And a billion years before that I inhabited a great rugose cone of a body, a living organism that was in fact a member of the Great Race that settled on Earth in unthinkable

296

abysses of the past. I've seen the cruel and world-spanning empire of Tsan-Chan three thousand years in the future, and beyond that the great dark vaults that loom at the end of time. I've talked telepathically with the super-intelligent mollusks of Venus' shallow soupy oceans, which will not support even the most primitive life for another half-billion years; and I've swum in those same seas ten million years later when they were sterile, after a great plague had destroyed all life on the entire planet. Why, I've come close to seeing the very birth of the universe, and almost its death! And all of these wonders and others exist still, just beyond the thin mists of time and space.

'This clock of mine sails those mists more bravely and surely than any Viking's dragonship ever crossed the gray North Sea. And you ask me what I mean when I talk of another trip, one involving yourself?

'When I return to Elysia, Henri, to the home of the Elder Gods themselves in a dimension bordering upon Orion, there will be a place for you in my sky-floating castle there. Indeed, you shall have a castle of your own, and dragons to bear you to the great festivals! And why not? The gods mated with the daughters of men in the old days, didn't they? And won't you only be reversing the process? I did, my friend, and now the universe is mine. It can be yours, too!'

PART THREE

1

# *At the End of Time*
### *(From de Marigny's recordings)*

It would verge upon the impossible to attempt a description of the actual sensation of time travel, de Marigny. Frankly, while traveling through time – and I have done that aplenty since last I saw you – there is very little *time* to think about it! The mind, you see, has to tune in, to become one with the machinery of the space-time machine, to cleave psychically to the very being of the clock. As you know, I was once telepathic to a degree; well, this talent has recently returned to me tenfold. It has been strengthening in me ever since leaving Blowne House on that night of the winds so long ago.

I was and still remain highly psychic; I pick up vibrations which are beyond the sensory perceptions of most other men. Most people are psychically blind, and how may one explain colors to a child blind from birth? Similarly I am unable to explain this sixth psychic sense of mine, or how I managed to control the clock by meshing with its psyche. If I make it sound as if the thing is not a machine but a being in its own right, well, it very nearly is . . .

However, most of that is well away from the point, which is that I am unable to explain the sensation of time travel. Even the precise control of the clock still eludes me. Mind you, I am particularly clever at piloting the thing through space – on that I pride myself – but it is a far different matter to pilot a vehicle through time, which is completely against man's nature.

And of course it was for this reason that our first

299

attempt at traveling together in time was so nearly disastrous. I had very little idea really how to begin to use the clock. I am astonished now that I dared even try it, and you knew even less of the thing's mechanics. You knew only what I had tried to tell you about it. To think that we dared to brave such an adventure, and that we both lived to talk about it!

But anyway, it took me all my time – again that word, though frankly it conveys very little to me now – merely to hang on mentally to the element of the omniverse which the clock became; to try to grip the 'controls' of the thing with my inadequately trained mind while it slipped and slithered on a careening course to and fro across the fabric of the entire space-time spectrum. And whereas the clock itself was built for this kind of work – it is quite simply a vehicle for transdimensional travel – man never was intended to endure such stresses. I had to fight against all the forces of order, forces which were bent upon keeping me in my correct and designated place and time, determined not to let me break away from my own sphere of existence. And moreover, I had to try to keep you with me, de Marigny.

Finally, when I was beginning to believe that I could hang on no longer, when I had almost given up trying to bring the clock under my control and was about to let go and the devil take everything, then I sensed that my vehicle had abruptly steadied itself, that it was hurtling now on a straighter, truer course. I knew then that I had been attempting to exert too great a measure of control, like the novice driver whose lack of dexterity causes his shiny new car to leap and bound. This craft had been designed for a gentler touch than mine, but at last I seemed to be gaining, albeit fractionally, in my understanding of its many and complex subtleties.

And that was when I realized that you, de Marigny,

were slipping away from me. In turning my attention to this mental symbiosis of man and machine I had relaxed my grip on you. I cried out to you to stay with me, to follow me, to mesh your mind with mine and become one with me and the machine, but it was too late, for you were already gone!

I had no idea how to check my machine. It was a demon steed bounding through the years, and having no reins I could but cling grimly to its streaming mane. You were gone, lost in the seas of time, and I could not even begin to know where or how to search for you. And almost as if you had been a human anchor chaining the time ship to your own age, now that the chain was broken it leaped along the timestream ever faster, its vibrations attuned to the rushing, dizzying currents at time's very rim!

Now I turned all my psychic perception to a greater penetration of the clock's being and, despite my horror at your loss in unknown voids, I found a mad euphoria in the sensation of sheer speed as the centuries sped by with the ticking of a clock or the beating of my straining heart. Now my more mundane senses came into play, though in a thoroughly extramundane fashion, for projected through the sensory equipment of my vessel, which I later came to think of as scanners, I saw the known constellations flying through space in a terrifying spiral, speeding up even as I watched until their tracks were blinding whirls and the passage of alien galaxies showed as stupefying tracks across the sky.

I knew then that at this rate of acceleration eternity itself must soon rush to a close, and no sooner had this terrific thought dawned on me than for the first time I heard Tiania's voice. You have heard her voice, Henri, when Ithaqua attacked us in the void. Just as she warned us against the Wind-Walker, which I thought a mere

301

mental projection of the CCD, so she warned me as I rushed ever faster into the future.

'*No, my love,*' she said. '*You are too rash! Stop! Stop now! Only the End lies that way!*'

A guardian angel? The mind of the clock in which I ate the æons speaking to me telepathically? A voice of madness, my own, ringing in my head as my mind crumpled under stresses and visions never before experienced, never meant for experiencing by a mind of man? All of these things I considered, all flashing instantly through my thoughts – all rejected. You have heard that voice, Henri . . .

I heard it. I knew it was Love and Beauty and Truth, and in that same instant I commenced a frantic mental search for my vessel's brakes.

Now, Henri, sit yourself in an automobile, get it in gear, top gear, then push the accelerator down to the floor and watch while the needle creeps up and up until it moves off the scale and the road becomes a blur beneath your wheels. Then take your hands from the steering wheel and throw all your weight against the brakes. This, in effect, is what I did!

Of course, given the circumstances I have just described, you would very likely die. Almost certainly you would be a hospital case and your car would be wrecked, but whatever the end results they would all be physical. My journey, however, was along no merely mundane road, neither was I subject to inertia or gravitational stresses as we know them, nor could I be said to actually feel the result of the abrupt temporal deceleration in any physical way, *but mentally . . .!*

There was no windshield for my body to hurtle through, no hard concrete surface to receive me. Welded to my machine, I simply decelerated along with it, but at the instant that deceleration began all my perceptions shot

302

dizzily forward in time, to the limit of time itself, affording me glimpses of the dead black tombs which wait for all matter and energy at the very end!

I perceived it, I recognized it and in the next moment, like an elastic band stretched almost to breaking point and then released, my psyche snapped back into place within its fleshy house; and in that same instant I let go all control and surrendered myself to what I knew must be death.

But of course I was wrong. It was not death; I was merely stunned. The mind of the clock, with which my own mind had been in some sort of symbiotic rapport, had taken the brunt of the shock. No, I was simply unconscious, suffering from . . . from a badly bruised psyche, if you like.

When I came to I was very cold. I was dressed quite lightly, just as I left Blowne House, in slacks, a silk shirt and a smoking jacket, and the cold seemed to be penetrating through to my very bones. My face lay in dust. Turning, I saw that I lay half in, half out of the clock, in a dust bowl of a valley between low hills whose crests were gray against a dark blue sky.

At first I thought it was late evening and that a great, swollen moon hung in the sky at the zenith, but an orange moon?

*And something was nuzzling at my neck!*

I cried out and rolled away from whatever it was, leaping to my feet and immediately staggering and falling as my senses whirled in an attack of nausea. The clock remained open, enigmatic as ever, its aberrant ticking strangely faint. Something crawled slowly in the purple pulsing light from its open panel.

The thing was some eight or nine inches long, deeply furred like a great caterpillar, featureless as far as I could see. The scene swam momentarily before my eyes. I carefully felt my reeling head and drank air deep into my lungs, or at least I tried to! Now what on Earth was wrong with my lungs? Nothing, it was simply that the air was very thin. Then I must be high in some mountainous region, which alone might explain the cold and the rarity of air. I was far in the future, that much I knew, but how far?

The crawling thing, moving very slowly, was now levering its furry body up and into the pulsing interior of the clock. Whatever it was, this creature, it seemed to have done me no harm. I certainly wished it none. Unless one is prepared, the clock can play hideous tricks. It is not only capable of traveling in space and time, it can also transmit matter into space and time while remaining stationary itself! I somehow knew, I was aware, that I had nothing to fear from the furry creature; it was harmless as a kitten without claws. So before it could cross the threshold into the clock's transdimensional interior, I stepped forward and caught it up. Instantly it snuggled into my jacket like a cold kitten would, and I knew that my body's heat had been the attraction which had first drawn the creature to me. Instinctively I called it Puss, stroking its deep fur as I peered about at the twilight hills.

'Puss,' I told the creature, 'I would get a better view of things from the top of those hills. What do you say we climb them and see what's become of the world, eh?'

The soil of the hillside was very crumbly, flaky with a sort of gray-brown rust, but here and there small horizontal burrows offered footholds as I climbed the fairly steep incline. I saw two more of the furry creatures as I rose up out of the valley, and then another emerging from its burrow. Toward the crest of the hill an even larger group of them gathered about a greeny-gray shrub whose brittle, withered twigs and drooping leaves they appeared to be eating. I did not break my climb to discover how this was accomplished but placed my odd little friend among its cousins at the shrub and carried on until, heaving and gasping for air, I stood wearily upon the crest of the hill.

And that was when I felt the first pangs of an incredible fear, a dread that set my teeth to chattering even more than the numbing cold, and the hair to bristling at the nape of my neck. No, it was much more than merely fear. I actually stood in awe of immensities whose like I had only ever guessed at, which now lay behind me in the wake of my fantastic journey. For this was indeed the twilight of Earth. I stood at the deathbed of a planet, and if proof were needed then that proof now hung like a ghastly, leprous sickle low in the sky over distant mountains. It was the moon, and the pregnant orange orb directly overhead could only be the sun, once golden and fiery but dulled now and dying in its turn!

A faint, eerie wind stirred the dust of ages at my feet as I gasped painfully at the thin air, turning slowly in order to take in everything of this time-ravaged scene. My vantage point stood up a little from its immediate surroundings, as if I stood upon the rim of a crater, and I guessed that this could well be the nature of that declivity in which my machine now stood. Meteoric impacts must surely be far more frequent now that time had so attenuated Earth's atmospheric envelope. I looked back at the clock, behind and some distance below my position, and felt reassured at the sight of the weird purple glow in whose pool it silently stood, like some alien spacecraft in the valleys of the moon.

Then I turned my face once more to the incredible scene that lay outside the crater wall, that picture of a planet at death's door. As I have said, distant mountains supported a thin-horned leper-moon, but even the mountains seemed flattened somehow and lower than they

305

ought to be, as if weighed down by æons of gravity and worn away by the countless sands of time, until now they brooded like huge unmajestic humps on the far horizon.

Between myself and the mountains, beneath this hideous midday sun, a vast flat plain extended, gray-mottled and reddish in places as if rusted. Was not Mars once equally red in the eye of a childhood telescope? And had I not wondered if those great red sores had once been towns, and the straight and inexplicable lines between them highways?

Earth – this? The third planet from the sun, green and juicy and lush with life, howling in its season with nature's fury and lapped by giant oceans – this? This dry dust bowl of rust and weary lichens, of dumb, furry caterpillars, feeble winds and chill, lifeless air – Earth? Impossible! And yet I knew that it was so. And again I wondered how far, how many billions of years I had journeyed into tomorrow.

I shivered and blew into my cold, cupped hands. It was my intuition that I had not strayed far in space during my journey through time. I mean that while knowing my machine had advanced me fearfully far into the future, I believed that it had continued to occupy its original geographic location in space. If I was correct, then it seemed plain the machine must be fitted with some mechanism to make automatic compensation for planetary motion and alterations in surface levels, for surely in the absence of such compensation the clock might materialize anywhere at the end of a time-jump. High in the air, underground, even beneath mighty oceans as the continents rose and fell like the interminable waves of some leaden sea throughout the ages.

So I stood now not far from the spot where the walls of Blowne House had once sheltered me from the elements, even against those malign elementals of the air which tore our refuge down about us as we fled, you and I, de Marigny, into time. And here it was, noon, with the old sun directly overhead, and chilly as a London November! It was an awesome sensation, to stand there atop that crater's ridge, in a twilight land at the end of time . . .

As the cold worked itself deeper into my bones I started to beat my arms across my body, watching my warm breath crystallize as it plumed off into the thin air. I decided then to walk around the rim of the crater to its far side. Perhaps there would be a better view from there. At first I walked slowly, taking care not to fall and tumble down the steep crater wall, but shortly I began to hurry, as much as the thin air and my labored breathing would allow, as it dawned on me that hope sprang yet within me. What if . . . what if . . . supposing man lived yet within this withered husk of a world? Perhaps, deep down beneath the starveling crust, closer to the warm core, the spires and columns of great cities reared even now, their subterranean sidewalks teeming with life and, and . . .

My hopes for mankind sank abruptly low as I finally reached a point on the crater wall from which I could gaze south at what was once London, the greatest of capitals, now a great gray desolation! Then, to the west, twin fires blazed briefly in the dark blue sky, distracting me as they raced to earth. Meteorites at noon! My eyes followed their balefire to the horizon, then I turned my gaze southward again. What of the green downs of Surrey, Kent and Sussex? Away beyond the sprawling flat scab where once London had proudly stood, as far as my appalled eyes could see, stretched only that same endless gray wasteland.

I shuddered again as a feeble wisp of wind blew the dust of forgotten millennia over my shoes, and I felt an ache in my heart that I knew had little or nothing to do with the bitter chill of the air. It dawned on me then that

I could never leave this place, this future Earth, until I had satisfied myself against all hope that indeed she was barren of human life. With this in mind I began to slip and slide back down the inner wall of the crater to the clock. So far I had not tested the thing as a vehicle in the normal sense of the word, as a machine for traveling in three dimensions as opposed to four. Now would be as good a time as any.

My first trip was a very short one, more of a hop, really. I simply piloted my craft across the bottom of the crater. Of course there was no window I could look out of, and no controls as such. I merely plugged myself in mentally to the mind of the clock and moved it in the direction I wished to move. The clock's scanner system served me far better than any window would have done, for I could see far more clearly than through any Earthly sheet of glass. The whole process of the exercise was ridiculously simple, and the clock completed its first test trip by following a low mid-air trajectory and coming to rest without the slightest bump. Moreover, though I had witnessed the clock's movements in the mental scanner, I had experienced no physical sense of motion during the short journey. Patently my machine traversed space no less efficiently than time!

# 2

## *The Last Race*

*(From de Marigny's recordings)*

My second trip was somewhat more adventurous. I flew the craft up over the lip of the crater to the gray plain beyond. By now I was starting to experience a great pleasure in my increasing ability to control the clock, and so I determined to move on at once in search of . . . of what? Hope springs eternal, and I felt there had to be at least a chance that I could find the vestiges of mankind. Just what this need of mine really was, this suddenly insistent urge within me to find in this unthinkably distant future world some recognizable remnant of man, I cannot really say, unless it was simply the loneliness! No man before me, no Robinson Crusoe, not even the first lone astronaut, had ever been more remote from his fellows than I.

I *felt* remote. It shocked me to think that, by all normal terms of reckoning and depending upon how long I had lain unconscious at the foot of the clock in the crater, I had been in my home on the outskirts of a teeming metropolis only a few short hours ago. And yet it was billions of years since I was last in the world of men and in the company of a friend, you yourself, de Marigny, removed from me now by countless gulfs of space and time.

However, in addition to this insistent and poignant urge of mine to search the Earth for some revenant of man's lost glory, I now felt a desire to test the clock's vehicular speed. Fortunately I was wise before the fact in this latter trial. I took the clock up, way up out of harm's way, until in my mental scanner the now thin atmospheric envelope was plainly visible against the curve of the Earth. I must have risen to a height of some fifteen to twenty miles, and right across the indigo sky meteorites large and small were burning themselves out in fiery descents. Up there I set course to the left of the leper-moon and tentatively opened up my mental throttle. The Earth smoothly commenced rotating beneath me. As my speed picked up, in a sudden surge of exhilaration, I fed fuel to the motor of my machine – and much more than I intended!

Immediately the scanners blurred; the screen in my mind became indistinct and seemed to tremble with a rushing darkness shot with lines of fire. In that same instant, in something akin to panic and believing something to be terribly wrong, I canceled all of the clock's forward motion.

Again there came the mental shock of instant and complete deceleration, but in no way as devastating as that traumatic temporal shock I had known. Almost immediately my psychic scanner cleared to afford me an unobstructed view of the clock's surroundings.

We hung stationary, my vehicle and I, and my momentary terror was now completely forgotten in the breathless contemplation of what I had wrought with that one petty burst of overexuberance. I knew then that my scanners had been working all along, that things had only seemed to blur because of the fantastic speed I had achieved! All mathematical impossibilities to the contrary, the clock had defied Einstein himself! I had traveled, for something less than one second, at a speed which must have been in excess of that of light!

And this time my machine had followed no parabolic trajectory around the curve of the Earth. Why should it when I had not demanded as much of it? Indeed, my last mental instructions had directed the clock, albeit obliquely, at a spot ahead of me and to the left of the sickle moon.

And I had reached just such a spot!

To my right, half in black shadow, half in dull yellow and pinkish gray light, the moon's great pitted orb loomed huge, and away behind me Earth's grim gray disk floated like a tarnished coin in midnight vaults.

I knew then that I had a machine in which I might very easily fly out beyond the farthest stars and, despite all the unknown and unimaginable terrors of such a voyage, or perhaps because of them, I admit that I was sorely tempted.

But there was something I had to know first, about which I must be absolutely sure before I could contemplate any other adventures in this amazing craft of mine, and that was the question of man and his continuation or extinction. To my knowledge, there was only one place where the answer might be found; and so, more carefully this time, I set my return course for the gray disk of Earth.

How long I spent orbiting the Earth at a height of some fifteen miles and on a course designed to allow an eventual observation of the complete surface I cannot say. I know that I was completing each revolution in something less than two hours, and that therefore my relative speed must be in the region of fifteen thousand miles per hour, but I kept no count of my revolutions for my concentration was equally divided between control of the clock and observation of the transient terrain below. I know that toward the end of my search, when I believed that at least I had found what I was looking for, I was very tired and hungry and I had lost all sense of direction and orientation.

Below me it was late evening, and the very last rays of the dim sun, sinking over the curve of the Earth, struck silvery sparks from some mile-high object towering way down by the shore of an æons-dead sea.

I slowed my craft and swooped lower, hovering at a safe distance until the sun had set proper, before determining to bring the clock down for the night at a spot some five or six miles to the west of that gigantic artifact whose merest outlines I had glimpsed from on high. As I settled my craft down to a landing lighter than the touch of the most weightless feather, I searched the land to the east for lights. Surely, if the edifice I had seen was a building of sorts, the place would be illuminated at night? But there again, what if it was simply a deserted, unused entranceway, a vast construction guarding a door to those inner worlds I had envisioned deep within the dead crust and that much closer to the still-warm core of the planet? In any event, other than the transient flaring of frequent meteorites, there were no lights, and so I settled down to sleep in the warm interior of the clock, determining that in the morning I would fly to the strange structure and perhaps satisfy that craving of mine for knowledge of man's ultimate station.

And here I find that I must attempt something of a description of the clock's interior.

The clock is, well, its interior is – how might one describe it? – greater than its external dimensions might suggest. By that I mean that it reverses all the demonstrable laws of geometry. Its internal 'angles', like those with which the ancient Cthulhu spawn were familiar and which were used in the construction of their nightmare sepulchers, were non-Euclidean. It was my first thought that to achieve this compact enclosure of a large area within a smaller space, hyperspace principles must be involved. Such concepts make difficult and highly conjectural theories as Möbius-strip mathematics seem as easy as the ABC by comparison. In this, though there was no way I could have known it at the time, I was actually understating the clock's fantastic properties. While I myself can now visualize and understand its basic principles, still it is literally impossible for me to describe them in anything other than the most commonplace terms or by use of the feeblest analogies.

What I said before, about the clock being a matter-transmitter as well as a space-time ship, has some bearing upon it. And yet perhaps such a statement gives an equally incorrect impression. Let me say instead that the clock is linked with all points in space-time. If the universe consisted of a two-inch cube composed of eight one-inch cubes – the three mundane dimensions, plus time and four others – then the clock would *always* lie at the exact center of the two-inch cube, where the innermost points or corners of the eight hypothetical dimensions of time and space meet. A mental push will send the clock itself traveling along a line parallel to any four of these dimensions at the same time. Of course my illustration ignores the fact that there are an infinite number of space-time dimensions, just as there are an infinite number of stars in space, but the same principles apply.

So within the clock, where all these interdimensional lines of force are gathered together and concentrated, there an untrained or inexpert adventurer may 'take a step' or 'fall' in any of an infinite number of 'directions', while the shell of the vessel itself remains static at its focal point of existence. Psychically then, the clock *is* everywhere and everywhen, but it can only *be* somewhere physically when directed by a second psyche, that of its user.

I fear I've lost you, de Marigny, but don't let it worry you. I've chewed the thing over countless times and I still occasionally lose myself!

And still I haven't described the clock's interior, have

I? Well, picture the thickest London fog you've ever seen, a solid wall of swirling gray through which you can't see a hand in front of your face. Now then, take away the dampness that invariably accompanies such a fog, and similarly remove all the physical phenomena you usually associate with it. Finally, let the pavement beneath your feet gradually lose substance until it too is gone, but without incurring any sensations of imbalance or falling, and there you have it.

The clock retains a temperature as nearly that of the human body as makes no difference, and provided one can plug in to its psychic receptors, then one can be perfectly comfortable. You could pack an army into that clock, de Marigny, and you could make *all* of them comfortable! When I'm tired I imagine a couch, and I lie on it. Picture that, me asleep on a couch, in a hyperspatial dimension, at a junction of unimaginable forces, and all within the confines of something that looks just like a grandfather clock, albeit one which has very little to do with any chronological system devised by man!

But to get on with my story.

I was up at dawn, if that gradual lightening of the sky, in which the stars never quite managed to extinguish themselves above the monstrous desert of Earth, could ever be called a dawn. The waning orange sun was rising in the dark blue of the eastern sky. And yet, despite the fact that the sun was dying, still its rising was my undoing, for of course the enigmatic structure I so desired to investigate lay in just that direction, to the east. Pitifully dim though the sun was by the standards of this twentieth century, still it was bright enough to throw the face of that towering edifice into shadow. Because of this I found myself approaching the thing blind, as it were, and I did so to within a distance of some three and a half miles. The base of the skyscraper (so I had come to think of it, though its actual purpose was as much a mystery as ever) lay in something of a declivity, but for all that the thing must still have stretched a good three-quarters of a mile into the thin air, while its column was easily a third of that distance in diameter.

At this point something about the shape of the thing caused me to halt the clock's slow forward motion. It almost seemed as if I stood at the feet of a giant, and I had not yet made up my mind that this giant was friendly! Nor was this idea too far fetched, for indeed the shape of the thing, seen in silhouette, was somehow statuesque.

I decided to circle about it and thus observe it from a position where the dim sun would not be shining directly into my eyes, but no sooner had I taken this decision than yet another factor arose to deny me a clear, unobstructed view of the thing. The sun, climbing steadily now into the sky, was warming however remotely the tenuous air of the valley in which my giant stood. A fine mist was rising, clinging to and climbing the steep and strangely suggestive outlines of the structure, so that by the time I reached that point to the north from which I had hoped to view it, the combination of ground haze and rising, writhing vaporization had obscured all but its pointed summit. That summit, however, I could now see quite clearly: a great curve of a silvery hull and sharp prow tilted at the sky, sleek fins gleaming in the weak sunlight. A spaceship, held aloft in a giant's hand, symbol of man's domination of the stars and of his exodus from this dying Earth!

My heart gave a wild leap. This was more than I had dared hope for, better by far than the thought of the last members of the human race burrowing in the dry earth like so many miserable worms. Impatiently I waited while the sun completed its work and the feeble haze began to drift lazily down from the gargantuan it so thinly veiled. And soon those disturbing proportions I had noted before

315

began to emerge, but this time clearly and unmistakably to my shocked eyes!

My mouth went dry, my mind utterly blank in an instant. I could only stare . . . and stare . . . while my jaw dropped lower and lower and my hopes for mankind plummeted into unfathomable abysses. For perhaps a full half hour I stood there beside the clock, until, gripped by an emotion like none I had ever known before, I stumbled once more in through the panel of that purple-glowing gateway to forgotten times and places and carelessly hurled myself back, back into time, perhaps to a time when man lived and loved, fought and died and gloried on the green hills and in fertile valleys of Earth.

For the immense metal statue holding aloft that silvery symbol of galactic exodus was made neither by nor yet in the image of man. Vastly intelligent were its builders, yes, and plainly proud of their ancient heritage, a heritage which predated mere man and now patently antedated him . . . *It was a beetle!*

# 3

## *The Cretaceous*

### *(From de Marigny's recordings)*

Fortunately, de Marigny, prehistory and the flora and fauna of bygone ages were favorite subjects of mine in my younger days. I kept a tray of fossils at Blowne House for years, stony fragments I myself collected as a boy: ammonites and belemnites, a tiny bony fish from Eocene Leicestershire, a beautifully preserved 280,000,000-year-old trilobite from Permian Yorkshire, even *Archaeopterix* wing-fragments from the cycadeoid forests of the Jurassic. Traveling back through time in a blind panic-flight from the thought of those nameless beetle intelligences which at the last inherited the dying Earth and left a monument to indicate their galactic destiny, I had no idea that my more than average knowledge of the prehistoric world would be so soon put to practical use.

My plan – not really a plan as such, more an instinctive urge to get back to the eras of man – was simply to find a recognizable period of history. I would work my way back from there – perhaps I had better say work 'forward' – to my starting point, or even to a point a week or so after my departure in the time-machine. It all depended, of course, on if I was able to get the clock's mechanics down to such niceties! And while I talk about my panic-flight, still I was not in such a desperate hurry as to forget what happened toward the end of my first trip in time, when I almost overshot time itself. I was not about to make a second mistake of that nature, perhaps ending up in a mass of superheated plasma just recently hurled out from the sun!

Thus it was that after some time, rousing myself from a

state of morbid moodiness, I attempted to use the scanners. Now use of the scanners in normal circumstances – by that I mean during journeys in three-dimensional space – had proved to be comparatively easy, but traveling in time was a far different kettle of fish, and particularly traveling *backward* in time. Picture, if you can, a gigantic panoramic film run in reverse at many thousands of times its normal running speed and perhaps you'll understand what I mean.

I had taken my craft up out of Earth's atmosphere. The sun and moon were no longer distinguishable as such but had become continuous lines of light weaving in fantastic patterns through space, similarly the whirling constellations. I could discern nothing of the Earth beneath me but a constant flurry of fantastically transient cloud patterns and a tidal blurring of the coastal regions between oceans and land masses. I slowed down and brought the clock lower into the atmosphere.

The sky immediately turned black, only to be lighted up a second later by an impossibly hurtling full moon, mercifully bright and yellow as I had always known it, as opposed to that pitted, leprous horror at the end of time. And then came an incredible blaze of sunlight as the familiar flaming orb of Sol shot up from the *western* horizon to race east across the sky. In another second it grew dark again, and then once more the moon rocketed into view.

Here was an interesting point. Because I was not seeing all this with my eyes but psychically, there was no retinal image left to distort my view of Earth during the fleeting periods of darkness. It was because I saw something during this sequence of dark periods that I slowed down even further. I glimpsed a row of red and yellow lights blazing in a line that from my height seemed certain to be artificial, like some vast system of street lighting. I was wrong, and but for the clock's near invulnerability the end of my adventures in space and time would have come right there and then!

The Earth of course was stationary below. I mean that the clock was making its own compensations for planetary motion; it was rotating through space *with* the Earth, directly over that spot I had fled from in the now far distant future. So I plunged lower still through the dense stuff of what I took to be clouds. Too late I realized that this was not cloud but tephra, and that directly below me the throat of a monster volcano was belching lava-bombs, smoke and fire at me in a spectacular eruption. The row of lights was simply a great volcanic rift in the earth, from which at fairly regularly spaced points in its length the cones of active volcanoes thrust threateningly upward. Lightning flashed ceaselessly in the roiling tephra clouds, striking the time-clock again and again before I had recovered my wits sufficiently to move my machine laterally out of the way.

But about that volcano, de Marigny, and particularly about the lightning – just try to picture it! Of course I was still traveling backward in time, and so the lava-bombs were all hurtling up toward the clock from an area outside the actual radius of the volcano, to fall into its heaving, bubbling throat. And the lightning was not striking at me from the tephra clouds but seemed to be striking from the clock to the clouds! In any event I was unharmed, and the clock was barely scratched.

Once clear of the volcanic range I slowed my temporal speed more yet until the moon hung still and bright, if redly tinged, in a sky so dark that the stars seemed merely to flicker dimly above, and then only with difficulty. I brought the clock down to a landing there when I judged that dawn was not far away, but I stayed in the clock until the sun was fully up. My reason for doing this was very simple: using the clock's scanners I could see my immediate surroundings even in the dark, but once I left that strange vessel I would have to rely solely on my own five senses. So I waited for the sun to come up before opening the panel and stepping out into a weird, fascinating and deadly world.

And it was then, striking through all my wonder and delight – the origin of which I will explain in a minute – that I first realized just how hungry I was. Oh, I was tired, too, terribly tired, but it was purely a fatigue of mind now. The clock had taken much out of me, sapping emotions as hard work saps physical strength. Even so, despite this emotional weariness, I was astounded, amazed, yes, and delighted. Do you see, Henri? Now I knew where I was. Perhaps I should really say I knew *when* I was, for I was back, way back, deep in the prehistoric world of the Cretaceous!

The Cretaceous was the last period of the Mesozoic, one hundred million years ago! It was also the Age of Reptiles, when the dinosaurs were lords. When giant *Archelon* turtles and mosasaurs swam in soupy oceans that were not nearly as salty as they are now, and scythe-winged *Pteranodon* called hideously to his mate as he winged on creaking leather through rich warm skies beneath billowing, soaring clouds.

It was an age of primal things – colors, odors, sights, sounds and sensations – so that even the wind felt different against my skin. It was Earth in the glory of youth, with all of creation insane in a frenzy of experimental trial and error, building new life-forms and changing them, destroying and then building anew. And the thought of man had not even crossed Nature's mind, would not for another ninety million years!

Men? Why, Nature did not build things as puny as men in those days! They were the days of python-necked

*Brachiosaurus*; of tank-like *Triceratops*, beside whom a rhinoceros would seem the merest toy; of *Tyrannosaurus*, who bellowed and strode the land on powerful piston legs, king of all the dinosaurs, ruling his cycadeoid domain with a tyrant's lusts and rages. Even the mollusks were monsters in those days, like titan-valved *Inoceramus*, which dwarfed even the greatest of today's *Tridacna*. Oysters, too, proliferated in those youthful seas, producing pearls as big as a man's fist, pearls that the ages have since reduced again to calcium dust. It was on the shore of just such a Cretaceous coral sea that I now found myself.

I knew it was the Cretaceous, I recognized it as surely as I would King's Cross or the tones of Big Ben, without stepping more than a dozen paces from the open panel of the clock. It had chiefly to do with that fossil collection of mine that I've mentioned. Favorites among those fossils were certain ammonites from this period, hard, lusterless things, drab as gray pebbles on a beach; but there in that coral pool upon whose edge I stood played myriads of these very creatures, alive and glowing in a morning sun that already drew mist up from the damp sands. Weirdly coiled, octopoid *Helioceras*, unicorn-horn *Baculites* and intelligent-eyed *Placenticeras*, all were there, groping with tiny tentacular arms, darting on squid jets, swimming in crystal waters that teemed with uncountable struggling life-forms. And lifting my eyes to the crashing ocean beyond I caught a glimpse of spray-wreathed *Tylosaurus* as the head and back of that primal sea serpent broke the frothing waters. In distant skies enormous, fantastic shapes flitted: *Pteranodons*, flying reptiles, darting to snatch bony fishes from white-tipped wave crests.

Oh, yes, without the least shadow of a doubt, I recognized this age, the Cretaceous. And I knew, too, that my physical hunger, the emptiness in my belly, should not go long unabated.

Close by, within a hundred yards landward of the beach, a low volcanic vent was steaming, its lava lip glowing red: there was my cooking fire. And here at my feet great crabs and lobsters, creatures halfway between trilobites and crayfish, moved on segmented legs in jeweled waters. Palm-like trees with large, strange nuts grew further along the shore, cycads and flowering trees, too, doubtless bearing fruit. Even as I gazed a small furry mammal sprang down from one of the nearer palms, scampered to the next and up into its green shade. Oh, there was food enough here, more than enough. Why, if a man had a rocket-launcher, doubtless back beyond that low range of volcanic mountains, in the cycad forests, he could bring down ten tons of meat with one shot – if he had the nerve! I would be satisfied with a lobster, and fruit for dessert and perhaps the milk of a coconut to wash it all down. I might even find myself a spring, with water that never had to recycle itself to remove detergents or DDT.

Now then, was the tide in or out? I scanned the beach for a tidemark and found it, many yards down from where I stood. To the rear of the clock the sand was yellow, unwashed. Nonetheless the pool at my feet with its many denizens showed quite clearly that the sea had recently reached this spot. Perhaps the tides were irregular, perhaps they had not quite settled yet to the pull of the moon. I had best move the clock back, higher up the beach to where the first palms and cycads fringed the feet of the volcanic hills. The volcanoes themselves did not worry me greatly; a few lava-bombs lay scattered about but the majority of them were old. That line of livid cones I had passed over last night – the night to come? – lay some miles west, behind this lower range.

I found a spiked branch of coral and speared myself a large wriggling lobster-thing, killing it immediately with a rock that severed its head from its body. Then I carried my breakfast back to the clock. I moved inshore to the fringe of palms, and sure enough the ground held a scattering of great nuts. As I hefted one, there came a liquid swishing from within its globe. Fruits there were, too, and I tentatively tasted one that looked like a small pear. Its juice was sweet, tangy and pleasing but like nothing I ever tasted before. This was a primal taste, from which lesser tastes might later distill themselves. Indeed it was heady, that taste, so that later I sang as I roasted my lobster in its shell on a coral spit over the fiery breath of a volcanic blowhole.

Feasted as royally as any lord, feeling a contentedness of soul experienced all too rarely in a lifetime, I ambled back in the warm sunshine toward the clock where it stood shaded beneath swaying, coarse-grained palms. In an instant, as I passed where I had not walked before, I was brought back down to earth with a jolt. There, in the dark yellowish soil at the edge of the palm clump, was a footprint – no, a clawprint! Huge, it was, that deeply imbedded impression of a hind foot whose owner, I knew, towered twenty feet high and weighed as many tons. Three claws fore and one less prominent behind, the greatest carnivore the world has ever known had made his mark: *Tyrannosaurus rex*, king tyrant of the giant reptiles!

I have never been a coward, but at sight of that monstrous indentation the hair on my neck prickled in almost preternatural dread. Since the end of the Mesozoic the world has never seen such rampant, unbridled, sheer animal ferocity in any living creature – no, not even in man himself – as in *Tyrannosaurus rex*. This print was a powerful reminder that I trod ground other than familiar, other than the safest, where man never trod before. I knew that the longer I stayed the more certain would be my eventual meeting with the creature who made this mark or others like him. I decided on the instant that as soon as I had rested I would be on my way. I would move forward, forward in time to the age of man, leaping the æons in my time-clock and only pausing to check my progress and eat.

First, though, I would rest, and then I would collect a store of the great nuts and roast myself another lobster, perhaps two, to take with me. The last was imperative. Though I could foresee little difficulty in what I intended to do, who could say for certain that a future opportunity to replenish would present itself? Of course, the need might never arise, but . . . And before I went, why of course I must scour this shore for seashells, for half a dozen of each variety that I could find; and I had to pass over the mountains in my clock to see the primeval forests and their denizens, to fly above the lizard-lands in safety and watch the great beasts at play – and at war!

And yet when I awakened, though I had intended my sleep to last only until midafternoon, it was already late evening and far too dusky to think about gathering seashells, not on that shore, at any rate. There were too many things to worry about in the Cretaceous night. I had earlier set a pair of nuts down beside the clock; now, sitting in the late evening beneath the palms and gazing out over the moonlit sea, I pierced one of the nuts with a coral spike and drank its refreshing milk. In the morning I would drink from the other, then crack them both for their flesh.

The night was warm. The moon, while it was as bright as I had ever known it, seemed smoother somehow, faceless. The stars, though many of their constellations appeared amply familiar, were dim, due to volcanic ash high in the atmosphere. Of course, for explaining the unscarred surface of the moon, that lunar orb was too young yet to have gathered many craters. Indeed its haze might even suggest that it had a faint atmosphere of sorts, not yet drifted off into space . . . A fascinating place, this Cretaceous.

As it grew darker still I opened the panel in the front of the clock, allowing its eerie dappling to illuminate my seat on a large stone. Great moths, attracted by the light just as they are today, came to visit me, soon becoming a nuisance as they fluttered in the purple pulsing light. Then they became more than a nuisance.

I have never been a moth fancier, indeed most insects are offensive to me one way or the other, but in the Cretaceous some of these nocturnal lepidoptera had wing-spreads of eight inches and more. When I put my hand up to keep one of these from fluttering in my face its fur-edged wings stung me! Likely the creature lived on the poisonous pollens of strange night-blooming flowers. Enough of that! I retreated into the clock and continued to observe the weird night from the safety of its interior.

To my back, several peaks jutting up from the line of hills glowed with volcanic fires. Far along the shore down at the edge of the sea, some shadowy beast splashed and snorted. The sea itself was quiet, the wind of day having dropped to a gentle breeze. Though I rarely smoke, I would have vastly appreciated a good cigar right then, and of course I should dearly have loved a glass of good brandy. I had neither, but I did have one of those intoxicating fruits. Nibbling on this I eventually drifted off into a shallow, troubled sleep.

No, that may give the wrong impression. My sleep was not troubled by nightmares or those nameless fears that waken you in the night drenched with sweat and fright-ened but unable to recall the threat. In fact my dream was quite vivid and ineffably beautiful, I could say haunting. Indeed, it haunted me for a long time after. No, it was only disturbing in that I sensed, even dreaming, that this was much more than a dream . . . a vision! There were elements in it hinting of an almost telepathic communication, albeit an unwitting one.

I dreamed I was in a tremendous hall or room of fantastic angles and proportions. A curving, high-arched ceiling towered over me like the dome of some hollow mountain. Everything, the gargantuan-paved floor, the distant walls and clouded ceiling, the pillars whose ornate columns supported high balconies lost in rose petal clouds of mist, everything was of crystal. Milky crystal, mother-of-pearl crystal, pink and blood hues of crystal glowed everywhere, like the interior of a splendid conch of the seas of space, letting the light of alien suns shine through its translucent nacre.

Some vague titanic Eminence of similar hues stirred upon a vast seat or throne in a distant curtained alcove. I held my breath, knowing that this was what disturbed me so, this being whose misty form behind luminous pearl-dust drapes flashed fire from jewel-adorned members. I did not wish to see the being more clearly; I was glad that it sat far off, that its form was hidden by the crystal sheen emitted by the walls, roof and pillars of this, its palace. I knew, you understand, that this place I was in belonged to the Eminence upon the throne, that being whose presence filled me with a subconscious, psychic unease.

Then my attention focused on a figure in the center of the gigantic room. There a scarlet divan, low but of great surface area, like an enormous pillow, supported a figure at once human and inhuman. It was a woman, with her back to me, and I was glad that this was so for no face could ever hope to match the perfection of that body. I have known women in my youth. I remember beautiful women, but never has any woman I ever knew looked like this.

She was clothed in a cape of faintly golden bubbles, with a high collar laid back by the weight of hair cascading over it. That hair, it was . . . can green describe it? Highlighted by emerald mists and aquamarine coils, it massed in ringlets down her milk-of-pearl back to a waist delicate as the stem of a crystal wineglass. The cape concealed little. Of bubbles itself, it merely softened the outlines as bubbles do. She knelt, her legs drawn up beneath her and clothed in wide-bottomed trousers of the same spun-gold bubbles. Thigh and hip, waist and back, arms and slender neck and rich, glossy, emerald-flashing hair, all were encased but not enclosed, not concealed, by precious foam-of-gold. No man could look upon this vision and not gasp. Fires I had believed forgotten since my youth raced in molten streams through my body, driven by a furnace heat. And yet, even in my longing, I was sad. No woman's face however lovely could match the beauty of this woman's body. No, Nature herself could never conceive of such a face. But I had to know.

I moved forward, approaching until a perfume distilled of no rare orchids but the flowers of her own milk-of-pearl skin drifted to me. She was so close now that I could touch her. My fingers burned, tingled, ached to stroke that hair, turn that head to me; my eyes desired so to gaze upon that face, even though I knew I must be disappointed. I moved around her, passing over the huge cushion without feeling it, as one moves in a dream. Now I could see . . . her face!

I dared not cry out for fear she would hear me and flee, the thought of which I could not bear. I could no more bear that thought than I could bear the sight of her face, a sight mortal man was surely never intended to see. And yet I was seeing it: the pale pearl brow from which an

327

emerald ocean sent lustrous waves and wavelets cascading down the spun-gold strand of her cape; the huge eyes of deepest beryl, in which a man might drown, open wide and staring; the mouth, quite beyond my meager powers of description, with its perfect cupid's-bow of pearl-dusted rose, turned down now over teeth whiter than purest snow that bit the flesh of the bottom lip in distress. The whole lucent face was a slender oval, with arching emerald eyebrows almost long enough to melt into the verdure of temples, elfin ears like the petals of rare blooms, a nose so delicate as to go almost unnoticed. She radiated a distillation of Essence of Woman, human but quite alien. A woman – but a goddess, too!

Her eyebrows were drawn now in a frown, and still she bit her lip. The infinite depths of her eyes were worried. Her expression hurt me with concern for her, that she should ever feel the need to worry. She studied a great crystal set in the center of her huge cushion, a sphere of shining brilliance to which I eventually managed to drag my eyes from her face. I stared for a moment, and the crystal cleared to show a scene at first unrecognized. There were star-spaces streaked with a comet's blaze, but then that shooting star loomed close and I saw that it was no comet but . . . my clock!

Faster and faster the vessel fled down the void, speeding on an immaculately straight course down to a blackness that loomed in the crystal, a blackness in which no tiniest gleam of light showed. The stars were gone now, leaving nothing but an empty void ahead and an irresistible force that pulled the great clock faster yet toward some unknown doom.

'Kthanid!' the woman on the vast cushion cried, half glancing over her shoulder to where the hidden Eminence sat upon its alcove throne. 'Kthanid, I must go to him at once or he is lost, my beloved, who you promised me so long ago!'

She had spoken to the Eminence in a voice as wondrous as her face and form, and drawing breath to do so her perfect breasts had lifted, heaving in anguished agitation. Again I glanced at the crystal sphere. Faster still rocketed the clock, its shape beginning to distort, twist and flow. It was my clock, my vessel, and therefore the obvious concern of this goddess must be for me, but how? Why . . .?

In my dream – I will call it that, though I know now it was no such thing – the Eminence stirred behind its pearl-dust curtains, jeweled members writhing and tiny crystal bells chiming as drapes briefly billowed. It answered her, but with no voice of sound. In my head I heard the Eminence speak, and by her actions knew that she also heard.

'*Child – Tiania -- you must know this: if this man dies now – and if you are with him when he dies – then you may yourself be hurt even unto death.*'

'Wise one, if he dies I will die also, of a broken heart! That I know, for I love him. It is why I must be with him, why I must try to help him.'

'*He is most human, this man; the blood of his own kind is stronger than ours in him. His mind may not be able to guide his vessel away from the Black Hole. You may only join him in spirit – true – but such is the pull of the Black Hole that even your spirit may find itself fast. If you cannot help him – if you fail – then you go down to the Black Hole with him!*'

'I know it, yet I must go to him, now, before it is too late!'

'*And you desire my help?*'

'Oh, yes, Kthanid, yes!'

'*I cannot deny you, therefore I will help you. It has long*

329

*been my thought that he may be – great – this man. I sense
his presence even now. I suspect that you are his magnet
even as he is yours. If indeed he has the germ of greatness
within him, then it would be a matter of great neglect not
to help you. So ride the thought-winds, child – and hold
fast to this Great Thought I send you, to help you on your
way!'*

Instantly the lights in her eyes went out, her lashes
furled down like the silken sails of færie ships. She sighed
once, deeply, then gently curled herself about the crystal
sphere, its orb cloudy now and empty of visions.

And abruptly the scene contracted, shrank, as if a
giant's hand had snatched me up from it. The beautiful
creature curled upon the great cushion melted to a tiny
halo of life about a glowing seed-pearl; the alcove of the
Eminence dwindled and its misty drapes became as the
tiny, dew-spangled webs of dwarf spiders; I passed into
the vaulted ceiling of rose crystal and my dream collapsed
in the wake of returning consciousness.

I awakened in the clock with a cry of pain, pain that I
was separated from the woman of the dream.

Dream? Had it been a dream?

# 4

## Marooned in Prehistory

*(From de Marigny's recordings)*

Hours later, after I had breakfasted and flown the clock down to the wet sand where the sea now sullenly retreated, while I absentmindedly gathered gem-tinted shells unknown to man except as drab and colorless rocks, I still pondered the dream or vision, whichever it had been. So engrossed was I with it that I passed off the first trembling of the earth beneath my feet as normal volcanic activity; such seismic shocks must be frequent in an area literally riddled with volcanic vents.

With a thousand damp and glistening shells in the bowl of a broken nut, lifting my eyes from the contours of the conches to the line of smoking hills, I felt that pulse of Earth and strangely it set off chords of memory. The voice of the girl, the woman, the goddess in my dream had been . . . had been the same voice that came to me as I crashed headlong into the future in the clock, as I hurtled toward the End! It had been that voice of warning I heard even as I applied mental brakes against the closing of time! But who, where, what was she? And she had said she loved me . . .

Now why should I connect a warning of disaster from a beautiful creature of dreams with a volcanic rumbling deep in the ground? Was it simply a hangover from my past experience of the burrowers beneath, the automatic suggestion of danger in connection with any movements of the earth? Or was it something deeper, of the subconscious? Perhaps I had better get back to my clock.

Wasting no more time in pondering the enigma, I tucked my shell collection up under one arm and set off

331

briskly back toward the time-clock. Even as I started out there came again that subterranean trembling, accompanied this time by a low and ominous rumbling. Black smoke coiled up now from several pinnacles and crests along the line of low hills, and as I lengthened my pace to a clumsy run across the damp sand there came a loud explosion from out at sea, and then an even louder one, followed by a tremendous blast that threw me down on the sand while the earth commenced a violent shaking.

There followed such a hissing and crackling that I immediately turned my face toward the sea, to the source of these threatening sounds. A fantastic manifestation drew my awed attention. Something was beginning to happen out there, something preceded by a flash of lightning from a sky already darkly turbulent and accompanied by a mad swirl and rush of ocean, a sudden howling of wind and a column of smoke and tephra that reached up into the sky with astonishing speed. Then, through the smoke and abruptly hissing rain, I saw the outline of a tremendous bulk steaming up from the sea. A newborn island, crying out as it struggled from its watery womb!

Shuddering, jerking, a massive pinnacle of gray-black rock and slag was climbing from the boiling waters. And flame, too, gouting up redly in a sudden barrage of liquid rock from the emerging volcano, blasting down in the form of white lightning from a now blue-black sky. And water – a shock wave of panicked ocean!

The clock, my one means of returning from this place, from the Cretaceous back to the ages of man, lay directly in the path of a fearful wall of water that even now heaped itself up far out at sea to begin the awesome plunge landward. Despite the lurching of the earth beneath me as I struggled to my feet, despite the sucking of the wet, quaking sand, I tried to run. Perhaps I might have made it back to my vessel in time if yet another tremendous seismic shock had not chosen that exact moment to throw me down once more in the sand and pebbles.

And I was still there, some fifteen to twenty yards away from my coffin-shaped refuge, when the great wave crashed down on me, crushing me to the beach until I thought I must drown, then sucking me up and hurling me headlong on its rushing crest until finally I was thrown down again in a clump of great palms. There, as the first rush of water subsided, I managed to cling to the bole of one of the primal trees and so save myself.

There was no chance yet to spot my vessel amid the crazed howling of the elements. Stumbling out from under the lashing palm branches toward higher ground, it was all I could do to support myself against the tearing wind. Oh, of course my concern for the clock was of the greatest – I was filled with a terror of my vessel being lost forever – but even so the instinct for immediate personal survival was uppermost. Glancing back as I stumblingly climbed the gradual slopes, I could see that a series of secondary shock waves was already forming concentric circles about the island out at sea; it would not be long before they, too, rushed in to further flood the lowland areas.

Well, time passed. Though those lesser shock waves did not reach as high as the first, still they continued to form until well into the afternoon. Watching from my vantage point in the foothills, I saw them breaking all through the day in gradually lessening fury along the great curve of the beach in both directions. The ground rumblings had eventually ceased, too, as had the sporadic eruptions in the hills behind me. The newborn island stood steady now in the gray sea, sullenly smoldering.

A sort of lava dam had been created out in the ocean, forming a great basin in which those waters thrown

333

landward by the initial emergence of the volcano were trapped. Also, it seemed that the shoreline must have settled somewhat, for while the arms of this newly formed bay did not completely shut off the stretch of water between the new island and the mainland, still that water did not seem to be receding to its previous level. And if the ocean did not recede . . .

My God, Henri, but that was a monstrous thought! To be trapped here in the Cretaceous, with my time-clock lost beneath the shallow but viciously denizened waters of this volcanic bay, in a prehistoric world of great beasts and primal plants. What chance would a mere man have in a world ruled by dinosaurs, an age of constant struggle for survival? And there I was, stranded in those Cretaceous foothills, with afternoon all too quickly growing into murky evening.

As night drew near and the elements less wild, the hum of insects and raucous cries of bat-lizards began to come in to me from the surrounding wilderness of foggy heights and crags, particularly from the now heavily misted beach. Of course! Down there must be a wonderful feast of stranded fishes, mollusks and crustaceans for the *pteranodons;* indeed I could see large numbers of the flying lizards flapping in from over the ocean as the warm, heavy haze of the beach developed into a full blown fog.

Now, complementing the clinging clouds of moisture-laden air that rolled up from the sullenly washing ocean, there came the odor of things too long out of water, a far stronger smell than I had ever known in London's fish markets. Little wonder that the flying lizards had been attracted so soon to the scene of the recent upheaval. I would not be able to go back down to the beach tonight, perhaps not even tomorrow. But what was this? Here I was sitting in these foothills, surrounded by a rapidly thickening wall of fog while night quickly set in, dreaming like a madman of tomorrow! My God! Would there be another tomorrow for me?

Quickly I found myself a tiny cave in a steep escarpment of rock, large enough to cram myself into but leaving no room for anything so superfluous as comfort. Then, marking the location of my shelter, I left it again to search out a great palm leaf from which to strip a long, sharp, pliant splinter: a weapon against any unwelcome attentions I might attract from night-wandering beasts of prey. Still feeling far from safe, and while there was yet enough light, I sought out from the volcanic shale of those foothills a flat slab of slate about the size and thickness of a paving stone. A further twenty minutes of pushing and struggling saw me inhabiting my uncomfortable hole in the rocks, weapon in hand and pointing out through a narrow crack between the edge of my new slab door and the side of my tiny cave. As darkness fell, miserable though I was and – I freely admit it – desperately afraid, I finally fell into fitful slumbers.

Twice during that dreadful night I awakened, once to the eerie creaking of leathery wings overhead – a sound that had my nerves silently screaming for at least ten minutes before it finally faded into the background hum of night insects – and the second time when something tugged at my sharp fang of palm splinter where it projected slightly from its aperture. A nervous, involuntary thrust of this weapon as I awoke sent whatever creature it had been – possibly one of those tree-dwelling mammals I have previously mentioned, certainly nothing very large – scampering off unseen with a shrill cry of fear and pain into the night mists.

By midmorning the fog had dispersed and the sun was blazing down from a sky of purest blue. The last of the gorged *pteranodons*, their sac-like bellies grotesquely distended, had flapped away along the beach or out to sea. Behind me, higher up in the hills, solitary smudges of smoke drifted lazily above volcanic sources. It seemed completely impossible that only a few short hours ago Nature had displayed such a disastrous fury of elemental creation, and yet now a great new stretch of ocean lay flat and calm, lapping at the edge of those fringing palm groves that so recently had stood well back from the beach. I calculated that the waters had crept at least one hundred and fifty yards further inland from the level at which I had last seen my clock.

I made my way slowly down to the beach, picking a path through an appalling assortment of rotting, ravaged marine corpses of various sizes, from tiny translucent bony fishes to shark-like things up to eight or nine feet in length, to the water's edge. The sea, as I have said, was flat and blue, mirroring the sky. An occasional fish could be observed to leap clear of the warm waters in a burst of desperate acceleration as it fled from greater dwellers in those sparkling shallows. Even as I watched a particularly ugly, square, serpent-like head viciously broke the surface only a few score yards out from where I stood.

I shuddered despite the fact that the weather was so nearly tropical as to drench the deteriorating rags of my clothes in perspiration. I had been thinking of swimming out there, of making a series of dives until I found my clock. It was out of the question – I might make twenty-five yards if I was lucky! On the other hand, why couldn't I build a raft and simply paddle out until I could actually see the clock in those crystal waters? That way I would only have to risk one solitary dive. I refused even to consider the possibility that my vessel might not work under water! But if I did build a raft, would I find the time-clock in the place where I believed it to be? What if yesterday's upheaval and tremendous shock waves had moved it, perhaps even burying it beneath the silt of this shallow seabed?

Well, that last was a distinct possibility certainly, but it was no kind of thought to dwell on for any length of time. A raft would at least enable me to find out one way or the other.

I looked around with more purpose now. Following yesterday's violence the sea, despite whatever life-and-death turbulence there might be beneath the surface, had grown singularly calm. All along its quiet edge giant palm branches were strewn; it should not be too difficult to lash two or three of these together.

A sudden rage came over me and I cursed the newborn volcano, shaking my fist at it where –

The creak of leathery, membranous wings drew my instantly terrified eyes from their angry contemplation of the smoldering infant cone standing out in the sea's blue expanse to the skies directly above me. Winging down in a narrowing spiral came one of those hideous, hammer-headed scavenger-lizards, a *pteranodon*, blotting out the sun with its shadow as it descended directly toward me. Without a doubt, I was the thing's target; it uttered a hungry, raucous cry and its eyes, red as the pits of hell, burned unblinkingly on me as it fell from the sky. I felt the cooling fan of its great wings, with a span all of twenty-five feet, and then I ran wildly, desperately along the edge of the water.

Closer yet the wings of that pursuing horror beat at the air, until one of them struck me like a leather club as I zigzagged amid the rotting refuse of the recent upheaval, sending me sprawling with my head and shoulders penetrating the spear-like fronds of a fallen giant palm branch. Quickly I scrambled into the shade of the branch, pressing my body to the wider stem and peering up through the lesser leaves at the sky-lizard as it settled in a violent stirring of rancid seaweed and damp sand to lean its evil head inquiringly forward in avid contemplation of my refuge.

As I pressed closer to the great palm stem the *pteranodon* saw the movement of my body through the umbrella of fronds directly above me. Quick as thought, its murderous beak came down to slam into the thick branch, ripping away a strip of coarse bark and missing my head by inches. I smelled the horror's vile exhalation of breath – perhaps I even tasted it, so thick was the overpowering fetor of decay – but then, before that dreadful beak could descend again, a shrill screech and fanning of air announced the arrival of yet another sky-lizard. Now there were two of them, with but a single thought in their tiny minds.

Then, crouching beneath that fallen palm branch while two of the prehistoric past's most terrible children battled for the right to devour me, I saw what might just be a means for survival. Sooner or later one of these great flying reptiles must win the fight outright or at least frighten the other off, and then it would not be long before I fell to a vile, darting beak. But right now I saw a refuge that might just be a little more difficult to penetrate than the comparatively flimsy green foliage now protecting me.

There, where tiny wavelets washed coarse grasses only fifty feet or so away from my temporary shelter, a great coiled shell like some vast ammonite lay, but empty now of whatever species of octopus had built it. The bell-like mouth of this monster was like a small calcium cave, well over two feet in diameter. Now, keeping one eye on the battling *pteranodons* while their horny lizard feet hopped and stamped and their beaks darted in angry conflict, I scrambled out from under the fallen branch. I took my chance to make a run for the coiled shell, and . . . it moved!

I skidded to a trembling halt as the great shell swiveled on the grasses at the edge of the sea. A huge plated claw extended from the shadow of the bell mouth to snap shut with a pistol-shot report only inches in front of my chest. One stalked eye, then a second, edged out warily from behind the massive claw, the two swaying and observing me intently where I stood transfixed with terror. A hermit crab, by God, the biggest of its species I could ever have imagined!

Now the pink, hairy, paddle-like arachnid legs curled out from under the stalked eyes and over the lower rim of the shell's mouth. They touched and felt the ground beneath, spread themselves and braced against it, then with hideous speed the thing scuttled forward, bearing the vast shell with it!

In that moment I knew that I was done for. To this day I don't know exactly what happened to prove me wrong. The claw, I could have sworn it, was actually closing on my head and upper body when once again I was sent sprawling by a blow from a flapping leathery wing. One of the sky-lizards must have noticed my flight from beneath the palm branch and had hopped after me. Doubtless it regarded the attack of the crab as a threat to its own proprietary rights. There again, perhaps I flatter myself. It could be of course simply that the *pteranodon* preferred crab meat to my own untried, completely conjectural texture and taste. Whichever, the great crab saw the danger it was in, snatched itself back and its walking appendages commenced a rapid, jerky retraction – but not rapid enough.

The fetid beak darted over my stretched-out form to pluck the soft-bodied crab from its shell in one lightning-like snatch. The writhing victim screamed hideously, harshly as, in the next instant, its juices squirted where the flashing beak split its black-veined body-sac. I was drenched in nameless muck as I gathered my wits sufficiently to scramble unceremoniously, and completely uncaring of the fate of its most recent resident, feet-first into the safety of the great shell's bell mouth.

I slithered backward, and as I went I snatched up from the sand a long, dagger-like *Baculites* shell, holding its sharp point outward. Further back yet I forced my body, until the curve of the thick shell shut off my view of the outside world, until my hips would go no further down that smooth, vacant throat. Then, trembling in a fever of reaction and terror, I waited for whatever was to come next.

The crab was still screaming, but weaker now. Its harsh, rasping emissions soon turned to a quiet rattle and a lessening, sporadic clicking of claws. Then there was only the splintering of shell and rending of flesh, and the occasional indignant squawk or threatening, hissing cry. Obviously the two sky-lizards were sharing the crab, however unwillingly. I hoped that their tiny minds would forget all about me in the general festivities.

It must have been all of an hour later when I heard the heavy flopping of wings and fading, raucous cries that announced the departure of at least one of the *pteranodons*, perhaps both of them. I waited for half an hour longer, hardly daring to breathe, before squirming my body forward until the curve of the shell's mouth formed a crescent of light with the curving main body of the shell itself. A crescent of daylight, with a distant palm bending in a freshening breeze off the sea. I used my elbow to edge myself forward a few inches more, and froze!

Sitting there waiting for me, wings folded back, its head cocked expectantly on one side and its evil red eyes gazing unblinkingly, almost hypnotically into mine, was the second *pteranodon*! Oh, no, it had not forgotten me, this creature. Perhaps its now departed colleague had filled itself with the doubtless succulent flesh of the crab, but this one had obviously not been satisfied, would not be until I, too, had been made a meal of . . .

But not if I had anything to say about it.

I slid backward again until I could only just see the sky-lizard, then hurriedly further back as it experimentally tried its head in the mouth of the shell. No, I was safe for the moment, it was unable to reach me. The great wedge-shaped head and beak simply could not maneuver within the shell's mouth. In fact as the *pteranodon* pushed harder, twisting its head as it sought to close with me, that huge wedge of head and beak jammed. In something of a panic the sky-lizard attempted to withdraw, actually rocking the vast ammonite before its head came free. For a moment or two then there was silence, but in the next instant my head was ringing to the reverberations of a series of savage blows on the exterior of the shell. Within those hollow acoustical confines the sound was deafening, a burst of machine-gun fire!

God almighty! Could the shell hold out against such a battering? The whole coil seemed to be vibrating about me. Surely it would shatter into a thousand pieces at any moment, exposing me like a bark-bug in a cracked cocoon to the beak of a hungry woodpecker! But mercifully the sharp blows soon ceased.

Following a long period of silence, thinking that per-haps the creature had given up at last and moved away, I eased myself forward again. He was still there, peering at me just as intently, his head cocked on one side as before. As I stared back at that monster I couldn't help but think of a line from *Aepyornis Island* by H. G. Wells: 'A great gawky, out-of-date bird! And me a human being, heir to the ages and all that.'

341

Oh, I know, the creature in Wells's story was a true bird and mine was a reptile; but my plight was much the same as that of Wells's hero, infinitely worse, in fact. He at least had been located in his own time: *Aepyornis Vastus* had been the odd-bird-out.

So the afternoon crept by. At intervals I would ease myself forward to peer out from the mouth of the great shell, invariably to find my *pteranodon* antagonist still laying siege on that exit with what seemed to me the patience of a prehistoric Job. Occasionally, too, there would come a burst of staccato pecking at the outer wall of the shell, to which I soon grew accustomed. And strangely enough, apart from my slight hunger and thirst, and not to mention the horror awaiting me outside, I found the coiled shell very much preferable to that pebbly crevice of the previous night. It dawned on me that I was perfectly safe where I was. Following fast on the heels of this realization my state of extreme nervous tension, the rigors of which, by then, had been sapping me for over twenty-four hours, subsided into a relaxed weariness that soon gave way to sleep.

Suddenly there came an assault upon the shell that almost tipped me from its bell mouth before I was properly awake and bracing myself against the sides of the cavity. What had it been, this rude awakening? My sleep-dulled mind could not quite grasp it. There had been a rumble as of distant thunder, then a vast stirring of the ground that tilted the shell on its side, almost tipping me out. This had shaken me roughly awake, and –

Again the ground rocked, jolting the shell wildly up and down, shaking me violently and threatening to cast me loose from my position against the curving walls. There came a frightened squawking from outside in the night and a lurid orange glow shone dimly even through the coils of my ammonite refuge. This could only mean volcanic activity, a second eruption!

Above the low rumblings of the earth there came then a frantic flapping of leathery wings and the sudden *hisss* of swirling waters. I could hear the *pteranodon* squawking and blustering as it rose high in the disturbed air, and as I crawled from the mouth of the mammoth ammonite I saw the sky-lizard's wildly fluttering shadow cast by the glare from the distant mountains.

Out at sea the volcano was on the move again, sinking this time as secondary cones broke the surface much further out. A rush of cool water swirled about my feet, lifting the huge shell and floating it away along the beach. Hastily, with the water rising quickly to my knees, fearing a shock wave of water such as had left me in my present predicament, I backed up the beach to slightly higher ground. The expected shock wave did not come, however; instead, the disturbed water quickly subsided.

Out near the cone the whole surface of the sea sprayed up suddenly in foaming white crests, and I could see that the new volcano was quite definitely sinking. Way out beyond the reef it had formed, at a distance of what must have been five or six miles, many fires shot the darkness with lurid light, hissing and roaring as they spouted flames from the sea. Plainly I had slept all through the night, for already dawn was showing on the horizon. Even as I watched, the edge of the sun crept up to illuminate a fantastic scene.

The sea was on fire! For mile upon mile the surface of the water was lit by submarine explosions; geysers of superheated water shot into the air; turbulent waters tossed and rushed in an utter confusion of currents. Behind me the hills seemed to burn as rivers of lava began

343

to course down them. Away to my right these lava streams had already reached the water, sending sheets of steam hissing and searing skyward. And then a wonderful thing happened.

The last of the waters washing about my feet began a hurried retreat and, as the sun rose higher and the volcanic activity out at sea grew more furious, that retreat became an absolute rout of receding waters. Down went the reef in a sundering of ocean, back to its watery origins, and the blazing cone with it. A tremendous cloud of steam rose up then that turned the sun into a pink glow, washing the entire horizon in rose and blood tints.

The whole beach jerked and tossed now, no longer in violent spasms but rather in short, spastic rhythms that kept me adjusting my balance as I watched the spectacle of the red, retreating waters. They were in full flood now, leaving the beach bubbling and slimy and scattered with gasping fish and flopping shapes behind them. Why, at this rate –

At this rate the time-clock would soon be exposed! Somewhere out there in the mud and pebbles my time-machine lay, just waiting for the retreating waters to leave it high and dry.

I started down the beach in the wake of the fleeing ocean, beginning to run across the coarse wet sands as the sun rose up above the volcanic mists to turn the entire Cretaceous scene pink and gold. The sand sucked at my feet and various stranded creatures snapped at me in their death agonies as I sloshed past them. To my left a huge shadow grew up from the misty beach to flop awkwardly in a shallow pool. I barely gave it a second glance, however, barely recognized it as a vast *tylosaurus*, as a second shape, one with which I was far more familiar, suddenly appeared in a swirl of black, receding water.

The time-clock! There it was, half buried in wet sands, its narrow end pointing at thirty degrees to the sky, its face buried deep in muck. My vessel, my gateway to the future, to the world of men!

Through a pool of warm water I splashed and struggled, dimly aware that something huge splashed after me, but I was interested in one thing only: to regain my clock and find a way to dig it from the clinging muck. Now I was almost upon it, falling beside it as finally I tripped and sprawled in the trembling, quaking sands. My hand touched the clock's peculiar wood-like texture. I trembled then in a cold sweat of frustration and fear. It would take me hours to dig the thing out, assuming that I was to have the chance!

Far down the beach seaward a massive wall of water was gathering, piling itself up for a titanic onslaught on the land. But I must at least try. Even as I began scrabbling at the wet sand and pulling uselessly at the heavy bulk of the clock a shadow fell upon me and a primal scream tore the salty, misted air.

I hurled myself flat and headlong as a monster flipper slapped down at the spot where I had crouched, spraying me with slimy pebbles and mud and half lifting the clock from the grip of the sand. The great jaws of the stranded *tylosaurus* struck at me, missed, fastened in terrible anger on my half buried vessel. Balanced on its massive foreflippers, the creature slammed its rear quarters time and again down onto the sand to assist its jaws in their action of tearing the time-clock up from its boggy bed. At last the time-machine came loose, was tossed a dozen yards as easily as a man might fling a light chair, landing on its back, face up.

As the ground began to rock more violently and the *tylosaurus* again turned to snap at me, I scrambled after the clock, diving on it and groping for the hidden mechanisms that would open its panel. The great sea beast flopped after me, its body thudding down on the wet sand with each convulsive heave of gigantic flippers.

For some time a roaring had been growing in my ears, and even as the frontal panel of the clock swung silently open I looked up to see an awesome wall of water bearing down on me like some monstrous express train! That wave was all of fifty feet high, white-crested, curling and roaring and hissing like all the demons of hell and quite as fearsome! I hurled myself in a headlong dive into the clock's eerily illuminated interior, and as the panel clicked shut behind me felt my vessel picked up like a toy and carried away on the crest of the wave.

The *tylosaurus* was gone at once in the mad torrent of water. An instant more and my mind had meshed with the clock's and I was climbing up, up to the clouds while below me, viewed in the scanners, the great wave crashed inland, carrying all before it . . .

Three days later I left the Cretaceous and set course for the future. During the intervening time I managed to collect a marvelously representative selection of shells to replace the collection lost at the onset of that first disastrous volcanic outbreak. I undertook the task this second time far more carefully, choosing a beach far from volcanic regions. I also gathered an ample supply of the great nuts, to sustain myself should my journey prove to be a long one.

Ah, if only I could have guessed just how long it would take to return to my own era. But there, I could never have guessed, could not possibly have had any idea.

On the third evening following the recovery of my vessel, as the hot disk of the sun sank down behind wild and primal mountains, then I said my silent farewells and took leave of the Cretaceous forever. I had seen as much as I wanted to see of the vast and teeming swamps and forests, jungles, lakes and oceans; and certainly I had had my fill of that prehistoric world's denizens. All scientific interests aside, my own time called to me from across future ages.

So it was that lifting the time-clock up again to the skies, I meshed my mind and psyche with those of my vessel and turned the prow of that fantastic vehicle in the direction of tomorrow.

# PART FOUR

# *Introductory Note*

Since it has been part of my task in the preparation of this work to divide it into its various parts, chapters and sections, and to provide titles, and since the following part (despite its length) is composed mainly of fragments, I have chosen for it simply that title, 'Fragments'. I have however subtitled separate sections within the whole.

This has been necessary due to the fact that while my safe at Miskatonic University was more or less fireproof, it was not completely waterproof. The flames that devoured the old university during the Fury did little harm to the tapes, but the flood waters of the freak storm which later deluged the ruins most certainly did! Whole sections of the tapes, I fear, complete and complex statements of not inconsiderable length, have been lost.

I have used the usual system of ellipses, three or four periods to mark breaks in what I judge to be sentences and paragraphs; I have similarly prefaced new paragraphs apparently springing from the broken narrative. Excessively large or long breaks I have marked with a line of asterisks and/or comments.

With the opening section of the following part my task was not so difficult, as the tapes were more or less complete. In general, however, this part of my work toward preparing the manuscript for publication was by far the most trying, particularly for one whose interests prior to this task were anything but literary.

Arthur D. Meyer

# Fragments

*(From de Marigny's recordings)*

## 1 The Thing in the Vat

. . . And that, de Marigny, was when I first met up with the Hounds of Tindalos. Yes, those same Tind'losi Hounds of the Cthulhu Cycle: vampires of time that haunt the darkest angles of the fourth dimension, foraging abroad from the temporal towers of wraithlike Tindalos to hunt down unwary travelers.

I knew them of course through my familiarity with the pantheon of the Cthulhu Cycle and its legends, remembering them from the references they are afforded in the old occult works. Nevertheless, and though I ought to have been at least partially prepared by such knowledge, when I sensed them about my time-ship, and particularly when I actually first saw them in my scanners, they were so patently evil that my very soul shuddered!

And yet they are so difficult to describe. They are what one might expect to find if all goodness were taken away: an uncleanliness without living form, and yet embodied in vaguely batlike shapes, flapping rags of evil, vampirish drinkers of life itself. Of course, if we are to take the olden records as gospel, then in certain circumstances the Hounds are capable of materializations in three-dimensional space. I can only say that I have known innumerable clashes with them since that first time, but not once have they followed me out of time into normal space.

They exist, you see, in time itself, 'amid time's darkest

angles', as it were. Which means of course that they exist at a different temporal speed from life as we know it. Ah, but when one travels in time, then one moves in their element.

. But that first meeting.

As I have said, I had set my course forward from the Cretaceous, toward the present era, intending to slow down and stop at intervals of time until I reached a period subsequent to that of our departure when we fled from Ithaqua's elementals of the air. In this way I hoped to avoid the obvious pitfalls of temporal paradox.

It was as I was about to make my first halt in time that I became aware of the Hounds.

They were like shadows in the scanners, distant tatters that flapped almost aimlessly in the voids of time; but as they in turn sensed me their movements became imbued with more purpose! As they drew closer, I saw that in fact they had shape and size and even something approaching solidarity, but that despite all of these attributes there was still nothing about them that even remotely resembled what we know of life. They were Death, the worms in a dead man's skull, the maggots fattening in a rotting corpse. They were the Hounds of Tindalos, and once recognized they can never be forgotten!

Now they swarmed toward the clock, ethereal wasps attracted by a juicy apple of time in which I was the succulent core, and as they fluttered darkly about my hurtling vessel I heard their hellish chittering. They were batlike, and they communicated with batlike voices. Or were their chitterings simply expressions of delight that here they had found some unsuspecting traveler in time? Knowing instinctively that they were evil – I knew it as surely as I knew that they were the Hounds of Tindalos – I nevertheless thought myself safe in the body of the clock. Very soon, however, I discovered that this was not the case.

If my time machine were a sphere, Henri, then I might have been safe, for the Hounds fear perfect curves. But of course the clock is of hard angles, and the Vampires of the Void are one with all the angles of time. There are ancient Greek documents which, along with certain esoteric translations, might explain all of this far better than I ever could. What I am saying essentially is this: the Hounds could reach me, even through the incredibly hard material of the clock's walls. The first I knew of it was when smoke seemed to pour from all the interior angles of my vessel, angles I sensed rather than saw, you understand. And then awesome feelers entered into my refuge to fondle me with their chill, a chill that threatened instantly to draw off all of my body's heat – all of my life-force – and leave me stiff, frozen and dead!

I instantly accelerated, only to discover that the Hounds were endowed with that same power. They, too, were capable of controlling their rate of passage through time. Similarly, when I hastily slowed down and turned to race into the past again, they were amply capable of pacing me, closing with the time-clock once more to recommence their foul gropings and draining of my life-force.

Desperately, while yet hurtling backward through time, I further maneuvered my vessel in space. That is, I consciously sought to avoid the Hounds of Tindalos, whose element is time, by throwing my vessel through space. In this my blunder was twofold. One, I lost myself hopelessly. Two, my ploy did not succeed. Certainly I had fled through space, but I had still been traveling in time as I did it!

One cannot avoid the Tind'losi Hounds in time. There is only one way to escape them: the time-traveler must revert back to the three mundane dimensions. I should have known it at once, but it's useless to cry over spilled milk. When, at the very last moment, I did revert back into normal space, it was to find myself utterly and hopelessly lost! Gone the Hounds, and with them any chance of an early return to my own time, my own place.

I had no way of judging, you see, how far I had accelerated into the future, no way of knowing how many æons I had traversed in my flight back into the past. And when you consider the fantastic leagues, the light-years of space that the clock can consume in mere instants, why, I could be out beyond the Milky Way, while back on Earth the ice sheets might even now be reaching out from polar regions to freeze the woolly mammoth on the plains of Siberia.

I repeat, I was utterly, hopelessly lost.

From then on, for what I judge now must have been a period of at least a year of normal time – I find difficulty now, you know, in thinking of time as in my old pre-transition period – I wandered the space-lanes, and occasionally the corridors of time, seeking some clue, some signpost to the planet of my origins. It was toward the end of this period that I again braved time in a direction I hoped would take me toward my own era. I was actually searching for a period in which I might recognize the constellations, which in turn might lead me home. Instead, I again chanced upon a foraging party of the Hounds.

I say chanced upon them, and yet it is more than probable that in fact they were lying in ambush. Yes, it seemed they were waiting for me, and I became aware of them only in the last instant, as they were actually fastening on the clock! To be surprised like that is disconcerting to say the least, de Marigny. Picture yourself in a car, driving down an empty street, when suddenly a child steps off the curb only a few feet in front. Your brakes are out of the question; you are too close to the child. You hold the steering wheel in your hands, however, and while your foot is reaching for the brake you are able to turn the wheels.

I was in a vaguely similar position, except of course that it was my own life I had to save. My immediate reaction, I suppose, should have been to switch out of time into the mundane three dimensions. To this day I do not know why I did not do so, unless the Hounds have that same ability of the greater powers of the CCD to get into men's minds and dull them or turn them to their own purposes. Anyway, I turned my 'steering wheel' instead, and sought a path through the massed ranks of the Tind'losi Hounds. And indeed there seemed to be a path, a clear route through time that they had not blocked.

Fleeing down this sole avenue of egress, I saw my mistake too late: there were more of them waiting for me behind dark angles. Yet again I was obliged to fly both in space and time simultaneously, and yet again I found that in the end all escape routes were blocked. Only then, it seemed, did I remember the three mundane dimensions and revert back to them, and only then did I discover how cruelly the Hounds of Tindalos had fooled me!

They had maneuvered me into a perfect trap, forcing me to revert to normal space – or at least reminding me that I could do so – at that exact second of time most propitious to their cause, which I knew then was to destroy me completely! Hurtling out of time but yet speeding through space, I emerged in three dimensions to discover myself already rushing down upon the surface of a gray world. The vast bulk of the planet was there directly before me. There was no time even to think – an automatic application of mental brakes had but minimal effect. The lower atmosphere rushing by in a stream of sparks that formed a flaming tail, I plunged, a meteorite, tightening my mental controls of the time-clock, but it was already too late. The bulk of the world below rushed up to embrace the clock, to flatten it to its bosom of mountains and plains.

I threw my hands up before my face, at least, I think I tried to . . .

I became aware of a vast room filled with a variety of machines and obscure electrical mechanisms for all the world reminiscent – no, the very duplicate – of some mad scientist's laboratory out of those old horror films of the thirties and forties. Over the tiled floor of this tremendous laboratory, in and about and all around the towering consoles of incredibly complicated instruments, trundled a squat, rubber-wheeled robot of multiple appendages and faceted electrical eyes. It paused every now and then at one bank of dials and levers or another to make speedy but delicate adjustments. The whole scene was soundless and I seemed to view it through some distorting element, like faintly frosted glass. Either that or my eyes were not functioning properly.

My mind, too, was very foggy. Snatches of memory were there, I recall, from all my years of youth and middle age, but much was missing. For example, while I knew dimly who I was, I did not know where or how I came to be where I was. My awareness, which had seemed to be instantaneous, was incomplete, as if I were a machine, suddenly switched on but not yet warmed to the task of existing.

Then it dawned on me that I was hardly aware at all. I could not feel my body, could not close my eyes or even blink. I felt no sensations whatever. Where, for instance, was the tightening and slackening of the chest that goes hand in hand with breathing? Where was the sense of flowing blood, the pulse, which I personally have always been able to feel or hear in my head? But I was given very little time to ponder these things. In any case, such questions would all soon be answered.

All at once, as far as I could make out, having paused to observe the readings on a metal mushroom of gleaming dials and flashing lights, the robot spun quickly about while its faceted eyes all swiveled in my direction. The thing looked at me. Then it rushed toward me, its rubber wheels blurring over the tiles while the upper appendages of its metal body became suddenly galvanized into fantastic tremblings. Three of its five eyes flashed through an astonishing range of color combinations.

The thing came right up to me until, achieving some sort of perspective and clarity of vision at last, I could see that it stood almost man-sized. It reached out an appendage toward my eyes, a rubber-tipped claw of sorts. As this tool began to close over my right eye I tried to scream, to turn and run, to throw up a protective arm before my face, and nothing happened! My brain was pouring commands to every part of my body but –

My body? Had I been capable of laughter then indeed, at that exact moment of time, I might have laughed hysterically, though I think it more likely that I would have screamed. For as the mechanical claw steadied itself to close gently on my right eye and shut out sight in that orb, so my left eye witnessed this action reflected in the many facets of the robot's own five crystal lenses. It also saw the vat of electrolytic fluids bubbling and the thing the vat contained: a thing like a flattened, wrinkled, elongated bladder. It saw the glowing plastic tubes that protruded from the grayly pulsing mass in the vat, and also the naked organs with which those tubes were tipped. In short I saw myself, the mortal remains of Titus Crow: *a brain in a bowl, with stalked, lidless, bloodshot eyes!*

The human mind, despite its circumstances, or perhaps because of them, is mercifully equipped with a means to shut out sensations and sights which are completely unbearable. Happily what remained of my brain in that robot laboratory upon an alien world still retained this facility. A blackness engulfed me in which I was to know no dreams but only a long drawn out longing for death rather than the ultimate horror and madness of the thing in the vat.

## 2 Robot World

So began my transition, de Marigny.

My next awakening was one of longer duration but no less horrible, though this time the climax did not cause my mind to shut down, seeking safety in unconscious oblivion. As it happened, the shutting down was done for me, automatically. But in many other ways that second awakening was very different from the first. For one thing, the scene in the great laboratory was now accompanied by sounds, the sounds one might expect to hear at the heart of a giant computer: a mechanical clicking, as of a thousand typewriter keys; a whirring and fluttering, similar to the shuffle of programming cards; the hiss and sputter of controlled electrical energies and the distant, subterranean thrummings and vibrations of great engines.

When the robot – custodian? – of the place saw that I was once again conscious, it approached in far less agitation than before and, astonishingly, spoke to me, in a neutral but not unpleasant English! 'I see that you are aware.' Two of its eyes swiveled down to peer steadily at something below my sphere of vision, then joined the other three in staring at me in a manner more than merely mechanical. I detected an air – I could swear it – of something approaching pride in the metal scientist, for such the robot later proved to be.

'Yes, you are aware, and you hear me, but do not try to answer. You will not have a voice until much later. At that time we will be able to talk, but until then I must rely upon the intelligence imparted to me by your friend here. He is guiding me in your reconstruction and we are making slow but steady progress.'

My friend? I found that with a little effort I could move my eyes, making them follow the direction clearly indicated by a movement of one of the robot's upper appendages. There in a cleared space, its back to the wall of the laboratory, stood my time-clock. It was undamaged, as far as I could tell, and as I saw it many memories rushed in to fill the blank spaces in my mind, particularly the memory of falling in the clock like a meteorite to the surface of a gray world!

But what had the robot meant by calling the clock my friend? I was not to find that out for some time.

'I am told,' the robot continued, its voice remarkably human if hollow, 'that life-forms such as yourself suffer certain disturbances of mind originating in diseased or damaged members or organs of your bodies, and that such disturbances are known collectively as pain. This condition, I am led to believe, is as distressing to you as rust or lack of lubrication would be to me; indeed more distressing, for you are incapable of disconnecting the offending member or organ or of switching it off from your brain while the necessary corrections are performed. Moreover, I am assured that this pain is quite capable of bringing about a general debility in your entire system. Since it is important that you are not further damaged during this period of your reconstruction, I would like to know if you are now experiencing pain. If so I will switch

358

you off immediately until I can find and remove the source of such distress. So that I may do these things, you may reply in the affirmative by moving your eyes to the right, or in the negative by moving them to the left. Are you in pain?'

Immediately, and with less effort this time, I moved my eyes to the left, then back again to stare at the robot. I could feel no pain whatever. Indeed I could barely feel my eyes, while the rest of my body remained a mere vacancy. (All this time I had kept my eyes averted from any shiny surface in which I might see unmentionable things reflected.) But now the robot's upper appendages were trembling and quivering; its faceted eyes were swiveling here and there like those of some freak, hybrid chameleon; its voice, when at last it spoke again, was full of what might only be called, well, if not emotion, certainly an unprecedented machine excitement!

'You . . . you see, you hear and you reason! You . . . you really *are*!' For a moment longer this weird metal creature exulted, then said, 'But there remains much to be done, and once more I must consult your friend before continuing my work. It were better, I think, if I switched you off.' He – already I thought of the robot as a male entity – reached out an appendage toward an area to one side of me and to the rear of my sphere of vision, pulling into view a large mirror on wheels. 'But before I do I would like you to see how we have progressed, your friend and I!'

I tried to close my eyes then but found that I could not do so. The attempt was an automatic reflex which, if I had been able to bear the sight revealed by the mirror, if I had looked closer, I would have seen to be impossible anyway. One cannot close eyes that have no lids! Instead I remembered the robot's words of a minute or so earlier and simply moved my eyes, all too slowly, to the right.

'Pain!' The robot actually seemed to gasp, recognizing my signal on the instant. Then he turned and sped rapidly away to operate a red switch in the center of a nearby console. Once again darkness descended, but not before I had fearfully, in dreadful but irresistible curiosity, turned my eyes back to the mirror.

Oh, yes, much had been done. Work upon my reconstruction was truly progressing:

My eyes were attached to my brain as before (the latter was now much more brain-shaped), but now they had been embedded in nubs of living flesh, in rudimentary sockets. There were twin, raw, wrinkled orifices, one at each side of the brain, with metallic cones attached to them by slim copper wires: my ears, I supposed them to be. There was an esophagus of flexible plastic, supported at the back by the first bones – or were they, too, plastic? – of a spine, which in turn had hanging before it a black, baglike thing that I took to be my stomach. Lungs, liver and kidneys were there, all artificial and none seeming to be working, all loosely attached to one another in a network of gristly filaments of synthetic protoplasm or plastic. And where my heart should have been, there hung a cluster of connected plastic balls, five of them spaced evenly about a shining metal nucleus. The whole visceral obscenity, with the exception of the stalked eyes and the metallic cones, swam or floated in a large transparent tube of yellow fluids.

And so my transition progressed. Periodically I would be made to awaken, to be shown my latest physical acquisitions, the most recent steps in my path toward completion. It seemed to me that my robot super-surgeon worked lovingly, and with tremendous pride in his craft. I watched myself grow in his mirror, saw my body gradually taking shape. Step by step I was brought back to full existence in that laboratory, and I marveled as each bone

– many of them plastic duplicates, for most of the originals were ruined beyond redemption – was made to fit into place within my semi-synthetic body. I saw my limbs take shape, and felt memories waking as my damaged brain healed itself or was repaired. And always and ever the robot talked to me, explaining how all this had come about, how it was that my jigsaw puzzle being was in process of reconstruction in his laboratory.

It seemed that my disastrous arrival upon the surface of the gray world had been witnessed by the robot, who at the time had been on a lone interplanetary expedition in search of life! His own planet, a world of subterranean hives and corridors, utterly devoid of organic life, was fifth from the sun in a system of six worlds and eleven moons. That was where I was now, on the fifth planet, but the gray world whose surface had so rudely received me had been the second from the sun, 680 millions of miles away toward the system's center. The robot had transported all of my parts and the clock, too, to his home world. There he had commenced . . .

. . . but in any case it had been my good fortune – no, let me not understate the matter. It had been a fantastically fortunate coincidence – not only that the robot had seen me crash to the surface of that gray planet, but also that he had been perhaps the one and only mechanism of his race who could ever have . . .

. . . T3RE, however, possibly by virtue of his years of random thought and his inbuilt capacity for endless physical and theoretical experimentation, had developed his own ideas with regard to organic life. His theory of the origin of species was that robots were not there in the beginning, but that they had been created originally by and in the service of superior organic life-forms. In short, I suppose you could call my friend a mechanical Darwin!

Eventually there came a time when I could no longer

be completely switched off, when only my conscious mind would respond to T3RE's control. This simply meant that my brain was whole again. Moreover, my id must be intact – I could hope, I could dream! And during those periods when the robot scientist labored his labor of love – and in the case of T3RE I am sure that so utterly unmechanical a phrase is not at all out of order – when of necessity my surface consciousness must be closed down to spare me the embarrassment of pain, then indeed I did dream.

As often as not the dream was recurrent, but though the main setting was known to me of old, this time it came to me that I *only* dreamed, that these subconscious sensations were merely pictures out of my own mind. They were not, as had been their prototype, of telepathic intensity. There was of course a vast crystal hall and a gossamer-clad goddess who cried crystal tears, while the rumbling thoughts of some being great beyond words fumbled to comfort her grief-stricken mind, and misty drapes trembled before a huge, alcoved throne upon which the Eminence himself stirred in emotional agitation. Such dreams were not good.

Then came that long-awaited awakening when I found myself with a working voice (I had already had several that did not work) and at last I was able to put to T3RE all of those questions I had saved up during my period of enforced muteness. Of course, it was a great moment for the robot, too, for at last he had a genuine, self-attestable specimen, albeit a reconstructed one of sentient organic life. Soon he would be able to . . .

'. . . as I myself am – was – organic.' I told him. 'We called them presidents and prime ministers and dictators and kings. They were all human beings. At least here you are all equal.'

'An equality leading to the utmost boredom, at least

until I found you!' he answered. 'And make no mistake, you are still organic, the greater part of you. But tell me more about this world of human beings. Were there no robots, no computers?' He was vastly interested.

'Oh, yes, there were computers. There were robots, too, though none so advanced as you,' I told him.

'And the machines existed in companionship with you human beings?'

'They were' – I was forced to admit it – 'man's slaves. Men made them.'

'Slaves? They were not companions? Men made them?'

'They were machines, as you are a machine, but they were simply not individual enough to be companions. They were heading that way, though. Certainly I knew men who loved their automobiles!'

'Ah! I see. They were of a low order, these robots, as are the T6's and T7's.' He turned from me where I hung in my complicated life-support tube. For a moment his crystal eyes stared across the laboratory at my time-clock, then he turned back to me. 'And yet your robot, the time-clock that brought you across time and space, is of an exceptionally high order, higher, I would say, even than a T2. It surprises me that he deigns to talk to me at all.'

'Oh, yes, the clock is a high-order machine, all right,' I answered. 'But it was made by organic beings of *such* a high order that by comparison I am not much better than those lowly, single-celled organisms and primitive animals which you tell me you have found on distant moons.'

At this revelation T3RE grew very excited. 'Then my theory may very well be correct! I have long suspected that it is a basically illogical presumption that we robots were here in the beginning. We have no sexual reproductory apparatus; we are incapable of generation by fission, though that is certainly the nearest we get to organic reproduction; we devise new models for specialized tasks,

363

of course, but these have to be assembled from components which are, as separate units, insensate. Who, then, built the first robot?'

'We have a similar theological problem on my world,' I answered, as T3RE turned from me, switching off my conscious mind as he trundled almost absently away to ponder, no doubt, his last question. 'But there on Earth,' my subconscious mind continued to itself, 'there we ask ourselves who made God!'

It was not until very much later, during a period of wakefulness when T3RE had once more called me up from the netherworlds of subconscious mind to his robot laboratory, that I thought to ask him how long he had worked on me. The answer was not immediately forthcoming as we had to work out a satisfactory chronological system. It was based on the speed of light, in units of the length of time it took light to race from the primary of T3RE's system to his home planet. Finally I discovered I had been in the robot's care for no less than forty-seven years. Of all that time I had spent perhaps one hour awake, and of that hour all of fifteen minutes had been taken up in mutual conversation!

It had taken T3RE ten years merely to duplicate his first living red corpuscle. My nervous system had taken much longer, was still in process of reconstruction. My brain, too, had been a major problem: not its repair and assembly but the replacement of lost memories and complex nerve and motor areas. In this T3RE had relied solely upon my friend the time-clock.

What I had never known – what I could never have guessed – was that during my journeys in the clock through time and space, not only had I been one with the clock's psyche but the clock had recorded in its own memory banks all of my memories and thoughts! I have never discovered just why this was done; I fancy that it is normal procedure, that time-clocks such as mine always retain copies of the psychic identities and memories of their users.

At any rate, T3RE had fed these recordings back into my reconstructed brain using an infinitely delicate electronic system devised by the clock and himself. Now my body was almost complete, a composite but nearly perfect Frankenstein built mainly of synthetic parts, but yet retaining all of its original passions and humors, hopes and aspirations, pleasures and fears.

And in another twenty-three years, perhaps three or four hours of consciousness, I was ready. Ready for T3RE's final tests, when he would link up in a series of operations all of my millions of synthetic circuits and give me back my body. Then I would be lifted free of my life-support tube complete again as a man, a man like no other.

'When you have undergone all your tests,' he told me toward the end, 'when you are ready to recommence your journey, for your friend the time-clock tells me you are destined to complete a great journey, then I will . . .'

. . .'And what of yourself?' I asked him. 'Your future?'

'I do not matter. I have no God. My emotions are based mainly upon your own, which I tried to duplicate electronically within myself before you first regained consciousness. The clock explained these emotions to me. It was not a very successful experiment: I cannot even dream! You are superior, you and your clock, both of you. He can dream; he has many memories, even those of many beings before your time, he tells me. He has, yes, a psyche, an id. I do not matter, no – but you? – both of you must go on, to your journey's end.'

# 3 The Transition of Titus Crow

When I awakened next it was to a sort of chaos in the laboratory of T3RE. Other T3's were everywhere. Many of them moved about the laboratory, three or four clustered around my tube. At least half of them were almost indistinguishable from T3RE himself, while others had different arrangements of appendages and were obviously constructed to perform different tasks. Finally the robot directly in front of me spoke and I recognized him.

'That was your first test!' T3RE told me. 'You woke up yourself, without stimulation. Is there pain?'

'No, but there is – I have feelings! I can feel my arms and legs, my fingers. Is it finished?'

'It is finished,' cried T3RE in a sort of mechanical delight. He was a robot for sure, but in that instant he seemed more human than any real person I had ever known. He was whirring nervously on his wheels back and forth in front of me, his upper appendages waving, his five faceted eyes all aswivel; he acted for all the world like some excited schoolboy with his first model airplane, about to propel it on its maiden flight. And, more amazingly, his enthusiasm seemed to have infected his visitors!

'I am communicating with them on radio wavelengths,' he explained. 'They cannot speak in your tongue, indeed they have no tongues as such. Nor had I before I built into myself the necessary components. Even so, they are not as efficient as your organic vocal chords. Now we must see if the rest of you is equally efficient!'

I felt myself being lifted, tried to turn my head to see

what was going on, and my head turned! A sort of dazed disbelief enveloped me then; I felt quite drunk. At last I was back in control of my body! But what degree of control did I have? In an instant I was trembling in the grip of many emotions, and fear was not the least of them. Often before I had compared myself with the Frankenstein monster of fiction, but what if I should prove to be no less a monster? A stiff-limbed, mechanically jointed, uncoordinated mass of synthetic muscle and plastic parts?

A harness of some soft material lifted me from the tube and set me slowly down on the tiled floor of the laboratory. Though my feet touched the floor, and I actually felt them touch it, the harness lowered me no further. 'Is something wrong?' I inquired of T3RE.

'I will lower you slowly,' he answered, 'to give your body a chance to orientate. If anything goes wrong, tell me.' He moved a lever on a nearby console and the harness lowered me a few more inches.

Now I braced my feet against the floor and stood upright. I shrugged my shoulders free of the harness. I lifted my hands and looked at them, then tried a spontaneous whoop of joy and relief – and nothing came!

'My . . . my voice!' I gasped. 'What . . . what is wrong with my – ?'

'You must first learn to breathe if you wish to expel air violently,' T3RE told me. 'You have lungs, but from now on they will only be of use to you in speaking. I decided long ago that yours was a most inefficient circulatory system, and that – '

'Are you trying to tell me that I don't need air?' I cut him off.

'Only for the activation of your vocal cords,' he answered. 'But come, this is nothing to worry about. In fact your new system is far more efficient. You will be

367

able to exist unprotected in all but the most corrosive atmospheres. I thought this would be better for you, in view of the journey you have ahead. Come, now, there are other, more important things to be tested. Walk, run, jump – try out your body! I need to see you function. Breathe if you wish, if it seems normal to you. The atmosphere in here has been adapted to suit your old constitution; see what your taste buds think of it. And then I have food for you, and drink: synthetic proteins and carbohydrates extracted from the oils of the earth!'

I sucked air into my lungs, tasted it, expelled it – and suddenly I exulted! Strength filled my body, I could feel it: an abundance of vitality, the sure knowledge that I was a new man, quite literally! I turned to the great mirror that stood beside my now empty tube and stared at myself.

Oh, the man who stood there, reflected in that mirror, was Titus Crow, little doubt of that, but he was a younger Titus Crow, revitalized. And he was complete! I knew that, just staring at myself. And yet I was more than complete. Not perfect, not by any means, for despite the wonderful blend of synthetics and flesh and metals and bone and plastics and hair that I now was, despite all this I was still human. And human beings are far from perfect. But I was a damn sight nearer perfect than had been the old man who fled the Tind'losi Hounds and smashed himself to pulp on the surface of a dead gray world!

'T3RE,' I finally said, 'you have worked a miracle. Many miracles. There is no need at all to test this body of mine; I know that it is an excellent body. And there is no way for me to thank you for what you have done.'

'You have thanked me enough,' he answered, 'in that I now know that my theory . . . all these colleagues of mine: they, too, are now aware that . . .'

\* \* \*

. . . had known any practical way to get T3RE into the time-clock at that time then possibly he would have come along with me. As it was we said what we could of farewells, and so I took my . . .

. . . for where I was headed: well . . . list of possible three-dimensional directions which just might take me back to Earth. The route was designed, in any case, to send me close to galaxies and star clusters and nebulæ where, with a bit of luck, I might suddenly recognize some constellation or other and thus find my way home.

Such a route-card of interstellar space seems quite ridiculous, I know, but nevertheless that's the way I tried to do it. Not quite 'turn right at the blue dwarf with the tri-planet system and head for the binary with the spiral nebula at its left', but pretty much that sort of thing. Yes, I suppose it must seem ridiculous, until one considers the sort of speeds my craft could accomplish. If you are working with speeds in the region of tens of thousands of miles per hour, then of course you require a very accurate scientific course to get you and your target arriving at the same spot at the same time. Not so with the time-clock! I could simply pick a star in the sky and go there, and at almost that speed!

But of course there is only one Earth, and I soon discovered that the planet of my birth might just as well be the proverbial needle in the haystack as far as instant success was concerned. One thing I did have, however, and that was patience.

# 4 Roman Britain

. . . in the end, can wear extremely thin, and I proved to be no exception to this rule. Not that my journey could be said in any way to be boring. On the contrary, for I had my pick of alien worlds to explore, and many of them were beautiful beyond words. Others, I must add, were frightening beyond words.

. . . as close to Venus, and not only in time, for . . .

. . . wonderful as any that the science-fiction writers ever dreamed of; more, because they were real! But the telling would take so long that it must wait until another time. Perhaps, de Marigny, if ever you decide to join me in Elysia, and I'm sure you will, then we'll be able to swap adventures with each other. And if . . .

. . . back on Earth. And I *knew* it was Earth. Third from the sun, with a moon I knew and loved as every human lover since the beginning of time has loved it; green and beautiful as no other planet except perhaps Elysia, which isn't really a planet anyway, is beautiful. Oh, it was Earth, and not too far removed from my own time at that, for England's shores were sharply etched against the blue of the sea as I fell toward . . . could see that there was a . . . fields of the North . . .

. . . boy herding sheep. In my excitement as I brought the clock in to a landing I had not bothered to pay attention to my exact geographic location; I only knew that I was somewhere in Yorkshire. No doubt the lad with the sheep would be able to put me right . . .

. . . to run away! Perhaps he had seen me land and thought me some sort of flying monster. A minute later I had managed to catch up with him and bring him to a halt. I held his shoulders and looked him straight in the eyes, letting him see that I was only a man, if a somewhat weirdly dressed man, for I was clad only in a soft leathery loincloth, a leaf torn from an alien palm on a tropical planet.

And yet by then I had discovered that the shepherd boy's own garment was no less surprising. It was formed of little more than a body sheet of rough cloth, with a few stitches to hold the thing in place, like a crude poncho. He kept rolling his eyes longingly toward a far-off huddle of stone towers and outlying huts with smoke rising into the blue summer sky, and trying to pull away from me while crying out in a tongue which at first I did not recognize. Then I caught the fact that he wanted to go home. Home to – to *Eboracum*!

Eboracum! The name given by the Romans to York! I was home on Earth, in the very land of my birth, but hundreds of years too early, in Roman Britain! You can have no idea . . .

. . . boy further. Once he was used to the idea that I meant him no harm, and hearing my stilted, rather poor Latin, he soon regained his composure. The governor of Britain, I discovered, was Platorius Nepos, and three years earlier work had commenced 'far to the north' on Hadrian's Wall. Roman Britain in the year 125 A.D.! . . . that I was so close to home, the merest hop through time in the clock, and –

Ah, but it was not to be. Close to where I had landed stood a villa, and now that I knew *when* I was I realized why, when I had flown the clock down close to the place, the building had struck me as being rather Old Mediterranean in style. Later I was to discover that the villa was the retreat of a retired Roman senator, one Felicius Tetricus, and that because of a local uprising some miles to the northwest he had stationed sentries and watchmen in and around his villa's grounds. These men were of his own household and very loyal to him, which was my downfall. Perhaps if they had . . . course they were on the lookout for just such persons . . .

. . . talking to him. At any rate I saw this fellow in a jerkin and leather skirt, with sandals on his feet and a shortsword at his belt. He seemed friendly enough, despite an evil scar across one cheek, but as he came up to me and started to speak I saw his eyes flicker strangely and, simultaneously, heard the shepherd boy's cry of warning. Someone behind me! I whirled, saw a second man leaping – and then the heavy pommel of his sword crashed down upon my temple and I fell, unconscious, to the heather.

When I came to I was in a bed of silks and linens, in a room whose balcony overlooked a paved veranda surrounded by a garden of flowers. From my bed I could look out and actually see the garden. I could smell the flowers' heady perfume. There is no other smell in the entire universe as sweet as the flowers of Earth, unless it is that fragrance of my own Tiania's slender neck.

Well, I was eventually attended by a physician in a purple toga, an elderly man who would not talk but simply clucked and bathed my head, applied some cooling liniment and changed my bandage. Finally, before he left me, he told me that I must rest. I had been in Tetricus' villa for three days, and at first the master of the house had despaired of my life.

'You can consider yourself lucky,' he told me obscurely, 'that you resemble Titus Tetricus so well!'

My mind was all foggy, in fact I was in a fever, and so perhaps I didn't entirely know what I said when I answered: 'But I *am* Titus!'

When he heard this the old physician turned quite gray, then backed away, mumbling to his gods and making a series of esoteric symbols in the air with a forefinger. Not long after this, before I could drop back off to sleep, Felicius Tetricus himself . . .

. . . was a period when I kept swimming up out of my fever for a few minutes and then sinking slowly back. During one of my semiconscious bouts I heard old Tetricus and someone else – I think it was the gnarled physician – talking about me in lowered tones. Tetricus remarked on my likeness to his own dead son, Titus, killed in a chariot race across the moors and buried these three years. The bereaved father had offered up prayers to all the gods of earth, air, fire and water – particularly the latter, Sul, who seemed to be Tetricus' patron deity – that his son be returned to him. And now? Could it be that his prayers had at last been answered?

Might this stranger not indeed be Titus, returned from the land of the shades to his doting father in the form of this stranger? And was this man really a stranger? Had he not admitted that his name was Titus? True, he was older than Titus Tetricus had been at his death, but that had been three years ago. Did the shades, too, age then? The man had an athlete's body, of that there could be little doubt, and he was no simple Briton. Patently his was a noble . . .

. . . more Felicius had looked upon my troubled, feverish face and form, the more sure the old Roman was becoming that I was his son reincarnate, that . . .

. . . came to proper. I found Felicius at my bedside. My fever seemed much abated and my head much clearer, and I remembered what I had overheard of the old man's superstitious half-belief in his son's resurrection in my body. I determined that if it seemed in my favor to do so, I would put Felicius' fancies to my own use. By that I mean that it . . .

. . . thing I asked about, therefore, was the clock, which I called a 'shrine' to all the gods of the air. I did this just in case those assailants of mine who had knocked me down and brought me here, nearly caving my skull in with their enthusiasm, had actually seen me land. It seemed to me . . .

. . . had it brought into the villa, though he had seen little use for so inordinately heavy a thing. Now, however, he was glad. If it was indeed a shrine, then he would offer up prayers to it that I had been delivered unto him. But what was I really, and where did I hail from?

Well, I obviously could not tell the truth. For one thing I doubted if Tetricus, a very down-to-Earth man for his sort, could even grasp so completely outré a concept as time-travel. Instead I feigned loss of memory: all I could remember was my name, which was Titus.

. . . hear nothing of my moving out of bed. I was to spend a further week in enforced recuperation, until my head was fully healed. In fact my head was already fully healed, and long before the end of the week Felicius caught me pacing to and fro in my room and asked me what was wrong. I told him I needed to worship, that he must take me to my clock. He skated around the subject, walked me around the villa and its grounds, literally gave me free run of the place, except for certain locked rooms in the . . . servants. There, too, I was introduced to Thorpos, a huge Nubian whose . . .

. . . absolutely no way! More and more it seemed that Felicius was becoming enamored of the idea that I really was his son, and I had to play along with him. That seemed to me the only way I might ever. . .

. . . while they hadn't seen the clock actually arrive, they had seen me step from it! Felicius was no fool; he certainly did not intend that his son, recently returned to him from beyond the pale, should ever be recalled! He wasn't going to let me anywhere near that clock, not as long as he could help it. So what was I . . .

. . . unwilling to use force against the members of the noble's household, and so I tried at first to bluff my way past the ever watchful Thorpos. I might as well . . . failed, I then attempted to bribe the Nubian. He was very polite – I was his master as much as any man could be – but his orders came direct from Felicius Tetricus and they were . . .

The big black must have informed Felicius that I was still trying to get to the clock, for the next day I was called to the old man's chambers and chided over the matter. If I wanted to offer up prayers, I was told, there were temples in Eboracum I could visit, not to mention Felicius' own private shrine in the grounds of the villa itself.

For a fortnight then I was completely obedient to the old man's whims, simply biding my time and trying to allay his fears that perhaps I desired to leave the hospitality of the villa. This was in no way easy, for . . . and in the end I made the fatal mistake of letting Thorpos find me wandering in the servants' quarters, trying the doors in the middle of the night. I simply wasn't made to be stealthy. And how could I possibly make out after that that I was not trying to get away from the villa, away from Felicius Tetricus?

Some few days later I heard it whispered among the servants that my clock had been taken out and buried on the moors. I made what worried, discreet inquiries I could, all useless, and it didn't take long for me to understand that Felicius had put a terrible price on the head of any man who dared even mention the clock to me! That was that, then. Since it seemed I . . .

. . . simply continue to bide my time and hope that eventually I could talk the Roman noble into revealing the clock's whereabouts, I settled to my far from uncomfortable existence in Felicius' household.

And it was that way for the better part of a year. I waited and tried my best to ignore the ever-present anxiety that nagged at my insides, that the clock might be lost beyond redemption, and only . . . good at subterfuge, the type of trick I've never much cared for, but I . . .

. . . many months. For a period I was even driven to consider violence upon the person of Felicius Tetricus himself, but when the opportunity came I could not bring myself to do it. And by then the old man was absolutely convinced that I was his son, Titus Tetricus, returned to him by the gods.

And yet the year had not been wasted, for I had struck up a firm friendship with the Roman philosopher, Lollius Urbicus (not to be confused with Q. Lollius Urbicus, who was to become Antonius Pius' governor of Britain in 139 A.D.) whose truly remarkable erudition and magnetic personality suited my own mental attitudes very well. At the same time, yet on an entirely different level, I had managed to find many outlets for that physical abundance built into me by T3RE. I was a man in my prime, with the strength and stamina of three men.

Much to Felicius' alarm I had taken up chariot racing and wrestling, all the sports of the games, and I had quickly grown to excel in them all. I had been tutored in the use of the shortsword and in the heavier British blade, even in the Scottish and Pictish long-handled ax. There came a time when it seemed that there was no weapon I could not master, but all of . . .

. . . instincts and love of knowledge always took me back to the sparse household of Lollius Urbicus, and there I would bury my frustrations in long hours of discussion and simple contemplation of the nature of . . .

Oh, certainly Felicius Tetricus tried to win me over. There was, for instance, always a party at the villa; the women he made arrangements with for my amusement ran from the wives of officers engaged on supervisory duties at the Wall to expensive local whores whose wares would have tempted any man, except perhaps one whose dreams were haunted by the face and form of a goddess. No, try as he might to make me his son, the weeks found me spending more and more of my time with Lollius Urbicus, with whom I had developed scholarly links completely transcending two thousand years of time and vast differences of creed, society and similar mundane concepts.

And it was in this affinity of mine with the Roman philosopher whose book, *Frontier Garrison*, back in the . . . seeds of a dilemma within a dilemma were sown, and they were seeds that grew and blossomed strangely in the end.

# 5 The Great Race

. . . that this Earth of ours was inhabited by many intelligent races before Man, some of them malign, as the Cthulhu Spawn, others benign and . . .

. . . in the writings of the elder Peaslee, Wingate's father, particularly in what he wrote of his peculiar amnesia during the years 1908-13 . . . that one of Wingate's principal interests had always lain in the Great Sandy Desert. Of course I can see that you are wondering just what all this has to do with my life in the villa of Felicius Tetricus in 125 A.D.. I will tell you.

I have mentioned this almost psychic affinity of mine

with the Roman philosopher Lollius Urbicus, the similarity in our thinking and the primal puzzles to which our minds were drawn as one. Now I want you to picture, way back in the dim mists of time, a great race of scientists dwelling upon the primordial landmass of Australia, which was yet to sink beneath the waves and rise again several times before the first man walked the Earth. This race is lost to man except in the most ancient of desert ruins, whose hints of an antediluvian super-civilization are mind-staggering.

These beings, creatures of multiple appendages that walked in much the same manner as garden snails and talked by clicking great claws, stood ten feet tall and were ten feet wide at the bases of their rugose, conical bodies. They had developed instruments through which they could send their minds out into space, or into the past or future, to displace the minds of other sentient beings and replace them. When this happened the displaced minds took up habitation in the conical bodies of the usurping Great Race. In this way scientists of the Great Race collected knowledge of all future and past civilizations, of every planet within range of their mind-swapping machines. And always they were on the lookout for fresh bodies to inhabit, young races into which, should the need arise, they might project their own minds en masse. As to . . .

. . . but Lollius! How it happened I will never know, but where it had undoubtedly been their intention to reach out from the dim past of 500,000,000 years ago to exchange a mind with my philosopher friend, well, the Great Race got me instead! To be a man, deep in silent contemplation the one minute – and in the next to find oneself inhabiting the body of some monstrous slug! The shock was tremendous, and were it not for the sheer stability of the shape of my new body I am sure I would have fallen over in a faint. There was no suggestion that this might be a dream or an hallucination; I knew immediately that it . . .

. . . to record the history of my own civilization, the Roman race, and in that instant I knew that I was the victim of a terrible mistake: I knew that Lollius Urbicus should be there in my place. But what to do? And what would become of me if these beings should suddenly discover that I was not the Roman philosopher they thought I was? I decided that for the moment I would attempt to bluff my way through, at least until I could see which way the . . .

. . . minds of divers races from every conceivable epoch of Earth time, and from hundreds of inhabited planets scattered throughout . . .

. . . conversed with the group-mind of members of a hybrid polyp race whose home world had been a moon of Mercury ages before it was drawn into the sun's destroying furnace; with the minds of two intelligent reptile creatures from dimly fabulous Valusia; with the utterly alien consciousness of a semi-vegetable entity whose hibernating body slumbered at the core of a vast comet which would not end its journey for ten million years, when at last its passenger would awaken. I talked with the mind of a Cimmerian chieftain, Crom-Ya, of prehistoric Northumberland; with that of Khephnes, an erudite Egyptian of the Fourteenth Dynasty; and with the mind of Wolfred Herman Freimann, who fought the Romans in the passes of the Teutoberger Wald. There were intelligences from . . .

. . . but that eventually . . .

. . . through me as easily as a windowpane. In a state of terrific apprehension I was taken before a council of scientists whose prime purpose and task was the correlation of the ages, the Masters of the Archives. And when they began to question me, then I knew that my problems were only just beginning. They wanted to know who I was and from which era of Earth's future. Then, when I answered, they desired to know how the mind of a man from the twentieth century could possibly have been drawn back from Roman Britain in the year 125 A.D.? . . . nothing else for it but to tell them of my travels through time and space in search of my own era, which I had fled in the face of insuperable adversity. And so . . .

. . . the time, during my examination, I was conscious of a kind of derision in the council members, frankly of their disbelief. Obviously they had made a great mistake, and plainly my story was one huge fabrication. Perhaps I was the philosopher they had sought, but the business of mind-transference had driven me insane. This was surely the only reasonable explanation, for even with all the technological advances the Great Race had made in the course of a million years of migration across the universe, not even they had discovered how to project their *bodies* through time, only their minds. How then could so rudely fashioned a being as myself have . . . and then built a machine with which to . . .

And that was when I broke in on them. I think I would rather be struck in the face than ridiculed, de Marigny, for . . . be made sport of by these vast intelligences, even knowing them to be incredibly superior intellectually to any man, was just too much to bear. I told them that I was not the builder of a machine for traveling through time, but that I had simply discovered the machine and learned its intricacies over many years. This interested them. What form did this machine take, they desired to know, and how had I discovered its use? And so I . . .

. . . such confusion! At first I couldn't understand it, but then it dawned on me that these mighty beings actually stood in awe of me! It had been when I mentioned

380

the hieroglyphs about the time-clock's face, and the weird sweep of its four hands. That was when they had started to sit up and listen. And no wonder, for . . .

'. . . of the Elder Gods themselves!' said their spokesman. 'If you have learned to use one of their devices, then you yourself are of their kin. Only the finest of minds are capable even of knowing of their existence. We know of them, and we are to them what microbes are to us.' Then this great cone-creature began to cast patently fearful glances all about the great auditorium in which I stood. 'They are all-seeing, all-knowing,' he told me. 'They may be watching all that happens here even now!'

And the idea of these tremendous beings trembling at the thought of being observed about their business by the Elder Gods, and thrown into a panic that perhaps in the transference of my mind they had erred against the will of those Elder Gods, made me quickly reply: 'Yes, they probably are, and I don't think they'll be at all happy about this!'

'But you should have mentioned this earlier!' the spokesman protested. 'You have been here for three days now, and – '

'Three days of my time wasted, of their time!' I shot back.

'Will you allow us to make amends?' the agitated being asked me. 'We will send you back to your rightful body immediately.'

And that was when a wonderful idea occurred to me, a frightening idea, too, for I wasn't at all sure that it could work. But it was at least worth a try. 'I do not wish to be transferred directly back to my body,' I told them. 'I want you to transfer my mind back to the time-clock!'

'But surely this time-clock you have mentioned is a machine, without the necessary – '

'It has a mind!' I cut in.

'And do you know its location, relative to your own at the time we interfered?'

'No, only that it was close, buried somewhere under the earth.'

There followed a hurried discussion among the council members. Finally the spokesman turned back to me. 'We can try, but you must help. Your mind can only – live – for so long unbodied. If between us we cannot find this machine of yours, then you will perish. I will explain.'

And he did explain. I was told that after the transference, if I wished to wander mentally and unrestricted by flesh in 125 A.D., then I could do so simply by willing it. I would be almost, well, a ghost. In the meantime my body's present inhabitant would be snatched back into his own body far in the past. This would leave my human shell empty, a husk of flesh without a will, without a mind or spirit. Gradually, then, my free-wandering mind would lose its ability to move of its own accord, and soon my body would die. If I could not find the clock, and if I did not get back to my body in time . . .

The body is the battery, you see, Henri? And the mind is the power. Without the power the battery is flat, dead. Without the battery the power must escape, dissipate. The dangers were . . .

. . . they would attempt in the interval of transference to find the mechanical mind that powered the time-clock, and then to enter my mind into it. That, too, was something they had never done before: inserting a mind alongside another in the same body. Looking back now I can see that the risks were enormous, but at . . .

. . . arrangements had been made and I was to . . . energy . . . projection . . .

# 6 Back to the Clock

. . . that obviously they had not been able to locate the clock. I was back in my own body, back where I started in the villa of Felicius Tetricus. I was in the old man's chambers and he was seated at a table writing. He looked up thoughtfully, and he looked right through me!

No sign of recognition, no glimmer to even hint of my presence showed on his face. Was he ill? 'Felicius,' I began, stepping forward, but I heard nothing, and instead of moving on my own two feet I seemed merely to drift! And in that instant I became aware that indeed I had no body! My mind was free, not clothed in flesh, and somewhere within this household my empty husk must even now be dying for want of a governing spirit!

. . . such mental panic . . .

. . . old physician entered with a powder for Felicius. The ex-senator looked up at him and said, 'Septimeus, have you seen Titus?'

'He went out to walk on the moors, I believe, Felicius. He has been strangely unsettled these past few days, as you know, but today he seemed much more his old self. He seemed, when I saw him, full of life and curiosity. He'll come to no harm.'

'Huh!' the master of the house grunted. 'Doubtless he's off to visit with that simpleton Urbicus. Can't understand what he sees in that fellow!'

Lollius Urbicus! Could it be that my body lay at his house? But that was some miles away. I must hurry! Unaccustomed to this unbodied condition of mine I moved toward the open door, and as I did so Septimeus stepped in my way. I passed through him before I could bring myself to stop! But I should have known it: a bodiless mind can know no barriers. Behind me as I passed out through the wall in the direction of Urbicus' place I heard Felicius say:

'You went quite white then, Septimeus. Is something wrong?'

And I heard the old physician's answer: 'I . . . it was as if someone stepped on my soul!'

Then I was on my way to the house of Lollius Urbicus, drifting in what seemed to me to be agonizing slowness over the moors toward the valley where his modest dwelling nestled. Worse than this frustrating inability to force myself to move faster, the thought came to me that indeed I was slowing down fractionally! What had that spokesman for the council of the Archives said to me? That if I did not return to my own body at once I would gradually lose my ability to move about? In a passion of frustration and dread, I finally came to the house of Lollius Urbicus, only to discover that he was not in, that I – or rather my body – was not there either!

Rapidly weakening now, or perhaps it was only my morbid imagination, I started back for . . .

. . . villa, I headed straight for Tetricus' chambers. There I found the old noble again in earnest conversation with Septimeus. 'Do you think it possible?' the ex-senator had asked at the moment I entered.

'It may well be,' replied Septimeus. 'And it would certainly explain his never-ending visits to Urbicus' place. The two of them would have to be in it together. The shrine was buried deep – I saw to that myself – but two of them working at it secretly could soon exhume it, I think. That is always assuming, of course, that they have discovered the shrine's burial place.'

Felicius' face darkened as he climbed to his feet. 'It would be most ungrateful of Titus,' he said. 'Come, gather

384

a few of the servants together: Thorpos and Valerius and a handful of others. We'll go, you and I, to where the shrine is buried. If they are there I shall be most angry!'

Was it possible? The clock and my body both . . . I followed the two Romans as close to heel as a dog as they quickly prepared for a visit to the buried shrine. But by then I knew indeed that my strength was failing. The power of my mind was dimming, waning, I had difficulty in concentrating. But I must . . .

. . . over the moors. We were only a handful – rather, they were only a handful, for of course I was less physically than a puff of wind – Felicius, Septimeus, Thorpos and four others. Mercifully I found that simply following them was comparatively easy. It required very little conscious effort on my part to allow their embodied spirits to draw mine after them; but I had to fight off a constant weariness now, the urge to simply fall asleep. I knew that this was a sleep from which I could never awaken!

. . . perhaps two miles. I knew the little valley, for it was a place I had often visited during walks . . . wonder that I had never guessed that here my clock lay hidden, for its tomb was deep in the heart of a hazel grove beside a small stream . . .

. . . dimly now, only very dimly aware that here I must . . .

. . . . Septimeus' voice, all shuddery, saying that if ever a place was haunted, this must surely be that place. And Felicius must have agreed, for even as my dying essence began to permeate the ground, sinking down into . . .

. . . sensed that the group was moving away, returning by an alternate route to the villa. But by then I did not care; nothing had meaning any longer. A great peace seemed to be falling over me like a cloak of darkness.

My spreading, disintegrating spirit sank ever slower

into soft earth, all sentience radiating outward and disappearing in abysses of disembodiment, drawn toward Earth-heart whose warmth is that of the cradle of all souls, and –

And however weak, however insignificant, something of the spirit of myself, some infinitely tiny particle of the intelligence of Titus Crow penetrated or was absorbed into the time-clock.

And simultaneously there came a pinprick of light in Stygian darkness, and an infinitely distant voice cried out to me: 'Titus, oh my Titus – let the clock help you! Only ask of it, seek out its being with your mind, even with a tiny spark of your mind. The clock is yours to command!' And as quickly as it came the voice was gone, leaving only . . .

. . . Tiania! And her voice crying out to me had awakened and aroused all that was left of life, even disembodied life, in me. 'Seek out its being,' she cried: 'the being of the clock, its mind, its psyche. Seek it out and command.' And I did!

The pinprick of light became a floodlight, a magnificent expanding beam of light and knowledge and reason that dispelled darkness and left my spirit whole, intact, with the clock once more mine to command more properly – but buried still! And somewhere my poor body lay, even now growing colder, colder, its capacity to support life dwindling, blood congealing, brain gelling . . .

. . . urgency gripped me, I . . . must be very loosely packed. The question remained: would my time-clock be able to surface, push the tons of earth above out of its way and . . .

. . . with the merest pressure of my mind! It must have seemed like an eruption. Tons of earth geysering to the sky, and the time-clock a lava-bomb that . . .

. . . had doubtless seen the aerial display, indeed were

386

even now staring up at me, or rather at the clock, as I flew my machine in a great circle, desperately scanning the whole area of moors for sight of my empty shell of a body. All of them gazed skyward, fear staring straight out of their faces, terror in the trembling arms they threw up before their eyes. All except Felicius himself who knelt, oblivious of all else, on a path that wound in gorse and heather. And beneath his hands and bowed head, hidden almost in the white folds of his flowing toga under which his shoulders moved in unmistakable emotion as he sobbed shamelessly – a motionless form!

. . . my body down there, and if Felicius and his party had not come across it first then I might . . . to set the clock down close by. All others fled, even Thorpos, save the Roman noble whose faith . . .

'. . . gave you back to me,' he said, 'that you are theirs to take away!' He turned to the clock and cried: 'Merciful and almighty shades, whose wisdom . . . eternal and dwell . . . but only give him life again . . . this shrine!'

What better time then to attempt what must now be attempted? If I succeeded, Felicius would be at peace in the belief that the shrine had taken me off again to the land of shades, and that he had been instrumental in his prayers for my deliverance from Earthly death and decay. And if I failed? But in any case, I had no time left to . . .

And so I once more left my body behind, although on this occasion it was a body fashioned of no woman's womb but the hands of alien gods of Eld. I projected my mind or psyche or what you will out through the portal of my vessel, which opened at my command, even though that was unnecessary, and into the still cold form of that flesh which had been Titus Crow.

Instantly I felt my body about me, like the shelter of a room entered out of a storm. Felicius immediately jerked his hands from me and I heard him gasp. I opened my eyes and looked at him, at which his jaw fell while his white crown of hair seemed to stand straight on his head. He staggered back from me as I climbed easily, smilingly to my feet. I marveled at this body T3RE had given me that life should spring so readily in organs which, by human standards, should surely already be falling into corruption!

'. . . no fear, Father mine, who has brought me back again from death's dark door that I may now return to the land of shades, there to live in peace and glory. But promise me this: that never more will you try to call me back from them whose shrine this is.' I turned toward the clock. 'And I . . . that you, too, will live out your span of years in peace and tranquility of mind and spirit, until you are called in your turn to the great beyond.'

Now I could not honestly say where the inspiration sprang from to use those exact words, but wherever . . .

For Felicius threw himself down before the clock to bathe a moment in its eerie rays, and as the door swung silently shut on me I heard him say, 'This I promise!'

It was only later, as I sailed the time-stream for home, that I thought to ponder . . . and of course I had known all along that Urbicus had been one and the same man as that author of *Frontier Garrison*, in which he had told his story from the viewpoint of . . . Only the fact that I had not wished to tamper with the past, and that . . .

. . . is it not written, among many other strange things, that there occurred in that year a mysterious volcanic eruption of soil and stones in the vicinity of a villa some five miles from Eboracum, which sent a cloud of dust and pebbles and soil almost half a mile into the air and shook the moors over an area of many miles?

It *is* written, de Marigny, and thus it was.

# 7 The Black Hole

So I had set course for the future, and this time I had
dared hope that my journey might not be long. Indeed, it
should not have been long, less than nineteen hundred
years! Never since leaving Blowne House to fall in ruins,
as Ithaqua's elementals of the air beat at the place with
their hurricane wings, had I been so close to my own age.
Nineteen hundred years? It was nothing! Had I not
journeyed through hundreds of millions of years of time,
traversing whole epochs as if they were mere minutes?
And had I not crossed limitless light-years in my venturings in the voids of space?

Ah, but Cthulhu and his hosts were also aware that I
was moving quickly toward journey's end, and it was not
part of their plan that I should succeed in returning to my
own time. Since they were in constant telepathic contact
with those vampires of time, the Tind'losi Hounds, and
since time was the element I must cross in order to regain
my own period, it would not be too difficult for them once
more to thwart my efforts. It was *not* difficult.

Of the Hounds themselves, one might almost be willing
to return to a belief in the so-called supernatural when
confronted with them; but since we know that there is a
supernatural, and that it is merely the phenomenon of an
alien science wherein mundane concepts hold little
water . . .

. . . were herding me, those nightmares, a great flock
of them and I was the only sheep. No unlikely analogy,
that, for it really was as though a multitude of wolves
chased one lone sheep, myself, and that soon they must
bring me down.

Forgotten now was any dream of returning to my own time; it would be sufficient to come out of this alive, my soul intact! It dawned on me that to escape them I might simply halt my clock's motion in time, but that might mean a crash such as I had known when pursued by the Hounds to the world of robots. They might be simply maneuvering me into just such a position again. Then I had not known that I might also fly my craft through solids, even through the hearts of suns, with impunity. Instead, knowing that I must crash I *had* crashed, for my mind was linked with the clock and I had instinctively ordered it to halt, literally to crash against the surface of the robot world. Now I knew differently, that I could have driven right through that planet if I had wanted to, but such belated knowledge had not helped me then.

And supposing that the Tind'losi Hounds had now arranged a similar surprise for me in the universe of three dimensions? No, not until it was absolutely necessary dared I . . .

. . . me utterly! Why, this was Tindalos – Tind'losi – itself! There, sailing the time-winds, doomed to the temporal mists of the fourth dimension just as the Flying Dutchman was doomed to sail the foggy seas of Earth, there was the ghost city; the black-spiraled citadel and seat of these disembodied vampires! They had driven me to their place, shepherding this frightened sheep to the slaughter; and out the butchers came to meet me, pouring from the dark turrets and black corkscrew towers of a city wandering in time. I have described them before, de Marigny, and you assure me that you yourself have seen them in monstrous dreams. Still, the memory is awful, even now!

What to do? How to avoid them, escape from them, when even now their flapping, pulsing, poisoned feelers sought me out through the fabric of the clock? Immaterial themselves, the substance of the clock's shell was no barrier to them. They came through it like, like ghosts through a solid wall. For of course they were ghosts, disembodied entities doomed to sail a city over the temporal tides!

They were the same black rags of yore: rags with glinting eyes, flapping threads of wings and groping, soul-sucking feelers. And now those feelers were upon me, in my mind, fastening on my soul, sapping my life as Arctic ice draws all feeling from flesh and leaving me quite as numb. And then Tiania's voice came to me as so often before. This time, however, she had no advice, could offer no succor but only add her own mental cries of horror to my own.

Weakening, feeling my life-strength sapped and dimming like the flame of a candle in a bell jar, suddenly I saw my chance. They had closed in on me, the Hounds, clustering to my coffin-ship like bats to the walls of a cave, but beyond them the void of time lay clear before me in one direction. In that direction rode dark Tind'losi itself, empty now of its hideous inhabitants, and so I used up what was left of my rapidly waning mental strength to ram my faltering craft in that direction, scattering the Hounds in a flurry of fluttering, chittering rags behind me. Straight for their damned city I drove, straight to its heart and out the other side like an arrow through misted cobwebs – and knew too late that yet again they had tricked me!

Driven to this point in time, trapped and on the point of being mentally devoured, I had seen one egress and had taken it, but the Hounds of Tindalos had left no egress! I knew it as soon as I felt that nameless power, that force that pulled the clock now faster and faster, against all my efforts to rein it back. But wait! This was a force that must exist over vast distances of time; surely it was so, for even now I was hurtling over the aeons. Did it also exist in three-dimensioned space? Dare I now stop the time-clock's temporal rushing, reverting back to those three dimensions of my natural heritage?

Shrieking their mental fear, helpless as moths caught in the candle's flame, a dozen rag-things which had thought to follow too close behind me whirled past, tumbling head over heels, as it were, in the grip of the same tremendous force that held me. If these beings that dwelt in time could not fight this awful attraction, then what chance did I stand?

I slowed the aeon-devouring flight of my vessel until it emerged into the mundane three dimensions, but not in any mundane place! For still the clock hurtled, not through time now but space, and yet drawn on by that same dread attraction. Faster and faster yet it plummeted, falling through space.

Falling? Gravity!

I was caught in a gravitational field of incredible force, which of course had extended in time as well as space. But in all my traveling in space I had never experienced this before; no sun, no giant star I had ever passed by in the clock had affected the course of that vessel of mine in the slightest degree. What, then, was the source of this enormous power?

The Hounds of Tindalos were gone now, left behind in time, their enforced habitat, their prison forever, and yet I saw that I was in no less a . . .

. . . Behind me the stars, shrinking in the awful voids of space; ahead of me an empty blackness, a midnight that grew as I plunged headlong down its throat of pitch. All my power over the time-clock seemed dead, departed, as if it had never been. I could move my vessel neither up nor down, left nor right, and all efforts to slow the clock in its rapidly accelerating rush were useless.

One by one the stars behind blinked out, until blackness stretched in all directions. I had passed into a region where it seemed as if light was bent back upon itself, a region of such ferocious gravitational attraction that nothing might escape its lunatic pull! As this thought passed in a twinkling through my mind I knew suddenly where I was, and I remembered that dream I had known so long ago. I remembered those words uttered by the Eminence as it sat upon its alcove throne behind curtains of crystal and pearl-mist:

'*If you cannot help him – if you fail – then you go down to the Black Hole with him!*'

The Black Hole! And now other memories flooded my mind: of scientific concepts and theories I had known in my own time, particularly the popular one of a black hole. The theory describes how a giant star, collapsing in upon itself to a tiny diameter, develops a density of billions of tons per cubic inch of matter; this incredible mass would exert a gravitational field from which not even light itself might escape!

That was a black hole, and here I plummeted headlong into one!

Already my velocity must be enormous! And now I began to feel the tremendous strain on the clock and my own mind and body. If I could only swing my vessel to one side of the center of this unthinkable attraction, use its speed, like the swing of a giant pendulum, to fling myself away into free space on the other side. The idea caught, was immediately rejected. I was grasping at straws and . . .

. . . ridiculous thought; why, plainly . . .

. . . twisting, distorting, the time-clock's very atomic pattern commenced an elongation, a liquid flowing apart, and I knew my being, my human body, must also be

393

subject to this horrid atomic viscosity. Was this the end, then? The clock's mental scanners were dimming – not that it mattered greatly for there was absolutely nothing to see outside the vessel's shell – but the symbiotic sensitivity of their feel was dying in my mind's eye. I was rapidly losing all control, all contact with my time-ship.

What use to fight any longer? Toward the end of this last trip together, the clock and I would simply spread out, become an almost two-dimensional rain of component chemicals falling still toward the gravitational center. We were doomed, the clock and I!

*'No, my love, my Titus, there is a way!'*

The voice of the goddess, and more than a mere voice this time: a presence, a spirit! 'A way?' I asked, hope springing eternal within me, even as time itself slowed down with my velocity. 'What way?'

*'You have not explored all the possibilities, my love. Kthanid has explained it to me: your vessel is not restricted to time and space alone.'* I could almost feel her marvelous green tresses against my cheek, her urgent lips against my ear.

'But how can I – I don't understand!'

*'You have taken control of the vessel with your mind. Its controls are in your mental grasp, but you have not yet mastered all of them!'*

'Other controls?' I answered. 'Yes, I believe there are other controls. But they are meaningless to me.' I could feel the time-clock spreading out about me, and the very atoms of my body with it. 'I don't understand the other controls, can't use them!'

*'The controls you do understand are useless to you here. Release them! Do it now, love, before it is too late. Then take possession of those unknown controls. It is the only way!'*

The only way! I released what remaining mental grip I had on the . . . she had said, could it be so? Had I been

394

merely taxiing a plane around the airfield, never once attempting to fly? . . . meaningless they might be, and their purposes . . .

And if I failed? Then the spirit of my goddess would go down to the Black Hole with me!

Freed now from those previous mental restrictions I had been imposing, the vessel sped faster still; wider its sundering atoms spaced themselves, and mine too. Desperately I sought to manipulate, activate those sections of the clock's complex psyche hitherto avoided. No good! My mind was human; this damned device, this impossible vehicle had been built by gods! And goddesses?

And then, knowing that I turned to her for help, she spoke to me again. And now she, too, was desperate: '*Not that way, Titus! There are dimensions other than the four you know. Do not try to draw back from the Black Hole, nor yet to circumvent it. Simply move . . . away from it!*'

At last I had the answer, and now I meshed myself deeper still into the clock's inhuman being. We were one again, the clock and I, and finally I recognized an escape route – no, a hundred escape routes *away* from the fiendish pull of the Black Hole. I chose one of them barely in time, melted into it!

Instantly the scanners opened like windows in my mind, affording me one fantastic, horrific glimpse outside the clock before I sent my vessel darting into yet another previously unsuspected alleyway between dimensions. For in that first there had been a blue ocean of light filled with drifting figures of rainbow hues and starkly geometric design; and in and about these aimless, helpless patterns ambitiously dark and slender cylinders had roved, snapping up the slower shapes as large fish devour small ones. My flight from that place is most easily explained: those black cylinders had been immediately aware of the clock, and even as it appeared among them they had darted in my direction!

Ah, but whatever they were, they could not follow me between dimensions!

Only then, emerging into that second parallel dimension, did I realize that my goddess had left me once more. I heard her beautiful voice, retreating in my mind, its telepathic echo bidding me farewell:

'*I go now. Kthanid sends me a Great Thought to guide my spirit home. Take care, my love, that we may be one in Elysia!*' And then she was gone. I sent my thanks silently after her, to follow her through what I guessed must be many eternities to her home in Elysia.

Now I could look about me at this new place, ready on the instant to slip away again between dimensions should danger threaten. But no, no danger here. Here I moved through vast orange spaces in which, afar, scarlet jewel stars twinkled against a background of red-tinged infinities. Flat disk-shapes with the diameters of worlds but no apparent thickness whatever, spun by; between them tiny, flat diamond shapes moved in obviously intelligent journeyings. A cluster of these diamonds were . . .

. . . this strange dimension, to a place which I hoped would be many light-years away from the monstrous Black Hole of my own universe. Only then would I dare make the trip back through the dimensional barriers, which my vessel penetrated like sunlight through shallow water.

When at last I fancied that . . .

. . . hopeless! . . .

. . . to starvation. Such was my hunger by then that I cared not a damn whether I set the clock down on an alien world in an alien time, or on some prehistoric . . .

. . . own longed-for universe of three dimensions, no,

four, for now I accepted time, too, as my element. And thus, no worse for my many ordeals, I . . .

. . . not Earth, however, nor had I the remotest idea in which direction my home planet lay. Still, there . . .

# 8 Of Alien Life-Forms

. . .hinted at . . . those many worlds of wonder I visited after leaving the Cretaceous . . . different again, with . . . tell you?

De Marigny, you know how there are creatures that dwell in the most inaccessible, inhospitable places above, on and under the Earth and in her oceans? I am talking about life-forms you can find in any handbook of zoology, as opposed to those fearsome beings of the Cthulhu Cycle with which we are now so familiar. Well, there are also creatures which exist in the most obscure and random corridors and corners of time, in lost and unthinkable abysses of space, and in certain other twilight places which are most easily explained by referring to them as junctions of forces neither temporal nor spatial, places which by all rights should only exist in the wildest imaginings of theoreticians and mathematicians.

. . . wonder how this can possibly be; one might as well ponder Hans Geisler's photographs of great burrowing bivalves which suck up sustenance from the aeon-deposited muck of the Taumotu Trench, six miles deep in the sea; or the microbes that thrive in the mud of boiling geysers. And if one considers . . . multiverse . . . impossible?

Suffice to say, then, that there are extreme forms of life within and without this universe of ours. And I know it to be so for I have seen or learned of many such forms.

For instance:

. . . intelligent energies in the heart of a giant alien sun who measure time in ratios of nuclear fission and space in unimaginable degrees of pressure! There are wraithlike biological gases which issue at the dark of their moon from the fissures of a fungoid world in Hydra, to dance away their brief lives until, exhausted, they die at dawn, scattering the sentient seeds of mushroom minds which will sprout and take root, and whose crevice-deep roots will in turn emit at the dark of the moon euphoric, spore-bearing mists of genesis.

There is a dying purple sun on Andromeda's rim whose rays support life on all seven of its planets. On the fourth planet there are exactly seventeen forms of life, or so it would appear. On closer inspection, however, a zoologist could tell you that these forms are all different phases of only one life-form! Consider the batrachian and lepidopterous cycles of Earth life and this might not seem too astonishing, until I tell you that of these seventeen phases two are as apparently inanimate mineral deposits, six are aquatic, two others amphibious, three land-dwelling cannibals, three more are aerial and the last is to all intents and purposes a plant while all of its preliminary stages (excluding the mineral phases) were animal! And to . . .

. . . the time-stream of a distant and utterly alien universe, a one-dimensional entity argues continually with its past and future selves on the improbability of space! And beyond . . . life as a terminal disease?. . .

. . . I mention all of these things, Henri, to help you in the first instance to understand the diversity and tenacity of life, but mainly as an introduction to what I . . .

NOTE: Here the contents of almost a complete tape have been lost.

ADM

## 9 The Lake of Doomed Souls

. . . Hyades, though I did not know that then. Indeed I knew nothing of the whereabouts of my present refuge, neither in time nor in space. When a man flees for his life in the dark he takes whatever route is open to him; he only looks before leaping if he has time. One thing I knew for certain, though: this was not Earth. Never in any period of our planet's prehistory that I know of has it looked like that! And God forbid it ever look that way in the future.

There were moons, Henri, strange moons whose orbits were about other moons as well as the parent planet, so that they seemed to circle or spiral across the sky. And the stars – they were black! I suppose, looking back on it now, that those things alone should have told me where I was, but my mind was so badly battered and bruised that I was hardly capable of knowing anything, merely of accepting. And one thing I accepted gratefully: for the nonce I was again free of Them, the vampires of time, the Tind'losi Hounds.

Well, I was exhausted and I slept. In that dreamless sleep, still ephemerally attached as my dormant mind was to the psyche of the clock, I knew that day had come and that a sun, or suns, had walked the sky, and that now night was once more upon this weird world. Surely enough, when I awakened I saw in the scanners that black stars hung again in the sky; the ashen moons were spiraling in sulfurous, ocher heavens.

I knew instinctively that I dared not leave my vessel, no, not for an instant, for the atmosphere of this world would kill me as surely as immersion in sulfuric acid. Not a comforting thought, that . . .

. . . of oppression. How may I describe it? It was a feeling as vague really as the dim and nighted landscape, and yet ominous.

Suddenly it came to me that I must not simply sit there waiting for something to happen. I knew, you see, that sooner or later something *would* happen. It was the type of feeling you get standing too close to the lip of a vast cliff gazing out over far horizons. No, not vertigo but rather a presentiment, the sudden realization of infinity and one's own insignificance, an awareness of the presence of vast powers. And even with the shadows lengthening grayly, then shortening, constantly and weirdly dividing and uniting under the spell of oddly orbiting moons, still I did not know where I was. Not even as I lifted my clock up and forward, to drift lazily over that pallid, alien, fog-masked landscape . . .

. . . that the milky fog now rolled like the waves of an ocean, a sea of undulating fumes white as the snowy domes of *Amanita phalloides*, and just as deadly, rising from some mordant sea. No, not a sea, a lake.

I saw it as my vessel passed into a region where the cloud-waves rolled less densely: a lake of murky depths the very sight of which, so still, without a ripple to stir its surface, tugged at the roots of memories that slumbered uneasily but would not waken.

A numbness was on my mind, Henri, engendered of unplumbed mysteries, mysteries not alone of the lake. That was only a part of it. I felt perhaps as a dying man feels in that moment before death; or as a baby before it is born; or a soul before it is reborn. Yes, this world, or more accurately this lake, might easily be the rebirthing place of souls – *or their graveyard*!

Ah, now I knew this place – as Alhazred knew it in the

desert, and Castaigne in New York; as Schrach, Tierney and others have known it – as every dreamer knows it at least once in life. And once is as much as most can bear, too much for many. Rearing in horror then above those depths, mentally lifting my coffin-clock up through an agonizingly leaden atmosphere, a succession of names and associations of half-remembered elder myths and monstrous legends flooded my mind.

I thought of Demhe and Hali, and knew it was the latter lying beneath me even as I rose slowly to the sky. I seemed to hear the songs Cassilda's dead voice sings, but knew them to be only the eerie ululations of someone, something else! I sensed the dread approach of the King in Yellow, knowing that his scalloped tatters still shrouded Yhtill; and, seeing a sudden swirl of mottled yellow far down near the milky shore of the lake, I knew also that my torpor had dissipated only just in time. Then, lifting higher and more freely, I saw behind that flapping yellow mote down on the shore the shadows of a moon, and behind those bloating fungi shades the jagged towers of lost Carcosa!

Then came the real horror, that which I had most feared. For rising up now behind me in that mordant lake from which, in the words of the poet, '. . . dreamers flee in nameless dread,' a great tentacle stretched, dripping bubbling acids as it lashed viciously in the wake of my fleeing vessel. It was a Cthulhoid tentacle, I knew, belonging to that prime evil's half-brother, the whistler of Cassilda's songs. Hastur had reached up from the depths of the prison Lake of Hali, sending a pseudopod to trap me but mercifully sending it too late!

Faster I climbed, completely free now of the morbid mental sloth that shortly before had held me in its languid arms, until red rays reached out to me from over the rim

401

of the prison planet and massive Aldebaran bathed my time-clock in the warmth of her ruddy light.

And now with the horror of Hali behind me, as I sped out into the Hyades, it dawned on me that indeed I was not far from the planet of my birth. Not far? No, a mere sixty-four light-years, but a moment of concentration. Ah, but in which direction? I was sure that my very rudimentary . . .

NOTE: At this point another lengthy part of the narrative, consisting of a third of a spool of tape, is lost.

ADM

# 10 Atlantis

. . . Sidney-Fryer's translations from the Atlantean of Atlantarion? Man, I was there when they were written in the original! In that same period, something like fifteen thousand years ago, I saw the foundering of Atlantis. Saw it? I was very nearly part of it . . .

. . . awesome cataclysm, de Marigny! It saw the end of a land, of a people, of an era – the end of a period of poets who knew the true meaning of beauty, whose like can never be known again. I may say that of all . . .

NOTE: Here the break in the narrative is not so extensive, and my opinion is that the lost matter is not of great importance. In any case the narrative from this point on is more or less complete.

# 11 Outside!

. . . that at last they had succeeded in hounding me into a place of utmost evil. I sensed it in the same instant that I passed between incomprehensibly layered zones of hyper-space-time into that other place. There had been a sudden, short-lived blast of mental exultation, of fiendish delight, from the pursuing Hounds; their echoes seemed to follow me as I slipped sideways away from those fluttering, chittering rag-things into that parallel dimension. And their unholy . . . anticipation, warned me that here . . . something which, while it must be allied to the Tind'losi Hounds in hideous purpose, in the overall alliance of evil forces, even they stood in awe . . . A power so monstrous that . . .

. . . dread; I had heard again as so often before Tiania's voice crying in my mind. And oh, the hopelessness that rang in that beautiful telepathic voice before it, too, was cut off:

'*Not there, my love. I cannot follow you or help you there. I cannot even penetrate the veil in Kthanid's crystal! Not even a Great Thought can follow you there, and there is no returning from –*

'*No, Titus! NO!*' . . .

. . . could not stay here, and yet I could not leave!

It had been contrived that I might place myself in a region from which I could not escape; and once again, in fear and loathing of the Hounds of Tindalos, I had obligingly done just that. But what else could I have done?

Desperately now I sought to plumb those depths of my vessel's psyche wherein I knew lay the controls to open the gates between dimensions, those same controls I had manipulated to break through into this place, as I had used them to escape the Black Hole and other horrors. But now they were . . . gone! There was only an emptiness where they had been.

And outside, exterior to the clock, there stretched an infinite darkness. No stars hung in that all-embracing wall of seemingly solid jet. It was comprised of a blackness without the tiniest glimmer of illumination, as if suddenly I had been plunged into the heart of some titanic block of black marble, and yet not like that. For black may be defined as a color and this was an absence of color, an absolute absence of light. No, it was more even than that: it was the absence of everything. It came to me that there was quite literally nothing beyond the walls of my vessel, neither time nor space. This time I had gone – *away* – from everything; the time-clock – and I had quite literally moved *outside*!

Why, I asked myself, should these restrictions suddenly have been placed on the clock's previously unlimited capabilities? My vessel was now like an ocean-going liner confined to port, and an alien port at that. Desperately I attempted to burrow even deeper into the time-clock's . . .

. . . perceived that there was something out there after all, a movement, a disturbance in the darkness far away. This impression came to me through the clock's fantastically sensitive scanners. There being nothing else in that whole immense blackness to detect, the scanners had finally sought out this most distant disturbance to bring to my attention. But in this I was made aware of several other things, namely: if the source of the disturbance was distant, then this place did not have an absence of space. Therefore, since it is an irrefutable law that space and time go hand in hand, time also existed here. And yet I knew somehow that this was a very different space, a very different time, a space-time continuum like no other.

The realization was instantaneous and went no further than that, for now the disturbance was closer, growing, seething in the scanners, its outlines beginning to make themselves clearer. For another instant I gaped, then drove my vessel away from the thing as it grew with fantastic speed from a distant amoeba outlined in eerie blue radiance to a spreading blot that put out groping, bubbling pseudopods. And along these pseudopods the thing seemed to shoot itself toward me, reminding me of some hideous octopus with its quick, jerky movements. But by then I knew that it was no octopus. I knew exactly what it was and where I was.

A different space, a different time – different because of an alien juxtaposition to nature – a place utterly outside nature, synthetic, manufactured! A dimension parallel with all four mundane dimensions but impinging on none of them, 'coexistent with all time and conterminous in all space' but locked outside nevertheless, behind barriers only the Elder Gods might construct. But barriers constructed to enclose what?

What else but that soul-symbol of most abysmal evil, that father of darkness, that frothing, liquescent, blasphemous shapelessness that masks its true horror behind a congeries of iridescent globes and bubbles; that primal slime seething forever 'beyond the nethermost angles', the Lurker at the Threshold – the noxious Yog-Sothoth!

I knew then that I was dead, de Marigny, finished, that already my life was used up and that all I had aspired to must come to nothing. My soul was lead within me, plumbing the very depths of despair, for there I was face to face with a being whose only peer in monstrousness is dread Cthulhu himself.

Face to face? Yes, despite the fact that I had in the

405

previous instant driven my vessel away from the thing! Certainly, for how might one escape a being who is conterminous in all space? I had no sooner hurled my craft in a direction away from that frothing obscenity than I found myself rushing toward him as he placed himself in my path! Time was no refuge either, for flinging my clock madly into the future I found the horror already waiting for me – no, rushing with me along the time-stream – and always, inexorably, drawing closer to me!

To and fro in space, forward and back in time. And through all of that silent, nightmare rush my hurtling vessel's scanners sought to obtain for me a clearer picture of the thing lurking behind those protoplasmic bubbles and globes. I caught insane glimpses of a purplish blue mass: a titanic primal jelly of wriggling ropes, bulging eyes and tossing, convulsing pseudopods and mouths . . . a super-sentient but nevertheless ultra-evil anemone from the deepest seas of screaming nightmare!

Closer still the horror came, while my attempts to avoid it grew ever more frenzied, ever more useless. Forward and back in time I plunged, then further back yet; to and fro and around and about in space. Faster and ever faster the pace grew, and closer the looming horror of Yog-Sothoth. All of those lightning mental reflexes built into me by T3RE were being taxed to their very limits, strained to the breaking point as I flung the clock through space and time in ever more intricate four-dimensional patterns. And through all of this those myriad bulging eyes of the monster stared and lusted. Its convulsing mouths drooled and chomped vacuously, and the mass of its throbbing body loomed over the clock as if to enclose it within some unmentionable amoeba.

It was hideous, indescribably hideous! Then suddenly, driven almost to insanity, gibbering and clawing at my hair in an attempt to force my mind to react faster and faster yet to the perils of that impossible chase, finally it happened. I drove my time-clock in two directions at one and the same time!

Impossible? Fantastic? Even I did not immediately understand. I, too, believed it impossible, believed that I had finally gone mad. Even now I do not completely understand the how of it, but I think I know the why:

I was hemmed in by Yog-Sothoth in space, enclosed in time. Driven finally to a frenzy of mental agitation surpassing any state of mind I had ever known before, torn between a number of choices of directions in which to flee, I had chosen two simultaneously. And I had hurled both the clock and myself in *both* of them! And wonder of wonders, the Lurker at the Threshold could only follow me in one! Bemused as I flashed both forward and back in time, Yog-Sothoth paused, and I took that chance to allow the split psyches of the clock and myself to flow back together again.

But in that last statement perhaps I mislead you. I brought the two materializations of man and vessel back into one phase, yes, and in so doing I repaired that rent I had made in the fabric of infinity; but the reparation was almost involuntary. It was simply a correction of something I knew could not be, made the instant after realizing that it could be and was. In any event, I then found myself free of the lord of that black demesne, but not for long.

The breathing space I had given myself, however short, was at least time in which to consider the implications of the foregoing phenomenon. Now, you must understand, Henri: it was not as if I had been two men in that brief instant of split personality. No, I had been one man, thinking as one man, reacting as one man, but existing in two places! A difficult concept even for me, but in that concept lay the seeds of my salvation.

If I could move in two temporal directions at once, into

407

both past and future simultaneously – is that a contradiction of terms? – could I also remain in the present simultaneously? Could I, in the present, move here and there simultaneously? And similarly in the future, and in the past? If this vessel of mine existed, however hypothetically, everywhere and everywhen, couldn't I with the application of my human psyche and superhuman mind – for indeed T3RE had given me a superhuman mind – be able to make the time-clock physically omnipresent?

I know what you are thinking, Henri, that only the gods are capable of such things. But didn't gods, the Elder Gods, build this craft of mine? Think of it: here was Yog-Sothoth, a prime member of the Ancient Ones, a being with the ability to reach any given location in the space-time of his own dimension almost instantaneously, but not several locations simultaneously! Only I had that ability, and in that I had the monster's measure.

Now, doubtless recovered from his initial surprise, he was coming for me again, walking the black voids on his pseudopod arms like some thinking slug of space. Well, if he wanted Titus Crow so badly he would have him! *He would have one million Titus Crows, and each and every one of them capable of a further million branchings, enough to fill this entire dimension end to end and top to bottom – a superabundance of Titus Crows!*

Throwing all caution to the wind then, uncaring of what cosmic calamities might accompany my next action, I achieved an instant and complete psychic meshing with my vessel. I became a sort of superhuman polyp as I commenced to divide in that instant, subdivide and divide again in all my manifestations to a point not far short of infinite. I became one mind governing a billion materializations, one psyche with the omnipresent awareness of a billion psyches. And in the next instant of time – the next few millions of years of time; for of course I had spread my materializations through all of Yog-Sothoth's time-dimension – a number of things happened.

First, the Lurker at the Threshold curled up on himself, writhing horribly and visibly shrinking. His telepathic anguish filled me with a mental agony that was almost physical. Yog-Sothoth was mortally afraid! Confronted with an enigma as unthinkable as this, I yet found myself capable of compassion. More than that even, I felt a tearing, sickening, intensely burning empathy for the horror, exactly like that which I had known as a small boy when a friend of mine poured salt on a snail!

Second, even as I realized that the devastating explosion of my myriad manifestations had torn a gaping hole in the fabric of Yog-Sothoth's prison dimension, so a voice called to me from the other side of that awesome gap. The mental voice I had heard before in what I had taken to be dreams. I recognized the voice of the being in the great alcove behind the enigmatic drapes in the hall of crystal: Kthanid, guardian of my own guardian angel! *'This way, born of woman, you, Titus Crow. You have opened the gate, now come through it!'*

And finally, drawing back my own and the clock's countless identities into the one original id, into one body, one vessel, I flew as bidden out through that fantastic rent from which issued now a beam of purest light – that same beam you saw me use against the Wind-Walker, Henri, or at least a beam issuing from a similar source. This ray, so pure and dazzling white as to strike physically, like a solid shaft, flashed over and beyond my darting vessel at something behind me. In my scanner I saw Yog-Sothoth, bloated again to his former titanic loathesomeness, rushing to escape his interminable punishment. He fell back, stricken as the beam hit him. And as he fell the portal I had torn in his prison wall slammed shut again, closing on him and locking him in as securely as ever.

All of these things happened, Henri, and one more thing. It was simply that flooding my entire being there came the realization that at last I was one with the Elder Gods, a lost sheep returned to the fold, a wanderer come home.

*Home to Elysia!*

# PART FIVE

# 1
# *Elysia*
## *(From de Marigny's recordings)*

The voice of Kthanid, a supreme being, had called me from vile vortices of nether-existence to Elysia, a true garden of heaven! Elysia was home of the Elder Gods – of which Kthanid doubtless was one – and home, too, of the goddess whose telepathic guidance had succored me through a score of danger-fraught situations.

Elysia is not a planet, or if so it is the most tremendous colossus among worlds. There was, for example, no horizon that I ever saw. Even from on high I could testify to no visible curvature of the surface below me in the great misted distances. There were beautiful mountains, between and behind whose peaks the spires and columns of delicate cities clustered. Beyond those golden balconies and fretted crystal balustrades silver rivers and lakes tinkled; and far and away behind all this, misted by distance, yet more mountains thrust upward – and yet more fairy cities sparkled afar – but no horizon! Instead distance vanished in a pearly haze beneath skies that were high and blue. Flying machines soared or hovered in those skies or simply hung motionless. And through tufted drifting clouds golden creatures like benign, majestic dragons pulsed on wings of ivory and leather.

Some of these dragons were harnessed and bore proud riders through dizzy heights of air, riders whose scales or feathers or crests or iridescent skins set them aside from mere humanity, or rather, set them in a higher mold. These were the Elder Gods themselves, or their minions, and not one of them displayed the slightest interest in my time-clock as I passed between them now on an arrow-straight course beyond an emerald ocean toward the steep spires of blue mountains.

Completely numb from head to foot – awash with awe and wonder and pinching myself to make sure this whole experience was not simply some fantastic dream – I made no motion, no mental effort to check the flight of the clock as it rushed out of the utter blackness of Yog-Sothoth's realm into this place. And yet now I perceived that I passed at a very leisurely pace over fields of green and gold, and dizzy aerial roadways that spread unsupported spans city to city like the gossamer threads of a spider's web.

How could this be? How was it that while I had made no conscious effort to slow the clock we yet paced the skies so steadily? I reached mental fingers into my vessel's motor areas, its psyche or mind, and recoiled as a sort of slow, frozen electrical charge burned me! The time-clock rejecting me? I tried again, but to no avail. My machine, my time-clock, did not want to know me now, not at this exact moment of time. I knew instinctively then that I must not interfere, must make no attempt to pilot the clock or guide its course. Nevertheless, out of sheer human stubbornness, I tried yet a third time – only to meet a blank mental wall. I was no longer master but passenger, shut out of the engine room, not even allowed on the bridge.

T3RE's words came back to me in that moment: 'You have a great journey before you, you and your time-clock . . . he has told me it is so . . .' My clock had been like some lean hound, lost and wandering alone. I had found him, befriended him. We had roved and adventured together and now, by accident, we had come into his homeland. He knew and recognized the place. No use my hand on the leash, for he scented the hearth of home. If I tried too hard to curb him then he might turn on me, for even now his mistress called him.

His mistress . . . and perhaps mine?

Slowly the scanners dimmed. All my connections with the time-clock were breaking now, each joining thread parting. Now I was simply a man in a box, alone in the deepening darkness.

My last glimpse of Elysia before the scanners went completely blank was of the blue mountain spires, much closer now, lifting up to pierce cotton clouds. Then the darkness was complete and I was journeying blindly toward an unknown destiny in an alien, beautiful world.

After some little time I felt the slightest jolt as the clock came to a halt, and almost immediately the door before me swung open on a corridor that stretched away into softly silver distances. A corridor lined with . . . with time-clocks, just like my own!

No, not quite like mine. Certainly they were machines governed by a similar principle – the clocklike faces with their strangely erratic, twin-paired hands and curious hieroglyphs were ample proof of that. But these machines, the majority of them at least, were designed for forms other than those of men. There were some identical in every respect to that clock of mine, which I had mistakenly believed to be unique, but of the rest . . .

There were machines of silver and gold, others of glass or crystal, some of stone or at least of a material indistinguishable from stone, and at least one of a delicate bronze wire mesh. Some were quite tiny, no more than seven or eight inches in height; others were wide and tall, towering a fantastic thirty feet or more toward the glowing ceiling of the vast corridor. I could not help but wonder what sort of creatures might have need of these latter machines.

Then, as I gazed along the corridor of clocks, I saw that

I was not alone. Moving toward me strode a plumed, bird-headed being whose saucer eyes regarded me with an ancient intelligence. Costumed in a cloak of gold and wearing padlike sandals of golden mesh on his clawed bird feet, he drew close and paused to address me in softly clucking, inquiring tones in answer to which I could only shake my head. Rapidly then and with many a gesture the bird-man tried several different tongues on me, all without avail. His demeanor, despite his utterly alien aspect, was the very soul of polite friendliness. Eventually, after listening to a long sequence of hissing cachinnations, I said, 'It's no use. I'm afraid I don't understand a word you're saying.'

'Ah!' he replied at once. 'Then you'll be the Earthman Tiania is expecting. Stupid of me, I should have known at once, but it's been a long, long time since a man of Earth was here in Elysia. Let me introduce myself. I am Esch, Master Linguist of the Dchichis and adept in all known tongues, including the electric hum of the D'horna-ahn Energies. Whenever I meet up with a stranger I take the opportunity to practice my art. Right now, though, I am off to Atha-Atha VII to learn the language of the sea-sloth. Perhaps we'll meet again. Do excuse me.'

He turned to a globular clock whose base resembled, not surprisingly, the woven bowl of a metal nest and was about to enter when, as if on an afterthought, he turned and added, 'Oh, but I almost forgot. A lithard is waiting for you outside, sent by Tiania.'

'A lithard? Outside?' I answered uncertainly, staring about me. 'Thank you.' I began to take a tentative step in the direction from which the bird-man had approached.

'No, no, no!' he called out. 'I walk only for the exercise. You have no need of exercise.' He quite openly admired my muscular torso, then cocked his head on one side and gave a piercing whistle from his ridged beak. 'There we

are. Now just you wait a moment and your lithard will
come for you.'

'But – '

'*Auf Wiedersehen! Au revoir! Saph-ess isaph!*' he chir-
ruped, waving a vestigial wing and entering into the nest-
shaped clock. The machine immediately faded and disappeared from view.

Again I was alone in the corridor of clocks, but not for
long. At first the sound was a mere – susurration, a
murmur as of small winds or the sound of a distant ocean
in a conch's sounding coil, but in a twinkling it grew to a
regular throbbing, a beating of great wings. My lithard
was coming for me!

To my left the corridor stretched into softly silvery
distances as before; to my right a mote danced afar in the
air between the glowing ceiling and the floor of the
corridor, passing above the receding rows of space-time
machines. Rapidly the mote grew to a shape, a winged
outline preceded by outstretched head and neck. Just as
quickly I began to feel the air stir on my cheek as the
dragon – for the moment I could only think of the creature
as such – flew toward me with a majestic beating of its
great wings. A moment more and it alighted before me
on the floor of the corridor, a living fragment from one of
Earth's oldest mythologies. Here was the green and
golden dragon of the Tung-gat tapestries, a beast such as
might play in the Gardens of Rak! There it stood,
*Tyrannosaurus rex* with leather wings and serpentine
neck, a *draco* out of the Asian hinterlands but magnified
many times over, and all of a natural green and gilt
iridescence. It was harnessed in black leather where neck
joined body with a saddle of hammered silver and reins
of spun gold!

The massive lizard head towered high above me while
huge eyes observed me, then a great rear leg bent to

415

lower the creature's bulk, forming two scaly steps each half the height of a man. Amazingly, with a dull rumble, the creature spoke: 'Tituth, Tituth Crow! Tiania ith waiting.'

A lisping lizard! A . . . lithard! Could this possibly be the source of the naming of such creatures? I doubted it, but laughed nevertheless at the thought. There was no malice in my laugh, however, and as if it knew my thoughts the huge beast before me laughed too, throwing its head back on its scaled neck and booming until I thought the high ceiling must surely come down on us both.

When the creature was quiet I reached up and patted its great head, gazing in wonder into the huge black eyes. For a moment longer we studied one another, man and dragon, and then the lithard began again: 'Tiania ith – '

'I know, I know!' I cried. 'She's waiting for me.' Then, with all my senses dizzy and rushing, almost as if I was half drunk on the wine of pure joy, I put all other thoughts aside but those of the goddess. Leaping on my mount's knee, and from there to the ridged back where I swung easily into the saddle, I cried: 'Lead on, my scaly friend!'

The great head turned to regard me more soberly. 'Thcaly friend named Oth-Neth!'

'Bravo, Oth-Neth!' I slapped the great neck. 'Now take me to your mistress.' And mountain of flesh that he was, he stretched his great wings and we lifted up, impossibly light as a feather, and I gripped the reins hard as the corridor of clocks began to speed by beneath me . . .

The corridor of clocks stretched away and away, but before long Oth-Neth turned and flew into a side shaft that rose at about thirty degrees and at right angles away from the silvery main corridor until it emerged from the subterranean place into daylight. I had not been dreaming when I flew the time-clock – or rather when it flew me – over the fields and aerial roads and cities of færie Elysia. The same fantastic view now spread below me as before. Behind us were the blue mountains, in the heart of which lay the corridor of clocks, and before us the vast and splendid landscape of a world of opium dreams! A fragrant wind whipped my hair and lifted my soul to heights rarely if ever experienced before.

A sudden thought came to me and I stood up in my saddle to stretch myself out along the ridged neck of my mount. I shouted into one of Oth-Neth's tiny ears: 'Oth-Neth, I fear I'm hardly in any fit state for audience with Tiania!'

My hair was long and unkempt; my beard was wild and uneven; my naked body, while brown from the rays of several suns, was not nearly as clean as I would have liked it. Oth-Neth turned his head slightly and rolled back a great eye. 'Do you with to bathe?' He wrinkled a nostril. 'You thmelly?'

'Yes, I think I am rather . . . smelly, and I would love to bathe,' I answered him, somewhat abashed at his more or less accurate perceptions. 'And perhaps clothes . . .?'

But now the dragon seemed uncertain. The beat of his wings became fractionally less steady, then stilled completely as he drew them back and fell forward into a breathtaking, gliding swoop.

'You would bathe . . . thoon?' he asked. 'Before we get to houththold of Tiania?'

'Yes, before we get to the household of Tiania,' I answered.

'Then there ith only . . . lithard pool. If that will do, I altho bathe. Later . . . bring you robeth.'

'That will do very nicely,' I told him, wondering what, exactly, the lithard pool could be but not wanting to appear ignorant.

'Good!' he seemed greatly relieved. He turned one wing into the wind, pulled his head up and transformed his dive into a circling, soaring climb that took us up, up to the cotton clouds and through them. Then he turned his head slightly to ask inquiringly: 'Do you fear . . . the high platheth?'

'No, I'm firm enough in the saddle.'

'And do you like . . . thpeed?'

I thrilled to the idea of riding a speeding dragon through the skies of an unknown world. 'I love speed!'

He blinked his great eyes. 'Tiania, too, like fly . . . fatht!' And with that his wings stretched out and back, doubling the speed of their beating in a moment. In but another moment we were caught up in a thermal current that whipped us faster and faster along dizzy paths of upper air in a thrilling, nerve-tingling ride that I wished might go on forever!

All too soon, however, it was over. Then we plunged down, down through the clouds and between the higher spires of a scarlet city, then down again toward a distant glittering blue patch in fields of green. The patch soon became a lake – the lithard pool.

Young dragons splashed in the shallows of glittering waters under the watchful eyes of warty matrons, while farther out more mature creatures raced above and below the surface, to and fro, with wings folded back almost in the manner of Earth's penguins. Occasionally they would leap up from depths near the center of the lake to burst fully into view in rainbow cascades of water that caught the warm sunlight and scattered it. Then they would spread their wings to climb high before plummeting again to the cool pool below. This then was the lithard pool, a lake of sporting dragons!

We settled in the shallows where Oth-Neth put down his great hind legs and spread his wings across the surface of the pool. All the younger lithards backed away to stand watching us. Their eyes were saucer-wide and, among the very young ones, a little frightened. In a matter of seconds all the excited activity of the pool had died down and all lithard eyes were upon us. Only the matrons politely turned their backs on my nakedness.

'What's wrong?' I questioned Oth-Neth. 'Is something . . .'

'Very rarely,' he answered, 'do mathterth bathe . . . in lithard pool.'

'Is it taboo, then?' I asked. As a stranger in Elysia I hardly wished to go against the grain.

'Not taboo, but . . .'

'You mean the masters frown upon it?'

'Not mathterth . . . lithardth!'

'But you didn't mention this be – '

'For you,' he cut me off, 'ith different.' Then he lifted up his voice and boomed deafeningly across the pool what must have been some sort of explanation of my presence. I caught only the name 'Tiania' in all he said. By the time the echoes of that dragon-cry had died away, however, the play was on again in full swing, and some of the younger lithards splashed over to us as I slid from Oth-Neth's saddle into the blue crystal waters.

One of these young ones, big as myself, covered with a soft velvet leather the color of marble, kept pace with me as I slipped easily into the motions of a powerful crawl. Closer he came, eyeing me intently, then he dived down beneath me to lift me up bodily sprawled across his neck. High out of the water he tossed me, letting me fall back with a splash. Indignant, I rose to the surface, only to find the bawling infant undergoing a thorough booming tirade from a vast and blotchy matron.

'No, no!' I cried at once. 'He was only having fun.' Oth-Neth, paddling over like some gorgeously painted

Loch Ness monster, translated loudly. From out near the center of the pool there came a noisy and concerted booming from an audience of more mature lithards.

'They approve of you . . . Tituth Crow!' Oth-Neth informed me. 'Now you bathe. I go . . . fetch robes.' Without another word he sank down into deeper waters, to emerge a moment or two later in a breathtaking fountain of spray. His great wings unfolded in the air and he was off, lifting ponderously at first, then more certainly, finally climbing to the sky and disappearing in tufted clouds and rosy sunlight.

So there I was, left alone for the duration to the tender mercies of the strange lithards, and never could I have imagined that to bathe in a pool of dragons might be such wonderful sport! No sooner had Oth-Neth taken his departure than a pair of young beasts came to me from the middle of the lake, hoisting me up out of the water and bearing me bodily to where a host of adult males and females splashed and cavorted. I became the ball in a game of catch, but such was the gentleness of the friendly lithards that I received not even the smallest bruise.

Then, tiring of hurling me through the air one to another, they formed a floating bridge of arched necks along which I ran, while one of them splashed and boomed after me in the water, trying to dislodge me from each successive scaly perch. Finally slipping from a great neck, I swam to the bottom of the pool, staying there for many minutes to study the decorative beds of freshwater oysters with their huge black pearls. As I rose in a slow spiral to the surface, two young adults grabbed me. They were males, booming in turn what were obviously questions, in answer to which I could only shake my head. A pity that all the lithards were not versed, like Oth-Neth, in English.

Then one of the lithards thrust his head beneath the

surface of the lake, whipping it out an instant later to display bulging eyes and panting, lolling tongue. He repeated this performance, but on the second occasion when he withdrew his head he plainly suffered no discomfort whatever. The whole thing had been a mime and now I knew the creature's meaning: he had asked me whether or not I found any difficulty in staying under water for long periods. In answer I allowed myself to sink slowly down into crystal depths, tickling scaly legs and staying down until my two new friends came after me. For this was one of the benefits of having a custom-built body, as it were. I needed lungs only for talking, and who wants to talk under water?

Plainly the two young lithards wanted me to follow them when they set off down toward the deepest part of the lake, their great rear legs sending them speeding into silent fathoms. Then, when they noticed how far behind they were leaving me – their speed was quite phenomenal – they circled back to grab me with their small forelegs and carry me effortlessly along between them. Down we went, down to depths I had not suspected, and in through a sunken portal whose interior was lit with a mother-of-pearl radiance. This glowing light apparently sprang from shoals of tiny organisms that swam in that entryway, luminous clouds that parted like opening curtains to allow us access to the mysteries beyond.

Deeper still we swam, through waters strangely warm and growing warmer, until suddenly the narrow neck of the channel opened into a great cave. There we surfaced, emerging into air in a cavern whose domed ceiling, adorned with sparkling stalactites, covered an area of what must have been at least an acre. Globes of artificial light hung near the ceiling, invisibly suspended in the air, sending down a dappling of green and mauve rays to give the place an appearance of soft contours and quiet, submarine shades.

We emerged from the pool onto a wide shelf where rested several matrons whose task, I soon saw, was the tending of hundreds of huge eggs – dragonspawn! The eggs rested in rows in hollows all along the sandy shelf, each perfect oval perhaps nine inches long and each one beautifully speckled in blue and gold. Under the watchful eyes of the matrons my lithard friends guided me down a path between the rows of eggs. Soon we stopped where the two dragons crouched to admire a pair of gold-flecked ovals, their subdued and reverent booming hinting to me that they must be the respective fathers of these hatch-lings-to-be. After a minute or two of what seemed to me rather proud and boastful booming together, nevertheless undertaken in lowered tones, my friends indicated that it was time to go. I kneeled to touch the speckled surfaces of the eggs just once, to feel their smoothness, then the lithards led the way back past the matrons and again we entered the water, returning through the narrow neck of the cave to the surface of the lake.

Spying Oth-Neth on the far bank, I first said farewell to my new friends and then swam over to him. While drying myself in the sun I told the lithard what I had seen below the lake.

'You thingularly honored,' he answered. 'The Cave of Hope . . . it ith for lithardth alone!'

'The Cave of Hope?'

'Yeth. Not many eggth hatch. Elythia ith not Thak'r-Yon. Thak'r-Yon . . . home world.'

'Then why are you here?'

'Thak'r-Yon gone . . . ecthplode when thun nova. Elder Godth have pity on lithardth. Bring here. But Elythia ith not Thak'r-Yon.'

When I was dry at last, Oth-Neth handed me a pair of

soft boots, dark silk trousers straight out of the Arabian Nights, and a light cloak of some golden material whose wide fastenings crossed my body to buckle into the belt of my trousers. The collar of the cloak was decorated with large brass studs inset with black buttons. Oth-Neth explained the purpose of these studs: they were antigravity devices by means of which the wearer of the cloak might control himself in marvelous flight. Then the dragon pointed out similar studs and buttons set in his own harness. within reach of his short forelegs.

'All lithardth fly with . . . antigrav. The Elder Godth gave . . . when they brought uth from doomed Thak'r-Yon. Thak'r-Yon had low grav. But you try cloak . . . later. Now, Tiania ith waiting.'

'But my beard.' I tugged at the untidy growth. 'And my hair. I was never very vain, but to appear before a goddess . . .'

'Ah, yeth. Forgot,' he replied, drawing from his harness pouch a small jar of cream and a silver comb. The cream was a most efficient depilatory; my face was soon clean and smooth and I was able to set about combing the knots and tangles out of my hair. Finally, and before I could stop him, Oth-Neth produced a tiny spray and liberally doused me with a faint, not unpleasant perfume.

As I jumped into the saddle I said, 'Well, if I wasn't "thmelly" before I most certainly am now!' At which Oth-Neth threw back his head and boomed jovially. He sobered quickly.

'One more thing,' he said. 'Tiania not goddeth but . . . one of Chothen.'

'The Chosen?'

'Chothen of the Godth!' Then, and without a single further word, the great lithard stroked the row of studs set in his harness and bounded into the sky in a fanning of leather wings.

# 2

## *Tiania*

*(From de Marigny's recordings)*

There are times in a man's life, no matter what previous wonders he has known, when the feeling comes that everything is a dream and he must pinch himself to wake up. I had known this feeling before, when faced with horrors too grotesque to be real – though they were! – and again on a number of occasions when realization of marvels beyond words had suddenly burst upon me.

Now it was this dragon-ride of mine toward a destiny I knew had called me all the days of my life – the feel of my healthy, strong body, alive and burning bright, seated in the saddle of a fabulous beast snatched straight out of Chinese mythology; a journey more fantastic than dreams themselves. I was actually riding a dragon through the skies of an alien world, enroute to the household of Tiania, Chosen of the Gods in her sky-floating, garden-girt castle high in the cotton clouds of Elysia!

Down below, the fields formed a giant patchwork quilt on which some child of the djinni had thrown his toy cities of crystal, with yellow and silver ribbons for roads and bright pieces of broken mirrors for lakes and pools. I laughed with the heady exhilaration of it all, and Oth-Neth laughed too, baring his teeth and booming into the tiny clouds that flew apart at the unspoken command of his thrumming wings.

Then ahead I spied an island in the sky. It was literally that, an island, a massive slab of rough rock floating in a sea of air. It looked for all the world as if it had just crashed down from some titanic cliff in space, except that its topside was planted with lush grass, trees and flowers,

424

and its precipitous edges were walled and grown with orchid-sprouting creepers. And set back in a garden of fountains and pools, where strange lilies exhaled exotic perfumes, there rose a granite-walled, wide-windowed ornamental castle. Sweet-smelling stables stood at the rear, close by a clover field in which a group of sated dragons slumbered in the shade of mighty trees. The household of Tiania. A world of its own that looked down upon Elysia even as the great soaring birds of the upper air look down upon the fields and cities of Earth.

We alighted first on a cobbled path before the outer walls; with a single bound Oth-Neth carried me in beneath a high archway, coming to a halt in a tiny courtyard. Trembling suddenly, filled with emotions and passions that blazed within me as they never blazed in my Earth-youth, I got down from Oth-Neth's back and stood waiting . . . I knew not what for. Intricately wrought and inscribed glass doors stood open in the granite face of the inner wall; beyond them a maze of mosaic-adorned rooms strewn with cushions glowed in the beams of sunlight striking through a thousand tiny crystal windows all set about the wider casements.

With a sudden snort of impatience and a toss of his dragon's head, Oth-Neth thrust me awkwardly forward. Numb though my legs felt, at least I found them answering my commands, sufficiently to allow me to walk in through the glass doors to the maze of mosaic rooms. Behind me the doors silently closed; one by one the crystal windows, large and small, glowed, then turned opaque; from somewhere a chiming music as of færie bells and sighing strings faintly sounded. Now the light grew dim, until quite suddenly the vaulted ceiling glowed with a fluorescence which, while faint, seemed to act upon and fill the maze of rooms with sparkling wineglass translucency.

I stood still, not daring to move lest I ruin the magic by

my intrusion. Gradually the mosaics of the walls faded to be replaced by perfect mirror surfaces in which a thousand images of myself were reflected. Vain as it may seem now to say it, I was not displeased with the looks of these myriad caped giants. Then, even as I stared at the mirror images of myself, suddenly I was not alone. The image of Tiania – a thousand images – gossamer-clad and supple as willow-wands, appeared beside my own.

The sight was enough to burn the retina like a naked sun, containing a beauty to destroy a man's sight forever. At the very least it would make him an addict, drawn forever to seek the purest bliss of such sheer unbelievable beauty, or driven to the dark oblivion of suicide in its absence. A thousand Tianias, but which one was real? Every fiber of my body, my soul and even, I thought, that mechanical heart of mine, ached.

I held out my arms. 'Tiania, which of these dreams is really you?'

'This one,' her warm, trembling voice answered. Then her cool arms were suddenly about me and her eyes, in which I knew I could happily drown, gazed gorgeously into mine. No man of flesh and blood could ever withstand so tremendous an assault on his senses; I made no attempt to but instantly bent to kiss her.

Quickly she put delicately tapered, trembling hands to my lips. Her eyes were wide; her face, even as mine, full of wonder. 'Titus Crow . . . do you love me?'

'Tiania,' I answered, or perhaps my soul answered for me, 'I have loved you forever . . .'

To this day I cannot recall that first kiss. I remember that before we drew apart in mutual wonder the maze of rooms had darkened again, and that Tiania's eyes were veiled jewels in the darkness. Their fire was finally put out beneath fluttering lashes. For a moment we stood like that, until she almost seemed to faint against me. All about us then, as I fiercely caught her up and she as fiercely responded. the færie music swelled to match the beat of incensed pulses . . .

Thus Tiania became mine, and she will remain mine forever.

The morning was synthetic, prepared by the castle itself under instruction from its mistress, for there is no night in Elysia. Gradually the crystal windows lightened, as if dawn glowed beyond them, and slowly the maze of rooms and their mosaic walls began to take on form in the darkness. The twittering of small birds filtered into the castle from the ivied walls outside.

I cannot really say whether I was asleep or not when Tiania's absence impressed itself on me; most likely I was in that half-world between dream and waking. I roused myself. dressed as full daylight returned to the maze of interconnecting rooms and made my way to the open glass doors. In the courtyard a spiderlike creature of roughly human proportions but with an abundance of hairy legs and other appendages moved swiftly, almost nervously about. It was armed with an arsenal of brooms and brushes, dusting, sweeping, polishing the hard cobbles and whistling to itself what sounded like a thoroughly human tune.

Despite the fact that the creature was obviously harmless. a member of Tiania's household, nevertheless I found a certain disturbing similarity between it and certain of the robots on T3RE's world. This was surely, I told myself, only the thing's spindly-leggedness. As I watched, a second spider twitched rapidly into view from around the curve of the castle wall and made straight for the glass doors where I stood. It paused in patent confusion when I made no move to get out of its way.

427

'Er, excuse me,' I said, smiling in what I was sure must be a very foolish fashion. 'Where is Tiania?'

It whistled questioningly, the antennae above its soft brown eyes trembling in peculiar agitation. Then the pitch of its whistling fell. 'Tiania?' it repeated in fluting tones. 'Bathing.' It made to get by me but I stood my ground.

'Bathing, you say? Where is she bathing?'

'Lithard pool,' the spider answered. Then, after a further moment of indecision, it gently but firmly picked me up in surprisingly strong arms to set me down again on one side and out of its way. It shuffled about nervously, awkwardly, peered at me wonderingly and gradually resumed its whistling. Then, as if I no longer existed, apparently satisfied that it had done the right thing, the spider twitched on past me into the maze of rooms within the castle. In another second, in addition to its whistling, I could hear the sounds of its sweeping and brushing as it moved rapidly through the rooms. After that I paid these curious menials no further attention, except to get out of their way when they were busy!

Tiania had told me about Elysia's constant day during our long 'night'. Elysia's dwellings incorporate marvelously intricate computers which make special mornings, evenings or nights to order for their owners. Depending on the worlds of origin of their inhabitants, the dwellings also work all kinds of atmospheric wonders; together with an unlimited combination of special lighting effects and weather conditioning, the homes can be programmed to suit every mood and need. Still, I was surprised and it registered as a shock when I saw that the 'sun' stood as always at its zenith.

Then, shielding my eyes against the orb's brightness, I saw a speck rapidly growing larger among fleecy cotton clouds, and shortly the speck became the outline of Oth-Neth with the glowing form of Tiania on his back. Her wonderful hair, catching the wind, billowed about her shoulders where she stretched out full length along the dragon's neck. As they circled high above the courtyard I could hear her laughter and the joyous booming of her mount. She was clad in a garment that glowed with faint mother-of-pearl, with huge bell-bottoms at her sandaled feet, a top that left her arms and shoulders bare, and a wide belt of silver glowing about her waist. As Oth-Neth commenced hovering above the courtyard like some enormous hawk in the sunlight, she stood up on his neck and put her hands to her belt where the buckle would be – then stepped free of the lithard into thin air!

Down she plummeted like a falling arrow, feet first, her emerald hair a meteorite's tail streaming green fire up from her head. Horrified, I rushed forward, holding up my arms to catch her, knowing that from so extreme a height she must surely kill herself and probably me too. At the last instant I closed my eyes, certain she would smash me down onto the freshly cleaned cobbles of the courtyard. Instead there came only her beautiful voice in worried inquiry, and from on high the beat of great wings and a familiar but questioning booming. As I opened my eyes in disbelief she settled into my arms gentle as a feather.

'Titus, your face . . .' She put the palms of her hands to my temples. 'Are you ill?'

'No,' I answered, realization beginning to dawn, remembering what Oth-Neth had told me about the use of antigravity. I lifted her up and gently shook her. 'I'm not ill, just terribly angry!'

'But why?'

I folded her into my arms. 'I thought you would kill yourself!'

'Surely Oth-Neth told you of the devices we use to – '

'Yes, but I had never seen one used, except by Oth-Neth, and that was different. I certainly wasn't thinking of such devices when I saw you step from his back.'

'And you really feared for me?'

I lifted her up above me again, so that she looked quizzically down at me, wide-eyed. 'I've only just found you,' I told her. 'But I don't ever want to lose you!'

'You will never lose me, Titus,' she answered quickly, excitedly. 'We are one now and none may put us asunder. While I bathed Oth-Neth went to see Kthanid far in the frostlands. He sends us his blessing and says that when you have seen Elysia we are to go to him. Kthanid it was who first told me of you; indeed, it was he – '

'Who promised me to you?' I finished for her, smiling.

Her sweet mouth fell open. 'But how do you know that?'

'Oh,' I teased, 'I know many things. Simple Earthman I may be but – '

She laughed at me and kissed me as I put her down. 'No, Titus, Simple Earthman you are *not*!' she said. 'But still you don't know everything!'

I asked her meaning but she shook her head. 'No time now to bother with all that. You shall know later. But this . . . evening' – she formed the word carefully, unused to its sound in a world where natural evenings did not exist – 'many friends of mine are coming to meet you and eat with us. Before then I must show you how to use your flying cloak, and I will need to talk to the computer to ensure that the . . . evening is perfect. So much to do. First you must learn to fly!'

And so I learned to fly! Tiania showed me how I must cross my hands over my chest in front of me, like an Egyptian mummy in his sarcophagus, to reach the buttons set in their brass studs in the harness of my cloak. And she taught me which buttons and combinations of buttons to press in order to achieve elevation, lateral and transverse flight and many other more awkward maneuvers of aerial agility that might have taxed the dexterity of a fly. Because I reveled in this new art I learned quickly, and at last Tiania decided I knew enough to allow me to fly with her over the precipitous edge of her sky-floating island. I took the initiative to speed like an arrow before her, while Oth-Neth hurtled after us and boomed his approval as we tumbled through the sky like human bats in a fantastic game of tag.

Then, as I turned sharply to speed beneath the sky-floating island itself, I heard Tiania's cry of warning and slowed until she flashed up beside me. 'Careful, Titus! See there.' She turned on her side to point out for me a series of vast brass disks, at least a dozen of them, set in the rough rock base of the floating island. Each disk had a black center like an iris, and central in each of the irises was a luminous area that sent a slim white ray of light earthward. These beams soon petered out, but they were plainly visible where they issued from the luminous areas.

'Oh, yes!' Tiania told me later, as we sat beside a fountain. 'The antigravity power which the disks exert is so powerful that to fly into a ray too close to its source would be to die instantly, flattened in a moment and hurled to the fields of Elysia far, far below.' She sipped iced wine from a tiny glass. 'Those engines are tremendously powerful. Just think, they float my entire island here in the air as if it were a feather!'

And then, towards 'evening', Tiania took me with her to the center of the maze of rooms and showed me the computer that governed the life of her castle in the sky. It was quite different from anything I might have expected: a gadget like a large microphone beneath which Tiania sat while she spoke her commands out loud. She explained that really there was no need for her to speak

431

at all but she wanted me to hear what kind of evening she had in mind for our party. Her orders would have been understood and carried out had she merely sat still and thought them to the machine. The device could obey instructions no matter what sort of creature used it, for telepathy knows no distinction between races, creeds or species. Thought is thought.

The evening was to be exotic. No, that simply would not do to describe it. It would be fantastic! Twin moons, one gold, the other silver, would sail the night sky while small warm winds would play all about the castle. Stars as big as a man's fist, so close one might try to pluck them from the firmament, would seem to light up the sky with their twinklings, and meteorites would blaze like fireworks as they fell down from the heavens. Music would play softly in the background, the most beautiful tunes of a hundred worlds, and there would be dancing and singing and good things to eat and drink until 'morning', which would be equally fantastic. The party would go on all through the synthetic night.

When Tiania was finally satisfied, she stood up from beneath the programming device and I took hold of her hands. 'It will go on all night?' I smilingly asked.

'Yes,' she answered brightly, then noticed the look in my eyes and blushed. 'But when our friends have gone then we shall have another night, a long one, to enjoy together. But you must not listen when I tell the castle's computer the arrangements for that night!'

And so we bathed in an indoor pool, dressed and went to the walls to watch for the arrival of our guests. If anything, these arrivals were more fantastic than both the evening to come and the morning put together. First came members of that bird race of linguists, the Dchichis, a member of which, Esch, had been the first being to greet me in

432

Elysia. Next came a tiny couple that I thought to be small children when I first saw them flying afar. They arrived completely naked and alone, without the aid of dragons or antigravity belts. Only when they actually alighted beside us was I able to see that they themselves were winged, with twin-paired gossamer membranes that gleamed all the rainbow's hues before the little people folded them down along their backs. Then, too, I saw that they resembled insects more than anything else, with slender bodies and limbs and softly furred faces that smiled and blushed as Tiania greeted them warmly, introduced me and then directed them to the castle.

Next came a terrifically tall manlike being in a cape that covered him in fiery mesh from his neck to his feet, if he had any; he climbed up the winds of night to us, Tiania declared, using powers of levitation generated by his mind alone. He was Ardatha Ell, a white wizard from demon-doomed Pu-Tha, who had made his way to Elysia alone. He greeted us in a deep, sonorous voice which, while I studied him intently, I could swear did not issue from his pale lips but yet was not telepathic in the sense that I understood telepathy.

And so they came, creatures and beings from all the worlds of fantasy that a man might ever dream, and all of them plainly loved the woman, the girl, the goddess whose heart was mine. There were two hundred of them, per-haps more, none of them of the Elder Gods proper but all of them chosen ones, Chosen of the Gods. And there were some among them who, like Tiania herself, were very nearly human and yet more than human: beautiful creatures so delicate of form and feature, so exotic in styles and mannerisms, but yet radiating over all such auras of purest love, like Tiania, that they transcended mere humanity.

Of that computerized night, of the party itself and the

wonders and mysteries I saw and had explained to me, I will not even attempt descriptions. It is enough to say that despite their various, vastly differing forms and origins, despite the fact that of those who had tongues only a very few of them spoke languages I could understand, despite their coming to Elysia from all the ends of time and space, still a camaraderie of joy and friendship existed between all of them. It existed and grew through the long night, including myself as few friendships have ever included me during a lifetime on Earth. In the utter absence of fear and hate there can only be joy and love!

And so the night, long as it was, came and went. Time flew by and the most beautiful morning I ever saw grew into day, until finally our guests departed. I sorrowed when they went until, as she had promised, Tiania made another night for us, beside which all the beauty and wonder of the last paled to insignificance . . .

# 3
## World of Wonder

*(From de Marigny's recordings)*

All too soon came the time when, perhaps sensing a germ of restlessness in me, Tiania took me away from her castle in the sky to see Elysia. What little I knew of the home of the Elder Gods was the merest fraction of an amazing total. Tiania told me that if I lived a thousand years and traveled Elysia far and wide I could never behold half of her wonders.

Indeed our travels occupied us for quite a long period. Often we stayed at the houses, castles, nests – on one occasion a hive – of Tiania's friends; at other times we flew back to the castle in the sky. Sometimes we rode Oth-Neth, when there were places and people the dragon particularly wanted to visit. And yet despite the never-ending marvels, the incredible scope and beauty of that world of wonder, always there nagged at the back of my mind an uneasy feeling of frustration. In all truth I was not sure . . . I did not *know* what the nagging feeling was.

How could one know frustration in Elysia, where all of a man's dreams might come true and all fears are put away, dispelled in the atmosphere of well-being that the Elder Gods themselves radiate? And yet there was this worry that I had left something undone, something very important. And just as a forgotten word sits for hours on the tip of one's tongue, so that inchoate thing lurked at the edge of my mind, slipping away whenever I attempted to focus on it.

No, it was not really frustration. Guilt, then? But of what could I possibly deem myself guilty? Had the Elder Gods themselves not found me worthy? Had not Kthanid, the Eminence in the Hall of Crystal and Pearl, bestowed his blessing upon Tiania and her Earthman? No, it was not guilt. What it was of course eventually dawned on me – perhaps I knew it all along but simply did not wish to recognize it, hence my feelings of guilt and frustration – but by then the remedy for this peculiar uneasiness of soul had already been decided.

That, however, is all away from the point. I have seen Elysia; I will now attempt, with totally inadequate words, to describe some of that world's wonders.

There is, for instance, the vast and aerial city of the Dchichis, an aerie of lava crags and spires honeycombed with burrows, silk-lined nests and communal incubators. But if that sounds like some rather grand and elevated North Sea bird sanctuary do not be misled: this island city floats many miles in the sky above Elysia, held aloft by enormous antigravity disks. Its nests are no less comfortable and well appointed than the rooms of Tiania's own castle, and its denizens, Esch's people, are more civilized and sophisticated than any race of Earth ever was or will be. The Dchichi hatchlings, even in their shells, commence learning the arts and sciences – particularly the tongues, the linguistic and other modes of conversation and communication – of dozens of the races and civilizations of an eternally expanding universe. The adults are fearless voyagers in space and time, seekers after knowledge in the fullest meaning of the words.

I saw and was awed at the sight of the Thousand Sealed Doors of the N'hlathi, hibernating centipedes whose slumbers have already lasted for five thousand years and will not be broken for as long again. These great circular slabs of magnificently inscribed basalt, where they line the feet of the Purple Mountain in the Vale of Dreams, are thirty feet in diameter and barred with massive bands of a white metal that no caustic liquid may ever corrode. They are the portals to the burrows of the dreaming N'hlathi, who sleep until the great pale poppies bloom again on the slopes of the Purple Mountains. Only then will they emerge from their deep cavern sanctums, for their food is the seed of the giant poppy which blooms every ten thousand years and then, like the N'hlathi themselves, falls once more into centuried hibernation. And none in Elysia save the Elder Gods remember the ways of these cryptogenic slumberers at the roots of the Purple Mountains, for theirs is a history that was never written and their tongue has never been understood. Not even the Dchichis, whose greatest linguists and calligraphers regularly convene in the Vale of Dreams to ponder the inscriptions of the Thousand Sealed Doors, have been able to decipher their mysteries.

In the mountain-girt Gardens of Nymarrah, Tiania took me to meet the Tree. By then I no longer questioned her with regard to the denizens of Elysia, nor about other matters which had initially bothered me, though certainly there were many questions I could have asked. I had discovered that it was far simpler to wait and see; the answers invariably presented themselves in their own time.

The Tree was a very special friend of Tiania's. She had played in his branches as a child, when he stood to the west of the Gardens of Nymarrah, and had visited him often during his slow journey east. Now he stood in the center of the Gardens, a towering emerald giant twelve hundred feet tall. He had a classical brandy-glass shape, all beautiful yard-long leaves of lush green, with creeper-like tendrils hanging in festoons beneath the branches, and ridged brown bark a foot thick. Serene, silent and sentient!

437

The trunk of this titan must have been all of one hundred and fifty feet through and through, and as Tiania and I approached him, walking barefoot and hand in hand through knee-deep grasses, the outer branches sighed and bent down and the soft furry edges of giant leaves touched us. At the same instant I felt a thrill of strange awareness deep in my every fiber. A question had been asked, had passed from one living, thinking being to others, but as yet the empathy between the Tree and myself was incomplete. Tiania, on the other hand, had known the Tree all her life.

'It is I!' she cried at once, answering the Tree's question. She darted forward into the shade of massive branches and beneath suddenly mobile tendrils, pressing herself to the rough bark of the great bole and spreading her arms wide as if to encompass that massive girth. 'It is Tiania!'

Should a man be jealous of a tree? No, not even a tree as magnificent as this one. Tiania turned and took my hand as I approached the trunk less hastily. She spoke, but not to me: 'This is Titus, my Earthman.'

Again the Tree sighed and tendrils like slender snakes tentatively brushed Tiania's waist, then wrapped themselves about her. I was watching this so intently that I did not notice the second group of tendrils until I actually felt the first fumblings at my waist. With a startled cry I pulled back against the Tree's touch, and instantly the tendrils sprang away and the leaves above my head furled in on themselves and drew back.

'No, no, Titus. That is not the way,' Tiania chided. 'The Tree loves me, he loves all living things in Elysia and would love you, too, but you must not frighten him!'

Frighten him? I looked up into dim distances of receding green, dappled here and there by soft sunlight penetrating from outside, where shafts of gold showed a myriad scented motes dancing in the air. Beneath one tree, I stood in the green heart of a forest!

'Frighten him?' I asked out loud.

'Certainly. He is very shy.'

'I meant no harm, no discourtesy, but . . .'

'Then you must think of him as a person in his own right, like Oth-Neth or Esch, not just a tree. He is *the* Tree, and he is a very beautiful person!'

Well, no doubt about that last. He was quite beautiful, and indeed as I had pulled away from his tendrils, I had felt in the thrilling energies that filled me a sensation of . . . hurt? So what was wrong with me? I could happily mesh my mind with a machine, the time-clock; feel comradeship toward a robot, T3RE; laugh and swim with dragons and ride one across alien skies. And yet now, this living, thinking – yes, person – shrank from me.

I reached to stroke the edge of a leaf where it curled uncertainly above my head and with my mind I said, '*You are very, very beautiful, and if you love Tiania then love me also for we are one*.'

A sigh that grew into a great soughing of branches filled the Tree as he reached down his tendril arms to lift us up in joy into his midst, swinging us high like bobbins on threads and passing us tendril to tendril all the way up his fantastic length. It was breathtaking, and more so for the fact that now the Tree's empathic aura, its radiations of emotion, were reaching me.

And all the Tree knew or was interested in was beauty! Beauty poured from the titan's soul, enveloping all, swelling out to set the very air trembling in sympathetic joy. And in the center of all that wonder Tiania and I were rushed dizzyingly aloft to finally perch in the topmost branches, there to listen to the Tree's songs of love and joy and beauty.

Peering through those highest branches and leaves,

439

almost a quarter of a mile above Elysia's soil, I could see a wide gray path away to the west. The great path seemed to lead arrow-straight to the Tree, drawn as if by a ruler, except that this ruler would have to be many miles long. As the Tree's songs finally died away in a vast sighing, I knew suddenly what that great swath of dry sandy soil was: nothing less than the track the Tree had made in his long journey from the west.

'Yes,' Tiania told me when I asked her, 'you are right. The Tree leans almost imperceptibly to the east; he sends out new roots in that direction. To the west, where the soil is dead, there the old roots die. And so the Tree turns himself, ever so slowly, and turning he moves forward. As the new roots turn to the west they grow old. And always the Tree leans toward the east, moving and turning, turning and moving, ever so slowly. He calls it his dance. Such is his size that he requires much nourishment. The earth he feeds in is dead and dry when he moves on, and he sorrows for the dead earth he leaves behind him. But he sorrows rarely and usually only when he is alone. When people visit him, then he fills out with joy.'

As she finished speaking I saw that there were tears in her eyes. I took her in my arms. 'Tiania, why do you cry?'

'The Tree tells me,' she answered, 'that there is a sadness in you. I have known you were restless but did not think it must come so soon.'

'A sadness in me?' I was astonished. 'You did not think it would come so soon? I don't understand, Tiania. What do you mean?'

She threw her arms around me and sobbed openly on my shoulder. 'You do not even know, my love, you have not realized it; but Kthanid said it might be so. You searched so long and hard for your Earth before you found Elysia, that you still – '

440

'*No!*' I denied it, angrily shaking my head.

She pushed me away and sprang to her feet on the naked branch high above the Gardens of Nymarrah and her hands flew to her belt. 'There must be no pain here . . . the Tree . . .' And drawing back from me as fresh tears flooded her eyes, she flew out through the leaves and was gone.

'Tiania!' Rising in anger – angry because I knew that she was right, and yet still not understanding, or not wanting to understand – I rose to leap after her. The Tree immediately cast quivering tendrils about me, holding me fast. All the fibers of my soul read the Tree's message, which was love, and a great sadness filled me.

'I love you,' the Tree told me, 'and I love Tiania. She loves you, and you . . .?'

'I love her, too,' I answered, 'and always will, but she is right. For a little while at least I must leave Elysia!'

And then I sat down again in that high place and the Tree stroked me with the furry edge of a great leaf and sang songs to my innermost being, songs as sad as my troubled soul, which would not have been soothed by all the joy in Elysia . . .

And so we went to Kthanid, the Elder God who was Tiania's guardian. His palace of crystal and mother-of-pearl lay in the heart of a glacier, in a region where the sun shone far off, as if it were about to sink down behind Elysia and disappear. Warmly wrapped we went, in furs and boots, riding a gravity-defying vessel of silver whose curved crystal screen kept the biting cold from us.

We approached Kthanid's demesne from the sea, across an expanse of blue ocean where icebergs sailed majestic and serene. There, far ahead and glittering in the rays of the distant sun, Tiania pointed out the vast and eternal glacier whose heart housed Kthanid's palace. It was a solitary place, as are all the seats of the Elder Gods, where Kthanid might ponder whichever problems he desired or do whatever he wished in peace eternal.

'I will ask him,' she told me as we flew in through the crevasse that guarded the entrance to the ice-enveloped palace, 'if I may not go with you to your Earth. Perhaps it is possible that – '

'Even if he agreed,' I cut her off, 'I would not take you. There are terrors in the voids of space and time that you must never know face to face. You have risked too much for me already.'

As we alighted from the flying machine at the head of a series of magnificent ice steps she stamped her booted feet, and not, I thought, solely because of the cold we could now feel biting through our furs. 'Are you so soon bored with me then, Titus Crow?'

'Little one,' I told her, my own anger rising, 'Kthanid's palace or not, and him your guardian and all, if you once more hint that I could ever find boredom in your arms – or you in mine, for that matter – then you'll go across my knee! Why, girl, I – '

But she was crying, and if ever a sight was designed to bend, to break my heart, then it was the sight of Tiania in grief. Comforting her while the tears froze on her cheeks, I pulled her furs closer and picked her up in my arms to carry her down the first sweeping flight of ice-hewn steps. Above us the crevasse walls swept up to meet in a splendid arch of icicles, which looked for all the world like the roof of some titanic ice-beast's gaping mouth, but soon this entranceway had dwindled to a mere triangle of light at our rear.

Finally, after descending many flights of the steps cut in ice and arriving at the foot of that tremendous staircase, I saw that we had reached the polished bedrock of the mountain ravine. An ice tunnel, its granite floor worn smooth by centuries of glaciation, stretched away into the heart of the glacier. Sweeping along this passage there came strange and exotic scents the like of which I had never known before, all carried by a warm breeze. It blew upon the face of the now drowsy girl in my arms and caused her to stir. She kissed me, which told me that all was well, and I placed her gently on her own feet. Then, with my arm around her waist, we continued.

As the distance we covered increased, so did the warmth. We soon shrugged off our robes and proceeded clad only in the accustomed dress of Elysia's warmer climes. I would have flown but Tiania stopped me, saying that mortals should show humility in the presence of the gods.

We walked another mile or so until quite suddenly the dim blue light grew brighter, as if here a great source of illumination was hidden behind the soft sheen of ice walls. Then those walls themselves became granite and finally we arrived at a hanging curtain of crystal beads and pearls threaded on gold. Such was the number of golden threads thus adorned that the curtain was quite thick; in width it extended right across the tunnel. Even so, each individual thread of that precious veil was fine enough to allow the whole curtain to move in the warm draft that issued from its hidden side.

'The throne room of Kthanid,' Tiania told me, 'whose wisdom is unequaled and unchallenged among all the Elder Gods!' She parted the curtain and held it open for me, beckoning me to enter. I slipped through the opening . . . into a scene remembered from my dreams!

For of course this was the Hall of Crystal and Pearl, the Palace of the Eminence, the inner sanctum wherein a great being thought Great Thoughts upon its throne in a curtained alcove! It was here that I had stood beside an anguished, frightened girl/woman/goddess who had not known I was present, to watch myself hurtling down to the Black Hole in the time-clock. But while that had been a dream – or at best a vision engendered of some aeon-spanning telepathic empathy between Tiania and myself – this was real, here, now! My mind reeled in the grip of fantastic paradoxes.

Standing just within the curtain, Tiania at my side, I gazed dry-mouthed all around me. I recognized the tremendous hall, with its weird angles and proportions and high-arched ceiling, the titan-paved floor of massive hexagonal flags and the ornate columns rising to support high balconies that seemed obscured in a haze of rose quartz. Everywhere were the remembered white, pink and blood hues of multicolored crystal, even the vast scarlet cushion with its centerpiece that resembled nothing so much as a huge, milky crystal ball. Everything was as I remembered it . . .

No, not quite. There were two things, at least, that were new to me. One of these was that the walls, where they rose up on all sides from the flagged floor, had a regular series of tunnels cut into them. These passageways were similar to the pearl- and crystal-draped shaft which Tiania and I had just used to enter into this great cathedral of a hall. No use, I supposed, to wonder where these tunnels led. The other difference did not become noticeable until Tiania led me to the center of the hall, where the vast silken cushion lay. From there a great wide trail of what looked like jewel-dust was quite conspicuous. It led from the cushion to the huge and curtained alcove wherein I knew the Eminence stirred even now.

This brilliantly twinkling path was at least fifty feet wide, and I felt strangely uneasy just looking at it. It was like –

'Kthanid has been using the viewer,' Tiania told me, her eyes, too, turned to the twinkling path. And I knew then that I had been right: that the jeweled track between the silken cushion and the curtained alcove was nothing less than the – dare I say it? – snail-trail of the Eminence, and my uneasiness returned twofold.

# 4

## Kthanid

### (From de Marigny's recordings)

No sooner had the outré realization dawned on me – that
I stood now truly in the presence of a being strange and
mighty almost beyond the imaginings of the world of men
I had left behind – than the curtains of the great alcove
billowed slightly in response to a hidden inner movement.
And then Kthanid's awesome mental voice spoke in our
minds, addressing Tiania but not shutting me out:

*'So, child, it is as I said it would be: for a while you must
lose your Earthman. But I have looked into the viewer on
times to come, and though the possible futures are many I
have seen that all the factors that guide probability point to
his return. However, since you yourself do not appear in any
of this man's most immediate tomorrows, you will not
accompany him but wait in Elysia until he returns.'*

'But why may I not go with him, Kthanid?' she cried.
'Perhaps you have not seen all the possible futures in the
viewer; perhaps if he stays a little longer in Elysia the
futures will change, and – '

*'I have not seen all of the possible futures, no, for that
itself is impossible – as you well know, Tiania. And no use
to argue, child, Titus Crow may not stay longer. Indeed,
he sets forth in a very short time to return to his Earth.
Even now his machine is being readied. I have seen to it
that a weapon is fitted, by possession of which during his
journey he need not so greatly fear the minions of evil,
though certainly they will yet attempt to lure him astray
from his path. Indeed, even equipped with the weapon, his
return to Earth will not be an easy one . . . When the
machine is ready, it will come for him.*

446

'Now I would speak to Titus Crow alone. Tiania, play with the viewer and find yourself a joyous future to look upon in its depths while we talk, for there are many questions your man would have answers to, and time grows short.

'You, Titus Crow, come and stand by the curtains and I will tell you the things you need to know.'

'But, Kthanid – ' Tiania started forward, and immediately her figure stiffened, then as quickly relaxed again. The contrary frown on her face fell away and she smiled, turning to step up onto the scarlet cushion and throw herself down in its center, head on hands to gaze into the swirling, milky depths of the crystal ball.

It seemed to me that in my mind I heard a sigh, then Kthanid's mental voice saying: 'She is only a girl, yet more than a woman. I delight in her for she is of my own flesh. Now come to the curtains.'

And so I walked the space between cushion and alcove, noticing as I did so that the massive flags of the floor were blank now, that the brilliant track which had told so elegantly of Kthanid's passing this way had faded and disappeared. I stopped and waited at the softly billowing curtains, almost hypnotized by the reflected luster of scintillant points of light and color. At once the voice of the Eminence came again:

'Yes, you have been patient and there is much you desire to know. There is much that you should know and little time for the telling. We who are known as Elder Gods, however, have a way of communicating many things in a very short space of time. Were you an ordinary man so vast an amount of concentrated knowledge would surely blast your mind if I attempted to pass it in such a way. But you are no ordinary man.

'Now steel yourself, Titus Crow, and know these things.'

\* \* \*

447

That command of the Eminence, to steel myself, gave me barely sufficient time to brace my mind before I found it suddenly submerged in a tidal wave of intense telepathic transmissions. I was well able to understand, as my consciousness reeled under that mental assault, how any ordinary man's being might well be blasted! With incredible rapidity a series of facts imprinted themselves on my mind, coming in no recognizable order but simply flashing on me as brilliant bursts of knowledge and often of inspirational truth.

'*Know these things*,' the Eminence had told me, and now –

I knew why in the beginning and after the Great Uprising the Elder Gods had retired to Elysia from all the worlds of space. For the CCD had been Elder Gods too; yes, even the Great Old Ones, but they had realized their power. And their power had been so very nearly absolute that they had been absolutely corrupted.

Then the Elder Gods had locked away their brothers who had grown evil. Lest others of them fall prey to corruption, they had decided to remain and live in Elysia. And knowing that they alone were responsible for the evil they had bred in all the worlds, they elected to take all necessary precautions: the imprisoned forces of evil *must* remain imprisoned and never again gain the upper hand over the various sentient races which inhabited the worlds.

And so the Elder Gods watched over the prisons of the CCD from afar, that the forces of evil might never again prey among the emerging races of the worlds. But as the æons passed those new races grew in wisdom and in folly. Influenced little by little by the mind-sendings of the evil ones imprisoned in or adjacent to their worlds, they began to worship them and seek ways to free them from their prisons.

The Elder Gods were aware of all this, and they knew what they must do. Capable of miscegenation, they would go out and plant their seed in the flesh of the children of all the worlds and thus disseminate their essence down the ages. But in this they had to safeguard their pattern's genetic perpetuation, without allowing their various forms to be repeated in those races with which they intermingled. And in this, too, they were adept.

Thus a subconscious strength – springing of the Elder Gods' own wanting to overcome the evil of the CCD – would always lie dormant in the beings of the children of all the worlds. When strength was needed to oppose the insidious wills of the captive forces of evil, then they would find it within themselves. And yet the Elder Gods had to be careful, for they wished all the races and civilizations to grow according to their own natures, and therefore the seed of the Elder Gods must not be sown too thickly.

And so on Earth the Elder Gods mated with the daughters of men, and there were giants in the world in those days. And among all the spheres they mingled with the children of the worlds, to ensure that when they returned to Elysia there would still be warders to guard the prisons of their brothers lost in great sin.

And I knew that I myself was a throwback to just such matings between the Elder Gods and the daughters of men, that in my blood and body and being an ancient genetic pattern had returned, had swung full circle. I was a man, but part of me had roots in Elysia! I knew that there were many like me, and that one of them was my own Tiania, but Tiania was a very special case for she was also of the Chosen Ones.

Born of man and woman but not on Earth, Tiania had been raised in Elysia when her parents had traveled there from Earth. Her father had been a great scientist of drowned Mu and her mother a Thenopian lady whose blood was imbued with all the æon-spanning properties of the great Beings of Eld. And they had journeyed to Elysia at the foundering of Mu in no vessel but using the power of their minds alone, a power only the Elder Gods had known before them, for in Mu they were far, far ahead of their own time on Earth. Unbeknown to them they had been assisted by Kthanid, who sent them a Great Thought to guide them forward through time and space to Elysia. In his action in this matter the Eminence had felt an obligation, for it was none other than his blood which flowed in the veins of Tiania's mother, and his genetic pattern which, repeating down the ages, shaped her inner being.

Tiania's parents had found favor in the eyes of the Elder Gods and, desiring to do their will, were sent out into the worlds to do wondrous works. So as a child Tiania was left in Elysia and Kthanid watched over her, and thus she grew to strange, beautiful womanhood, more strange and beautiful even than the drowned flowers of Mu . . .

But even as she grew Kthanid had known that the time would come when one of Elysia's young men – of which a small number were of worlds similar to Earth and of very human form – would desire her. This had troubled him, for while the Chosen of the Gods were beautiful in all their diverse forms they were often weak – not in spirit or intelligence or character, not even physically weak. But they were weak in that they had never known the meaning of adversity; their strength had never been tested.

So he had looked into his crystal sphere – that viewer whose surface was a window on a universe of universes, just as the time-clocks are gateways on all times and places – and he had seen a man fighting the immemorial fight against the powers of evil. Following this man's life

450

in his viewer, Kthanid had seen that there was a possible future when he might reach Elysia, and so he had brought the man to the attention of Tiania. And she had looked into the viewer at Kthanid's bidding and had seen this man. And he had been old. Then Kthanid told her, '*Look into his futures, for there is one such future when he might come to you in Elysia, but not as an old man.*'

So she had looked again, and saw the same man grown young and strong, and Kthanid made her a promise that if ever he came to Elysia (for the possible futures were many) then she should have him. That promise was made to a child of twelve tender years who, from that time on and for ten long years more, was to wait patiently for her Earthman in Elysia.

And often she had begged the great being Kthanid to send her mind and thoughts out to this man when dangers threatened him on his long journey to the secret place of the Elder Gods, even when the Earthman went down to the Black Hole. She would have gone to him, too, when he penetrated the blackest veil of all and was driven into Yog-Sothoth's prison dimension, but such was the evil of Yog-Sothoth that not even a Great Thought could carry her there. And so she waited still, unknowing if he lived or died, for Kthanid's crystal could not see into that dark demesne. (Or at least Kthanid would not allow it, lest Tiania see something which might break her mind and soul.)

And Kthanid himself had despaired, for the man was after all only a man despite his heritage. Then the veil was rent and Kthanid called out to the man to come into Elysia. And Kthanid also used the great power of the Elder Gods to throw back the monstrous Yog-Sothoth, who would have followed the man into Elysia . . .

All of this knowledge and much, much more crowded my mind, de Marigny. I knew that you, my old friend of

451

– of how many ages ago? – had lived on when I had thought you dead and gone in unlit abysses; found that even now you were alive and well on old Earth. And I knew why Tiania had never once mentioned your name to me, though she too must have known that you lived. If I was going to leave her to return to my home planet, she was not going to hurry me with any such inducement. But in any case I could not blame her, for even knowing all of these things, I also knew how much she loved me.

And it was as if I looked into Kthanid's crystal ball myself, for I saw that my return to Earth would be hard, despite the ever watchful Tiania, and despite whichever weapon the Elder God Eminence had given me. But I knew now that you, your mind, would be there like a bright beacon to guide and speed me into a safe berth, Henri.

My mind absorbed this knowledge like a dry sponge absorbs water. I knew finally and was ashamed of my own and man's cowardice. Strange knowledge blossomed from depths and storehouses of my mind unguessed, telling me things I had always known but refused to recognize, facts that lie dormant in the beings and souls of all men. I had been a coward, all human beings are; but I knew now that mankind's terrors, since mankind dawned, have never been physical, tangible things.

Make no mistake, what I say is true! Our fears are all of the mind, implanted there by other minds that rule our dismal destinies. Cowards all, I said: we have looked outwards, yes – but how often have we looked inside?

Few minds have been strong enough to bear even a single glimpse. Alhazred, who might have been one of the greatest of men, went insane, and others before and since his time. And some simply died rather than go on living knowing what they knew – their purposes in life! Those few who looked, who saw and yet retained their sanity, they were brought down by the night, destroyed by the atavistic fear of others, fears that lingered on from a time before recorded history. They are no more.

I am speaking of the works of the CCD, yes, and of the fear that the entire world of men knows in the face of them. And that is not as it should be. Their seed is in us all, the seed of gods and the seed of demons of Eld, but we are the new generation of the universe and we ought to decide our own futures. Cthulhu and all the others of his dreadful cycle, they should dance man's tune! Perhaps, in the Wilmarth Foundation, the true foundation is laid at long last.

Finally I knew all of these things and many, many others. The full meaning of Kthanid's sendings burst upon me then, illuminating my whole mind, but in that mental sunburst one fact stood out above all others: I knew why the Elder Gods had not destroyed the CCD after they had put them down in their great sin. Do we murder our poor unfortunate lunatic brothers? No, we lock them up and set keepers over them for their own and everyone else's safety.

The Elder Gods are not their brothers' keepers! Man is the custodian, the warder of all the gibbering horrors of Earth and space. I will tell you what we fear, Henri, and why we are cowards. We fear the awesome task we have been given, for we and no others are guardians of the universe!

With this last revelation, without waiting for his permission or even asking it, I stepped forward through the magnificent curtains that draped Kthanid's alcove, and I stood at the foot of his throne. I gazed at him.

Staggered in spite of having guessed what I must find, I was at first amazed, then horrified. Finally I felt my lips pull back in the beginning of a scream, the hair stiffen at the back of my neck and my flesh creep in shudders . . . I gazed on the face and form of Kthanid, the Eminence, the Elder God guardian and progenitor of my own Tiania.

And madness sprang up in me as I tottered on paralyzed legs within the curtain of the great alcove, gazing at the thing on the throne – at the massive body, the wings folded back, the great head with its proliferation of face-tentacles. For this, except for those eyes, might well have been Cthulhu himself! Kin to the Lord of R'lyeh this being most certainly was, and close to him at that, so that only his eyes saved me from the rushing madness. The very soul of goodness and mercy, those massive golden eyes were lucid depths through which passes all the love and compassion of a father for his children, all the joy of a great artist at the perfection of his composition.

And he reached down to me and touched me, and all fear and awe, all terror of the unknown, all uneasiness of soul and psyche fled me at his touch. When I went out to Tiania where she gazed enraptured into joyous futures that floated on the surface of the crystal ball, I was a man at peace with all things . . .

When Tiania and I retraced our steps, when we climbed the ice staircase to the mouth of that great crevasse in the glacier, we found our flying machine just as we had left it. Beside it, its panel open and softly illumined in a pale blue lambency from within, my time-clock waited.

I kissed Tiania once and promised I would return, and no change came into her bright face, but I saw a tear forming in the corner of her eye. Before that tear could swell and roll down onto her cheek, I entered the time-clock and took my vessel up into icy atmosphere. And below me in the scanners a tiny dot stood by a mighty glacier and watched me go, and thus I began my return to Earth . . .

# PART SIX

# De Marigny's Choice
### (Random excerpts from de Marigny's diary)

Feb. 28

Today I can hardly believe it but last night I looked
down on Earth through the scanners of the time-clock,
and the lights of the cities were like tiny candles on a
gigantic cake. Yet now I can't help feeling that the cake
is made of plastic, false and tasteless.

Still, today's mood can't completely spoil the memory
of how we flew up high above the world and looked down
on the cities of men. Titus showed me how to reach out
my mind telepathically and touch the mind of the clock.
It was frightening, awesome, exhilarating! I actually flew
that fantastic machine out to the moon and back, but
Titus took the controls again to land the clock right back
in the study. That sort of thing, he tells me, involves a
technique which employs 'a step sideways in hyperspace-
time', something that takes practice to master. I'll take
his word for it; the alternative would have been for me
simply to drive the clock in through the wall or roof!

When we got back we had a brandy – I must say I
needed it! – over which Titus mentioned how I should be
well pleased with myself; my practice flight hadn't gone
badly at all. He seems to think it's all decided now.
Perhaps it is . . .

Mar. 2

For the last four days Titus has been away roving the
countryside in a rented car. He said he didn't know when
he'd get the next chance to 'have a look at Old England.'
I can't help wondering if he'll ever get another chance!

While he's been away I've given a lot of thought to what he's told me about his amazing travels. The world seems a very drab place compared with Titus Crow's description of Elysia. It's a funny thing, but the more I try to enumerate them the fewer ties I seem to have here on Earth. And there's a certain phrase of his that keeps repeating in my mind: 'a gateway on all space and time . . .'

Mar. 4

Tonight I'm to try my hand at using Crow's flying cloak, the antigravity device he brought back with him from Elysia. He tells me that it's the most wonderful experience. We must, of course, wait for darkness; it wouldn't do for me to frighten the life out of people by flying over London in broad daylight, like some great vampire bat at noon.

Mar. 7

Crow has gone back to Elysia. I woke up this morning to find his bed empty, barely slept in, a note left for me on the pillow:

Henri –
Forgive me for not letting you know that I was returning to Elysia so soon; I didn't know myself until half an hour or so ago. I couldn't sleep, got up and made myself a coffee, then wandered into your study.
The clock's hands were more than normally erratic; I opened the panel and stepped inside. Immediately Tiania's voice came to me, and her message was in the form of a pretty enigmatic warning from Kthanid. In short, it's imperative that I return to Elysia now, within the hour. Tiania wouldn't tell me what the trouble is, Henri – Kthanid had forbidden it – but something pretty big must be in the air and obviously they don't want me involved in it!
I shouldn't feel torn two ways like this, for while Earth is my

456

home world so is Elysia now, and a goddess waits for me there
. . . As Kthanid once told me, she is only a girl, but she's a
strange, strange woman – and to me she's a goddess.

I wouldn't wake you, Henri – farewells never come easy
between friends such as you and I. And in any case I plan to see
you soon, in Elysia.

I've left you my flying cloak; you know how to use it and it
may come in handy. I'm leaving you the clock, too, for I don't
need it now, except as a gateway to the gardens of Elysia. My
mind has *opened*, Henri! The possibilities are infinite . . . I've
told you all I can of the clock and its workings, and I've
instructed the Old Fellow to wait for you for four days before
returning to that vast corridor of clocks in the heart of the Blue
Mountains. At that time the panel will open of its own accord,
and by then you will know what to do.

You will be welcome in Elysia, Henri, but of course you must
make your own way there. You are not yet one of the Chosen.
It may well be a dangerous voyage; it will certainly be difficult.
But at least you have a weapon that I never had when I first set
out in the clock. And when there are obstacles, when you need
a helping hand, well, we'll be watching in Elysia. And if you are
where I can't reach you without aid, then I'll ride a Great
Thought to you. Oh, yes, the pitfalls of time and space are
many, but the rewards will be great.

Worlds without end, de Marigny, and all time and space at
your fingertips! Strange dimensions and nighted planes of existence -- places of myth and legend, dream and fantasy – and all
real, existing here and now and within your reach. All this, or
Earth, the choice is yours.

You are a lover of mysteries, my friend, as your father before
you; and I'll tell you something, something which you really
ought to have guessed before now. There's something in you
that hearkens back into dim abysses of time, a spark whose fire
burns still in Elysia. And one more thing you should know:

I have mentioned places of fantasy and places of dream, and
all of them are as real and solid in their way as the ground
beneath your feet. Ah, but there are dreams and there are
dreams, and there are dreamers and dreamers. Your father was
a great dreamer, Henri. *He still is – for he is a lord of Ilek-Vad,
where his old friend Randolph Carter is a just and honored king!*

I intend to visit them there one day, in that land of dreams.
When I do you can be with me, we two and Tiania – for I know

457

she'll never let me leave Elysia on my own again – and perhaps one other. Who can say?

Yes, the choice is yours, but one more thing I ask you to remember. There once was a time when man's remote forbear swam in warm, soupy oceans and never dreamed of walking on dry land. And then there was a time when he walked and gazed awestruck at the birds which flew. And then he flew in his turn and looked on the moon, the planets . . . In ten thousand years, perhaps, men might have their own Elysia right here on Earth, but you have not got ten thousand years!

Remember, the clock will open. That will be when you must make the final decision.

I will not say goodbye –
Titus.

Mar. 9

I seem to be spending more and more time these days here in my study, and the old clock is really becoming something of an obsession with me. I find myself listening to its ticking, trying to sort out some kind of pattern in the crazy sweep of its four hands. And despite the promise I made myself only yesterday morning – that whatever happened I would remain here on Earth – well, today I've packed all my recordings of Crow's adventures, together with my notebooks and assorted papers, into a strong cardboard carton. All that remains now is to place this diary in the carton with the rest of the stuff and address it. Mrs Adams will do the rest when she comes back. She hasn't been near the place since discovering that Crow was here!

Yes, I'll send all this stuff to Peaslee and . . .

But all this, of course, depends on whether or not I decide to change my mind about going . . . about not going? *God damn that clock's insane ticking!*

Mar. 10

A letter this morning from Mother Quarry, more a note really. She knows Crow's gone again, and she echoes his words when she says, 'Something big is in the air.' But what? I feel it, too, the lull before the storm, a disquiet, an ominous mental depression, an uneasiness of psyche. And I may as well admit it now . . . I've made my choice.

Mar. 11

The door in the clock has opened, Wingate, and I've no time to do more than wish you all the best –

HLdM

# Epilogue

At midnight, March 25, 1980, some fourteen days after de Marigny left Earth for Elysia in the time-clock and five days after Wingate Peaslee received de Marigny's parcel, Project X was finalized . . . and the CCD struck back! The unprecedented fury of the destruction that they wrought was Cthulhu's answer to the attack on Cthylla, Dagon and Hydra, for the project of course, had been the attempted destruction of all of these beings. A nuclear-powered burrowing device was sent four and a half miles deep into the earth beneath Innsmouth's Devil Reef and exploded down there by remote control. That atomic explosion, occurring just before midnight, had triggered Cthulhu's direst wrath.

No, that last is an understatement: the prime member of the CCD was not merely wrathful, he was absolutely insane with rage, berserk! Of course he was, for his Secret Seed, Cthylla, in whose darkling womb he planned to rise up again one day reborn, had been threatened. And I fear that she was not destroyed, for if she had been then surely the Fury would have been that much worse. As it was it lasted for three days and nights, a mental and physical onslaught that stopped as abruptly as it began. Foundation telepaths – those few who dared open their minds at all during that time – detected something still alive deep. deep down beneath shattered Devil Reef, something that mewled a demented telepathic threat of revenge as it moved off wounded, finally to disappear into the deeps of the North Atlantic.

The Fury lasted for three days and nights. The mental

effects of it were world wide, while its purely physical phenomena were very much localized. Of the former, the hateful telepathic outpourings from R'lyeh and other sunken Pacific sepulchers of the Cthulhi were such as to cause the most frightening outbreaks of unbridled, raging mass lunacy in all the world's mental institutions. Even the most passive inmates became possessed with hideous homicidal urges beyond all the powers of their keepers to control. In more than one hospital home the responsible authorities had to resort to the use of firearms to protect their own lives, but in many others the warnings came too late. Escaped lunatics marauded in the streets of Lisbon, Chicago, London and Köln before the Fury finally, abruptly ceased on the evening of the third day.

By then, too, the old Miskatonic University was no more. Brought down by the earth tremors that shook New England, nowhere more severely than Arkham, Miskatonic was first of all flayed by a tornado to end all tornadoes, then became the center of an incredible electrical storm. I escaped the holocaust by pure luck; many of my colleagues were less fortunate . . .

So the old university burned to the ground, and with it went most of the amassed lore of the Wilmarth Foundation, a vast storehouse of esoteric knowledge concerning the CCD, their minions and their dark works against mankind and the universe. And while Miskatonic blazed Innsmouth suffered a simultaneous and duplicate destruction, in which poor Wingate Peaslee and his team gave up their lives for the safety and sanity of a world they had fought to protect against direst evil.

Even then, however, Cthulhu was not appeased, for on the third day he sent the torrential rains that flooded ruined Innsmouth and Arkham and burst the banks of the brooding Miskatonic in a flash flood that cost many lives before the waters subsided. This was the Fury, in which the whole of New England became a disaster area to rival any other in living memory.

It was not my intention, however, when I first decided to publish this work to chronicle details of the terrible loss of life and the destruction caused by the Fury. Its manifestations were later more than amply discussed in several scientific magazines and journals under the completely inadequate misnomer of unusual meteorological phenomena. And so I will say no more on the subject. What I would take this opportunity to speak about is a matter which at the moment seems to be the standard topic of conversation. It is not only constantly debated among the junior ranks in our ever-expanding Wilmarth Foundation, but also among a minority of the heads of those several governmental departments which we serve and which know us and the importance of our work.

Speaking plainly, Titus Crow and Henri-Laurent de Marigny have been slandered in the cruelest manner by people who choose to see them as cowards and traitors to the Foundation's cause. Titus Crow, particularly, is seen to have fled the Earth at a time when he alone was in possession of a weapon against which the CCD could not stand. Indeed, one of the reasons why those forces of evil were so determined in their efforts to prevent Crow from returning to this world must have been that they themselves feared that he would use his newfound powers against them.

Still I say that these two men have been slandered, and so they have. Both de Marigny and Crow fought the most hideous battles with the CCD behind the scenes long before many of us even knew the Ancient Ones existed. How can one describe such men as cowards or traitors? And yet I have spoken to several people who are dissatisfied with Crow's 'desertion', and it seems obvious to me that festering seeds of suspicion have certainly been sown in their minds – *but by whom?*

Do I have to remind Foundation members of the fact that our fight is far from over? And must I add that just as surely as we are pledged to thwart every effort of the CCD to free themselves from the immemorial prisons of the Elder Gods, so are they equally determined in the discovery of new ways to achieve just that end? And if one of these ways is to breed distrust in the minds of men . . . what then? I am afraid, we are *all* afraid, and in Titus Crow's own words I will tell you what we fear: We fear the awesome task we have been given for we and no others are the guardians of the universe . . .

Always remember, Cthulhu lives and dreams on, yet seeking to rule the minds of men; and through them all of space and time – *and I say to you that already he has gained certain victories*!

Arthur D. Meyer
New Miskatonic,
Rutland, Vermont

# THE CLOCK
# OF DREAMS

For Barzai
the Not-so-Wise,
who proved – however
involuntarily – that what
goes up need not
necessarily
come down
again.

# Introduction

Myself, I've never been much of a dreamer, never traveled far past Ulthar; but I have watched caravans fording the Skai, and I have sat in the smokeroom of the Inn of a Thousand Sleeping Cats and listened to the tales of my betters. I suppose most dreamers have. It's true, though, that there seem to be fewer of us around these days. Time was when a man of the waking world could guarantee that if he boarded at an inn in the land of Earth's dreams, sure enough he would find a fellow dreamer or two from the world of waking mortals; and wouldn't the tales fly thick and fast then? Yes, they surely would.

You would hear magical names of men and places – names to set your pulses pounding and your imagination tingling – and thrill to the telling of tales of heroic and fantastic deeds. And someone would be bound to mention Kuranes or Randolph Carter . . . or Richard Upton Pickman. And while you might shudder at the hinted fate of the latter, certainly you would also gasp in awe at the adventures of the others. Ah, those were the dreams . . .

Still, I suppose I shouldn't complain too bitterly, for when I come to think of it I heard two of my favorite tales quite recently, and as coincidence would have it I heard them at the Inn of a Thousand Sleeping Cats . . . in Ulthar.

The first was a strange tale and complicated, a tale of all the worlds of space and time, of strange dimensions and planes of existence beyond the ken of most men. A tale of motes in the multiverse swirling beyond barriers neither spacial nor temporal, nor of any intermediate dimension recognized by mortal man except in the wildest theories of science and metaphysics. A tale of paths between the spheres, dim corridors leading to equally dim and conjectural lands of elder myth . . . And yet all of these seemingly inaccessible places were just around the corner to the time-clock.

Indeed 'time-clock,' as Titus Crow had long since recognized the fact, was a completely inadequate misnomer for that – machine? A plaything of the elder Gods come down the ages from lands beyond legend, from a time beyond time as men reckon it, the clock was a gateway on – on everything! It was a door to worlds of wonder, joy and beauty – but it was also a dark pothole entrance to caves of innermost, alien evil and shrieking, unnameable horror.

The first tale I heard was the story of how the clock came into Henri-Laurent de Marigny's hands in the first place, and it is a tale already told. But for the sake of the unacquainted I will briefly reiterate it before taking up the second of the two stories proper. Before even that, however, I had better tell what little is known of the time-clock itself.

Certainly the clock's history is strange and obscure enough to whet the mental appetite of any lover of mysteries or would-be sounder of unfathomable wonders (which you must be, else you would not be reading this). First, tracing the existence of the weird – conveyance? – back as far as possible in the light of incomplete knowledge, it seems to have belonged to one Yogi Hiamaldi, an Indian friend of the ill-fated Carolina mystic Harley Warren. Hiamaldi had been a member, along with Warren, of a psychic-phenomenist group in Boston about 1916–18; and he had sworn before all other members of that group that he alone of living men had been to Yian-Ho, crumbling remnant of eons long lost, and that he had borne away certain *things* from that grim and leering necropolis.

For reasons unknown, the Yogi had made a gift of the clock to one Etienne-Laurent de Marigny (perhaps the greatest ever American occultist and the father of one of the heroes of the story to follow), who kept it at the New Orleans retreat where his studies of the arcane sciences formed his primary purpose in life. How much he discovered of its secrets remains unknown, but after the elder de Marigny died the clock was sold, along with many another antique curiosity, to a French collector.

Here there is a gap in the history, for while many years later Titus Crow bought the clock at an auction of antique furniture in London, all of his subsequent attempts to discover the whereabouts of its previous Parisian owner were doomed to failure; it was as though the man had simply vanished off the face of the Earth.

Now then, of Titus Crow himself – a man with a positive genius for the discovery of dark lore, lost legends, and nighted myth-patterns, who will also feature prominently in my tale – much is known; but for now suffice it to mention that his protracted studies of the clock over many years of his life were such that the device became something of an obsession with him. Often in his earlier years Crow would sit in his study in the night, his chin in his hands as he gravely pondered the enigma of the peculiar, coffin-shaped, oddly-ticking monstrosity in the corner of the room; a 'clock,' of sorts, whose four hands moved in patterns patently divorced from any chronological system known or even guessed at by man, and his eyes would rove over the strange hieroglyphs that swept in intricate designs around the great clock's face.

When he was not at work on less baffling cases, always Titus Crow would return his attentions to the clock, and though usually such studies were in vain, they were not always complete failures. Often he believed himself on the verge of a breakthrough – knowing that if he were right he would finally understand the alien intricacies governing his 'doorway on all space and time' – only to be frustrated in the final hour. And once he actually had the doubtful privilege of seeing the clock opened by two men of equally doubtful repute and intent, whose affairs in the world were fortunately soon terminated . . . but then at long last there came a genuine clue.

It was while he was working for the Wilmarth Foundation – a far-flung body of erudite men whose sole avowed intent and purpose was to rid the world, indeed the entire universe, of all remaining traces of an aeon-old evil, the surviving demonic forces and powers of the Cthulhu Cycle of Myth – that Titus Crow visited Miskatonic University in Arkham, Massachusetts. There, in one of the carefully guarded, great old occult volumes in the university's world-renowned library, he finally recognized a sequence of odd glyphs which at first he was startled, then delighted to note bore a striking resemblance to the figures on the dial of his huge clock. Moreover, the book bore translations of its own hieroglyphed passages in Latin!

Armed with this Rosetta-Stone knowledge, Crow had returned to London, where soon he was at work again disinterring many of the clock's centuries-buried mysteries. And he had been right, for that incredible device was indeed a vehicle: a space-time machine of sorts with principles more alien than the centers of stars, whose like we may at least conjecture upon.

Of his work on the clock at this time, he wrote to his friend and colleague, Henri-Laurent de Marigny: 'I am in the position of a Neanderthal studying the operational handbook of a passenger-carrying aircraft – except I have no handbook!' And Henri was unable to assist his learned friend, for while his father had once owned the selfsame clock, that had been when he was a boy, and he could remember nothing of it. Titus Crow, however, was never a man to be denied anything once he set his mind after it, and so he had persevered.

And little by little he discovered all of the clock's peculiar secrets. He learned how to open its frontal panel, without suffering any of the many possible consequences, allowing the strange lights which invariably illumined its interior to flood out in eerie shades that dappled his study with alien hues. He knew how to attune himself 'telepathically' to the device's sub-ethereal vibrations: how to 'make himself one,' as he had it, with the clock. He was aware of the nature of the 'commands' he must give to the clock to guide it on its journeyings through temporal and spacial voids, so that the time soon came when he believed he might attempt his first flight in the weird vehicle.

All of this knowledge came to Titus Crow in the very nick of time, for no sooner was he psychically ready to test his theories than just such a test was forced upon him. It happened when he and his young friend de Marigny (also a member of the Wilmarth Foundation) were staying at Blowne House, Crow's sprawling bungalow home on Leonard's Heath in London.

The two of them had grown to be very painful thorns in the sides of the deities or demons of the Cthulhu Cycle, and at last the prime member of that cycle, dread Cthulhu himself, had discovered a way to strike back at them. Dreaming hideously in R'lyeh, his 'house' drowned somewhere in the vast Pacific, Cthulhu worked his evil plot through Ithaqua the Wind-Walker, Lord of the Snows. For while Ithaqua himself was unable to go abroad beyond barriers immemorially imposed by the Elder Gods – that is, while he was restricted in his movements to the Arctic Circle and its adjacent environs, and to strange Boreal starlanes and alien worlds – nonetheless he was still undisputed master of all the world's winds. And now he sent elementals of the air

471

from the four corners of the sky to attack Titus Crow's home.

Left with no choice but to risk the doubtful sanctuary of the time-clock – as eerie shapes of evil formed beyond the shattering windows, monstrous forces that pounded at the shuddering frame of his bungalow retreat until Blowne House fell about his ears – Crow stepped beyond the open front panel of his vehicle and bade de Marigny follow him. And when that 'freak localized storm' had expired and the house was discovered in ruins, perhaps not surprisingly no trace could be found of the two friends; neither of them, nor of the weird clock.

Well, to cut a long story short, Titus Crow made good his escape from those monstrous minion winds of Ithaqua into the far future, traveling almost to the End of Time itself before finally he mastered the clock's many intricacies to control its flight. But as for de Marigny, he was not the adept that his friend was. Barely was their craft 'out of port,' as it were, before de Marigny was 'washed overboard' into terrible temporal tides – to be fished from the Thames more dead than alive *ten years later!* Though the flight in the time-clock had seemed to last mere seconds, and while Crow's younger friend had aged not at all, nevertheless ten years had sped by; which caused de Marigny to wonder *just how far* his friend had finally traveled – and was he perhaps still traveling?

It was not long before he was to learn the answers to these and to other questions.

Upon recovering from his fantastic ordeal, de Marigny went back to his old London home, and there one night a short time later Titus Crow also returned to the world of men. Ah, but this was a much-changed Titus Crow, for he had undergone a transition. Younger, stronger, wiser (though de Marigny found the latter hardly credible), the new Crow had seen marvels beyond belief, had traced his own lineage back to the very Elder Gods themselves. And now he had returned to Earth for one reason only: to offer Henri-Laurent de Marigny the opportunity to join him in Elysia, the home of the Great Gods of Eld. As an inducement, if such were needed, this is how Crow had told his friend of his adventures:

'. . . I've been trapped on the shores of a prehistoric ocean, Henri, living on my wits and by hunting great crabs and spearing strange fishes, dodging the dinosaurs which in turn hunted me. And a billion years before that I inhabited a great rugose cone of a body, a living organism which was in fact a member of the Great Race that settled on Earth in unthinkable abysses of the past. I've seen the cruel and world-spanning empire of Tsan-Chan, three thousand years in the future, and beyond that the great dark vaults that loom at the end of time. I've talked telepathically with the super-intelligent mollusks of soupy Venusian oceans, which will not support even the most primitive life for another half-billion years; and I've stood on the bleak shores of those same seas ten million years later when they were sterile, after a great plague had destroyed all life on the entire planet . . .

'Why, I've come close to seeing the very birth of the universe, and almost its death! – and all of these wonders and others exist still just beyond the thin mists of time and space. This clock of mine sails those mists more bravely and surely than any Viking's dragonship ever crossed the gray North Sea. And you ask me what I mean when I talk of another trip, one involving yourself?

'When I return to Elysia, Henri, to the home of the Elder Gods in Orion, there will be a place for you in my palace there. Indeed, you shall have a palace of your own. And why not? The Gods mated with the daughters of men in the old days, didn't they? And won't you only be reversing the process? I did, my friend, and now the universe is mine. It can be yours, too . . .'

Soon after that Titus Crow took his departure from

Earth yet again, but this time he used the time-clock more properly as a 'gateway,' passing through it but yet leaving it behind until de Marigny should make up his mind one way or the other. If he decided to brave the machine's dark unknown, the way would not be easy. De Marigny knew that. But visions previously undreamed of had opened in his mind, and wonders beckoned and enticed him more magnetically than ever the Sirens lured Ulysses.

For de Marigny was a lover of mysteries no less than you, the reader, and as such could he possibly refuse the proffered challenge? Could you?

# 1

## *The Call of Kthanid*

De Marigny had first flown the time-clock two weeks earlier under Titus Crow's expert tutelage. Now Crow was gone – back to Elysia and the incredible girl-goddess he loved there, Tiania – and de Marigny had decided to follow him, alone.

Crow had done a marvelous job of instruction during the brief flights he had shared with his friend in the clock, and de Marigny was by no means lost in regard to controlling that fantastic machine. It was simply a matter of 'meshing oneself' with the thing, so that the clock became an extension of its passenger's body and mind, an extra limb or sixth sense . . . or both.

Thus, while half the world slept and darkness covered the land, Henri-Laurent de Marigny set out to prove himself worthy of a new and higher life in Elysia; and he did so in the only way open to him, by pitting himself and his vessel against all the currents of space and time. The world, all unawares, dwindled behind him as he cruised out into the void in his strangely hybrid craft, his almost 'human' machine, and a wild enthusiasm and exhilaration filled him as he piloted that vessel in the direction of Orion. Somewhere out there – somewhere in the distant void, behind invisible hyperdimensional barriers – he knew that faerie Elysia waited for him, and it seemed only reasonable to de Marigny that since Elysia lay 'adjacent' to Orion, that star should mark his starting point.

On one thing de Marigny had already and irreversibly made up his mind: though Titus Crow had told him that

475

in the event of insurmountable difficulties he could always contact him through the clock, he would not do so unless his life itself were threatened. From what he knew of it there seemed to be only one way into Elysia for a creature not born to it, and that was the way of peril. Only those who deserve Elysia may ever enjoy her elder wonders, and de Marigny did not intend to be dependant upon Titus Crow for his – birthright?

His birthright, yes – Elysia *was* his birthright, Crow had hinted as much. What was it his friend had said to him? 'Lover of mysteries you are, Henri, as your father before you. And I'll tell you something, something which you really ought to have guessed before now. There's that in you that hearkens back into dim abysses of time, a spark whose fire burns still in Elysia. And one more thing you should know.

'Those places of fantasy and dream I've mentioned – they're all as real and solid in their way as the very ground beneath your feet. The Lands of Dream, after all, are only dimensions lying parallel to the Worlds of Reality. Ah, but there are dreamers and there are dreamers, my friend, and your father was a great dreamer. *He still is – for he is a Lord of Ilek-Vad, Counselor to his great friend Randolph Carter, who is himself a just and honored king!*

'I intend to visit them there one day, in Ilek-Vad deep in Earth's dreamland, and when I do you can be with me . . .'

Musing on these things that Crow had told him, physically and emotionally weary now that the initial stage of his flight was successfully completed and the journey safely underway, de Marigny lay back and watched with his mind's eye – which was now a part of the time-clock's equipment, a mental 'scanner' of sorts – as the stars visibly moved in the inky blackness about him, so tremendous was the velocity of his craft as it hurtled through the airless, frozen deeps.

'As real and solid as the very ground beneath your feet,' Crow had said of dreams. Well, if Titus Crow said it was so, then it was so. And hadn't Gerhard Schrach hinted much the same thing back in the thirties, and other great thinkers and philosophers before him? Certainly they had. De Marigny could remember Schrach's very words on the subject:

'. . . My own dreams being particularly vivid and real – to such an extent that I never know for sure whether or not I am dreaming until I wake up – I would not like to argue which world is the more vital: the waking world or the world of dream. Certainly the waking world appears to be the more solid – but consider what science tells us about the atomic make-up of so-called solids . . . and what are you left with?'

And with thoughts such as these swirling in his head, and the fascinating panoply of vasty voids sprinkled with a myriad jewels in his mind's eye, de Marigny bade the clock speed on and drifted into a sleep; a sleep which seemed eagerly to open its arms to him, and one which was far from dreamless.

Beyond the slightest shadow of a doubt the slumbering de Marigny's dreams were not natural ones, and but for his previous knowledge of Elysia, passed on to him through Titus Crow – particularly of the Hall of Crystal and Pearl, wherein Kthanid the Elder God Eminence had his seat in an inviolable sanctuary beneath a great glacier – certainly he must have considered himself the victim of vilest nightmare. For the thing upon which he suddenly found himself gazing was a shape of primal horror, the blasphemous shape of Cthulhu himself – except that it was not Cthulhu but Kthanid, and where the former was black as the pit the latter shone with the light of stars.

Thus, while his subconscious body hurtled through the star-voids within the spacetime-defying matrix of the great

477

clock, de Marigny's dreaming mind was present in that very Hall of Crystal and Pearl which Titus Crow had described to him in so much detail. And he saw that Crow had painted an almost perfect picture of that magnificently alien palace beneath the ice of Elysia's 'polar' regions.

Here was the massive high-arched ceiling, the Titan-paved floor of great hexagonal flags, the ornate columns rising to support high balconies which glowed partially hidden in rose-quartz mists and pearly hazes. And everywhere were the white, pink, and blood hues of crystal, strangely diffused in all those weird angles and proportions that Crow had spoken of. Even the hall's centerpiece – the vast scarlet cushion with its huge, milky crystal ball – was just as Crow had described it. And of course, Kthanid was there, too . . .

Kthanid the Eminence, Elder God and cousin to Great Cthulhu – indeed of the same strain of cosmic spawn that bred the Lord of R'lyeh – moved massively in the Cyclopean hall. His body was mountainous! And yet his folded-back, fantastic wings trembled in seeming agitation as Kthanid paced the enormous flags, his great octopoid head, with its proliferation of face-tentacles, turning this way and that in what was plainly consternation.

But for all that this Being was alien beyond words, what might easily have been horrific was in fact magnificent! For this great creature, bejeweled and glittering as though dusted with diamonds, stared out upon the hall through huge eyes that glowed like molten gold; eyes filled with compassion and love – yes, and fear – almost impossible to imagine as existing within so terrible a fleshly house. And those eyes returned again and again to peer intently at the lustrous crystal upon its scarlet cushion.

It was because of Kthanid's eyes that de Marigny knew – was certain – that there was nothing to fear here, and he knew too that this was much more than merely a dream. It was as if he had been called into the Elder God's presence, and no sooner had this thought occurred to the dreamer than the Eminence turned and stared straight at him where his disembodied being 'stood' invisible within the vast subterranean vault.

'Henri-Laurent de Marigny,' a rumbling but infinitely kindly voice spoke in the dreamer's mind. 'Man of Earth, is it you? Yes, I see that it is. You have answered my summons, which is good, for that was a test I had intended to set you before – before –' The mental voice faded into uncertain silence.

'Kthanid,' de Marigny spoke up, unsure as to how to address the mythical Being, 'I see that you are . . . disturbed. Why have you called me here? Has the trouble to do with Titus Crow?'

'With Titus, yes, and with Tiania, whom I love as a father. But come,' the great voice took on urgency, 'look into the crystal and tell me what you see.'

Disembodied, nevertheless de Marigny found that he was capable of movement. He followed Kthanid to the edge of the great cushion, then moved on across its silken expanse to the center. There the huge, milky crystal ball reposed, its surface opaque and slowly mobile, as a reflection of dense clouds mirrored in a still lake.

'Look!' the Eminence commanded yet again, and slowly the milky clouds began to part, revealing . . .

The dreaming de Marigny gazed upon a scene that filled him with icy dread, a scene he could understand even less than he could believe it. The crystal on its scarlet cushion now burned with red fires of its own, and dark shadows danced as flames leaped high above four hugely flaring, blackly-forged flambeaux. These torches stood at the corners of a raised dais or altar, atop which a great reddish mass – a living, malignant jewel at least three feet across – pulsed evilly as it reflected the ruddy light of the torches. The thing seemed to be an impossibly vast ruby; and guarding it, patroling the round-cobbled square in which

479

the dais stood, were several squat, strangely-turbaned figures with awful wide-mouthed faces. At their belts these guardsmen wore viciously curving scimitars, and as they moved about the foot of the raised altar de Marigny saw that they paused occasionally to torment two ragged figures whose limbs were roped to irons hammered into the steps of the dais.

The horror and sick shock that de Marigny experienced had its source in these two figures; for one of them was certainly his great friend of olden adventures, Titus Crow, while the other – ruddily illumined in the light of the flaring flambeaux, fantastically beautiful even in her present distress – must be the girl-goddess Tiania, late of Elysia. Then, as suddenly as it had come, while de Marigny tried desperately to commit all the vision's details to memory, the milky clouds rolled back across the crystal's surface and all was gone.

Away in the time-clock, still hurtling through the star-voids half a universe away in space and time, de Marigny's recumbent form sweated, tossed and turned; while in the great Hall of Crystal and Pearl his disembodied sub-conscious turned imploringly to Kthanid the Eminence to ask: 'But what does it mean? Where are they? And how did this –'

'*Hold!*' The great Being turned abruptly and for a moment his huge eyes were slits, glittering with something other than compassion or love. Kthanid was every inch a God, and de Marigny sensed that for a moment he had been very close to witnessing the release of awesome energies. The Elder God's frustration was a living force that the dreamer felt as surely as his waking body would feel the warmth of sunlight or the chill of a bitter wind. Then the golden eyes blinked rapidly and Kthanid's towering form trembled violently as he fought to bring his emotions under control.

'Hold, de Marigny,' the mental voice finally rumbled

again, this time less forcefully, 'and I will explain all. But understand that every wasted moment increases their peril . . .'

Then the great voice seemed almost to become resigned, as if giving a telepathic shrug. 'Still, what other way is there? I must tell you as much as I know, for of course you are their one hope of salvation. Indeed, you will be the *instrument* of that salvation – if you are able. Have you the strength, de Marigny? Are you the man Titus Crow believes you to be? Would you really presume to enter Elysia? I tell you now, I am not unjust – but I love those two. Bring them back to me, and I will welcome you to Elysia as a son. Fail me, and –' again the mental shrug, 'and you remain a child of Earth all your days – *if* you live through your ordeal!'

'Whatever needs to be done to help Titus Crow – yes, and his Tiania – I'll try to do it,' the dreamer fervently answered. 'Wherever I need to go, I'll go there.'

'You will need to do more than merely try, de Marigny, and indeed there is far to go. When I have told you all I am able to tell, then you must be on your way – immediately.'

'And my destination?'

'Earth!'

'Earth?' the dreamer gaped. 'But –'

'Earth, yes, for your own homeworld is the only safe steppingstone to your ultimate destination, to the place where even now Titus Crow and Tiania face unknown terrors.' For a brief moment Kthanid paused, then he turned his golden eyes in the dreaming de Marigny's direction. 'Obviously your mind is receptive to telepathic attraction, man of Earth, else I could not have called you here to Elysia. But tell me, can you dream? Can you truly dream?'

'Can I dream? Why, I –'

'Your father was a great dreamer.'

'Titus Crow has told me much the same thing, but –' de Marigny began, then paused as an astounding thought came to him. 'Are you trying to tell me that Titus and Tiania are –'

The great Being nodded: 'Yes, they are trapped in Earth's dreamworld, de Marigny. To find them, free them, and return them to Elysia unscathed, that is your quest. One man against all Earth's dreamworld – which is also the land of her nightmares!'

# *Dreams of Doom*

'There is a way,' the Eminence continued, 'by means of which I can rapidly impress upon your mind all that I know of your . . . destination. It may be unpleasant in that you could be left with a headache, but other than that it is not dangerous. There is also a way to speed the process up immeasurably, and . . . But no, I fear your mind is not ready for that. It would probably destroy you.'

'Crow has told me how you – *revealed* – certain things to him,' de Marigny answered. 'Right here in this hall, I believe. I am ready for whatever it is you have to do to me.'

'Titus Crow's capacity was unbelievably high, even taking into account the fact that the strains of Eld ran strong in his blood. With him the process was very quick, almost instantaneous, but I would not dare to attempt such a process with you. That is not to belittle you, de Marigny: it is simply that if you are incapacitated, then nothing can save Titus Crow and Tiania. But in any case, your education will not take too long; my knowledge of Earth's dreamland is regrettably limited. The reason for this will soon become amply clear to you. Now come to me . . .'

As the dreamer drifted toward the alien Eminence, so that great Being's face-tentacles seemed to reach out to touch his disembodied mind. 'Steel yourself,' came Kthanid's warning in the instant before contact was made.

. . . *And immediately gates of strange knowledge opened in de Marigny's mind, through which streamed fantastic visions of nighted myth and legend, released from Kthanid's mental storehouse of lore concerning Earth's dreamland. And though it was perfectly true that the Eminence knew comparatively little of that subconscious dimension, still it seemed to the disembodied Earthman that the Elder God must surely be omniscient in the ways of human dreams.*

*For as rapidly as his mind could accept it, de Marigny became heir to a wealth of information previously known only to certain seasoned travelers in dreamland, a dimension whose very fabric existed for and was sustained only by the minds of Earth's dreamers. He saw the continents, hills and mountains, rivers and oceans of dream, her fabulous countries, cities, and towns, and he saw the peoples who inhabited those ethereal regions. Amazingly, he even recognized some of the places he saw, remembering now adventures believed forgotten forever in olden dreams, just as the night is forgotten in the light of dawn's rays.*

*And so knowledge passed from the mind of the great Being into the mind of Henri-Laurent de Marigny. He was shown the Cavern of the Flame where, not far from the gates of the waking world, the bearded, pshent-bearing priests Nasht and Kaman-Thah offer up prayers and sacrifices to the capricious gods of dream that dwell in the clouds above Kadath. Yes, and an instant later, whirled away to the Cold Waste, he even glimpsed Kadath itself, forbidden to men, but was offered no guarantee of that hideous region's location. Not even Kthanid knew for certain in which area of spacetime Kadath lay.*

*Snatched away from Kadath in the space of a single heartbeat, de Marigny traversed the seven hundred steps to the Gates of Deeper Slumber; and beyond those steps the Enchanted Wood with its furtive Zoog inhabitants was made known to him. He was given to understand how the Zoogs – small and brown and indeterminate as they were – might be very important to his quest, for they were not unintelligent and their knowledge of Earth's dreamland* was prodigious. Moreover, the Zoogs were reputed to have access even to the waking world, knowing the two places where the dimensions of dream and reality merge; though mercifully, in consideration of their doubtful appetites, they could not journey far beyond the mysterious places of their own dimension.

Then the Enchanted Wood and its burrow-dwelling Zoogs were gone, and de Marigny was shown the resplendent city of Celephais in the valley of Ooth-Nargai beyond the Tanarian Hills. And he knew that Kuranes, himself once a legendary dreamer, reigned in Celephais, and that King Kuranes was renowned in all the lands of dream as the only man ever to transcend the star-gulfs and return sane. Gazing down upon Celephais from on high, de Marigny saw the glittering minarets of that splendid city and the galleys at anchor in the blue harbor, and Mount Aran where the ginkgos swayed in the breeze off the sea. And there was the singing, bubbling Naraxa with its tiny wooden bridges, wending its way to the sea; and there the city's bronze gates, beyond which onyx pavements wound away into a maze of curious streets and alleys.

But de Marigny was given precious little time to study Celephais, for no sooner had he glimpsed the city and its surrroundings than he was whirled away, high over the Cerenarian Sea, whose billows rise up inexplicably to the heavens. There, among fleecy clouds tinted with rose, he was shown sky-floating Serannian, the pink marble city of the clouds, builded on that ethereal coast where the west wind flows into the sky; and he marveled at dream's wonders as he saw below, through breaks in roseate clouds, hills and rivers and cities of a rare beauty, dreaming gorgeously in brilliant sunshine.

And once again the scene quickly changed – so rapidly, indeed, that de Marigny was thrown in an instant from daylight into darkness – and now he knew that the land below him was none other than the icy desert plateau of

Leng, and he saw the horrible stone villages whose balefires flared up so evilly. Then, coming to him on an icy wind that seemed to freeze his very soul, he heard the rattling of strange bone instruments and the whine of cursed flutes, while a distant chanting of monstrous implications chilled him further yet.

For a moment, peering down in starkest horror, he thought he saw some inhuman thing writhing and blazing upon a stake in the heart of one of these balefires, while in the red shadows around monstrous figures jerked and cavorted to the hellish, wind-whipped music. De Marigny knew that the thing in the fire – whatever it was – screamed hideously as it roasted, and he was glad that the icy, howling wind kept those screams from him; and more glad when suddenly he was rushed away once more to other, less terrible visions.

Now he was relieved to behold the templed terraces of Zak, abode of forgotten dreams, where many of his own youthful dreams lingered still, gradually fading as all dreams must in the end. But before he could look too long or wistfully at Zak's dim visions, he felt himself borne irresistibly onward, to pass beneath twin headlands of crystal which rose up to meet high overhead in a resplendent arch; and then he found himself above the harbor of Sona-Nyl, blessed land of fancy. But since it could not have been deemed too important that he should look long upon Sona-Nyl, once again he was snatched away, without pause, on across the Southern Sea toward the Basalt Pillars of the West.

Now, some say that splendid Cathuria lies beyond the spot where those black columns tower from the ocean; but wiser dreamers are sure that the pillars are only a gateway, one which opens to a monstrous cataract where all dream's oceans fall abysmally away into awful voids outside the ordered universe. De Marigny knew these things at once, and he might have had the answer to the enigmatic problem *had he not found himself once more suddenly and without warning whirled away to the Enchanted Wood. Patently there was something else in that dark place that Kthanid would appraise him of, for now he found himself in an exceptionally unfrequented part of the wood, where even the Zoogs rarely ventured . . . and he was soon given to understand the reason for their caution.*

*Here the great squat oaks were very much thinned out, all of them dead or dying, and the whole area seemed covered wtih unnaturally luxuriant fungi, springing up from the dead ground and the mush of fallen, rotten trees. And there was a twilight and a silence here such as might have existed since time began; and in a sort of clearing a tremendous slab of stone lay on the forest's floor, bearing in its center a Titan iron ring all of three feet in diameter.*

*As de Marigny was shown the strange moss-obscured runes graven into the vast slab's surface, so the timeless quiet and oppressiveness of the place seemed to swell beyond endurance. He gazed upon those graven runes and, finally understanding, shuddered; for while one set of the glyphs was patently designed to keep something down beneath the slab, a second rune seemed to have the power to cancel out the first.*

*Then de Marigny's very soul shrank down within him, as if some monstrously alien symbol had been held out to it. And now he seemed to hear his own voice repeating a warning couplet from Abdul Alhazred's abhorrent Necronomicon: 'That is not dead which can eternal lie, and with strange aeons even death may die . . .' And he knew that there must be something singularly evil and damnable here, a connection between this hideous slab lost in an ensorcelled wood . . . and all the dread demons of the Cthulhu Cycle of Myth!*

*De Marigny was already more than well-acquainted with the CCD (the Cthulhu Cycle Deities, so designated by the Wilmarth Foundation) and now in an instant, faster than Kthanid might have implanted such knowledge in his mind, there flashed through his memory the pantheon as he knew it:*

*First there was dread Cthulhu, prime member of the CCD, prisoned in drowned R'lyeh somewhere in the vast and unknown depths of Earth's inscrutable Pacific. Then there was Yogg-Sothoth, the 'all-in-one-and-one-in-all,' a creature hideous beyond imagining – so monstrous indeed that his true shape and aspect are forever hidden, behind a mask or congeries of iridescent globes – who inhabits a synthetic dimension created by the Elder Gods to be his eternal prison. Since Yogg-Sothoth's prison dimension lies parallel to both time and space, it is often obscurely hinted of him that he is coexistent with the entire span of the former medium and coterminous in all the latter.*

*Then, high and low in the ranks of the CCD and their minions, there were the following: Hastur the Unspeakable, an elemental of interstellar space and air, and allegedly half brother to Cthulhu; Dagon, an ancient aquatic survival worshipped once in his own right by the Philistines and the Phoenicians, now lord and master of the suboceanic Deep Ones in their various tasks, chiefly the guarding of R'lyeh's immemorially pressured tombs and sunken sepulchers; Cthylla, Cthulhu's 'secret seed,' his daughter; Shudde-M'ell, Nest-Master of the insidious Cthonian Burrowers Beneath; the Tind'losi Hounds; Hydra and Yibb-Tstll; Nyogtha and Tsathoggua; Lloigor, Zhar and Ithaqua; Glaaki, Daoloth, Thamuth-Djig, and many, many more.*

*The list was a long one and contained, along with these actual, physical representatives of Cthulhu's cycle, several purely symbolic figures endowed with equally awe-inspiring names and attributes of their own. Chiefly, these were Azathoth, Nyarlathotep, and Shub-Niggurath, which symbols the Wilmarth Foundation had explained away thus:*

*Azathoth, the 'supreme father' of the cycle and described*

as a 'blind idiot god' – an 'amorphous blight of nethermost confusion blaspheming and bubbling at the center of all infinity' – was in fact the devastating power of the atom. It was nuclear fission, particularly the great atomic explosion that changed the perfect peace of the primal NOTHING into a chaotic and continuously evolving universe: Azathoth – the Big Bang!

Nyarlathotep – as his imperfectly anagrammatical name had early suggested to Titus Crow (albeit that this fact was entirely coincidental) was none other than the power of telepathy, and as such was known as the 'Great Messenger' of the CCD. Even after the rampaging members of the Cthulhu Cycle were put down and 'imprisoned' or 'banished' by the Elder Gods, Nyarlathotep had been left free to carry the messages of the CCD one to the other between their various prisons. How may one imprison purely mental power, telepathic thought?

Shub-Niggurath – known in the pantheon as a god of fertility, the 'black goat of the woods with a thousand young' – was in fact the power of miscegenation inherent in all the CCD since time immemorial. For in the old days did not the gods come down to mate with the daughters of men?

So, de Marigny saw again in his mind's eye all of these things and knew the truth of them, these and many other facts concerning the CCD. And he knew, too, why Titus Crow had braved the trans- or hyper-dimensional voids between Elysia's and Earth's dreamworlds – a voyage undertaken in the past only by two great seekers after knowledge and one fool, of which trio only one returned sane – for Crow's errand had been of the utmost importance. It had been to put an end to Cthulhu's incursions into the dreams of men. For since men first walked the Earth as true men they had dreamed and peopled the parallel dimension of dream with their own imaginings; and Cthulhu, seizing early upon his opportunity as he lay in dark slumbers of his own in sunken, blasphemous

R'lyeh, had achieved a certain mastery over dreams long before man mastered the mammoth.

But from the start Earth's dreamland had proven alien to Lord Cthulhu and had resisted him; for his were dreams of outer voids beyond the comprehension of men, and as such could invade human dreams only briefly. Also, many of dreamland's inhabitants – not the human dreamers themselves but the living figments of their dreams – were friendly toward men of the waking world and abhorred those concepts Cthulhu would introduce into their strange dimension of myth and fancy.

So the Lord of R'lyeh cloaked his schemes concerning Earth's dreamland in mysteries and obscurities, patiently going about his aeon-devised plan in so devious a fashion as to wear away the barriers of men's dreams, even as great oceans wear away continents. In this way he gradually introduced many utterly inhuman concepts into the dreamland, nightmares with which to intimidate the subconscious minds of certain men in the waking world. Thus, while Cthulhu himself could enter the dreamlands briefly, the evil concepts of his minion dreams would fester there forever; his, and those of his likewise 'imprisoned' cousins of the same dreadful cycle.

All of these things concerning Cthulhu and the CCD flashed through Henri-Laurent de Marigny's mind in a split second, but in the next instant he was snatched away yet again to visions just as strange if not so fearsome. And yet these, too, were fearsome enough.

He saw Ngranek's peak, and the great face carven in the mountain's gaunt side. He saw the hideously thin and noisome outlines of horned bat-shapes with barbed tails, flapping not altogether vaguely about the mountain, and he knew that these were the night-gaunts that guard Ngranek's secret. Then, as some of them flew closer, he saw that which made him shudder horribly: they had no faces!

But the bat-shapes did not acknowledge his presence,

*and before they could draw too close he was rushed away
again over the Peaks of Throk, whose needle pinnacles
are the subject of many of dream's most awful fables.
For these peaks, higher than any man might ever guess
or believe, are known to guard the terrible valleys of the
Dholes, whose shapes and outlines are often suspected but
never seen. Then he soared down, down, and down, until
his ears were filled with a vast rustling of Dholes amidst
piles of dried-out bones . . . He knew then that this place
he had swooped down to was none other than the Vale
of Pnoth, into which ossuary all the ghouls of the waking
world throw the remains of their nighted feastings; and
he trembled violently as the rustling ceased momentarily
– almost expectantly – just as the chirruping of crickets
ceases at the tread of human feet.*

*But now the things de Marigny was experiencing were
hastening one after the other through his mind at a dizzy
pace, blurring as they went down upon his memory in
fragmentary, erratic fashion. He was snatched up and
out of the Dhole-infested Vale of Pnoth and away across
dreamland in a frantic rush. In rapid procession he saw
the oaken wharves of Hlanith, whose sailors are more like
unto men of the waking world than any others in dreamland
– and ruined, fearsome Sarkomand, whose broken basalt
quays and crumbling sphinxes are remnant of a time long
before the years of man – and the mountain Hatheg-Kla,
whose peak Barzai the Wise once climbed, never to come
down again. He saw Nir and Istharta, and the charnel
Gardens of Zura where pleasure is unattainable. He saw
Oriab in the Southern Sea, and infamous Thalarion of a
thousand demon-cursed wonders, where the eidolon Lathi
reigns. He saw all of these places and things and many more
. . . and then there came a terrific, sickening whirling of his
soul* – following which de Marigny found himself dizzy and
utterly disoriented back in the throneroom of Kthanid the
Eminence in Elysia.

# 3

## *Journey Into Dream*

'But why?' de Marigny asked the great Being. 'Why did Crow go into Earth's dreamland, and how? And what possessed him to take Tiania with him? And where *exactly* are they? I need to know these things if I'm to –'

'Hold, man of Earth,' Kthanid cut him off. 'As to your first question: I had thought to make that amply clear in what I have shown you, but obviously I failed. Crow went into Earth's dreamland to put an end to Cthulhu's insidious fouling of the dreams of men. He went where it was his birthright to go, just as it was his birthright to enter into Elysia. He went because the Lords of Elysia – which you know as Elder Gods, of which I am one – cannot go there themselves. We would be just as alien in your dreamland as is Cthulhu, and for that reason we will not enter it. If ever the time arrives when we *must* enter it, then the visit will be as brief as possible – as brief and unobtrusive as we can make it. There are reasons other than those I have mentioned, and one of them is this: the gateway between Elysia and the world of Earth's dreams has two sides. If we entered from Elysia, who can say what might or might not follow us back through the gate when we returned?

'As to why Titus Crow took Tiania with him, she would not let him go without her! And it will be to my eternal sorrow if aught of evil befall them, for it was I laid them to sleep here, and I assisted their dreaming minds across nightmare voids to your Earth and its dreamland.' As he spoke, Kthanid moved across the great hall to a small and curtained alcove. He drew aside the drapes to show de Marigny the forms of a man and woman where they lay in crystal containers, their heads resting upon silken cushions.

As his spirit eagerly drifted forward, it was as much of a 'physical' shock as it could be to the disembodied de Marigny to gaze upon the recumbent form of the man with whom he had shared so many strange adventures . . . and upon that of Titus Crow's woman, the girl-goddess Tiania. Despite the fact that he knew what he had seen of them in Kthanid's crystal was only a dream manifestation of the two, nevertheless it was an eerie experience to see their living, breathing bodies here in the Hall of Crystal and Pearl. Recovering himself, he moved closer.

Crow's handsome, leonine face and his form were well enough known to de Marigny, but Tiania was very new to him, a stranger. He looked upon her, awed. Kthanid felt the awe of de Marigny and understood the emotions the Earthman must feel. He knew that no mortal man could look upon Tiania and not be moved. And he was right. Tiania's figure and face were indescribably beautiful. Her eyes were closed now in dreams that brought troubled lines to her pale-pearl brow, but de Marigny was almost glad that she slept this uneasy sleep. He felt sure that to gaze into her eyes would be to drown quite helplessly. He knew that he could never forget her, that he would know her wherever and whenever he saw her again.

Her hair was a lustrous emerald ocean, cascading down the spun golden strand of her cape, and her mouth was a perfect Cupid's bow of pearl-dusted rose, lips parted slightly to show the whitest teeth de Marigny had ever seen. The girl's face formed a slender oval in which arcing emerald eyebrows melted into the verdure of her temples. She had elfin ears like petals of rare blooms, and a nose so delicate as to go almost unnoticed. She radiated a distillation of the very Essence of Woman, human and yet quite definitely alien. She *was* a woman, yes, and not a goddess – but certainly the stuff of the Gods was in her. And she was the same woman he had glimpsed in Kthanid's crystal, helplessly staked out on the steps of the ruby altar in the distant world of Earth's dreamland. And just as she lay here now in this strange casket, so she had lain on those basalt steps – side by side with Titus Crow.

De Marigny turned suddenly to Kthanid to implore: 'But why don't you just wake them up? Surely that would get them out of there?'

Seeming quite human now, or as human as he could in his alien form, the great Being shook his head. 'No, de Marigny, it cannot be done. I have at my command every physical and psychical means by which such a recovery could be attempted, but they cannot be awakened. Do you think I have not tried? Something has them trapped there in Earth's dreamland, a force which defies every attempt I make to recall them. Here their subconscious bodies lie, rapt in evil dreams from which I am powerless to rouse them. The problems are many, de Marigny, and they are rare. First there is this unknown force that binds them to Earth's dreamland. Then there is the fact that they are separated from Elysia by vast alien voids of dream and all the horrors such voids harbor, and finally –'

'Yes?'

'We do not know their exact location. The same force that binds them to dream prevents detailed observation. I cannot name the region in which they are trapped. And Earth's dreamland is vast, de Marigny, wide-ranging as all the dreams of men have made it.'

'Then where do I begin?' de Marigny asked, perplexed. 'When? How?'

'Do not be too eager, Earthman. And, yes, perhaps I myself am too fearful for the safety of Tiania and your friend. What you saw in the crystal was a possible future, a possible occurrence yet to come. It has not gone so far, but in all the worlds of probability it will. I have searched the possible futures of Earth's dreamland as far as I dare, but only that one future ever presents itself for my viewing, and that one future draws ever closer. It is most certainly the same force that binds Titus and Tiania in dream that threatens their very existence.'

'Their very existence? But how can any real physical harm come to them when their bodies are here? I don't understand.'

Again (sadly, de Marigny thought) Kthanid shook his head. 'You seem to understand very little, Earthman.'

'You have to remember, Kthanid, that I'm not a great dreamer.'

'No, you are not,' the Eminence answered, again sadly. Then the great Being's thoughts brightened. 'But your father was; indeed he still is. And I believe that one day you will be, too.'

'That's all very well – and I thank you for your faith in me – but with all due respect, it doesn't help us much right now, does it? Look, you keep mentioning my father. I don't remember a great deal of him, but if it's true that he lives on in Earth's dreamland, well, surely he would be able to help me.'

'Etienne-Laurent de Marigny? Oh, yes, doubtless he would help you. Indeed, I am certain he would find a way to go to the aid of your friends – if he were able.'

De Marigny waited for Kthanid to continue, then shook his head at the great Being's silence. 'I still don't understand. My father is a lord in dreamland, surely. Trusted counselor to Randolph Carter, and –'

'Yes, that is so,' Kthanid interrupted, 'but there is a problem.'

'A problem?'

Kthanid offered what de Marigny took to be a nod, then continued. 'Ilek-Vad, where Randolph Carter wisely rules – and not only Ilek-Vad but Celephais and Dylath-Leen

495

too – they are beyond my power to scan. This was not always so. Until quite recently, an Earthyear or so at most, I could look upon Ilek-Vad and Celephais in my crystal, but no longer. Dylath-Leen is different. For many years there has been some sort of screen about Dylath-Leen. Of two of these forcefields – I suppose that is what they must be – those about Ilek-Vad and Celephais, I know only this: that nothing gets either in or out. I do not wish to alarm you, young man, but for all I know of those places their inhabitants are no more, they may well have been stricken from the dreams of men. As for the third city, Dylath-Leen, I believe that the same force which obstructs me in attempting to locate Titus Crow and Tiania is also responsible for my inability clearly to scan Dylath-Leen. Yes, perhaps there is a connection there, de Marigny. Perhaps –'

'Perhaps that's where they are, in Dylath-Leen.'

'It would seem possible. You must look into it as soon as you can. Meanwhile, listen well to what I have to say. Remember that there are levels of dreaming, de Marigny, and that our lost friends must be in the very deeps of dream. A man might waken easily from the shallower levels, and he may be awakened even as he sinks into the abysses. But Titus and Tiania have penetrated to a region from which – for some reason as yet unknown, perhaps that *force* I have mentioned – they cannot escape unaided.

'In effect, this means that right now Earth's dreamland is more real to them than the waking world. Wherever they are you must find them; you must rendezvous with them there in the possible future that you saw in my crystal. It will not be easy.'

'Then let's waste no more time. Tell me how to go about it.'

'Yes, yes, in a moment. But before that there are certain things you must commit to memory. Firstly: in

Ulthar there is a very ancient man named Atal. Seek him out and ask him what you will. He is wise almost beyond wisdom and good beyond goodness. Secondly: beware of manifestations of Cthulhu or his devil's brood that you may come across, and remember that in the dreamlands even purely symbolic concepts may take form. Be particularly wary of Nyarlathotep! Thirdly: remember that you have Crow's flying cloak, and you have the time-clock, too. These should prove to be great weapons against any terrors dream may confront you with. As for the clock: why, Titus Crow can use that device in ways that confound even me! Finally: never forget that while many things are far simpler in dream, others are maddeningly difficult, almost impossible. Now, do you think you can remember these things?'

'Yes, and everything else you've showed me.'

'Good. As to how you may reach Earth's dreamland: first you must return to the time-clock, which you will then pilot back to Earth. I will of course assist you in your return to the time-clock, but from then on you will be on your own. I suggest you go into orbit about the planet Earth, after which . . . you will simply go to sleep. But as you drift into sleep you will command the clock to carry you *in the direction of dreamland!* Then you will sleep – and you will dream, de Marigny, you will dream.'

The Eminence paused, and after a moment de Marigny asked: 'And is that all?'

'That is all. Anything else would be a waste of time, superfluous, possibly dangerous. I do not know enough of your dreamland to say more. Now you must go back to the clock. Your quest begins, de Marigny. I wish you luck.'

Suddenly the great Being's face-tentacles spread outward from his face like the rays of a bright sun, and the lights of stars blazed in his eyes. De Marigny – or rather his Ka, or whatever it was of him that Kthanid had called to his glacier palace in Elysia's frozen regions

497

– was instantly dazzled. When finally he could see again, the scene before him was rapidly shrinking, dwindling down to nothing, so that soon even Kthanid was only a tiny, alien, jeweled creature that finally shrank away and vanished. Then there was nothing but a rushing darkness that seemed to last forever; and yet he knew when the rushing stopped and he found himself once more within the matrix of the time-clock that his journey had taken less than a second. Indeed, it had been instantaneous.

Without wasting a single moment, he turned the clock about and raced back through the voids of space toward the world of his origin. His heart began to beat wildly and his head started singing with exhilaration as he thought of the quest before him, and the reward at quest's end – to enter Elysia! Not once did he contemplate failure . . .

Some time later, in the Hall of Crystal and Pearl, Kthanid stood where de Marigny had last seen him. Now, however, no bright fires lit his golden eyes, and the lighting of the vast chamber itself was greatly subdued. Within the Eminence an unseen battle raged, and he trembled violently as he sought to calm himself. Of course he had done the right thing . . . or had he? After all, he owed no loyalty to the Earthman de Marigny . . . but then, neither was the man an enemy. Nor was his willingness to be faulted. Yet, if the problem was looked at in the right perspective it was immediately apparent that in the great scheme of things Henri-Laurent de Marigny was utterly insignificant. On the other hand . . .

For what must have been the fifth or sixth time since he had sent the disembodied de Marigny back to his Earthly body in the time-clock, Kthanid went to the huge cushion with its milky crystal and peered into translucent depths that quickly cleared to his gaze. And as before he drew back from the scene which repeated itself within the crystal's all-scanning eye. It was that same cruel scene de Marigny had gazed upon earlier, at least in all the details of its background. But whereas before two figures had lain stretched out on the basalt steps of the ruby dais, now there was only one. Kthanid could see the man's face quite clearly, and once more he trembled mightily as the battle within him welled up again. The fear-filled yet grimly determined face in the crystal was that of Kthanid's most recent visitor – Henri-Laurent de Marigny!

Finally, something gave within the great Being's heart; a decision like none he had ever made before was made. He uttered a word which only the Elder Gods themselves might ever repeat or understand, then snatched his eyes from the scene in the crystal. And in the next instant his golden eyes blazed brighter as, tapping the tremendous sources of his body's alien energies, he sent his mind racing out on a Great Thought across strange transdimensional gulfs and light-years of space.

Straight to the time-clock where it raced in orbit around the Earth Kthanid's mind sped – but too late. De Marigny was already fast asleep in the warm womb of his weird vessel. And while that vessel registered his body's presence, Kthanid knew that the real de Marigny was somewhere else, inhabitant now of Earth's mysterious dreamland. It was as it should be, as Kthanid had planned it to be, and yet . . . What use to call him back from dream now?

Feeling within himself a treachery as alien to his emotions as they were to those of the Earthman he felt he had betrayed, the Elder God rushed in a fury back to Elysia. There he closed his palace and his mind to all would-be visitations and sat alone in the vast Hall of Crystal and Pearl.

# The Quest Begins

Night merged slowly into dawn in dreamland. To the east the very faintest of flushes tinted the sky gray, which was as well, for otherwise the night, except where it was studded with the bright jewels of fireflies, was of the very blackest.

At first de Marigny was disoriented, dazed; a lassitude was upon him. It was pleasant to do nothing but stand and admire the night and the first stirrings of a distant dawn. Then, as he drifted deeper into dream, he felt the night's chill and shivered at the luminous mist that began to swirl up eerily about his ankles. Then, he remembered his mission, and realized his supreme mistake. He was . . . alone! True, he still had Titus Crow's flying cloak about his shoulders, but where was the time-clock?

Suddenly complete realization of his plight filled him. He was lost in a nighted mist in some unknown region of Earth's vast dreamland, with only the fireflies for company and a ground mist that lapped at his ankles. And somehow he had lost his greatest hope of ever completing his mission; somehow he had left the fabulous time-clock behind him in the waking world.

How had it happened?

What was it Kthanid had said he must do? Yes, the Eminence had said: 'Command the clock to convey you in the direction of dreamland.' Well, he had done just as Kthanid had directed . . . hadn't he? Then, remembering, de Marigny groaned and cursed himself for a fool. The instructions he had given the clock had been wrong. He had simply ordered it to *transport* him to dreamland. And it had done just that. Without really knowing what he was doing, de Marigny had discovered Crow's method of using the clock more truly as a 'gateway.' For right now that alien vehicle was still in orbit around the Earth where he had left it, and de Marigny was stranded in dream just as surely as the friends he had come to rescue.

Perhaps if he had kept his head – if he had given the problem a little more studied thought – he might have seen a solution. For he was not yet too deeply drowned in dream to strike out for the surface, to waken himself up. Things are rarely perfectly clear in dream, however, and de Marigny was not an expert dreamer . . .

As the sky gradually lightened and the fireflies blinked out one by one, the adventurer found himself at the top of a great flight of steps that went down into a sea of mist. De Marigny knew those steps from older dreams forgotten until now, and more recently from his telepathic session with Kthanid. They were the seven hundred steps to the Gate of Deeper Slumber, beyond which lay the Enchanted Wood and those regions of dream which he sought.

De Marigny gritted his teeth and pulled Crow's cloak more warmly about his shoulders. Somewhere down there, beyond that wood at the foot of the steps, somewhere in those dreamlands spawned of the fantasies of a million dreamers, Titus Crow and Tiania of Elysia were or would soon be in desperate need of help, in peril of their very lives. There was only one course of action open to him.

Cautiously de Marigny descended the seven hundred steps and passed through the Gate of Deeper Slumber, and as the mist began to disperse and dawn grew more strongly beyond the trees, he set out through the groves of great gnarled oaks toward the far side of the Enchanted Wood, where he knew that the Skai rushed down from Lerion's slopes to Nir and Ulthar on the plain. Often as he pushed on through the wood, de Marigny heard the sounds that Zoogs make, but he saw not a one and was glad for that.

Often, too, he stumbled upon places where the trees were fallen into decay, and the ground was soggy with its burden of rotten oaks and alive with phosphorescent fungi. He would skirt these diseased areas, knowing that in one of them a massive slab of stone set with an iron ring of fantastic girth stood sentinel over nameless Cthonian things of hideous connections.

The wood was a fearsome place indeed, but while de Marigny was tempted again and again to use his flying cloak to climb above its suspected but unseen terrors, he refrained from doing so. He could not say what eyes might be watching him; he did not wish it known that a dreamer with a strange and wonderful flying cloak had entered dreamland. In any case, the sun was up now and the fears of the dark wood were disappearing along with the last wisps of mist.

It was a bright morning when he finally, wearily came out of the wood and set off across the rolling plains for Ulthar. He skirted Nir late in the morning, and as the sun approached its zenith crossed the Skai by means of an ancient wooden bridge. Hungry now, he was tempted to stop and rest at one of the many farms that dotted the plain; he had little doubt but that the friendly folk of these parts would find a meal for him. He did not stop, however, for the urgency of his mission was driving him relentlessly onward. And he did not know how long he had to effect the rescue of Titus Crow and the girl-goddess Tiania.

And so de Marigny came to Ulthar, the City of Cats, where an ancient ordinance has it that no man may kill a cat. It was quite obvious to the dreamer that this was indeed Ulthar, for even the outskirts were crowded with felines of every variety. Sleek females sunned themselves atop sloping roofs; young, careful-eyed toms kept cool while guarding their territories in shaded doorways; kittens tumbled comically in the long grass of the ornate gardens of rich personages. He paused very briefly in the suburbs to watch some of the kittens at their play; but then, having questioned a shopkeeper as to the whereabouts of the Temple of the Elder Ones, he hurried on into the city proper.

The Temple of the Elder Ones stood round and towering, of ivied stone, atop Ulthar's highest hill; and there, just within the temple's vast outer door, de Marigny was politely questioned by three young priests as to his purpose at the temple. He answered that he was from the waking world, that he sought audience with Atal the Ancient on very important matters. And when, in answer to further questioning, he told them his name the young priests grew wide-eyed indeed. One of them went hurriedly off into the dim and mysterious heart of the temple to seek an audience for de Marigny with the ailing high priest.

Finally the dreamer was taken to an inner sanctum where in a bed of finest silks lay the frail and weary shell of dreamland's wisest and oldest inhabitant. Now the younger priests departed, bowing themselves from the presence of their master and his visitor. Atal very gently propped himself up on his pillows to beckon de Marigny closer. When he could see the man from the waking world more clearly, he smiled feebly to himself, nodding in silent acknowledgment.

Eventually the ancient spoke, and his voice was like the rustle of late autumn leaves. 'Yes, yes – you are truly the son of your father.'

'You knew . . . you *know* my father?'

'Aye. Etienne-Laurent de Marigny, Lord of Ilek-Vad and Advisor in Chief to the king, Randolph Carter. He *is* your father, is he not?'

De Marigny nodded in answer, studying the trembling ancient where he lay. Atal's face was like a tiny wrinkled walnut; his head had a sparse crest of white hair; a long and voluminous beard like a fall of snow flowed down over

503

the covers of his bed. And yet the eyes in the wrinkled face, faded as they were to the point of being colorless, had lit with an inner intelligence as they recognized the dreamer's lineage.

'Aye,' Atal continued, 'he came to see me once, your father, when first he entered dreamland to dwell here. A wise dreamer, and a fitting counselor to Randolph Carter. He came merely to see me, to honor me, but you –'

'I come to seek your help,' de Marigny promptly answered, 'in order to discover –'

'I know why you are here, my son,' Atal whispered. 'And I know who sent you. Am I not the high priest of the temple, and is this not the Temple of the Elder Ones? When the light of life flickers out in this old, old body, then it is my hope to move on to greater marvels, to immortality in Elysia, where I may continue to serve forever the elder Intelligences of my faith.' The old man paused to peer again at de Marigny where he stood by his bed. 'It is true that *They* sent you, those elder Beings, is it not?'

Once more de Marigny nodded, and when Atal spoke again his voice was very low, as if he wished to conceal his words even from the air of the room. 'Aye, I knew you were coming – you, instrument of Kthanid, great Voice of all the Gods of Eld – and I know where your friends are!'

'Titus Crow and Tiania?' De Marigny leaned closer, his eyes intent upon Atal's, aware of the ancient's fragile and trembling form.

Now it was Atal's turn to nod, and when he spoke again his voice was a low, fearful, broken whisper. 'They are on their way to Dylath-Leen, of which place I . . . I fear to speak. They are held prisoners of creatures whose very presence in dreamland is a blasphemy!'

'When will they get to Dylath-Leen? Is there a way I might intercept them en route? Who are these creatures that hold them captive, and where is Dylath –'

504

'I know much of Dylath-Leen.' Atal's dry whisper cut him off. 'But there is one who knows much more. He was once a dreamer, just like you, but now he is an inhabitant of Ulthar. He dwells here with his wife, two fine sons, and a daughter of great beauty. I can tell you where his house is – but, de Marigny –'

'Yes?'

'I have a feeling that time is running out quickly for your friends.' For a second or two the ancient's eyes seemed to gaze through the dreamer, as if they looked upon distant things, but then they focused upon him once more. 'Now you must eat. The food here at the temple is plain but wholesome. You are welcome to take a meal, but then you must be on your way. Please clap your hands for me; my own are not very strong.'

De Marigny clapped his hands once, and almost immediately one of the young priests entered the room. Atal told him to arrange a meal for their visitor, then lowered himself down once more onto his pillow. The audience was over.

Then, as the dreamer began to follow the young priest out of the room, Atal called out: 'Oh, de Marigny – I almost forgot. I have something for you, which you must take with you.' He reached beneath his pillow to take out a small, strangely shaped vial.

'It is a very potent liquid brewed here in Ulthar, in this very temple. Unknown in the waking world, and rare enough here in dreamland, it has the property of awakening dreamers from even the deepest slumbers. One sip will return a dreamer to the waking world in seconds – aye, and all he brought through the gates of dream with him. To the true inhabitant of dream, however, the potion is a deadly poison; for of course it "awakens" such inhabitants to a world in which they do not exist! It can be seen that they must quite simply . . . disappear.'

For a moment de Marigny looked stunned as the

505

implications dawned on him – then he cried out: 'What? A potion to awaken dreamers? Then I could take a sip right away, return to the time-clock, and then –'

'No, my young friend.' Atal held up a quieting hand. 'The potion is not yet quite ready. It has to ferment. I had it brewed as soon as I knew you were coming, for it came to me in a vision that you would need it. But you must wait for at least another day and a half a day before it will be safe to use. By that time, if good fortune goes with you, you ought to have found your friends.'

Later, as the first stars came out in the evening sky, de Marigny walked the cool streets of Ulthar to the house of Grant Enderby, late of the waking world. Enderby was the man who could tell him about Dylath-Leen, perhaps help him in his search for Titus Crow and Tiania.

Dylath-Leen . . . The very name conjured up strange pictures in the dreamer's mind, and as he walked the darkening streets and watched the lights coming on in friendly, small-paned windows, he wondered why Atal had been so loth to speak of the place. Well, before the night was out doubtless he would know well enough.

Following Atal's directions, de Marigny soon came to the path that led to Grant Enderby's house of red stone and dark oaken beams. And the red stone walls about the garden bore testimony to Enderby's calling here in dreamland, the fact that he was a quarrier, and his sons in his footsteps. The walls were broad and straight and strong, as was the man who built them.

And so the dreamer knocked upon the oaken door and was welcomed into the home of this one-time man of the waking world; and after his host's family were all to bed, de Marigny sat alone with Grant Enderby and listened until the wee hours to the following story . . .

# PART TWO

# *Grant Enderby's Story, I: Litha*

Three times only have I visited basalt-towered, myriad-wharved Dylath-Leen, three curious visits which spanned almost a century of that city's existence. Now I am glad that I have seen it for the last time.

I went there first in my late teens, filled with a longing engendered of continuous study of such works as *The Arabian Nights* and Gelder's *Atlantis Found* for wondrous places of antique legend and fable and centuried cities of ages past. And my longing was not disappointed.

I first saw the city from afar, wandering along the river Skai with a caravan of merchants from distant places, and at first sight of the tall black towers which form the city's ramparts I felt a strange fascination for the place. Later, lost in awe and wonder, I took leave of my merchant friends to walk Dylath-Leen's ancient streets and alleys, to visit the wharfside taverns and chat with seamen from every part of Earth's dreamland – and with a few, I fancy, from more distant places.

I never once pondered my ability to chatter in their many tongues, for often things are far simpler in dream, nor did I wonder at the ease with which I fitted myself into the alien yet surprisingly friendly scene; once attired in robes of dream's styling, my looks were not unlike those of many of her peoples. I was a little taller than average, true, but in the main Dylath-Leen's diverse folk might well have passed for those of any town of the waking world, and vice versa.

Yet there were in the city others, strange traders from across the Southern Sea, whose appearance and *odor* filled me with a dread loathing so that I could not abide to stay near where they were for long. Of these traders and their origin I questioned the tavern-keepers, to be told that I was not the first from the waking world whose instinct found in those traders traces of hinted evil and deeds not to be mentioned. Randolph Carter himself had once warned Dylath-Leen's peoples that the traders were fiends not to be trusted, whose only desire was to spread horror and evil throughout all the lands of dream.

But when I heard Carter's name mentioned I was hushed, for an amateur at dreaming such as I was at that time could not dare aspire to walk even in the shadow of one such as he. Why, Carter was rumored to have been even to Kadath in the Cold Waste, to have confronted Nyarlathotep the Crawling Chaos, and to have returned unscathed from that place! How many could boast of that?

Yet loath though I was to have anything to do with those traders, I found myself one morning in the towering tavern of Potan-Lith, in a high barroom the windows of which looked out over the Bay of Wharves, waiting for the galley I had heard was coming to the city with a cargo of rubies from an unknown shore. I wanted to discover just what it was of them that so repelled me, and the best way to decide this, I thought, would be to observe them from a safe distant and location at which I, myself, might go unobserved. I did not wish to bring myself to the notice of those queerly frightening people of unguessed origin. Potan-Lith's tavern, with its ninety-nine steps, served my purpose admirably.

I could see the whole of the wharfside spread beneath me in the morning light; the nets of the fishermen drying, with smells of rope and deep ocean floating up to my window; the smaller craft of private tradesmen rolling gently at anchor, sails lowered and hatches laid back to

508

let the sun dry out their musty holds; the thag-weed merchants unloading their strongly-scented, dream-within-dream-engendering opiates garnered in exotic Eastern parts; and, eventually appearing on the horizon, the sails of the black galley for which I so vigilantly waited. There were other traders of the same race already in the city, to be sure, but how could one get close to them without attracting unwanted attention? My plan of observation was best, I was certain, but I did not know just what it was I wished to observe – or why.

It was not long before the black galley loomed against the entrance of the bay. It slipped into the harbor past the great basalt lighthouse, and a strange stench driven by the South Wind came with it. As with the coming of all such craft and their weird masters, uneasiness rippled all along the waterfront as the silent ship closed with its chosen wharf, and its three banks of briskly moving oars stilled and slipped in through their oarlocks to the unseen and equally silent rowers within. I watched eagerly then, waiting for the galley's master and crew to come ashore, but only five persons – if persons they truly were – chose to leave that enigmatic craft. This was the best look at such traders I had so far managed, and what I saw did not please me at all.

I have intimated my doubts with regard to the humanity of those – men? Let me explain why.

Firstly, their mouths were far too wide. Indeed, I thought that one of them glanced up at my window as he left the ship, smiling a smile which only just fell within the boundaries of that word's limitations, and it was horrible to see just how wide his evil mouth was. Now what would any eater of normal foods want with a mouth of such abnormal proportions? And for that matter, why did the owners of such mouths wear such queerly moulded turbans? Or was it simply the *way* in which the turbans were worn? For they were humped up

509

in two points over the foreheads of the wearers in what seemed especially bad taste. And as for their shoes: well, they were certainly the most peculiar footwear I had ever seen, in or out of dreams. They were short, blunt-toed, and flat, as though the feet within were not feet at all! I thoughtfully finished off my mug of muth-dew and wedge of bread and cheese, turning from the window to leave the tavern of Potan-Lith.

My heart seemed to leap into my mouth. There in the low entrance stood that same merchant who had so evilly smiled up at my window! His turbaned head turned to follow my every move as I sidled out past him and flew down the ninety-nine steps to the wharf below. An awful fear pursued me as I ran through the alleys and streets, making my feet fly faster on the basalt flags of the wider pavements, until I reached the well known, green-cobbled courtyard wherein I had my room. But even there I could not get the face of that strangely turbaned, wide-mouthed trader from beyond the Southern Sea out of my mind, nor his smell from my nostrils. So I paid my landlord his due, moving out there and then to head for that side of Dylath-Leen which faces away from the sea and which is clean with the scents of window-box flowers and baking bread, where the men of the taverns rarely venture.

There, in the district called S'eemla, I found myself lodging with a family of basalt quarriers who were such good, cheerful, charming folk that later, when I became an inhabitant of dream proper, I too chose quarrying for my trade. The head of the house was named Bo-Kareth, and he provided me with my own wide-windowed garret room, with a bed and a mattress of fegg-down; so that soon it was as though I had been born into the family, or might have seemed had I been able to imagine myself a brother to comely Litha.

Within the month I was firmly settled in, and from then on I made it my business to carry on Randolph Carter's work of warning, putting in my word against the turbaned traders at every opportunity. My task was made no easier by the fact that I had nothing concrete to hold against them. There was only the feeling, already shared by many of the folk of Dylath-Leen, that trade between the city and the black galleys could bring to fruition nothing of any good.

Eventually my knowledge of the traders grew to include such evidences as to make me more certain than ever of their evil nature. Why should those black galleys come into harbor, discharge their four or five traders, and then simply lie there at anchor, emitting their foul odor, showing never a sign of their silent crews? That there were crews seems needless to state; with three great banks of oars to each ship there must have been many rowers. But what man could say just who or what such rowers were?

Too, the grocers and butchers of the city grumbled over the apparent frugality of those singularly shy crews, for the only things the traders bought with their great and small rubies were gold and stout Pargian slaves. This traffic had gone on for years, I was told, and in that time many a fat black man had vanished, never to be seen again, up the gangplanks into those mysterious galleys to be transported to lands across uncharted seas – if, indeed, such lands were their destination!

And where did the queer traders get their rubies, the like of which were to be found in no known mines in all Earth's dreamland? Yet those rubies came cheaply enough, too cheaply in fact, so that every home in Dylath-Leen contained them, some large enough to be used as paperweights in the homes of the richer merchants. Myself, I found those gems strangely loathsome, seeing in them only the reflections of the traders who brought them from across nameless oceans.

So it was that in the district called S'eemla my interest in the ruby traders waxed to its full, paled, waned, and finally withered – but never died completely. My new interest, however, in dark-eyed Litha, Bo-Kareth's daughter, grew with each passing day, and my nights were filled with dreams within dreams of Litha and her ways, so that only occasionally were my slumbers invaded by the unpleasantly-turbaned, wide-mouthed traders from unknown parts.

One evening, after a trip out to Ti-Penth, a village not far from Dylath-Leen where we enjoyed the annual Festival of Plenty, as Litha and I walked back hand in hand through the irrigated green valley called Tanta toward our black-towered city, she told me of her love and we sank together to the darkling sward. That night, when the city's myriad twinkling lights had all blinked out and the bats chittered thick without my window, Litha crept into my garret room and only the narg-oil lamp on the wall could tell of the wonders we knew with each other.

In the morning, rising rapidly in joy from my dreams within dreams, I broke through too many layers of that flimsy stuff which constitutes the world of the subconscious, to waken with a cry of agony in the house of my parents at Norden on the northeast coast. Thereafter I cried myself to sleep for a year before finally I managed to convince myself that my dark-eyed Litha existed only in dreams.

## Grant Enderby's Story, II: The Ruby Horror

I was thirty years old before I saw Dylath-Leen again. I arrived in the evening, when the city was all but in darkness, but I recognized immediately the feel of those basalt flagstones beneath my feet, and, while the last of the myriad lights flickered out in the towers and the last tavern closed, my heart leaped as I turned my suddenly light feet toward the house of Bo-Kareth. But something did not seem right, and a horror grew rapidly upon me as I saw in the streets thickening groups of carousing, nastily chattering, strangely turbaned people not quite so much men as monsters. And many of them had had their turbans disarrayed in their sporting so that protuberances glimpsed previously only in books of witchcraft and the like and in certain biblical paintings showed clearly through! Once I was stopped and pawed vilely by a half-dozen of them. As they conferred over me in low, menacing tones, I tore myself free and fled. For they were indeed those same evil traders of yore, and I was horrified that they should be there in my City of Black Towers in such great numbers.

I must have seen hundreds of those vile creatures as I hurried through the city's thoroughfares; yet somehow I contrived to arrive at the house of Bo-Kareth without further pause or hindrance, and I hammered at his oaken door until a light flickered behind the round panes of blue glass in the upper sections of that entrance. It was Bo-Kareth himself who came to answer my banging, and he came wide-eyed with a fear I could well understand. Relief showed visibly in his whole aspect when he saw that only a man stood upon his step. Although he seemed amazingly *aged* – so aged, in fact, that I was taken aback (for I did not then know of the variations experienced by different dreamers, variations in the passage of time between the waking world and dreamland) – he recognized me at once, whispering my name:

'Grant! Grant Enderby! My friend – my old friend . . .! Come in, come in . . .'

'Bo-Kareth,' I burst out, 'Bo, I –'

'*Shhh!*' He pressed a finger to his lips, eyes widening even further than before, leaning out to glance up and down the street before pulling me in and quickly closing and bolting the door behind me. 'Quietly, Grant, quietly. This is a city of silence now, where *they* alone carouse and make their own hellish brand of merry – and they may soon be abroad and about their business.'

'*They?*' I questioned, instinctively knowing the answer.

'Those you once tried to warn us of. The turbaned traders.'

'I thought as much,' I answered. 'And they're already abroad, I've seen them. But what *business* is this you speak of?'

Then Bo-Kareth told me a tale that filled my heart with horror and determined me never to rest until I had at least attempted to right a great wrong.

It had started a number of years earlier, according to my host (I made no attempt to pinpoint a date; what was the point when Bo-Kareth had apparently aged thirty years to my twelve?) and had involved the bringing to the city of a gigantic ruby. This great gem had been a gift, an assurance of the traders' regard for Dylath-Leen's peoples, and as such had been set upon a pedestal in the city's main square. But only a few nights later the horror had started to make itself noticeable.

The keeper of a tavern near the square, peering from his window after locking the door for the night, had noticed a strange, deep, reddish glow from the giant gem's heart; a glow which seemed to pulse with an alien life all its own. And when the tavern-keeper told the next day of what he had seen an amazing thing came to light. All of the other galley-brought rubies in the city – the smaller gems set in rings, amulets, and instruments, and those larger, less ornamental, almost rude stones owned purely for the sake of ownership by certain of the city's richer gentlemen – had glowed through the night to a lesser degree, as if

514

in response to the greater activity of their bulky brother. And with that unearthly glowing of the gems had come a strange partial paralysis, making all the peoples of the city other than the turbaned traders themselves slumberous and weak, incapable and unwanting of any festivity and barely able to go about their normal duties and business. As the days passed and the power of the great ruby and the less regal ones waxed, so also did the strange drowsiness upon Dylath-Leen's folks. And it was only then, too late, that the plot was seen and its purpose recognized.

For a long time there had been a shortage of the fat black slaves of Parg. They had been taken from the city by the traders faster than they came in, until only a handful remained; and that handful, on hearing one day of a black galley soon due to dock, had fled their masters and left the city to seek less suspicious bondage. That had been shortly before the horned traders brought the great jewel to Dyath-Leen, and since that time, as the leering, gem-induced lethargy had increased until its effects were felt in daylight almost as much as they were at night, so had the number of oddly-shod traders grown until the docks were full of their great black galleys.

Then, inexplicable absences began to be noticed; a taverner's daughter here and a quarrier there, a merchant from Ulthar and a thagweed curer and a silversmith's son. Soon any retaining sufficient willpower sold up their businesses, homes, and houses and left Dylath-Leen for Ti-Penth, Ulthar, and Nir. I was glad to learn that Litha and her brothers had thus departed, though it made me strangely sad to hear that when Litha went she took with her a handsome husband and two strong sons. She was old enough now, her father told me, to be mistaken for my mother; but she still retained her great beauty.

By this time the hour of midnight was well passed and all about the house tiny red points of light had begun to glow in an eerie, slumber-engendering coruscation. As

Bo-Kareth talked, his monologue interrupted now with many a yawn and shake of his head, I tracked down the sources of those weird points of radiance and found them to be rubies.

The curse was just as Bo-Kareth had described it – rubies! Ten tiny gems were set in the base of an ornamental goblet; many more of the small red stones enhanced the hanging silver and gold plates; fire-flashing splinters of precious crystal were embedded in the spines of certain of my host's leather-bound books of prayer and dream-lore – and when his mumbling had died away completely I turned from my investigations to find the old man asleep in his chair, lost in distressing dreams which pulled his gray face into an expression of muted terror.

I had to see the great gem. I make no excuse for such a rash and headstrong decision (one does things in dreams which one would never consider for a moment in the waking world) but I knew I could make no proper plans nor rest easy in my mind until I had seen that great ruby for myself.

I left the house by the back door, locking it behind me and pocketing the key. I knew Bo-Kareth had a duplicate key, and besides, I might later need to get into the house without delay. The layout of the city was well known to me, and thus it was not difficult for me to find my way through labyrinthine back streets to the main square. That square was away from the district of S'eemla, far closer to the docks and quays, and the nearer I drew to the waterfront the more carefully I crept.

Why, the whole area was alive with the alien and evil traders! The wonder is that I was not spotted in the first few minutes; and when I saw what those hellish creatures were up to, thus confirming beyond a shadow of a doubt Bo-Kareth's worst fears, the possibility that I might yet be discovered – and the consequences such an untimely discovery would bring – caused me to creep even more carefully. Each streetcorner became a focal point for terror, where lurking, unseen presences caused me to glance over my shoulder or jump at the slightest flutter of bat-wings or scurry of mice feet. And then, almost before I knew it, I came upon the square.

I came at a run, my feet flying frantically, all caution thrown to the wind. For I knew now for sure what the horned ones did at night, and a fancy had grown quickly on me that something followed in the dark; so that when I suddenly burst from that darkness into a blaze of red firelight I was taken completely by surprise. I literally keeled over backwards as I contrived to halt my flight of fear before it plunged me into the four turbaned terrors standing at the base of the dais of the jewel. My feet skidded as I pivoted on my heels and my fingers scrabbled madly at the round cobbles of the square as I fell. In truth it could scarce be termed a real fall – I was no sooner down than up – but in that split second or so as I fought to bring my careening body under control those guardians of the great gem were after me. Glancing fearfully back I saw them darting rat-like in my wake.

My exit from that square can only properly be described as panic-stricken, but brief though my visit had been I had seen more than enough to strengthen that first resolve of mine to do something about the loathsome and insidious invasion of the traders. Backtracking, bounding through the night streets I went, with the houses and taverns towering blackly on both sides, seeing in my mind's eye that horrible haunting picture which I had but glimpsed in the main square.

There had been the four guards with great knives fastened in their belts, the dais with pyramid steps to its flat summit, four hugely flaring torches in blackly-forged metal holders, and, atop the basalt altar itself, a great reddish mass pulsing with inner life, its myriad facets catching and reflecting the fire of the torches in a mixture with its own evil radiance. The hypnotic horror, the malignant monster – the great ruby!

Then the vision changed as I heard close behind me a weird, ululant cry – a definite *alert* – which carried and echoed in Dylath-Leen's canyon alleys. In rampant revulsion I pictured myself linked by an iron anklet to the long chain of mute, unprotesting people which I had seen only minutes earlier being led in the direction of the docks and the black galleys, and this monstrous mental image drove my feet to a frenzied activity that sent me speeding headlong down the dark passages between the city's basalt walls.

But fast and furious though my flight was, it soon became apparent that my pursuers were gaining on me. A faint padding came to my ears as I ran, causing me to accelerate, forcing my feet to pump even faster. The effort was useless, if anything, *worse* than useless, for I soon tired and had to slow down. Twice I stumbled and the second time, as I struggled to rise, the fumbling of slimy fingers at my feet lent them wings and shot me out again in front. It became as one of those nightmares (which indeed it was) where you run and run through vast vats of subconscious molasses, totally unable to increase the distance between yourself and your ethereal pursuer; the only difference being, dream or none, that I knew for a certainty I was running for my life!

It was a few moments later, when an added horror had just about brought me to the verge of giving up hope, that I found an unexpected but welcome reprieve. Slipping and stumbling, panting for air, I had been brought up short by a mad fancy that the soft padding of alien feet now came from the very direction in which I was heading, from somewhere in *front* of me! And as those sounds of demon footfalls came closer, closing in on me, I flattened myself to the basalt wall, spreading my arms and groping desperately with my hands at the bare, rough stone; and there, beneath my unbelieving fingers – *an opening!* – a narrow crack or entry, completely hidden in jet shadows, between two of the street's bleak buildings.

I squeezed myself into the narrow opening, trying to get my breathing under control, fighting a lunatic urge to cry out in my terror. It was pitch black, the blackness of the pit, and a hideous thought suddenly came to me. What if this tunnel of darkness – this possible gateway to sanity – what if it were closed, a dead end? That would be a dead end indeed! Then, as if in answer to my silent, frantic prayers, even as I heard the first squawk of amazed frustration from somewhere behind me, I squirmed from the other end of the division to emerge in a street mercifully void of the evil aliens.

My flight had carried me in a direction well away from Bo-Kareth's house; but in any case, now that my worst fears were realized and the alarm raised, it would have been completely idiotic to think of hiding anywhere in the city. I had to get away, to Ulthar or Nir, as far as possible – and as fast as possible – until I could try to find a way to rid Dylath-Leen of its inhuman curse.

Less than an hour later, with the city behind me, I was in an uninhabited desert area heading in a direction which I hoped would eventually bring me to Ulthar. It was cool beneath a full, cloud-floating moon, yet a long while passed before the fever of my panic-flight left me. When it did I was almost sorry, for soon I found myself shivering as the sweat of my body turned icy chill, and I wrapped my cloak more tightly about me for I knew it must grow still colder before the dawn. I was not particularly worried about food or water; there are many water holes and oases between Dylath-Leen and Ulthar. No, my main cause for concern lay in orientation. I did not want to end up wandering in one of the many great parched deserts! My sense of direction in open country has never been very good.

Before long, great clouds came drifting in from a direction I took to be the south, obscuring the moon until only the stars in the sky ahead gave any light by which to travel. Then, it seemed, the dune-cast shadows grew blacker and longer and an eerie sensation of not being alone waxed in me. I found myself casting sharp, nervous glances over my shoulder and shuddering to an extent not entirely warranted by the chill of the night. There grew in my mind an awful suspicion, one which I had to resolve one way or the other.

I hid behind a dune and waited, peering back the way I had come. Soon I saw a darting shadow moving swiftly over the sand, following my trail – and that shadow was endowed with twin points at its top and chuckled obscenely as it came. My hair stood on end as I saw the creature stop to study the ground, then lift its wide-mouthed face to the night sky. I heard again that weird, ululant cry of alert – and I waited no longer.

In a passion of fear even greater than that which I had known in the streets of Dylath-Leen, I fled – racing like a madman over the night sands, scrambling and often falling head over heels down the sides of the steeper sandhills, until my head struck something hard in the shadow of a dune and I was knocked unconscious.

But it seems that I was not too deeply gone in dream to be shocked back into the waking world, and I was fortunate enough to wake up before my pursuer could find me. This time I was far from sorry when I leapt shouting awake at my home in Norden; and in the sanity of the waking world I recognized the fact that all those horrors of dream and the night had existed only in my slumbers, so that in the space of a few days my second visit to Dylath-Leen was all but forgotten. The mind soon forgets that which it cannot bear to remember . . .

# Grant Enderby's Story, III:
## The Utterer of the Words

I was forty-seven when next – when last – I saw Dylath-Leen. Not that my dream took me straight to the basalt city; rather, I found myself first on the outskirts of Ulthar, the City of Cats. Wandering through the city's streets, I stooped to pet a fat tom as he lazed upon a doorstep, and an old shopkeeper seated outside his store beneath a shade called out to me in a friendly, quavering voice:

'It is good, stranger. It is good when a stranger pets the cats of Ulthar. Have you journeyed far?'

'Far,' I affirmed. 'From the waking world. But even there I stop to play when I see a cat. Tell me, sir, can you direct me to the house of Litha, daughter of Bo-Kareth of Dylath-Leen?'

'Indeed, I know her well.' He nodded his old head. 'She is one of the few in Ulthar with as many years to count as I. She lives with her husband and family not far from here. Until some years ago her father also lived at his daughter's house. He came out of Dylath-Leen mazed and mumbling, and did not live long here in Ulthar. Now no man goes to Dylath-Leen.'

But the old man had soured at the thought of Dylath-Leen and did not wish to talk any longer. I took his directions and started off with mixed feelings along the street he had indicated; but only halfway up that street I cut off down a dusty alley and made for the Temple of the Elder Ones instead. It could do no good to see Litha now. What use to wake old memories – if indeed she were capable of remembering anything of those golden days of her youth? And it was not as though she might help me solve my problem.

That same problem of thirteen waking years ago: how to

avenge the outraged peoples of Dylath-Leen, and how to rescue those of them – if any such existed – still enslaved. For there was still a feeling of yearning in me for the black-towered city and its peoples of yore. I remembered the friends I had known and my many walks through the high-walled streets and along the farm lanes of the outskirts. Yet even in S'eemla the knowledge that certain offensive black galleys were moored in the docks had somehow always sufficed to dull my appetite for living, had even impaired the happiness I had known with dark-eyed Litha, in the garret of Bo-Kareth's house, with the bats of night clustered thick and chittering beneath the sill without my window.

As quickly as the vision of Litha the girl came, I put it out of my mind, striding out more purposefully for the Temple of the Elder Ones. If any man could help me in my bid for vengeance against the turbaned traders, Atal, the Priest of the Temple, was that man. It was rumored that in the temple he had keep of many incredible volumes of sorcery. His great knowledge of the darker mysteries was, in fact, my main reason for seeking his aid. I could hardly hope to engage the forces of evil controlled by the hell-traders with physical means alone.

It was then, as I left the little green cottages and neatly fenced farms and shady shops of the suburbs behind me, as I pressed more truly into the city proper, that I received a shock so powerful my soul almost withered within me. It is a wonder that I was not driven to seek refuge in the waking world, but a vision of vengeance made me cling desperately to dreamland.

I had allowed myself to become interested in the old peaked roofs, the overhanging upper storeys, numberless chimney pots, and narrow, old cobbled streets of the city, so that my attention had been diverted from the path my feet followed, causing me to bump rudely into someone coming out of the narrow door of a shop. Of a sudden the air was foul with shuddersome, well remembered odors of hideous connection, and my hackles rose as I backed quickly away from the strangely turbaned, squat figure I had chanced into. The slightly tilted eyes regarded me curiously and a wicked smile played around the too wide mouth.

One of *Them!* Here in Ulthar?

I mumbled incoherent apologies, slipped past the still evilly grinning figure, and ran the rest of the way to the Temple of the Elder Ones. If there had been any suggestion of half-heartedness to my intentions earlier there was certainly none now! It seemed obvious to me the course events were taking. First it had been Dylath-Leen, now an attempt at Ulthar. Where next? Nowhere, if I had anything to say of it.

I found the patriarch I sought, Atal of Hatheg-Kla, Atal the Ancient, in the Room of Ancient Records low in the great tower that houses the Temple of the Elder Ones. He sat, in flowing black and gold robes, at a centuried wooden bench, fading eyes studiously lost in the yellowed pages of a great aeon-worn book, its metal hasps dully agleam in a stray beam of sunlight striking in from the single high window.

He looked up, starting as if in shock as I entered the musty room with its tall bookshelves. Then he pushed his book away and spoke:

'The Priest of the Temple greets you, stranger. You *are* a stranger, are you not?'

'I have seen Ulthar before,' I answered. 'But, yes, I am a stranger here in the Temple of the Elder Ones. I come from the waking world, Atal, to seek your help.'

'Huh!' He was calmer now. 'You are not the first from the waking world to ask my aid, nor the last I fancy. How are you named and in what manner might I assist you? – *if* I choose to assist you!'

'My name is Grant Enderby, Atal, and the help I ask is not for myself. I come in the hope that you might be able to help me rid Dylath-Leen of a certain contagion; but since coming to Ulthar today I have learned that even here the sores are spreading. Are there not even now in Ulthar strange traders from no clearly named land? Is it not so?'

'It is so.' He nodded his venerable head. 'Say on.'

'Then you should know that they are those same traders who brought Dylath-Leen to slavery – an evil, hypnotic slavery – and I fancy that they mean to use the same black arts here in Ulthar to a like end. Do they trade rubies the like of which are found in no known mine in the whole of dreamland?'

Again he nodded: 'They do – but say no more. I am already aware. At this very moment I search for a means by which the trouble may be put to an end. But I work only on rumors, and I am unable to leave the temple to verify those rumors. My duties are all important, and in any case, these bones are too old to wander very far . . .' He paused for a moment, then continued.

'Truly, Dylath-Leen did suffer an evil fate, but think not that her peoples had no warning. Why, even a century ago the city's reputation was bad, through the presence of those very traders you have mentioned. Another dreamer before you saw the doom in store for the city, speaking against those traders vehemently and often; but his words were soon forgotten by all who heard them and people went their old ways as of yore. No man may help him who will not help himself.

'But it is the presence of those traders here in Ulthar which has driven me to this search of mine. I cannot allow the same doom to strike here – whatever that doom may be – yet it is difficult to see what may be done. No man of this town will venture anywhere near Dylath-Leen. It is said that the streets of that city have known no human

524

feet for more than twenty years, nor can any man say with any certainty where the city's peoples have gone.'

'I can say!' I answered. 'Not *where*, exactly, but *how* at least. Enslaved, I said, and told no lie. I had it first from Bo-Kareth, late of Dylath-Leen, who told me that when those traders had taken all the fat black slaves of Parg for those evil stones of theirs, they brought to the city the biggest ruby ever seen – a boulder of a gem – leaving it on a pedestal in the main square as a false token of esteem. It was the evil influence of this great jewel that bewitched the people of Dylath-Leen, bemusing them to such a degree that in the end they, too, became slaves to be led away to the black galleys of the traders. And now, apparently, those traders have . . . *used up* . . . all the peoples of that ill-omened city and are starting their monstrous game here! And Bo-Kareth's story was true in every detail, for with my own eyes –'

'A great ruby . . . hmmm!' Atal musingly cut me off, stroking his face and frowning in concentration. 'That puts a different complexion on it. Yes, I believe that in the *Fourth Book* there may be a mention! Shall we see?'

I nodded my eager agreement, and at Atal's direction lifted down from a corner shelf the largest and weightiest tome I had ever seen. Each page – pages of no material I had ever known before – glowed with burning letters which stood out with firefly definition in the dimness of the room. I could make out nothing of the unique ciphers within the book, but Atal seemed thoroughly familiar with each alien character, translating easily, mumbling to himself in barely discernible tones, until suddenly he stopped. He lurched shakily to his feet then, slamming the priceless volume shut, horror burning in his ancient eyes.

'So!' he exclaimed, hissing out the word. 'It is *that!* The Fly-the-Light from Yuggoth on the Rim, a vampire in the worst meaning of the word – and we must make sure that it is never brought to Ulthar!' He paused, visibly taking hold of himself before he could continue.

'Let me tell you:

'Long ago, before dreams, in the primal mist of the predawn Beginning of All, the great ruby was brought from distant Yuggoth on the Rim by the Old Ones. Within that jewel, prisoned by light and the magic of the Old Ones, lurks a basic avatar of the prime evil, a thing hideous as the pit itself! Understand, Grant Enderby, it is not the stone that induces the hypnotic weariness of which you have spoken, but the thing *within* the stone, the evil influence of the Fly-the-Light from dark Yuggoth on the Rim. Few men know the history of that huge jewel and its monstrous inhabitant, and I do not consider myself fortunate to be one of the few.

'It is told that it was discovered after coming down in an avalanche from the heights of forbidden Hatheg-Kla – which I can believe for I know much of that mountain – discovered and carried away by the Black Princess, Yath-Lhi of Tyrhhia. And when her caravan reached her silver-spired city it was found that all Yath-Lhi's men at arms, her slaves, even the Black Princess herself, were as zombies, altered and mazed. It is not remembered now where Tyrhhia once stood, but many believe the centuried desert sands to cover even its tallest spire, and that the remains of its habitants lie putrid within their buried houses.

'But the ruby was not buried with Tyrhhia, more's the pity, and rumor has it that it was next discovered in a golden galley on the Southern Sea twixt Dylath-Leen and the Isle of Oriab. A strange ocean is the Southern Sea, and especially between Oriab and Dylath-Leen; for there, many fathoms deep, lies a basalt city with a temple and monolithic altar. And sailors are loth to pass over that submarine city, fearing the great storms which legend has it strike suddenly, even when there is no breath of wind to stir the sails!

'However, there the great jewel was found, aboard a great golden galley, and the crew of that galley were very beautiful even though they were not men, and all were long dead but not corrupt! Only one sailor, mad and babbling, was later rescued from the sea off Oriab to gibber pitifully the tale of the golden galley, but of his fellow crewmates nothing more is known. It is interesting to note that it is further writ how only certain people – horned people who dance to the evil drone of pipes and the rattle of crotala in mysterious Leng – are unaffected by the stone's proximity!' Atal looked at me knowingly. 'And I can see you have already noticed how strangely our traders wear their turbans . . .

'But I digress. Again the jewel survived whatever fate overtook the poor seamen who rescued it from the golden galley, and it was later worshiped by the enormous dholes in the Vale of Pnoth, until three leathery night-gaunts flew off with it over the Peaks of Throk and down into those places of subterranean horror of which certain dim myths hint most terribly. For that underworld is said to be a place litten only by pale death-fires, a place reeking of ghoulish odours and filled with the primal mists which swirl in the pits at Earth's core. Who may say what form the inhabitants of such a place might take?'

At this point Atal's eyes cleared of their faraway look and turned from the dark places of his tale to the present and to me. He placed his rheumy hands on my shoulders, peering at me earnestly.

'Well, so says legend and the *Fourth Book of D'harsis* – and now, you say, the great ruby is come again into the known places of Earth's dreamland. I believe it, for over the years there have been vague rumors. Now hear you, Grant Enderby, I know what must be done – but how may I ask any man to take such risks? For my plan involves not only the risk of destruction to the mortal body, but the possible eternal damnation of the immortal soul!'

527

'I have pledged myself,' I told him, 'to avenge the peoples of Dylath-Leen. My pledge still stands, for though Dylath-Leen is lost, yet are there other towns and cities in dreams which I would dream again – but not to see them corrupted by horned horrors that trade in fever-cursed rubies! Atal – tell me what I must do.'

Atal then set himself to it, and there was much for him to be about. I could not help him with the greater part of his work, tasks involving the translation into language I could understand of certain tracts from the *Fourth Book of D'harsis*. Even though many things are simpler in dream, those passages were not meant to be read by any man, neither awake nor sleeping, who did not understand their importance.

Slowly but surely the hours passed, and Atal labored as I watched, putting down letter after letter in the creation of pronounceable syllables from the seemingly impossible mumbo-jumbo of the great book from which he drew. I began to recognize certain symbols I had seen in allegedly 'forbidden' tomes in the waking world, and even began to mumble the first of them aloud – '*Tetragammaton Thabaite Sabaoth Tethiktos*' – until Atal silenced me by jerking to his feet and favoring me with a gaze of pure horror.

'It is almost night,' he remonstrated, striking a flint to a wax candle, his hands shaking more than even his extreme age might reasonably explain, 'and outside the shadows are lengthening. Would you call *That* forth without first having protection? For make no mistake, distance is of no consequence to this invocation, and if we wished we could call out the Fly-the-Light even from here. But first you must cast a spell over Dylath-Leen, to contain the thing when you release it from the ruby; for certainly unless it is contained it will ravish the whole of dreamland. And you, the caller, the Utterer of The Words, would be one of the first to die – horribly!'

I gulped my apologies and sat silently from then on, listening attentively to Atal's instructions even as my eyes followed his scratching pen.

'You must go to Dylath-Leen,' he told me, 'taking with you the two incantations I now prepare. One of them, which you will keep at your left, is to build the protective Wall of Naach-Tith about the city. To work this spell you must journey around Dylath-Leen, returning to your starting point and crossing it, chanting the words as you go. This means, of course, that you will need to cross the bay; and I suggest that you do this by boat, for there are things in the night sea that do not take kindly to swimmers.

'When you have crossed your starting point the wall will be builded. Then you may use the other chant, spoken only once, to shatter the great gem. You should carry the second chant at your right. This way you will not confuse the two – a mistake which would prove disastrous! I have used inks which shine in the dark; there will be no difficulty in reading the chants. So, having done all I have told you, your revenge will be complete and you will have served all the lands of dream greatly.

'No creature or thing will ever be able to enter Dylath-Leen again so long as the Wall of Naach-Tith is there, nor leave the place, and the Fly-the-Light will be loosed amongst the horned ones. One warning though, Grant Enderby – *do not watch the results of your work!* It will be as was never meant for the eyes of men.'

## Grant Enderby's Story, IV: The Wall of Naach-Tith

I came through the desert toward Dylath-Leen at dusk, when the desert grasses made spiky silhouettes atop the dunes and the last kites circled high, their shrill cries telling of night's stealthy approach. Night was indeed coming, striding across dreamland in lengthening shadows which befriended and hid me as I tethered my yak and made for the western point of the bay. I would start there, making my way from shadow to shadow with the wall-building Chant of Naach-Tith on my lips, to the opposite side of the bay; and then I would see about crossing the water back to my starting point.

I was glad that the moon was thinly-horned, glad the desert was not more brightly illumined, for I could not be sure that there were no sentries out from the unquiet city. Whatever joys Dylath-Leen may once have held for me, now the place was unquiet. No normal lights shone in its streets and squares; but, as night came more quickly, there soon sprang up many thousands of tiny points of evil red, and in one certain area a great morbidly red blotch glowed in strange reminiscence of Jupiter's huge eye-like spot, glimpsed often in my youth through a friend's telescope. Empty though the city now was of all normal life, that poisoned jewel in the main square still filled the town with its loathsomeness, a terror ignored by the abnormal traders as the statues of past heroes are ignored in saner places.

Halfway round the city's perimeter there came to my ears the strains of music – if such evilly soul-disturbing sounds warrant placing in any such category – and leaping fires sprang up in Dylath-Leen's outer streets, so that I could see and shudder at the horned figures that leapt and cavorted round those ritual hellfires, observing disgustedly the way their squat bodies jerked and shook to the jarring cacophony of bone-dry crotala and strangled flutes. I could neither bear to hear nor watch, and so passed quickly on, chanting breathlessly to myself and feeling about me a weird magic building up to a thrill of unseen energies in the night air.

I was more than three-quarters towards the eastern side of the bay when I heard far behind me a sound that stiffened the short hairs on the back of my neck and brought a chill sweat to my brow. It was the terrified cry of my yak, and following that single shrill scream of animal fear there came another sound – one which caused me to quicken my pace almost to a run as I emerged from the dunes to the washed pebbles of the shore – the horrid, ululant cry of alarm of the horned ones!

Stranded on the beach, its bottom festooned with barnacles, was a small one-man craft as used of old by the octopus fishers of Dylath-Leen. Frail and unsafe though this vessel looked, beggars cannot be choosers, and thus thinking I leapt within its tar-planked shell, offering up a prayer of thanks to the night skies when I found that the craft still floated. I found the old round-bladed paddle and, still chanting those mad words of Atal's deciphering, made strongly for the black outline of the far side of the bay. And, ungainly though my craft had at first looked, it fairly cleft the dark water as I drove furiously at the paddle.

By now there were squattish outlines on the shore behind me, dancing in anger at my escape to the sea, and I wondered if the horned ones had a means of communication with which more orthodox creatures such as men were unfamiliar. If so, then perhaps I would find monstrous welcomers awaiting my beaching on the western point.

Halfway across the bay things happened to make me forget the problem of what might wait for me on landing. I felt a tug at my paddle from the oily water and a dark mass rose up out of the depths before my boat. As that unknown swimmer came alongside and the thin moonlight lit on its sharp teeth, I lashed out with my paddle – taking a very deep breath when the horror turned slowly away and silently submerged.

I continued then with my frenzied paddling and chanting until the western point loomed out of the dark and the shallow keel of my boat bit sand. Leaping overboard into shallow, night-chilled water, I imagined soggy gropings at my legs and ploughed in an agony of terror for the pebbles of the beach – and in that same instant, as I touched dry land, there loped out of the dark from the direction of the city the squat forms of a dozen or so of those foul, horned creatures whose brothers dwell in nighted Leng! Before they could reach me, even as their poisonous paws stretched out for me, I raced across my starting point and there came a clap of magical thunder that hurled me down face first into the sand. I leapt up again, and there within arm's length, clawing at an unseen barrier – the merciful Wall of Naach-Tith – were those thwarted horned ones of elder dreams. Hateful their looks and murderous their strangled intent as they clawed with vile purpose at thin air, held back by the invisible spell of Naach-Tith's barrier.

Without pause I snatched out the second of those papers given me by Atal and commenced the invocation of the Fly-the-Light, the spell to draw forth the horror from the ruby. And as the first of those weird syllables passed my lips the horned ones fell back, unbelievable terror twisting their already awful features.

'*Tetragammaton Thabaite Sabaoth Tethiktos –*' As I chanted on, by the dim light of that thin-horned moon, the snarls of those creatures at bay turned to pleading mewls and gibbers as they began to grovel at the base of the Wall of Naach-Tith. And eventually I spoke the last rune, and there came a silence which was as that quiet that rules at the core of the moon.

Then, out of the silence, a low and distant rumble was born, growing rapidly in volume to a roar, to a blast of sound, to an ear-splitting shriek as of a billion banshees – and from the heart of Dylath-Leen a cold wind blew, extinguishing in an instant the hellfires of the horned ones. And all the tiny red points of light went out in a second, and there came a loud, sharp crack, as of a great crystal disintegrating. And soon thereafter I heard the first of the screams.

I remembered Atal's warning 'not to watch,' but found myself unable to turn away. I was rooted to the spot, and as the screams from the dark city rose in unbearable intensity I could but stare into the darkness with bulging eyes, straining to pick out some detail of what occurred there in the midnight streets. Then, as the grovelers at the wall broke and scattered, *It* came!

It came – rushing from out the bowels of the terrified town – bringing with it a wind that bowled over the fleeing creatures beyond the invisible wall as though they had no weight at all . . . and I *saw* it!

Blind and yet all-seeing – without legs and yet running like flood water – the poisonous mouths in the bubbling mass – the Fly-the-Light beyond the wall. Great God! The sight of the creature was mind-blasting! And what it *did* to those now pitiful things from Leng. . . .

Thus it was.

Three times only have I visited the basalt-towered, myriad-wharved city of Dylath-Leen – and now I am glad that I have seen that city for the last time.

# PART THREE

# 1
# *Shadow Over Dreamland*

'And it is still your intention to enter Dylath-Leen? Deliberately, despite all I have told you?' Grant Enderby's voice showed his incredulity. He stood up to pace the floor of the room wherein he and Henri-Laurent de Marigny had so firmly cemented their friendship through the hours of darkness. Enderby's tale had taken until the wee hours in the telling, and since then the two men had talked of a variety of things. Their discourse had covered many subjects, some of them centering upon de Marigny's quest, others touching upon the general air of malaise, of a strange impending doom that seemed to hang like a dark shadow over most of dreamland.

'Yes,' de Marigny answered, 'I must enter Dylath-Leen; my friends are there and they are in trouble.'

'But, Henri, if the Elder Gods themselves are incapable of helping your friends, then what can a mere man do?'

'You ask me that? And you, a "mere man," once built the Wall of Naach-Tith about Dylath-Leen, destroying all of the horned traders in the city.'

'I was lucky,' the older man grunted. 'Without Atal's help I could have done nothing.'

'But I, too, have been helped by Atal,' de Marigny pointed out. 'And I have my flying cloak.'

'Huh!' Enderby grunted grudgingly. 'Still, you do not know what you go against, Henri.'

'Oh, but I do. You have told me what I go against, Grant, for which I am grateful. There is something further, however.'

'Oh?'

'Yes. You explained how you built the Wall of Naach-Tith about Dylath-Leen, but you said nothing about its removal. How can you be sure that things are once more as they were – that Dylath-Leen again suffers the contagion of the horned traders?'

Enderby shrugged. 'There are reasons. Travelers have strayed too close to the city, never to be seen again; others have been lucky enough to escape. It is rumored that two such men have stumbled away from the city in the last five years, two out of dozens lost forever. Then there is the vision you saw in Kthanid's crystal: the square in the center of Dylath-Leen, where once again the horned ones have set up a great ruby which doubtless pulses out its evil, debilitating radiations even now . . .

'As to how the horned ones regained Dylath-Leen – how they chained the Fly-the-Light from Yuggoth on the Rim, prisoning it again within this new ruby they have brought to the city from across the Southern Sea – of these things I can only guess. And anyone's guess is as good as mine. Remember, Henri, that there was a rune to build the Wall of Naach-Tith, and another to splinter the great ruby and free the Fly-the-Light. Why not a third to remove Naach-Tith's barrier, and yet another to prison the horror from Yuggoth?

'It is after all a Fly-the-Light, which, during the hours of day, must find a dark sanctuary or perish beneath the sun's rays. If man – or monster – knew the correct runes, it would be an easy task to trap the vampire during the hours of daylight.'

Wearily de Marigny stroked his forehead. 'Whichever way it is,' he answered, 'I'll find out soon enough for myself.' He stood up and stretched, and his host immediately apologized.

'I fear I've kept you up talking too long, my friend. Let me show you to your room now. You have come a long way and will probably need all the strength you can

536

muster. When will you tackle Dylath-Leen?'

Following Enderby upstairs to the tiny guestroom, de Marigny answered. 'I intend it to be tomorrow night, and of course I will fly into the city. That way the journey will be one of minutes, a half hour at most. With luck I should be in and out of Dylath-Leen before your horned traders even suspect that I am there. I won't need much more equipment than I have already: a rope – a sharp knife, perhaps – a little blacking for my face.'

'Ah, well, Henri, go to your bed now,' his host answered. 'We'll talk again tomorrow, when you are fully rested. If only I were a young man again, I –'

'No, no – you've done enough already, Grant, and I am extremely grateful.'

'My boys, too,' Enderby nodded, ushering the man from the waking world into the guestroom. 'If you were going afoot, I would find it difficult to dissuade them from going with you. You will understand why I am glad you are flying to Dylath-Leen.'

De Marigny nodded. 'Of course I understand, but in any case it's best I go it alone. Goodnight, Grant.'

'Goodnight, my friend. And may your dreams within dreams be pleasant ones.'


The following evening, as twilight deepened and the first suggestions of stars began to glow dimly in the sky over Ulthar, de Marigny set out. People who saw his shadow and the shape that cast it flitting high over the rooftops would later talk of a great bat; or perhaps it was a night-gaunt – though night-gaunts were extremely rare in these parts.

As the dreamer passed swiftly through the darkening sky he retraced in his mind's eye the comprehensive map of Dylath-Leen which Grant Enderby had drawn for him. It was of the utmost importance that he remember all of the routes from the square of the ruby dais to the outskirts of the city, and from the outskirts to the desert. It would not be too difficult to reach that square, where by now Titus Crow and Tiania might well be suffering the none too tender attentions of the squat horned ones. But it could very well be a different story again to escape from the place.

De Marigny had upon his person a stout rope with a noose, a sharp knife in a leather sheath, and the precious vial given him by Atal. Nothing more. He hoped that nothing more would be necessary, for he dared not weigh himself down too much.

Out in the desert he paused briefly to alight and tie his rope to a boulder that must have weighed as heavy as two men. With the other end of the rope fastened to the harness of his cloak, he attempted an ascent into the night. His spirits dropped when, as he had feared, he found the cloak incapable of lifting the additional weight. He found a second boulder only half so great as the first and repeated the experiment, feeling a little of his confidence returning as the cloak bore its burden slowly but surely up into dark skies.

The cloak could manage two people without being taxed beyond its capabilities, but not three. That was more or less as de Marigny had expected, but he had hoped –

No, he checked himself, hope was nothing without strength and determination. He untied the smaller boulder and wound the rope about his body once more. Then, slitting his eyes against a wind that blew high above the desert, following the winding course of a river of stars reflected in the night-dark Skai, he once more headed for Dylath-Leen.

Fires surrounded the city, spaced out to form a horse-shoe pattern whose mouth was the bay of Dylath-Leen, where the land met the currents of the Southern Sea. Seeing these fires from afar, de Marigny rose higher in the sky until he could plainly make out the shape they formed. Then he flew up higher still so that there could be no chance of his being observed as he soared above the watchers who kept those fires burning.

There were other lights in the city, but they were not the healthy, welcoming lights of any normal town. There was no physical warmth in them for all their redness, and de Marigny knew that these crimson glow-worms were only smaller versions of the great malignancy in the central square, the horror which even now pulsed out its red rays, glowing like the evil eye of an alien Cyclops. And seeing from on high that great unwinking glow, de Marigny believed he knew now for sure the source of all the unease in dreamland.

# 2

# Rescue

To the three squat creatures whose task it was to guard the two dreaming humans spreadeagled upon the steps of the ruby dais, the night was a welcome, beautiful thing. Most of their fellows were asleep now, for there were no longer any of the normal inhabitants of dreamland left in Dylath-Leen with which to amuse themselves. It had been thus for many a year, unless one cared to count the occasional unwary wanderer who might stumble mistakenly upon Dylath-Leen from out of the desert. This night, however, should prove a rare diversion – in the shapes of these two very important intruders from the waking world of men.

The grotesquely alien trio that formed the nightguard about the dais of the ruby would have to be patient, though, waiting until they could be sure that they would not be disturbed in their pleasures. Lots had been drawn for their 'duty' this night, and the trio had been the winners. The prize must surely be enjoyed to the full, and it would be a pity if the cries of these two captives should attract jealous-minded colleagues to spoil their amusements.

The male captive would provide hours of sport, though he must not be *too* severely damaged. Nyarlathotep, emissary of Great Cthulhu himself, was coming to dreamland to speak with Titus Crow personally. It would not be meet if the Crawling Chaos should find the man a babbling idiot before he could question him – though doubtless he would be just such an idiot by the time the interrogation was over! As for the female . . . Ah! But *there* was a thought . . . They would have her one at a time, right there upon the dais steps, where her male companion could see and hear all that occurred. And later, before the morrow, they would have her again, perhaps all three at once!

As night deepened and the city grew quieter still, the three horned ones joked of such things and ensured that their captives overheard them – never knowing that upon a high, nearby rooftop a third party also heard them, nor that the unseen stranger grew livid with rage at their vileness!

The figures of the two captives tied to the dais steps were pitiful in their helplessness. Titus Crow, normally so proud and leonine – with eyes that spoke the secrets of strange ways walked unafraid, a man whose deeds had rocked the seats of the Great Old Ones themselves before taking him to the home of the Elder Gods in Elysia – now lay like a man already dead, naked and ready for the shroud. The ridges of the basalt steps bruised his back and cut into his flesh; his head lolled drunkenly; the only spark glowing behind his eyes was one of horror and shame. Shame that he was helpless now to protect the incredibly beautiful girl-goddess whose love for him had led her to this hideous place, this unthinkable fate.

The two gazed at each other, and for a moment their love blazed through all the misery. 'Oh, Titus,' the wondrous girl's equally wondrous voice, weak now and terrified, spoke to her Earthman. 'Is this really how it is all to end?'

'Tiania,' Crow's own voice plumbed the depths of wretchedness and shame, 'I would not have –'

'Hush, my Titus,' she shook her head, 'for I would have it no other way. If we are to suffer and die, then we suffer and die together. Do you think I would even want to live without you?'

Before Crow could answer, the rattling, rasping tones of one of the squat, alien guardsmen crackled harshly in the still air. 'Hah! The two lovers converse! See how they gaze upon one another and mumble their sweet nothings!' The speaker turned to his comrades. 'What do you say, brothers? Is it not time we found ourselves a morsel of pleasure with these two?'

'Indeed,' one of the two he addressed grated impatiently, 'if you two had listened to me we'd have been at it an hour ago. I want the girl – and I want her now!' The great wide mouth in the speaker's evil face widened even further in a ghastly grin as he stared at the writhing figure of Tiania upon the basalt steps.

Hearing this horned one's words, Titus Crow struggled wretchedly, helplessly with his bonds, gasping: 'By God, I'll –'

'You'll what, dreamer?' With his scimitar, the same horned one carelessly drew a thin red line down Crow's rib cage.

'Hold!' cried the third of the aliens. He approached Tiania and reached out a vile paw to snatch away the tattered square of silk which alone covered her perfect breasts. 'We haven't yet decided who's to be first with the girl, have we?' He took from his belt a pouch, and from this removed a ten-sided die. 'Highest score takes her first, lowest last. Agreed?'

His two companions nodded, at which he flipped his gamestone into the air. It fell, bounced, and the three horned ones crowded about it where it lay. 'Ten!' crowed the thrower, delighted with his luck.

The next guardsman threw only a four, at which he grunted a low curse. But the third also threw a ten. To break the tie, the first thrower took up the die a second time, at which his opponent said:

'Throw it higher this time. I don't trust you and your die.'

542

'High as you like,' chortled the other, flinging the gamestone into the air. It did not return to earth.

The three looked up into the night for a little while, shading their eyes against the lurid glow of the great ruby, then peered puzzledly at each other and frowned uncertainly. And in this moment of indecision a noose snaked down out of darkness and settled about the shoulders of the lost gamestone's owner.

The noose swiftly lifted and tightened about the guardsman's fat neck, drawing him inexorably up from the ground. He disappeared into the sky, choking and gurgling and kicking wildly. Stunned, his companions gaped at one another – for a second or two only. Then, before they could make a move, the now inert body of their hanged comrade crashed down again from a great height, dashing one of the two remaining horrors to the ground with a broken back.

At that, the legs of the third member of that loathsome trio were galvanized into frantic activity. It seemed to the astounded, delighted, almost disbelieving pair tied to the dais steps that the remaining alien tried to run in at least three directions at one and the same time. But then, before the lone survivor of the unknown vengeance from the night sky could even cry out, as finally he made to bolt from the cobbled square, down swooped a great, black-faced bat-shape that struck him from his feet and was upon him, knife glinting redly, all in one fluid motion. A second later, it was all over. De Marigny had acted with a murderous efficiency born of utter horror and loathing. He felt not the slightest repugnance at the fact that he had so ruthlessly destroyed these three abominations of darkest dream.

Without pause the avenging dreamer leapt to the steps of the dais, where it was the work of seconds to cut the captives loose. All this time Titus Crow had spoken not a word. His mouth hung half open in amazement and his eyes were wide in disbelief. Finally, as de Marigny helped the two to their feet, averting his eyes as best he could from Tiania's nakedness, Crow blurted: 'Henri! De Marigny! It's you under that blacking! But how? You, here in dreamland? God! But I've never been more –'

'Later, Titus,' de Marigny cut him off. 'Heaven knows we've little enough time right now. I'll take Tiania first – the cloak can't manage three – but I'll be back for you immediately. Better grab yourself one of those scimitars in case more of these beasts come on the scene. I'll be as quick as I can.' With that he turned to Tiania, who in turn looked to Crow for guidance.

'Trust de Marigny, Tiania,' the bruised and bloodied man told her. 'He is the greatest friend a man ever had.' He gave the girl into his friend's care, and the latter, more than ever aware of Tiania's nakedness and unearthly beauty, wrapped her quickly in a wing of his cloak. Without further pause he took firm hold of her and flew up into darkness. They sped quickly to a tall unlighted tower about a mile from the dais of the ruby, and there de Marigny quietly deposited Tiania behind the balcony of the flat roof. Before he could fly off again she caught him by the arm.

'Titus has told me much of you, Henri-Laurent de Marigny,' she whispered. 'I understand now why he left me alone in Elysia to return to your green Earth. Friends such as you are singularly rare. He loves you as a brother, and from this time on so do I.'

She leaned forward and kissed de Marigny lightly upon his mouth. A moment later, as he soared off again into the night, his heart also soared within him. And de Marigny knew that come what may he had already been rewarded fully for whatever risks he was taking here in Earth's dreamland.

A minute or so later de Marigny picked up Titus Crow

from the square of the ruby dais, and then it became obvious to him just how much the latter's ordeals had taken out of him; scimitar grasped in one hand, Crow was barely capable of hanging on as they flew up into the night. De Marigny asked his strangely fatigued friend how long he and Tiania had languished upon the steps of the dais.

'Since noon, Henri, but we were weak enough before ever we got to Dylath-Leen. They brought us to the city in one of their vile black galleys, and never a bite to eat in three days. I was drugged and only half-conscious all of that time, but even wide awake I could never have eaten the unnameable slop they offered us! And don't forget that we've been tied beneath that monstrous abnormality in the square for nigh on eleven hours. That alone has robbed me of more energy than the three days spent in that galley rolled into one.

'Tiania is amazing. There's more of the Elder Gods in her than you'd ever guess – even taking into account her unearthly beauty – and I fancy that's what saved her from being greatly affected by proximity to the great ruby. As for me, all I need is a bite of plain, decent food, a little rest, and I'll soon be my normal self again. Or my *ab*normal self, if you will. I don't suppose you brought a bottle of brandy with you, Henri? By God, that would cheer me up no end!'

In spite of all his worries, de Marigny had to grin. This was typical of the Titus Crow he knew, a far cry from the forlorn and desperate figure so recently tied fast to the steps of the ruby dais. Indeed, Crow had not been understating that vast jewel's debilitating influence, and as the distance between the flyers and the ruby increased, so something of Crow's former strength and zest began to return. De Marigny knew that when that strength had returned fully, then indeed would Titus Crow be a force to reckon with, and it would certainly be a dark hour for the evil influences at present operating in Earth's dreamland.

And de Marigny understood what his friend had meant by referring to himself as being 'abnormal.' During his adventures in space and time, on his way to Elysia, Crow had crashed the time-clock into an alien world. Rescued from oblivion by a robot doctor, T3RE, Crow had been rebuilt from the pulp of his human body by a science beyond anything even guessed at by the doctors and scientists of his mother world. He was immensely strong and fast; he could stay underwater without mechanical aids for indefinite periods; his skin was impervious to all but the most corrosive atmospheres; and, perhaps most amazing of all, he had been built in the image of himself as he had been twenty to twenty-five years earlier! Even Crow's mind had been altered! He had found himself able to do completely inexplicable and unbelievable things with the time-clock, using it in ways never conceived of by its original builders, the Elder Gods themselves.

De Marigny banished all such thoughts and memories from his mind as he caused the cloak to drop them down to the roof of the tower. With a little cry of relief Tiania threw herself into Crow's arms. He stroked her for a moment, then turned to their rescuer:

'Well, Henri, what do you have in mind now? We're not out of the fire yet, my friend.'

'I know that, but –' de Marigny began, then paused and put a finger to his lips as suddenly sounds of activity began to drift up from the nighted city. Below, some distance away, freshly lighted torches flared redly. The man in the flying cloak turned a wide-eyed look to his companions. 'That sounds like trouble. It looks like they've discovered your escape!'

# 3

# Night-Gaunt

'They'll soon alert the whole city,' de Marigny continued in haste as he tried to rearrange his plans. 'Titus, how many of them are there in Dylath-Leen?'

'A thousand, possibly more,' Crow answered. 'We saw a regular fleet of their black galleys in the harbor.'

'Then we've no time to lose. Same as last time, I'll take Tiania first and see if I can get her to a safe place beyond the watchfires at the perimeter of the city. Then I'll be back for you. Lie low, Titus, until I get back.'

Crow clapped his friend on the back and wished him luck, then squatted down behind the tower's parapet wall. A second later de Marigny was once again airborne, with Tiania wrapped in a wing of his cloak. As they flew on high, looking down at the squares and rooftops of nighted Dylath-Leen, they could see that indeed the horned horrors from Leng were beginning to throng the city's streets.

With the fingers of his free hand upon the studs that controlled the cloak's antigravitic forces, and his other arm wrapped firmly around Tiania's tiny waist, de Marigny coaxed the clock up higher still into the night air. The girl clung tightly to him, but though the swiftflowing air was chill, their height above the ground fearful, and the tension increasing with each passing moment, not once did she tremble.

He believed she must be thinking about Titus Crow, left behind now atop the tower in the middle of an unquiet city, and to divert her mind from any morbid train of thought, he said: 'You're a brave girl, Tiania.'

She immediately turned her head toward him and smiled through the rush of dark air, and de Marigny believed he could see the worry and fear swiftly fading from her lovely, almost luminous face. 'I'm not really brave,' she said. 'In the care of two such as you and Titus, what can there be to fear?'

It was de Marigny's turn to smile; but a second later he frowned, asking: 'Why in the name of all that's wonderful didn't you two bring flying cloaks with you to dreamland? I should have thought that –'

'But we did bring cloaks,' she cut him off, 'and would have brought a time-clock, too, except that it would give the game away. Our cloaks were taken from us by those horned beasts when they trapped us. The fools, they threw them away with the rest of our clothes!'

'They didn't know what they were?'

'No. Creatures such as they are could never dream of flying. Their very souls are earthbound.'

'And how were you trapped in the first place?' de Marigny asked, noting that the watchfires were slowly falling away to the rear. He stared ahead into darkness, hoping to find a good place to alight.

'That is a long story, but I will try to be brief . . .

'When first we came here there were many things we should have done. We ought first to have visited Atal the Wise, and perhaps Kuranes of Ooth-Nargai beyond the Tanarian Hills. But there seemed so many wonders to see – almost as many as one might find in Elysia – and it was the first time I had ever been in an alien world, even a dream world. Also, I wanted Titus for myself for a little while. And so I persuaded him to spend just a day or two in idle wandering from town to town, spending the nights at tiny inns and taverns. To me it was just a game, you see. I did not know . . .

'Anyway, Titus agreed to my silly ideas, saying it would be a good way to acclimatize ourselves, to get the feel of dreamland. We used our cloaks very discreetly, usually traveling in the hours immediately before dawn. Thus, distance was no problem.

'Those first two days were wonderful; then in Ath –

'Ath is an unpleasant little place bordering on Istharta. Neither Titus nor I liked it much and we did not stay there long. But while we were there Titus was given a lead to follow. It was a false lead, but we did not know that then. We were told by a man of dreamland – a traitor, in league with the dark forces of nightmare, a dupe of powers unnatural in dream who must have somehow known who we were and why we were here – that we should go to the Isle of Oriab, across the Southern Sea. He told us to go to Baharna, the great seaport, where we would find a black galley whose captain would be able to tell us all we needed to know of the troubles besetting dreamland, perhaps even how to deal with those troubles.

'We went to Baharna, arriving late in the evening when the wharves were all in darkness. The captain of the black galley, a squat little man who kept himself in the shadows, told us to go to a certain tavern, that he would meet us there upon the morrow. The tavern was a wharfside place, none too clean and somehow depressing, where furtive figures seemed to hide in dark corners. But our room was the best in the house, and the food and wine seemed excellent . . . The food, the wine too – they were drugged! We woke up captives of the black galley, and . . . but the rest you know.'

De Marigny nodded. 'Well, it's all over now. And look there!' he pointed sharply down into the darkness. 'That's it, that white rock there. It's not too high or steep for you to climb down from should . . . should anything happen. And it's a landmark I can't miss when I return with Titus. Down we go, Tiania.'

He caused the cloak to drop them gently down to a wide ledge halfway up the peak that jutted stark and white from

the desert's sands. There he deposited Tiania, telling her
that it would not be long before he brought Titus to her,
and then that they would all three be in Ulthar in time
for breakfast. It was not to be so, but de Marigny could
not know that.

To Titus Crow, waiting behind the parapet wall of the
tower only a mile from the unquiet center of Dylath-Leen,
it seemed an inordinately long time indeed before de
Marigny came silently winging down once more out of
the night to alight beside him like some great bat. 'Henri,'
Crow whispered, 'is all well?'

The low hush of his voice was not unwarranted. The
streets below were alive with torch-bearing search parties,
so that Dylath-Leen was a maze of redly flickering flames
and leaping shadows – and now from all directions could
be heard the hideous, ululant alert-cries of the horned
ones from nighted Leng. Indeed the sound of hurrying
footsteps even echoed up to them from the street directly
beneath their tall refuge.

'So far so good,' de Marigny breathlessly answered.
'Tiania is safe for the moment. I think we're just about in
the clear, Titus. This flying cloak of yours must take all the
credit, though. Without it I could have done nothing.'

'The cloak is yours now, Henri – you've earned it. Here,
tuck this sword into your belt. Now, just let me get a firm
grip. Right, up we go!'

More slowly this time, feeling the burden of Titus
Crow's greater weight, the flying cloak lifted the two
friends into the night air over Dylath-Leen, and both
men were greatly relieved when the flickering torchfires
had dimmed and fallen away below and behind them. It
was not long then before other fires sprang up in red relief
to their front, and soon after that they were flying high
above the watchfires at the rim of the city.

'A mile, perhaps two miles more,' said de Marigny.

'There's a jagged fang of white rock sticking up out of the desert. That's where I left Tiania. We'll be there in another minute or so.'

'And what then, Henri – a series of short hops to Ulthar?'

'Something like that, I think, yes.'

'Good. And as soon as we've rested up a little and found safe lodging for Tiania, then we're off to Ilek-Vad. I want to know just exactly what's going on there. Yes, and you might even find time to tell me what the devil you're doing here in Earth's dreamland, when by all rights you should be well on your way to Elysia.'

'I *am* on my way to Elysia, Titus. This is the only way I'm ever likely to get there. Kthanid asked me to come, telling me that you and Tiania were in trouble. I'll tell you the whole story later. As for Ilek-Vad: yes, I, too, would like to know what's going on there. After all, that's where my father is. I don't remember a great deal about him, but –'

'There's your white rock dead ahead!' Crow suddenly cried, cutting his friend off short. He pointed eagerly. 'And there's Tiania, I can see her waving. Oh, well done, Henri. You're not an inch off course!'

Controlling the cloak's descent, de Marigny brought them drifting down toward the ledge where the girl-goddess waited. She waved again, reaching out her arms to them as they approached out of the darkness.

It was only then – as the two men felt a rushing blast of air, a buffeting gust much stronger and quite different from any normal draught they might expect to meet during their steady flight above the desert – that they realized something was greatly amiss. The freakish, turbulent eddy tossed them to one side, so that they crashed shoulders-on into the sheer wall of the rock at a point some thirty feet to one side of Tiania. Here the drop was sheer to the desert's floor, and de Marigny had to manipulate the cloak's studs to draw back from the white rock's jagged face. As he did so he heard Crow's sharp intake of breath, and following his friend's horrified gaze he saw and recognized a huge gray shape that passed noiselessly by, circling the rocky spire on membrane wings.

'Night-gaunt!' cried de Marigny, fighting to regain control of the cloak as it was caught again in the wash of the creature's wings. 'A great gray gaunt!'

'Put me down on that ledge, quick!' Crow shouted. 'That damn thing must be after Tiania! Look — here it comes again!'

For the third time they felt the turbulence of the huge night-gaunt's wings as they flapped in leathery sentience, suspending their rubbery owner directly over the girl who now crouched terrified on the ledge of the white rock. Now they were able to get a reasonably clear view of the thing, better by far than de Marigny's previous look at such creatures received through Kthanid's telepathic knowledge-imparting.

The horror, while being twice as big as any of its loathsome species viewed before, was nevertheless endowed with the same noxiously thin outline as lesser gaunts and wore precisely the same aspect. Horns sprouted from its faceless head; it was barb-tailed and bat-winged; its skin looked rubbery, cold, and damp – and, possibly worst of all, it was utterly silent.

Then de Marigny was rushed abruptly aloft as Crow let go his hold on the cloak's harness to leap to the ledge close to Tiania. Yet again struggling to bring the cloak under his control, de Marigny all but missed what followed next. As it was he heard Crow's cry of rage and horror . . . and he saw the gray shape of that giant among night-gaunts as it lifted skyward on silently beating pinions, bearing aloft the wriggling, shrieking, slender form of Tiania grasped in prehensile paws!

# 4

## *Atal's Elixir*

On the wide ledge of the white rock's peak high above the desert, Titus Crow raged silently in the night and shook his scimitar at the diminishing gray shape that flapped away against a background of strange constellations. By the time de Marigny had landed beside him, however, the naked giant had recovered his equilibrium sufficiently to cry out in a half-choked voice: 'Quickly, man, out of the cloak! Hurry, Henri, I must get after that monster!'

Seeing instantly how useless and time-consuming it would be to argue – aware that the cloak was designed to operate at maximum efficiency with only one passenger and that it was Titus Crow's prerogative to pursue the huge night-gaunt and rescue Tiania, if such was at all possible – de Marigny immediately unfastened the cloak's harness and helped Crow into it. Then, without another word spoken, Crow grabbed his friend around the waist with one arm, his other hand flying to the collar studs that controlled the cloak. Another moment saw de Marigny deposited none too gently on the desert's sandy floor.

Rising again into the night, Crow called: 'Can you find your way back to Ulthar, Henri?'

'I know the way,' de Marigny shouted back. 'Five miles or so from here I pick up the Skai and simply follow the river. No need to worry about me, Titus. I'll see you in Ulthar . . . both of you! Good luck!'

'Thanks. I fancy I'll need all the luck I can get,' Crow's answer came back from the heights. 'Take care, Henri.' For a moment or two he was a vague batshape against the blue crystal stars, then he was gone.

Half an hour and a little more than two miles later, as he strode out over the desert dunes in the direction of Ulthar, led on by the sweet scent of night-blooming flowers on the banks of the Skai, de Marigny glanced for the tenth time apprehensively over his shoulder. It was his imagination, of course, but for the last twenty minutes or so, since shortly after he set out from the foot of the white rock pinnacle, he had had the feeling that he was being followed. Yet each time he looked back there was nothing to be seen, only the low dunes and occasionally the rock jutting starkly against the night-dark sky.

Climbing to the top of a high dune, he glanced back yet again and this time spied in the distance the darkly looming basalt towers of Dylath-Leen. No healthy lights showed in the city, only a dull glow from the watchfires at its rim. It shocked de Marigny to be reminded how close he still was to that nightmare-cursed city, and he determined there and then to increase his distance from it as rapidly as humanly possible. It did not seem likely that the horned ones could be on his trail already, and yet –

He shuddered and felt the short hairs rise at the back of his neck, a reaction not alone engendered of the desert's chill, and turned once more toward friendly Ulthar; but even as he turned he saw a movement in the corner of his eye. Something had slipped silently from shadow to shadow less than a hundred yards to his rear. Now he remembered something Grant Enderby had told him – about how expert the horned ones were at tracking their prey – and he shuddered again.

Quickly de Marigny slid down the side of the dune and looked about for a vantage point. He ran for a boulder that lay half-buried in the sand and hid behind it. As he went to his knees in the shadows he heard a distant but distinct wail rising in the night air. The cry reached its highest note, quavered inquiringly, then died into eerie silence. It was almost immediately answered by a second call, from a point de Marigny judged to be just beyond the tall dune; and while these were not the ululant alert cries with which he was now familiar, nevertheless the dreamer knew that they were given voice by those same horned horrors from Leng!

Now de Marigny shot frantic glances to left and right, his eyes searching the desert's starlit gloom for areas of deeper shadow that might hide his onward flight toward the river. And as he did so there came to his ears many more of the inquiring cries – except that now certain of the creatures who uttered those hideous bayings obviously flanked him! Indeed, one of those cries had seemed to come from somewhere *behind* where he crouched, from the direction of the Skai itself. And this cry had been different in that it had seemed somehow – triumphant?

So intent was he upon gauging the exact directions whence these latter sounds had issued that he almost failed to hear the soft footfalls in the sand. Too late, he did hear them, and he turned with a single gasp of horror in time to see only the jeweled hilt of a scimitar in the instant before it struck him between the eyes . . .

When de Marigny regained consciousness he believed for a moment that he had somehow returned through the barriers of dream to the waking world. But not so. Though the sun stood at its zenith and hurt his eyes behind his fluttering eyelids, the dreamer knew that indeed he was still a prisoner of dreamland; more than ever a prisoner, for the buildings and towers that loomed blackly upwards before him, and the steps that sent knives of pain lancing into his spine where he was tied to them were a basalt quarried in dreamland. This could only be Dylath-Leen; and sure enough, if he tilted his head right back at an angle he could see – the great ruby!

'Ah, our friend from the waking world of men has finally

returned to us – with a very sick head, no doubt!' The squat speaker leaned carelessly on the hilt of his scimitar, its point digging into the rough grain of the steps and its blade curving uncomfortably close to de Marigny's rib cage. The coarse black silk of the horned one's baggy breeches was stained and grimed, the red sash at his waist festooned with knives. He wore huge rubies in the rings on his fat fingers and an evil grin upon his face, in which veiled, slightly slanted eyes regarded de Marigny almost hungrily.

And suddenly the dreamer was aware of his pain. His skin felt completely dehydrated, baked dry under the noon sun; his back, which through long hours of unconsciousness had lain across the sharp corners of three of the dais steps, felt as though it might break in pieces at any moment; his head ached abominably and felt grotesquely swollen. Naked, his entire body was bruised from being brutally dragged across miles of desert sands; his lips, tongue, and throat were parched, and leather thongs cut into his wrists and ankles where they were tied.

'Dreamer, we are going to kill you!' This time the speaker emphasized his words by idly kicking de Marigny's bruised ribs. De Marigny barely held back the cry of agony that sprang to his lips, managing at the same time to lift his head up high enough to see that he was ringed by perhaps twenty of the horned ones. Their leader, the speaker, wore no shoes, and de Marigny knew that the extreme pain he had felt when his tender ribs were kicked was due to the fact that his torturer had hooves instead of feet.

'We are going to kill you,' that monstrous being said again, 'but it is entirely up to you how we do it. You can die slowly, very slowly, losing first your hands, then your feet, and your so-called manhood. Then your ears, your eyes, your tongue at the very end. It would take at least a day, perhaps two. *Or you could die the hard way!'*

He paused to let that last sink in, then continued: 'On the other hand, we could be merciful.'

'I doubt,' de Marigny groaned, 'if your sort know the meaning of mercy.'

'Ah, but we do! For instance, it would be merciful to lop off your head with a single stroke – but before you are granted that boon, there are several things I want to know.'

The horned one waited expectantly but de Marigny made no answer.

'If I have your eyes propped open with slivers of wood, and your head tied back, you would very quickly, very painfully go blind. The sun is singularly unkind to those who stare so at her. But before that becomes necessary –'

'– You want to know something.'

'Correct! You have been listening to me. That is good. There are several things I wish to know, yes. One: how did you come into Dylath-Leen so secretively, and manage to kill three of our colleagues so efficiently before they could even raise the alarm? Two: how were you able to smuggle your friends so cleverly, so swiftly away, when you yourself were later caught? Three: where are your friends now, for we must bring them back here in order that they may keep an important appointment. And finally, four: what is in this vial, which was all you carried other than your knife and a length of rope?'

The elixir! De Marigny gasped involuntarily as his questioner mentioned Atal's elixir. He had forgotten about the vial until now. The horned one heard the dreamer's gasp and was quick to note how his eyes had widened fractionally, however momentarily. 'Eh?' he grunted. 'Something I said? About this strange little bottle of liquid, perhaps?' He held the vial out, between thumb and forefinger, where de Marigny could see it.

'A man, with no food, no water, coming out of nowhere

with nothing but a knife, a rope, and this – and yet you somehow succeeded in rescuing your two friends. Amazing! And such a little thing, this vial, to sustain the three of you across the desert to Ulthar. What does it contain?'

De Marigny's brain whirled as he sought an advantageous way to answer the horned one's question. 'A . . . a *poison*,' he finally offered. 'It contains a deadly poison.'

His questioner lifted his scimitar, allowing its point to scrape slowly up the line of de Marigny's ribs, and peered intently at its shiny blade. For a long moment he was silent, then: 'Oh, no, no, no, my friend.' His voice was low now, oily, deadly; his eyes glittered dangerously. 'That will never do. A little vial of poison – no more than a dozen or so drops – to murder an entire city?'

De Marigny writhed both physically and mentally, like a great intelligent moth pinned to some entomologist's card. He had hoped that his interrogator would make him drink his own 'poison' – which by now should have properly fermented – but the ruse had not worked. Then, like a flash of lightning illuminating the dark clouds of the dreamer's mind, there came a scene remembered from his youth. From a book, perhaps, or a cartoon viewed in some moviehouse of childhood. It was the picture of a rabbit: Br'er Rabbit! And suddenly de Marigny believed that there might after all be a way out. He could but try.

'If I tell you what is in the vial – if I reveal the secret of the magical potion it contains – will you swear to set me free unharmed?'

The horned one pretended to give de Marigny's proposal some consideration, fooling the dreamer not at all, then grated: 'Agreed. After all, it is not you we want but the two you stole from us. If what you have to tell us has some bearing on their present whereabouts, then we will set you free.'

Now it was de Marigny's turn to feign deliberation.

Finally he said, 'It is an elixir to increase one's strength tenfold. One sip of the potion – one drop – and a man may leap the tallest dune at one bound, stride over the desert to Ulthar in the space of a single hour, fight like ten men to overcome tremendous odds, aye, and never once feel the effort.'

The horned one folded the vial carefully in his fat fist and stared at de Marigny intently. 'Is this true?'

'How else do you suppose I came out of the night, without provisions, defeating your three guardsmen like so many children to be tossed aside? How else do you explain the utter absence of the two I rescued, gone now like the wind over the desert? Doubtless they are even now in Ulthar, at the Temple of the Elder Ones, where Atal –'

'*Atal!*' hissed his interrogator. 'What do you know of Atal?'

'Why, it was Atal gave me the elixir, to speed me on my quest!'

A murmuring swelled in the crowd of horned ones standing about, mutterings of hatred, of awe and amazement – of greed for the magic elixir, if elixir it was. Now de Marigny's questioner opened his fist once more to stare lustfully at the tiny bottle it contained. Then his expression grew very sly.

'No, I do not believe you. I think that after all it is perhaps a poison, and that you would trick me into tasting it. If so, then –' He quickly unstoppered the vial and thrust it toward de Marigny's face. The dreamer, expecting that this might happen, lifted up his head and opened his mouth wide, straining his neck to reach the tiny bottle.

Immediately the horned one snatched back his arm. He grinned evilly. 'So your story *is* true! It . . . must be.' His grin was quickly replaced by a look of strange anticipation. He licked his wide lips and his hand actually trembled as once more he studied the vial with wide eyes.

'Let me try it, Garl,' came a guttural rasp from one who stood behind the leader.

'No, me,' another voice demanded.

'Hold!' Garl held up his hand. 'There is still one question unanswered.' He turned his gaze once more to de Marigny's face. 'If indeed you tell the truth, how was it we caught you so easily? Why did you not escape, like your friends, by leaping away over the dunes and speeding to Ulthar?'

'Simple.' De Marigny attempted a shrug as best he could. 'I neglected to heed Atal's warning.'

'Which was?'

'Too much of the elixir affects a man like too much wine, slowing him down and dulling his senses for a while. After freeing the other two dreamers, thinking to make myself stronger and faster still, I took a second sip of the elixir. Before I knew it –'

'We caught you. Hmm! I believe you, yes. And I also believe that with the aid of your elixir we might even recapture the ones you freed. But first the elixir's powers must be tested.'

'I'll test it, Garl,' came a concerted babble of cries from the crowding horned ones.

'Me!'

'No, let me be the one, Garl!'

De Marigny's inquisitor turned on his colleagues. 'What? You'd all like to be stronger than Garl, would you?' He laughed and shook a fat finger at them. 'None of that, my lads. The elixir is far too precious to waste on fools and hotheads. Later, perhaps, I'll handpick a raiding party – and tonight we'll look for certain absent friends in Ulthar – but right now I myself will test the illustrious Atal's elixir! Stand back, all of you!'

Though the sun blazed high overhead, it was not the heat of that golden orb that brought fresh streams of sweat to de Marigny's brow but the slow and deliberate way in

which Garl of Leng lifted one hand up to his alien face –
that and the way his other hand lifted high his scimitar.

'If you have lied to me, dreamer, then at least you'll
have earned yourself a quick death. That is the only bonus
such lies will bring you, however. And now –' He barely
touched his lips to the rim of the tilted vial.

First a look of puzzlement changed the horned one's
features, then a frown. 'A not unpleasant taste,' he began,
'though somewhat –' Then he reeled drunkenly backward
down the dais steps, his scimitar falling with a clatter
from a suddenly spastic hand that clawed its way to his
throat. He swayed at the foot of the dais for a second
only, bulging eyes fixed upon the vial still clenched in
one shaking hand.

Then his outline wavered; he seemed to puff outwards
as his flesh became a mist; finally his clothes fell in a
silken rain to the cobbles of the square. The vial fell too,
cushioned by the coarse silks. Hanging in the air, all that
remained of Garl was a rapidly diminishing echo, a thin
squeal of outrage and horror!

Then de Marigny's hoarse laughter broke the stunned
silence. Hearing the derision in the dreamer's voice, the
awed crowd of horned ones was galvanized into activity.
As one of them stooped to snatch up the fallen vial and
others fought over the remaining silks, the rest ringed de
Marigny on the steps. Scimitars whispered from scabbards
and flashed in the sun, and for a moment the dreamer
thought that he was done for. Then –

'Hold, lads!' shouted the one who had snatched up the
vial. 'I, Barzt, now lead you – and I claim the right to
avenge Garl myself. But first there is something I must
know.' He tickled de Marigny's throat with the point of
his scimitar. 'You, man from the waking world, dreamer.
Where have you sent Garl with your dark magic?'

'He's gone to a hell worse than anything even you could
imagine,' de Marigny chuckled. 'Worse by far than any

torture you could apply to me. You see, the "elixir" was a poison after all, the key to a gate which opens to the blackest hells. Even now Garl screams in eternal agony, where he will curse me in his torment forever; but I am safe from him here in dreamland. Kill me now, if you will, for I am satisfied that Garl has paid for the deaths of my two friends from the waking world. They, too, drank of the poison rather than suffer the indignities of your vile paws. Kill me – kill me now!' He offered up his throat. 'Only –'

De Marigny paused, as if biting his tongue, feigning sudden horror. Then, to the crowding horned ones, it seemed as if he attempted to cringe into himself upon the dais steps. 'No!' he forced a strangled cry from parched lips. 'No, not . . . not *that!*'

'Wha –?' began the frowning Barzt. Then he noticed how de Marigny's terrified eyes had fastened upon the vial he held so gingerly away from his vile body. And Barzt's eyes lit at once with a fiendish delight.

'So!' he cried. 'Garl will curse you in his torment forever, will he? Well then, go to this hell you speak so eloquently of, dreamer, where you, too, may suffer its eternal torments – *and* Garl's tender mercies!' So saying, standing on the dreamer's hair to hold his head still, he stooped and touched the vial to de Marigny's lips.

But no sooner was the oddly shaped bottle at his lips than he licked its moist rim with a darting tongue. Barzt sensed that he had been fooled, but it was too late. In the space of another second or so de Marigny seemed to fill out like a limp balloon suddenly inflated with air, and even as his form wavered and disappeared the horned ones noted the look of glad triumph that lit in his eyes.

And in the wake of his vanishing they heard the echoes of joyous laughter.

# PART FOUR

# 1

# *Beyond the Peaks of Throk*

Subduing his raging fury as best he could, yet totally incapable of curbing the sick feeling of horror that lay thick in his stomach like bile – horror for Tiania in the clutches of that flying beast-thing that soared somewhere ahead in the darkness over the desert – Titus Crow leaned into the wind and rode his cloak like a great bat through the night. He followed the occasional shriek from Tiania, dread draining him every time he heard her cry out, until at last he realized that she was deliberately screaming, creating a trail by means of which he could follow the flightpath of the great night-gaunt.

And it dawned on him too that, plucky girl though she was, she might save some of her breath for later – when perhaps they might both have more need of screaming. Indeed, the flight of the night-gaunt seemed arrow-straight, and Crow's instinct told him where the beast was headed. Then, as its outline momentarily obliterated a great whorl of stars hanging low in the sky ahead, he caught a glimpse of the thing and knew he had been correct. Unlike its cousins, the common gaunts, by virtue of its gigantic size, nevertheless this faceless terror of the night made for a region of dreamland where Titus Crow knew that the lesser gaunts proliferated. He put on a burst of speed to shorten, if possible, the monster's lead.

Out over the Southern Sea sped the great gaunt, and far below Tiania could see all the stars of the night sky reflected in black mirror waters. Normally she would have found such a sight beautiful indeed, but now, dangling from the rubbery paws of this clammy creature as it soared silently through the upper air of dreamland, she shuddered and cried out yet again. She knew that Titus Crow must be somewhere behind the great night-gaunt, knew too that her cries must eventually guide him to her; for while the gaunt could not fly on forever, Crow's cloak was utterly tireless.

Behind her now, Tiania could make out the dim lights of small towns spread along the coast of the Southern Sea, and briefly from far below there came drifting the song of a lone fisherman at the helm of his night-becalmed vessel. Doubtless he was singing to ward off the dark spirits of the night waters, which legend had it walked on the glassy surface of the deep when the nights were calm.

Then, far to the east, Tiania saw the first thin gray line of light curving on the distant horizon. True dawn was still hours away, but the promise of a new day was already aborning. She wondered what the new day would bring, and she thought with longing of faerie Elysia, many dimensions away in space and time. Love of Elysia was strong in Tiania, but love of Titus Crow was stronger. Though she was no longer afraid, she cried out yet again in the darkness, praying that her voice would ride back to her Earthman on the night wind. He would not answer, dared not alert the monstrous creature that carried her high above the Southern Sea of his presence, but as certain to Tiania as the beating of her own pure heart was the knowledge that he was there.

Thus the hours sped by, until chilled and weary, utterly depleted by her adventures, the girl-goddess fell asleep in the grip of the great gaunt. And perhaps fate smiled at Tiania in her innocence, for a warm wind from far exotic lands found her there where she lay between the night-gaunt's clammy paws, lulling her into dreams within dreams which were not at all nightmarish.

Titus Crow, too, saw the thin gray light on the horizon,

and he urged still more speed from his cloak and stream-lined himself to cleave the air more cleanly. He believed that with the dawn the huge night-gaunt would find a cave or crevice in which to sleep and while away the hours of daylight, like less fabulous nocturnal beasts of the waking world. And he wanted to be in view of the creature when it went to ground.

For some time now he had listened intently for Tiania's cries coming back to him on the wind, but in vain, and while he was fairly certain of the direction in which the great gaunt headed, nevertheless he would dearly love to hear the girl's golden voice confirming his guess. Then, as dawn turned the horizon into a gray mist, he spied the vapor-wreathed Isle of Oriab ahead, and against the pale of dawn a nightmare shape that fell down and down toward far Ngranek.

Crow's spirits immediately revived. He had been right, then. The great gaunt's destination was indeed Ngranek, haunt of all the lesser gaunts of night. Now he flew more carefully, keeping his presence secret, for he was closer to the monster than he had dared hope. Down toward Ngranek's peak spiraled the gaunt, with Titus Crow behind it, down toward the mouths of certain caves that opened to the cavernously honeycombed interior of that mountain.

Now Crow could see the strange face cut in vast outlines on that side of the peak forever hidden to Oriab's peoples, the face carved more in the likeness of a strange god than a man. And looking down from on high he saw far beneath those carven features the sterile lava abysses which marked the wrath of the Great Gods of Eld . . . even here in Earth's dreamland! Now, seeing for himself this proof positive of a mighty battle long forgotten and beyond the meager imagination of men, he knew indeed that Ngranek was a peak ancient beyond words.

But Titus Crow had little enough time to study these

things or ponder their import. He had seen the great gaunt settling on high-arched wings toward a black cave mouth, and now he flew his cloak as swiftly as he could in that direction. Around and about this cavern entrance flew a flock of lesser gaunts in apparently aimless circles, and for all that they were more than twice the size of a man they scattered in terror as Crow hurtled through their midst. Then, after he had passed by, they hung in the brightening dawn air in sleepy, faceless bewilderment. And down, down into Ngranek's inner darkness went Titus Crow, flying blind now and of necessity more slowly, following only the muffled throb of vast and leathery wings.

It seemed to the cloaked dreamer that he flitted down through inconceivable gulfs of night; but then, as his eyes grew more accustomed to the gloom, he saw that the dark air was semiluminous with a gray phosphorescence. Moments later he descended into reeking clouds of mist that may well have had their origin in Earth's core.

And now, high above, a monstrously vast ceiling of stalactites stretched away into dim distances, while below marched the ominous needles of spires which could only be the fabulous Peaks of Throk. Down and down, ever deeper the cloak carried Crow into this underworld of dream, until the stark gray Peaks of Throk reached up immense and ageless on all sides. And then the needle tips of those peaks were lost in legendary heights and their feet in darkest depths, so that it seemed to the dreamer he fell between numberless pillars going down to infinity. And always he followed the throb of tremendous, rubbery wings.

Then, for what seemed an interminable time, there came buffeting, howling winds that blew Crow far off course; and struggle as he might against this unexpected maelstrom of air, he could do nothing but pray that he would not be hurled against the granite pillars that loomed on all sides. Now, too, he found his view obscured by clouds of sulphurous ash and smoke; but at last the winds calmed down, the smoke cleared, and far away the dreamer saw the Peaks of Throk receding into flickering, pale-blue death-fires. Then there was only darkness and a distant, weary-sounding throbbing of monstrous wings.

Knowing that by now he could only be in the fabled Vale of Pnoth, where the enormous dholes dig their burrows and pile their cairns of bones, Crow felt something of the unreasoning terror that all dreamers know in the face of nightmare. For this was that place where all the ghouls of the waking world are reputed to throw the remains of their graveyard feasts. Titus Crow desired to meet neither ghouls nor dholes, and so he put on a burst of speed in the direction of the now fading throbbing.

Again he was flying blind, in near-solid darkness, but his instinct did not desert him; and as he rushed through reeking ebony vaults he reminded himself over and over again that many things are far simpler in dream. But then he uttered a short, harsh sardonic bark of self-derision as he wondered why, if this were really so, he was finding things so difficult!

Beneath him now as he flew he could hear a dry rustling, which he guessed must be the sound that dholes make in their singular bone-heaping occupations; and once he brushed against something that loomed up vast and slimy in his path. Then ahead he saw a bright point of light that soon grew into a painful white glare. Approaching the source of this harsh illumination, he saw that it was a natural cave that led back into the face of a sheer wall of granite. A moment later a great gray shadow flitted eerily and silently along the path of white light to disappear into the cave beyond.

Titus Crow's mechanical heart seemed to give a great leap within him then, for at the last he had seen a limp, slender form hanging from that shadow's tiredly drooping paws! Now, reassuring himself, he fondled the hilt of his scimitar where it hung from the belt of his cloak's harness, and he allowed himself a low grunt of grim anticipation as he drove for the bright cave's entrance.

It was then, as he entered into a tremendously vast white cavern, that the disaster occurred. Fortunately for Titus Crow the thing came immediately after he cleared the cave's entrance, when he was flying only a few feet above the white sands that floored the fantastic cavern. If he had been at a greater height . . . it did not bear thinking about.

For without warning his cloak suddenly disappeared, vanishing utterly and without trace in an instant, leaving him prone in thin air, diving forward in a downward curve that could only end in the white sand! A second later came the shock of impact and momentary oblivion, then painful consciousness. He spat out sand and picked himself up; shaken and awed, he stared all about. The cloak had quite definitely vanished, so useless to worry or wonder about the hows or whys of it – and anyway there were other, more important things to think about.

Staring across the desert of white sand, Crow's eyes narrowed as he picked out a vague movement in the middle distance. Instinct warned him that there were terrible dangers here, for himself as well as the girl-goddess, and if Tiania of Elysia was to be rescued unharmed from this unknown place, then he must face those dangers alone, naked and on foot . . .

## *Perchance to Dream*

De Marigny came joyously awake in the time-clock, whirling in orbit high above the Earth. His awakening was instantaneous, without any of the usual transitory dullness of mind and physical sloth, so that he immediately remembered all that had happened. Indeed, his *removal* from dreamland to the waking world was so complete that its effect upon his senses was more a physical than a purely mental thing; for a few moments he felt that his body as well as his mind had been transported. Then the truth of the matter sank in, and as his somewhat shaky laughter terminated in a ringing shout of triumph, he realized that his ploy against the horned ones in Dylath-Leen had been completely successful.

It was only when this initial euphoria began to wear off that de Marigny saw the several rather less than pleasing circumstances of his escape. One: he was wearing the flying cloak, which could only mean that Titus Crow no longer wore it. Then he remembered what Atal had told him about the elixir – how one sip would immediately transport a dreamer back to the waking world, *along with anything he had brought into dreamland with him!* Knowing that in all likelihood Titus Crow depended upon the cloak for his own and Tiania's lives, de Marigny found this last train of thought too unpleasant to follow up. Instead he turned to problem number two: his main reason for wanting to wake up had been to return at once to dreamland, this time taking the time-clock with him. How might he do this now, when he had never felt more fully awake in his entire life?

Now, furious that everything he did seemed to be working out adversely, he cursed himself soundly. Atal's elixir, as far as Henri-Laurent de Marigny was concerned, had performed its function marvelously – but its effect now was that of a strong stimulant, and there seemed no guarantee at all that this effect would soon wear off. He cursed himself again. Of course, it could hardly have been foreseen, but it would have been so simple to ask Atal for something, some drug or 'potion' with which he might return himself to dreamland.

Then de Marigny's eyes lit with inspiration and he snapped his fingers. A drug to return him to dreamland? Why, he knew of something that could do the job admirably. Alcohol!

He was not a great drinker, but he did enjoy a glass of brandy. A double invariably quickened his mind. Another, taken immediately after the first, usually made him tingle. A third would dull his senses considerably, and a fourth –

Half a bottle should see him back to dreamland almost as quickly as he could drink it! One of his few, hasty, last-minute provisions prior to setting out for Elysia had been to load the time-clock with three bottles of the very best cognac. These had been for Titus Crow, for good brandies were Crow's one weakness. Now he opened one of the bottles and took a long, deep draft, coughing and spluttering as the first 'bite' of the fluid inflamed his throat. Crow, he knew, would have called him a barbarian; but doubtless he would also have agreed that the deadly serious nature of the situation demanded a rapid solution, however drastic.

Halfway through the bottle, de Marigny felt his head begin to spin quite independently of the whirling timeclock (the motion of which, impossibly, he was beginning to believe he could now actually feel) and suddenly he found himself incapable of repressing a short burst of uproarious laughter. Also, a haze was definitely creeping over his brain, but much too slowly. He took another mouthful of the warming, heady fluid, and yet another. Then, as he removed the bottle from his lips, he staggered.

Now, he knew that it was quite impossible for him to physically stagger inside the clock. While Titus Crow could use the machine both as a gateway into all space and time and as a vehicle proper, de Marigny simply was not yet adept enough for that. Indeed, his one effort in that direction had been completely involuntary, almost disastrous. Therefore he recognized the fact, however vaguely, that he had 'staggered' mentally. In short, he knew now that he was very nearly drunk.

By this time only an inch or so of brandy remained in the bottle. De Marigny peered at it curiously for a moment, swilled it about – then yawned. No more than twenty minutes had elapsed since he started on his solitary binge, but he grinned lopsidedly and began to sing, finishing the bottle off between repeated bursts of the following four lines:

> 'Oh, carry me back to dreamland,
> That's the way to go, to go.
> Carry me back to dreamland,
> You space-time so-and-so!'

The minutes passed steadily and de Marigny's singing occasionally faltered, picking up intermittently as he struggled to keep the song going. Finally the bottle slipped from his fingers – but he was not aware of it.

Outside the clock, had there been someone to observe it, it would at that moment seem that the stars themselves blurred, if only for a moment, and that the disc of Earth trembled in its inexorable orbit of the mighty

571

solar furnace. It might seem, for a moment, that the entire scene were viewed through smoke or warm, rising air – and that then, in the next instant, things were once more as they had always been.

But they were not . . .

# 3

## Creatures of the Cave

White crystal sands shifted beneath Titus Crow's naked feet. He stood under a great white roof that formed a sky reflecting the whiteness of the desert. And the floor of the vast cavern surely was a desert. Miles of bleached sand stretched to the limits of vision in dunes and hills, and the only relief in this blinding monotony was a dark dot moving in the middle distance.

The dreamer had no idea where the blinding light of the place came from – that brightness which so garishly illumined every feature of what ought to have been one of the underworld's blackest pits – but in any case he was far more concerned about other things. One of those things, the one uppermost in his mind, was the agitated motion of the distant dot.

He found his scimitar where it had fallen from the belt of his disappearing cloak, then turned to face in the direction of the peculiar movements. He watched the disturbance grow with a startling swiftness. Soon the single moving shape split amoeba-like into two – one up and one down – and in only a few seconds more the two took on definite forms. Spiraling up from the lower form he could see regular white puffs of sand.

The hairs at the back of Titus Crow's neck suddenly stiffened. At first he had thought that the moving object must be that great gaunt which had carried off Tiania; now he could see how wrong he had been. There were in fact three – creatures? One flew, the second rode upon the Flyer's back, the third ran beneath . . . and all three were things of sheerest nightmare!

573

Of the three as they drew closer, Crow found the tripedal Runner the most fantastic. Though its two outer legs were thin and bent like those of some monstrous spider, nevertheless they were powerfully muscled; they acted as springs or pistons. The inner or center leg was three times as thick as the other two together, straight and horribly hammerlike. The Runner looked like a great freakish three-legged race, with its center leg slamming forward and down, to be hoisted up again and thrust forward by the springy power of its twin companions. The – foot? – at the end of that middle limb was awesome: hugely splayed and webbed, as wide at least as any ten normal feet, clublike. Why! That great foot would crush muscle and bone to pulp as easily and utterly as would a falling northern pine!

Tall though Crow was, the Runner stood at least half as tall again. It had short, stumpy arms – useless appendages to Crow's keen eyes – and a slender neck. But the *face* above that neck! The dreamer shuddered. He had seen similar things in nightmares as a boy: the red, bulging eyes, the dripping fangs in grinning, wide-slit mouths . . .

By now the creatures were much closer and slowing their pace, but still eagerly craning their necks in Crow's direction, obviously appraising him before a concerted attack. The Runner uttered a hideous cry – like the rasp of a file upon an edge of glass, or a giant chalk on a slate – before moving off to one side from beneath the Flyer and its Rider. Crow did not have to turn to follow the creature's movements; the thudding vibrations of the sand under his feet positioned the Runner exactly in his mind's eye. Instead he concentrated upon the other two.

The Flyer was a monstrous, slender worm, with no eyes that Titus Crow could see, just undulant body and gaping beak. Yet, somehow he knew that the thing sensed him keenly and knew of him as he knew of it. The Rider, seated to the rear of the bat-worm's wings, was worse still. A

574

skull-like head set with glaring green eyes surmounted a thin and wiry body, scaled and mottled in squamous shades, with arms of fantastic length hanging like coiled whips at its sides.

Studying these beings of nightmare Crow tightened his grip on his sword. He was aware of their subtle, edging approach. He would have preferred them to come on at their original headlong pace, when he would have relied upon the superb reactions built into his semisynthetic body by the robot T3RE, but they had seemed to sense his tremendous speed and strength and were wary. Indeed, Crow's strength had returned, and now it redoubled as he reconciled himself to battle. It seemed that this was to be the only way he could get on with his pursuit of the great gaunt and Tiania: first, to do battle with these three creatures of the white cavern.

The Flyer and its Rider were still twenty feet or so from the dreamer when he had his first taste of the fight to come. The Rider took first blood when, catching Crow off guard, a razor-clawed tentacle lashed out like the tongue of a chameleon, cutting his cheek. The cut almost touched his eye and caused him to cry out in outrage at the unexpected pain. The tentacle was withdrawn well out of range before he could even bring his scimitar into a defensive position.

Instantly, at sight of the red blood on Crow's cheek, the Rider began to laugh: '*Rhee, rheee, rheee-eee-eee!*' And as the hair of Crow's neck again reacted to this hellish sound, so he sensed the rapid approach of the Runner – from the rear!

Second blood, with a lightning stroke of the scimitar, went to the embattled dreamer. For having perceived the Runner's cowardly rear attack through the shuddering of the sand underfoot, Titus Crow turned and made a headlong dive to one side. And as the Runner pounded by mere inches away, so the scimitar leaped up in Crow's hand to sever at the knee the creature's right outer leg.

The rest of the fight was chaos and nightmare combined. All three of the hideous guardians of the cavern were screaming, particularly the pain-crazed, crippled Runner. The latter was now slewing mindlessly about on its own axis in a welter of gray ichor and white sand. Half blinded by his own blood and that of the Runner, Crow flailed about with his sword, knowing from the deafening cries of the Flyer and its razor-tentacled rider that they were near at hand. He felt his sword arm suddenly caught in a tentacular grip and wrenched at an odd angle, felt the scimitar fly from fingers part-numbed as his forearm almost broke. And then he took his strong square teeth savagely to work on the slimy tentacle coiled crushingly round his arm.

With his free arm he protected his head, all the time working at the tentacle with his teeth and feeling upon his shoulders and back the agony of ripping cuts from the Rider's second vicious appendage. But suddenly, as his mouth filled with a vile fluid from the rubbery limb, he felt himself jerked off his feet and dashed down in the sand. The movement had been convulsive and he guessed that his teeth had found a ticklish nerve. But he had lost his sword.

Free now, he rolled automatically – feeling the burning sting of sand in his torn back, groping for his sword, not knowing where or even in which direction it lay – until his hand came into contact with something solid. He clenched his fingers about the unknown object and rolled onto his back.

There, immediately above him, lancing down, came the vicious beak of the blind Flyer. Just how the awesome bat-worm knew his exact position he could never have guessed, and he had no time for guessing. He jerked up the object grasped in his hand and thrust it between himself and the descending beak. He saw then that his shield was nothing less than the shorn leg of the Runner, which the Flyer at once tore from his grasp and tossed to one side.

Yet, even as Crow gave up his gristly shield he came to his feet, swinging one fist in a deadly arc to smack shatteringly against the side of the lunging beak. The 'bones' of Crow's arms and hands were shaped mainly of an incredibly tough plastic, but the bat-worm's beak, however effective as a weapon, was only of shell-like bone. That great beak cracked open like a hammered egg, and marrow and yellow juices slopped out to further drench the bloodied dreamer.

The Flyer went mad then, shrieking in its excruciating agony, worm-body coiling and whipping, flinging its harshly gibbering Rider down onto the white sand. Crow had but a second to collect his scattered senses as the dazed and suddenly silenced Rider climbed to its feet, but in that second he saw his sword sticking pommel-up from a patch of slimed sand.

The weapon lay directly in the path of the Runner, which was again heading, in an erratic and lumbering fashion, for the gore-spattered dreamer. Crow saw the thing's approach as a last desperate effort to bring him down before the seepage of its vile life's juices stilled it forever; he saw, too, the possible destruction of his sword beneath that lopsidedly pounding hammer-leg.

Without the scimitar he was done for, and so he hurled himself frantically across the sand, fingers stretched wide and reaching. Even as his hand grasped the hilt of the curving sword, Crow knew he had run out of time. The huge, pounding leg of the Runner was already in the air, its own thrust compensating for the missing outer member. Down came that great hammer toward his head – and then, a miracle!

With a bubbling shriek something shot over Crow's

spread-eagled body on tortured wings to smack blindly into the towering Runner. Bat-worm and Runner alike crashed down onto the sand as Crow rose with the scimitar in his hand, unable to believe that he still lived. The Runner lay there – mad fangs gnashing in its hideous face, its remaining outer leg limp but its hammer continuing to pound away at the air – and the half-crippled Flyer flopped mindlessly about on the sand, its fractured beak dripping evil-smelling liquid.

The dreamer knew suddenly the means by which that bat-worm had known his whereabouts during the fight. The thing had somehow been guided by its Rider – that Rider which held the reins *in its mind* rather than in its hand! The two had existed in a weird symbiosis. But now, without its Rider, the Flyer was truly blind! No wonder the tentacled Rider was even now crying out harshly to the wounded monster, trying the while to climb once more onto its back.

'To hell with that!' Crow roared, leaping forward to swing his sword in an awesome blow that cut into and through the neck of the bat-worm, sending its evil head flying to spatter the already fouled sand. Yet again the half-mounted Rider fell as the body of his beast-brother commenced its last, convulsive spasm and fell to sprawl on the white sand beside the now motionless Runner.

And now the Rider saw that he was indeed on his own. With an alien cry of rage and hatred he sprang to his feet, uncoiling his tentacular arms, drawing them back whiplike onto the sand behind him. Crow knew that in another moment those viciously claw-tipped weapons would be at him; his superb reactions took over almost unbidden. In one lithe movement he leaned forward, throwing the scimitar like a knife straight at the Rider's black heart.

The point ran home and the weight of the curving blade carried it through the Rider's thin body. Surprise grew like a pale stain on the creature's face, then his tentacular arms wrapped themselves spastically around the length of his body, head to toe. The hideous form trembled violently for a moment and gave one final shriek of hatred and frustration before falling slowly over backward onto the churned and stained sand. In a count of ten, bar the dreamer's hoarse shout of triumph, the white cavern was still again and silent.

For a few seconds more Titus Crow swayed over the bodies of the defeated trio, every flesh-and-blood muscle in his body aching and his arms like lead. Then he lifted his eyes to peer undaunted across the white waste. Somewhere here, somewhere in this glaring white nightmare, Tiania of Elysia was even now in dire need of him.

He had not a moment to spare.

# 4

## *The Clock in Flames!*

Three hours had elapsed in Dylath-Leen since Henri-Laurent de Marigny's disappearance from the dais of the ruby. During the interval there had been some little turmoil in the city. Barzt, the new, self-appointed leader of the horned ones, had himself very recently been removed from power. His position had been disputed; a fight with knives had decided the matter positively in favor of his opponent. That opponent, Eriff, now licked his wounds and supped muth-dew with his cronies in a rotting tavern near the seafront.

There was much for Eriff to consider now that he was a leader; a good deal of thinking – an art for which he had no great aptitude – was required. He was uncertain now, for example, whether or not his usurping of Barzt's pretensions to leadership of the horned ones had been a wise move. Nyarlathotep was coming to Dylath-Leen, expecting to interrogate (whatever form such interrogation might take) the man and woman of the waking world. That prize pair, however, were no longer here. Even the unknown dreamer who freed them had made his escape, albeit into oblivion. On top of all this, disturbing reports were beginning to reach the horned ones in their basalt city, reports hinting that the insidious incursions of their agents into the healthier cities of dreamland were being inexplicably checked, particularly in Ulthar, which had been their next objective.

No, Eriff was not at all happy with the situation, and what little he knew of Nyarlathotep only went to increase his apprehension. Perhaps it were better, he was beginning to reason, that the ancient compact between the horned ones of Leng and the prisoned Great Old Ones of the Cthulhu Cycle had never been. Better, perhaps, if all of Dylath-Leen's horned ones now took to their black galleys and sailed away across the Southern Sea. Better for Eriff, certainly; for what had he now to offer that mighty emissary of Cthulhu, the dread Nyarlathotep? Utterly emptyhanded, how might he greet the Great Messenger?

So Eriff grumbled over his muth-dew and nursed his bruises and cuts. And this was the brooding, pensive mood he was in when they came from the square of the great ruby to find him, bringing him the news that even now a strange, silent, enigmatic visitor stood in Dylath-Leen's central square on the cobbles opposite the ruby dais. The thing, they said, was tall and oddly figured, like a mummycase of olden Ohlmi. Of wood or a material like wood, it was very heavy and hard, and in its upper part four hands swung about a common center in wholly inexplicable motions. Would Eriff not come and say what must be done with this object, which had appeared as if from thin air?

In the heat of the afternoon Eriff left his cool drink and made his way with his retinue of cronies painfully to the square of the ruby dais. And it was just as he had heard it: there, facing the dais almost as if it scrutinized the monstrous ruby atop the basalt steps, stood the unknown object from another world. Eriff, for all his ignorance, saw one thing immediately: that indeed this thing was not fashioned of dreamland's skills. Staring at the time-clock, his unnatural features quickly took on a cautious, a suspicious look.

How did this thing get here? What was it? Why was it here in the square of the ruby? He had been told that it was of wood, and certainly it appeared to be. Well then, why take chances?

'Either carry it away, out of the city, or burn it!' he ordered. 'Use old timbers, doors, and furniture from the city's houses. Build a pyre for the thing, whatever it is. I don't like it . . .'

'But Eriff, it appears to be a box of some sort!' one of his brothers protested.

'And what's inside it?' he asked.

'We don't know, but –'

'And can you open it?'

'Not yet, but –'

'Then burn it and be on the safe side!'

And so a pyre was built around the time-clock, of furniture from the old uninhabited houses and timbers from other habitations long fallen into ruin; and when the time-clock was completely obscured from view by the flammable materials thus heaped about it, then torches were brought and the fire lighted.

Within the clock, whose shell was impervious to all but the most incredible temperatures and pressures, in an indeterminate limbo which might best be described as the place where all the 'corners' of space and time meet, Henri-Laurent de Marigny was ill. He was as drunk, more drunk than at any previous time in his entire life. That is not to say that he had never before consumed a whole bottle of brandy – he had, but in a civilized manner. Never in such barbarous haste!

And yet he knew that he had a mission . . . if only this dark universe would stop revolving long enough to allow him to remember what that mission was! It had to do with Titus Crow, and it had to do with Tiania . . . And with the time-clock.

The time-clock! De Marigny's mind fastened avidly upon that concept.

Time-clock! Of course! He was *inside* that peculiar device, that space-time vehicle, right now – in a warm womb between the worlds. He had only to reach out his mind, and – but that would be too much of an effort. It would be better simply to fight the flooding nausea within himself, the sickening spinning and whirling of vast black voids within and without him. Oh, yes – much better to sleep until the alcohol had burned itself out of his system.

Alcohol?

Sleep . . .?

Alarm bells clamored distantly in de Marigny's inner being. Alcohol – sleep – *dream!* That had been his mission: to sleep and to dream. And he had slept, he knew that. Why, then, was he not dreaming?

The answer was obvious: he was not dreaming because as he had fallen drunkenly asleep he had released his mental contact with the time-clock. Where was the clock now? Had he in fact managed to pilot his fantastic vehicle to the desired destination?

Now he put himself to the effort so recently rejected, meshing his besotted mind with that of his machine – and instantly the scanners opened in his mind's eye.

An inferno – all the fires of hell blazing about the clock – the inner cone of some primeval volcano during an eruption – the fiery surface of the solar orb itself! *Where the devil was he?*

Panic clawed momentarily at de Marigny's insides as he instinctively threw up his arms to ward off the heat that he knew could never penetrate the clock's shell. Then, fleetingly through the flame and smoke, he glimpsed the ruby dais and the horned figures that cavorted around the bonfire in demoniac glee, and he knew where he was. He was back in Dylath-Leen, in Earth's dreamland. Now too, however drunkenly, he remembered what had gone before.

Then, fighting to hold the time-clock's scanners steady in his staggering mind, de Marigny attempted to focus his blurred thoughts on the horned ones, on their present activity. What were they doing now, these wide-mouthed monsters? Plainly, they were trying to burn the time-clock! Anger began to expand within de Marigny's breast. He glared at the creatures from Leng with a fiery hatred that burned in his veins to match the heat of the brandy.

These vile inhabitants of the forbidden plateau had perpetrated enough horrors in the lands of Earth's dreams. They, or their fathers before them, had brought down Dylath-Leen in the first place; they were responsible for the dissemination of much that was abominable in dreamland; they were the foul sores of Man's subconscious, in league with the Powers of Darkness, particularly with the prisoned Cthulhu spawn of the waking world. And on top of all this they had recently humiliated Titus Crow, Tiania, even de Marigny himself.

Tiania they would have violated – unthinkably. Crow would have been put to terrible tortures; indeed, de Marigny's friends would eventually have been handed over to Nyarlathotep, the Great Messenger of the CCD. And here in dreamland Nyarlathotep had been given monstrous form by the massed telepathic sendings of his immemorial masters. The more the dreamer's foggy mind dwelled on the CCD – and on the horned ones, their minions in dreamland – the more angry he became. And now those minions were trying to burn the time-clock, with de Marigny inside it!

His anger suddenly boiled over into a rage that drove back his alcoholic nausea and brought him into awesome action. It was high time these Leng-spawned horrors were taught a lesson, and one that would not be quickly forgotten . . .

584

# 5

# *Weapon from the Waking World*

It was, of course, the habit of the horned ones of Leng – who were cannibals whenever the opportunity to eat the flesh of sentient beings presented itself – to leap and dance about their ritual fires. In this way in ages long lost they had thought to propitiate the elemental spirits. Therefore, the knowledge that an enemy – a thing alien to their monstrous conception of normalcy, in the shape of the time-clock – was burning in the center of their bonfire was sufficient to set them dancing. Had they been roasting a man, then they would have leaped in time to his screaming, invoking the spirits of the feast. In the case of the clock, they danced to thank the spirits of their fathers, which had delivered this enemy unto them.

Eriff, lightly wounded in his fight with the unfortunate Barzt, sat on the steps of the ruby dais and clapped his hands, accompanying the musicians who rattled chalk-dry crotala and played upon whining flutes. All the while, other horned ones darted in and out between the encircling dancers, feeding the flames with the looted furniture of olden Dylath-Leen.

Then there was an astounding occurrence: the strange, coffin-shaped object at the fire's core started to spin, fanning the flames of the fire outward.

Instantly the dancers backed away, the dreadful cacophony of the musicians faded, and Eriff stopped his clapping to stand up on the dais steps, his too-wide mouth falling open and his slanted eyes bugging. Faster the time-clock whirled, until a wind began to roar outward from it that hurled blazing brands in all directions. Now

585

the horned ones broke and scattered, screaming and gibbering, many of them beating frantically at themselves as their coarse silken clothes caught fire.

And up rose the spinning clock from the blackened cobbles, the winds of its whirling bowling over the fleeing horned ones, hurling great timbers about like straws, its shrieking voice that of the storm-demon and its wild gyrations increasing from moment to moment. Then, high above the square, it tilted, seeming to aim itself directly at the basalt dais – at the massive ruby!

Finally Eriff, recovering his slow wits, made to flee from the steps of the dais – but too late. Such was the speed of the clock as it drilled down through tortured air to slam into, *through* the splintering jewel, that for a second it seemed simply to elongate itself.

Eriff was shredded as he tried to run from the steps, blasted into crimson pieces by the bombburst of ruby fragments; and the clock drove on, wildly slewing to one side, tearing a great hole in one of the square's buildings before coming to a shuddering halt in the debris. For a moment or two there was silence in the square of the dais.

Within the clock de Marigny fought down the rising tide of nausea within him, a sickness born not only of his alcoholic condition but also of the devastation he had wrought in the space of the last few seconds. For of course he had seen the results of his great anger, and drunk or sober such slaughter was not to de Marigny's liking. Not now that his original passion of rage was dying down. It was one thing to do away with such as the three who had so direly threatened Titus Crow and Tiania when they were tied to the dais steps, even coldbloodedly, but quite another to go unaffected by the scene in the square as it was now.

Corpses literally littered the smeared and slimed cobbles, many of them with limbs missing, torn like Eriff in the explosion of ruby shards; others lay in smoldering rags or trapped beneath still-burning timbers. And there were some who still lived, crawling across the square, mewling dementedly both in fear and in the agony of their wounds . . .

Finally, shakily, de Marigny took control of the clock once more, freeing it from the rubble of the collapsed wall and turning it toward the now empty dais. As he did so he saw several of the horned ones, apparently unharmed, climbing to their feet and backing away in utmost horror from the center of the square. At first he could not make out what it was that they so patently feared. It was not de Marigny's coffin-shaped weapon from the waking world; indeed, they appeared to be ignoring the time-clock completely. Then –

There atop the dais steps, shimmering faintly in the cleansing sunlight, a shape gathered. Even as he focused the clock's scanners upon the thing, its form began to solidify, its outline to fill in. And at last de Marigny knew what the thing was.

The Fly-the-Light from Yuggoth on the Rim – a vampire molded of the malignity of the Cthulhu Cycle Deities themselves – a thing of *Their* manufacture! In shattering the great ruby, he had freed the demon from that multifaceted prison, loosing it for the second time upon Dylath-Leen . . . except that this time the sunlight poured down upon it from a clear mid-afternoon sky, the blessed light from which it must either flee or die!

De Marigny saw the horror, but still could hardly believe his own eyes. He remembered Grant Enderby's ambiguous description and knew now why the man had phrased it so. For how might one describe this monster except as Enderby had described it? Blind and yet all-seeing – limbless and yet mobile as some vast, mercurial amoeba – with poisonous mouths that gaped and drooled in its bubbling mass! The only thing

Enderby had left out of his tale was the thing's size. It was *huge!*

And it was screaming – shrieking and writhing in agony under the rays of the sun – melting and shrinking visibly as great black clouds of smoke poured from it. Then it 'saw' the half-dozen or so horned ones that cringed away from it as they tried to slink unseen from the square. And it was just as Enderby had said: the Fly-the-Light moved after them like flood water, pouring down the dais steps and soaking them up in an instant. When the frantic, awful screaming had stopped, finally the thing 'saw' the time-clock.

By then its bulk was greatly reduced, despite the *sustenance* so recently and hideously derived from the six or seven horned ones, whose bones now gleamed wetly in small heaps about the square. Black smoke still roiled from it; its quakings were awful to watch; the screaming sounds it made had risen so far up the sonic scale as to be almost inaudible. And yet, when the horror suddenly made for the time-clock, de Marigny sensed that it was far from done for. He sensed, too, that the thing knew what the time-clock was, its fantastic function. The vampire had purpose now, its movements were no longer hopeless; it seemed to exude an essence of eager – anticipation!

Then an incredible suspicion set de Marigny's flesh to creeping. What if this thing of blackest nightmare was capable of entering into the time-clock? Suppose it could *come through* the clock's outer shell? Titus Crow had told him that the Hounds of Tindalos could do this quite effortlessly. Was it completely inconceivable that this thing from the great ruby might possess the same power? De Marigny in no way intended to put his suspicion to the test. He backed his vehicle hurriedly away as the Fly-the-Light rushed upon him, lifting the vessel up high into the sunlight over the square in an effort to avoid contact with the horror.

He was astounded and terrified when the vampire flashed skyward after him! The thing did not recognize the restrictions of gravity!

By now it was much smaller – a pulsating fireball of greenly drooling mouths that trailed a pall of foul black smoke. But it moved at a lightning pace that de Marigny, still drunk and completely off guard, found difficulty in matching. It was not that the clock could not outrun the vampire, rather that the man within the clock was off guard, by no means recovered yet from his overdose of alcohol.

Then, his dulled senses shocked into positive action, at last de Marigny made to flee the Fly-the-Light's advances at full speed – only to discover that the demon was not prepared to let him go! A numbness fell over his mind like an icy shroud; a great white fog obscured his brain; and pouring from behind this awful mental mist, penetrating it, came the mind-commands of the thing from the ruby:

*'You will not flee. Stand and accept me. You have not the strength to flee. You are weak, as all mortal creatures are weak, and I am strong. Even now I am stronger than you, but I will be mighty once more. Therefore you must obey me. Stand – you may not flee – you have not the strength to flee!'*

Over and over the message repeated in de Marigny's mind, and while he was dimly aware of what was happening, still the dreadful paralysis held him in an unbreakable embrace. This was that debilitating force with which the ruby-creature had whelmed Dylath-Leen's peoples many years ago, the vampiric power that had drained even Titus Crow of his strength. And now, freed from the prisoning ruby, the former gem-dweller was concentrating that power in its last bid for life.

The thing was depleted and quickly dying, but still the mental sloth it generated gripped de Marigny's mind as it moved, carefully now, toward the time-clock. And the paralyzed dreamer knew that indeed the clock would be the horror's salvation, for once inside the weird vehicle – and as soon as its present master had been dealt with – then the thing would be truly free to ravage among all the dark dimensions of a limitless multiverse. That must never be.

As the horror closed with him, de Marigny groped for the clock's controls with blunted senses. It was quite hopeless. He could find nothing. The time-clock was completely immobilized. The Fly-the-Light sensed this too, and thrust itself triumphantly upon its prey in one last surge of waning strength. In that final moment, still desperately groping in vague, unfeeling abysses, de Marigny came across a control which had absolutely nothing to do with the clock's mobility. It was a trigger rather than a control proper, the trigger that powered a weapon Titus Crow had brought back with him from Elysis!

De Marigny squeezed that trigger.

Instantly the alien numbness was flushed from his mind. The vampire dwindled in his scanners, dwindled and boiled as a beam of purest light flashed from the clock's dial to strike it squarely and thrust it back. The beam lengthened as it forced the shrinking horror away, until finally the dying thing was pinned by that shaft of light to the basalt dais amidst shards of shattered ruby.

There, at last, in a blaze of purest white light, the creature expired, became nothing. And still de Marigny played his weapon's beam upon the spot where it had been. Shortly the dais itself began to melt and bubble, the very basalt to run like water. Only then, when the dais was a misshapen hummock of glowing rock, did de Marigny release the mental trigger.

Wearily then, thankfully, the dreamer set the clock down in the silent, scorched square. And yet, exhausted as he now felt and still by no means sober, he remembered Titus Crow and Tiania. Indeed they were now uppermost in his thoughts. What terrors were they facing even now? And what was he doing, wasting his time here in Dylath-Leen?

He grasped his vehicle's controls with his mind and lifted it up, however tiredly, unsteadily, to the skies. But where to go? Where was Titus Crow now?

No sooner had the unspoken question passed through de Marigny's mind than the clock trembled and strained like a great hound tugging at its leash, and simultaneously a scene of startling clarity flashed upon the dreamer's inner eye. He saw Titus Crow, naked, pacing a great white sandy expanse, scimitar in hand, head hung low. The vision began to fade – but not before Crow had looked up startled, frowning and peering puzzledly about.

His face was dusted with white sand, caked at the corners of his mouth, and his weariness was plainly great. Even as the vision receded once more and vanished from de Marigny's mind, he saw Crow's lips form the question: 'Henri! Is that you?'

And de Marigny *knew!*

Of course! There had always existed between the two men a strange psychic link – a connection which the time-clock had momentarily picked up and magnified. Indeed, this was how Titus Crow had found his way back to Earth from Elysia, by using de Marigny's mind as a beacon. Well, why shouldn't the method work just as well in reverse?

He released his mental grasp upon the clock's controls by all but the merest contact, then transmitted the following message to that vehicle of the Elder Gods: 'You know where Crow is. He's here within my mind – within *our* minds! – and he's in trouble. It's up to you now. Go to him – *go to Titus Crow!'*

And like a great hound hearing its master's call, freed from the restraining leash, away the clock raced across the skies of dreamland . . .

# 6

## *At the Pits of Nightmare*

The white sand tugged at Titus Crow's naked feet; fine
particles of white dust stung his eyes and clogged his
nostrils. His scimitar seemed to weigh a ton and he felt
as though he had walked a thousand miles. He allowed
himself a derisive snort and cursed whichever fool had said
that things were often far simpler in dreams. If that were
really so, then it was high time things began working in
favor of Titus Crow!

For hours now – or what seemed like hours – he
had been making his way toward what looked like a
continuous geyser of concentric rings of steam or vapor,
rising, expanding, and dispersing high in the atmosphere
of the great cave. He had first seen this phenomenon
shortly after setting out across the desert and had automatically headed toward it. These distant smoke rings,
rolling swiftly up at regular intervals from some unknown
source, had been the only sign of life, however inorganic,
in the entire cavern. His instinct told him that this was
where he would find Tiania.

And at long last he had almost reached his destination.
Just across a range of low dunes lay the source of these
puzzling eruptions of vapor. The sand now transmitted
to his naked feet a steady hammering as of massive
subterranean sledges, and he saw that the rising rings
of vapor soared skyward in perfect synchronization with
these poundings. These were not, Crow was certain,
purely natural phenomena. Then, mounting the crest, he
saw how right his instinct had been.

The scene was alien and fantastic. Beyond the dunes a

deep valley opened to Crow's eyes; in its center a crater, with sides of fused sand, went down like the mouth of some vast funnel into indeterminate abysses of earth. To one side of this gaping hole, from which issued the billowing smoke rings, a structure like some enormous asymetrical birdcage stood, of intertwining metal bars half rotten with a leprous gray oxidization. Within the cage, which was open at its very top, a motley collection of dreamland's diverse peoples, men, women, and children, stood or reclined upon the sandy floor. Many of them were plainly distraught, wringing their hands and crying out in horror at their plight, beating frenziedly with bloodied hands at the metal bars of their prison. Others simply lay on the sand in attitudes of exhaustion, or sat blankly staring at nothing through eyes glazed with shock.

There were other . . . *things* . . . to be seen: the Keeper of the Cage, for instance, seated on a throne of boulders; and the great gaunt, perched now upon the Keeper's shoulder. But for the moment Crow's eyes sought elsewhere. They swept the crowded cage until finally they rested upon Tiania. And within that singular prison she was even now in danger of hideous outrage!

Two horned ones were trapped in the cage along with all the rest, and they were trying to dislodge Tiania from where she clung halfway up the cage's wall in a latticework of silver bars. They were climbing after her, laughing loudly and gutturally as they snatched at her naked feet to bring her down.

All common sense, all caution went out of Titus Crow then. Strength born of a raging bloodlust surged in his veins and the purr of his synthetic heart became a snarl deep within his chest. His cry of rage was almost animal; he saw nothing but blood – the blood of the horned ones from Leng – as he raced with all speed down the dune. He ignored utterly, as if they did not exist, the creatures that kept the cage. Skirting the crater, running like the wind, he came to the cage and put his terrible strength to bear upon the bars where they seemed most rotten. In a rending of rusted metal he was inside the cage, leaping the prostrate forms of weeping inmates and dodging the beseeching embrace of others as he raced across the sandy floor.

Another moment saw him directly beneath the horned ones who climbed after Tiania; and then, because he could not climb and carry his scimitar easily at the same time, he put down the sword and swung himself swiftly up into the framework of bars. By now the horned ones had seen him – Tiania, too.

'Be careful, Titus!' she cried.

Dodging a kick from the lower of the two horned ones, he grabbed the creature's leg and hauled mightily. The thing from Leng gave a shriek and tried to hold on to the bars; Crow shook him like a hawk shakes its prey, tore him loose and threw him down to the floor fifty feet below. Then, hauling himself higher, he came face to face with the second of Tiania's tormentors.

The horned one had made himself fast in a secure position; he stabbed at Crow with a curving knife. Crow caught the creature's wrist, twisting until its snarls became cries of pain. Then he swiftly twisted the other way, slamming an elbow of hard flesh with a core of harder bone and plastic into the horned one's face.

That face was smashed in an instant. Teeth crunched and blood flew. The nose disintegrated, the wide mouth became a red gash, the slanting eyes glazed over. Crow released his grip on the horned one's wrist, caught him by his neck, and jerked him free of the bars into empty air. A moment later came the crunch of bones from below. Then Crow reached for Tiania where she clung naked to the bars just a few feet higher.

Before their hands could meet there came a buffeting of air and a shadow fell across them. Crow cried out a sick denial as the great gaunt soared down through the open roof of the cage to snatch the girl from her precarious position. Tiania screamed and struggled as she was lifted up, up and out of the cage, carried high into the white cavern's atmosphere. There the great gaunt found the thermal current rising from the crater and glided in wide circles in the rising air. Below the gaunt where it soared with its wriggling captive, the smoke rings went down in concentric circles to the crater-like vent that issued them; the thundering, as of massive, monstrous engines, pounded up through leagues of earth and sand to make the very air shimmer and vibrate.

With horrified eyes Titus Crow watched the circling gaunt, certain with every passing moment that the blank-faced bat-thing would drop Tiania into the throat of the mysterious vent. Then the Keeper of the Cage spoke:

'Come down from the cage, man of the waking world. Come and speak to me.' The voice of the gigantic, manlike figure was loud to match its dimensions but flat and utterly void of life. It was as if some colossal zombie had spoken, a thing brought back from the dead against its will, without emotion.

Titus Crow dragged his eyes from the high-circling gaunt and stared at the Keeper where it sat upon its throne of huge boulders. It was as naked as Crow himself, hairless, with skin the color of death. Its eyes were lusterless yellow orbs that never blinked, through which it seemed to stare straight into Crow's very soul.

'I'll come down,' Crow shouted his answer, clambering down the bars of the cage, 'and I'll speak to you – but order your hideous pet to bring my woman down to safety!'

'Your woman? No, she is mine now, and when I am ready she will go down into darkness to fuel the nightmares of certain awful dreamers. You, too, are destined for the pits of nightmare. But not until I have spoken with you.'

By then Crow had left the cage through the hole he'd made in its rotten bars. He ran to the feet of the Keeper of the Cage and waved his scimitar futilely up at the giant. 'Why?' he shouted. 'Why will you do these things?'

'It is my reason for being. It is why *They* put me here. Long and long ago I was a man of the waking world, like you. But I learned the mysteries of the Great Old Ones and became *Their* priest. Then, when I tried to use *Their* power to my own ends, *They* destroyed me on Earth and put me here to serve *Them* in Earth's dreamland. *They* gave me great size and amazing powers to command. Then, mockingly, *They* robbed me of my will, left me emotionless. I am almost omnipotent, almost immortal, and yet I am *Their* slave, powerless to do except as *They* will be done.' Even saying these things the huge figure showed no emotion; the tone of his voice remained unvaried.

'If the Cthulhu spawn did these things to you, then Cthulhu is your enemy no less than mine,' Crow cried. 'Yet you have given yourself over into his service – you are his slave. I would sooner die than be slave to Cthulhu, but I'll fight as long as there's life in me!'

The Keeper answered: 'Ah, but *They* thought of that, too. I might also fight, might also believe death preferable to this existence *They* plotted for me – had *They* not increased tenfold within me the human instinct for survival. All I have is an unquenchable desire to survive – and to survive I must obey.'

With that the massive, white-fleshed creature leaned forward and scooped up Titus Crow in one hand before he could move. Crow struck time and again at the great hand that held him, but his blade drew no blood from the deathly flesh.

'Now,' the Keeper continued, 'stop your pointless striving and tell me who you are, why you are so different from other men. You are strong beyond belief for a mortal dreamer, and strange, too, I fancy.'

'And if I tell you these things will you set the woman free?'

'No, no. You and she must both go down to nightmare. Down there in the pit, where the Engines of Horror pound, your souls will feed the darkest dreams of the Great Old Ones, and the nightmares *They* send to plague human dreamers will be that much more horrible.'

'Then I'll not speak to you. I'll speak only to . . . Nyarlathotep!' Crow cried, desperately.

'Nyarlathotep?' No emotion but a certain hesitation entered into the Keeper's voice. 'What do you want with Nyarlathotep – and what makes you think that the Great Messenger would want anything of you?'

'He wants to . . . to see us,' Crow insisted. 'I don't know why.'

'If what you say is true, then I was right and you are indeed an extraordinary human being. I believe you.' With that, the Keeper lifted up a great dead white arm and beckoned, and the circling gaunt immediately flew down and settled on his shoulder, still holding fast to the wriggling form of Tiania.

'I have the power,' the Keeper continued, 'to contact *Them* in *Their* immemorial slumbers. Perhaps *They* will send Nyarlathotep directly to see you.'

'No!' Crow gasped.

'Oh? Were you after all lying, then?'

'No, but –'

'But you don't really want to see Nyarlathotep? I see. His plans for you are not to your liking, that is it. I will contact *Them*. But meanwhile my familiar must be about his work. See, you have freed all of my prisoners. They have escaped through the hole you tore in the cage's bars.'

Crow saw that the Keeper was right. The last of the

escapees was just hurrying over the crest of the sandhills out of sight. Again the Keeper gave a signal, and Tiania fell from the great gaunt's clutches and slid with a cry of alarm down over the Keeper's leprous chest and onto his lap.

The Keeper placed Crow in his lap, too, and at that moment, as the great gaunt flapped aloft to soar after the fleeing people from the cage – then came an amazing diversion!

# 7

## *Dreams of a Diseased Mind*

Out of the sky, from above the white horizon of sandhills, a beam of purest white light struck at the great gaunt, shredding one wing into a swirling gray mist of fine particles. The beam was cut off instantly at its as yet unseen source, leaving the crippled gaunt to spin madly down, down the funnel of concentric smoke rings to where it struck the curving mouth of the pit, bouncing and tumbling like a bundle of rags before plummeting out of sight into the abyss. And not once did the creature voice its agony; no cry escaped it as it went down to the pits of nightmare.

'Whatever this is,' said the Keeper, 'plainly it is not intended to benefit me. Someone seeks perhaps to rescue you, or to destroy me, or both. If the intention is to rescue you, then your rescuer must first destroy me. Therefore I give your would-be rescuer no chance!' Even as the vast pale creature spoke – even as he snatched up Titus Crow and Tiania in one massive hand, holding them high over the throat of the great pit – so the white beam came again, lancing out of the sky to strike him square in his leprous chest.

The Keeper sprang to his feet and reeled at the edge of the pit. His strange eyes stood out huge and round in his face, and from his suddenly scarred and seared chest there came a deep and plainly audible wheezing. Now he slowly opened his outstretched hand, so that the dreamers had to scramble up onto his palm, clinging to each other above the vapor-belching pit.

'If he strikes me again, whoever or whatever he is, then

he strikes all three of us,' the Keeper said, pain in his voice but still no emotion. 'For you will fall as surely as I, but you will fall into deepest purgatory. You see? It is my instinct for survival . . .'

By now the time-clock was plainly visible, racing in wide circles at some considerable height above the cage and its Keeper. Titus Crow knew that only Henri-Laurent de Marigny could be at the machine's controls, and hope sprang up in him as he watched its circlings. The Keeper followed Crow's eyes to the clock and he asked: 'What kind of device is that?'

'Right now it's a weapon,' Crow answered. 'From the waking world. A weapon against all the Cthulhu Cycle Deities and their minions!'

'You are . . . stranger than I thought, dreamer,' the vast being said, his voice now faltering, an echoing croak that crackled like muted lightning. His great palm, upon which Crow and Tiania crouched, trembled mightily. They threw themselves down to lie prone across the huge fingers.

Suddenly the Keeper fell to his knees, the ground trembling as all the tons of his weight crashed down upon the sand. But still he held out his hand, palm up, above the great glassy abyss. Now the time-clock was stationary, poised threateningly on high, its dial turned toward the fantastic tableau below.

There at the lip of the infernal funnel, from whose nightmare throat those exhalations of obscene vapor puffed upward unabatedly, the Keeper kneeled, plainly injured. Crow and Tiania hung on grimly to his great fingers as his huge frame trembled, rocking to and fro. Beside him the now empty cage was an oddly woven lobster pot of gleaming metal and scabrous gray rust, and on all sides the white sand formed a dazzling, sterile backdrop to the entire scene. The time-clock fell from on high, moved closer, and became motionless again.

'It is my belief,' came the Keeper's broken voice,

drawing Crow's fevered gaze back from the time-clock, 'that for all your woman's strange beauty you, dreamer, are far more important in the great scheme of things. That being so, I will now let her fall into nightmare, saving you until later. But unless you send your aerial weapon away, you will surely follow her.'

'If you let her fall,' Crow shouted, a conflicting mixture of horror, rage, and desperation in his voice, 'I'll order your death immediately!'

'And your own?'

Crow knew what the Keeper meant: if the white ray struck him down, then Crow must fall from his hand into the pit. He answered, 'And my own.'

'Bluff.' The Keeper's free hand moved out over the pit, thumb and forefinger reaching for Tiania. She threw her arms about her man.

'Wait!' Crow slashed uselessly at the threatening fingers with his scimitar. 'Even if I were bluffing, what about Nyarlathotep? He wants to see us. Had you forgotten? Even if you escape with your miserable life – if my weapon from the waking world fails to kill you – how will you explain the woman's death, my death, to your masters?'

'Her death? Oh, but she will not . . . die, not immediately, not for a . . . long time. You do not . . . know as much as you . . . pretend, dreamer,' the Keeper wheezed shudderingly on. 'Nyarlathotep is . . . *Their* messenger, the Great . . . Messenger of my masters. Embodied or . . . disembodied, he is . . . *Their* messenger.

'Ask yourself who it is that carries Cthulhu's nightmares to . . . influence the dreams of mortals. It is . . . Nyarlathotep! You desired to . . . see him? So you shall – at the pits of nightmare. There your souls will fuel the engines of horror, for long and long before . . . you are . . . finished; and Nyarlathotep will disseminate all the . . . horror of your shrieking minds and souls among the reams of . . . other mortals. But enough! The woman first!'

Suddenly Tiania, breathless and frightened but brave as ever, freed herself from Crow's arms to throw back her emerald hair in a defiant gesture. Her beautiful voice trembled almost unnoticeably as she spoke up in her own right.

'You would do this to Tiania of Elysia? Then you are surely doomed in this land of dream and in all others. You should know, creature, that I am beloved of the Elder Gods – beloved of Kthanid himself. Beware!'

'The . . . Elder Gods? Kthanid?' For the first time there was, or appeared to be, a trace of emotion – fear – in the Keeper's steadily disintegrating voice. 'You are of . . . Elysia?'

The vast being's frame rocked more wildly yet, and for a moment his hand swung to one side, so that the pair huddled upon his palm suddenly found themselves above sandy ground and not the gaping maw of the glassy-throated pit. In one movement Crow grabbed Tiania and carried her into space in a coiled-spring leap; and in that same instant de Marigny, seizing upon his one opportunity, applied pressure to the mental trigger that controlled the time-clock's weapon.

Again the white ray reached blindingly, unerringly out, stabbing at the Keeper and striking him between the eyes. He fell back upon his haunches, clawing at his face and jerking spastically, toppling against the cage, which crumpled beneath his great weight.

Titus Crow hit the ground a second later, holding Tiania above him, deliberately cushioning her with his body as she fell upon him. It was a fall of at least thirty feet and would certainly have broken the bones of any normal man. Crow was not normal, however, and had fallen in a spot where the sand was soft and deep. Nevertheless, he was momentarily winded, so that it was several seconds before he drew himself to his knees to take the badly shaken Tiania in his arms. They had been lucky: a distance of only a few feet separated them from the smooth, curving lip of the pit, from which those regular exhalations went up inexorably as ever to the great cavern's roof. There, at the edge of the pit, clinging together, they saw a terrible sight.

The time-clock, flying in tight circles about the Keeper's gigantic, leprous, reeling form, was pouring a constant beam of white light down upon him, and wherever the ray struck his body oily black smoke gushed out from steaming pits to form darkly drifting cloudlets in the throbbing air.

It could not last for long. With one abrupt, flailing motion, the mortally wounded Keeper lurched to his feet. He glared from a single bulging eye – its twin now a gaping, blackly bubbling hole – and took a single, stumbling step after his aerial tormentor. Then he swayed to a halt. His mouth fell open and he spoke, signaling at last his recognition of doom, the fact that for all his instinct for survival, his lust for life even in the hell that Cthulhu had given him, he was done for.

'I know this . . . *power!*' he cried, his voice a monstrous bell with a cracked clapper, tolling a cacophony of horror. 'I . . . know it. It is . . . that power which . . . even *They* fear. It is . . . the star of Mnar – the love of the . . . Elder Gods – the Good before which all Evil . . . flees. And it is . . . my . . . death!'

He staggered wildly, then spun about, throwing his arms wide to form an unholy cross. And again the beam of white light reached out. But this time de Marigny aimed it out of mercy. The beam played upon, passed *through* the Keeper's body, finally expending its potent energies harmlessly in the sand. The giant uttered one last incoherent cry; his arms fell uselessly to his sides; his head snapped back with a loud crack. He toppled forward, it seemed almost in slow-motion, crashing headlong down the glassy funnel to hell.

Titus Crow and Tiania, fleeing wearily toward the sandhills, were hurled flat by the hurricane rush of displaced air and stinging sand as the colossus fell. When they regained their feet again he was gone, and for several minutes there were no more rings of vapor rising over the white sands . . .

Cresting the dunes, they came to where de Marigny stood at the open door of the time-clock. He was deathly pale, trembling; he leaned unsteadily, balancing himself by holding onto the clock.

'Henri,' Crow said, taking his arm. 'Without you we were finished. You'll never know how I felt when . . .' His voice tapered off and a frown creased his brow. He put his face closer to de Marigny's and sniffed suspiciously. The frown deepened. 'Man, I do believe you're drunk!'

'No, no, Titus,' the other managed a sickly grin. 'I'm almost sober now. But you should have seen me an hour or so ago! Here.' He passed Crow an unopened bottle of brandy. 'I don't care if I never taste a drop again.'

'What? Brandy?' Crow turned to Tiania and hugged her, showing her the bottle. 'Even in Elysia there's nothing quite like this, Tiania. What a man, eh? Twice he's rescued me in ten minutes!' Then his voice took on a more serious note. 'But we'll celebrate later. Right now all I want to do is —'

At that moment there came a deep subterranean rumbling that shook the ground and made the trio stumble to keep their balance. It seemed suddenly darker, as though clouds had gathered to obscure the sun, though no such healthy orb illuminated the great cavern. Again the ground shuddered, and they felt a series of dull detonations far below. A moment more and there came a roaring blast from the mouth of the pit, and almost simultaneously a huge black ring of smoke hurtled up into view – and with it the vilest stench imaginable.

'Right now,' said de Marigny, finishing what Crow had started to say, 'I reckon we ought to be getting out of here!'

Crow nodded in agreement, bundled de Marigny in through the clock's open panel and Tiania after him, looked once more upon the awful landscape of the white underworld, whose light was now visibly failing, then entered the clock himself.

As he took the vessel's familiar controls and lifted it up into the cave's atmosphere, Crow saw massive cracks opening in the floor of the desert. Dimly in the distance he perceived through the clock's scanners the impending death of this subterranean vault: the fall of great chunks of rock, stalactites and smaller debris from the shuddering ceiling. Of the diverse peoples so recently escaped from the Keeper's cage, there was no trace. Then, as the cavern grew darker yet and the pace of its disintegration accelerated, he raced the clock across the desert and out into the nighted places of deeper dream . . .

Later, high over the Southern Sea and under a sky that was beginning to fill with evening, as they sped for Ulthar and the haven that the City of Cats offered, de Marigny thought to ask of Crow: 'What was it, that place?'

Tiania answered him. 'It was one of those places where Cthulhu manufactures nightmares with which to terrorize dreaming mortals.'

Crow nodded. 'Yes, and there must be a number of places like it in dreamland. Factories where Cthulhu employs the Machineries of Horror to amplify his loathsome dreams before transmitting them to the minds of sensitive dreamers. Tiania and I almost became the raw materials such factories consume. Yes, we were very nearly part of it, Henri. *Aegri somnia vana!'*

'"Dreams of a diseased mind,"' de Marigny translated with an involuntary shudder. 'Ah, well – that's one factory I wasn't sorry to close down, Titus. No, not at all.'

# 1
# *Ilek-Vad*

After three days of somewhat crowded but contented recuperation at the home of Grant Enderby in Ulthar – three days of almost complete peace and quiet, marred only by the knowledge that soon they must once more be about the task in hand – Titus Crow, Henri-Laurent de Marigny, and Tiania of Elysia convened at the Inn of a Thousand Sleeping Cats, taking a secluded table in an alcove where they could talk in utmost privacy.

They were dressed now in rich robes of dream's styling. Tiania wore a low-cut flowing gown of mother-of-pearl whose mobile, greenly glowing tints matched her hair perfectly; Crow sported a short jacket of yellow silk, with matching Eastern-styled trousers supported by a wide black belt; de Marigny had chosen a single-piece suit of scarlet satin, throwing his black flying cloak carelessly about his shoulders. In their cool alcove they relaxed, toyed with their food, which at the Inn of a Thousand Sleeping Cats is the best in all dreamland, and sipped exotic liqueurs.

Eventually, almost reluctantly, Titus Crow opened the conversation. 'Now, Henri, how did you get on at the temple of the Elder Ones yesterday evening? Was Atal able to offer any more help?'

'Well,' de Marigny began, 'first of all I told him how well things had worked out: about our escape from Dylath-Leen, the destruction of the great ruby and the Fly-the-Light, the death of the Keeper and his – pets – and more or less everything else that happened in between. He was particularly pleased that his elixir had served me so well.

607

'Then I told him how we planned to go Ilek-Vad . . .' He paused and shrugged. 'I'm afraid I drew something of a blank there, Titus. Atal could only repeat what Kthanid told me in the Hall of Crystal and Pearl: that there is some sort of screen about Ilek-Vad, one that lets nothing in or out.'

'Drawn a blank, eh?' Crow repeated after a while. 'Maybe, and maybe not. I'm inclined to look on the bright side. Look at it this way: a screen has two sides, Henri. True, it might have been built, this screen, by enemies of dreamland, to keep people from knowing what was going on in there. But on the other hand, might it not have been built to keep Cthulhu's invasion forces out?'

'You think that perhaps Randolph Carter and my father –'

'That they built this screen? I think it's possible. As to what they're doing behind it, in Ilek-Vad, that's another matter. It's something we'll have to find out for ourselves. And there's really only one way to do that.'

'We're going to Ilek-Vad!' Tiania put in, excitement in her beautiful voice.

'No,' said Crow, 'not you, Tiania. Henri and I – *we* are going to Ilek-Vad.'

'Titus,' she answered, 'I'm not letting you out of my sight again, not for a moment. There are too many terrors in this dreamland of yours. What would I do if any harm befell you?'

'And what would I do if harm befell you, Tiania? No, you stay here in Ulthar, at Grant Enderby's house. I'll know you're safe there. It will only be for a day or two, until we know what's going on, then we'll be back. And don't argue. You might be able to sway Kthanid, but not me.'

Tiania pursed her lips and sat back, eyes flashing angrily. De Marigny coughed and hastily asked: 'When do we set out?' He was already beginning to feel his stomach tighten as the Unknown loomed once more before him.

'Tomorrow morning, at dawn,' Crow answered. 'We're known to be here in dreamland now, so it's useless to attempt any sort of stealth. We leave at first light, in the time-clock.'

'Then you two will have to excuse me,' said de Marigny, rising to his feet.

'Oh? An early night, Henri?' Crow asked.

'No, I'm meeting with . . . someone.'

'I have seen the way she looks at you!' Tiania laughed mischievously, her disappointment already forgotten.

'She?' Crow frowned. Then his face brightened. 'Oh, you mean Litha, Grant Enderby's daughter.' He too laughed, then warned: 'But remember, Henri, that beautiful as she is with those huge dark eyes of hers, she's only a dream.'

'I'll endorse that heartily,' de Marigny answered, turning away to hide the sudden flush that suffused his face. 'She is a dream, isn't she?'

And so Titus Crow and Henri-Laurent de Marigny set out at dawn's first light, leaving Tiania behind at the friendly house of Grant Enderby in Ulthar. And by midday they were well out over the twilight sea.

They could have traveled at a greater speed, certainly, but Crow was fascinated by the topography of dreamland. He had closely scanned all of the rivers, towns, lakes, islands, and villages as they passed in endless procession beneath the time-clock. Now he silently appreciated the calm, peaceful, scintillating surface of the twilight sea.

For the twilight sea is a vast inland ocean (whose name derives from a perpetual serenity reminiscent of that of lonely lakes on calm summer evenings) far to the west of dreamland's third greatest continent. There, on a high promontory of volcanic glass that reaches far out over blue waters, stands Ilek-Vad – city of fabulous towers, domes, and turrets – once seat of a proud line of ancient kings, palace-city now of King Carter, late of the waking world.

Below the time-clock as it sped high over the wavelets, Crow and de Marigny could make out the coral-like labyrinths of the bearded and finny Gnorri, industrious dwellers in crystal depths. And it was as they scanned the marvelous intricacy of the Gnorri's incessant subaqueous labors, while yet Ilek-Vad lay a good ten miles distant, that the time-clock suddenly began to act very strangely indeed. Refusing to obey Crow's commands, the vessel veered to one side and began to fly in a wide circle which would eventually carry it *around* Ilek-Vad but no *closer* to that splendid city.

After a minute or so of wrestling with the clock's mind-controls, Crow grunted: 'Huh! Well, there's your screen, Henri, and a damned effective one at that!'

'That's amazing!' de Marigny replied. 'It must be similar to the Wall of Naach-Tith that Grant Enderby told me about. An invisible, impenetrable wall. A force-screen. But how . . .?'

'Science, Henri – or sorcery. Remember that this is Earth's dreamland, and men have been dreaming of such devices for a long, long time. In any case, what does it matter? The wall exists, and we're on the wrong side of it.'

'Do you suppose,' asked de Marigny, thoughtfully, 'that the barrier goes down under the twilight sea?'

'We can soon find out,' Crow answered, and he caused the time-clock to dive down, down into blue waters where the Gnorri swam and ogled and constructed their calcium caves and labyrinths. And there they once more came up against the invisible wall. But here there was a strange thing: the Gnorri were unobstructed in their submarine activities! For them the barrier did not exist, and they swam without hindrance to and fro across the invisible line.

'Well, now,' Crow mused. 'And I wonder how the birds fare?'

Up he took the clock and out of the calm waters with barely a splash. And there in the sky they waited until a cloud of white birds like geese, with a harsh, surprised gabble of inquiry, parted to fly around the clock and on through the invisible barrier.

'And the clouds themselves,' said de Marigny, watching in the scanners the passage of fleecy clouds into regions where the clock was forbidden. 'I don't understand . . .'

'I think I do,' Crow said. 'The Gnorri, the birds and clouds, they are all, well, *natural* things. They are the harmless, everyday, commonplace realities of dreamland, with no special allegiances to any powers, good or evil. The clock, on the other hand – yes, and its passengers – we are the aliens here.'

'But Atal, and Kthanid before him, said that *nothing* could get in or out of Ilek-Vad,' de Marigny protested.

Crow shrugged. 'What would they know about birds or clouds or the Gnorri, Henri? No, Ilek-Vad is only forbidden to alien things and to things which would fathom her secrets. Forbidden to alien scanners on alien worlds, and to alien Elder Gods that use such scanners. Forbidden to the shew-stones of dreamland's magicians – black or white – because shew-stones are not natural but supernatural, alien. Forbidden to the minions of the CCD, and to Nyarlathotep, *Their* messenger and agent.'

'And to us,' de Marigny added, 'because of the clock, no doubt. A device of the Elder Gods and alien to dreamland.'

'Oh, the clock is alien, all right,' Crow nodded, a stubborn frown wrinkling his forehead. 'It's damned ingenious, too. I don't think this barrier will stop us for too long, Henri.'

'Titus, I don't see –'

'Listen, my friend. In this clock I've escaped from the awesome pull of a black hole in space, an omnivorous freak of nature from which not even light may flee. I did it not by going around the black hole but simply by moving . . . *away* from it! You see, the clock isn't only a space-time machine but a gateway between intermediary dimensions, too. The proof of that statement lies in the simple fact that the clock is here in dreamland right now, in that you yourself have used it to travel between dimensions, Henri. For dreamland after all is only a parallel dimension existing on a level compatible to the subconscious mind of man.

'But I didn't only escape from a black hole; I've also been safely into and out of the prison dimension of Yog-Sothoth, the Lurker at the Threshold, where not even one of Kthanid's Great Thoughts could follow. Yes, and from there into Elysia itself! Why, the clock slips between dimensions as easily as it flies through space and time!' He paused. 'But there, we've wasted enough of the latter, now let's see just how resourceful the time-clock really is.'

In the space of the next ten minutes Titus Crow piloted the clock into as many again parallel dimensions, using the semisentient machine in a way which might baffle even the Elder Gods themselves. De Marigny was astounded at the view the scanners gave him of these remarkable planes of existence. Some of them seemed darkly-gaseous, nighted places, where vague shadowy shapes moved inexplicably; others were riots of primal color, to the apparent exclusion of all else. In two more there were definite geometric shapes, but Crow was quick to leave the latter planes; he was leery of the interest certain sharply-angled shapes displayed in the time-clock.

What most surprised de Marigny, however, was the fact that in several of these parallel universes the barrier about

612

Ilek-Vad – or rather, the barriers about corresponding areas in the alien spaces and times – was not only extant but visible. In one it showed in the scanners as a vast, silvery shimmering sphere, in another as an opaque pyramid of enormous proportions. But in all its various manifestations one thing about the barrier remained constant: to the time-clock it was impenetrable.

Then, as Crow switched dimensions yet again – to emerge in a scarlet glare through which thin bars of green light appeared to shoot in every conceivable direction without ever colliding – he gave a cry of triumph. 'This is it, Henri, our gateway into Ilek-Vad. The barrier doesn't extend into this subdimension, the scanners show no trace of it. We simply move forward, in a physical sense, like this –' The alien universe outside the clock seemed momentarily to whirl. 'And then we slide back through the intermediate dimensions to dreamland!'

There followed a kaleidoscopic confusion of weird colors, shapes, and motions as Crow returned the time-clock sideways through a dozen intervening planes of existence; and at last they emerged again above the twilight sea. All was as it had been, except that now they were moving forward, toward Ilek-Vad, and they were at last within the ten-mile boundary line of the invisible force-screen.

And there ahead and below was Ilek-Vad itself, fabulous city of towers, turrets, and domes rising up from the hollow glass cliffs wherein its foundations are housed, straddling the volcanic promontory beneath whose heights the Gnorri labor ceaselessly in the twilight sea. The afternoon sun shone down on Ilek-Vad, reflecting brilliantly from windows and bright metal statues, and in the city's squares and gardens brightly garbed crowds gathered to watch the approach of the weird aerial visitor.

As they drew even closer to the city, de Marigny's attention was drawn to what looked like a huge mirror at the very tip of the glassy promontory. At the base of this device, at what looked like a control bank, a pair of helmeted – soldiers? – busied themselves. Then, all around the rim of the city, many apertures appeared simultaneously in rampart walls, and out from these openings trundled more of the great mirrors.

'Titus,' de Marigny began, 'I don't think I quite like –' But before he could finish, suddenly Ilek-Vad seemed to disintegrate in a blinding flash of light that bloomed outward from the great mirrors. Actually the city had suffered no harm whatever, and as quickly as it had come the blinding glare died down – only to repeat a moment later as once more the vast mirrors hurled forth their incredibly bright beams of light.

The answer was now obvious, and Crow gave voice to de Marigny's unspoken thought:

'Those things are weapons, Henri!' he cried. 'And damn it, *they're firing them at us!*'

# 2

## *Warlords of Dream*

Half-a-dozen times at least the clock was caught in a crisscross of blinding rays from the projector-batteries about the city, before an astonished Titus Crow even thought to make a move to avoid them. By then such a move would have been superfluous; it was obvious that the beams of dazzling white light were neither damaging nor impeding the clock.

The troops manning the projectors saw this too, and moments later a second screen – this time a flickering, redly coruscating dome of purely physical energies – went up to enclose the city proper.

'No good, my friends,' Crow grinned. 'That's not going to keep us out either.' He flew the time-clock forward and, as if the redly flickering screen did not exist at all, the vehicle of the Elder Gods passed through the curtain of energies without pause.

Into the heart of the city Titus Crow flew the clock, slowly and carefully now, not wishing to alarm Ilek-Vad's inhabitants more than was absolutely unavoidable. Finally, after hanging motionless for a few seconds over the gardens of the central palace itself, he set the clock down between tinkling fountains and exotic flowering shrubs.

Shortly thereafter a thousand soldiers, attired in lightly armored suits with shining metal helmets, emerged from new, barrack-like buildings in the outer gardens to surround the time-clock and take up defensive positions. They wore swords and carried shields which bore in their centers small versions of the mirror-like ray projectors.

None of these troops came any closer to the time-clock than thirty or forty feet, and once they were in position behind their shields they made no further threatening move. Crow and de Marigny were content for the moment to remain in the complete safety of their vehicle and await developments – which were not long in coming.

Escorted by some two-dozen personal guardsmen, approaching on foot and dressed in splendidly opulent robes of silver and gold cloth, a strange, slender personage came from the direction of the palace itself. The soldiers around him were patently men of Ilek-Vad, and they had obviously been selected for their task. But while they were noticeably taller than the average inhabitants of dreamland, nevertheless the man they protected stood head and shoulders taller than the tallest of them.

'That man,' said de Marigny. 'He's as tall as I am. Is he young or . . . old? I can't quite make up my mind. And surely he's –'

'A man from the waking world?' Crow asked it for him; and answered: 'Yes, he is, Henri. And unless I'm very much mistaken, we're singularly honored. Oh, yes, see? He recognizes the time-clock! And so he should, for he used it long before I even knew it existed.'

'Randolph Carter!' De Marigny nodded his acknowledgment, awed in spite of himself. 'King Carter of Ilek-Vad!'

Now the king waved his guardsmen back and came right up to the clock. His face was pale, slender, that of a young gentleman, but his shoulder-length hair was white and his eyes old with incredible wisdom. Amazement shone in those eyes now and, as Titus Crow had noted, recognition. He reached out his hands and touched the clock, saying:

'Whoever you are, please come out now. I know that you mean no harm, for if you did, then by now my city would be falling around me. You have my word that no harm will come to you in Ilek-Vad. See, I know your vehicle well . . .'

As King Carter's hands moved expertly along the clock's sides there came an odd clicking from some hidden mechanism. The tall man stepped nimbly back as the clock's front panel swung silently open beneath the weird, four-handed dial, and his eyes scrutinized the clock's passengers minutely as they emerged.

Then, plainly perplexed at some as yet unknown thing, after taking Crow's hand in a somewhat cursory greeting he grasped de Marigny's shoulders and stared hard at him. The frown deepened then on his own face and he shook his head in mystification.

'For a moment I thought that . . . you look so very much like . . . someone.'

'I know who you are,' answered the object of the king's scrutiny, 'but I'm pretty sure we never met – or if we did I was only a very small child at the time. I am Henri-Laurent de Marigny, and this is Titus Crow.'

Now the king's lantern jaw fell open in an unashamed gasp of astonishment. His grip tightened on the other's shoulders. 'Then you *are* a de Marigny! By all the lands of dream, I should have guessed it! Who could possibly look more like his father than a son? Only a twin, I think, and believe me you *are* the twin of Etienne as he was . . . how long ago?

'But this is unforgivable of me. I have guests from the waking world – the son of my trusted friend and counselor, Etienne-Laurent de Marigny, and your friend here, Mr. Crow – and here we stand chatting in the garden! Forgive me, forgive me, and come with me please to the palace. There is much to talk about. I don't know why you're here, but I feel it's a good omen – and by the Sign of Koth, dreamland needs all the good omens she can get!'

\* \* \*

'So,' said the king much later, after they had dined and when he knew all about his visitors – from their initial encounters with the CCD, through Titus Crow's venturings in space and time and de Marigny's attempt to find Elysia for himself, right up to the present moment – 'then I was right. It was an omen, your coming here. You could have chosen no more opportune time, for at this very moment we prepare for war against dream's minions of the CCD, against the nightmares of the Great Old Ones themselves.

'In you two we have powerful allies, and already you have struck telling blows against the evil in dreamland. Yes, great allies indeed! Why, you, Titus Crow, have seen Elysia, and for all my wanderings I never found my way there!'

'But your name is known there,' Crow answered, equally gallant. 'And as for encounters with the CCD: what other man has sought out, even confronted Nyarlathotep? And escaped sane!'

'That was long ago,' the king modestly answered, 'and I was by no means as great a dreamer as the stories have it. No, my adventures in dreamland were often ill-advised. I was lucky, believe me. Nyarlathotep will not let me go so lightly next time.'

'And you think there may be a next time?' de Marigny asked.

'It seems more than possible,' King Carter nodded. 'There are warlords stalking dreamland even now, and war itself cannot be far behind.'

'Warlords?' Crow questioned.

'Myself and Kuranes, yes, and others, too. And then, of course, there are also our enemies, the warlords of the CCD! Of the latter you know as much, possibly more than I do.' He paused for a moment of contemplation, then went on:

'Like myself, Kuranes trains his generals; and in the

sky-islands about cloud-floating Serannian he builds a great armada of sky-yachts and yearns for the day when he may once more return to the throne in timeless Celephaïs. Until that day Celephaïs remains behind its own force-screen, safe for now from the CCD, dreaming more wondrously than any other city in all dreamland.'

The king laughed wryly before continuing. 'Strange, I was hardly a warlike man in the waking world, but I shall command armies in dreamland! Mind you, it will not be the first time I have commanded the legions of dream, but those were strange dreams indeed.' He paused again. 'However – I would like you two to assist me, to be my generals. Certainly you know more of such matters than I, as your very presence here testifies. To have fought so long and hard against Cthulhu's hideous brethren – and to survive the unending battle! I fear, though, that new phases of that eternal conflict are in the offing.'

'Sir,' said Crow, 'we would gladly join you, but there are many things we should like to know. Neither one of us is a great dreamer, and –'

'I understand,' King Carter nodded, 'but do not under-estimate your ability to dream, my friends. Dreams are all things to all men, and men must shape their own dreams just as they shape their destinies in the waking world. Now, what is it you wish to know?'

'I want to know about my father,' de Marigny immedi-ately answered. 'While we dined you mentioned his absence. If he is not here in Ilek-Vad, where is he?'

The king smiled. 'Ah, Etienne. Where is he, you ask? Where indeed? He set out some years ago, before this latest trouble in dreamland began. His destination? Who can say? Let me explain that Etienne has become the greatest of all human dreamers. His dream-quests are unending; they have carried him beyond hitherto undreamed of regions – not only in Earth's dreamlands but in those of distant worlds and dimensions.

'He will return – of course he will – but I cannot say when. There was a period of peace in dreamland when he left, but it did not last. I would have gone with him . . .' he shrugged, 'except that my adopted people are here in Ilek-Vad. So, at the moment I am both king and counselor. But make no mistake, Henri, your father will return. Someday . . .

'However, if you would be satisfied merely to see his *physical* form – why, that is simple! Come –'

The king led the way to one of the palace's inner sanctums where, upon a marble divan covered with rich silks and soft cushions, reclined the motionless form of Etienne-Laurent de Marigny. Wan and breathless, seemingly frozen in death, but undecayed, the spirit merely – absent – for the moment.

'He –' de Marigny broke the hush, 'he is as I remember him. And this trancelike state of his: you and Tiania share this same type of sleep, Titus. You looked so much like this when I saw you in Elysia.'

'Don't disturb yourself, Henri,' Crow quietly said, sensing the depth of his friend's emotion. 'It's simply a very deep form of dreaming. Worlds without end at his fingertips, my friend, and your father one of the greatest seekers of all time. Who knows what wonders he may be seeing even now? Would you really call him back?'

De Marigny made no attempt to answer.

For a long while the three men stood looking at the silent figure on the divan.

# 3

## *The Curse of Cthulhu*

The next morning after breakfast King Carter of Ilek-Vad set out to tell his visitors of the shadow over Earth's dreamland, the curse of Cthulhu. Since Crow and de Marigny were aware of the general threat, the king confined himself to specific areas of the peril. He explained the defenses which he and Kuranes and several others had set up before it, detailing the forces they intended to throw against it.

The threat itself was of course the insidious encroachment of Cthulhu's minions into dreamland, bringing His Word with them and spreading horror and evil wherever they were permitted to infiltrate men's dreams. If they were not stopped, eventually dreamland would be simply a barren place of nightmare and abomination, and the dreams of men would belong to Cthulhu to do with them as he desired. Following that, of course, the Lord of R'lyeh's next step would be an invasion of the waking world itself, the control of the conscious as well as the subconscious minds of men.

Against this threat – which King Carter himself had warned of long ago while yet an inexperienced wanderer in dreamland, though even he had not realized how far the cancer might spread – certain barriers had already been raised, behind which preparations had forged ahead to thwart, even repel the creeping invasion. Of these barriers two were believed to be completely impassable to anything tainted by the curse of Cthulhu: the force-screens about Celephais and Ilek-Vad. But even so, the inhabitants of those cities took no chances, for they were sworn to defy this persecution by Cthulhu's alien dreams. Hence the ray-projectors with which the Ilek-Vadians had bombarded the time-clock.

And behind the force-screens the armies of dreamland were being trained and its armadas built, strange weapons devised and plans for great battles laid. The King of Ilek-Vad had five thousand soldiers who would fight for him to the death, and in cloud-floating Cerannian Kuranes had built fifty great sky-yachts and was presently building fifty more.

Even before the arrival of Crow and de Marigny plans had been laid for an assault on Dylath-Leen. The intention was to rid the city forever of the horned ones of Leng, then to hold and protect its boundaries. Eventually the place might once more support the honest folk of dreamland, who would then patrol and protect the city's boundaries themselves.

Thus would Dylath-Leen become an outpost against the horned invaders, who would receive short shrift if ever they dared sail their abhorrent vessels into its harbors again. With the glad news that Carter's visitors brought, however – that the power of the horned ones in Dylath-Leen was destroyed, however temporarily, and that in all likelihood they had already fled the city in their great black galleys – now it would be only a matter of days before the first of Kuranes' anti-gravity boats with its complement of Ilek-Vadian soldier-crewmen departed for Dylath-Leen.

Nor would the reclamation of dreamland's cities, those fallen into evil ways, end with Dylath-Leen. There were other suspect places lying far to the west, along the coast of the great Southern Sea. Zak, for instance, with its terraced temples wherein forgotten dreams fade and slowly vanish, seldom to be resurrected, would be an ideal haunt for Cthulhu's emissaries: there they might experience all the dreams of Man's youth, and thereby perhaps determine the course of dreams yet to come.

Then there was infamous Thalarion, the Demon City of a Thousand Dark Wonders, reigned over by the eidolon Lathi whose fleshly avatar was rumored to be of the Cthulhu Cycle Deities themselves! Surely, in a place where images of the CCD had been openly, immemorially worshipped, there would be many unwholesome things to root out and destroy. And what of the Charnel Gardens of Zura, land of pleasures unattained; and Sona-Nyl, a region of fancy where, legend had it, future dreams were shaped and implanted like seeds in the receptive minds of certain waking men, there to blossom and grow into full-fledged dreams in their own right? What a marvelous coup *that* would be for Cthulhu's minions!

As to how the friends and enemies of dreamland might be recognized one from the other, King Carter said that the true men of dreamland were dreamland's true friends, of whom only a handful were under Cthulhu's evil spell. The horned ones of Leng were not true men – indeed, they could hardly be said to be men at all – but were of the dreamland of a dark dimension paralleling Yuggoth on the Rim, whence the CCD had brought them when the dreams of men were very young.

And apart from true men and pseudo-men there were also the utterly inhuman creatures of dream, some sentient and others barely so. The loyalty of these beings was more often than not highly suspect. The 'G' creatures, for instance, were especially suspicious – the gugs, ghasts and ghouls – and only slightly less sinister were the others: the shantaks, dholes and zoogs.

King Carter had had much to do with all such creatures in his youth, and in some of them he had found very strange allies indeed. The cats of Ulthar all knew and loved him; the zoogs of the Enchanted Wood were not disinclined toward him. He had even befriended the ghouls of dreamland's nether-pits, whose leader was a special acquaintance of his.

623

As to the ghasts and gugs, mercifully they were usually content to remain in their own realms. The ghasts were least bothersome in that real light destroyed them. They were rarely to be found outside the lightless Vaults of Zin, where they were hunted by and in turn hunted the gigantic gugs.

Night-gaunts, however, were not to be dealt with so lightly. Though faceless, they were nevertheless believed to be the secret eyes of Cthulhu's minions in dreamland. Moreover, many of dream's people still believed that the night-gaunts held great power over all of dream's lesser creatures. And certainly the vast and hippocephalic shantak-birds were mortally afraid of them. Chiefly to be found near the summit of Ngranek on the Isle of Oriab, night-gaunts also guarded the grim gray peaks dividing Leng and Inquanok, where they spent the drab daylight hours in caves that scarred the topmost pinnacles. In the night, though, gaunts flew far and wide throughout dreamland, and their secretive nature was such that indeed they would make ideal spies for the CCD.

One of the first tasks for Kuranes' sky-yachts, once Dylath-Leen was secured, would be to destroy the night-gaunt stronghold atop Ngranek, then to block all of those entrances leading down into the black and reeking abyss beneath. In this manner that area of the underworld and all its terrors would be shut off forever from saner, upper regions of dream.

And so the armies of dream would go from strength to strength. Eventually there would be great battle-fleets upon the Southern Sea, barring access to the black galleys of the horned ones; vast stone fortresses would be built and manned along the border of Inquanok and Leng, ensuring that the horrors of the latter tableland might forever remain remote. Finally, a way would be sought to destroy those black places in dreamland – the evil foci of CCD influence – where Cthulhu's engines of nightmare pounded detestably, poisoning the healthy dreams of Earth's mortals.

Such places were known to exist in the Enchanted Wood, in certain green deeps of the Southern Sea, even in the perfumed and often beautiful jungles of fabled Kled; others were rumored to lie in subterranean vaults beneath Zura's elusive temples, and in the hinterland of ruined, primordial Sarkomand. There were many, many places to be freed or cleansed of the curse of Cthulhu; great battles to be fought and won; temples of evil to be razed and healthy frontier cities founded. And all to free Man's subconscious mind from the canker of CCD-inspired nightmares.

For unless Cthulhu's creeping incursion into dreams could be put an end to, neither the waking world of men nor the universe itself would ever be truly safe from the horror inherent in His aeon-devised design for the utter destruction of all sanity and order.

Such were the grim and doom-fraught subjects covered by King Carter through all of that long day; but in the evening a banquet was prepared in honor of the visitors from the waking world, and as they sipped the clean red wine of Ilek-Vad so their apprehension for dreamland's future eased a little. Later, reclining in silk-cushioned couches that swung gently to and fro beneath the crystal-clear dome of the city's highest tower, gazing out across the placid twilight sea where all the stars of night gleamed in a darkly fluid firmament, Crow and de Marigny talked a while and then fell silent. Both of them were thinking the same thing: they knew now all they had wanted to know of Ilek-Vad. It was time to move on.

The next morning King Carter wrote a letter of introduction for his visitors, a warrant authorizing their new ranks as Generals of the Armies of Dream, telling briefly of their origins and their present importance to all dreamland.

They were to take this letter with them to Kuranes in cloud-floating Serannian, the pink marble city of the clouds; for the pair had intimated their desire to be once more on their way, and Serannian was to be their next stop.

Thus, at noon of that same day, the dreamers said their farewells to the king and flew up in the time-clock over the city. And as the powers that sustained the great invisible dome of hyperdimensional energy were momentarily revoked by Ilek-Vad's wizards, they sped away over the twilight sea in the direction of Serannian.

'Titus,' said de Marigny as they gained speed, 'things seem to be working out very well.'

'At the moment, yes. Does it bother you?'

'Something bothers me. But it's difficult to pin it down. I mean, everything seems so easy now – the obstacles are behind us.'

'Perhaps they are.'

'And yet I somehow feel an urgency, a need for greater haste.'

Crow nodded. 'I feel it too. My instinct tells me that all is not as well as it might be.'

'And there are still many questions,' de Marigny went on. 'For instance, the weapons we've seen so far. Are they magical or mechanical?'

'A bit of both, I suspect. But that takes us back to an old argument, Henri: just what *is* magic? This is Earth's dreamland, remember? If you had been to Elysia with me, then you might finally be able to put that word "magic" behind you. In Elysia there are islands that float a mile in the air, just like Serannian. Surely the science that holds such islands aloft is little short of "magical"? What you must remember is this: whether in the waking world or the world of dream, if man wants something badly enough to be, he will *make it be!* Is a sky-yacht any more fantastic than an airplane? Are King Carter's ray-projectors any

626

stranger than lasers? Dreamland and the waking world are two different spheres, Henri, certainly – but both were shaped in the minds of men, sleeping and waking alike!'

De Marigny frowned, then suddenly burst out: 'Star-stones! That's something else that's been bothering me – are there no star-stones in dreamland? I had one hanging from a chain around my neck when I set out from Earth, but I'm damned if it's there now!'

'Ah!' Crow smiled. 'But the star-stones came to Earth from an alien universe, Henri, an alien dimension. Dreamland guards her boundaries well; she does not gladly suffer that which is not of Earth and Man's own dreaming.'

'But what of Cthulhu and the CCD?' de Marigny argued. 'What could possibly be more alien? And yet their emissaries are here.'

'Sentience!' Crow answered. 'They are here because Cthulhu wills it, just as we are here because we will it.' He shrugged. 'Quite apart from which, of course, Cthulhu is a master of dreams. And it could be argued, too, that we are the aliens on Earth and not the CCD. After all, they were here first – millions of years before man. Perhaps Cthulhu himself has put this stricture on the star-stones of ancient Mnar, that they may not exist in dreams. It has certainly taken us long enough to remember them and question their absence.'

'Hmph!' de Marigny grunted. 'It's very odd: one minute everything seems so easy, the next – impossible!'

'That's the way of it, Henri,' Crow agreed. 'Often things are far simpler in dreams – but then again they can be a damned sight more difficult, too.'

627

# 4

## *Serannian*

At first sight, even knowing he was dreaming, de Marigny found Serannian almost unbelievable. He had seen it before, certainly, in those telepathic visions showed to him by Kthanid in hyperdimensional Elysia, but the reality was a far greater thing. A cloud-washed coast of pink marble that seemed to stretch away to its own horizons; and built upon the shore, a splendid city that looked out over an ethereal sea of glowing cirrus and cirrocumulus.

Far below, glimpsed through roseate mists and pink-hued clouds, the Cerenarian Sea's white-tipped billows washed towards a distance-hazed land where Mount Aran was only just visible. That mountain, the dreamers knew, formed one of the valley-walls of Ooth-Nargai, where timeless Celephais reared her splendid domes, towers, and minarets beneath a dome of energy like that which protected Ilek-Vad. But because Celephais and Serannian both came under Kuranes' wise rule, trade went on as of old between the Timeless City and the Sky Islands; except that now the force-screen about the former must periodically be relaxed, allowing the sky-galleys that brought the latter's supplies free passage out onto the Cerenarian Sea.

Indeed, the galleys they saw riding to the horizon, where they sailed skyward on rose-tinted mists, had recently put out from Celephais. Awed by the beauty of all they saw – marveling that the subconscious mind of man could dream such wonders – the travelers in the time-clock followed one of the galleys into the harbor of Serannian; and when

Crow set the clock down on the walls of the pink-marble docks, they marveled again that Serannian had ever been built here, on this ethereal coast where the west wind flowed into the sky.

Moored in the harbor, floating impossibly on pink cloud-crests, the dreamers spied twenty-five of Kuranes' fleet of fifty war vessels; along their decks, port and starboard, were single rows of mirror-bright devices that reflected sharp shafts of sunlight as the ships bobbed up and down. These were ray-projectors, like those they had seen in Ilek-Vad. In the distant sky, riding out on the west wind, the other half of the fleet was under sail.

Standing beside the time-clock on the dockside – which was deserted now, for sailors and dockers alike had quietly melted away into the wharfside taverns as soon as the time-clock had landed – Crow and de Marigny watched the receding sails of the ships until a voice informed: 'They go out to practice the arts of war, arts which will soon be put to good use in Dylath-Leen and other places.'

Turning, they came face to face with Kuranes, a man once of the waking world, now Lord of Ooth-Nargai, Celephais, and the Sky around Serannian. They knew him immediately from a description furnished by King Carter. Slightly built but regally robed, gray-bearded but sprightly and bright-eyed – and wary – Kuranes had with him a retinue of pike-armed guardsmen. He gazed briefly upon his visitors before continuing.

'Rumors have been reaching me for days now of a strange flying machine come into Earth's dreamland.' He made a motion with his hand and the guardsmen clustered closer, moving between the two dreamers and their machine. Crow and de Marigny found themselves inside a circle of sharp pikeheads.

'I have wondered,' Kuranes went on, 'whether this device, this flying machine, was benign toward dreamland

629

or – malignant.' Again he beckoned, and his guardsmen laid restraining hands on the two strangers.

At last Crow spoke. 'Lord Kuranes, we understand your apprehension perfectly, but you may put your mind at ease simply by reading this letter.' He produced the carefully folded document. 'It is from Randolph Carter in Ilek-Vad.'

'A letter from Randolph Carter?' Kuranes' eyebrows went up and he seemed surprised. 'Randolph, you say? Are you so familiar, then, with the King of Ilek-Vad?'

'My father was King Carter's counselor,' de Marigny quickly answered, 'before he took to exploring in undreamed of places. I am Henri-Laurent de Marigny, and this is Titus Crow.'

As Kuranes read King Carter's letter, so the attitude of alert wariness fell from him. Finally he smiled and waved his guardsmen aside, clasping first de Marigny's hand, then Titus Crow's.

'Gentlemen,' he said, 'I am at your service.'


A few minutes later, on their way to Kuranes' 'palace' – which, astonishingly, they saw at a distance to be nothing less than a great Gothic manorhouse with a gray stone tower, typical of lordly English dwellings Kuranes had known in the Cornwall of his youth in the waking world – a servant of the Lord of Serannian approached in great haste. This man, a whiskered butler attired in typically English livery, though patently he was a denizen of dreamland, probably born and bred in Celephais or Ulthar, handed Kuranes a tiny metal tube.

Kuranes took square-framed spectacles from his robe and put them on, then unscrewed one end of the metal tube and carefully extracted a tightly rolled strip of extremely thin paper. 'James,' he asked of his butler, 'what color was the bird that delivered this?'

'Pink as Serannian's clouds, my Lord,' the butler answered, in an accent which was not quite Cornish.

'Hmm . . . Then it came from Atal in Ulthar. I wonder what he wants.'

On hearing Atal's name spoken, the two dreamers exchanged quick, speculative glances. Then de Marigny's suddenly taut features relaxed and he shrugged, murmuring: 'It can have nothing to do with us, Titus. No one knows we're here.'

'Oh?' exclaimed Kuranes, his sharp ears catching de Marigny's remark. 'But you are wrong, my young friend! It does concern you – both of you. And as to how Atal knew you would be here – none in dreamland is wise as Atal. Did he know you were going to Ilek-Vad?'

The two nodded in unison.

'Then it would not be hard to guess your next port of call.' His eyes went back to the paper. 'It says that you should return to Ulthar at once, that many of Leng's horned ones are in the city disguised as foreign traders, and that a man called Grant Enderby is worried about strange figures seen lurking near his house in the dead of night.'

'Anything else?' Crow's voice was tense.

'Yes. Atal says that although there are no true soldiers in Ulthar – that is, no real force for the protection of the public – he has sent several young priests from the Temple of the Elder Ones to keep a discreet watch over Enderby's house. Hmm! And that's all there is. It seems to have been penned in some haste.'

He handed the letter to Crow. 'Take it, by all means, but you'll have to take my word for what's in it. It's written in an obscure glyph with which only a few in dreamland are familiar. Atal knows that I am one of the few.'

'Lord Kuranes,' said de Marigny, his voice urgent, 'you must understand, we have loved ones in Ulthar. It's more than possible that our mutual enemies intend them harm.'

'Yes,' Crow continued when de Marigny paused. 'It seems we must take our leave of you sooner than we expected. Immediately.'

Kuranes nodded. 'I understand. It's a pity, for I was looking forward to a long talk. It's rare now that I have distinguished visitors from the waking world. You will go in your flying machine, of course?'

'Yes,' Crow answered, 'but as soon as we get another chance we'll be back to try your hospitality, Kuranes.'

'You won't find it wanting,' the Lord of Serannian promised. 'But listen, I have an idea. This could be my chance to exercise my armada a bit more realistically. It's known that the horned ones have a number of sky-galleys of their own. In fact, they once kidnapped King Carter to dreamland's moon – which is not like the moon of the waking world – in just such a galley. This could be how they plan to make their getaway from Ulthar once their dirty work, whatever it is, is done there. It's not unlikely that they've hidden one of their foul galleys somewhere on the coast, to which they'll flee when they're ready. How would it be if I sent a dozen of my sky-yachts, with full complement of trained crew-men, to follow you to Ulthar?'

'It's a very kind offer,' Crow answered, 'but the time-clock travels at an incredible pace. We'd leave your ships far behind. Still, I think it would be a good idea to send some of your vessels to Ulthar, perhaps to station them there permanently. There have always been a few horned ones in the city, or so I'm led to believe, and we can never tell what nests they may have built for themselves. Why not let a handful of your best ships and their crews form the city's first soldiery, a police force to guard against the subversion of the horned ones?'

'I'll do it!' Kuranes cried. 'Even if my ships can be of no assistance to you two, still they can perform a useful service for the peoples of Ulthar. In any case, I can only send a handful of ships, for I'm short of crews. I'm to draw upon Ilek-Vad for most of my crewmen. Now then, I can see that you're eager to be off, so I won't hold you. Off you go – and the very best of British luck to you!' He waved after them as they turned and hurriedly retraced their steps in the direction of the harbor.

To the young priest who anxiously scanned the skies from the roof of the temple's ivied tower, the coming of the clock into Ulthar was an awe-inspiring experience. Having seen many marvels as an initiate and acolyte at the Temple of the Elder Ones, he was used to wonders, but this was somehow different. There was no clap of thunder, no darkening over of the skies, none of the phenomena with which he was used to associating the onset of occult or paranormal occurrences. And yet surely this flying clock was a magick of the first water.

Out of an early afternoon sky touched with fleece the time-clock raced – at first a dot spied among the distant clouds, then a dark oblong shape that flew upright, finally a coffin shape that slowed and fell out of the sky – down past the tower so that the young priest could see the four hands that moved irregularly and in exotic sequences about the great dial. His warning shout had barely echoed down to the square in front of the temple's entrance, where three of his fellows awaited the clock's coming in their robes of priesthood, before the space-time vehicle alighted and its passengers stepped forth.

They were immediately ushered into the temple, along a maze of corridors, until finally they came to that inner sanctum where Atal the Elder reclined upon his bed of silks. Extreme in age and fragile as he was, warm recognition still showed in the patriarch's faded, almost colorless eyes as he welcomed the two dreamers into his presence. His trembling, whispery voice was urgent as he gave them the grim news:

'My young friends . . . it is terrible . . . terrible!' he quavered. 'Sinister creatures in the city in greater numbers than ever before. Three of the temple's young priests bloodily slain – the lady Tiania of Elysia and the girl Litha Enderby of Ulthar kidnapped and carried off – and an almost tangible oppression settling like a shroud over the minds of all Ulthar's decent citizens. I set a dozen of my pigeons to seek you out – to Nir, Serannian, Hatheg, Sona-Nyl, and Baharna; even to Ilek-Vad, though I was not sure that the bird would be able to fly into the city – and I am only sorry that you . . . were not found . . . soon . . . enough . . .' He came to a faltering, panting halt.

'In your own time.' Titus Crow calmed him, quickly seating himself beside the centuried high priest, cradling his head and shoulders against his own strong arm. 'Now, from the beginning –'

And so, slowly and with many a pause, Atal told them how on the previous morning it had been noticed that there was an inordinate number of the strangely turbaned traders in the city, those squat beings of ill-legended Leng. Ulthar had never found it necessary to totally ban such creatures – only the trading of their blasphemous rubies was forbidden, and usually the horned ones were merely passing through the city on their way to less discerning places – but nevertheless Atal found this sudden increase in their numbers greatly disturbing.

He made discreet inquiries, discovered that furtive groups of the horned ones had been seen in that district where Tiania of Elysia was staying, and immediately his concern trebled – particularly when Grant Enderby himself later complained that he had seen suspicious evening shadows where none had been before, shadows that melted quickly away when he attempted to approach them.

Enderby had been sure that the horned ones were watching his house, and certainly his wide experience of these beings was such as must make him something of an expert on them. Thus he conveyed his concern for his exotic house guest to Atal, who in turn sent three priests from the Temple of the Elder Ones to watch over Enderby's house through the night. At the same time Atal gave orders that a dozen carrier pigeons were to be prepared for release to distant lands and cities, and with his own trembling hand he wrote the cryptograms to be tied to the legs of those blood-hued birds. All to no avail.

The straight, short ceremonial swords of the temple – with which the three young priests were not familiar in any other than esoteric connections – had been useless against the viciously curving blades of the horned ones, as the headless corpses of those priests had all too mutely testified the next morning. Enderby himself was lucky; he had been knocked unconscious from behind as he patrolled the walls around his house and garden. Mercifully his wife and sons had been away, visiting an ailing relative in a nearby hamlet.

At dawn, when the quarrier had achingly regained consciousness, he had found the decapitated priests lying in his garden where they had been dragged by their killers. Tiania of Elysia and Enderby's daughter Litha were nowhere to be found.

'And that,' Atal brought his tale to an end at last, 'was the way of it. Who can say what the rest of it will be?'

# The Legions of Nightmare

As Atal finished speaking, Crow laid the patriarch's head gently back on the pillows and stood up. A wild rage shone in the dreamer's eyes and his whole attitude was that of a lion crouching before springing to the attack.

'De Marigny,' he grated, 'if ever I've felt sorry for my enemies before – if ever I've been guilty of feelings of sympathy for the CCD in their eternal banishment, or their dupes and minions caught up in the foul schemes of their prisoned masters – then may my soul *rot* before I ever shall again!'

And Henri-Laurent de Marigny, white and trembling with fury and horror, made his own vow. 'Atal, we leave the Temple of the Elder Ones now – and we shall not return until these great wrongs are righted and their authors punished in full . . .' He paused, then turned despairingly to Titus Crow. 'But where can we even begin to look for them – and for Litha and Tiania?'

Before Crow could answer, Atal spoke. 'Wait, wait! I have sent out birds, dozens of them, the temple's pigeons, to all towns and hamlets in the vicinity of Ulthar. If the horned ones have passed by any one of fifty places, we shall soon know of it. Indeed, some of the birds have already returned, but as yet they have brought no word. You will fly off in your time-clock, I suppose, but if you have no success before evening, call back this way. By then we may know something. The priest at the top of the tower . . . will be kept . . . fully informed . . .' And once more exhausted, he again lay back on his pillows.

Without another word, the two grim-faced dreamers

turned and left Atal's room, passing into the maze of corridors and making their way quickly out of the temple.

They split up, Crow taking the time-clock and de Marigny his anti-gravity cloak, flying outward from Ulthar in opposite directions to begin their aerial search of the surrounding regions. Crow headed for the coast, thinking that perhaps Kuranes had been right about a hidden sky-galley in which the horned ones would attempt an escape; and de Marigny followed the Skai down to distant Dylath-Leen, deserted now and strangely drab in the mid-afternoon sunlight.

Both dreamers were to find only bitter disappointment . . .

Titus Crow sought the sails of ships as he flew out over the sea – particularly ships headed for the horizon, where they might suddenly lift into the sky, bound perhaps for Kadath, Leng, or even dreamland's moon itself – and, sure enough, after searching for over an hour he spied sails, but these were already airborne. And they were not the ominous black galleys of the horned ones but the colorful battle-yachts of Serannian, on their way to Ulthar as Kuranes had promised.

Briefly Crow landed on the deck of the lead ship to inquire of the captain if perhaps anything had been seen of black galleys sailing the seas below. He was told that nothing had been seen at all to arouse any suspicion, neither on the Cerenarian nor on the Southern Sea. Crow quickly related what he knew of the recent trouble in Ulthar and took off again.

De Marigny, making ever widening, concentric sweeps about Dylath-Leen and eventually winging out over the great deserts, spied a caravan in an unseemly hurry and approached with some caution until he flew directly above it, unseen by its masters. But no, these were only honest merchants of dream about their business, and their haste was probably due to the close proximity of Dylath-Leen, whose gray towers reared in sinister fashion not too many miles distant. It would be a long time before that empty city lost its unenviable reputation in dreamland.

As the hours passed and afternoon began to grow toward evening, Titus Crow and Henri-Laurent de Marigny turned back for Ulthar. Over the City of Cats they spied one another across a league of sky, and winging down toward the tower of the temple both were attracted by the frantic waving of a priest behind the high, ivied parapet. They landed together on the roof, and as Crow stepped out of the time-clock de Marigny began to question the young, breathlessly excited priest.

Yes, at last there was news! A dozen of the horned ones, more furtive than ever, had been sighted in mid-morning on the outskirts of Nir. They had been making their way across the plain toward the Enchanted Wood, bearing two bundles like rolled carpets with open ends. And strange sounds had seemed to emanate from those bundles, like muffled cries for help. Later, a shepherd had found traces of the party in a cave, where they had doubtless rested out the night. Their journey must be very tiring; horned ones were not ideally structured for the carrying of heavy bundles, and they had no beasts of burden with them.

This news had come via one of the temple's carrier pigeons, sent back by a holy man in Nir, and it arrived just as Kuranes' sky-yachts had appeared over the city. With his vessel anchored firmly to the temple's high tower, the senior captain had alighted to learn of the kidnapping and of the route taken by the kidnappers toward the Enchanted Wood. The airborne ships had at once sailed off in the same direction, picking up a vengeful Grant Enderby and his sons on the way. This had occurred well over an hour ago.

'Into the clock, Henri!' Titus Crow cried. 'I believe I know what they're up to now, and if I'm right we haven't a moment to spare!'

'The Enchanted Wood, of course!' de Marigny exclaimed as the clock's door closed on them and they lifted to the sky. 'The Enchanted Wood – and that great slab with its massive ring and runic inscriptions!'

'Right,' Crow grimly affirmed, sending the clock racing across dreamland like a coffin-shaped blur in the sky. 'One of those places King Randolph Carter told us about – where Cthulhu's engines of nightmare pound away down in the black, reeking underworld, manufacturing madness with which to disease the subconscious minds of men and subvert them to his cause. It's a place like the one we destroyed beyond the Peaks of Throk, whose guardian was the vast and leprous Keeper. I only hope we're in time, that's all.'

Far down below, the grassy fields of the plain rushed by breathtakingly; then, ahead and to the left, Nir appeared, drew level, vanished behind in a twinkling; the singing Skai flashed for an instant like a narrow silver ribbon in the last rays of evening; Hatheg with its domed dwellings came and went. In the twilight they overtook the battle-yachts of Serannian and at last flew over the edge of the gloomy Enchanted Wood.

Then Crow reluctantly reduced the speed of their craft and brought it down to the level of the treetops in the rapidly fading light, and as the rush of the great trees beneath them slowed they covered another mile or so until they came to that shocking region of diseased oaks which was in fact almost a clearing of crumbling stumps, quaggy earth, and luminescent, bloated fungi. There Crow set the clock down and they alighted from its cleanly pulsating radiance into the rotten glow of putrefying foliage.

They carefully approached the center of that scabrous clearing, where lay the massive slab with its Titan ring. Eagerly their eyes searched the mold and mush-slimed edges of the great slab for signs that it had recently been moved.

'Thank all that's merciful!' cried de Marigny, his voice shattering the miasmal silence. 'It hasn't been moved. We're in time, Titus!'

Crow nodded in the semidarkness. 'Yes, if this is indeed their destination –' He suddenly cocked his head on one side and held up a cautionary finger. 'Listen! Do you hear it? What do you make of that, Henri?'

All was gloom, fetor, and uneasy, misted silence. De Marigny held his breath and listened for a moment. He could hear nothing. 'What is it, Titus?'

'Here, put your hand on the slab. Now do you hear it?'

'Yes . . . It's a pounding, deep down in the bowels of the earth.'

'Well, we were right about that at least.' Crow nodded in grim satisfaction. 'This is certainly the portal to one of Cthulhu's factories of nightmare. And –'

'*Shh!*' de Marigny suddenly whispered. 'Someone's coming!'

A moment later came definite sounds of disturbed underbrush not too far distant – immediately followed by an outraged cry from a female throat!

'Litha!' de Marigny choked, instinctively making to rush in the direction of the cry.

'Hold on, Henri,' Crow restrained him. 'Believe me I'm as eager to be at them as you are, but let's get the time-clock out of the way first and lie in wait for them. Let's see if we can discover just exactly what's going on here.'

No sooner had they flown the time-clock into a deep, dense patch of bramble at the edge of the clearing, closing its panel behind them so that the clock's weird light would not give away their presence, than from the opposite side of the clearing appeared the fugitive group of horned ones.

Between them – hands bound and shivering, with their clothes in tatters – staggered the two fiercely protesting girls, Tiania and Litha. Crow and de Marigny saw all of this very clearly, for two of the horned ones had lanterns that cast a yellow, penetrating light all about as they moved forward, dragging the women toward the great slab.

'Titus,' whispered de Marigny, his hand trembling violently on the other's arm, 'I can't –'

'Shh!' Crow cut him off. 'The girls are all right, Henri, just a bit roughed up, that's all. Let's learn what we can before we make a move.'

In the center of the clearing one of the horned ones moved forward, held up his lantern before him, and commenced to read from the runes graven into the top of the slab. Such sounds as he made could never be echoed by the vocal chords of man, but the horned one was totally fluent in this unearthly tongue. And in response to the chanted rune, suddenly, with a harsh grating and shuddering, the great slab began to tilt upon some hidden spindle. As the horned one continued his weird chanting, so the girls were bundled forward.

'All right, Henri,' Crow snapped, urgently gripping his friend's shoulder. 'Now see what you can do to slow things down a bit while I bring the time-clock into play!'

De Marigny needed no more urging. He bounded aloft in his cloak, swooped down from on high, and crashed headlong into three of the squat creatures from Leng. One of these flew with a shrill shriek straight into the reeking gap where the edge of the slab had now lifted to reveal an inky hole beneath; a second was dashed to the mushy earth where he lay still; the third jumped to his feet – only to be grabbed about his fat neck and hoisted aloft as de Marigny flew his cloak up into darkness. A moment later and this third horned one's gurgling cry was cut off short as his squat body fell with a snapping of bones against the steadily tilting slab.

A few seconds more and de Marigny flashed out of the sky again – but this time they were ready for him. Four of them were still awkwardly struggling with the girls, doing their best to push them into the hole showing beneath the slab while keeping a nervous watch out for de Marigny. The other five slashed with their scimitars at the dreamer's hurtling form as he swerved over their heads.

Then Titus Crow took a hand in the matter. The time-clock crashed forward out of the brambles at the clearing's edge; and even as the horned ones saw that strange vehicle of the Elder Gods, so Crow triggered the clock's awesome weapon.

A beam of purest, dazzling light flashed forth from the four-handed dial, slicing first into those five horned ones whose blades were drawn against de Marigny, scything them down in an instant. The four who held the girls let go of them at once and turned to flee. Crow cut three down with another slashing beam of light, then, with that same beam, tracked the fourth – who immediately darted behind the now almost vertical slab!

Crow's beam struck the great slab . . . and the next instant the whole clearing shook with an ear-splitting roar as that monstrous door to the underworld shattered and flew asunder. It was sheer luck that the two girls, stumbling away toward the edge of the clearing, were not hit by the boulder-sized chunks of rock that hurtled in all directions; but they were not, and when the smoke cleared they stood clinging together, half-swooning, until de Marigny alighted beside them and hugged them to him.

Only then, when it appeared that the immediate danger was past, did the true horror of the situation become apparent.

For as de Marigny stood with his arms protectively about the two girls – and as Crow in the time-clock surveyed the scene in the clearing, ill-lit now that the lanterns of the horned ones were extinguished – so there came a subterranean rumbling and a geyser of slime and foul gases from the yawning pit. Hurriedly, half-carrying the girls with him, de Marigny backed away from that awful orifice; but Titus Crow, protected by the almost totally impervious shell of the time-clock, eased his vessel forward until it poised on the very lip of the pit.

Using the clock's scanners he gazed down into a dim and reeking abyss . . . *from which, suddenly and without warning, there burst a noisome stream of horrors straight out of a madman's blackest nightmares!*

Ethereal the things might well have been, but still they seemed solid enough to cause Crow to back his clock hastily away from the pit's edge. Dozens, hundreds of them, out they poured like pus from a ruptured abscess, an endless tide of monsters created by Cthulhu's machineries of madness, released now to plague the subconscious minds of mortal dreamers. And they were, quite literally – *nightmares!*

Misty, wraithlike, utterly malignant and malevolent, they swirled and billowed about the poisoned clearing while their shapes seemed to take on more form, more substance. Here were vampires, ghouls, werewolves and witches, monsters of every sort imaginable and others quite unimaginable. Burnt-out eye-sockets leered from melting faces; mad fangs gnashed hideously in mouths that drooled and chomped vacuously; eyestalks twined and twisted while leprous claws and stumps of fingers scrabbled spastically. The stenches of a thousand open tombs issued up from that hellish pit, and its gibbering depths reverberated with a throbbing cacophony of completely lunatic, utterly inhuman laughter.

And the worst was still to come, for de Marigny and the girls had no protection at all against these nightmares from the pit, which now swarmed about them in ever thickening, ever more threatening hordes. Illumined in the rotten glow of phosphorescent corruption, Crow saw the faces of the three convulse in ultimate horror, watched them quite literally going mad in the face of unthinkable, unbearable nightmare.

Again and again, frantically he triggered the clock's weapon, lighting up the clearing in blinding flashes of white light, shredding the monsters from the pit in their hundreds. But as quickly as they steamed off in vile evaporation others rushed from the hole to replace them. Then the unimaginable happened: suddenly Titus Crow himself was on the defensive!

At last he recognized his peril and cursed himself that he hadn't seen it sooner. These things were *nightmares*, and even in the dreamlands they were not 'physical' but 'psychical' phenomena. As such they were not subject to mundane laws of time and space. He could no more keep them out of the time-clock than he could keep from dreaming. Dreams come and go ignoring all walls and barriers – and so do nightmares!

Again he triggered the clock's mighty weapon, again, and yet again . . . until at last he felt his brain gripped and wrenched and squeezed by incredible terror, and knew that finally they had breached the time-clock's polydimensional walls! Then everything seemed to dissolve in one vast cataclysmic bombburst of flame and light . . .

# 6

## Nyarlathotep

For a single moment only – which Titus Crow reasonably believed might be his last – the blinding glare filled the clearing with its light, leaving a cascade of illusory fireworks dripping white fire on his retinae . . . and leaving his mind completely free from nightmare!

Instinctively, in complete astonishment, he had time enough to merely glance into the clock's scanners before turning from them to avoid suffering the glare again. For in the night sky above the Enchanted Wood he had seen a glad, fantastic sight: six battle-yachts in line, their ray-projectors aimed threateningly down into the heart of the nightmare-ridden clearing. The clearing itself had looked much as before, except that now the mist was that much denser through absorbing the ectoplasmic stuff of which a thousand defunct nightmares had recently been composed.

De Marigny, Tiania, and Litha had been stumbling to and fro, their hands to their heads, still suffering the mental aftermath of that concerted attack of blackest nightmares; and even as Crow had snapped shut his scanners to avoid the blaze of a second salvo from the ray-projectors, he had seen that the gaping, steaming pit still issued a vile stream of threatening, abyss-spawned horrors.

Flying blind but using all the skill with which his long experience of the time-clock had endowed him, he flew across the clearing, skirting the pit to fetch a halt close to the stricken trio. As he made to leave his exotic, hybrid machine – even within its hyperdimensional shell – still

Crow felt again that blast of awesome illumination as the aerial gunners opened up on the nightmares from the pit a second time; then he quickly stepped out of the clock, snatched up Tiania, and pulled her to safety. He did the same for Litha and finally de Marigny, and no sooner was the clock's door shut than yet again there came a concerted blast of purifying light from the sky.

Only then did Titus Crow use the scanners again, and as he lifted the clock up out of the clearing he saw that the rush of nightmares from the subterranean abyss was greatly reduced. A few seconds later he landed his vessel beneath the mainmast of the lead ship and assisted his rapidly recovering passengers out onto the deck.

'Titus,' de Marigny caught his elbow as he turned back to the clock. 'What are you doing?'

'I intend to finish this job once and for all, Henri. Don't worry, I'm not going down into the pit. I just intend to close it up forever – if I can! These shipboard ray-projectors are fine used en masse, and their powers must be very similar to the clock's own, but I think you'll find they're only good for short bursts. This job will require more than that.'

Without another word he entered the clock and flew it back down to the clearing, hovering directly above the pit. Only a thin trickle of nightmares was issuing from that ghastly hole now, and keen-sighted gunners on the battle-yachts were picking them off as fast as they appeared. Crow tilted the clock slightly, lining up its four-handed dial with the mouth of the pit, then triggered his weapon in a long, continuous burst.

And Titus Crow was right, for while in unison the ray-projectors were indeed a force to be reckoned with, as individual weapons they simply could not be compared with the marvelous power of the Elder Gods. Directly into the mouth of the pit he played that unbearably pure beam, illuminating incredible depths that seemed to go down forever, perhaps to the vaults at dreamland's core. For thirty seconds or more that stream of concentrated purity – the very Essence of Benevolence, the evil-destroying Light of the Elder Gods themselves – played into the pit, and slowly but surely the desired metamorphosis was brought about.

First the mushy ground in the immediate vicinity of the pit began to glow with a radiance of its own, a light that throbbed like the beating of a great luminous heart. And this radiance spread outwards until it encompassed the entire clearing, pulsing ever faster, almost hypnotically, in a strange strobic splendor.

At the height of this activity – from which at its onset, as from a suddenly erupting volcano, the six sky-yachts had sailed off to a safe distance – without warning the ground in the clearing began to bubble and boil, flowing like molten lava and streaming into the pit. On the heels of this phenomenon came others as the entire clearing and the diseased oaks around it suddenly trembled, then heaved and bucked in a seismic convulsion as muffled explosions sounded from deep down in the underworld. Then, blowing outward from the spot where the pit had been, there came a howling, madly rushing ghost-wind that hurled the six sky-yachts back across the sky like so many autumn leaves, a torrent of winds that continued long after Crow released the trigger of his awesome weapon. The ground in the clearing still steamed and bubbled, and it retained a little of its luminosity – in which eerie light Crow now witnessed the beginning of this strange drama's final act.

Slowly at first, then rapidly widening, a crack appeared in the glowing earth where the pit had been sealed off, and emerging from this ominous fissure came a rotten, greenish glow that seemed to ooze upward into the clearing. At first Crow was tempted to use the time-clock's weapon yet again, without waiting to see what this new threat might be, but his human curiosity got the better of him. Despite his recent experience with the nightmares from the pit, his faith in the clock's imperviousness remained all but unshaken; whatever this green glow was he did not believe it could harm him. In any case, it would be the work of the merest moment to bring his weapon to bear upon this unknown thing, for its 'trigger' was in his own mind. He flew the time-clock down to a spot which he reckoned was at a safe distance from the as yet unidentified phenomenon.

The glowing sphere of green light slowly lost its opaque quality until Crow could make out a figure standing at its center – a human figure! And as the green glow grew dimmer yet and the winds ceased their frantic outward rush, so he made out the physical details of this unexpected apparition.

Tall and slim, clad in bright robes and crowned with a luminous yellow pshent, the figure seemed to become more solid as its heralding green glow died away. It was a man with the young, proud face of a Pharaoh of ancient Khem – but whose eyes were those of a dark God, where lurked a languid, sardonic humor.

'So you are the man Titus Crow,' the figure finally spoke in rippling mellow tones. 'A mere man – and yet much *more* than a man . . .'

On hearing that languorous voice – despite detecting a trace of malice in the emphasized word, which ought to have alerted, galvanized him – a creeping numbness fell over Crow's brain. Too late, he started to reach out a mental finger, intending to activate the time-clock's weapon, only to discover that halfway to the trigger his hand was stayed, his will frozen solid. An iciness like the chill of the deeps between the stars pervaded his whole being, robbing him of all volition. And at last Titus Crow recognized the newcomer, knew also that he was face to face with Doom, that he could not possibly survive the encounter. For this handsome young Pharaoh was none other than Nyarlathotep, the Crawling Chaos!

'Ah, yes!' The voice came inside Crow's head now. 'You know me, Titus Crow, for we've had dealings before, you and I, when you've seen me in some of my thousand other forms. And you are one who knows me for what I really am, and you know the nature of my masters . . .

'Well, dreamer, it is at an end. Only a very few men have caused my masters so much concern, and doubtless you would go on to cause more trouble if you were not curbed. For you are impetuous and wild and do not understand my masters, who are great and glorious beyond all greatness and glory. So I have sought you out in dreams, and have brought about this meeting which will set your feet on the road to a greater destiny: to be one with my masters out among the stars and in the hidden places of the waking world!

'For they would like to know you, Titus Crow, more intimately. They would like to watch your reactions to terrors greater than any yet conceived by your race, and would taste of the entire range of your passions when, at the end, they scatter the shreds of your subconscious being to the very corners of existence. But never fear, Titus Crow, for they would not destroy you immediately. No, for there are punishments far worse than those imposed upon my masters by the so-called Elder Gods, and surely a suitable one will be found for you . . .

'Now come, dreamer, out of your time-clock and embrace me. Come, for we have far to go and must leave at once . . .' And Nyarlathotep beckoned, smiling sardonically and opening his arms wide as if welcoming an old friend.

Like a doll on the strings of a master puppeteer, Crow opened the clock and stepped out of its purple-glowing interior. He approached Nyarlathotep wide-eyed, moving like an automaton, and as the distance closed between them so the green glow began to return, springing up and deepening around the slim Pharaoh-like figure.

Behind the dreamer as he moved inexorably forward, the weird purple light from the open door of the time-clock grew deeper as its pulsing slowed; the glow itself expanded until it completely encompassed the clock and a wide area around it, finally matching in size and intensity the green and rotten luminescence about the form of Nyarlathotep. Abruptly in Crow's frozen mind a second commanding voice now resounded:

'Man of Earth, you, Titus Crow, *stop!* Turn about!'

Falteringly, zombie-like in his movements, the dreamer turned. A vast nebulous face was growing out of the purple glow about the clock, a face in which huge golden octopus eyes glared out in a terrible rage. Face-tentacles lashed and the entire visage of the Elder God shook and trembled in the spasms of a towering passion.

For this was of course the image of Kthanid, Tiania's guardian and Titus Crow's patron in Elysia – Kthanid, who now used the time-clock more truly as a gateway between dimensions to intrude on Crow's behalf in this his moment of direst peril.

'Titus Crow, come to me!' ordered Nyarlathotep, his mental voice slightly less mellow, less certain now. Obediently, the dreamer began to turn away from the clock.

'No!' came Kthanid's urgent denial. 'Get out of the way if you can, Titus, so that I may strike him. I have a power here greater even than the time-clock's own. But it will destroy you, too, if you stand before it!'

'He can't disobey me, fool!' Nyarlathotep laughed, his voice quickly deteriorating to a bass croaking in Crow's mind. 'Come to me, Earthman – NOW!'

At that precise moment, down from the sky a bat-cloaked figure flew, hurling the stumbling, hypnotized dreamer from between the two beings in the clearing. Immediately the spell was broken; Crow shuddered as he clung to de Marigny and they lifted up above the treetops of the Enchanted Wood. Then, rising rapidly toward the sky-yachts, the two dreamers stared down at a fantastic scene.

A tremendous booming voice came up to them, a mental voice that reverberated in their minds as Kthanid addressed his Enemy: 'You have threatened those in my protection – even Tiania who is flesh of my flesh – *and now you must pay!*'

Simultaneous with the last word, twin beams of pulsating golden light flashed from Kthanid's great eyes to penetrate the green glow of corruption and strike the figure of Nyarlathotep with their full force. He staggered, that Great Messenger of the CCD, then swelled up huge and bloated. 'Damn you, Kthanid! Let me . . . *go!*'

'Not until you have suffered . . . and would that I could make you suffer a thousand times more!' Again the twin beams leapt from his eyes to the grotesquely bloated figure of the Pharaoh – which instantly reformed itself into . . . *something else!*

A vast, monstrous congeries of iridescent globes and bubbles shifted and frothed where the bloated human figure had stood, and Kthanid's cry was glad and triumphant as he hurled his beams directly into this seething mass. Those sizzling golden beams struck home – and for a moment the two dreamers floating high above were afforded a glimpse of the *Thing* that lurked behind those globes and bubbles: a Titan primal jelly of wriggling ropes, bulging eyes, and tossing, convulsing pseudopods and mouths – an ultraevil, supersentient anemone from deepest oceans of horror!

'Ah, Yog-Sothoth! So, you have helped Him in this, have you? A joint effort, was it? And who else hides behind the lying mask of Nyarlathotep, how many more of the thousand forms?' Again the searing golden beams lashed out, and another metamorphosis immediately took place. Gone now the liquescent, purplish-blue loathsomeness of Yog-Sothoth, and in his place a towering black anthropomorphic outline that stood on great webbed feet and gazed with carmine stars for eyes!

'Ithaqua, too!' boomed Kthanid. 'The Thing that Walks on the Wind. Well, begone, Ithaqua, and let us see what others there are . . .'

Then, in rapid succession, using his twin golden beams like great knives, Kthanid peeled away the outer layers of telepathic consciousness that shielded the innermost, ultimate blasphemy. Many members of the CCD there were that Crow and de Marigny recognized, and many they did not know at all. Shudde-M'ell was there, the dreaded burrower beneath; yes, and fiery Cthugha and tentacled Hastur, too. A single, shocking glimpse of slimy Yibb-Tstll; and one of Yig, Father of Serpents; and Zhar, Chaugnar Faugn, and many others. And finally – Cthulhu!

Cthulhu, the dread Lord of R'lyeh, dreaming but not dead, sending his dreams from drowned R'lyeh to infest and desecrate the sacred lands of Earth's human dreamers. He was almost the twin of Kthanid, but where Kthanid was golden Cthulhu was leaden, where the former was Good the latter was absolute Evil. Evil writhed and twisted in twining face-tentacles, leered out of kraken eyes, and twitched convulsively in vastly arched wings. Evil glowered hideously, unblinkingly at the shining image of Kthanid – until once again, for the last time, twin beams of pulsating yellow fire reached out to strike the monster dead center.

'Get you gone from here, Cthulhu,' boomed the Elder God, 'back to R'lyeh where you belong. Will you never learn to keep your mad dreams to yourself? Begone!'

Then there echoed up from the clearing a tremendous, rumbling explosion like a great clap of thunder, and when the dazed dreamers flying high above next dared to look down Cthulhu was indeed gone. Gone, too, was Kthanid, and the time-clock stood alone and issued its softly pulsing glow in a clearing that lay blasted and barren and silent, where, in the morning, birds might safely sing as they never had since time immemorial . . .

# *Epilogue*

Ah, yes, the Inn of a Thousand Sleeping Cats, in Ulthar!

Of course, I didn't hear all of the tale that one evening, merely snatches of it that reached me from the fabled group at the head of the massive banquet table. The Enderbys were there – with dark-eyed Litha seated blushingly alongside Henri-Laurent de Marigny – and Tiania of Elysia, side by side with her Earthman, Titus Crow; and all around the table were dignitaries from all of dreamland's districts and counties and cities. Yes, even Atal of Hatheg-Kla. And all of them come to applaud the exploits of the adventurers from the waking world.

As to the tale's total veracity: well, I for one would swear to it. Have I not myself visited the Enchanted Wood and chatted with the Zoogs, all of them telling me of that night when the wood was bright with strange lights, following which the birds returned to nest in the great oaks about the place where once had rested a monstrous slab of stone graven with strange runes?

Aye, and there are other proofs. I have already booked passage on a galley out of Theelys bound for Dylath-Leen, and who would once have braved that place? And what captain dared to sail his ship there? Too, bright sky-yachts float above dreamland's cities and patrol her farthest borders, reporting their findings back to ever-watchful Kuranes in Serannian and King Carter in Ilek-Vad. And I'm told that so far they've had precious little to report, for which I'm glad.

But it must not be believed that the Forces of Evil are finished in dreamland. No, for beyond the frontiers of sanity there still lie lands of ill-legend and temples of terror. Leng breeds her horrors as of old on the borders of dream, and Kadath broods gray and gaunt in the Cold Waste. Aye, and man is an infant in dreams compared with great Cthulhu, who slumbers on eternally in R'lyeh, waiting . . . waiting.

And what of the heroes of the story now? Well, I have it on good authority that de Marigny is dreaming a white-walled villa in timeless Celephais, to which he'll return one day when at last he's traveled the road to Elysia. And Tiania and Titus Crow?

Strange visions wake. Fearsome starlanes and the gulfs between dimensions beckon. How long before even the marvels and wonders of dreamland pall and the lure of the Unknown calls Crow and his love away again? Who can say?

Worlds without end.

# Demogorgon

## Brian Lumley

### HELL IS RIGHT HERE ON EARTH

Charlie Trace, professional thief, is no stanger to deceit and violence. But nothing in all his life of petty crime could have prepared him for the horror of . . .

### DEMOGORGON

The guardian of a creature centuries old, who walks the Earth in the guise of a man, Demogorgon is the very Essence of Evil. And yet it is merely a watchdog for the ONE who commands it. And all down the centuries, and across all the nations, it has watched him sow the seeds of hell! Now the seeds are coming to fruition, the children are called home, and Demogorgon's power grows with every soul devoured. Charlie Trace is the one man who can stop it, and if he doesn't . . . he could be the next victim!

ISBN 0 586 07031 1